A
Garland Series

VICTORIAN
FICTION

NOVELS OF FAITH
AND DOUBT

A collection of 121 novels
in 92 volumes, selected by
Professor Robert Lee Wolff,
Harvard University,
with a separate introductory volume
written by him
especially for this series.

SIR ROLAND ASHTON

Catharine Long

MARY SPENCER

Anne Howard

Garland Publishing, Inc., New York & London

1975

Copyright © 1975
by Garland Publishing, Inc.
All Rights Reserved

Library of Congress Cataloging in Publication Data

Long, Catharine Walpole, Lady, d. 1867.
   Sir Roland Ashton.

   (Victorian fiction : Novels of faith and doubt ;
v. 41)
   Reprint of 2 works originally published in 1844:
the 1st published by J. Nisbet, London; the 2d published by Seeley, Burnside, and Seeley, London.
   I. Howard, Anne. Mary Spencer. 1975. II. Title. III. Series.
PZ3.L85Si5 [PR4891.L6]   823'.8   75-489
ISBN 0-8240-1565-7

SIR ROLAND ASHTON

Bibliographical note:

this facsimile has been made from a copy in the
British Museum
(N.2433)

SIR ROLAND ASHTON.

LONDON:
PRINTED BY MOYES AND BARCLAY, CASTLE STREET,
LEICESTER SQUARE.

SIR ROLAND ASHTON.

A Tale of the Times.

BY

LADY CATHARINE LONG.

"He deemed it incumbent upon every individual, however humble, to offer the tribute of his influence and example, if they amounted but to a mite, on the altar of his God."—*Private Life.*

IN TWO VOLUMES.

VOL. I.

———————

LONDON:

JAMES NISBET AND CO., BERNERS STREET.

MDCCCXLIV.

My dear Lady Carnarvon,

I DEDICATE this Work to you as a memorial of the friendship and affection which have subsisted between us for so many years, and which time, it is pleasant to feel, not only cements, but gives continually to increase.

Your idea is also particularly associated with it in my mind, for you are fully acquainted with the motive, wholly distinct from personal considerations, which originally induced me to think of writing, and you were among the very first to encourage me in the undertaking.

I know there are many most excellent people who do not approve of religious sentiments being brought forward through the medium of fiction, and who think that works of that nature are not calculated to produce good effects. But my experience has taught me decidedly the contrary, for not only have they often been instrumental in awakening and exalting spiritual feelings, but in some instances they have been the means, in God's hands, of conveying vital truth to the soul.

I am fully aware that my hero is not perfect, nor have I endeavoured to make him so, for perfection is not to be found in man; but I have endeavoured to prove, as far as fiction can prove any thing, that religion has power greatly to overcome the natural faults of disposition, and to strengthen and sustain the soul under the trials and temptations of life. The tale flows on "from grave to gay, from lively to severe," pretty much as real life does to those who, though not of the world, are constrained to live much in it; and I have not thought it necessary, in the least, to lower the tone of innocent cheerfulness, or of natural feeling and affection; on the contrary, I have endeavoured to represent love in its very highest degree, believing that in the very noblest characters it will always hold that place, and also thinking that it gives the love of God a much higher triumph to represent it as capable, which it truly is, of subduing the lofty and vehement feelings of men, than as able merely to control the tame and placid emotions of commonplace character.

In dedicating my Book to you, I am not afraid of compromising you in any way, for, though we may not always feel the same on religious subjects, yet we both know that the difference lies merely in the depth of tone, and not in the nature of the colouring; and you therefore have not feared allowing yourself to be associated with my wholly untried work, while I do not dread, by any sentiments brought forward in it, bringing a shadow of discredit upon a name so justly dear to me.

Believe me ever,

My dear Lady Carnarvon,

Your truly affectionate

CATHARINE LONG.

Spa, June 18, 1844.

SIR ROLAND ASHTON:

A Tale of the Times.

CHAPTER I.

" Now in thy youth beseech of Him
Who giveth, upbraiding not,
That His light in thy heart become not dim,
And His love be unforgot ;
And thy God in the darkest of days shall be
Greenness, and beauty, and strength to thee."

BERNARD BARTON.

"'*Voyager c'est un triste plaisir,*'" said Sir Roland
Ashton to Lady Constance Templeton, as he walked
with her in the garden at Claverton, just before he
started for the Continent.

Claverton, the seat of Lord St. Ervan, Lady Constance's father, was situated in Cornwall, very near the
coast. Only a few miles distant from it was Sir
Roland Ashton's residence, Llanaven, which was a
magnificent place, and surrounded by an immense
property ; which, together with an ancient baronetcy,
Sir Roland had inherited from his father when only
fifteen years of age. His mother had been a most

intimate friend of the late Lady St. Ervan's; and a
similarity in feeling and principles had drawn the bonds
of amity between the two families very close. Lady
St. Ervan's death (which took place when her youngest child, Lady Florence, was about three years old)
robbed Claverton of half its attractions for Lady Ashton; yet her friendship for Lord St. Ervan continued
unabated, while the motherless state of his two little
girls formed a new claim on her sympathy and kindness; and when, a few months afterwards, she lost
her own husband, her deep grief found a partial relief
in the almost maternal care she bestowed on the children of her friend, who, with her own two sons, Sir
Roland and his younger brother Henry, formed the
solace and charm of her existence.

The children of the two families had grown up
together on terms of the fondest intimacy. Their
homes were so near, that they continually saw each
other; and during absence at school or college, or
when Henry, who was in the navy, went to sea, constant communications between them had prevented
their ever being separated in heart; and letters were
as frequently exchanged between Lady Constance and
her absent friends, as between them and their mother.
She had ever felt for them the confiding love of a
sister, and Henry returned her affection in like manner;
but Sir Roland's feeling had gradually deepened into
one of exclusive love and attachment. Having, however, on one occasion, hinted his wishes to Lord
St. Ervan, the latter had begged him, for a time, to
defer making them known to their object, considering
her too young (she was but in her seventeenth year) to
know her own mind on such a subject. Finding it

extremely irksome to continue near, and yet be obliged
to repress the feelings which were ever hovering on
his lips, Sir Roland determined to go abroad for a
year, trusting he should be permitted at the expiration
of that time, to open his heart to her in whom all his
affections centred ; and the day on which this story
opens was that on which he was about to commence
what he considered a dreary exile.

After quitting Llanaven, he had to pass the park-
gates of Claverton ; and, having taken leave of his
mother at the former place, he could not resist paying a farewell visit at Lord St. Ervan's. He found
Lady Constance in the garden, and was taking a last
walk with her, when he made the exclamation with
which this chapter commences, — " *'Voyager c'est un
triste plaisir !'* — at least, so it seems to me," he continued, " when it begins with partings such as these.
Dear Constance, I cannot bear to go. Does it not
seem like madness to hurry away from what one loves
best on earth, *'pour aller là ou personne ne vous
attend.'* "

" I am sure you will enjoy it when once you are
abroad," said Lady Constance ; " but parting is always
sorrow, and never even ' sweet sorrow,' I think, though
Shakspeare calls it so. It is bitter sorrow to me, I
know, parting with you, dear Roland ; " and she burst
into tears.

" Constance, dear," said Sir Roland, in great
agitation, " do not, I beseech you, — I cannot bear those
tears ! "

" Oh ! they are only for a moment," she answered,
smiling through them ; " and selfish tears too, for I

know you will enjoy your travels so much ; but just at the time ——" and again her tears burst forth.

Sir Roland abruptly left her, and threw himself down on a seat in a summerhouse near ; he could not trust himself with her at that moment. She soon, however, joined him with an April face, and, sitting down by him,—

" There," she said, smiling, " I have wiped my tears away, as you had no compassion on them."

Sir Roland could not answer.

" You will write very often," she continued ; " we shall delight in tracing every step of your journey. It will be so dull when you as well as Henry are away."

" Well, let us enjoy our last five minutes now," said Sir Roland. Yet he leant his head on his hand in a manner that betokened any thing but enjoyment. Then, looking up hastily, he said,—

" Oh, yes ! I will write continually, and you will write to me,—all of you. Do not forget me. Constance," he added, a deep seriousness resting on his countenance, " will you grant me one favour ? "

" Gladly, if I can."

" Then meet me every night, at midnight, before the throne of God. It will be a solace to me to know that there, at least, we shall be together."

" I will," said Lady Constance ; " and pray for me, Roland—pray that my weak faith may be strengthened, and that I may continually grow in grace."

" Every prayer I offer up for you will be a selfish prayer," he replied.

" No, you have not a selfish thought in your whole heart," she exclaimed, not perceiving his meaning.

" And I ! What shall I pray for specially, — for you ? "

" All blessings on yourself, Constance ! " he replied, for a moment forgetting his caution ; then checking himself, he added, —

" Pray for me, that I may be preserved from, and in, temptation. I go where God is not much honoured or regarded ; pray that my love may not become cold. I do not fear it," he added, with a sigh, " as regards my earthly feelings ; but I dread as the worst evil,—yes, truly as the *worst* evil, coldness of heart towards God. I rejoice that you have made this appointment with me, Constance, it takes away some of the sting of parting ; God will surely bless our meeting in His presence, and I shall long for the quiet night-hour, for then I shall know your heart is with me."

Lady Constance held out her hand to him, and smiled through fresh-springing tears.

" Oh ! I hear those hateful wheels," she cried, starting up ; "·why did you order the carriage round so soon ? "

" I must not be late," said Sir Roland ; " and the sooner we part, the sooner will this terrible pain be over. Do not come with me to the carriage, Constance ; I cannot say farewell before others. I shall like to think of my last look of you here in your own flowery summerhouse. You will often think of me, my dearest ? "

Lady Constance could not speak. Sir Roland looked at her for one moment, then, kissing the hand she had held out to him, turned, and was gone.

CHAPTER II.

" So spake the seraph Abdiel, faithful found
  Among the faithless, faithful only he ;
  Among innumerable false, unmoved,
  Unshaken, unseduced, unterrified,
  His loyalty he kept, his love, his zeal ;
  Nor number, nor example, with him weigh'd
  To swerve from truth, or change his constant mind,
  Though single."   MILTON.

OF all the characters that the imagination of genius
had ever sketched, the one that had most delighted Sir
Roland, even from his boyish days, was that drawn
with the master-hand of Milton, and quoted above;
and often had he prayed that he might be enabled to
follow the bright example of the glorious being there
portrayed. God had heard and recorded the aspirations of his youthful servant, and had given him a
strength of character rarely met with. Continual,
indeed, were the failings and evils he found in his own
heart; but the knowledge of his infirmities ever led
him to throw himself with greater self-abandonment on
Christ, for all his strength and all his salvation ; and
thus, like the fabled Antæus of old, he rose the stronger
from every fall. The light of holy truth had early shone
upon him, and the blessing of God had borne him,
almost harmless, through scenes that too often wreck

both the virtue and the peace of youth.   Though entering with the kindest sympathy into the feelings of
others, his own heart seemed lifted above the world,
and continually dwelling in the presence of God; and
in him was realised, to a most unusual degree, the
power of a living faith, evidencing the truth of Scripture, "Thou shalt keep him in perfect peace whose
mind is stayed upon Thee."   The generality even of
true Christians pay, as it were, but visits to the throne
of grace, and are too apt to suffer themselves at other
times to be overcharged with the cares and affections
of this world.   But with Sir Roland the peace of God
abode, for his soul was stayed upon his heavenly
Father.

On leaving Claverton he proceeded direct to London, where he was joined by a friend whose mind was
wholly congenial to his own, and who had agreed to
accompany him in his travels.   Mr. Scott (for that
was the name of this friend) was three years younger
than Sir Roland.   He had not been blessed, like him,
with parents, who had trained his youth in the ways of
piety and usefulness; but, having been brought up for
the world, he had pursued its pleasures and dissipations,
and, sooth to say, its vices too, with eagerness and
delight.   His mother died early, and his father, though
he had thrown his son into the society he thought most
advantageous in all worldly points of view, yet when
he saw the evils it led him into, mourned over that
which his own hand had done.   He died when his son
was about twenty, and during the previous seclusion of
a long illness, he learned the insufficiency of earthly
things to bring comfort and peace in the hour of death;

and bitterly did he then regret the life and strength he
had wasted on the things of this world.   His son's dissipated life filled him with alarm and self-upbraiding.
When he spoke to him on the subject, he would laugh,
saying, "he must live as others did;" that "young
men must be young men," &c.

But when his father's illness assumed a dangerous
aspect, it seemed to sober him at once.   He was most
attentive and kind, and seldom left the house.   Yet
there seemed no conviction of sin, no awakening of the
conscience, or turning of the heart to God; and the
unhappy father had to leave the world under the agonising apprehension that the son, whose late unremitting attentions had made him dearer to him than ever,
was a stranger to God, and wholly given to the follies
of the world.   He had neglected to commend his young
years to his Maker, and now he had to leave him alone
in the world, without one human counsellor to assist
him, and wholly ignorant of Him in whose service
alone there is true wisdom.

After the first feelings of natural grief and mourning
had subsided, Mr. Scott, having nothing within to sustain and comfort him, naturally fell back to the companions with whom his life had been spent.   In very
kindliness they tried to raise his spirits, after their own
fashion, by leading him to "drown care" in renewed
folly and dissipation; and he entered into the snare
with the *gusto* of one who takes up again a favourite
enjoyment after having been for a time debarred from
its pursuit.   But he soon became surprised at finding
that these things had not the charm for him that they
formerly possessed.   He no longer returned from the

haunts of folly or vice light-hearted, reckless, and cheerful ; but a weight and oppression hung over him, and his heart, uneasy and disappointed, felt no peace.

Still, however, he went on, and even plunged deeper and deeper into sin and folly, in order to stifle the voice that was speaking within. Though he had never been convinced by what his father had said to him, yet his conversation had brought new subjects before his mind, and when he began again to mix in the world the aspect of things seemed changed to him, and he gradually lost all power of enjoyment in scenes that had once seemed so enchanting. Yet still he knew of nothing better, and his old associates could in no way help him, they " being tied and bound with the chain of those sins," which he began so earnestly to desire to shake off.

Just when his mind was in this state, one of his cousins, who had been abroad for some years, returned to England. He had seen but little of him before that time ; but, as soon as he became well acquainted with him, he took an extreme liking to his society, which his near relationship gave him frequent opportunities of enjoying. Mr. Singleton was one whose principles and pursuits were wholly at variance with those of his young cousin, yet hoping to do him good, and feeling a great regard for him, notwithstanding his many faults, he let him be as much with him as he chose ; and an extreme intimacy thus grew up between them. He was several years older than Mr. Scott, and of a most commanding style of countenance and character. He was very desirous to be of use to his cousin, but he determined not to press the subject of religion too much upon him. He felt sure, from what he saw, that his mind was unsatisfied with his present pursuits, and

he thought it best to let him feel his misery fully, before he tried to relieve him from it, by pointing out the
only path of peace and happiness.   With every one he
would not have acted in this way ; but he was well versed
in reading human character, and he saw so much of
determination and indomitable energy in Mr. Scott, that
he felt convinced that if he commenced the attack, the
other would never willingly relinquish the defence of
any point.

One morning thoroughly out of humour with himself and all the world, Mr. Scott threw himself on a
sofa in his cousin's room, exclaiming that " he was a
miserable wretch ! "

" I shouldn't wonder," said the other, coolly, continuing a letter he was writing.

" Why so ? " said Mr. Scott, rather indignant at the
readiness with which his assertion had been received.

" You seem to me to labour under many disadvantages," said his cousin.

" I am generally considered," returned Mr. Scott,
now apparently set upon making himself out to be
remarkably happy, " to be rather an enviable fellow,
and to possess an unusual share of advantages in the
world."

His cousin was silent, and pertinaciously plied his
pen.

" Why should you fancy I was miserable ? " said
Mr. Scott.

" One reason was, that you said you were," replied
his cousin.

" Oh ! one often says things one doesn't mean."

" Does one ?—I don't."

" What an odious fellow you are, Singleton ! "

" I suppose 'one is saying what one doesn't mean
now," replied his cousin quietly sealing his letter.

" No, I do mean it. I hate you when you are in
these humours."

" In what humours?" asked Mr. Singleton, extin-
guishing the bougie, and turning to his cousin in an
attitude of patient attention; " I have finished my
letter now, and can attend to you and to your misery
—or happiness. Which is it to be?"

Mr. Scott was excessively provoked,—the more so
that he could not help laughing.

" I shall not talk any more to you," he said, starting up; " but leave you till you are in a better mood."

" I assure you I am in quite a sweet mood," said
Mr. Singleton, " so let us discuss leisurely this very
interesting, and seemingly rather obscure point."

" I wish it were made law," said Mr. Scott, " to
strangle people who provoke one on the spot."

Mr. Singleton laughed loud and long; so loud and
so long that his cousin could not refrain from joining
him; and all preliminaries being thus brought to a
happy conclusion, they entered on the business under
discussion.

" Well, why, I ask you once more, should you
take upon you to imagine that I am miserable; and
why do you say that I labour under disadvantages?
What are they?"

" Your misery we will let rest upon your own assertion. The disadvantages rest on mine, and I am
prepared to name and prove them. You are young,
rich, clever, agreeable, fashionable, idle, and godless."

" I am not going to dispute the latter points," replied
Mr. Scott, with rather a heightened colour; " but

how, with all your love of paradoxes, will you make
it out that being (as you obligingly fictionise me to
be) rich, clever, agreeable, and fashionable, is to be
labouring under disadvantages.   They are things
usually rather coveted than otherwise."

"My sayings," replied Mr. Singleton, "are perfect
as *wholes ;* I cannot be answerable for them in fragments.   I again assert, that a man endowed with all
the attributes and qualifications I have named, united
together, labours under great disadvantages."

"I suppose you mean, that to a godless man, as
you are liberal enough to call me, the things first on
your list act as snares."

"I do mean that, my dear Willy," said the other,
kindly ; "the freight that would be very valuable if
God were at the helm, tends but the more to sink the
ship when Satan steers."

This pious but eccentric man then proceeded to lay
before his cousin many valuable views of himself, and
of God ; and the result of many conversations, of many
hard-fought battles, and of much patient exertion on
his part, was that, by the blessing of God, Mr. Scott
was brought to see things as the Almighty sees them ;
and not only to lament, but entirely to give up, his
former mode of life.   The energy of character which
had made him go farther than many in the pursuits of
the world, made him now surpass most others in the
diligence with which he subdued the evils of his own
nature, and sought occasions of mercy and kindness
towards his fellow-creatures. It was after this great and
happy change had taken place, that he became acquainted with Sir Roland, whose mind was not less
energetic than his own in all good things ; and the

similarity in their habits and feelings produced between them a strong and lasting friendship.

Though Sir Roland was so much attached to Lady Constance Templeton, yet his reserve was so great on this subject, that he and Mr. Scott had travelled together for some time before the latter became at all aware of the state of his feelings; and then it was by accident more than intention that the secret of his heart escaped him. He nursed it as a treasure too delightful, too sacred, to be laid open to common eyes; though, after it had once been mentioned, he often found a solace in speaking of his future hopes.

After spending some months in the more southern parts of Europe, the two friends went to pay a visit to Sir Roland's uncle, Lord N——, his mother's brother, who was then ambassador at one of the northern courts, and who was delighted to see his nephew, and invited both him and Mr. Scott to remain in his house during their stay at ——.

On Sir Roland's arrival, he found that the secretary of embassy, Mr. Anstruther, an old acquaintance of his, had been dangerously ill, and was consequently unable to fulfil the duties of his office. He had, indeed, wholly resigned his employment, as he had been told that his best chance of recovery was going to a warmer climate, which he purposed doing as soon as he should have regained a little more strength. This was a great trouble to Lord N——, who had been long accustomed to him, and who had none but young thoughtless *attachés* about him, in whom he could place but small reliance. The person who was appointed to the vacant post was at that time in a distant part of the world, and some months must necessarily elapse before he could enter on his new situation, and, in this dilemma, Lord N—— asked Sir Roland to act as secretary till the one newly appointed should arrive, if government would consent to his doing so.

Sir Roland, anxious to continue his journey, and longing to be again at home, felt very averse to complying with this proposal ; but his uncle was not young, and had much important business on his hands, and he felt that it would be selfish to refuse his assistance in such an emergency ; so he sacrificed, as was his wont, his own pleasure to the gratification of others, and yielded to his uncle's wish for him to remain for awhile with him at ——.

He expected to find his new situation extremely irksome, accustomed as he was to perfect freedom of action, and to associating chiefly with such friends as he liked ; but it was galling to him beyond all that he could have conceived. In the midst of a dissipated capital, and living in the ambassador's house, he found that a very different course of life and of conduct was expected from him than any to which he had ever before been accustomed, and which it was totally impossible for him to adopt. His upright mind was shocked continually at things which occurred in the course of the business he had to transact, and he ventured to mention to his uncle several matters, which seemed to him to bear far away from the open, truthful conduct, which had hitherto been his only line of action. Lord N—— smiled at his nephew's " unnecessary scrupulosity," as he called it, and which he attributed solely to his inexperience in the ways of the world ; for long as he had known Sir Roland, he had not yet penetrated into the recesses of his noble

mind. He was, perhaps, of a rather reserved temper;
but this, though proceeding partly from natural disposition, was much increased by finding few who could
understand the exalted Christian characters written on
his heart. They were like hieroglyphics to the people
of the world; therefore to such he unconsciously closed
the volume, while to those who knew him well, and
were able to appreciate his feelings, every line of his
bright and godly character was open for perusal.

　The old Machiavellian style of policy is now happily much exploded from our councils; but Lord
N——, though of an upright, honourable character
in ordinary life, was a man of the world, and retained
much of the old routine of conduct which formerly was
thought necessary in his situation. To disguise his
wishes, rather than make them plain, was, he thought,
the grand desideratum; while no art was considered
dishonourable that could tend to the discovery of the
secret intentions of the powers with whom he had to
act. Sir Roland, however, stated at once that it
would be impossible for him to use falsehood or deceit
in any way. He did not, of course, fancy that he was
to dictate what measures were to be adopted, such
things depending on persons much higher in power
than himself; but in carrying out those measures, as
far as he was intrusted with their conduct, he assured
his uncle he could not act otherwise than with candour
and honesty; and he felt convinced, he added, "that
openness would, in the end, be found to answer the
best, even in this world's estimation."

　"I must let you take your own way, I suppose,"
said Lord N——, good-humouredly; "but you will

soon have had enough of truth-telling in this lying world."

"Truth is, surely, the least difficult of all positions to attain and to defend," replied Sir Roland. "'The worst part of telling *one* lie,' some one said, 'is the having to tell so many to uphold it.' Now, without approving the morality of my friend of the single lie, yet the correctness of his position is, we well know, matter of history and experience."

"It may be so," returned his uncle; "but the first lie in diplomacy was told such centuries ago, that I confess that I quail under the attempt at cleansing this Augean stable. If Diogenes was forced to take a lantern to find an honest man in his day, I am sure it would need a Bude light to discover one now, at least amongst our ranks. And I suspect you will find one very necessary, too, in your pertinacious search after truth, which lies, they say, at the bottom of a well."

"*Lucerna pedibus meis verbum tuum,*" said Sir Roland with a tranquil smile; "that is the only light which guides to truth—all others lead astray. Scripture warns us, also, that it were better to cut off the right hand than to let it cause us to offend."

"Cut off your own hand, by all means," answered Lord N——, "if you have any particular predilection that way; but pray remember that you have your country to consult as well as your own fancies, and don't be like the lady, who, determining to have her own way with the loaf, cut herself through and the footman behind her."

Sir Roland laughed, and was about to speak, but

his uncle continued, " Your country will not feel
very grateful, I can tell you, if you sacrifice her interests to follow some phantasm of your own, which
no one can understand when they have got it—probably not even yourself. You may, perhaps, think it
your duty in private life, to go about telling people
how frightful and disagreeable you think them; but
that will not do here. When there are conflicting
duties, we must reconcile them as well as we can."

There was much in the contemptuous tone of his
uncle which was unpleasant to Sir Roland, but his
usual self-command did not desert him. His uncle's
age would have prevented any quick reply, even if
otherwise he might have been tempted to have given
way to one, and with great temperance he answered,
" I cannot but think it is an error, though I know it
is a common one, to talk of ' conflicting duties;' such
cannot surely exist. There can be but one line of
action at one time that is right, all others therefore
must necessarily be wrong."

" All that sounds vastly pretty, and amazingly
conclusive," answered Lord N——; " but I conceive,
with all due deference to your greater experience,
that it may so happen that what is well to do at one
time is ill to do at another. Truth is a very good
thing, where it will achieve the purpose we have in
hand; but even the truth will not bear telling at all
times, or in all places. If these rascally fellows saw
we had set our hearts upon any thing, do you think
they would let us have it? Not they. It would be
putting whip, spur, and bit into their hands, to use
as they pleased on us. No, no, depend upon it, it is
not your four-footed pig alone who must be told we

are taking him to Fermoy if we would get him to Kilkenny."

" But if all act on the same plan," replied Sir Roland, " we may also find ourselves at Kilkenny some fine day without intending it."

" There is that danger to be sure," answered Lord N——; "but we must have our wits about us, and only sleep with one eye at a time. It is useless, if you really want a thing, to act in such a way as to cut up your own project by the roots. In the prosecution of a great end, smaller interests must give way."

" As was the case with the unfortunate *Princes Mediatisés* at the time of the peace, I suppose," said Sir Roland, archly.

Lord N—— shook his head at him, though a smile lurked at the corners of his mouth. " You are quick enough at finding out the faults of your betters, I see," he said; " but if you are so malapert, I shall give you double work to do to keep you quiet. But I'll answer for it, you are just like your father; there never was any persuading him to do a thing like other people. Sometimes when we were boys together — and a bold boy he was — aye, and a noble fellow too — he would be wanting perhaps to do, or to have something or other (reasonable enough, I dare say) and would be always for going directly to ask his father about it, who was one of the most capricious bodies that ever lived. I used to say to him sometimes, ' Wait a little, and see what sort of a humour he is in.' But, ' No,' he would answer, looking very fierce and virtuous, ' if it is a right thing to do, it is a right thing to ask for at all times! I hate your deceit.' So off he went, going bolt up to his father — at a time when no man in his senses would have ventured to have spoken to him, even to tell him that he had had a fortune of twenty thousand a-year left him — and out he comes at once with his request. 'It needs no ghost' to tell what was the invariable result. 'Well,' I would say, when he returned, 'you have got your wish, of course.' 'No,' with a sigh of resignation, 'but I dare say there is some good reason why it is refused me.'"

"My dear father!" exclaimed Sir Roland involuntarily, his heart glowing at the recollection of him.

"Yes, he was a very dear father and a very good father," said Lord N——; "and a good husband, and a good man. And your mother is just such another spirit. Honest, open, truth-telling people, both — worthy and excellent — and intellectual too, especially your father; but they would have ruined the interests of any nation in a fortnight. Happy thing that they settled quietly in the country! I cannot wonder," he continued, looking slily but kindly at his nephew, "that you are no better than you are, considering from whom you spring."

Sir Roland smiled gratefully at the implied compliment to himself and to his parents, while his countenance lighted up with the beauty of filial love. "The thought of them is, indeed, most cheering to me," he said, "shewing what single-minded faith in Christ will do. Yet I must confess I do not quite agree in my father's boyish sentiment; for if you do want a thing, it is best to take all lawful measures to obtain it; if it is a matter of indifference, it were best not to irritate the other party, by mooting the point at all. I think he should have waited till his father was in a mood, quietly and reasonably, to judge of his request; and not have asked it of a person who, to all intents and purposes, was at the time *non compos*. We are told to use the wisdom of the serpent as well as the simplicity of the dove."

"Well, well, my dear boy, that is just what I have been saying. If you have a point at heart, gain it — honestly of course, if you can."

"Nay, nay, my dear uncle," replied Sir Roland; "I say, be honest, and gain your point, if you can. A Christian does not reckon that he can gain a point with other than honest weapons."

"My young Solomon," said Lord N——, "we must beat our enemies with their own weapons, if we expect to beat them at all."

"'Duties are ours, events are God's,'" said Sir Roland, gravely; "no Jesuit should be allowed to creep into our counsels. It was one of my father's sayings, I remember well, 'that the path of duty is generally clear to those who have no secret wish to turn aside from it.'"

"Well, have it your own way, for a headstrong, wilful boy, as you are," said Lord N——, who, nevertheless, could not help secretly admiring what he considered his nephew's chivalrous romance of character; "ask the light then, of your chosen lamp on the subject."

"You will think I am determined to gainsay all your advice," said Sir Roland, good-humouredly; "but I cannot ask counsel on a point where plain commands have been laid down. It would be like Balaam, going to inquire of God, in hopes of being allowed to curse where God had pronounced his determination to bless."

"Upon my word, young gentleman, you are rather strong in your language," said Lord N——.

"I beg your pardon, my dear uncle," said Sir Roland; "I did not at the moment perceive the strict application of the words; for nothing would induce me wilfully to say a disrespectful word to you. But still, dear sir, if you would but only consider the matter, I am sure you would see it in this light; we know that all insincerity is condemned by God, and He certainly pronounces any thing but a blessing upon it."

"No one, as you well know, Roland," said Lord N——, mildly, "disdains a lie more, as man to man, than I do; but I assure you, in public business you will find it is absolutely impossible to do without it."

"I cannot believe it," said Sir Roland; "nay, it is impossible it should be the case. Is it not God's intention that nation should have intercourse with nation? Most assuredly, then, such intercourse can be, and should be, carried on in accordance with His most truthful laws."

"Well, I see you are determined to beat me out of the field," said Lord N——, puckering up his eyebrows into a tremendous frown, from beneath which his quick, clear, grey eye twinkled with the most good-humoured expression; "there is no such thing as reverence for the wisdom of age in these degenerate days; so I shall hand you over to George Anstruther. *There's* a scholar who has far outstripped his master! And you will be quick indeed, if you are able at all times to give him a 'Roland for his Oliver.'"

So saying, and shaking hands kindly with his nephew, he left the room.

"Strange," thought Sir Roland, when alone, "that

Satan should have such unlimited range through this
world ! Well is he called the 'prince of this world,' ' the
prince of the power of darkness.' But a day will come,
and that soon I trust, when his power shall be cast
down, and the Lord of truth shall reign throughout
His earth."

CHAPTER III.

" That keen sarcastic levity of tongue,
The stinging of a heart the world has stung."
Phantasmagoria.

Mr. Anstruther was, indeed, an apt pupil of Lord N——'s in the arts of diplomacy; or rather, he might more properly be called, his active master; for bold, unscrupulous, and full of resource, he led, rather than followed, his nominal chief. Lord N—— made use of deceit in his way of carrying on affairs, in submission to the supposed necessities of the case; but Mr. Anstruther rejoiced in it as an exercise of ability and ingenuity. To him the keen encounter of wits in these matters was a most exhilarating exercise; and he seemed to have little amusement at any time but in playing with the weaknesses and sins of his fellow-creatures; yet, notwithstanding that this was his well-known character, he possessed such a power of fascination that, when he chose it, he could unlock almost every heart, and wind its most secret feelings from the unsuspecting mind. Penetrating to the keenest degree, he delighted in reading the thoughts of others. He quickly perceived if there existed in any one a dislike towards another; and by a judicious throwing in of now a little praise, now a little censure of the obnoxious personage, would bring out all the unkindly feelings that lurked in the heart of his companion, and not unfrequently create a vast deal more than had before existed.

He amused himself, too, in diving into the heart's secrets, as regarded its likings, as well as its *dislikings ;* and it might be said truly of him, '*qu'il aimait planter le couteau dans le cœur d'un homme, pour en faire sortir ce qu'il y avait.*' If he wished to ascertain the state of any one's feelings, he would casually mention the name of the person towards whom he suspected a preference; or more frequently, perhaps, say something disparaging of them, in order to elicit a burst of feeling. If he were desirous of observing secretly the effect of his words, he would let his eyes fall vacantly upon his companion, in the midst of the conversation, gathering at that one, apparently listless glance, worlds of knowledge; or if he wished to obtain power over him, by letting him see he was master of his secret, he would, when he was in the height of the turmoil his observations occasioned, suddenly fix his dark, keen eye upon him, in a way from which there was no retreat, and with an expression which told him plainly that his heart was wholly open before him. He delighted in boasting of the various arts he practised; yet such was the ability with which he made use of them, that few were aware of his designs when directed against themselves.

His mother had been a great friend of Lady Ashton's, for they were kindred spirits. Not so their sons! If there was a being in the world who was distasteful to Sir Roland—if there was one whom he could have

looked upon with a well-defined wish of never looking
on him again, it was George Anstruther! For his
mother's sake he kept up his acquaintance with him,
though chosen companions they had ceased to be for
many years. As well might the frozen Laplander and
the heated denizen of the tropics expect to flourish in
the same temperature, as George Anstruther and Sir
Roland Ashton to find breathing-space in the same
moral atmosphere, — each poisoned the air for the
other. There was something in the reckless want of
principle — the daring disregard of all things sacred —
the wily reasonings, and cool, playful contempt, of
Mr. Anstruther — mingled too, with a careless, gaily
good-humoured manner, under cover of which he gave
vent to the most biting sarcasms, that seemed to paralyse Sir Roland's very heart and soul; while there
was that in Sir Roland's real dignity of mind and uprightness of principle — in his keen discernment, and
calm, penetrating eye, under which Mr. Anstruther
writhed and shrunk like a victim under the knife.

There was one point, and one only, which seemed
to be a link between their common natures; and that
was the devoted love which Mr. Anstruther bore to the
memory of his mother. She had died when he was
yet a child, and he seldom spoke of her; but when he
did so, the whole current of his being appeared for the
moment changed; the evils of his nature seemed driven
back to their own dark abodes, and feelings, scarcely
natural, almost angelic, for an instant flooded his mind.
To the very outward eye his appearance was changed
at these times, and his marked and handsome features
wore a heavenly expression, in place of the repellent,
harsh restlessness, which was their general character.

It was strange, that to Sir Roland alone did he ever shew these intense workings of feeling.   Never would he voluntarily have revealed them to any living soul,—it was no relief to him to do so,—no comfort did he seek, in speaking of her he had loved with so intense a love; but when the remembrance of her took full possession of his mind, he seemed to realise her very presence, and to be borne away as by a resistless flood; and though old recollections, by associating Sir Roland's idea with the loved remembrance of his mother, might have somewhat to do in accounting for it, we must seek its chief cause in the secret, unacknowledged, even unsuspected influence, which his truthful character and deep feeling exerted over him. He felt, intuitively, that with him all secrets would be safe—that he would never make his feelings subjects of ridicule, or even of conversation with others; and therefore, though in the presence of any one else he would probably have preferred dying in the effort to suppress emotion, yet with him, the restraint being a shade less powerful, the sluice-gates of his soul would at times give way, and all the feelings of a naturally affectionate heart would " burst forth in one wild flood;" though, when he regained power to pen them back again, he hated him the more for having been witness of their outflowings.

But on Sir Roland these scenes had a far different effect—they awakened in him an interest which not all the horror he felt of Mr. Anstruther's general tone of feeling could wholly do away. They kept alive a hope within his heart that the awful fiat might not yet have gone forth against him as against Ephraim of old: " He is joined to his idols—let him alone."

He therefore determined to keep up a kindly inter-

course with him, how disagreeable soever to himself, in
the hope that, sooner or later, he might be enabled to
shew him "the way, the truth, and the life," which
were now so wholly hidden from his eyes. He knew
what must be his eternal portion unless his heart were
changed and his sins pardoned through the blood of
Christ; and, not for even his worst enemy, could he
have brooked to think of the horror of everlasting
death.

> "Then marvel not if such as bask
> In purest light of innocence
> Hope against hope in love's dear task,
>   Spite of all dark offence.
> If they who hate the trespass most,
> Yet, when all other love is lost,
> Love the poor sinner, marvel not;
> Christ's mark outwears the rankest blot."

Yet, for all his kindly wishes, it was with a heavy
step that he now proceeded to pay the invalid a visit,
which he feared would be a painful one in every way.

Mr. Anstruther had been so weak hitherto that he
had been unable to see any one; but the interdict was
now taken off, and a few of his most intimate acquaintances were allowed to visit him. He lived in Lord
N——'s house, in apartments just over Sir Roland's;
so ascertaining from his servant that he was ready to
receive him, the latter mounted the stairs and entered
his room. It was partially darkened, and Mr. Anstruther, who was reclining on a sofa, lay with his back
to the light. Serious, and almost fatal, as had been his
illness, his vanity was still in full exercise, and he could
not endure the idea of any one's perceiving the great
ravages that sickness had made in his looks. One point
of his ambition had ever been to be supposed superior

to the common weaknesses of human nature; therefore, to have been sick and ill, like any ordinary man, was a terrible downfal to his vanity, and galled immensely his arrogant spirit. In receiving the visits of his acquaintance (friends he had none—Sir Roland and Lord N—— forming probably the sum-total of those who took any real interest in him) he assumed the most animated spirits, though often suffering severely afterwards for the efforts he was so ill calculated to sustain.

"Roland, my fine fellow, how are you?" he said, holding out two fingers as Sir Roland approached him; "where have you been disposing your person since last we met? You see me here in a new character. I had got tired of all the old ways, or rather they of me, I suppose, so they tossed me over to a sick-bed by way of something new. However, they knew their man, and gave me the only really gentlemanlike, aristocratic illness in the world—the only illness I could endure to die of. Inflammation on the lungs has something really romantic in its sound; as if one had nothing more gross or material about one than the breath of life—the ethereal and only point on which one was vulnerable. Then the 'sleepless night,' the 'fluttering pulse,' the 'hectic colour,'—are all so interesting! The very sounds are euphonious, and flow so well from the lips of the Clementinas and Seraphinas who hover about your door in spasms of anxiety, and mourn your untimely fate in laced and scented handkerchiefs. But now, Sir Baronet, recount all your exploits since last we parted."

He waited for Sir Roland's answer, glad to avail himself of the opportunity of rest; for even such small exertion nearly overcame him.

"I have been travelling very soberly," answered
Sir Roland, "over many kings' highways, through
France, Italy, &c., '*doing* all the sights' that other
people do." He then proceeded to "say where he'd
been, and what faces he'd seen," as far as he thought it
might amuse his auditor, who lay with his eyes shaded
by his hand, looking the picture of death. He was
much shocked by his appearance, and in a short time
rose to depart, saying he thought he had already stayed
too long.

"Not at all, my dear fellow," said the sick man, in
the most vivacious tone. "Charmed to see you; only
those stupid fellows of doctors have kept the room so
dark for some time, that the light oppresses my eyes
now. Sit still, as long as ever you like——What! you
will go? Well, come in whenever you choose—do not
stand on any ceremony with me."

Sir Roland could scarcely repress a smile at the
condescension with which he was given the *entrée* to a
stifling sick-room in the bloomy time of spring, when
every thing without offered him freshness and fragrance;
in company too, with the man least tolerable to him of
any on earth; (though that, perhaps, was not known
to his patronising friend, though probably suspected;
for we seldom cordially hate another without having
some faint idea of the dislike being reciprocal.) But
controlling his features, he merely said that he would
come and visit him again the next day; and glad of the
release, he returned to his own apartment.

CHAPTER IV.

" Spring, on thy native hills again,
     Shall bid neglected wild flowers rise,
And call forth, in each grassy glen,
     Her brightest emerald dyes !
There shall the lovely mountain rose,
Wreath of the cliffs, again disclose;
* * * *
The mountain rose may bloom and die,
—It will not meet thy smiling eye!"

        MRS. HEMANS.

WHEN Sir Roland entered his room, he was glad to
find Mr. Scott waiting for him. "Put on your hat,
and come out with me," he said. And they strolled together out on the ramparts. Taking a long deep
breath of the heavenly air, "What a relief!" he said:
"what a change of atmosphere, moral as well as
physical!"

" Why, where have you been?"

" In Anstruther's room, oppressive to both soul and
body. But now—shall we ride?" and ordering their
horses, they were soon far from the city, amidst scenes
where mere existence was luxury, and where their young
buoyant hearts swelled up with earth's ten thousand
voices to the Giver of all the beautiful things which
surrounded them. It was spring-time; and the very

hedge-rows were pictures, with the red shoots of the
rose, the early honeysuckle, the hawthorn, and maple,
with all their various tints of green.

"If God has made such a world for His enemies,
what must be that world He has prepared for His
friends!" Such, or some such, were the feelings of
the two beings who, with their reins upon their horses'
necks, wandered about through woods fragrant with
the smell of the early foliage; where the larch hung its
slight pensile boughs like verdant fountains all around,
and the beach unfurled its fairy banners to the breeze,
with many other trees, all adding beauty to the scene,
and sending out their leaves so fast, in the warm bursting air, that the shade seemed really deeper when they
quitted the precincts of the woods than when they had
entered them. Deep, indeed, it might scarcely yet be
called, for the young silken leaves but faintly obstructed
the rays of the sun,—it was softened light rather than
shade.

But lovely was that bright spring day, and fully
did the two friends enjoy it, though Sir Roland's fancy
would often turn to his own deep woods, now in their
first flush of green, with the sparkling ocean seen between; and to his mother—and to her who was to his
heart as " April dews, that softest fall, and first;" and
that sick yearning of the spirit for those we love, ever
felt most, perhaps, at such seasons, began to steal over
him, and turn his enjoyment into regret. " How irksome it is," he exclaimed, " to be kept away from home
at this season, for I had hoped to see my own leaves
unfold this year; and instead of being with those who
are all truth and sweetness, I am kept perpetually
battling with the falseness and selfishness of these

people. I feel as if my mind were stiff—as one's arms and chest become with swimming against a current. I long to be at rest and peace, and to be at home again. But it is a shame," he added, rousing himself, " to sully this pure air with one breath of discontent; so let us gallop across the plain, and leave all gloom behind.

' Shame on the heart that dreams of blessings gone,
*   *   *   *
When nature sings of joy and hope alone,
Reading her cheerful lesson in her own sweet time.' "

" I must beg to decline your obliging offer of violent exercise this hot day," said Mr. Scott; " but if you wish for it, don't let me detain you; you can play at El Djereed around me, if it please you, ' but leave, oh! leave me to repose.' "

" You are the idlest dog I ever saw, Scott, and always like basking in the sun."

" I'll be revenged for that," said Mr. Scott; " and torment you now by telling you I heard you very much abused the other day, and by a lady too. A quotation you made a minute ago just reminds me of it in good time for that purpose; though, after all, I dare say you are one of those vain fellows who had rather be abused than forgotten."

" Perhaps I am," said Sir Roland; " but now, what was I abused for? and by whom?"

" Oh, ho! you can ride quietly now, can you, and bask like others in the sun?"

" I can always be quiet if there is any thing to be got by it," said Sir Roland, good-humouredly; " so now tell me."

" I thought you felt no interest about any one here?" said Mr. Scott, in a quiet way.

" I feel interested about myself every where, at all times, and all seasons," replied Sir Roland.

" Well, that is honest, and a great exertion for a hot day, so I think I will tell you ; though I am afraid you will be disappointed, when I say that your fair traducer was only my respected aunt, Lady Wentworth !"

" *Only* Lady Wentworth ! But Lady Wentworth is one of the last people here I should wish to be abused by, being one of the very few whose good opinion I think worth having ; or rather, I should say, one of the few who is capable of forming one (for every one's good opinion is worth having). Dear old lady ! though she is rather vehement in her anathemas sometimes, I would fain not deserve them from her. But what did she abuse me for ? "

" She abused you—but only to me, be it observed —for doing what you did just now, and what you frequently do."

" What ! quoting from the 'Christian Year ?'"

" Yes. 'I can't conceive,' she said—and the old lady waxed quite wroth—' how Sir Roland Ashton can quote any thing from such an author. I trust I have not been mistaken in him ; I trust he has no tendency to Puseyism !' But I assured her that she need be under no alarm about her favourite, I was sure you were as much opposed to those doctrines as she was herself."

" I am, indeed, no Puseyite," replied Sir Roland ; " but I quote from the ' Christian Year,' because ' out of the abundance of the heart the mouth speaketh ;' and I not only have much of the ' Christian Year' by heart, but I trust I have many of the sentiments it contains continually at heart. It is a lovely book of

poetry, and was my delight long before I thought any
thing about Puseyism, and indeed, before that fearful evil had shewn itself openly to any extent. I always
loved poetry; but amidst the beauties of the Greek
and Latin authors, there was ever a something which,
while it pleased, never satisfied me. Their writings
have a beauty that 'plays round the head, but touches
not the heart;' to say nothing of the many portions of
them that had better never have been written at all;
and few English poems, of any merit, have any thing
of real religion in them. Milton is indeed, most
sublime, but the parts relating to the Redeemer are too
much the productions of the poet's imagination to
satisfy a heart that requires realities to rest upon. But
in Keble's poems there breathes a spirituality of mind,
which stretches from the heights of heavenly lore to
the humblest walks of practical Christianity. In it, the
love of God, and love of man, are so forcibly, and
so beautifully, pressed on the heart, that I have found
it a most valuable book to me. I despise no good
thing, let it come from what quarter it may; and I
think, I confess, that *we* are often too apt to forget,
that though salvation is a free—thank God, wholly free
gift—yet that labour and love are the appointed paths
to heaven. Too many of us are satisfied with being
safe, without striving sufficiently to be holy. Satan is
sleepless and busy, whilst we are slothful and idle; and
to me, therefore, these poems of Keble's are particularly animating and arousing, for they bring our duties
as well as our consolations continually before us. I
always felt that there were in them expressions and
sentiments whose meaning was not clear to me, but I
left those for what was distinct in its truth, its depth of

piety, and heavenly lore. I can now trace portions of the leaven which has worked so fearfully in their author's mind ; but still I cannot reject the rest on their account, nor cease to value what God has so often blessed to me. But oh! to think of such a mind as that being brought again to look to outward things, to be involved in the mists of such error! It seems scarcely 'less than Archangel ruined ;' it shews the dire malignity of that poison, which can reach and corrode a mind like his. It makes my heart wretched, and my soul sick, to see this work of ruin going on!"

"Well, if my good aunt heard you now, she would be satisfied, I think."

"I had quite forgotten what brought me on the subject ; for, when it takes possession of my mind, I seem to lose thought of all else. It is so terrible to me to see Satan striving to satisfy the craving souls of men with something short of the righteousness of Christ, leading them to trust to their own works, and making them satisfied with a mere form of godliness. Dreadful it is to hear men, permitted to remain in the Church of England too, saying, 'that the Atonement is to be preached with reserve.' The Atonement preached with reserve! What, then, would they preach ? Where else can they find the 'glad tidings of great joy that are to be unto all people.' Grievously have they, spite of their cherished 'succession,' forgotten the principle of the Apostle : 'I am determined henceforth, to know nothing amongst you but Christ Jesus, and Him crucified.' Do they forget that 'out of Christ'—without His atonement—'our God is a consuming fire ?' Their doctrine, too, enforces no holy separation from the world in its vanities and follies, no consecration of

the whole being to God. In the morning at church—
at the midnight hour with the God-forgetting world, in
the dissipations and vanities of the ball-room. Fasting
one day—the next at all the abominations of the
theatre. What a sickening mixture! How contrary
to the spirit of the Gospel! how destroying to the
souls of men! setting completely aside our Lord's declarations, 'Ye cannot serve God and Mammon'—'the
friendship of the world is enmity against God.'"

  " You have reason to thank God, my dear Ashton,
from your inmost heart," said Mr. Scott (and a shade
of sadness crossed his brow) " that, though you speak
so justly of the things of this world, you know them
only by report. Its foolish dissipations eat out the very
heart of spirituality; and truly, though in happy ignorance of them, do you speak of the ' *abominations* of
the theatre.' They are amongst Satan's most approved
workshops; and you may be most thankful that you
had guardians of your young days faithful, and pious,
and wise enough, to keep you from ever entering their
unhallowed walls. Yours is, indeed, the whitest page
of the human mind I ever met with, ' the princely heart
of innocence,' and that it is which makes you so particularly delightful to me."

  " I thank you, Scott," said Sir Roland, with pleased
emotion; " but do not write vain things on the tablet
you fancy so pure, by your kindly flatteries. Remember that the heart within gives one enough to
do; and this experience it is which makes Puseyism
so fearful to me, for it leads man, from the inward
spiritual grace, to rest in outward forms and ceremonies. The only comfort I can derive from these
things is the additional proof they afford that the end

of this dispensation is at hand. The increased power permitted to Satan to deceive the nations, is one of the predicted signs of the Lord's second coming; and the rapid strides of this fearful apostasy make it, I cannot but think evident, that the evil one is exerting himself a thousand-fold, 'knowing that his time is short.' One would almost think that Keble prophesied of this very thing (in the fulfilment of which he himself is aiding) when he said,

> ' Foe of mankind, too bold thy race
>   Thou runn'st, at such a reckless pace
> Thine own dire work thou surely wilt confound :
>   'Twas but one little drop of sin
>   We saw this morning enter in,
> And, lo! at even-tide the world is drowned.'

It seems such a delusion, so monstrous, and of such rapid growth, too, that I feel lost in astonishment at it. Yet," he added, looking earnestly up, " 'Thou, O God, art in the midst of us, and we are called by thy name; leave us not!'"

" I was perfectly sure that you did not agree with these doctrines," said Mr. Scott; " but I really did not know that you felt so strongly upon the subject."

" I feel more strongly on the subject to-day than I did yesterday, and yesterday than the day before; for the evil hourly increases, and each time I hear of it, or think of it, it assumes a more awful aspect than before. But I have not of late much canvassed these things with you, for I like best to dwell on the bright and sunny side of all subjects; and there are so many pleasant views to take of the present times, that I turn to gaze on them rather than dwell upon the deepening shades of the twilight of error."

"It is certainly delightful," said Mr. Scott, "to have encouragement to believe that the 'time of the restitution of all things is at hand;' it makes even these dark spots bring comfort with them, though brighter and better things also tend to produce the same conviction.   Good, as well as evil, is a sign of the Lord's coming, and certainly true religion flourishes now to an unprecedented degree; and more has been done for the spread of the Gospel, within the last forty years, than in the eighteen hundred which had elapsed before.   That reminds *me* of Keble, where he says, in that splendid stanza,—

> ' Thus bad and good their several warnings give
>   Of his approach, whom none may see and live;
>   Faith's ear, with awful, still delight,
>   Counts them like minute-bells at night,
>   Keeping the heart awake till dawn of morn,
>   While to her funeral pile this aged world is borne.' "

"They are magnificent lines," said Sir Roland; "and one can but earnestly hope, that a mind so gifted as his must be who wrote them, a heart that seems really to have been touched with 'a live coal from the altar,' may be led to see the whole 'truth of God,' and not be permitted to use his heavenly powers to lead astray the souls of men.   Well; we may, perhaps, help in his rescue from error as well as in the general furtherance of God's glory on earth.   'The effectual fervent prayer of a righteous man,' let us remember, Scott, 'availeth much.'   We are I trust, both of us, though sinners in ourselves, amongst those who are 'counted righteous before God,' for Christ's sake; let us use our high privileges, and 'offer up our supplications out of a pure heart, fervently.' "

They passed on, through cheerful meadows, where the field-flowers sent forth an almost overpowering fragrance, and through stilly woods, where all was hushed, except the thronging notes of the innumerable birds, which at that season

> " Pour their forgotten multitudes, and catch
>   New life, new rapture, from the smile of spring."

Then issuing forth again, they crossed the plain, and entering the city—where their horses' feet echoed with ringing sound through the almost empty streets—they at length dismounted at the gate of the Embassy-house.

What was there in those two young beings to distinguish them from the generality of those around them? The one was certainly pre-eminently handsome; his tall figure, fine countenance, and dark meditative eye, might have caught the attention of the passer-by; but his companion had nothing but the bright animation of his look to attract a moment's notice : they might both have passed even as others. Yet on their youthful brows was set the "signet of the Lord;" unseen indeed by man, but recognised by Him who had Himself sealed them by His Spirit.

Side by side the children of God and the children of the world go through life; together perchance they quit this mortal scene : these tranquillised by the comforts of the Gospel, those sleeping under the delusive spells of Satan; but, oh! what a difference in the awakening! We may see two young sisters who, though brought up under the same roof, are totally different in their spiritual views and feelings. We may behold them perhaps, in the same chamber, stretched by the same disease, in the repose of the same death!

Their last words may have been words of love and sweet affection for each other; and they may have died each with the other's hand clasped fondly in her own. As far, therefore, as regarded each other, they may have been "lovely and pleasant in their lives," but in their deaths they *are* divided: the one soars to the realms of eternal day—the other sinks to endless night; for to the one the "Saviour was precious," while to the other His "cross was foolishness."

Or look, where a little space from the bloody plain of battle (Satan's much-loved work) two soldiers drag their wounded, suffering forms to the stream, to slake the agonies of their dying thirst. Together they stoop and drink,—together die! The impress of pain is alike stamped on each contracted brow; but the one loved the "Lord his righteousness," while the other would not have Him for his God. Therefore, between them thenceforth, "there is a great gulph fixed," which neither can pass. On the one side, hell "heaves her floods of ever-during fire," while on the other, are the realms of eternal life!

And when the day of the Lord comes, "as a thief in the night," of such—so undistinguished in outward appearance, but so differing in the "inward man"—the "one shall be taken and the other left"—left, to be swept away by the flames that must clear the path of the Lord of all those "who would not have Him to rule over them;" whilst the other is "taken"—"caught up to meet the Lord in the air, and so to dwell with Him for ever." "Oh! think of this, ye that forget God, lest He pluck you away, and there be none to deliver!"

CHAPTER V.

"It is a weary and a bitter task
  Back from the lip the burning word to keep,
And to shut out heaven's air with falsehood's mask."
                                        MRS. HEMANS.

SIR ROLAND made a point of going to Mr. Anstruther once at least every day; for he knew, notwithstanding the indifference which the latter pretended to
feel, that his visits were, in fact, great resources to him.
Solitude, to a mind like his, was any thing but exhilarating, and few of his gay acquaintance cared to waste
their time on one whom they neither esteemed nor liked.
His health continued to improve, though he was long
unable to leave his room.

One day he said to Sir Roland,—

" Your respected uncle has handed you over to me,
to be initiated in the noble art of diplomacy. Now,
what are the points on which you wish to be enlightened?"

Sir Roland smiled, and said, " I shall be much
obliged by your explaining some things to me—some
matters which I have to take up in the middle."

" The best advice I have to give," continued Mr.
Anstruther, taking no notice of Sir Roland's answer,
" is that you should conceal your own thoughts, meanings, and feelings, and set all your wits to work to find

out the thoughts, meanings, and feelings of others.
That, in few words, is the concentration of diplomacy,
like the poor gentleman's thirty Westphalia hams, reduced to one small bottle of essence ; take it, and use
it *à discretion*."

Sir Roland smiled, and shook his head.

" Now pray don't affect to be sanctimonious,"
continued Mr. Anstruther ; " for that is acting as well
as speaking a lie. We all lie—we all know that we
lie ; and the only one who speaks any truth at all is he
who confesses that he lies ; as to making faces about it
—that is childish—ridiculous !"

" I can understand its being extremely difficult,"
said Sir Roland, " to keep upright under such crushing
burthens; but it is certainly not impossible, and I hope
there are those who do so."

Mr. Anstruther turned his head, and looked at him
with an affected smile of surprise and inquiry. " Are
you so young, so very young, as to suppose that ?" he
said. " Well, I thought even you had more sense ;
though I know, as Willy Scott said the other day,
'that the making you a diplomat was more hopeless
than looking for the needle at the north pole !—the
most amusing idea he ever heard of !' Yet I was foolish
enough, I confess, to have some hope of you ; but I see
I am wrong, decidedly wrong. Not that you will be a
jot better than others—that I never expected" (with a
contemptuous smile) ; " but I perceive, if ever you do
become like them at all, it will be a sort of caricature
likeness—a something which one perceives is meant to
resemble something else, but is manifestly a failure.
I am sorry for you, for it is no use resisting : the world
will turn and twist you her own way, do what you

will; and if you will only go through the process
quietly, there may still be a chance for you. But if
you are to plunge and kick all the way through, you
will be mutilated in all manner of ways, literally *mit en
lambeaux.* You have heard, of course, of that ma-
chine, where your live sheep, put in at one end in the
morning, comes out from the other at dinner-time in the
shape of roast legs of mutton and men's coats ? So
will you be transformed—pure lamb, that you doubtless
think yourself at present—in you must go, and out
you must come: only your legs will be worse roasted,
and your coat worse cut, than that of others—that's
all ! But now to enter a little more into particulars,
after my fashion—for it would really give me prodi-
gious satisfaction to mould you a little into form—we
must first consider the ends we have in view, and then
the means whereby they are to be attained. Without
joking, what you have first to master is the secret intentions of your enemy : for all the people you have to
do with, must be considered as enemies — politically I
mean ; that is, all of them will pursue their own interest, without the slightest regard to yours, preferring,
indeed, rather to rise on your ruins than otherwise."

" It is a pity," said Sir Roland, " that people have
not as yet, in general, found out that what benefits one,
will probably in the end benefit another too ; and that,
on the other hand, by outraging others, we are sure
finally to injure ourselves : as a man, sowing thistles in
his neighbour's field, will find that in time the seeds
blow over into his own."

" We leave such vulgar considerations for those
whom they may suit," replied Mr. Anstruther, contemptuously ; " what we have to do is to set our point

before us, and follow it, *coute qui coute.* The pace
is too good to stop and 'pick up the bits' of those who
are overthrown in the scramble; indeed, if our horses'
hoofs were wholly to obliterate the features of a friend,
I am afraid—it is very horrid! but I really am afraid—
it would be rather a pleasant thing than otherwise."

" ' Hateful and hating one another,'" said Sir Roland, indignantly.

" Just so, if that is the view it amuses you to take
of it. But as I was saying, your first point must be to
find out what are the particular things which the enemy
wishes you not to find out. Now one very good way
is just to observe the subjects which, in your intercourse together, they treat as trifling, insignificant
matters. Depend on it those are their hidden treasures, there lie the golden eggs they are trying to
hatch. From them they will endeavour to draw off
your thoughts, just as the partridge flaps and flutters
away to draw you from her nest. There fix your eye,
and never take it off, for sooner or later you will find
the root of the matter to be in that quarter. But, probably, you would not be up to all that—at least not at
first," he added, condescendingly; " so your best way
will be to get round somebody, to tell you all about it.
I dare say you are a great adept in the arts of pleasing?"

" I have never yet put them to the proof," said Sir
Roland, laughing.

" You expect that I should believe that, of course ? "
said Mr. Anstruther.

" I do," replied Sir Roland.

" Then you ought to be ashamed of yourself, my
good sir, for the neglect of the goods bestowed upon
you! Why! with that 'preux chevalier' face of yours

I would have broken all the hearts in Christendom before this, and have joined the expedition to Central Africa, to find out new worlds to conquer. However, if you have so long neglected to manufacture your raw —I am afraid very raw—material, to meet the demand of civilised society, it is time you begin; so I advise you to make your apprenticeship with *la belle Louise,* the young minister's charming little sister. Her brother makes her the choice depository of all he knows, suspects, and invents; and a little judicious attention on your part will soon win all from her."

" Your first recommendation I am really much obliged to you for," said Sir Roland ; " but the other I beg to decline, as I have no wish to carry home a foreign wife, and have, moreover, no liking for *la belle Louise.*"

" You are really most unpleasantly matter-of-fact and obtuse of intellect!" said Mr. Anstruther—" distressingly so, indeed! Who talked of your liking—or even marrying—any one? I suggested neither of those painful predicaments. I merely proposed that you should do what many others of your calibre have found very useful."

" And then leave the poor victim to die of a broken heart; as George Stanley did last year to that pretty girl at ———.''

" As to dying, that is a matter of choice or accident, I imagine," replied Mr. Anstruther. " People do not die of love nowadays, even if they ever did—which I consider rather apocryphal. I suspect there was a ' feverish cold,' or something of that sort, added to the love, in that case. I do not give George Stanley credit for producing *une si belle passion ;* and I should not

much fear for *la jolie Louise*, I confess, in this instance.
I really advise you to try. A litle show of attention,
a few *petits soins* towards the sisters or daughters of a
minister, helps those uncommonly who cannot help
themselves."

Mr. Anstruther said this without the slightest idea
of Sir Roland's adopting his suggestions, but merely
with the desire of mortifying him, by appearing to
think him no better than the common run of unprincipled men of the world.

" Your code is mightily at variance with mine on
all subjects," answered Sir Roland, coldly. " I wonder
you can exist, Anstruther, with such a lining to the
heart and imagination as you must have."

" My codes and my linings have nothing to do
with the case," rejoined the diplomat. " I never engage in matters of that kind, for I do not need such
resources and assistances. I love no one—nor do I
affect it," and a sardonic smile curled his lip.

" I almost think that with you, Anstruther, the will
to love is wanting more than the power," replied Sir
Roland, with a kindly smile.

A strong emotion rushed suddenly over Mr. Anstruther's mind, but with a great effort subduing it,
he replied, coldly and carelessly, " Will and power are,
I imagine, pretty well synonymous with me. As regards
love, however," he continued, with a vivacity evidently
affected, " I have a thorough contempt of the article as
imported into high life; what it is amongst your boors
and savages I have yet to learn. But I rather like,
when I am *désœuvré*, and trouble myself at all about
such light matters, to amuse myself with contravening
the little outbreaks, and manifestations of liking, be-

tween the young and foolish of the world. The old I
leave to themselves, as they are best qualified to work
out their own absurdities, and to expose themselves unbidden in all the shapes of folly, which long use and experience enable them to command. But the '*chasse
à l'homme*' diverts me in every way. Now you, I dare
say, would rather foster all those pretty weaknesses,
and would think them uncommonly amiable! *Àpro-
pos*," he added, fixing his quick eye full on Sir Roland,
" how is my old friend the pretty Constance? Does
she favour your suit? or are you wandering here
in hopeless exile?"

Sir Roland's colour mounted to his temples, and
his dark eye flashed with a sudden expression of anger,
as he replied quickly,—

" Do you mean Lady Constance Templeton? for
if so, I beg you will speak with respect of her, as
of all my friends, and not affect an intimacy with
those who have scarcely ever honoured you even with
a bow."

" I really beg your pardon," replied Mr. Anstruther, in an affectedly soothing voice ; " I spoke quite at
random, I had no idea of there being any thing so
serious. I am exceedingly sorry to have annoyed you ;
but I assure you it shall go no farther—your secret is
perfectly safe in my keeping."

The confidential air with which this was said was
beyond measure annoying to Sir Roland, who rose and
went to the window ; he soon, however, replied in a
calm tone,—

" I especially dislike the impertinent familiarity
of the present day ; where men think it a mark of importance, I suppose, to 'Susan,' and 'Mary,' and

' Arabella,' every body whom they know by sight or name."

"I am sorry to have ruffled you, my dear fellow," rejoined Mr. Anstruther; "really very sorry. I had no idea the subject was of so tender a nature; but as I see now how the land lies, I will be more cautious for the future, and will not mention her again."

Sir Roland was about to reply hastily; but checking himself, he said, after a few moments' silence,—

"I do not mind who you talk of, only let it be in a proper tone. But my horses must be waiting for me now, so I shall take my leave; and will send my servant up with that book you wished to see."

Mr. Anstruther threw a compassionate smile into his countenance as Sir Roland crossed the room to depart, in hopes that the latter would turn and perceive it; but as he failed to do so, he let it fade away; and as the door closed, and he listened to his steps rapidly descending the stair, a sigh involuntary broke from him. "I am half sorry I vexed him," he thought, "for there are few like him!"

Though Mr. Anstruther had delighted in harassing Sir Roland on a point on which he knew he would be particularly susceptible, yet there was a feeling within him which would have made it impossible for him to have betrayed the knowledge he had so ungenerously obtained, to any other human being. His mind paid an involuntary tribute of respect to the noble qualities of his late companion, though he would not on any account that this feeling should have been perceived. He did not, indeed, acknowledge it to himself; for like many in this world, in order to deceive others, he tried first to deceive himself.

Sir Roland, having escaped from what was to him
as a scorpion's nest, gladly exchanged Mr. Anstruther's
society for that of Mr. Scott, with whom he generally
rode at that hour.

"It is very wise of me," he said, as they passed
into the pure and fragrant air, "to go through my
purgatorio just before my hour for going out and
being with you. I always go to Anstruther before my
ride, for I do not think I could sit down to my papers
immediately on leaving his room. My mind always
feels as if it had been rubbed up the wrong way, and I
need the air to smoothe it down again; and you gain,
too, prodigiously by the contrast, Scott—the foil sets
you off to admiration."

"I am much obliged both to him and to you; but
you seem more than usually rubbed up to-day, Ashton,
you look gloomy and wrathful. It is very odd, but
though every one that knows Anstruther agrees, that
not a word he says is worth attending to, yet every one
does attend to it; and he is so full of those 'reckless
sarcasms, those jests which scald like tears,' that he has
the power of sending every one from his presence with
a sting in their mind—a something which spite of
themselves irritates them whenever it recurs, fretting
the mental cuticle, as the needle arrows of the Lillipu-
tians tormented the corporeal epidermis of the unfortunate Gulliver. He either abuses your mother—or
praises your father with a 'but'—or tells some pleasant story of some one, 'who made himself so very
ridiculous,' quite forgetting, of course, till the end,
that it was all about your own brother,—laments the
'propensity' that the person he fancies you like 'has
to flirting,' &c.,—or repeats, or rather invents for the

occasion, something that your best friend has said against you—quite shocked, when he has done so, at his inadvertence—as he was 'particularly charged not to repeat it.'"

"Yes; he pretended to repeat something that you had said of me to-day; but 'il volpe soprafino,' over-leaped the mark there. Had he put it upon any one else, I might have fancied it true; but I certainly did not as coming from you."

"What was it?"

"Oh! merely something about my not being a perfect Metternich — nothing of any consequence; merely thrown out to give the pleasing impression that you talked to him contemptuously of me."

"Was it that which gave you your unwonted ruffling? Or had our experienced friend been fishing in deeper waters?" asked Mr. Scott.

"They must be deep waters, indeed, if they are deeper than those you swim in, as regards me," returned his companion, with a kindly glance, which, however, gave immediate place to a look of annoyance, and displeasure, as he continued, "But, perhaps, truth makes me confess it was the deepest depths that he disturbed to-day, for he spoke of *her*. But he did not abuse her, and that was being very gracious, and I was a fool to be so annoyed. But don't you know what a bore it is, for a person suddenly, with great eyes watching you, to name any thing—any one of that kind—and the light full in your face? No retreat — no burying your-self in a folio, or 'bending over embroidery-frames,' as distressed damsels in novels always do on such occasions!"

"No; I don't know what a bore it is," answered

Mr. Scott; "for I never had 'any thing, or any one of that kind,' whom I cared about being mentioned, even in the brightest sunshine. I often wish I had, for though your friendship satisfies me now, yet when you are at home again, I might have been one of the

' Scots wha hae wi' Wallace bled,'

for aught you would care."

"You are fishing for compliments now," said Sir Roland; "but you may as well put up your rod, for you will catch nothing to-day, nor get even a single rise out of me. The waters of my mind are muddy, and altogether at their lowest ebb. But without joking, I do feel greatly annoyed at having that feeling — which it was long before I could name even to you — touched by hands so rude as his."

"Ay, I remember it was a long time before you mentioned the subject to me; and then it was more by accident than good-will; for which I owe you a special grudge, dotted down duly — with mem.: to be paid off with aggravation, some fine day."

CHAPTER VI.

"Her lot is on you—silent tears to weep;
And patient smiles to wear through suffering's hour;
And sumless riches from affection's deep,
To pour on broken reeds a wasted shower;
And to make idols, and to find them clay;
And to bewail that worship,—therefore pray!"

MRS. HEMANS.

"Plant with earliest care
The seeds you most desire should fill the soil."

Walks in a Forest.

"I give thee to thy God—the God that gave thee,
A well-spring of deep gladness to my heart!
And, precious as thou art,
And pure as dew of Hermon, He shall have thee,
My own, my beautiful, my undefiled!
And thou shalt be His child."—MRS. HEMANS.

DAY after day did Sir Roland prosecute his labour of love towards Mr. Anstruther; and a labour of heavenly love it was—often a most irksome one. The physicians had informed Lord N——, that even if the invalid regained sufficient strength to enable him to remove to a warmer climate, and thus prolong his life for a time, yet that his lungs, naturally weak, had been so much affected by the violent attack he had had, that it was impossible he could ever wholly recover; and that they thought, indeed, that any fresh cold, or excitement of the chest, might speedily become fatal. With this knowledge, Sir Roland could not bear to neglect any means that might rouse the being, whose mortal life was so precarious, to a sense of his lost condition before God.

A character like Mr. Anstruther's is happily rare; but unhappily not wholly unknown in this world of varied sins. Some there are who even exceed him in intentional malice; for, though he took a feline pleasure in playing with the feelings of his victims, yet he was not always fully aware of the degree of pain he occasioned. There was a perpetual spring of irritation and virulence within himself, which vented itself recklessly on others, just as the Catherine-wheel, fretting round its own centre, dispenses its burning sparks on all around.

In order to account for the peculiarities in his character, we must look a little to his early years; for in his case, as in most others, the bitter fruits of evil proceeded more from the training than from the natural quality of the tree which produced them.

His mother, amiable and sweet by nature, had been educated in the purest school of Christianity, and had early learned its life-giving lessons; but far different was her husband in every way, though his real character was, for a length of time, wholly unsuspected by her. Her parents had died some years before, and she, an only child, had been left to the guardianship of her maternal grandfather, whose age and retired habits had long kept him aloof from all those who could have opened his eyes as to the character of the man who sought his grandchild's hand. Exceedingly handsome,

and very prepossessing where he wished to please, Mr.
Anstruther won upon the old man by his kind and
deferential manners; his conversation, too, was full
of animation and anecdote; and he would often
lament, with apparent candour and sincerity, the deficiencies of his own education in matters of religion.
But little did the old man, or the young maiden
suspect that these pleasing qualities were but cloaks
to hide the darkness of his heart, and that his
hours, when absent from them, were spent in the
society of persons of the worst and most unprincipled
description.

When in love with the rich and beautiful Miss
Gascoigne, he could with tolerable patience hearken to
her earnest conversation on religious subjects; for a
man, in such a case, will listen with pleasure to any
thing from the voice that is to him all melody! and
the attention thus yielded is often attributed, with ill-
placed modesty, to the weight of the argument rather
than to the charm of the preacher. "Affection is very
hopeful;" and Miss Gascoigne, with a facility which in
more cases than hers has been fraught with misery,
though she felt Mr. Anstruther was not a thorough
Christian in principle, yet believing that he was well
inclined, and that, under her influence and admonitions,
he would soon become all she could wish, in an ill-fated
hour consented to be his wife.

For some time all went on smoothly; and bright
was the dawn of the married life of this ill-assorted
pair. Mr. Anstruther still for a time continued to
listen patiently to the words of his wife; for it was
hard to refuse attention to one so lovely, and so earnest
in her zeal! But when the novelty of the thing wore

off, his patient endurance of themes so uncongenial to his mind departed also.

The birth of George, their first and only child, soon formed an excuse to the hitherto tolerably attentive husband to absent himself more than he had before done from his home; for, with his sweetest smile, he would tell his wife, that now, as she would not be alone, he would go again a little among friends he had long neglected, and who had often reproached him for his continued absence.

The young mother sighed to think that what had doubled the attraction of home to her should prove a reason for her husband's more frequently leaving her; but, strong in her confidence in him, she felt it merely as a loss of pleasure and comfort to herself.   Soon, however, she began to find a sensible alteration in his manner when he was with her; for he no longer exerted himself to be agreeable, or made any effort to restrain his naturally irritable disposition.   He was indifferent to his child, and morose to her; and she began to feel, with fearful force, the effects of her unfaithfulness to God in having united herself to one of an unconverted spirit.

Her doating fondness for her child served at times to beguile her from her sorrows; and in her husband's presence she always exerted herself to be cheerful.   She rarely now, however, ventured to speak to him on the subject of religion, but one day, when she had unconsciously adverted to it, she was surprised to see him not only appear calm, but with somewhat of his old accustomed kindness of manner, encourage her to proceed; and her heart beat with a flutter of happiness not to be expressed, when, as she continued with animated hope to speak on the subject, she saw him take her Bible in his hand, and, carefully turning its pages, seem to search for some particular passage. His long dark lashes completely hid the expression of his eye as he examined the holy volume; but after a few minutes, he raised his head, and turning the book to her, he pointed to the passage he had been seeking. There was a bland smile on his lips as he did so; but the look of dark malignity which glared from his eye so terrified his trembling wife, that she had scarcely power or senses left to see the words he marked.

"Read it," he said in a suppressed tone.

She read: "Be ye not unequally yoked together with unbelievers."

"May I ask," said Mr. Anstruther, in his smoothest manner, "whether those words had ever met your eye when you married me?"

Mrs. Anstruther, cast down as by a stunning blow from the bright happiness in which she had been indulging, was nearly fainting with terror as he asked the question, and was wholly unable to reply. Her husband, triumphing in the pain he was inflicting, again addressed her in his sweetest tone. She gave a trembling answer in the affirmative.

"And did you," he continued in the same voice, "consider me at that time what pious and excellent people would call—a believer? Answer me candidly, I shall not be offended." Still his unhappy wife could command no word.

"Did you," he resumed, in a restrained and concentrated voice, "consider me, at the time of our happy marriage, as deserving to be ranked by the devout amongst the number of believers?"

Mrs. Anstruther covered her face with her hands,

and, bursting into an agony of tears, answered,
" No."

He grasped her arm with violence, and his voice
trembled with passion, as he exclaimed,—

" Then never again dare to speak on the subject of
religion, or intrude your accursed cant upon me. You
should learn to obey before you preach, and not attempt
hypocritically to force on others the dull morality you
choose to spurn at your own convenience." *

So saying, he cast her from him, and left the room
with thundering tread. Mrs. Anstruther, more dead
than alive, sat rooted to her chair; her mind was in a
state of complete bewilderment, for unprincipled as
she had discovered her husband to be, he had till then
been tolerably respectful in his behaviour to her, and
she was little prepared for this outbreak of passion and
cruelty.

Bitterly did she, indeed, feel that the inconsistency
of her conduct had brought upon her this terrible trial;
and, also, that it had done discredit to the holy cause
she had so much at heart. " Be sure your sin will
find you out," rung in her ears, and smote upon her
heart with overwhelming force ; and with deep humiliation did she confess the justness of her punishment,
that it was " right she should be humbled," and by him,
too, for whom she had offended. Many had been the
struggles she had had with her conscience before she
had determined to marry Mr. Anstruther; but affection
had triumphed over faith and principle, and now she
had to eat the bitter fruits of her own planting.

---

* An incident, somewhat similar to the one here supposed,
occurred in real life, and is in print somewhere.

From that time she saw but little of her husband; and, when he did come home, it was but to harass and torment the gentle creature, whose oppressed spirit fast sunk beneath his unkindness. Her boy was her only earthly comfort, and richly did he return the love that was so overflowingly lavished on him. Yet, even on this last remaining spot of bliss, did the blight seem in part to have fallen. The child was often present when his father came home, and was therefore a frequent witness of the cruelty with which his mother was treated; and Mrs. Anstruther was terrified when she saw the effect of these things on his appearance. An expression of fierce anger would shoot from beneath his lowering brows, while he sat with closed teeth and clenched hand, as if ready to spring upon his father; and well as she appreciated the love that made him feel so strongly, yet her heart grieved to see in one so young the evidence of such violent feelings. He never, how-ever, mentioned these things to her, for he early shewed symptoms of that *tact* which in after-life was so remark-able a feature in his character; but after scenes of this kind, he would go to her, and strive to soothe her unhappiness by redoubling his own caresses.

His little couch was placed by hers at night, but often would he steal into her arms and slumber there. Her restlessness—the restlessness of an unhappy heart—taught him to be wakeful too; and often would he, in the darkness of night, put out his hand to stroke her face, and try with childish art to discover whether there were tears upon her cheek; and, when he found them there, he would creep closer still, and, putting his soft arms round her neck, would murmur words of love and fondness, till sleep again closed his weary eyes.

His mother loved him with an intensity scarcely to
be imagined by a happier spirit, and delighted in
early teaching him the things of God, and seeking to
fill his heart with the love of his Heavenly Father.
She delighted, long after the sweet days of babyhood
had passed, to be with him at that happy time when
the little wearied body seeks joyfully the repose to be
found in a mother's cradling arms; and when the
tranquil heart, soothed into forgetfulness of the more
boisterous pleasures of the day, is open to all the
sweetest emotions of love and tenderness—and then
would she speak to him of God.

In all the outward and visible scenes of creation
there is a voice which may remind us of inward
spiritual things. God does not send his gentle dews
upon the earth, when the noontide ray, with fervid
heat, would exhale them ere they had had time to
refresh the parched and drooping herb; but He sends
them silently down at the calm evening hour, when the
sun has ceased to exercise its burning force, and the
hushed winds are gone; and there they rest, sinking
deep into the heart of the grass and flowers, till, with
gentle influence, they have refreshed and nourished all
around. And thus should faithful parents watch for
the stilly hours of life to drop sweet, holy words into
their young babes' hearts, ere yet the world has made
them all its own!

Amongst the other evil habits in which George
Anstruther's father indulged, gambling found a place;
and before many years of his married life were past,
he had dissipated almost all the large fortune which he
had obtained with his wife. Without a moment's
warning, that unhappy woman found herself hurled

from affluence to almost absolute penury; and she retired with her child to a small obscure house in the country. Her friends, however, did not desert her; and amongst the most constant and attached was Lady Ashton, and many a month did she spend at Llanaven. But when George Anstruther was about six years old, grief and anxiety had made such fearful ravages in his mother's naturally delicate constitution, that it became evident that her life would soon come to a close; and for above a year before her death she was wholly confined to her own home, and was, therefore, entirely separated from all her friends. Her husband seldom visited her; and, when he did, it was only to vent upon her and upon her child that spleen which he dared not openly indulge in the world.

Precluded from the society of others of his age, the leading characteristics of George Anstruther's disposition became morbidly developed. His love for his mother was almost idolatry; yet was it scarcely a stronger feeling than his hatred for his father; and between these two strong passions his heart seemed completely divided. He had but few of the occupations and pursuits of childhood, for his mother's extreme weakness made her unequal to the task of carrying on his education; so that at seven years old he was an infant in learning—though a giant in feeling. At length the sad day of his mother's death arrived; "where the wicked cease from troubling, and the weary are at rest," there did that meek and suffering creature find peace and happiness at last.

For some time after this event Mr. Anstruther was obliged to have his child with him; but, finding that too great a restraint on his usual habits, he soon sent

him to school. The place he selected was not one
where much that was valuable was likely to be taught;
and there were none there who could in any way excite
feelings of affection in the boy; so that, though surrounded by a crowd, he still felt alone. His heart,
finding nothing to satisfy it, became bitter in its feelings;
and the lessons of heavenly love and wisdom he had
heard from his mother gradually died away from his
memory now that her voice was no longer there to
enforce them. During his holydays, his most unnatural
father used to amuse himself by taking him with him
into the haunts of folly and vice, and in teaching him
to gamble and drink, and take the oaths and words of
older sinners in his lips. But his ever-increasing de-
testation of his father was so far a happy thing, that it
made him hate all that he heard him praise, and taught
him to avoid, through all his after years, the sinful
excesses which he had witnessed in him; but it filled
his whole heart with a root of bitterness so intense and
engrossing, that he seemed almost incapable of any
other feeling; and the hatred which one being deserved from him but too well, extended itself to the
whole human race. It might, indeed, be said to reach
even to the Almighty; for his soul rebelled continually
at His decrees, and ever regarded the death of his mother
as a dispensation fraught with tyrannic cruelty. Could
he have borne to have cherished her remembrance in his
mind, it might have soothed his lacerated feelings, and
calmed his proud and troubled heart; and her heavenly
words, returning upon his soul, might have won him back
to love and peace. But the thought of her brought with
it an agony too great to be endured; he knew nothing
of her happiness in heaven—nothing of the love of

God—so no consolation came to mitigate the intensity
of his grief. A dark misanthropy took possession of
his breast, and, if he could ever be said to partake of
any pleasure, it was when he was disturbing in others
that peace which seemed to have fled his own unhappy
spirit for ever.

Such was the being with whose wayward mood Sir
Roland bore so patiently; for he knew somewhat of his
history from Lady Ashton, and felt a deep commiseration
for him.

Mr. Anstruther's father had so far done him justice
as to give him a good education at school and college;
and Lady Ashton, interesting herself in him for his
mother's sake, had induced her brother to take him
abroad as one of his *attachés.* His uncommon talents
and discerning mind made him most useful to Lord
N——, who, on a vacancy occurring, obtained for
him the appointment of secretary of embassy.

There was little in the present which could encourage Sir Roland in his self-denying task; but from
his knowledge of the past, he drew hope for the future;
and knowing from Lady Ashton's account of the
many prayers which the devoted mother had offered
up for her child, he looked forward with the hope of
faith to the fruition of those prayers—to the time when
this now dark heart should be wholly turned to God.
Mr. Anstruther's occasional bursts of feeling—coming
forth, like the flash of the volcano, from the cold bosom
of the earth—revealed the existence of good and strong
feeling somewhere in the depths of his being; and Sir
Roland trusted that he might be enabled, by the blessing of God, to open that fount of fire, and see its
flame, purified and sanctified, rise even unto heaven !

Impatient of his long confinement, Mr. Anstruther took advantage of one warm, lovely day to go out, and once again see the beauties of nature, from the enjoyment of which he had been so long debarred; but though balmy and soft, the outward air was too keen for his lungs, and brought on an increase of cough and of feverish excitement, which sent him again to his room and sofa. Sir Roland now saw that he must press on the work of the Lord. He had hitherto waited for an opening to be made visibly before him; but now he resolved boldly to bring forward the subject, and force it upon the attention of the being whose mortal span was so evidently coming to a close.

His uncle had not at that time much pressing business on his hands, and he might have obtained leave to visit England for a few weeks; but ardently as he desired to see his mother, and to return to Lady Constance, he could not at this juncture bear to desert one who seemed so wholly dependent upon him. He knew that he was the only person whose presence was at all valued by him, or who would speak to him any thing that might benefit his soul; and though it cost him a bitter struggle, yet he felt (like his great Master) that he came into this world, " not to do his own will, but the will of Him who sent him;" and resigning his own pleasure, he gave himself wholly to the work that God seemed to have set before him.

On visiting the invalid a few days after the exposure which had brought on so severe a relapse, he found him much exhausted, but still endeavouring to assume an appearance of gaiety and unconcern; though the expression of his countenance, when not speaking,

evidently betrayed that both mind and body were ill
at ease.

Sir Roland, who began perfectly to understand his
character, was aware that the ordinary mode of entering on religious subjects always utterly failed with
him.   Keen-sighted and wily, he detected from afar
any attempt to introduce the subject incidentally into
conversation, and instantly defeated the purpose of the
speaker.

The regular attack, too, was not more successful
than the " sap and mine ;" for he would not meet the
enemy, but peremptorily refused to enter on the
subject.   Sudden and strong remarks, and sayings
which could neither be anticipated nor parried, were
therefore the means Sir Roland determined to use,
hoping that—like a shell thrown into a citadel—(to follow out the military simile) they might fall and burst
upon him unawares, scattering the inmates that had too
long held possession of the place.

The sick man, in whose countenance there was
already more of death than life, was running on in his
usual reckless manner, when Sir Roland, with his eye
firmly, yet in sorrow, fixed upon him, said,—

" How can you, Anstruther, with the grave open
before you — which you know must so soon receive
you — ' death, and after that the judgment ! '—how can
you bear to think and talk on in such a way ? "

Mr. Anstruther had sometimes had a misgiving
that there was some danger in his case ; but his mind
had ever repelled the thought the instant it had arisen ;
and worldly friends, whose " tender mercies " are, indeed, in such cases most " cruel," had contributed to

keep apprehension from him, by talking of " the things he would soon be able to do"—of " the places he would soon visit with them," &c.; and though his physician, more faithful, had often insinuated his fears, yet with desperate self-delusion he would never give credit to what he said. When, therefore, he heard Sir Roland speak in so startling a manner, the shock which his mind received was too great to allow of his uttering a sound in reply. He knew him too well to suspect him of saying willingly one harsh or unfeeling word; and a voice from within his hollow and aching breast also rose up in accents that would not be silenced, and told him that it was all too true—that his days indeed were numbered ! Drops of agony burst from his brow, and the intense anxiety of his countenance was more than Sir Roland could bear to look at. In a few moments, however, he had mastered his strong emotion ; and asking Sir Roland for the *eau de luce* which stood near him, he remarked, with a faint but calm voice, that the heat was very great, and that a pain sometimes passed through his chest, which for a time took away his breath ; but " it was now gone," he said: " it was only a spasm, and of no consequence."

Sir Roland busied himself with a book which was before him, and desired him not to mind him, but to keep himself quiet. He saw that the bolt had sped ; and he was thankful that the effort, so painful to himself, had not been in vain. After awhile he read aloud a passage from the book he was looking at, which afforded an opportunity of saying something of the concerns of eternity ; but Mr. Anstruther, again assuming his reckless manner, turned his head away with affected nausea, and waving his hands deprecatingly, said,—

" No preaching, my good fellow, if you love me !
I have the greatest possible aversion to your preachers
and sermonisers. Bad enough in the open air, where
one may be lucky enough to lose half that is said; but
in this confined space, to fill the atmosphere with lugubrious warnings, and amiable consignments of your
friends to perdition, is quite overpowering, and enough
to ' vex the sick man dead.' Positively, my dear fellow,
if I am to admit you here at all, it must be on the well-
understood condition that there are to be no distasteful,
and to me unprofitable, lecturings. The thing is so
very vulgar and methodistical — quite discreditable !
Do oblige me, and keep all that sort of thing for the
exquisite, the evangelical Scott. I am quite unworthy
of it; and indeed, I must repeat, that if I admit you
here at all, it must be on condition of these subjects
being entirely excluded. Charmed to see you ! but
cannot have any preaching."

Sir Roland had walked to the window and was gazing at the beauty of the scene before him.

" If your eyes can bear the full light, Anstruther,
turn them this way a moment," he said, as he withdrew
the blind that shaded the landscape from his view.
The sun shone brightly, and it was indeed a lovely
scene he looked upon. Mr. Anstruther gazed for a
moment, then turned away with a sigh of sickening
regret.

" Why," he exclaimed sullenly, " am I to be shewn
the charm of things I cannot enjoy ?—But it is, I suppose, one of your saintly practices to aggravate men's
sufferings ;— for the good of their souls doubtless ; "
and he smiled with bitter scorn.

" No," replied Sir Roland, " it was not for that ;

but, if I am to continue visiting you at all, our intercourse must be put upon a right footing. You know
that our dispositions have never suited; our feelings—
in most respects, our thoughts, opinions, and principles
—are diametrically opposed to each other; and you
have for years been one whose society I have avoided,
as you have avoided mine. I bring these things before
you on the one hand, and I shew you the enchanting
loveliness of nature at this moment on the other, in
order that you may clearly and fully understand, that it
cannot be for my own personal pleasure that I leave the
free and perfumed air, and the society congenial to me,
for this sick room, with one—an alien from God, a
self-doomed stranger to peace and hope. If, therefore,
there are to be conditions respecting my visiting you, I
think it is for me to dictate them."

Mr. Anstruther's countenance underwent the most
violent changes while Sir Roland was speaking. The
firm, and even stern tenor of his speech, so unlike his
usual tone, completely thunderstruck him. Surprise,
pride, indignation, alternately swayed his mind; and
his heightened colour and furious look shewed the anger
that he felt. At length, with a bitter smile of derision,
he said, " I might have expected this, knowing you
were one of those who proverbially kick at the sick
lion."

Sir Roland's colour rose in his turn, and his eye
flashed with anger at this insolent speech; but restraining himself till his irritation had subsided (which
in his well-regulated mind it did not take many instants
to effect), and looking with sorrow on the worn being
before him, he answered calmly,—

" You are no lion, Anstruther—nor am I—an ass;"

and an irrepressible smile played over his countenance.
" We are both men of like passions, though not of
like principles !"

Mr. Anstruther's own gentlemanlike mind and feelings had made him feel shocked at the intemperance of
his last speech the moment it had passed his lips; but
he was too proud to apologise—so merely answered Sir
Roland's quiet reply by saying,—

" I wonder, then, that you cast your precious
pearls before such a reprobate as, doubtless, you consider me !"

" Far from it," said Sir Roland ; " it is because I
yet hope that you may prove not to be a reprobate, in
the Scripture sense of the word, that I continue to
visit you—because, as has been truly said, 'heavenly
love, though it makes one prefer to dwell with the
children of God, yet makes one also yearn over the
godless and profane.' I leave you now ; but if I
come again—remember the conditions must be of my
making."

CHAPTER VII.

" Where shalt thou turn ? It is not thine to raise
To yon pure heaven thy calm confiding gaze,
No gleam reflected from that realm of rest
Steals on the darkness of thy troubled breast.
*   *   *   *   *
Oh ! while the doom impends, not yet decreed ;
While yet the Atoner hath not ceased to plead ;
While still, suspended by a single hair,
The sharp, bright sword hangs quivering in the air ;
Bow down thy heart to Him who will not break
The bruised reed,—e'en yet awake, awake !
Patient, because Eternal, He may hear
The prayer of agony with pitying ear,
And send his chastening Spirit from above,
O'er the deep chaos of thy soul to move.
*   *   *   *   *
But seek thou mercy through His name alone
To whose unequalled sorrows none was shewn.
*   *   *   *   *
Call thou on Him, for He, in human form,
Hath walk'd the waves of life and still'd the storm."
MRS. HEMANS.

MR. ANSTRUTHER's mind, when he was left alone,
was in a perfect whirl of agitation and passion. Notwithstanding his abuse of Sir Roland's principles, he
had always internally respected him for them, and for
the consistency with which he had maintained them.
But he had been used of late rather to consider him as
one whose spirit wanted energy and courage ; (being

little aware that his patient forbearance towards him
was like that which a mother shews to the wayward
humours of a sick child) and he had, consequently, been
in the frequent habit of speaking to him in a contemptuous and overbearing manner. But his last
speech had been so unlike what he had ever heard
from him before, that he felt the current of his feelings
towards him suddenly and strangely changed; and
amid the tumult of his other contending emotions, the
conviction pressed itself upon his mind, that this last
stern remonstrance had been dictated, not by impetuous passion, but by calm, deliberate judgment, and
that Sir Roland, in fact, had said nothing in which he
was not fully justified;—and with this conviction his
respect for him rose immeasurably.

Sir Roland, indeed, had found that it was needful
to assert a supremacy over Mr. Anstruther's temper,
before he could hope to obtain a patient hearing of
those things to which he was so anxious to draw his
attention; and it was that which caused him to speak
as he had done; for he knew that if he were despised
—so would also be the message he had to deliver.

After a time — and when all indignation had died
away from Mr. Anstruther's mind—what had been said
on the subject of his danger took full possession of him;
and the many words of warning which his physician
had spoken from time to time, and which, till now,
he had always endeavoured to disbelieve, returned
to his memory, confirming the fatal fear which rose
before him, and filling his soul with terror.   Sir Roland's words, "The grave open before you!—the grave
open before you!" sounded again and again in his
ears, and rung like a knell through his heart.   He

heard it in his hollow cough—he felt it in the throbbing of his fevered temples—he saw it in his almost transparent hands! Like scorching lightning the conviction glared upon him—that he was dying! His brain seemed on fire! He clasped his hands to his head, and buried his face in the cushions as if to shut out from sight and hearing the terrific image that pursued him; but there it was—" Death!—and after that—the judgment!"

How long he lay there, he knew not, for a torpor of horror took possession of him.—He was aroused, however, after a time, by the sound of Sir Roland's voice. It was faint, but it came with thrilling power to him; and starting up, in spite of his weakness, he hurried to the window. It was open, for the heat was oppressive, and leaning against it to support himself, he gazed on the world before him. The sun had about an hour longer to run his course, and was streaming in floods of golden light through an opening in the dark and heavy thunder-clouds, which had begun already to send forth their indistinct mutterings. The mountains were crimson with the setting rays, and stood out in bright relief against the leaden sky, whilst the majestic river rolled its ample waters in light beneath; and nearer, and just below the walls, the *glacis* extended its lovely groves and gardens, lying in deepest shade. But these, and many other lovely things, were scarcely noted by the dying man, whose whole soul seemed riveted on one individual on the ramparts below. Sir Roland was standing there alone; but the sound of retreating steps shewed that some one had just been with him. He had taken off his cap, which with his riding-whip lay by his side on the grass, and he looked

unusually pale, while, from time to time, he passed his
hand across his brow to throw back his waving hair, as
if to cool himself. The beauties of the scene around
seemed lost also upon him, for his eyes were raised
above them all ;—yet not as in prayer, but as in abstraction—and his thoughts seemed troubled, for a sad
expression rested on his fine features. (He had had
letters from England, and they had brought all home
before his heart, and had left a feeling of depression on
his mind.) Mr. Anstruther would have given worlds to
have spoken to him—to have called him up—to have
clasped in kindness a hand, which till then had been
almost valueless to him. The yearning of his heart was
inexpressible, and his strong desire to speak to him almost
made him involuntarily pronounce his name, for he felt
as if he held life and death in his hands for him. He
controlled himself, however, and kept silence ; but it
was not without a feeling almost of despair that he saw
Sir Roland turn away without raising his eyes to his
window, and walk slowly across the little bridge which
connected the rampart with the ambassador's house.

He went early to rest that night, for he was quite
exhausted; but he could not sleep. As he tossed upon
his feverish couch, how desolate he felt ! Strong emotion had passed away ; but as his mind, in the vague
light-headedness of fever, wandered from thought to
thought, all seemed dull, and dark, and dreary ! He
was alone in the world ! no human being loved him !
— he had cut himself off by his own will and
choice from all the sympathies of his kind. For the
first time in his life he felt a terror of being alone ;—the
flickering lamp sent up strange figures and shadows

through the room, which his distempered wandering fancy shaped into demons and ill spirits brooding over him. Once and again he had his hand upon the bell to summon his servant to him, fancying that something living might be near; but, ashamed of betraying his weakness, he withdrew it and bore on, till at length a heavy, troubled slumber fell upon his eyes. His mind, however, still continued working, and the agitation of his countenance and hands, and his knit brow, shewed that strife was going on within.

The elements, too, without were busy. The storm, which had been threatening for some hours, drew nearer and nearer, and peals of continuous thunderings rolled round and round the city, like the roar of distant artillery. Still the sleeper was not aroused, though the sounds seemed to mingle with the images in his mind, adding to their fearful and oppressive nature. His frame became convulsed, and the damp dews stood upon his brow, and tremors shook him from head to foot, as the thunder grew louder and nearer; till at length one tremendous crash, which seemed as if the welkin itself were rent asunder, burst over the city. He started up wildly, and clasping his hands above his head he shrieked,—

" He comes ! Oh, God ! Not yet, not yet—have mercy—yet a little !" and he sunk back again breathless.

His servant, who had also been awakened by the storm, hearing his master's voice, hurried into his room, and advanced to the bed-side.

" Who are you ?" said Mr. Anstruther, in alarm, for his mind was still wandering and unsettled.

The servant spoke, and on recognising him the

invalid breathed a deep sigh of relief, and said, "The
storm awoke me, and my head is distracted!"

The man gave him something, and asked if he
should stay with him; but the proposal was made in
so cold and unwilling a tone, that he could not bear
to accept it; so dismissing him, he again laid his throbbing and fevered head on his pillow. "Yes, I am
alone," he thought; "not even he cares for me! and
why should he? I have never considered him but as
one paid to do unwilling service — as a tool of my
convenience; why should he care for me?" Yet
the thought added somewhat more bitterness to his
feelings.

He was too much shaken to get up early the next
day, and had, indeed, but just risen to his sofa when Sir
Roland's well-known, and now most welcome, footstep
sounded on the stair. How did his approach agitate
him! The blood rushed so quickly through his frame
that he could scarcely breathe, and no sound could
he distinguish but the rapid beatings of his pulse.
There was the being for whose presence he had so
much longed; who had seemed all the world to him!
He was at the door — in the room — and how was he
received? While his hand was yet on the unturned
lock, Mr. Anstruther felt as if he could have flown to
his feet; but the moment their eyes met — kind and
gentle as was Sir Roland's look — pride, indomitable
pride, unexpected even by himself, rose in Mr. Anstruther's breast, and cold and repellent was the glance
he gave him in return. His agitation, however, he
could not quell, nor stop the quivering of his lip. His
utterance seemed choked, and, to cover his embarrass-

ment, he affected a cough, which soon became but too natural, and it was long before his debilitated frame recovered from its effects. Sir Roland was deeply distressed at witnessing his sufferings, and did all in his power to alleviate them; but when the paroxysm was over, Mr. Anstruther thanked him coldly, and kept his head averted from him.

Sir Roland had, however, marked the feelings which agitated him at his first entrance, and was not daunted by his subsequent repulsive manner; he saw his own line of conduct now, and was determined steadily to pursue it.

" I was afraid the storm might have disturbed you last night," he began, after a while; " did you hear much of it?"

" No, not much; just the last clap or two; they were very loud."

" They were indeed terrific," said Sir Roland, " I never heard so awful a storm. The lightning was incessant; and I could not help thinking of the fire that must go forth at the coming of our Lord to destroy his enemies, and to cleanse this earth from ' all things that offend;' though doubtless it was but a faint image of that tremendous hour."

Mr. Anstruther shook with agitation, but he determined, if possible, not to betray it. After a few minutes he began, in a light tone,—

" It is lucky the storm came last night instead of this evening; such a display would be rather awkward amongst all the horses and carriages at Count ——'s to-night. What costume do you adopt for the occasion?"

" I am not going ; I dine out of town with Lord Wentworth."

" Oh, ay ! I suppose a select circle of the saints are to meet there, to shake their heads over the pomps and vanities of this wicked world, and to comfort themselves with the pleasing assurance, that all who dance to-night will be sure of suffering for it hereafter. You stay away from those innocent and cheerful amusements, I suppose, by way of what you call ' confessing God before men.'"

" No," said Sir Roland, " I have given that up ;— on consideration, I do not think that that will answer."

Mr. Anstruther looked round with unfeigned astonishment.

" You see," continued Sir Roland, " there are two parties to all arguments. Now our Lord has said, ' Whosoever will confess me before men, him will I confess before the angels of my Father who is in heaven.' Now I am not quite sure that that is the sort of company I should like to have about me through an endless eternity,— I rather think there would be something more *piquant* in the other—and only alternative. The company of lost souls—the lake of fire— evil spirits, ' the smoke of whose torment goeth up for ever and ever '—such are the things I choose for eternity ; and in order to secure them, I have determined to enrol myself now in the ranks of the ' Prince of this world,' who is also the ' Prince of the power of darkness.'"

Though Mr. Anstruther perceived in an instant that Sir Roland spoke ironically, yet he had no power to interrupt him ; the fearful images he presented to his mind, as he spoke in a rapid yet solemn manner, recalled so terribly the awful visions that had oppressed him during the past night, that his blood curdled in his veins. The fiery dart of conviction was in his heart, and every touch renewed its agonising torture. Yet still he attempted to speak lightly and contemptuously, endeavouring to hide from Sir Roland the effect of his words.

"Do you suppose," he said, "that you are speaking to a fool?"

"No," replied Sir Roland, in the deep earnestness of his fine voice; "'the fool hath said his *heart* there is no God;' you, Anstruther, say so only with your lips. Your heart acknowledges that there *is* a God, and at this moment you are feeling His tremendous power. 'The arrows of the Lord stick fast in you, and His hand presseth you sore.'"

"I will not tolerate this!" exclaimed Mr. Anstruther, with violent irritation; "what right have you to speak to me in this way—of these things?"

"I have," replied Sir Roland, "the right, which Christ gives to all who know His love, to proclaim it to others. Knowing, also, the terrors of the Lord, I would endeavour to persuade you; and as though Christ did speak to you by me at this moment, I do beseech you to be reconciled to God."

"I cannot endure this,—I cannot—cannot endure this!" exclaimed Mr. Anstruther, in frightful agitation. After a pause, however, he murmured, in a low and touching tone, "There was but one voice—but one—from which I could brook to hear such words; and that voice—those words—are lost for ever."

"Not lost!" exclaimed Sir Roland; "a Christian

mother's holy words and prayers cannot be lost. They
are treasured up in heaven as purest things ever had
in remembrance before God, and must either sink
the soul of the sinner into tenfold night, or bring
down, in God's good time, a blessing on the being so
fondly, faithfully cared for."

He spoke with deep emotion, and approaching Mr.
Anstruther, who lay on the sofa with his face turned
from him, kindly put his hand on his shoulder. Mr.
Anstruther buried his face in his hands, while his
whole frame trembled with excessive agitation. Both
were silent — at length Mr. Anstruther said, with much
feeling, —

"I cannot speak to you now, Ashton, but will you
come again ?"

He held out his hand and grasped that of Sir
Roland, who, promising soon to return, left the room.

As he could not well avoid fulfilling his dinner
engagement, Sir Roland gave up his ride that day
in order to be able soon again to return to Mr.
Anstruther ; and he sent to Mr. Scott to desire that
he would not wait for him. He regretted this trifling act
of self-denial the less, because he felt extremely averse
at that moment to speaking about Mr. Anstruther
even to Mr. Scott ; for though he had often lamented
to the latter the obdurate aversion of the other to
the things of God, yet that was matter of common
notoriety, and what any one might have remarked ;
but what had just passed he felt was wholly between
himself and the dying man, and, with proper delicacy,
he could not endure at that moment to make it matter
of discussion with any one else.

Mr. Anstruther, when Sir Roland had left him, felt like one in a dream. Indistinct images floated before his troubled imagination — thought chased thought—feeling crowded on feeling, in wild confusion. Remorse—hope—fear—joy—horrible forebodings— softened recollections — all in turn rushed over his bewildered mind, and almost maddened him. After many fearful conflicts, however, the terrors of avenging wrath seemed to give way to feelings of some undefined tenderness which overflowed his soul. For the first time for many years he allowed the thought of his mother to remain with him; and resting his crossed arms upon the table, he leant his head on them, and tears — long, deep floods of tears — burst irrepressibly from his very heart.

When he grew more composed, though much exhausted, there was a calm in his breast to which he had long been a stranger; for the God who knew what manner of spirit he was of, in mercy had sent earthly affection as a messenger, "to make ready his way before him," in a soul that would else, humanly speaking, soon have given way to the demon of despair, or to a spirit of proud defiance.

Undoubtedly the *whole* work of salvation is of God; from first to last it is the work of His Spirit! But, in the prosecution of His great and good designs, our Heavenly Father almost invariably makes use of means; preparing first the ground of the heart, and then cultivating it according to the nature of the soil he has formed. Some He draws by love—others He compels to come by fear. To some He makes His voice to sound above the storms of earthly affliction; while others, again, He wins from amid the fulness of earthly joy and affection; speaking to them of a love greater than earth's — of a tenderness surpassing even that which a mother bears her child. And thus should those, who desire to promote His glory on the earth, endeavour to make themselves, as St. Paul says, "all things to all men, so that they may *any how* win some."

When Sir Roland returned to Mr. Anstruther's room, the latter received him with grateful kindness, though he could not naturally, as yet, brook to shew him the full workings of his mind, and even strove to hide from him all traces of his recent strong emotion.

"It is most kind of you," he said, after an uneasy pause, "to come again so soon; I fear you have sacrificed your ride for me, and I know by old experience, how pleasant that is, after such irksome work as you have to do."

"I shall get some fresh air in driving down to Lord Wentworth's to dinner," answered Sir Roland, "so I shall do very well."

There was another pause: for though the heart of each was very full of the other, and a strong bond of sympathy had arisen between them, yet both were oppressed by that embarrassment which any strong display of feeling invariably leaves, when the excitement which drew it forth has died away.

"Your disturbed night," at length Sir Roland said, "has left you languid to-day, Anstruther, and talking is too much for you. Shall I read a little?"

This considerate offer was a great relief to Mr. Anstruther, who gladly accepted it, saying, "He was indeed, unfit for any exertion that day."

"What shall I read?"

" Any thing you like," he replied.

He could not bring himself to say "the Bible," though he thirsted for its hitherto almost untasted waters. He also recollected with shame, that he actually did not possess a copy of the Holy Scriptures, so entirely had he neglected even the appearance of religion ; and he could not have borne to have confessed this fact to Sir Roland. He was much vexed however, when the latter, taking up a commonplace book of fiction which was lying on the table, asked, " if he should read that."

" If you like it," he replied, in a tone of disappointment.

Sir Roland glanced his eye over a few pages, and then read some passages, which described one of the characters as labouring under great trial and sorrow. The author of the work (evidently knowing of no higher source of comfort) fed the mind of his hero with the flimsy consolations of earth, teaching him to turn again to the world for that peace which, though the world can take away, yet never can it give.

" How completely, even in a book like this," observed Sir Roland, " one feels the insufficiency of such modes of comfort as these ! Often, in reading even works of fiction, getting interested in those I read about, I feel an ardent longing to shew them the only source of real comfort — to lead them to that God who is ' mighty to save, and also mighty to console;' and though the next moment I feel that what I am reading is but imaginary, yet I cannot but remember, that there are thousands of real cases of anguish and unutterable sorrow, in which the afflicted soul knows not where to go for comfort. Many, under the tor-

tures of a late remorse, seem ready to exclaim, like
Milton's Satan,

> 'Me miserable ! which way shall I fly
> Infinite wrath and infinite despair ?'

yet find no hand to point to the cross of Christ — no
voice to pour His soothing, pardoning words within their
ear.   Even this poor tempest-tossed child of fiction of
whom we have been reading, when one is carried away
by the interest so as to forget that it *is* fiction, how does
one yearn to tell him that there is provided for him freely
—pardon for his sins, strength for his weakness, comfort
for his griefs !   How different from the world's, are
the consolations which the Gospel offers to those who
sorrow, either for earthly natural griefs, or of that
' godly sorrow which worketh repentance.' "

He drew from his pocket a small Bible, and read
several passages, striking for their beauty, and for the
comfort they conveyed.   Mr. Anstruther's eyes became
riveted on his eloquent countenance as he read these
things, so applicable to his own case; and his mind
inwardly thanked him for the delicacy with which he
touched the wounds of his heart, while speaking of the
wants of others.   He held out his hand for the book,
saying,—

" Will you mark those passages, and let me see
them ? "

" Willingly," said Sir Roland, who suspected that
Mr. Anstruther might not himself possess the volume ;
" I have marked many passages, in different ways, as
you will see;" and rising, he went to him.   " All
marked *thus* — are for consolation ; and *thus* — for
the necessity of holiness ; and *thus* — and *thus* — for
different subjects.   This plan assists me much, either

when I want these texts for my own comfort and instruction, or when I require them quickly in support of
argument with others.   I have a bad memory, and
these odd-looking landmarks easily catch the eye.   You
have, probably, not been in the habit of classing these
things in this way, or of proving Scripture thus by
Scripture, so keep this book, you will perhaps find it
useful, and I can get another; and perhaps, if I have
much business to occupy me, you will copy these marks
into the new one for me; and add any observations of
your own that you like, for they will be valuable to me.
Two heads are often better than one, even in heavenly
things," he added, smiling kindly.

He then left him, but said he would inquire of his
servant if he were still up when he returned from Lord
Wentworth's, and if so, see him again for a few moments, if he liked it; "for he knew," he said, "that a
little visit was often a relief in times of sickness and
solitude."

Mr. Anstruther thanked him, and said he was
sure to be awake, for that he seldom slept till the night
was far gone.

"And is this the man whom I have so long tried to
hate and to despise?" he thought, when the door
closed upon Sir Roland, and he was again left to the
stillness of his lonely chamber; "this the man whom I
have tried in every way to wound and to injure?"
He sighed heavily, as the contrast between himself and
Sir Roland forced itself upon his mind.

"He knows my heart, and yet how gently does he
bear with me, and talk of pardon and of peace!   But
what is the little which he knows, compared to what I
must appear in the sight of God,—of that Being whom

I have so long reviled, and striven to deny—even to myself—though vainly !"

Mr. Anstruther's mind, as regarded religious knowledge, was in the utmost darkness. The sacred books were almost wholly unknown to him, as for many years he had never willingly opened them ; and after the days of coercive attendance at church, when he was at school and college, he had seldom ever entered a sacred edifice. The history even of Christianity, and of the life and acts of its great founder, were therefore, excepting in their roughest outlines, novel matter to him ; and as now, for the first time for nearly twenty years, he read to himself the inspired word of God, his mind was overwhelmed with the immensity of the subjects presented to it.

It is not, perhaps, in the power of any to whom the Bible is at all familiar to form an adequate idea of the sensations thus produced in him ; for most persons of tolerable education, however dead they may be to the spirituality contained in the Scripture, are at least tolerably familiar with its holy words ; and when these are presented, for the first time, to the mind of one in full maturity, it is generally in the case of the illiterate savage, the ignorant heathen, or the still more debased occupant of the lowest grades of ignorance and vice in a nominally Christian land. But here was one of refined habits, most cultivated intellect, and naturally warm and generous affections, upon whom the glorious Gospel broke for the first time, in all the fulness of its light and beauty. True, he did not — could not, fully comprehend all its spirituality, its high acquirements, and its unbounded blessings ; but enough of these was revealed, to make him aware that a new and glorious region was opened to him, of which he had hitherto been in total ignorance.

Yet the feeling of admiration thus produced in his soul, was painfully mingled with a sense of deep depression on his own account. He felt astounded at the magnitude of his guilt! and the more gracious the promises—the freer the invitations—he met with in the Scriptures, the more heinous did his own sin appear, in having so long neglected to accept them. He felt as if the day of grace were past for him—as if, for him, all hope was gone; and the very things that should have poured peace and comfort into his heart sunk him in the deepest despair. The wilderness—the dreary wilderness of unsanctified feeling, bitter hatred, and murmuring discontent, was indeed past; but (like Moses at the end of *his* wanderings) though he saw from afar the blessed land of joy and promise, yet he felt that he was never to enter it—never to enjoy its "green pastures, and its still waters of comfort."

Yet this state of mind was preferable far, even as regarded his own sensations, to that in which he had existed for so many years; for, though a sad despondency sunk his spirits beyond what he had ever before experienced, yet his bitter enmity against God was gone, and he felt that he could now love and adore that Almighty Being whom he had begun to know, only, as he fancied, to lose for ever.

He was still intently studying the Scriptures when Sir Roland returned at night; but the latter, thinking that rest would be better for him than exciting conversation at that late hour, merely said a few kind and encouraging words, and then left him, promising to be with him again early the next day.

CHAPTER VIII.

" But never, never, when the mind once wakes ;
    Charmed back to slumber can it never be !
  When from the toils th' immortal spirit breaks,
    Vain is the attempt to bind—it must be free."
                    SIR ARCHIBALD EDMONSTON.

SIR ROLAND made the utmost despatch with his
business the following morning, and hastened to go up
to Mr. Anstruther.   On inquiry, he found he had slept
rather better than usual, but he was struck with the
increased pallor and languor of his countenance.

" Have you found my marks of any use ?" he asked.

" Not yet; I have been too much interested in
reading straight through. Ashton, my mind has made
rapid strides in the last two days. I have lived years
in them !—years of sorrow—years of regret ! Yet so
unlike the sorrow and regret of former times, that they
seem scarcely allied to them—scarcely of the same
nature ; only that it has all been pain.   My life has
been one drear reality of pain — I have known no
happiness, or joy, or repose ! A great change, too,
has been made in my heart, by finding that the man
whom I have ever treated most unworthily, is my
best — perhaps, my only friend.   This is much for
me to say," and the blood mounted in his pale cheek,

" but I have done with pride, and I shall be happier—
easier at least, when I can speak freely and without
reserve. There is but little time now remains to me,
and I feel to have much to say ; I seem filled with sensation of some kind, though I can scarcely say what,
for it appears to settle down upon my mind with the
shadowy weight of an oppressive dream."

" My dear Anstruther," said Sir Roland, " why is
this? Surely you find no gloom in the bright and
glorious volume you hold in your hand. 'Joy unspeakable' shines forth from its every page."

" To you, doubtless, it does—doubtless, it does,"
replied Mr. Anstruther, quickly ; " but what does it
say to me—to me, who have so long neglected even to
read it? Ashton," he added, throwing himself back on
his cushions, and shading his eyes with his hand,
" you will scarcely believe me when I tell you, that it
is nearly twenty years since I voluntarily took that
book into my hands."

Sir Roland could not speak for a moment; the
thought of that Saviour, whose love is so infinite, so
unspeakable, being still so " despised and rejected of
men"—struck him to the very heart.

" I knew you would cease to hope for me," said the
dying man, misconstruing his silence, and fixing his
anxious eyes upon him with a look in which the despondency of his soul was painfully depicted—" I knew
you must cease to hope for me when you knew all ;
though who can know all—all the frightful secrets of the
heart (and he shuddered as he spoke) but God alone?"

" I do not despair of you, Anstruther; I never did,
and do so less now than ever. 'The wicked have no

bands in their death;' they are not troubled, or I should rather say, blessed with thoughts like yours; they have no godly sorrow for sin, and no craving desire after God.   But what is it that weighs so heavily on your mind? what is it forms the chief subject of your bitter regrets?"

" I can scarcely say," replied Mr. Anstruther—"I can scarcely define my feelings, or bring to my mind any one thing that stands forward particularly as an object of regret; but my whole life, excepting, perhaps, a little glimmer at its early dawn, seems one black offence against God.   I cannot look into my former self, and see one thought that was not opposed to God. I know, therefore, that my condemnation is just; but still—to be cut off for ever! to be appointed my portion with the condemned—Ashton, it is more than human nature can endure!"

" But have you not," asked Sir Roland, "found in the Gospel 'a refuge from the wrath to come?'   Have you not read of Him, who took your sins upon Him, and suffered, 'the just for the unjust,' that you might be saved?"

" I read of Him who died for His people," replied Mr. Anstruther, " but how can I think that I am one of them?   Wherein has my spirit been like His?   What one thought of my wretched heart has ever been such as He could have approved?"

" But whom does it say that Christ Jesus came to 'seek and to save?'" asked Sir Roland.

" Remember, Ashton, I am still a novice in these things," said Mr. Anstruther, with somewhat of embarrassment; " I am not ready to answer every question.'

" He came," continued Sir Roland, " to 'seek and to save that which was *lost*.' Now are you not one of those who were lost ?"

" Surely — too surely."

" Then are you not one whom He came to seek and to save ?"

" It should seem so indeed," replied Mr. Anstruther, looking up with earnest attention.

Sir Roland continued, " ' The blood of Christ cleanseth from all sin'—from *all* sin, Anstruther; ' This is a true saying, and worthy of all acceptation, that Christ Jesus came into the world to save sinners ;' ' I came not,' says our Lord, ' to call the righteous, but sinners to repentance ;' ' He that cometh unto me I will in no wise cast out.'"

The light of hope had begun to dawn in Mr. Anstruther's heart, as Sir Roland repeated the three first of these texts ; but when he came to the fourth, he exclaimed bitterly,—

" But I have never gone to Him — never believed in Him — never sought Him !"

" But you believe in Him now, Anstruther ; why not seek Him now ?"

" I believe in Him as the Saviour of those who have done His will, but not as my Saviour—not as mine !"

" Anstruther, listen to me while I speak to you of the glories of the Gospel — of the greatness of Christ's salvation ; for though your soul is convinced of its sinfulness—though you are fully aware of your own lost estate, yet you do not see the plan and extent of the redemption procured for you by Christ. His sufferings and death form one great sacrifice, of such infinite value as to satisfy eternal justice for the sins of the whole world; and all who believe in Him, and seek pardon for His sake will undoubtedly be saved."

"But yet," said Mr. Anstruther, after a few minutes' silence, "this doctrine seems to open a wide field for sin."

"It opens no field for sin, Anstruther; none. The same word which tells us that, by Christ's merits *alone* can we be saved, also affirms that 'without holiness no man shall see the Lord.' The love of Christ which the Holy Spirit implants in the heart of every redeemed being, 'constrains us to live, not unto ourselves, but unto Him who hath loved us and given himself for us;' and the people of God are called 'a peculiar people, *zealous of good works*.' When you are better acquainted with the Scriptures, you will perceive how inseparable are a true faith in Christ, and a desire after righteousness; how completely free salvation and personal holiness go in hand in hand. Neither have we the least encouragement to defer the time of turning to God. Christ never invites us to come to Him on *the morrow*. He says, 'Behold, *now* is the accepted time; behold, *now* is the day of salvation.' 'We know not what one day may bring forth.' And we are also given to understand that, even while yet in the body, we may for our hardened neglect be 'delivered over to a reprobate mind.' God says, 'My Spirit shall not always strive with man;' and we are told, that 'Satan entered into Judas' while yet he was alive in the flesh, taking full possession of his miserable soul even in this world."

"How can I know that such is not the case with me?" exclaimed Mr. Anstruther despairingly,

" scarcely Judas betrayed his Lord more than I have
done ; I have rebelled continually against Him, despised
His people, and set at nought His commandments. Oh !
I have done the work of a demon on the earth, and I
feel that I am now justly abandoned of my God."

" I feel sure that such is not the case with you,"
returned Sir Roland, " for those who are abandoned of
God feel not as you feel. As I said before, they have
no ' godly sorrow for sin,' no love for their Heavenly
Father, no yearning for His favour ; and you have all
these."

" You try to pour balm into my wounded spirit,
Ashton, and God knows the unutterable love it makes
me feel for you," and the large tears gushed into his
eyes. " But I cannot feel the hope you do — I cannot
think that the iniquity of so many years can be cancelled in a moment."

" It is not cancelled at this moment," said Sir
Roland, who had been much affected by Mr. Anstruther's expressions ; " it was cancelled when Christ
bowed His head upon the cross and said, ' It is
finished.' Nay, it was virtually cancelled when the
promise of the Saviour was made to our first parents.
The whole work of salvation was *accomplished* when
Christ died ; for the whole work is Christ's—the whole
power—the whole glory ! God *is* a reconciled father
through Him ; our pardon *is* signed and sealed by
His blood ; and we have only ' to open our worthless
hands and to receive it.' And will you not receive it,
Anstruther ?"

" God knows how willingly, could I really believe
it offered to me."

" If you sincerely trust for all your salvation to

Him, and to Him alone," replied Sir Roland, " then His word is passed—to save you : ' Him that cometh to me I will in no wise cast out.' ' Behold,' He says, ' I stand at the door and knock ; if any man hear my voice, and open the door, I will come in to him, and will sup with him, and he with me.' Mark the word ' sup.' * The Lord does not mention the first meal of the day, which would denote, figuratively, the morning of life ; not the second, which would point to the time of energetic health and manhood ; but He says ' sup,' the last meal of the closing day, in order to shew that if, even at the last hour of life—' the eleventh hour'— we will open our hearts to receive Him as our Lord and Saviour, He will enter in and claim possession of those hearts, and ' no man shall pluck them out of His hand.'"

" Mighty love ! wondrous mercy !" sighed Mr. Anstruther ; " I can adore it, though I dare not realise it as for myself. You must pray for me, Ashton, that my faith may be enlightened, that I may indeed be enabled to see in God a Father and a Saviour. I can feel him now to be only a Judge, and a Sovereign ' who for my sins is justly displeased.'"

" I have often besought the Lord for you, and shall, doubt it not, continue most earnestly so to do. But your own prayers will be of more avail than mine."

" I cannot pray—I dare not lift my voice to God."

" Do you, then, never pray ?" asked Sir Roland, in astonishment.

" I have not for years. What could a heart seared as mine has been ask from God ? What could so rebellious a soul seek at His hands ?"

* Read the Rev. Henry Blunt's explanation.

" But now, Anstruther, you surely now desire His pardon and favour; and why not, then, now ask Him for them ?"

" I can only again repeat that I dare not. My eyes often, indeed, involuntarily turn to heaven, and my thoughts dart upwards to the mercy-seat; but they seem inexorably repelled, and a chill falls on my heart as if all hope for me were passed. A soul like yours, Ashton, cannot judge of mine. You can look back, young as you are, to a life of godliness, peace, and virtue, and to a trusting faith in Christ. But I can only look back to—sin ! Memory to me is a destroyer of rest, and peace, and hope !"

" But God says to the true penitent, that ' He retaineth not His anger for ever, because He delighteth in mercy.'"

" When you speak, Ashton, and repeat the gracious promises of God, my heart for a moment springs up, and a bright entrancing hope seems set before it, which, at times, I feel almost able to take hold of; but then a hand as from behind, seems to draw me back, and a voice to whisper in my ear, ' Not for you.'"

" That hand is Satan's, yield not to it, Anstruther; the voice is that of the enemy of your soul, who seeks to drive you from your salvation. Oh ! resist him, I beseech you, by earnest prayer; ' Believe in Christ and you must be saved,' spite of all the powers of darkness !"

Sir Roland spoke with passionate energy, for his spirit was stirred within him at seeing the so evident work of the evil one; and he felt almost as if he were combating with him hand to hand. His animated assurances seemed to breathe somewhat of hope into the heart of his friend, whose eyes kindled, and whose expressive countenance lighted up with eagerness — though his lip quivered, as he exclaimed, —

"And can it be — can it really be — that a simple belief in Christ as our Saviour can rescue from destruction?"

"It is Christ who rescues from destruction, my dear Anstruther," said Sir Roland, earnestly; "but it is belief in Him which, as the arm stretched out, lays hold on the salvation which He sets before us."

"But how, in this poor remnant of life that remains to me, how can I prove that my faith is sincere, that my repentance is genuine?"

"God sees the heart, and knows what He writes in it," replied Sir Roland; "but unless His Spirit teach," he added with a sigh, "all my words are vain."

He paused for a moment, inwardly imploring God's help, then continued, —

"Your own soul will be able to tell you whether you are really—truly enabled to believe that Christ, when dying on the cross, bore the punishment you deserve?"

"Oh, that I could believe it!" exclaimed Mr. Anstruther; "yet else, why did He take my nature upon Him?"

"Have you read St. Luke's account of the thief on the cross?" asked Sir Roland.

"I do not remember it."

"Then let me read it to you." And, taking the book, he read that touching portion of Scripture.

When he came to the earnest appeal of the repentant malefactor, "Lord, remember me when Thou comest into Thy kingdom," Mr. Anstruther involuntarily rose from his recumbent posture, and leaning upon his elbow—scarcely breathing—he fixed his eyes upon Sir Roland with agonised earnestness, as if he felt the answer were to be addressed to himself. And so, indeed, it was! God directed the words, " Verily I say unto thee, To-day shalt thou be with Me in Paradise," straight to his heart. He felt that the Saviour of that penitent was his Saviour!—that the gates of the same Paradise that were opened to him, were ready also to receive his pardoned soul! He spoke no word as this blessed conviction rushed over him, but gazing upwards for a moment, with a look that seemed to enter the very heavens, he sunk back, and closing his eyes, as if the prospect overpowered him, murmured, " Too great—too bright—too joyful!" while an expression of heavenly happiness rested on his countenance !

There was silence in that chamber for a time! but in heaven there was 'joy amongst the angels of God over that one sinner that repented;' and though their hymns of thanksgiving reached not the outward ears, yet were they echoed in the inmost souls of those two redeemed beings, who then poured forth the fulness of their hearts to God in love and praise.

It was long before Sir Roland spoke, for he saw what had passed in Mr. Anstruther's mind, and he would not interrupt the blissful emotions—the "joy and peace in believing"—which he knew his pardoned soul was then enjoying. But as he looked on the worn features and wasted frame of the man—once so uncongenial to him, now bound to him by so many ties— and felt how soon they must be separated for ever in this world, an uncontrollable gush of earthly sorrow mingled itself with the rejoicings of his spirit, and unwonted tears sprung from his eyes. His heart yearned over the being he had been the blessed means, in God's hands, of rescuing from everlasting destruction, and whose love and gratitude to himself was, he knew, so strong. But repelling the "wish that would have kept him here," he raised his thoughts to that world where death and separation are unknown, and where Satan can no more deceive, nor sin distress, the perfected soul !

> " Blest home ! no foe can enter,
> And no friend departeth thence !"

CHAPTER IX.

" My soul had drawn
Light from the Book whose words are graved in light!
There at its well-head had I found the dawn,
And day, and noon of freedom."

MRS. HEMANS.

WHEN Sir Roland had left Mr. Anstruther and returned to his own apartment, he poured forth his heart in warmest gratitude to God for the change which had taken place in the soul of his friend. He had never wholly despaired for him, though, for a long time, it seemed " through moonless skies" that he was gazing ; but now a dawn of no uncertain nature had appeared above the horizon, and never did the light of this material world give to shipwrecked mariner a joy more true, more full, than that which this zealous and devoted servant of the Lord felt, when he saw " the Sun of righteousness arise with healing on his wings" on the once benighted being in whom he now felt so deep an interest.

When next he visited him, he found him in the happiest state of mind, and ready to receive him with the warmest affection.

" Ashton," he began, holding out his hand, " I wish I had some new and unaccustomed words with

which to thank you for your excessive kindness to me,
—a kindness which might well have warmed a colder
breast than mine. How can I ever sufficiently bless
you for it—you, by whom God has led my erring
soul from death to life?"

"God has sufficiently blessed me by blessing you,
Anstruther," replied Sir Roland, with much emotion;
"you can now fully trust your salvation to Christ,—
can you not?"

"Fully—fully; I feel that He is my only—my all-
sufficient Saviour. And oh! how great a change
does that conviction bring with it! I seem like one
from before whose eyes a wall has been cast down, revealing a prospect of unutterable beauty! I feel as if
this world were nothing; eternity every thing! Well
might you tell me, Ashton, that 'in Christ Jesus we
were new creatures;' for most surely do I feel changed
in every pulse and feeling. And marvellous is the
change! though to you it could never have been the
same as to me; for though, doubtless, light increased
continually in your soul, yet you never knew the
blackness of darkness that I have known."

"Perhaps not," replied Sir Roland, "for I was
early trained in the knowledge of God. Yet well do I
remember (and it was accompanied by somewhat of
the same sensations you describe) the moment when I
first felt the sense of pardon in my heart."

"When was it?—do you mind telling me?"

"I had long had something of the fear and love of
God in me, and had chosen His service in preference
to that of the world; for I had lived with those in
whom I saw the happiness as well as the beauty of
holiness. Even in my early youth I remember it used

to surprise me, that when such pure and fresh springs of happiness were offered to men, they could slake the thirst of the soul in the foul and stagnant pools by the way-side; or, in plainer language, that they could choose the frivolous, and often debasing and vile pleasures of this world, rather than the exalted joys of companionship with God. Yet it was present happiness and present peace that I thought of, more than the glory of God, or the immortal well-being of my soul.

" But after a time (it was about eight years ago) my mind became much awakened on the subject of vital religion—of the real union of the soul with Christ. I found that I was far from being what I ought to be in God's sight; and not knowing the freeness of salvation, a miserable disquiet took possession of me, and I longed for something to rest upon. How vivid still is the remembrance of that hour when the Lord revealed Himself to me as the all-sufficient atonement, for whose sake God would accept and bless me !

" You have. not been at Llanaven for many years, Anstruther; but you remember it is near the sea, with downs and woods that feather, in parts, almost to the shore ?   I was one day lying on the grass, with that listless enjoyment which fine weather and beautiful scenery are so apt to produce, and my eye roved delightedly over the scene, so beautiful! that was spread out before me.   I thought with delight, and with a strong admixture, I fear, of vanity and earthly pride, of being the possessor of that lovely spot, and felt very great in my own estimation; when just at that time, the passing bell rung out from the tower of our old church.   I had heard it, of course, often before, when it had brought with it only a momentary sadness to my heart.   But

now it seemed so at variance with the bright look of
life that shone on all around, and taught a lesson so
contrary to the proud earthly thoughts I had been indulging, that it produced a sudden and painful revulsion of feeling within me.   Some lines on the subject
came into my mind :—

> ' There is a sound of sadness on our hill!
> Heard ye the moan of yon ill-omen'd bell,
> Solemn and slow, like messenger of ill
> Who weeping comes a heavy tale to tell?
>
> List to its lingering cadence, how it awes,
> Holding the spirit in a holy thrall!
> And what light heart thus questioned would not pause?
> For though one answer, 'tis addressed to all!
>
> *   *   *   *   *   *
>
> It warns a being from this troubled sphere,
> It calls a mortal to its parent clay,
> It rings the knell of hope's best promise here,
> It hymns a spirit on its heavenward way!'

" ' Its heavenward way!'" I thought, " would it be
such to me?

"My mind was much troubled, but Satan began
suggesting — what the self-sufficiency of the natural
heart is ever too ready to plead — its own merits.
'Did I not love God? was I not, in some respects,
better than my companions?' with many other such
insufficient sources of consolation.   But a spirit answered from within, ' That I had not loved the Lord
my God with all my heart, nor with all my soul,
and that I could not answer to Him for one of a
thousand of the things that I had said, or thought,
or done.'   This conviction humbled my very soul,
and filled me with dismay; an undefined fear took

possession of me, and the blood rushed throbbing
to my head, till all which had before appeared so clear
and calm around seemed disturbed and dizzy before
my eyes; and I remember shivering from head to
foot even under that summer sun. Still the bell went
swinging on, remorselessly, as it seemed to me, for
every stroke shook me to the heart, and I longed to
escape from its sound—but seemed chained to the spot.
At length the words, 'Thou hast destroyed thyself,
but in Me is thy help,' came to my recollection; and
passage after passage of comfort and hope flowed in
upon me, till the Holy Spirit opened my soul to the
joyful reception of the free, unpurchaseable salvation
of Christ. I can never forget the sensation I experienced at that moment! Before I had been, as it
were, walking on the earth, though looking up to
heaven; now I felt as if in heaven and looking down
upon the earth! For a time I was lost to every thing
around me. I no longer heard the knell of death
or the splashing of the waves, or saw any of the objects
that before had so much charmed me; my heart and
whole spirit seemed with God!"

He paused: while his upward glance appeared
again to seek the presence of his heavenly Father;
but after a few minutes' silence, which Mr. Anstruther
understood too well to wish to break, he resumed, with
a sigh,—

"Frail creatures we are here — incapable of retaining heavenly light! We can recall the remembrance of such feelings; but the excessive happiness
they produced will not glow again within us in this
world—though enough remains to fill these treacherous
hearts of ours with peace and joy."

"If such, then, was the effect of these things on your mind, Ashton, think what it must have been on mine—mine which was brought out of such darkness! You had ever had the love of God in your heart, though He had not been fully revealed to you as your Saviour; but I—my heart had been at bitter enmity with Him. You may be thankful that you were led to Him by the force of love, without seeing Hell opened beneath you as I did. Oh! what I suffered that night! But it has made Christ's salvation, if possible, the more valuable to me, by shewing from what depths of misery it has saved me. Would that my voice had a trumpet's power to arouse the souls of men, to warn them to fly from misery, and to turn to Him who is mighty and willing to save! But those who have known me through life, who have witnessed my cold contempt of every thing sacred, would think, perhaps naturally, that it was only the fear of death which had made me now alter my expressions and feelings: so that when I would— oh! how gladly—serve the Lord, I am justly shewn that He does not need me, and will not use me. But it is not fear that has changed me—I feel it is not fear."

"I believe you, Anstruther, for fear would not give you the peace and joy you seem to have," said Sir Roland.

"I did feel it once," continued Mr. Anstruther; "sunk under it nearly; but it is gone now, quite gone. Regret, indeed — deep, deep regret — do I feel for having so long offended one so merciful, so easy to be entreated; and I have a sorrow for sin which humbles me continually. And I would not have it otherwise: such feelings seem to befit one who has been so long and fearfully alienated from God; but far from teaching me now to despair or fear, they serve only to enhance my sense of God's long-suffering patience. The more I think of them, the deeper is my love for Him."

"I am very thankful, my dear Anstruther, to see you in this frame of mind," said Sir Roland; "and I know your joy is not the less deep and full for being chastened with regret; but still you must remember that all your sins are washed out, that Christ has borne them all in His own body on the cross."

"You are a gentle comforter, Ashton,—true servant of your Lord—true, true servant of your Lord. And if ever," he continued with the most earnest energy, "in the course of this uncertain life, trial or sorrow beset your path, think of this scene of death —of him whom you have been the means of leading to salvation, and you will find comfort." He paused, exhausted with his own emotions, but, after a minute, he added, "I rejoice in the thoughts of your being high in the kingdom of God; for myself, I feel sufficiently blessed in the hope of sitting on its threshold. It will be happiness enough through all eternity simply to dwell in the presence of the Lord, to see you employed about His throne—and again to behold—my mother."

His heart thrilled with joy as the last idea passed through it; and he closed his eyes, that their softened expression might not be read, even by Sir Roland. It was a feeling too sacred to brook the scrutiny of aught but heavenly eyes.

"It is strange," he said, after a time, "how completely all my feelings and thoughts are changed. I,

who never, in former times, could bear to think of
my mother, now dwell on her remembrance with the
most delighted happiness, whilst it is the thought of
my father now that is painful. I do not know where
he is; but, Ashton, if ever you should meet him, try,
will you? for my sake, to persuade him,—speak to him
as you have to me, and may God open his eyes as He
has mine."

"I will surely do what I can," replied Sir
Roland.

"Would it be too much to ask of you," continued
Mr. Anstruther, "now even, if you have any friends on
the continent (for I have reason to believe he is not in
England), to write and ask them if they have ever
heard of him or known him. I have been very neglectful in this matter; for he may be wanting my
assistance, and, God knows, I would willingly give it
now, if I knew but where to find him; and he might,
perhaps, when he hears how near I am to death, come
and see me once more."

"I will write this very evening," said Sir Roland,
"for I have many friends abroad, and I hope I may
be successful in discovering him. But tell me, Anstruther, have no thoughts of God ever since you
were a child,—no convictions of sin, ever crossed your
mind?"

"Often and often, but I repelled them instantly.
Yet amidst all my seeming indifference, spite of all
the rhodomontade nonsense I used to talk, so miserable have I been at times, that more than once (I
shudder at thinking of it now) I thought of putting an
end to my existence; but I was kept from it by an
intuitive feeling that I should then never again behold

my mother.* And thus mercifully did God restrain
my impious hand by the thoughts of her, whose
prayers for me had, doubtless, ‘ come up as a memorial before Him.’ ”

“ I know the outline of your history : but what
was it that preyed so particularly on your heart?—Yet
do not talk if it hurts you, you seem so very weak.”

“ It is a pleasure to speak to you while I can,” said
Mr. Anstruther, “ for my lips will soon be closed in
death;” and a quiet smile played over them as he spoke.

He then repeated as much as he himself knew of
the history of his parents (with which the reader is
already acquainted), and described the effect his early
trials had upon his heart. He said he was not with
his mother when she died—her death took place in the
night—and that when in the morning he was told that
she was dead, and entered her room, he felt relieved
to find her so little changed.

“ I used to go,” he continued, “ and read in the
room where she lay, and take my playthings there, and
sit for hours, for no one cared to disturb me. I had
no fear of death, for I had never witnessed it, till now,
in her who, dead, was worth all the living world to
me. I would amuse myself, I remember well, in
building bridges and towers, and things of that sort,
which seemed very beautiful to my childish fancy, and
then would look up for praise and kind words ; but
finding all remained still, as before, I would take them
down quietly one by one, instead of the noisy over-

* That gifted but eccentric being, Ugo Foscolo, while pouring
forth the sorrows of his heart on one occasion, said, that he had, indeed, thought of putting an end to himself; but, he added, in a peculiarly touching manner, “ Je crains de ne jamais revoir ma mère.”

throw which before used to be the crowning joy of all;
for, without knowing why, I felt there was a hush over
every thing around, and the least noise seemed to jar
in that quiet room of death.   And thus I went on for
some days, and was scarcely to say unhappy, though I
wearied for her sweet looks and gentle voice.   Strange
it is, that though I have not dared to recall these things
to my mind for years, yet now that I speak of them, the
smallest circumstance flows back upon my recollection with a force and clearness that makes the whole
seem as but of yesterday; and all my childish but
intense feelings return to my heart, fresh and natural
as when first they came.   It is like turning over the
pages of a long-forgotten volume !

"We were in the country, in a poor little house,
suited, I suppose, to our ruined fortunes, and we had
no friends near. The servants were kind to me, but
they spoke to each other in whispers, and often with
tears, and I did not care to ask them questions. I
knew my mother was dead, but I had then but faint,
indistinct ideas of what death was, and I dreaded hearing of something worse than what I saw. One day—
oh! can Eternity wash out the remembrance of that
hour!—on that day my father came down; he had not
been to the house before since my mother's death.
He must have felt, I imagine, as if every thing and
every body reproached him, and that probably chafed
his temper. The sadness of the people about made
him, perhaps, irritable and sensitive, knowing what
their thoughts must be, for they were all aware of
his neglect of my mother, and of her many sorrows.
He inquired where I was, and, being told I was in her
room, he entered in a sullen mood (for he always

resented any mark of affection shewn to her), and
bade me leave the place.   Frightened at his angry
look, I ran to the bed-side and clung to my mother's
hand, taking refuge with the quiet dead from the
violence of the living.   He advanced—I see him now,
his eyes flashing with anger — and seizing me, ordered
me to quit my mother's hand.   I could not do so, and
he dragged me away, I grasping her hand still with
the strength of despair.   Oh, God! what I felt at that
moment!" and he pressed his clasped hands crush-
ingly across his eyes, as if to destroy the recollection.
" The action made her move ; she seemed to follow me,
and I thought she lived.   I called on her to save me,
but with frantic violence my father tore my hand
from hers ; I heard her arm fall heavily on the bed—
and I heard no more.   When I awoke I was in my
own room, and a kind servant of my mother's was
watching by me, and in tears.

"I saw my mother once again.   I was feverish,
and was kept in bed ; but, having been left alone, I
crept out and stole into her room.   I did not see her
at the first moment, for they had placed her in her
coffin.   The sight of that mournful object filled me
with alarm, but I could not bear to return without
seeing her ; so I got on the bed on which the coffin
rested, and leaned over to look once more at that still,
pale face, so inexpressibly dear to me.   She was surrounded with flowers — the bright, gay flowers of
Spring.   I stooped to kiss her, and felt a rising agony
I had never known before, for I was sure they were
going to carry her away ; but my terror was so great
lest my father should return and find me there again, that
sorrow had not—happily perhaps—full sway over me.

I took up a flower which lay on her tranquil breast—
that breast, my precious mother, where I had been so
often hushed to rest—and in haste and fear crept back
to my own room. I never saw her after that, but
dearly did I cherish my stolen flower, and preserved it
with the greatest care. I have it now—it is in my
desk, sealed up with my mother's picture. Years—
many, many years have passed since I have borne to
look on either; but, Ashton, shall you think me quite
a child still, if I beg you to let that faded flower
be placed with me when I am in my coffin? I feel it
is a childish request," he added, as deep emotion flushed
his countenance, "but I somehow wish that what I
have so much treasured should not be cast away as a
worthless thing. Will you keep the picture? it is
very lovely—as she was;—and it may serve to remind
you perhaps of me; for though I had not her features,
or her beauty, yet some who knew her have said that
at times they saw a likeness between us. We have
indeed, been alike in some things," and he sighed
heavily; "for we have both suffered much, though
from what different causes! and she, too, died at
seven-and-twenty, cut off in her lovely prime. I
think I should like," he added, while his lip quivered,
"to look once more on those dear memorials; will
you kindly get them for me?—but no, I will not disturb
and melt my heart with the sight of them—I shall
need no remembrance to recognise her in the realms
of peace."

He paused for some time much exhausted, then
continued:—

"After a few days (during which I never saw
him) my father took me away with him, and soon

after sent me to school; but my heart found no resting-place in any of my companions, nor, indeed, ever has found one till now;" and he turned to Sir Roland with an expression of the deepest gratitude.

" I can scarcely wonder at the state of mind you used to be in, Anstruther," said Sir Roland, " yours was a terrible childhood ; how different to mine ! nursed as I was in the very lap of love and kindness ! and, while I was early trained in the ways of God, I have heard that you were exposed to every evil and temptation. It is surprising that your outward conduct should have been so free from reproach as it has been."

" My hatred of my father, I am sorry to say, served more to keep me from his vices than any thing else," replied Mr. Anstruther ; " besides which, I ever had a vanity in seeming to be above the weaknesses of other men, and should have lost my power of humbling them—my great delight I am sorry to say—had I debased myself to their level. But if I have had less, perhaps, than some of open audacious vice to reproach myself with, my heart, I feel, has been worse than mortal can conceive. It is appalling to me now to look back to what it was; my ' hand has, indeed, been against every man,' and justly has ' every man's hand been against me,' excepting yours, Ashton, and amongst all my companions or acquaintance, you were the only one I never could despise; I affected to do so—but I never really did. I tried, too, to despise your principles, but there, also, I could never succeed; the still small voice of other years echoed them in my heart, though so faintly that its tones were almost lost."

He paused, for his voice faltered; but after a few moments he continued, " I cannot now bear to think of what my feeling towards you used to be, Ashton, and happily I need not do so," and the finest animation glowed over his features; " for the deep, heart-felt love I bear you now has, I feel sure, blotted out the remembrance of it from your mind; and, thanks be to God, ' the blood of Christ cleanseth from all sin.' "

" *There* is, indeed, the point of comfort for us all," said Sir Roland, " for without that, ' who could abide the day of His coming, or who could stand when He appeareth?' But I have now no feeling but that of pleasure in thinking of you, Anstruther," and he kindly grasped the hand which the other had held out to him, " for our hearts and souls are now one, and will be so for ever. But I ought to leave you now, for you must need rest after the kind exertions you have been making to gratify my curiosity; you have talked too much I fear."

" It does not signify," said Mr. Anstruther, " I shall soon be quite at rest."

When next Sir Roland visited him, Mr. Anstruther, during their conversation, expressed a strong desire to see Mr. Scott.

" It is strange," he said, " how much one's heart feels drawn towards those who have the same hope with oneself. Scott, whom formerly I so much disliked—because I disliked his Master—I now feel so great a regard for."

" It is not strange," said Sir Roland, " for all true Christians are members of one body, of which Christ is the head; ' By this,' says our Lord, ' shall men know that ye are my disciples, if ye have love one to another.'"

" I have then, at least, that testimony of being His disciple," said Mr. Anstruther, " for I feel my heart warm up towards even strangers whom you name as being real Christians. Do you think Scott will mind coming again to this sick room ? — that he will forget my former cold rudeness to him ? "

" He would rejoice in nothing more, I am sure, than in seeing you as you are now, my dear Anstruther," replied Sir Roland : " all but that pale countenance ; and yet we must not mourn for that either, when we know how near you are to your rest."

" I have often in former times," said Mr. Anstruther, " heard of the bitterness and harshness of religious men ; but you, Ashton, have certainly none of that spirit, you are one of ' Comfort's true sons.' But there is one other thing I wished to speak of, which is — the Sacrament : I should much like to take it ; though," he added, with some embarrassment, while a flush passed over his pale features, " it will be for the first time, voluntarily in my life. Our Lord's words, ' Do this in remembrance of me,' haunt my mind, for I would fain obey him in all things."

" It is, indeed, a Christian's privilege to do so," observed Sir Roland.

" But there is one thing," continued Mr. Anstruther, " though I fear it is a weakness ; but I have a great dislike to the idea of taking the Sacrament from Roberts. I know, indeed, that the act is entirely between God and my own soul — that none can forward His blessing to me, or withhold it from me ; but still, I confess, I revolt from the idea of having, at that solemn moment, such a man as Roberts to administer to me even outward things. You know what he is—always was at least—frivolous, worldly, dissipated! and I cannot sufficiently divest myself of natural weakness to tolerate the idea of the feelings which I am sure would overcome me being witnessed by him."

"I can perfectly understand you," said Sir Roland, "and I confess that his presence with us here would much interfere with my enjoyment also, though the necessity of taking the Sacrament would remain the same. God's blessing rests on duty performed, not on enjoyment received; but I think, if we could get a spiritually minded man to officiate, it would be far better. Do you know Singleton—Scott's cousin? He is a true Christian, and I know Scott expected him here to-day or to-morrow; would you like me to ask him to come?"

"I should very much," replied Mr. Anstruther; "and his being a relation of Scott's would take away any appearance of rudeness or unkindness to Roberts, as he being chaplain to the Embassy it might seem otherwise, as if I ought to have sent to him. But, Ashton, if Mr. Singleton does not come, it ought not to be delayed—I have a monitor within which tells me —that time is not much longer for me."

Sir Roland soon after, when he saw Mr. Scott, told him of Mr. Anstruther's desire to see him. He had some time before informed him of the change which had taken place in the mind of his friend, which had greatly rejoiced Mr. Scott, who now said he should be most happy to go and visit him.

Sir Roland then mentioned Mr. Anstruther's wish,

that if Mr. Singleton arrived in time, he should be asked to administer the Sacrament to them.

" Singleton left this room not ten minutes ago," said Mr. Scott; " he arrived this morning, and is gone to look after his things, I fancy. I am sure he will be happy to be of use any where and any how. I often think it is a very good thing that that man has no settled avocation in life—or rather no living to settle down in; for his avocation evidently seems to be that of wandering over the face of the globe, doing good amongst the upper classes of society. He had an excellent living once, but gave it up for some reason or other which he never would explain. He is acceptable every where, even with the most worldly and unprincipled, and he always leaves them something to reflect on when he is gone. I have traced more good to him than to any man I ever knew, for he waits for no opportunity to be offered to him, but makes it for himself; yet with such judgment and such gentle earnestness, that what one is almost tempted at first to call rash courage is so invariably crowned with success, that it loses its rash character, and becomes matter of certain calculation. His playful, sidelong smile, too, seems to make it impossible for him ever to offend."

" I know him but little," said Sir Roland, " but that little makes me desirous of seeing more of him."

" I know him well," said Mr. Scott, with a glowing countenance, "and have as deep reason to love him as poor Anstruther has to love you."

" So I have heard you say," replied Sir Roland; " and it is a bond strong as delightful. One can imagine — or rather one can*not* imagine — what two souls, united by that tie, must feel when ranging the

wide fields of eternity together! Ah! how little do
those possess of real, ennobling happiness, who do not
know their high inheritance. How strange it seems
that Satan's power should be so strong, that he should
be permitted so much to delude the souls of men, and
tempt them to forsake their real bliss for the painted
gewgaws of an hour. Truly does our Lord say,
' What I do now thou knowest not;'—and how gracious is the condescension which makes Him add,
' But thou shalt know hereafter.' How comforting and
animating to be assured, that all which our insatiate
minds would fain know now, shall hereafter be spread
out clear and plain before us, and our powers be so
enlarged as to enable us to understand, approve, and
admire all."

" Our powers will then be boundless," said Mr.
Scott—" boundless to suffer—boundless to enjoy!
An awful thought as regards lost souls; but how delightful as regards those who are made perfect in glory!
Here, a very little joy suffices us, the least excess
becomes painful—indeed, the only expression of happiness at times is tears. But there our happiness will
be pure, perfect, and untinged by a single shade that
could sully it."

" We have indeed a glorious hope, ' full of immortality,'" said Sir Roland; "' Heirs of God and
joint-heirs with Christ.' What animating promises!
And how delightful is the earnest—the foretaste we
possess of them even here; proving that godliness has,
indeed, ' the promise of this world as well as of the
world to come.' How do earth's best joys sink beneath
these stupendous thoughts—and earth's brightest prospects! yes, even mine Scott, happy and delightful

as they are, how do they fade and vanish away before ' that day-spring from on high,' which reveals, though only now in glimpses, the perfect beauty of God's kingdom! What happiness it is to possess these hopes for oneself; what inexpressible joy to be the instrument in God's hand of imparting them to others —a glorious privilege!"

" When first I had these hopes for myself," said Mr. Scott, " I thought that I had but to tell others of them, to get them joyfully accepted by all. It seemed to me that a thing contained in three lines would bring all mankind, who heard it, to the foot of the cross."

" How do you mean ' contained in three lines?'"

" I mean that the gist of the Gospel lies in such small compass, that it need be a burthen to no memory : ' Man lost, justly, through his own sins; saved by the merits of Christ ; and constrained for His love's sake, through His Spirit, to do His will.' That appears to me the epitome of Christian faith and practice ; and it seemed so simple, when first I felt and understood it for myself, that I wondered all should not equally understand and feel it. But it is like a difficult riddle which none can find out of themselves, though the moment they are told it, it appears so clear, that they wonder they had never thought of it before. Melancthon, you may remember, says he felt just the same thing, and thought that all who heard him speak of the Gospel would immediately accept it; but, he adds, ' that he soon found old Adam was stronger than young Melancthon,'—and I am sure I have found it so too."

" Yes, every day's experience would serve to convince one of that," said Sir Roland, " even if Scripture

were silent on the subject; for no one can change the
heart but God. And yet how wonderfully is the conviction of the inefficacy of all earthly means, without
the Spirit's teaching, accompanied by the feeling of
the bounden necessity for working. It is extraordinary
that these two apparently contradictory feelings should
harmonise together so perfectly in the heart; yet they
do so—and most injurious is their separation, leading
us, on the one hand, to a presumptuous confidence in
our own endeavours, and, on the other, to a supineness
in God's work—as if there were nothing for us to do—
Satan by this delusion, so often bringing the blood of
souls upon our consciences. Well has it been said,
' Prayer without exertion is hypocrisy; exertion without prayer, presumption.' "

"Scripture condemns most forcibly the latter doctrine," observed Mr. Scott, " God himself being represented as saying, ' *All day long* have I stretched forth
my hands unto a disobedient and gainsaying people.'
And again, ' I have spoken unto you, *rising early* and
speaking.' And we are encouraged, too, so much to
work, as well as to pray, ' Cast thy bread upon the
waters: for thou shalt find it after many days.' ' In
the morning sow thy seed, and in the evening withhold not thy hand; for thou knowest not whether shall
prosper, either this or that, or whether they both shall
be alike good.' "

A hand laid suddenly on Sir Roland's shoulder
made him turn round quickly, when he met the " sidelong smile " of Mr. Singleton, who said,—

" If when last we parted it had been asked, ' When
shall we three meet again?' who would have said it

would be in the noble city of —— !   So little do we,
grand calculators as we think ourselves, know what on
earth is to become of us!"

"But, though unexpected, you are not the less
welcome to us," replied Sir Roland, shaking hands
warmly with him.   "I knew you were here, but what
fair wind was it which blew you our way?"

"I was on my way to Italy, through the Tyrol,"
replied Mr. Singleton, "and only a few days ago
heard that you and Scott were here; but, as you are
here, I think I shall set up my tent here too, till the
fidgets seize me again, and then I shall be off."

"Yes," said Mr. Scott, "as old nurses say, there is
no *set-still* in you.   You were born in the year of the
comet, and I always think its influence affected your
constitution, and gave you your erratic propensities.
'A wandering star' you certainly are, but not 'reserved
to darkness;'" and he looked at his cousin with the
greatest affection.

"Thank you, Willy," replied Mr. Singleton, with
a bright smile, "I hope not.   But what were you
talking of when I interrupted you? I heard something
about 'prospering,' and 'good,' so wanted to come in
for my share."

"Oh, it was only the old subject—sowing the
seed."

"Well, as Montgomery says, 'up hill, down vale,
broadcast it o'er the land.'   What field have you
found to cultivate here?   There is always enough every
where that needs the tilling, and you are neither of
you among those who put the hand to the plough and
look back; at least, I know you are not, Scott, and I
don't much think your friend here is."

"He has sown to some purpose just now," returned Mr. Scott, "and his shock is nearly ready for the sickle."

"Not sown, only watered," said Sir Roland; "but God has, indeed, given an almost unhoped-for increase. I was wishing to ask you, Mr. Singleton, to do a little act of kindness for us just now; which is, to give the Sacrament to a poor fellow up-stairs, whose sands are almost out."

"Up-stairs! who is he?"

"Mr. Anstruther. He was Secretary of Embassy here."

"Anstruther! I know that name. Is he a dark-eyed man, with high, marked features, and haughty, disagreeable manners?"

"He was such, certainly," replied Sir Roland, somewhat reluctantly; "but you will not recognise the latter characteristic in him now."

"What, 'the Word' has done its work has it? and brought down 'the high look of the proud.' Well, God be with him then! I shall be most happy to give him the Sacrament in that case; but I really could not have done so (as it is not my bounden office here) if he had been one of those who, having neglected religion all their lives, take this rite, at the last gasp, as a sort of moral or spiritual panacea; and place as much dependence on it as the deluded Papist does on the 'Viaticum' of his church. But to one who has really received the Lord in his heart, I greatly delight in administering it; it gives me such extreme pleasure to be enabled, in such a case, to lay a strong emphasis on the word '*thee*'—'That Christ's blood was shed for *thee*.' I know, indeed, that that most precious blood-shedding was for the sins of the whole world; but still, being available only for such as believe it was ' shed for them and are thankful,' to such only can I emphasise the word, or indeed, administer the outward sign at all with comfort. When shall it be? To-morrow?"

" To-morrow, if you like; as it is rather late to-day."

" So be it then. But I shall like to see him first."

" Will you come up with me now?"

" No, I will not go up *with you* at all, Sir Ro-land. Perhaps you will kindly go up by yourself, and ask him if he likes to see me; and then, when you are safe off the premises, I will go to him. I like such interviews always to be *tête-à-tête:* otherwise, one can only say odious commonplaces; or, if one does say more, one appears, to oneself at least, affected—and I don't know what. I do not mind the ministering angels hearing me, and I like that those evil beings who are ever at our sides, sick or well, should do so too; but I have a mortal aversion to mortal ears."

" And yet," said Mr. Scott, " I have heard you say, that you did not care how many thousands were pre-sent, when once you began preaching."

" That is quite another thing; one then addresses the world in general—looks at nobody, and thinks of no-body! one's whole soul is in one's subject; and I think sometimes I should hardly feel the difference, were I to die in the middle, so completely do I feel abstracted from the world—so in the spirit with God. Yet to be sure, there must be an immeasurable difference between preaching to the perishing souls around one, and being with the already glorified spirits of men in heaven; with the company of angels, and the presence of the blessed One himself! Well, all in good time—in God's own good time! Will you see now, Sir Roland, if I shall go to this 'lost and found' up-stairs?"

"If it will not be inconvenient to you, Mr. Singleton, I think I had rather you should put off your visit to him for a little while. He expressed a great wish just now to see Scott, so perhaps it would be best for him to go up first."

"I will go at once then," said Mr. Scott; and he left the room.

"You are looking ill, Sir Roland," said Mr. Singleton; "you have been anxious about this poor fellow, I dare say."

"I have certainly felt much for him," replied Sir Roland; "besides which, confinement in this hot weather is very trying. I am not used to being tied to business, and find it very irksome; and notwithstanding that being with Anstruther is very exciting, yet it is, in fact, my happiest time."

"I can believe it—well believe it," said Mr. Singleton. "There is scarcely any tie on earth like that which binds one to the soul one has been the happy means, in God's hands, of 'snatching like a brand from the burning.' One feels mightily complacent, at any time, towards those whom one has benefited in any way; which feeling is doubtless a boon from the Father of mercies to cheer one on. But when it is to the soul that one has ministered—then it is a stringent tie indeed—a tie strong as the 'seven-fold chords of light.'

A chain of adamant — and wreathed with amaranth too!"

"It is," replied Sir Roland. Yet a sigh escaped him as he thought, how soon the earthly portion of the tie which bound him to his dying friend would be dissolved.

"Stronger, I conceive," continued Mr. Singleton, "than that which binds the receiver of the boon to the imparter."

"I think," said Sir Roland, "that Scott—who has told me all he owes to you—loves you with a force, which your regard for him can scarcely exceed."

"Scott's heart is a most humble one—therefore with him it may be so; but the pride of our fallen nature generally makes us revolt from receiving favours, while it enhances the pleasure of bestowing them; and I fear there are few of us, who would take equal delight in the conversion, even of those most dear to us, if the Lord had made use of other instruments entirely, and had left us quite out of the work. Sin, in some shape or other, mixes with all our thoughts and feelings, sullying the stream which yet perhaps at first really did spring pure from the love of God. It is a sore and grievous work to trace the blight within which cankers all we do:—the thoughts from beneath which ' rise, like birds of evil wing, to mar our sacrifice !'"

Sir Roland and Mr. Singleton continued to converse as if they had known each other all their lives, for they were brothers in the great family of the redeemed, and such have always much in common.

After a short time Mr. Scott came down again from Mr. Anstruther's room.

"You found him much altered, did you not?" asked Sir Roland.

"I should scarcely have known him at first," replied Mr. Scott, "though it is not a month since I saw him—he is so fearfully changed! But in conversing with him, I frequently caught a resemblance to his former self, in the peculiar way in which he turns his eyes suddenly upon one when speaking. They seem to have such power now, as if they were all spirit. They were always peculiarly expressive; but now, from out of his death-like countenance, their force is almost overpowering—yet the expression so fine! If you could go to him, Singleton, about twelve to-morrow, he would like it; and then Ashton and I will come up when you are ready, and receive the sacrament with him."

"I shall be quite happy to do as he wishes," replied Mr. Singleton; "but have every thing ready, will you, before I go in. I hate those tiresome preparations, they always distract the mind. I suppose they always will as long as one is here—that is, as long as they are needful—for we shall want no such things up there (pointing to heaven); they are made irksome, I suppose, in order to remind us of that. Well, tell your friend to expect me precisely at twelve o'clock to-morrow, without any further notice; and you, Sir Roland, will, I am sure, kindly take care I shall have a clear field."

CHAPTER X.

"Under whatever subterfuges he may attempt to hide his error, the man who labours to expiate his own sin, by self-inflicted pains of the body, has lost his hold of the Gospel of the grace of God; he may be very devout, and very fervent, but the Gospel he has framed to himself is 'another Gospel,' and in fact is no Gospel;—it is not 'glad tidings,' but sad tidings." * * * *

"From that treacherous border the few would make their escape heavenward, as the few, in every age, have escaped from the false bosom of the Romish Church; but the many—the thousands of the people, would become the pitiable victims of this religion of sacraments."—TAYLOR'S *Ancient Christianity.*

As Mr. Singleton rose to depart, Mr. Scott's servant came in to ask if his master would see Mr. Roberts.

"By all means: ask him to come up.—Now, Singleton," added Mr. Scott, when the man had left the room, " do stay; this is our chaplain, and you may be able to say a word to do the poor fellow good, and I shall want you when he is gone; you can have nothing to do here but with me."

"Yes I have a great deal to do here with myself.—I want to look about me."

"Well, but wait till he is gone, and I will help you to look about you."

The servant now announced Mr. Roberts; and

Mr. Singleton, after bowing to him courteously, sat down again, as his cousin had wished.

"How are you, Roberts?" asked Mr. Scott.

"Half dead! I have been parading the streets with the town-crier all the live-long day, trying to detect some hidden parson to do my duty for me for a week or two."

"Why?—whither away?"

"Lord N—— has been kind enough to invite me to accompany him to ——, which I should be delighted to do, if I could only get clear of the abominable service here. I must go out again, I suppose—as one does to catch up a loose horse—with a little corn, and try to inveigle some one for hire and reward. I shall have it placarded up on every respectable, serious-looking bit of wall in the place."

"I don't want the corn," said Mr. Singleton, with great gravity; "but as I do not think the service very abominable, I will take it off your hands, if you like it. You do not seem to value it very highly, so perhaps, you will not mind intrusting its performance to a stranger."

"I am sure I am much obliged to you," answered Mr. Roberts, rather disturbed. "I did not know—I was not the least aware, that I was in the presence of a clergyman, or I should not ——"

"No excuses to me, my good sir," said Mr. Singleton, quietly; "what is fit for the Master's ear, is quite good enough for His servant's."

Mr. Roberts was excessively confused, and continued stammering out indistinct apologies; but Mr. Singleton stopped him by saying kindly —

"We will not talk any more of that just now; another time perhaps, when we know each other better, we can begin it in a soberer strain.——I suppose you do not often get leave of absence here, for there are but few clergymen who are such waifs and strays on the surface of society as I am ; but however, I am glad to have arrived just in time to be of use to you, for I well know the pleasure of a little liberty."

Mr. Scott looked with the utmost admiration on one whom he knew possessed all the thunders of eloquence, with which—had he chosen to put them forth—he might have confounded the thoughtless, undevout young man to whom he spoke, but who, in the gentleness of his wisdom, expressed kindly sympathy with his natural wishes, before he attempted to shew him the evil of his spirit; and Sir Roland also, with pleased surprise, gazed on the fine, kind countenance of the commanding being before him.

" When does Lord N—— set out ?" asked Mr. Scott.

" To-morrow morning," replied Mr. Roberts; "and I was beginning to grow desperate, but Mr. Singleton's kindness has made quite a new creature of me."

Mr. Singleton fixed his eyes upon the careless speaker, and his lips parted as if he were about to reply, but he restrained himself, and kept silence, though a sigh arose. He had been inclined to make a comment on Mr. Roberts's own expression of " being a new creature;" but he felt that this was not a fitting time or place; for a lecture before witnesses was, he well knew, a most unpalatable dose to any man.

" Are you lately from England, Mr. Singleton ?" asked Mr. Roberts.

" I left it about two months ago."

"Was anything particular going on? One never can believe the newspapers."

"Nothing very particular that I know of."

"The Puseyites seem flourishing—the vile hypocrites!"

"My good sir," said Mr. Singleton, quickly, "you will excuse me, but I must say, I think we should be acquainted with people very well, before we venture to fix upon them the blackest name in all the black calendar of sins."

"I am really most unfortunate to-day," exclaimed Mr. Roberts—"full of mistakes! I first find a clergyman where I least expected it, though that mistake his kindness has turned quite to my advantage (bowing to Mr. Singleton)—and then discover that he is a Puseyite! which I certainly should not have expected, considering the company in which I find him."

"You certainly mistake in supposing me one of the Puseyites," said Mr. Singleton, smiling; "for I am very far from being such, and highly disapprove their doctrines. But my young friend, I am some six or seven years older than you are, and by virtue of my bald head I claim brevet rank for six or seven more, so you will perhaps forgive my saying, that experience has taught me, that men may fall into all imaginable follies and errors without being hypocrites. You will remember who it is that says, 'Judge not, that ye be not judged,' and His commands are not lightly to be disregarded. We may be led away by a thousand corrupt motives—the winds of passion may blow us to all points of the compass; and the currents of self-interest, pride, worldliness, may pervert the judgment, and make the stream of life flow in any but the right channel. But deliberately to pretend to be what we know we are not, is what few have the consummate villany to undertake, or the bad boldness to carry through. That was why I objected to your calling these men hypocrites, though at the same time I have no hesitation in saying, that I believe them to be blindly carrying on a work of vast, incalculable evil in the world."

" You do not like to abuse them," said Sir Roland, " while you 'cry havoc! and let slip the dogs of war,' against their doctrines. Abuse certainly is not argument, and should always be avoided; but we are in general least inclined to cultivate that 'charity which thinketh no evil,' where it is most especially wanted: in thinking and speaking of those who differ from us either in opinion or action."

"Oh! I had much rather," said Mr. Roberts, "abuse people out and out, and 'make a clean breast of it' at once, than pretend a vast consideration for them, whilst I am smilingly drawing the bolt that is to send them to destruction. I like 'a good hater.' Your mild, mellifluous speeches are only the oiling of the point of the dagger, in order that it may go more easily to the heart."

" You are poetical, Roberts—that was quite a flight," said Mr. Scott; " but you must 'rein in your soaring genius, and clip the wings of your rampant steed,' before you can come down to the level of such poor sons of prose as we are."

" I think your 'rampant steed' has fully overtaken mine, Scott; so we two, at least, may tilt on equal ground. But I always observe that people who begin so killing sweet, always end so biting bitter. The 'choicest unkindnesses' always come from those who profess a vast consideration for your feelings; like Dr. Johnson in his memorable speech, when asked the profession of some one: ' I wish to speak evil of no man, but truth compels me to say—he was a lawyer.'"

" As if," said Sir Roland, " 'a man could not,' as Spencer Perceval—the minister said, ' serve his God as well in the law as in the church.'"

"I should think he might easily," said Mr. Scott, glancing significantly at the young chaplain.

" Or would you wish, Mr. Singleton," continued Mr. Roberts, without attending to what the others had said, " to keep singing the ' retournelle,' after the fashion of Anthony; and after abusing these men in every figure of speech, chant perpetually, ' But Pusey is an honourable man, so are they all—all honourable men? ' "

" Well ! I must say you bear our friend's impertinences very patiently," said Mr. Scott to his cousin.

" He certainly does not treat my grey hairs with all the respect I think due to them," replied Mr. Singleton; " but perhaps, he has an ugly trick of thinking his own opinion best; which I have observed some people have."

" I always think myself the wisest person in the world," said Sir Roland, smiling, and willing to relieve the embarrassment into which Mr. Scott's observation had thrown Mr. Roberts. " Where others agree with me, we are on a par; where they differ, my opinion, of course, is, *selon moi*, best; so there I am the superior."

" Well argued, and quite unanswerable," said Mr. Scott. "I imagine we all think the same though, it is what 'oft was thought, but ne'er so well expressed;' at least I have long had an idea that I was decidedly the nearest resemblance to Solomon that had appeared within our era."

"It is commonly observed," said Mr. Singleton, "that the most equally distributed of all gifts, seems to be good sense; as every one is satisfied with his own share of it."

"But still to return to the original subject," said Mr. Roberts, "if these men profess to believe things which it is impossible for any one in his senses to believe—they must be hypocrites, unless indeed you prefer calling them madmen."

"It certainly does astonish me," replied Mr. Singleton, "that men, otherwise reasonable, should be led away by what appear to me much gross errors. But still, till I know that they consider their doctrines as erroneous, I must not call them hypocrites for professing them. I think," he added, and a solemn expression filled his eye, "that they are 'given up to a strong delusion,' and that the mischief they are doing is woeful—unspeakable! Theirs is a doctrine 'which'—as the Bishop of Chester said, if I remember right, in one of his charges — 'ministers so much to the pride of human nature, that were it for that reason alone I should distrust it.'"

"I do not see that," replied Mr. Roberts, "excepting as to the clergy; for the poor laity are sorely rough-ridden and brow-beaten, I should say—ordered to keep silence 'even from good words'—to dispose of their intellects as best they may — and to swallow, without tasting either, whatever is set before them by their appointed 'pastors and masters.' 'Eat your pudding, slave, and hold your tongue,' seems the order of the day for them; though to be sure, even then,

their diet need not pall upon their appetites for want of
variety. It is by no means 'toujours perdrix;' for
when I was last in England, staying in the country,
there were within a walk four churches with, to my
certain knowledge, four different doctrines served up,
'all well defined, and separate' condiments, as distinct
in their 'savour' as the most sickly appetites could
desire. And yet the poor wretches are ordered not to
judge for themselves, but only to 'hear the Church.'
(Which Church—query?)

"They mean the Articles, &c. as the Church, you
know," said Mr. Scott.

"Yes; but each thinks he is giving the true explanation of them."

"You speak in rather a light way on the subject,
Mr. Roberts, though I cannot but agree in your meaning," said Mr. Singleton; "indeed I have often wondered that this discrepancy in the views of men who
have all derived their right of public teaching in the
Church, from the same imposition of hands, does not
stagger them in the belief of that act having any efficacy.
Indeed we see from the very first, that it neither bestowed light to guide, nor grace to sanctify; for one of
the seven deacons—those on whom the apostles first
laid hands, and who were consecrated, not only for the
administration of funds, but also for preaching, (at least
they certainly did preach)—was the author of that
dreadful heresy of the 'Nicolaitanes' which God twice,
in the Revelation, declares that 'He hates;'—which
shews, that though the laying on of hands could set a
person apart for the service of the outward, visible
Church; yet, that it had no efficacy in making him
either a faithful, or an efficient minister of Christ's real,

spiritual Church; and fearful experience teaches us the same thing through all stages of the 'succession:' so that I cannot myself attribute the slightest value to the present 'imposition of hands.' Do you remember that story about some one—I forget his name—who asked Louis the Fourteenth for a bishoprick, for some friend of his? 'Mais n'est-ce pas qu'il est Jansénist?' asked 'le grand monarque.' 'Du tout! Sire,' replied the applicant, 'Je le garantis moi athée—athée pur?' Can one think that God commits His power to such men as these? If others can, I cannot! But, with regard to what we were saying, of these things feeding the pride of heart in the laity as well as in the clergy, you will find, Mr. Roberts, that we all naturally like to exalt the body to which, in any way, we belong, though we may possess none of the power in it ourselves. Pride runs through all of us; therefore, as the good bishop said, 'we should distrust' what tends to foster the ungodly seed. It is a pleasant thing, by the bye, to see those two brother bishops—brothers in spirit, happily, as well as in blood—fighting so manfully, side by side, against the inroads of this fearful heresy; and, thank God, some other of the bishops besides, and many of the clergy, still remain untainted by its poison."

"As to the miraculous powers of the Church, where are they?" asked Mr. Roberts. "When the real apostles and others performed miracles, men saw them, and were benefited by them; but here, we are called upon to believe things contrary to what we see—and that upon the simple *ipse dixit* of men like ourselves."

"You refer, I suppose, to the change they believe to take place in the bread and wine at the sacrament," said

Mr. Singleton; "but you are aware that on that point they do not all agree; some going almost, if not quite, as far as the Romanists, in believing that the elements are converted, by the blessing of the priest, into the actual body and blood of the Lord Jesus; others, only believing in the 'real presence,' without attempting to account for it. I myself can only view that comforting sacrament 'as a continual remembrance of the sacrifice of the death of Christ;' and I partake of it in obedience to His express command, 'This do in remembrance of me;' expecting, of course, the blessing which attends every means of grace, if rightly used. I cannot feel that there is any thing miraculous, or mysterious, in it (further than that all God's ways of working in the soul are mysterious); or that the blessing which flows through it differs, either in kind, or—necessarily—in degree, from any of the other influences of God's Holy Spirit. Indeed I think of both the sacraments, that they are but —to use the words of a living author— 'instruments that God blesses in the using, not that He has blessed to a perpetual use; for then would the use be never separated from the blessing.'* We see also most clearly that no holiness in the giver of the rite can cause it to be beneficial to the receiver; for Christ, 'the Head of His Church,' gave it to Judas!—and was he benefited?"

"It is remarkable, I think," said Sir Roland, "that though our Lord generally added to all His injunctions some gracious, encouraging promise, yet in instituting the two sacraments, He merely gave the command, without any blessing being added. To secret prayer

* The Table of the Lord.—CAROLINE FRY.

He promised open reward—to congregational prayer, that He would ' be there in the midst of them'—to the pure in heart, that they should 'see God'—in short, I think, to the keeping of every other injunction, was a blessing promised, but none to the sacraments; and my soul can rest on nothing but a promise, though we know, that in ' keeping all His commandments, there is great reward.' Yet, notwithstanding this omission, such is the invincible tendency of the human mind to go astray, that upon these two simple commands, men have built the most wild and visionary hypotheses. It almost seems as if heavenly Wisdom, foreseeing the evils they would bring out of them, determined to leave them wholly without excuse for doing so. The real presence is inferred, I believe, chiefly from our Lord's saying, ' Take, eat; this is my body :' and again, in giving the cup, 'This is my blood.' But these words are surely not to be taken more literally than many other similar expressions made use of by our Lord. As here, He calls the bread ' His body ;' so in another place He calls Himself the ' true bread ;' He speaks of His body as a ' temple ;' He says He is the ' door of the sheepfold,' &c. Now no one, that ever I heard of, thought of taking these things in their literal sense ; why, then, should so forced a construction be put upon that one figure of speech ? Our Lord surely only ordained that sacrament as a remembrance of His death, whereby we should shew forth to the world continually our love to Him, and dependence on His merits, till He comes again ! He abolished the Jewish passover, of which He was then partaking for the last time with His disciples, and in its place instituted this bloodless memorial of our blood-bought

salvation. With regard also, to the priest's pronouncing
a blessing over the bread and wine, under the supposition of imparting any value to it—that is quite unscriptural.
The blessing which Christ pronounced had nothing in
it, evidently, of that kind.   Six times, it is said, 'He
gave thanks,' and only twice, 'He blessed;' and He
did just the same at the multiplying of the loaves and
fishes, and no one ever supposed that they were intended to be more than food for the body.   And where
St. Paul reproves the people for 'some being hungry,
and others drunken,' at the sacrament, and tells them
that 'they eat and drink their own damnation' (more
properly condemnation) 'not considering the Lord's
body,' I believe thoroughly, that he only meant, that
they forgot the sanctity and holiness of that Being, the
sacrifice of whose death they had met to commemorate,
and that they incurred His just displeasure by the in-
sult thus offered to Him.   With regard to baptism also,
it appears to me a great error to attribute the least efficacy to the mere outward act.   It seems to me only an
admission into the visible church of Christ, shewing forth
figuratively the washing and cleansing of our souls by the
Holy Spirit of God, and ordained by Christ possibly as
a sort of test, whereby the power of faith should be
proved; shewing, that not to the secret believer, but
to the open avower of his Lord, should salvation belong:
' For with the heart man believeth unto righteousness;
and with the mouth confession is made unto salvation.'
We then, enlist ourselves under the banner of the
Great Captain of our salvation—take His service
upon us—and look to Him for his blessing.
Adult baptism only is spoken of in Scripture; and
even then we are not borne out in the idea that the

gift of the Holy Spirit depended in the least upon it.
No!—the baptism which is available to salvation is that
of which John spake before when he said, 'I indeed
baptise you with water, but there cometh One * * *
who shall baptise you with the Holy Ghost.' Of that
also, our Lord spoke, when He made the promise to
James and to John : 'Ye shall indeed drink of the cup
that I drink of ; and with the baptism that I am baptised withal shall ye be baptised.' That baptism visibly
fell on them at the day of Pentecost, and it falls not
less surely, though now invisibly, on every child of
man who takes the Lord for his God.   That is the
only baptism for the remission of sins, I feel convinced!
St. Peter, too, when he saw that the Holy Ghost fell
on the household and friends of Cornelius, says, ' Then
remembered I the word of the Lord, how that He said,
' John indeed baptised with water, but ye shall be
baptised with the Holy Ghost ;' and he afterwards
exclaims, ' Can any man deny water that these be
baptised, seeing· they *have* received the Holy Ghost,
even as we ?'   We see plainly also, that the blessed
saving operation of the Spirit was by no means necessarily consequent on the outward act of baptism, even
at the very first outset of the Gospel ; for some of those
who had received the rite from the hands of the very
Apostles themselves (Ananias, Sapphira, and others)
proved utter reprobates and aliens from God! These
things appear to me unanswerable ! Indeed, in conversing with Puseyites, who have begun by asserting
that baptism—infant-baptism as well as adult—was necessary to salvation, I have asked them if they really
thought that infants born of Christian parents in some
place where, through unavoidable circumstances, no

clergyman could ever come—living a life of devoted
love to Christ and of faith in His salvation, and so dying
—whether such persons would, in their opinion, be lost
for want of baptism? and they have invariably been
constrained to say, 'that they did not think they
would!' (though the confession was, in each instance,
made with the most evident reluctance). Another
way I think I have, or I certainly might have, put it
to them. Worldly, perhaps openly vicious parents,
take their child to be christened merely for form's
sake, without one prayer of faith. That child they say
is saved! Other parents—true, devoted Christians—
are also bringing their child to the font, purposing
indeed to dedicate it to the Lord. Sudden sickness
carries it off before the rite is administered! Will they
say that that child is lost? The child of prayerful,
spiritual parents, condemned in its helpless infancy to
the fires of everlasting wrath! They dare not say it!
—therefore again—baptism is *not* necessary to salvation."

"Do you object then to infant-baptism?" asked
Mr. Singleton.

"Far from it; I like the idea of presenting our
children—dear as our own souls—to God, dedicating
them, as far as in us lies, to Christ, and imploring Him
to bestow upon them His Holy Spirit, and all the
blessed privileges of His redeemed. But as to supposing that the child is regenerated by that simple
sprinkling—that it is thereby made 'a child of God,
and an inheritor of the Kingdom of Heaven,'—I hold
that to be a fearful and most unscriptural error;
involving the destruction of the covenant promise to
those 'born again,' that they shall 'never be plucked

out of their Father's hand;' for the utmost stretch of
charity cannot make us believe that all who are baptised have been 'born again,' unless we choose also to
believe that we can be the redeemed children of God
one moment, and the accursed children of Satan the
next, or that the careless, ungodly, and profane, are
those whom God has chosen for himself to be 'a peculiar people'—though 'zealous' of anything but 'good
works.'"

"With respect to infants," said Mr. Scott, "I not
only think that baptism is not necessary for their salvation, but I believe that all infants are saved by the
blood of Christ, whether of Christian parents or not.
Scripture tells us that 'God was in Christ reconciling
the *world* unto himself;' and I believe, therefore, that
we are all 'born into a world forgiven'; and I firmly
hold, that the efficacy of the great atonement is
available for all those young things who die before
the age of reason. But the moment they are old
enough to sin wilfully against God, then, of course,
the whole requirements of the law come upon them (I
speak of those under the teaching of the Gospel), and
from the guilt of their actual transgressions they can
then be saved only by an individual appropriation of
the merits of Christ to their own souls, claiming the
benefits of His atonement for themselves, and laying all
their sins upon Him."

"I quite agree with you," said Mr. Singleton; "and
I think that you and Sir Roland have also disposed of
two points very satisfactorily. Have you studied as
deeply on the subject of the power of remitting sins,
now again claimed so fully for the Church?"

"My examinations of Scripture," replied Sir Ro-

land, " have made me reject that claim *in toto*. The
moment the soul believes in the Lord Jesus as its Saviour, that soul *is* pardoned, and 'no man can pluck it
out of its Father's hands.' 'Who shall separate us
from the love of Christ?' asks St. Paul; and if not
from his love—how can we be withheld by man from
his free and full pardon? 'There is,' indeed, 'one
Mediator between God and man, Christ Jesus the
righteous;' but thank God, there needs no mediator
between man and Him—the way to Christ is open for
all. If man does pronounce our pardon truly, Christ
must have pronounced it first—and that is all the soul
needs. If he pronounce it falsely—God does not pledge
himself to ratify it to the impenitent. When once we
have heard, ' Be of good cheer, thy sins be forgiven
thee,' sounding from the voice of the Spirit, through
the innermost recesses of the heart, all words of man
are superfluous—valueless! Besides, if any such power
was bestowed at all, it was not confined to the apostles.
It is said, ' When the doors were shut, where the *disciples* were assembled, for fear of the Jews, came Jesus
and stood in the midst; and saith unto them, Peace be
unto you * * * as my Father hath sent me, even
so send I you. And when He had said this, He
breathed on them, and saith unto them, Receive
ye the Holy Ghost: whose soever sins ye remit,
they are remitted unto them, and whose soever
sins ye retain they are retained.' Now the power
here given (even if any were really bestowed) was
most decidedly given, equally, to all who were
present on that occasion; and we know, from the
parallel passage in St. Luke, that the two disciples from
Emmaus were there, and others also—probably women

as well as men. Besides, far from being an exclusive
gift to the apostles, we know they did not even all partake of it; for the very next verse to those I have
been repeating tells us, that 'Thomas, one of the
twelve, called Didymus, was not with them when Jesus
came.' St. Paul also, most certainly was not present,
nor Matthias—as an apostle, though he might have
been there as one of the disciples. All persons, therefore, ordained through their line of succession, should
be considered, by the 'successionists,' as incapable of remitting sins; for how could these three men bestow
upon others a power which had never been bestowed on themselves? But I deny that the power of
absolution was given to any; firmly believing that
our Lord's meaning was, that the Gospel of truth
committed to them *all*, and through them to us, was
that which should be the means—by its reception, of
'remitting' sins, or—by its rejection of 'retaining' them
upon the soul for ever; as He says in another place,
' He that hath the Son hath life; but he that hath not
the Son hath not life, but the wrath of God abideth on
him.' And I believe the same meaning was attached
to what was said to St. Peter; and also that the 'rock'
upon which the Church was to be built was the truth
confessed :—' Thou art the Christ, the Son of the living
God;' and not the zealous, but unstable apostle who
made the confession."

" I believe your interpretation to be the true one,"
said Mr. Singleton, " and am pleased—for it is what
I have been convinced of many a long year."

" But how, Sir Roland, do you know that any women were there?" asked Mr. Roberts.

" Women always ranked high amongst the number

of our Lord's disciples," replied Sir Roland; " and in
the faithful boldness of their love, were, as Barrat
beautifully and truly says—

' Last at His cross, and earliest at His grave ;'

and as they are said to have been with the disciples
that very morning, it is most probable that some of
them were present when our Lord appeared and spoke
the words in question. But whether they were so or
not is a matter, I think, of no importance ; the point I
wish to establish is that no power was by our Lord's
words conveyed to the apostles, but what was equally
conveyed to all who were then present. We have,
however, full Scripture testimony to assure us that
women received the ' baptism of fire' on the day of
Pentecost, equally with the men ; the apostle's quotation from Joel sufficiently proves that. I have considered much about these things lately, because I
think it is of such very great importance that they
should be rightly understood, especially in these days,
when there is again being set up, instead of the religion of Christ, a ' religion of sacraments'—of forms
and ceremonies—of fastings and ascetic practices—in
short—of refined Popery !"

CHAPTER XI.

"A saint ! and what imports the name
Thus banded in derision's game ?
Holy and separate from sin,
To good, nay e'en to God, akin.

A saint ! oh, scorner ! give some sign,
Some seal to prove the title mine,
And warmer thanks thou shalt command,
Than bringing kingdoms in thy hand."—MARRIOTT.

"Yea, and why even of yourselves judge ye not what is right ?"—
LUKE, xii. 57.

"I will receive nothing without examining it, for I cannot think
my reasoning faculties were given to me to be hood-winked, and led
about in passive helplessness by those of other men."
Judah's Lion: CHARLOTTE ELIZABETH.

"While the toils are fast gathering around the English Church,
and while the younger clergy, if common report say true, are generally yielding themselves to the fascination, and while some who should
loudly express themselves, seem disposed to leave things to take their
course, and, at any rate, to be 'quiet,' there is a body at hand that
is not asleep, although mute, nor indifferent to the issue of the movement, however wary and discreet is the expression of its deepfelt joy.
The Church of Rome need not act or speak on the present occasion ;
her part is to wait her time."—TAYLOR'S *Ancient Christianity.*

"WELL, I have no objection to your doctrines, I am
sure," said Mr. Roberts, in answer to Sir Roland's last
observation, "if it were merely that it opposes those
proud, pragmatical, Papistic Puseyites ; whose only

motive in life, I believe, is to exalt themselves and their order, and to ride on the necks of the people."

"Why Roberts," asked Sir Roland, with some warmth, " will you deny to others that charitable construction which we probably all wish, and certainly all require, should be put on our own actions? Why will you indulge that spirit? However," he added, smiling, " I need not put myself into a rage about it, only it is so strange that you who are, in reality, one of the best-natured fellows in the world, always in conversation make yourself out to be a perfect Ogre."

" Why, you see, I have but a certain portion of sweets in my composition," answered Mr. Roberts, good-humouredly ; " so if I exhausted it all in ' honeyed accents,' my deeds might become dreadful !"

" Well, then, send out your bees and fill both hives," said Sir Roland. " But, with regard to the love of spiritual power in the Puseyites, I think it very likely that it does mingle itself with their other feelings, but we have no right to say that it is the main object which they set before them. It is certainly painful to see how their idea of the value of the ' apostolic succession' takes the place of more essential things in their minds; and nothing convinces me of the evil of their doctrines more than the change which I see them effect in many who formerly professed and acted upon evangelical principles. Those who were once ever wakeful to the necessities of souls, ever desirous to promote God's kingdom upon earth, seeming now, in many instances, intent only, or at least chiefly, on exalting the merits and power of the ' succession,' leaving the souls of men to fare as best they may. Returning too, in so many instances, to the vain and frivolous dissipation of the world, which once they had utterly renounced.   Oh! I have traced the effect of this poison in so many minds, and in some too, of whom my heart tearfully exclaims, 'Ye did run well, who hath hindered you?'"

"You will find, Mr. Roberts," said Mr. Singleton, "that grievous error has often been put forward by well-intentioned, honest, and even pious-hearted men. Indeed, it has been observed that most bad systems have been originated by good men—outwardly good, at least—Satan having sagacity enough to know, that, if wrong doctrines were preached by those of immoral character, the generality of people would instantly regret them. But the great evil is, that most of the followers of these men, adopting their errors, without holding to the chain of faith which, though slender, yet bound them to the truth, make shipwreck of conscience, and faith, and all things. I have heard a very excellent, but prejudiced man, say, 'that he did not think that any Puseyite could go to heaven;' but I cannot say that I agree with him in that awful opinion, for I believe, that amongst them may be found many (and among Roman Catholics also) who so sincerely desire to do the will of God, though not clearly perceiving wherein that will consists; and who also really trust to Christ for their salvation. But in both cases, there is so much of error mixed, that, I conceive, they must be saved in spite of the doctrine they hold, and not in accordance to what it teaches."

"Well then," said Mr. Roberts, "I hope I may be allowed, at least, to call these Puseyites the greatest fools that ever existed?"

"No," said Mr. Scott, "I shall enter my 'veto'

against you there, and quote, though not the Scriptures, yet the opinion of the wisest uninspired man that ever lived or wrote—Lord Bacon; who says (though I may not be quite correct in my words, perhaps, as I quote from memory) that, 'the Dervish who spins all his life on one foot in hopes of gaining Heaven, is a wiser man than he who takes no pains at all about it;' so if the matter were at issue between you and these earnest though mistaken men, or even between you and the spinning Dervish, Roberts, on which side would the learned authority just quoted have given his verdict?"

Mr. Scott looked at Sir Roland as he said this with a laughing gesture of deprecation; for he knew that the latter did not like the light tone of irony which he often used when speaking to Mr. Roberts; thinking it but ill calculated to create in the mind of that careless being, a respect for sacred things; or to awaken in him that due regard for "the vast concerns of an immortal state," which it was so desirable that he should feel.

Mr. Roberts, however, seemed but little discomposed, and replied contemptuously, "I do not pretend to be a saint, certainly; so I am afraid I must yield the palm both to my Puseyite and my twirling friends. I am not ambitious of such honours."

"You will, I am sure, forgive me, Mr. Roberts," said Mr. Singleton, in a grave but kind manner, for he felt that he ought not to remain silent, "if I say that the light way in which you speak at times pains me. These are high and solemn subjects, whether regarded as truth or error, and should not be approached with an irreverent spirit. Remember, if we are not 'saints' we are—what? Children of Satan! A saint is one who has been sanctified by the Spirit of God, and taught to accept in heart and soul the salvation of Christ; all who are not such, therefore, in a Christian land, must perish—wilfully perish—because they choose not to listen to Him who 'brought life and immortality to light.' I am sure if you will think of this in the solitude of your chamber, you will not wish to disdain so blessed a title, but rather earnestly desire to prove your claim to it."

He smiled kindly as he ended, and Mr. Roberts, whose spirit always hardened itself against Mr. Scott's playful but cutting remarks, was completely subdued. His colour rose, and he seemed both pained and embarrassed, and the expression of defiance which his countenance had previously worn, gave place to one of feeling and respect.

Sir Roland, whose considerate spirit felt for every one, willing to relieve his embarrassment, instantly resumed the conversation.

" I can easily comprehend," he said, " that persons who have habitually lived in ignorant and careless disregard of all religion, should be attracted by the doctrine of the Puseyites, and also by that of the Church of Rome. I had a friend who, having scarcely ever heard religion spoken of, and meeting with some zealous and amiable Roman Catholics, was induced to adopt their views, and become a Papist. Some one observed, ' It was a pity people were not contented with the faith of their fathers;' to which another answered, that, ' in this case, they would have been mighty easily contented if they had been.' To such persons, as I said before, I can well imagine that the doctrines and practices, of Rome and Oxford, may hold out great attractions—they knowing of nothing better. But that those who have once 'tasted the good things of God'—any portion of whose souls has been informed by the Holy Spirit of God—who have enjoyed in any measure 'the glorious liberty of the sons of God'—that such persons should 'leave feeding on this fair mountain, to batten on that moor,' is past my comprehension! I remember hearing of a speech which the old Lord Eldon made many years ago, in which he said, 'He could not think on a velocipede!' But the Tractarians have *un*-thought on a velocipede—and on one of tremendous power too—for in one moment, as it were, they have taken a backward leap of fourteen hundred years, and with desperate determination, have thrown their intellects into the darkness of the earliest ages."

"It is most marvellous!" said Mr. Singleton; "and they certainly strengthen exceedingly the hands of Rome, so that I do not wonder at the latter exclaiming, 'Beati sono i Puseiti!' But they have not yet found out the point at which infallibility is to rest. They say indeed, to us, 'Hear the Church,' and yet they differ from each other in every possible shade and degree, and 'hear the Church' themselves only on such points as they like."

"Yes, that has often struck me," said Sir Roland; "for if 'the Church' is to be received as an *infallible* guide (as the Papists *bonâ fide* receive their church) we must bow our judgments entirely to her, and not take upon ourselves to judge of any thing that she teaches; but this, though they inculcate it, they do not practise, for they venture to differ whenever they please; and if *they* object in *one* thing, *I* may—as far

as infallibility is concerned—object in a hundred. To
the Bible I can bow my whole soul, for that is the
true, unerring word of God; but I am afraid Dr. Pusey
would think me a terrible and audacious heretic were I
to say, that I adhere to the Church of England, not as
taking her for my guide, but as mere matter of preference. Indeed, a Puseyite friend of mine always tells
me I am not 'a churchman,' only a 'man who goes to
church'—not a bad distinction, and perfectly true according to their views."

"Do you prefer it then, merely as the best sect,"
asked Mr. Singleton, "or have you any value for it as
'the Church of England, as by law established?'"

"I value it as both," said Sir Roland.

"You are not then, for the voluntary principle?"

"Oh, no! I am totally opposed to that as a national rule. A Church—a settled State-church—I
think every nation is bound to maintain, if it hopes
for the blessing of God on it *as a nation*. Any government is inexcusable, in my opinion, which does
not, as a great 'Pater familias,' feed its children with
nourishing spiritual food; and our church, spite of her
errors, has been, and is, deeply valuable, as a preserver
of the uncorrupted word of God, and of much that
is excellent in doctrine and discipline. To her, therefore, shall I adhere as long as it is in any way possible.
If the Tractarians succeed, *as is their avowed and published wish*, in reuniting her to the Church of Rome,
by altering things so as to suit that church (some
concession also being expected from her) then I must
perforce, leave her—or rather she will have left me.
But I do not like to anticipate that evil day; if it

comes, may God 'give strength to His people, that they
may be faithful even unto the end.'"

" Amen !" said Mr. Singleton. " But if one thing
more than another could vex my soul, it would be, I
think, the having no fixed national church to go to.
Besides, I feel sure that, if the church depart from
God, God will depart from her, and from this—then
—fated nation. I almost fancy I have seen 'Ichabod'
written on her ever since the admission of the Catholics
into our national counsels; and whenever our church
becomes faithless, then indeed, shall I fully expect to
find that ' the glory of the Lord is departed.'"

" The same impression rests on my mind," said
Sir Roland ; " yet I can feel sincerely for the Roman
Catholics as men, and am glad that many of their dis-
abilities have been taken off; but never should they
have been admitted into parliament, and never either
ought we to have thought ourselves justified in voting
supplies for the instruction of those who were to go
forth and teach the people error."

" Ah ! it is a most difficult subject to manage,"
said Mr. Singleton ; " and I only wish we could have
come with cleaner hands into the combat, as regards
Ireland ; for though I do not believe that, in the whole
world, there are a set of men who labour as ' in the
fire,' as many ministers and others do at this moment
in that country, yet for how many years was the Protestant Church there a scandal and a disgrace to any
religion ?   It is a deep debt we owe to that unhappy
nation, and I almost fear the time and power for
paying it off is fast passing from us.   Truly ' Christ
has received fearful wounds in the house of His friends '

there, and even now, in many excellent people, I should
be rejoiced to see more of the ' sword of the Spirit,'
less of the *Spirit of the sword*, more conciliation to the
Papists themselves, though as deep an abhorrence as
they like to Popery. Of all the missionaries that I ever
read of, Felix Neff appears to me, for this very
reason, by far the most perfect—joining such temper, and gentleness, and discretion—to such high
clear views, and such unflagging zeal and devotion.
Labouring as he did, till he destroyed himself—and on
the very Valdensian spots, too, which had been so often
red with the blood of the persecuted and slaughtered
Protestants—yet he raised no enmity against, or among
the Romish priests and population which were about
him, but lived with them on the kindest terms; so
much so, that we are told in Gilly's memoir of him,
that the sub-prefect, a Roman Catholic, and many
others of that persuasion—to shew him honour—actually attended at the ceremony of opening the little
Protestant chapel at Violins; and that many also,
would often attend his sermons— Bibles and Testa-
ments being distributed too, for a length of time without interruption. Would—would that all were animated by the same heaven-born spirit ! that all—even
while devoting themselves as this young martyr did—
to teaching the most pure and spiritual truth, would
remember ' that the wrath of man worketh not the
righteousness of God.' "

"I have often wished that the Church in Ireland
could be put upon a different footing than it is," said
Sir Roland ; " though I dare say the attempt would be
found fraught with a thousand difficulties. It is very
easy to dictate what should be done, as one sits by

one's own fireside, but one must hold some of the reins of government one's self, I fancy, before one can justly estimate the difficulties that surround a minister, in the endeavour to carry out any great question. But I have long wished that tithes could have been entirely redeemed there, and a fund formed from them, out of which the clergy of the Church of England could be paid ; so that, dropping down, as it were from Heaven, in the midst of the Roman Catholics, they might spend and be spent amongst them, without drawing money from them in a manner which they feel, and naturally resent; and which is certainly calculated to prejudice them against these spiritual teachers; for it must be gallingly oppressive to them to have to pay for the maintenance of a church which they think accursed, and that, too, out of a fund which had for ages belonged to the ministers of their own faith. I think there has never been sufficient consideration shewn for these *natural* feelings of the Papists for what should we feel—and which perhaps, we may soon have to feel —were we obliged to pay our tithes to a Romish, instead of a Protestant church ?"

"As you are so very tender of them, Sir Roland," said Mr. Roberts, "you had better pay the Popish priests at once, as has been often talked of."

"I should as soon think of paying chemists and confectioners to sell poisoned drugs and sugar-plums," answered Sir Roland. "If people's *fancies* in religion are to be provided for, their *fancies* in other matters may as well be considered also, and there might be a provision for all sorts of absurdities. No, the use of a church is to instruct the people in the *truth ;* we must not pay to have such fearful error as Popery taught, though we may feel so much for the victims of delusion, as shall make us desirous of softening to their natural feelings all that may, and must seem hard, and difficult to be borne."

"I care not a rush for them or their feelings," exclaimed Mr. Roberts; "I should just like to string them all up in a row, like Ulysses's ill-behaved maids, with a bunch of Puseyites at each end, by way of tassels."

"And a sprinkling of dissenters too, Roberts," suggested Mr. Scott; "for I know you equally hate them."

"By all means, or a whole cluster of them, if you like it."

"What hangings, drownings, and burnings, you will have, my good fellow, when your sect of 'Nothingites' comes in; you, as the mighty 'Nil ipsissimum,' installed in the high chair of state!"

"When I am arrived at that desirable elevation, Scott, you may be sure I will give you and your dissenters some test which you will not be able easily to swallow; something which will bring you under all three forms of death."

"Are you particularly fond of the dissenters, Scott?" asked his cousin.

"I infinitely prefer standing by my own church to being a dissenter," replied Mr. Scott; "but when I see the great good those men have done in so many instances (Christian dissenters, I mean, not those who deny the Atonement, of course,) and how much God blesses their work, I am ready to say, as some good old divine did, 'What is good enough for Christ is good enough for me.' Many people seem to overlook the fact that it was, when in their unconverted state, that the apostles 'forbid' others doing good in Christ's name, 'because they followed not after them;' and they seem also, to have forgotten that our Lord answered, 'Forbid them not;' while St. Paul, *when converted*—even when speaking of those who preached of contention, said, ' Notwithstanding every way, whether in pretence or in truth, Christ is preached; and I therein do rejoice, yea, and will rejoice.' And I confess the apostle's feeling is my own."

" Well, Sir Roland, at least you will let me call Popish priests hypocrites?" said Mr. Roberts.

" Oh, in mercy do, Ashton," exclaimed Mr. Scott, with an imploring gesture; " he is under the influence of that word to-day, and we shall have no peace till he has had his fancy out. I really suspect, Roberts, that some one has been calling you ' hypocrite,' you seem so exceedingly anxious to pass the title on to some one else."

Mr. Roberts reddened, and Sir Roland answered, laughing—

" I am afraid I cannot grant your request, even here, Roberts; though I am quite grieved to refuse it, backed as it is by such cogent reasonings from Scott. But I will tell you why I cannot brand even these men, individually, with the name you wish me to give them."

" Particularly not those who assist at the liquefaction of the blood of St. Januarius—or at the bursting out of the statue of somebody or other at St. Peter's into a profuse perspiration—or who sew frogs up in lawn, and put them on the altar to leap about, pretending they are the devils they have just cast out of a shriven penitent, I suppose?" asked Mr. Roberts, triumphantly.

"You have not, after all, Mr. Roberts," observed Mr. Singleton, "named the worst of all impostures, the one, most horrible, probably, that the world ever produced—namely, the Greek fire."

"To say the truth," replied Mr. Roberts, "I never thoroughly understood what the Greek fire was, though I have often heard of it."

"It is this," replied Mr. Singleton. "The Church of the Holy Sepulchre at Jerusalem is, you know, built not only over the supposed site of our Lord's tomb, but over the—also supposed—house where the Holy Ghost fell on the disciples on the day of Pentecost. The Greek church, with awful profanity, pretend that fresh showers of the Holy Spirit descend on their priests every returning Whit Sunday. To prove this, they concoct a species of gas, or of phosphoric flame of some kind, called this 'Greek fire,' which they cause to issue forth at the appointed times, and, apparently, to fall on the assembled priests."

"Horrible!" exclaimed Mr. Roberts. "I did not think any such frightful atrocities could ever have been conceived."

"It is most lamentable, indeed," replied Mr. Singleton, "and scarcely is it less so, that the patriarch of this church should be regarded by the Tractarians with special reverence, as the 'immediate successor of St. James, the first bishop of Jerusalem.' At one time they endeavoured also to train a dove to descend; but the bird—more faithful to the nature God had given it than the men—proved refractory, and would

H 2

not descend properly, but flew hither and thither at its own pleasure, greatly discomforting the holy fathers, and finally obliging them to omit that scene in their profane farce."

"Can that be true?" asked Sir Roland.

"A perfect fact, I assure you," replied Mr. Single-ton, "though so dreadful a one, that I do not wonder at your doubting it."

"That is indeed worse than any thing I had ever dreamed of," said Mr. Roberts, who seemed really subdued by the frightful view of human nature presented to him.

"You have driven me hard, certainly, Roberts," replied Sir Roland, good-humouredly, "with regard to the Papists, though I won't yield yet. I am perfectly aware that in many cases the priests must know for certain that what they say is not true; and also that they pretend to do what they know to be impostures; but we must remember that their church teaches them that such things are calculated to do good, and to save souls; and if they once begin to doubt the lawfulness of the things she commands—that doubt would be, in their eyes, one of the most deadly sins they could commit: one not to be purged away without the severest penances; therefore, you see, the conscience itself becomes bound by this terrible system to such a degree, that, unless the all-powerful Spirit of God work irresistibly, the wretched slave of superstition is left to perish in the chain that reduces the whole soul to the most hopeless degradation. We have however taken extreme cases, for all are not commanded to perform such revolting impostures; but if I am right, you see

that the individuals themselves may even then be
wholly guiltless of the sin of hypocrisy, even in practising these pious frauds; though there is no doubt
that many delight in these things, and go far beyond
what even the church desires, for their own private
gain and advantage. But it is the system, Roberts,
that is so awful; and in nothing does the wily wisdom of its dreadful author shew itself more decidedly
than in thus terrifying men from venturing for one instant to use their own reason. Against the *system* of
Popery, it is impossible to feel too strongly."

"I see what you mean," said Mr. Roberts, "but
you really seem determined to make yourself ' un ange
de clémence,' for every thing in the world, good, bad,
and indifferent. You will end in being, like John
Huss, who, if you remember, when a woman rushed
forward with a lighted torch to be the first to set fire
to the pile that was to consume him, with wonderful
density of intellect, saw in the act only the simplicity of
her faith, and exclaimed, ' Sancta simplicitas !'"

"I don't know; I think I might have had my
doubts about that; though I might have been constrained to acknowledge her burning zeal."

"You making a pun, Ashton!" exclaimed Mr.
Scott; "' Proh pudor ! '"

"Very dreadful, I acknowledge," said Sir Roland,
smiling. "I cry you mercy, for the deed."

"But you really do appear to me," continued Mr.
Roberts to Sir Roland, " to waste your life in making
excuses for people."

"Wasn't it Lord A—— who said of some friend,
that he was a sort of man who frittered away his
money in paying tradesmen's bills?" asked Mr. Scott;

"your observation, Roberts, would serve beautifully as a 'pendant' to that witticism."

"Ah, well, I daresay I have you all against me; so I shall content myself with saying, as regards all Papists, and Puseyites — and dissenters, too, to please you, Scott — what the Swiss republican said respecting all the kings of the earth: 'Je voudrais bien, qu'ils avoient tous une chaîne autour de leurs cous, et qui moi, je la tenois!' and a pretty tight strain I should give it, you may be sure."

"My good friend," said Mr. Singleton, "it seemed mighty easy to Jehu to say, 'Come, see my zeal for the Lord,' when that zeal consisted in slaying the prophets of Baal; but when called upon to surrender one heart-sin, how far did it carry him? I think we have all great need of bearing that example in mind."

"I am afraid I shall come quite within the sweep of Roberts's virtuous indignation," said Sir Roland, "if I say that there are really some things in which I think the Puseyites have done good. I like, I confess, the restoration of the old church architecture, and the beautifying of churches, where not overdone; I highly approve a greater degree of church-discipline than has been attended to for a length of time; wishing earnestly that it would extend itself so as make the bishops who are opposed to the doctrine conscientiously and effectually suppress its preaching and teaching throughout their dioceses. Then I like, also, the more frequent services in towns, and the improvement in music; and the attention to education is most praiseworthy, though I cordially dislike and disapprove the exclusive principle on which it is carried on; which, however, naturally grows out of

the erroneous and unscriptural ideas they have formed
of the power and sanctity of their particular church."

"Well, if you take my advice," said Mr. Roberts,
"you will let them and all their practices alone. Depend upon it, if you begin by admiring *one* thing in
them now, and adopting it, you will never end till you
have gone to the 'ultima Thule' of all their absurdities
and abominations."

"I am too old, Roberts," replied Sir Roland,
shaking his head—while his young countenance lighted
up with the most sparkling smile—"to start at shadows.
No," he continued more gravely, "I am glad to accept what is good from any hand; for we are told to
'prove all things, and hold fast that which is good.
You shall hear what a wiser man than I am says on
this subject, for I have here an extract from a work of
that excellent man and pure theologian, Bickersteth,*
who, in his 'Divine Warning to the Church,' says,
'Let us beware of opposing any thing really good, because it comes from those whose general principles we
are constrained to condemn. Let us rather gladly
promote that which is really excellent whoever sug-
gests it. Thus we shall not only add strength to our
own testimony against their errors, but take away
the strength of error in conjunction with important
truths, by which alone the consciences of really good
men are retained in its defence. In short, let us realise the words of St. Paul, 'that ye may approve

---

* There is a slight literary anachronism here, as Mr. Bickersteth's work was only published in 1843; and this conversation, from
the construction of the story, must necessarily have taken place four
or five years before. Indeed, it must be confessed, the whole tenour
of this conversation is rather antedated.

things that are excellent, that ye may be sincere and
without offence till the day of Christ.' But see how
well he guards his liberality from the charge of care-
lessness by an after passage, which I have also noted
down here, and a magnificent passage it is too ! warning us of the approach of the troublous times, which
seem, indeed, near at hand. He says, 'Let us not mistake
halting between two opinions, for a peace-making,
peace-loving spirit, but, remember, that heavenly wisdom is first pure, then peaceable. Let us never think
to promote true peace by clothing unfaithfulness to
God and His truth with the names of judgment
and discretion. There is no judgment or discretion
equal to that of being on the Lord's side, and undergoing suffering for righteousness' sake ; and eternity
will make this clear to all creation. Let us then well
count the cost of being a real Christian, all the hazards
and dangers, all the shame and cruel mockings, all the
sacrifices and heavy losses, to which we may be soon
exposed. But then let us look to that treasury we
have in Christ Jesus to meet all this cost, and at that
recompense of reward and that crown of life which He
will bestow.'"

"It is a very beautiful passage, I will confess,"
observed Mr. Roberts, "and I don't know that I should
quite object to being like the man who wrote it ; but it
is the process of becoming like such persons that is
odious and insupportable. *Figurez vous* : the flapping
of wings, the struggling of legs, the writhing of antennæ,
before the butterfly can emerge from its chrysalis state !
I fancy we should all be tolerably resigned to being
perfect, if perfection could be achieved as easily as
renown was, by *that* man, who said ' that he got up one

morning and found himself famous!' But the transition state—that must be hideous!—When considerate, well-intentioned friends (like the present company) recommend perfection to me, it is extraordinary what an amiable, engaging fit of timidity comes over me. I retreat a step, and, courteously waving my hand, beg my friends to go first."

"And with true Chesterfieldian politeness, they have, I think, Roberts, obeyed the invitation," said Mr. Scott, with an arch smile.

Mr. Roberts laughed away a rising flush, and replied—"That is no disgrace, you know, Scott, when one has voluntarily yielded the *pas ;* and remember, that though Lord Chesterfield got into the carriage first, his majesty still remained king."

"I wish your majesty would make me a gracious donation of some of your royal modesty," said Mr. Scott.

"Perfectly welcome to the whole of it, my dear fellow! for I never make the slightest use of it myself."

"Really, Roberts," replied the other, "I do wish you were a good man, for I must confess, you have a vast deal to say for yourself, and might be of great use in a good cause."

"I am very well satisfied," replied Mr. Roberts: "'accordez moi la tète, et pour la cour, je vous l'abandonne !' But now I really must be off."

"What! without a lingering Parthian shot at the Puseyites?"

"Yes, *j'ai vidé ma carquoise,* and have only to entreat, that if Sir Roland gets installed in state amongst them, he will insure me a merciful death at their hands when they begin their 'auto-da-fés.' Depend upon it, when one of the first half-hatched chirps, out of the scarcely chipped egg-shell, is, that they 'approve of penances for differences of opinion,' they will not be full-grown and full-fledged, without making those penances pretty severe. That is a prospect which it is particularly disagreeable to me to contemplate; for though I may not be all Mr. Singleton would wish me to be (perhaps it would be better if I were), yet I hope I should be ready at any time to go to the stake rather than subscribe to what I felt was false. These Puseyite opinions suit 'la jeune église,' and the present bench of bishops is not throughout affected by them; but such will probably not be the case with the next, and—remember my words, and see if they come not true:—if ever these men get the staff in their own hands, they will make use of that 'argumentum baculinum' in a way difficult to be borne; and if some strong measure is not taken to keep them out of the Church of England *now*, depend upon it—that day will soon arrive. I warn you—and when you are smarting under their blows, remember me! There Scott, I have been able, after all, to produce one arrow more, and having 'drawn it to the head,' I take my leave;" and shaking hands with his two friends, and bowing with great respect to Mr. Singleton, he left the room.

"You don't take the right way with that young man, Scott," said Mr. Singleton, as soon as Mr. Roberts was gone; "you should not talk so lightly to him."

"There! I was sure you would begin a 'tirade' against me the moment he closed the door; I was very near going away with him to avoid being torn to pieces, for I know, Ashton is thirsting for the on-slaught."

"No, no, one at a time," said Sir Roland. "I leave you in very excellent hands, so good-bye;" and nodding kindly, he left the room.

"I wish he had stayed," said Mr. Scott, with some-what of an embarrassed laugh, "for I had much rather have had a general 'mêlée' than have to sit down for your solemn single-handed reproof, Singleton, and all your detestably unanswerable arguments."

"I will defer what I have to say then, if you like it, or suppress it altogether if you had rather not hear it."

"No, no—go on," and he took up a book and busied himself in turning over its leaves.

"I am not going to be very severe, Willy," said Mr. Singleton, smiling, "so don't put on that angry look."

"I am not angry," said Mr. Scott, raising his glow-ing countenance to his cousin, with a look of so much good feeling and affection, that the latter, looking at him for a moment with an expression of great love said, "I like to have a fault to find with you every now and then, Scott, it brings out such a bright side of your character; there are few who can bear as you can to have it hinted that they are not 'quite perfection.' However, I forgot, I was not going to praise—but to blame you—wasn't it?"

"I know pretty well what you would say," observed Mr. Scott; "you would tell me that I am wrong, both in laughing at Roberts, and in laughing with him."

" Quite right. Go on."

" No, no, I am not going to mix my own draught, and take it too; that is more than can be expected of mortal man! You must prepare the ingredients for the cup; and mind you make them very palatable if you mean me to swallow them."

" I object to your laughing at Roberts, then, because ridicule opens no man's heart; it is the utmost that the best temper can do just to bear it; no one can like it, or at the moment, can feel complacent towards the person who uses it. It is not a Christian weapon, and should be put out of our armory. Ridicule in writings may occasionally do good, as people reading what is said quietly to themselves, may perhaps, be led to see the folly of what they have professed or done, more by this means than by solid argument, and may secretly take their own measures for alteration, without their pride being hurt by having confessions to make, or by being forced to say what has caused the change. But in conversation, it should invariably be avoided, for the reasons I have mentioned. To such as you and I, who have both of us such an awful eye for the absurd in life, it is a great temptation; and hundreds of times have I given way to it, and hated myself the next moment. But of late years I have kept such a tight hand over myself in this respect, —especially where any thing of religion is concerned— that, my mind, ceasing to cater for its amusement in that way, really does not perceive the absurdity of many things that would have convulsed it in former days. I can now more sympathise with Sir Roland, who, I can see, feels distressed if any one makes himself ridiculous. How many times I observed him to-day draw off attention from Roberts, when he saw him embarrassed. You have no jealousy in you, Scott, so I do not fear praising your friend before you."

"It is impossible to praise him enough," said Mr. Scott, with great energy; "you don't know what that man is, nor half the sacrifices he has just made to be of use to Anstruther, whose conduct to him used to be unsufferable, poor fellow!"

"That he is your chosen friend is enough to prepossess me in his favour," said Mr. Singleton; "but I certainly like most extremely what I have seen of him. But with regard to laughing *with* that young fellow, I think if any thing it is worse than laughing *at* him, when you reflect that by joining him, you encourage him to speak lightly of serious matters. Good nonsense is a very good thing sometimes, as long as it is an innocent exercise of wit, and fun, and cleverness; but as soon as it verges towards that

' Mirth unblest,
Drowning God's music in the breast,'

which is so much condemned both by Scripture and good feeling, it ceases to be 'good'—and becomes 'bad' nonsense. 'Wisdom should ever be the under-current of your wit.' That young man, Roberts, has a very quick, clever, discerning mind, with a wonderfully good judgment, and great penetration; and I do not think there was a single view of the present fearful state of the church, in which I did not fully and entirely go with him; but his tone of feeling I could not approve. He seems to have been brought up entirely in, and for the world, and much excuse is therefore to be made for him; and we who think—who know—that we possess a better knowledge than what this world can teach, should never let him talk slightingly of those things whose inestimable value we are acquainted with. I am convinced he might be easily checked, for though conceited and presumptuous, he is not hardened; and if all the true Christians with whom he converses were faithful, Willy, and consistent, God might give a great blessing to them and to him.——Now put on your hat, and come and shew me about your fine city here."

CHAPTER XII.

" I was not ever thus, nor prayed that Thou should'st lead me on !
I loved to choose, and see my path, but now—lead Thou me on !
I loved the garish day, and spite of fears
Pride ruled my will,—remember not past years !
    *   *   *   *   *   *
              Those angel faces smile
Which I have loved long since and lost awhile ! "

AT twelve o'clock on the following day, Mr. Singleton, as had been agreed, went to Lord N——'s house and walked straight up to Mr. Anstruther's room, where he found all prepared for the Sacrament, and the invalid alone, as he had requested. The excitement of his feelings had lent an unusual glow to Mr. Anstruther's countenance; and a deep flush had settled in one bright crimson spot—the hectic of consumption—on his cheek. His large dark eyes shone with a force of expression which health seldom presents; yet was there nothing of the painful restlessness and anxiety which had formerly so strongly characterised them, but rather an earnest, settled look of exalted peace. The dignity of an adopted child of God had greatly delivered him from the fear of man, and had overcome the diffidence and embarrassment which he would otherwise have felt in seeing those who had

formerly known him under such very different circumstances. He had, with a noble frankness, asked forgiveness of Mr. Scott for the contemptuous rudeness
of his former manner and conduct; yet in doing so, no
false shame had caused his eye to shrink from that of
the other, who met him with the utmost kindness, and
shewed an interest and regard, that was most touching
to him. With equal openness, when Mr. Singleton
entered the room, he held out his hand to him, and
thanked him for coming so readily to a stranger.

" You must not consider yourself a stranger, Mr.
Anstruther," said the other. " None who are looking
to Christ for salvation can be strangers to those who
are enjoying the same inestimable hope. You are
truly resting on Him, are you not ? "

" Most truly."

" ' The Holy Spirit testifying with your spirit that
you are one of the sons of God ? ' "

Mr. Anstruther looked up with a countenance so
beaming with the bright hope that was within him; that
before he could answer, Mr. Singleton stopped him,
saying, " I want no words—save your poor lungs—a
higher language has told me all ; the testimony of the
Spirit shines too clearly through those speaking eyes
for me to need more.   You are a happy man—so near
the possession of your inheritance ! "

" I am indeed happy," replied Mr. Anstruther; " not
even the remembrance of my sins can disturb me now ;
for when I begin to think of them, the sense of God's
forgiving mercy rushes in, and sweeps all before it."

" Ay," returned Mr. Singleton; "it is like a nauseous
pill so wrapped in sweets that its bitterness is lost."

Mr. Anstruther smiled at the quaint comparison,

and said, " It was indeed true, for all bitterness was
lost in the sweetness of God's love."

" And now, my good friend," said Mr. Singleton,
" you shall talk no more. My mind is satisfied about
you, and I will gladly administer the Sacrament to you,
in remembrance of Him ' who has indeed redeemed you
to Himself by His precious blood-shedding.' "

Then ringing the bell, he desired Mr. Anstruther's
servant to request Sir Roland and Mr. Scott to come
up-stairs. The moment they approached the table, he
commenced the service which the peculiar circumstances under which it was given, rendered unusually
solemn. Mr. Anstruther was excessively affected, and
leant his head on the table the whole time, for he
was too weak to sit up. When it was concluded
however, he held out his hand to Mr. Singleton, and
thanked him with a countenance which proved that
the " peace of God," which had been so sincerely prayed
for, had entered indeed into his soul; and that " the
blessing of the Father, of the Son, and of the Holy
Spirit," rested abundantly upon him.

(In after times often did Sir Roland recall that look,
and never without a thrill of thankful joy passing
through his breast.)

" Are you tired, Anstruther," he said, after the
others had left the room, " or shall I stay with you
a little ? "

" Stay, by all means ; for even if I cannot talk
much, I delight in seeing you there."

" If I tire you, you must tell me, but I had something to say to you. A little while ago you asked
me how, in your short remaining time, it would be
possible for you to prove the reality of your con-

version. You have evidenced it by the complete change in your whole self; or rather, the Spirit has shewn forth its power and work in you in a manner visible to all who see you. But there is yet one exertion with which I think God would be well pleased if you felt equal to it."

"I shall be only too thankful to be enabled to shew forth His glory in any way."

"But your bodily powers might not be equal to it," said Sir Roland.

"Then I can have no choice. But what is it?"

"It is to speak to some of the young and thoughtless creatures around you, and try to arouse them to a sense of their own danger, and of their ingratitude to God. I have myself endeavoured to say a word to them from time to time, but I seldom see them, and, besides, every thing from me comes, you know, like an ' ex-parte' statement."

"It is from me, certainly, that it should come; for I have been too long a strengthener of Satan's ·hands as respects them, by my total disregard of religion, and by the contempt I have so often thrown upon it. And they could not think that I had any sinister motive in contradicting my former self, and speaking in favour of Him whose service I once so wholly cast off. Ask Seymour to come to me, will you, when he is at leisure. I may not be able to speak much to all, though I should like to take leave of them; but to him I could speak best; he is of a soberer, kindlier nature than the rest, and he might not, perhaps, mind repeating to them any message I might give him. Ah! how I now regret the time which is past, lost for ever! What a blessing I might have been to those young

things, so full of life and spirits, but giving all their
fresh and bright affections to this world! Instead
of which I have been a curse—a blighting, fearful
curse to them; teaching them to despise their God,
and trample upon His laws. Send the poor boy to
me now, will you, Ashton, if you can find him. Time
presses, and my proud heart might shrink from the
task if I thought long about it. It is not pleasing to
flesh and blood to say, 'I have been wrong;' but God
will not suffer me to fail, I trust, in this duty, and
joyful, indeed, should I be, if He would bless my
words to any who hear them."

Sir Roland went in search of Mr. Seymour, who
was one of Lord N——'s *attachés*, and who lived in
his house, and having found him, begged him to go up
to Mr. Anstruther.

When he entered his apartment the latter received
him most kindly, saying, he wished much to see him,
and take leave of him. The young man was much
affected at this kindness of manner in one, of whom, in
former days, he had always stood so much in awe;
and whose visibly dying state made his words fall
solemnly on his ear. Mr. Anstruther did not spare
himself, but lamented the rebellion of his former life
against the great Being who had created and redeemed
him, and entreated his young friend to give his
heart's best affections and earliest love to his Father
and his God.

He subsequently, in a similar manner, took leave
of all his young associates, most of whom seemed, for
the time at least, to be much affected by his repre-
sentations.

Each day now brought a change to the dying man,

who suffered agonisingly from weakness and difficulty in breathing; but seldom did an impatient sound pass his lips; or if one did occasionally escape, the eye, quickly turned towards heaven, shewed that he supplicated pardon, and sought the blessing of the Holy Spirit, that "patience" might have "her perfect work."

"You are a strange fellow, Roland," said Lord N——, when he had returned from his short excursion with Mr. Roberts; "a little while ago you could not bear George Anstruther, and now I have asked for you ever so many times since I came home, and am always told you are 'in Mr. Anstruther's room.' However, it is very kind of you, though I am afraid it is an irksome confinement."

"Far from it; I prefer being with him, to being elsewhere just now. His mind is much changed, poor fellow, of late."

"Oh, what! 'the sinner was sick, the sinner a saint would be,' I suppose."

"No," said Sir Roland, though he was pained at the way in which his uncle spoke, "I am convinced that it is no feeling of that kind with Anstruther. I believe him truly changed, and I rejoice the more because his days are well-nigh spent, I fear."

"Do you think him in immediate danger?" asked Lord N——, much alarmed.

"I do; I think a few weeks, or even a few days, may see it all at an end."

"I had no idea," said Lord N——, "that he was so very ill; I have not seen him lately, and during my absence I fear he must have got much worse. I

am sorry I spoke so heedlessly, poor fellow, for I am
truly grieved for him, and am shocked at what you
tell me; I did not think his danger was nearly so
great."

"This last week has been a very trying one to
him in every way," replied Sir Roland; "but his mind
is now at peace, though his health sinks fast."

"My dear Roland, you are young, and very enthusiastic (in which your friend Scott, by the bye, helps
you not a little) and I am sure I do not wish to
deprive you of any encouragement you may have in
your laudable exertions; but do let me warn you not
to imagine that real changes take place in people's
character in this sudden and wonderful way, for the
days of miracles are past. Go on in your own way, by
all means, for you have been a good boy from
your birth, and no doubt you will go to heaven
and have your reward. But don't expect an old man
like me to believe that, just because a body gets ill, and
is forced to lie in bed, that therefore, he becomes
a saint all of a sudden. I dare say he gets frightened,
just as a naughty boy does at the sight of the rod, and
exclaims he will be good; but when you have lived in
the world as long as I have, you will find that your
virtuous bed-ridden folks turn out as great rogues
as others, when they can walk alone again."

"I fear, indeed, that what you say is too often
true," replied Sir Roland; "but cases do, undoubtedly, sometimes occur in which the Spirit of God
touches the heart, even in the closing hours of life;
and as soon as they are led by Him to see their own
sinfulness, and to accept of Christ's free salvation, they
must, according to God's promise, become His child-

ren. And this real change it is which has, I truly
believe, taken place in poor Anstruther."

" Of course," replied Lord N——, " a man, at
such a time, when he thinks he has nothing to do but
to die, is vastly glad to be told he shall go to heaven
without any merit or trouble of his own ; *c'est tout
simple*, and very pleasant hearing."

" But, my dear sir, it really is not so *simple*—so
much ' of course' as you think. Many, even at that
hour, cling to ideas of their own righteousness—thanking God they have always been upright and religious,
or always done their best, &c.—the enemy soothing
them to the last with hollow hopes built on a wrong
foundation ; while others, sometimes not only virtually,
but actually—fearfully deny the name and existence of
Christ the Lord."

" Well, my dear nephew, if they do so, it is very
sad ; for after all, I don't think we have much to
boast of, any of us. And in truth, I do the poor fellow up-stairs a great injustice by classing him with
notorious sinners ; for though he has never been a religious man certainly, yet he has been under my roof now
nearly six years, and I don't in my conscience think that
even your life, Roland, has been a purer one than his, nor
one more free from vice of every kind. And yet, I
don't know how it was, but he was never liked ; the
vicious were afraid of him, I believe—and the virtuous
too, I fancy, for that matter—for he was so mighty
haughty and disdainful, and came into the room with
his chin in the air, looking so gentlemanlike and
disagreeable, that, truth to say, I would fain many a
time have conveyed my own person out of the way if I
could have done so unobserved : but that, of course,

'*sub sygillo confessionali*,' not to be breathed to ears profane."

"It is that unamiable spirit which he now so deeply regrets," said Sir Roland, "proceeding as it did, from enmity of the heart to God. But I always had a hope that the time would come in which the better part of his disposition might be brought out, and his heart reconciled to God."

"And why were you to have that hope about him particularly? or do you charitably feel the same for every body—even for your old reprobate uncle?"

Sir Roland smiled, and answered—"I cannot I am sorry to say, feel that hope for every one, however much I might wish it; but he had a mother once——"

"Well, and every body 'had a mother once,'" said Lord N——, interrupting Sir Roland quickly, whilst his bright grey eye twinkled with a merriment which even the gravest subjects could scarcely ever subdue— "you need draw no very exclusive ground of hope for him on that account, methinks."

"My dear uncle," replied Sir Roland, laughing, "I think I must really give up talking to you on these subjects at all. You are one of those who would make 'the scaffold re-echo with the joke,' and would delight in causing even 'death's ribs to shake with laughter,' I believe, if you could. I know you do not mind what I say, but, in truth," he added, with a sadder expression, "I do so much feel for poor Anstruther—so very much;—and am so filled with gratitude to God on his account, that though I could not help laughing at your interruption, yet it grieves and disquiets me to have the subject treated so lightly."

"Well, well! but I really am very sorry for the

poor fellow, and will go and see him in a few minutes,
though I shall not know what to say to him. We were
never on a very familiar footing—speaking terms, but
no more—business ended, so ended our conversations
generally. But still to know that one who has been so
long with me, and so young too," he added feelingly,
"is sinking so rapidly into the grave, is a very appalling, a very painful thing. But what were you going
to say just now?"

"Oh! I was only going to say that his mother,
whom you know, was a great friend of my mother's,
was a truly excellent woman, and taught him in early
youth much that was good, and I knew that he retained for her feelings of the deepest love; and it was
that which always made me hope for him, for I trusted
that what she had taught him—what she had sowed
with, I fear, many tears (for hers was a sad fate)
might, at length, be reaped with abundant joy; God's
promises are so full to faithful parents!"

"My dear Roland, I am sure your parents' faithfulness is abundantly repaid in you," said Lord N——
with a glistening eye, "for you are the best—the very
best creature I ever met with; and though I do sometimes abuse your vagaries, yet, when I come to hear
you fairly out, I find you as sober and steady as a
rock, and no wonder, for all you say is 'founded on a
Rock.' There, you see, I know a little bit of Scripture
as well as you, though I dare say, you thought I did
not know Aaron from Achilles. You good people
always fancy no one knows any thing but yourselves;
though I must confess, there are a monstrous number
of things which, if you do understand, *I* certainly *do
not.* They don't suit a stupid old fellow like me."

" What things do you mean, my dear sir?" inquired Sir Roland.

" Oh, many things! A mighty deal that you say is
utterly incomprehensible to me.   There are your *con-
versions* and *convictions,* and con—all sort of things,
which to my mind, end in a complete *con-fusion.* They
puzzle my old brain as much as all your new-fangled
names for old-fashioned flowers, which are enough to
distract any man.   If one goes nowadays to a gar-
dener's and asks for—let me see—a tropœolum, for
instance, expecting to get something very fine and new,
he gives you nothing but the old nasturtium, which
your grandmother pickled the seeds of a century ago;
and so on with all the rest.   And I dare say, when I
come to discover the meaning of your fine high-sound-
ing terms, I shall find them only to be some beautiful
paraphrastic mode of conveying some plain, sensible, old
distich, such as,—' Speak when you're spoken to ; do as
you're bid.'   It is dreadful to live in such an age as
this !   One can't open one's mouth, if it is but to say,
' What a fine day !' but out comes some moral aphor-
ism, or knock-me-down piece of virtue, which one
can't recover from for the next half-hour. And the moment one's back is turned one is sure of being held up
as a ' mournful example!'   It is the case with the whole
set of you !   You remind me of the French caricature
where the old school-dame has been reading a fairy
tale to her children, which ends with stating, ' that
when the princess was cured of all her faults, she became very beautiful and rich, and so forth, and married
a sweet young prince;' from whence she drew this
apt deduction — with skinny finger lifted high : " Ceci
vous montre mes chers enfans, qu'il faut toujours

manger du pain avec son fricot, ne jamais mettre
les doits à la bouche,' &c. Now is not that just the
way with you all—spoiling our fables with your dull
morals?"

"Which character of myself am I to walk away
with?" asked Sir Roland, good-humouredly; "just
now I was 'the best creature you ever saw,' now
I am a sanctified bore and a driveller! The very next
civil thing you say, I shall be off directly, for fear of a
reversal of the sentence."

"Then I shall go on abusing you on purpose to
keep you here," said Lord N——, "for I must say,
I greatly like to see the sort of fights that go on in
your mind when I traduce you or your people—wrath
and fury, struggling with good-nature and patience, but
never quite getting the better. You are like the bull,
and I the matadore. You let me fling at you what
darts I will, and flourish my taunting flags in your
eyes; but though I have at times seen the front of the
'noble beast' flush up, shewing there was a commotion
within, yet I have never succeeded in getting a single
roar or toss out of him yet."

"That will do very well," said Sir Roland; "and
now I am off."

"No, no, stay you here, I have a vast deal more
abuse in store for you. But first, I really have a
fancy for knowing what you *do* mean when you talk of
people 'being converted,' or 'having convictions,' and
such like terms. It reminds me of Lord ——'s boy.
Did you ever hear that story? A religious tutor crept
in unawares at one time into that infidel house, and
produced some good effect on one of the boys, which
one of the others, observing, rushed into his mother's

room, exclaiming, 'Do you know, mamma, brother has
got religion!' as if it were the measles or scarlet
fever! And now, pray tell me what you *do* mean by
those fine terms of yours."

"I will answer you in better words than my own.
'The conscience becomes disquieted, and this is *con-
viction ;* the heart and its affections are given back to
God, and this is *conversion.*'"

"And a mighty long journey it must be for the
hearts of some men to get back to God," observed
Lord N——. "Yes, that is indeed *conversion,* for our
affections are generally running in a far different channel from that! And of course, you will tell me too, that
it is only by the power of God that we can be so
changed—so converted. I believe you—I fully believe
you, Roland, for I have been trying at it, in my poor
way, for this half century, and have never yet got one
inch nearer to heaven, nor been able to track a path in
my heart that did not lead away from God."

"The Almighty promises not only to help us in the
work," replied Sir Roland, "but to do it for us—in us,
if we supplicate Him for His powerful blessing. But
one part of the explanation I quoted, you seem, my
dearest uncle, to have known by experience."

"Ah! you mean 'conviction,'" said Lord N——;
"but I am not going to make my confessions to you,
my young master, so do not think you are going to
have the triumph and satisfaction of putting me into
the right way as you think it. I do not mean, to be be-
holden to such a Will o' the Wisp as you. But now,"
and he sighed heavily, "I will go up to poor Anstruther, and you—for it is about your hour—are going to

ride—always with Scott, I suppose. You select him, I imagine, by way of contrast in appearance?"

"I do not think Scott at all ill-looking," said Sir Roland.

"And how do you know that it was not you that I meant as the ill-looking one?" exclaimed Lord N——. "Well, if ever I heard a speech of more consummate vanity and conceit! And so *you* are 'the glass of fashion, and the mould of form—the observed of all observers,' are you? *You* are 'the faultless monster that the world ne'er saw!' Upon my word, if that is not the quintessence of coxcombical impertinence!"

Sir Roland coloured excessively at the unintentional vanity of the speech he had made; but laughing at his uncle's vehement philippic, he said,—

"I am bound you know, my dear sir, to believe all you say; and how often have you told me that I was a vastly good-looking fellow!"

"A sad mistake indeed," said Lord N——, shaking his head; "and the worst is, that the good lady's recipe for some hideous but estimable man—of turning him inside out—would not benefit society much in your case; for with you the one is as bad as the other. But that fellow Scott!—he goes about all day, I am told, poking his nose into prisons, and hospitals, and other pestiferous places; mounting garrets, diving into cellars, threading labyrinths of filth—besmeared, vice-begrimed alleys! Well, '*tot homines quot sententiæ!*' I rather wonder, however, where he gets all the money he spends; for I am told he gives away enough to bribe the priests of Juggernaut to surrender the 'mountain of light.' I rather suspect that

he has a mighty long arm, *ce monsieur là*, and that,
whilst he is perambulating about in all directions, he
keeps his hand in somebody's pocket, not a hundred
miles from this room."

Sir Roland was confused for a moment; but then
with upright simplicity answered —

" Scott has a good fortune, but not one equal to
the largeness of his heart. It can be nothing, you
know, my dear uncle, to me to give away money for
which I have really no other use. The difficulty of
true charity is the personal labour required, and that
Scott most freely and devotedly bestows."

" Whilst you are pleasing yourself to your heart's
content in the manner most particularly delightful to
you, in reading crooked hearts, writing business-letters,
and casting up the sum-total of human vice—and of
your uncle's wishes!—Well! God forbid that I should
seek to bring you down from your '*good* eminence,' to
the level of the trifles—aye, and I fear," he added
with an involuntary sigh, " often worse than trifles of
this world. Go on—go on—*dans un si beau chemin,
il ne faut pas s'arrêter;* though I suppose in time,
you will rival Abdol Motalleb, and spread food on the
tops of the mountains for birds and beasts!" And
nodding kindly to his nephew, he left the room to pay
his dreaded visit to Mr. Anstruther.

CHAPTER XIII.

What Lord N—— had said of himself was perfectly true.   He had been for years ' feeling after God
in the dark ;' and virtuous sentiments, and holy truths,
had always found something of an echo in his breast.
He had been in the world all his life—thrown, from a
boy, into scenes the most bewildering to the heart,
the most searing to the conscience; yet throughout
all, he had maintained a fair character, and had been
beloved and respected by all his associates.   But good
and evil were so mixed together in his mind, and his
judgment was so warped by supposed necessities of
action, that though truth was ever making some feeble
efforts to be heard, yet he really knew not in what
direction it pointed, nor what it would have him do.
His mind was not sufficiently enlightened to make him
see that he could do nothing of himself, and therefore
he had never humbly applied to God for His effectual
teaching.   He had moreover, a great deal of heart-
pride to contend with ; not the pride which feels itself
superior to others, nor the pride of rank, and wealth,
and power—for no one was more affable and unassum-
ing than he was—but it was that pride which makes it

difficult to confess that any thing is wrong, or that any
help is required. He delighted in Sir Roland — was
vain of him beyond measure as his nephew — drank up
his praises as if they had been nectar, and doubled
them by encomiums of his own. But though he felt
his vast superiority to most others, he did not choose
to shew that he thought him superior to himself. He
endeavoured by all sorts of stratagems, jesting questions, and pretended misconstructions, to draw out his
principles and sentiments; really anxious to learn and
profit by them, but most extremely unwilling that his
aim should be observed; and though, at times perhaps, he would unguardedly make confession of his
own weakness and inability, yet the next moment he
would pass it off as a joke, and pretend to treat the
whole matter with contempt. But, in his heart he
treasured up all he heard; and the mists of error began
by degrees to roll off from his mind. He was exceedingly respected in the high situation which he occupied; and, though particularly familiar in his manner
to all ranks, and all ages, yet he had something about
him which kept off all familiarity from others; and it
was often observed, that though he passed his jests
freely on all, from the prince to the peasant—yet
that nor king, nor emperor, was ever known to jest
with him. He was looked up to by all with whom he
had to do, for he was keen, shrewd, and observant;
and though too often led into the crooked paths
thought necessary to success in his plans, yet his word
once pledged, was known to be inviolable.

His natural feelings were most kindly; but long
contact with the most worldly portion of the world,
had taken away much of their strength, and continued

absence from his family had weakened to a great
degree all habits of affection.   Strong emotions were
to him so unusual and so unpleasant, that he put them
aside as much as possible, and never, if it could be
avoided, mixed himself up with scenes of sorrow or
distress.   Not that he was incapable of sympathy, but
that he was selfishly unwilling to have his peace and
comfort disturbed, by the real compassion and regret
he was certain to feel.   Nothing therefore, would have
induced him to have gone to Mr. Anstruther in his
dying state, but the fear of seeming unkind and neglectful; and his reluctance to do so was so great—
the dread of what he had to encounter was so strong—
that even after he had mounted the staircase, it was
long before he could summon up courage to enter the
chamber.   Never had death visited his own house
before, and he felt a nervous apprehension of the
whole thing, that was most distressing ; and which
might perhaps surprise those who have not observed
how very much quiet habits of self-indulgence, enervate
the bold mind of man, and make it a feeble and a
timorous thing.

Long did he pause at the ante-room door—then
take a few turns on the stone landing-place ; then,
with a desperate effort put his hand on the lock—then
withdraw it, and again pace up and down—till at last
he had worked himself up to such a state of excitement and agitation, that in all probability he would
have entirely given up the effort, for that time at
least, and have gone down-stairs again—had not Mr.
Anstruther's servant, suddenly opening the ante-room
door, just as he was about to turn from it for the last
time, obliged him to summon up courage, and, for very

shame's sake, to ask the man if his master could see
him; and receiving an answer in the affirmative, he
reluctantly entered the chamber of death.

As soon as he had closed the door however, his
nervous tremours entirely ceased—overcome by feelings of real pain and distress. Mr. Anstruther lay
there supported by pillows, in his bed—for he could no
longer bear the fatigue of being moved to the sofa—
his eyes were closed—for he was at that moment particularly exhausted—and his countenance was so utterly
colourless, that at the first moment Lord N——
thought he was gone. The faint exclamation of horror which escaped the latter, however, roused Mr.
Anstruther from his torpor; and opening his languid
eyes he looked towards the door to see who entered.
On perceiving it was Lord N——, the colour rose in
his cheek, and his eyes became animated with an unusually full and strong expression. He had not seen
him before, since the great change in his views and
feelings had taken place; and a crowd of confused
emotions rushed over his mind. He made an effort to
raise himself, but could not do it.

"My dear Anstruther," said Lord N——, advancing to the bedside and taking his hand, "my dear
fellow!" He could say no more, for a choking pain
rose in his throat.

"I am quite easy now," said Mr. Anstruther, returning the kindly pressure of Lord N——'s hand,
"only weak. But my cough is better, and that is a
great mercy; it used to tear me to pieces; but it
seldom troubles me now. My dear lord," he continued, looking gratefully up at Lord N——'s agitated
countenance, "I doubt not you are shocked to see

this rapid change; but I am not dismayed—it must soon end, and then all pain and trouble cease."

"There may yet be hope," said Lord N——, after a time; "your youth—your regular way of life, are much in your favour."

Mr. Anstruther shook his head, while a quiet smile rested for a moment on his lips.

"No," he said, "there is no hope of life; but thank God, the bitterness of death is past. My lord, I have wished much to see you, that I might express my deep sense of your continued kindness to me. But for that I might have been a homeless outcast." He paused, while his labouring breath betrayed his weakness and his agitation. "I wished also," he continued, after a few minutes, "to express my deep regret — for the many ways in which I am conscious that I have not received—or returned, your kindness as I ought. My pride, and—and faults of many kinds —I am now painfully sensible of—though too late to prove it to you; but God knows that my regret—can cease but with my life."

"My dear fellow," said Lord N——, whose tears now flowed down his cheeks unrestrainedly, "why do you speak so? You have been most faithful and conscientious to me through all our intercourse together; you have saved me every trouble in your power, and no one fault have I ever had to find with you since you entered my house; and deeply—truly shall I regret you."

"I thank you, from my heart, my dear lord, for your kind and considerate words; but they cannot blind me to the truth—nor reconcile me to myself— though the kindness that dictates them I feel most deeply.——I cannot speak much—but Ashton will tell you any thing you may wish to know—about one—who has ever been so unworthy of your favour. Ask him— oh! my lord — ask him," he continued with energy beyond his strength, " the grounds of the peace I now enjoy—and may it be yours too."

He closed his eyes in utter exhaustion, and signed that he could speak no more. Lord N—— was equally incapable of replying; and after a few minutes, laying his hand with kindly pressure on Mr. Anstruther's shoulder, he seemed in that manner to take leave of him. Mr. Anstruther's eyes followed him to the door, kindling with grateful and softened expression, and Lord N——'s feelings again overcame him, as he turned to take a last look of one who was thus early " passing away." That look—so full of mutual kind- ness—was the last they ever exchanged! Lord N—— had to leave—again the next day for a short time, and ere he returned, his young friend had entered into his eternal rest.

When Lord N—— had left Sir Roland, the latter had still some letters to finish before he rode out. While employed on them, some one knocked at the door, and Wilson, Mr. Anstruther's servant made his appearance.

" What is it, Wilson?" said Sir Roland, rather alarmed. " Is your master worse?"

" No, sir, no, my master is not particularly bad just now; but I wanted to take the liberty of speaking to you, Sir Roland. Sir, my master is very ill——"

" Well, Wilson, but is he worse?" asked Sir Ro-

land again, looking up from the papers over which he
had been running his eye; " shall I go to him?"

" Not at all, Sir Roland, not at all; but, in fact, to
make the matter short, I was to have been leaving Mr.
Anstruther about this time, and somehow I feel very
unwilling to do so."

" I do not wonder at it," answered Sir Roland,
rather coldly.

" You see, Sir Roland, my warning was given
before my master's last attack came on, when he was
getting better; and, sir, master used to be very hard to
bear with at times. Not that I ever had a bad word
from him, Sir Roland, never; but then, I never had a
good one; and masters don't know how far a good word
goes with a servant. Master never was a riotous liver
sir, never — never heard an oath from his mouth;
never gambled, never did any thing to set a servant
a bad example; but there was something, Sir Roland,
so uncommonly cutting in his way. Take what pains
I would, there was never a ' thank-you,' never a word
of praise — only a gruff, ' that'll do,' — ' put it down.'
So when master was a little better — before he became
so ill again — I thought I would try another service,
and so gave warning. But I have been with master
now these six years, ever since he came here, and I
know all his ways, and how he likes things done, and I
should be uncommonly loth to give him over just
now to the hands of strangers, who don't know him
scarce by sight. So I was thinking, Sir Roland, if
you thought proper, and master was agreeable, that I
should have no objection to staying on, and doing
what I could as long as he is here;" and the poor man

moved about nervously, and cleared his voice once or twice.

"I think you are quite right," said Sir Roland, kindly; "and to say the truth, I thought it rather odd, Wilson, that you had not made this proposal before; for it must strike any one, that it would be very irksome and painful for a dying man to have strange faces and new ways about him; and I think too, from what I can observe, that your master is not so 'cutting,' as you express it now, but that any one might bear with him. Sickness is very trying you know, Wilson, to us all; and for a young man like your master, to be confined to his room — dying — whilst others of his age are enjoying themselves in health and spirits — without parents too, or relations to cheer him — it must seem a heavy trial."

"No doubt, Sir Roland — no doubt it must," replied Wilson, feelingly; "but it is strange, sir, that the worse he gets, the better he is to do for. He'll often thank me now, and say 'he's sorry to be so troublesome.' But dear me, Sir Roland, I don't mind trouble, if one's only treated like a Christian; and ever since he's been like that, I've been wanting to say, I should be glad to stay and do for him to the last; but I never plucked up courage till just now, when my lord went in to master; and so I thought I would make bold to step down and speak to you."

"I think it is a very good arrangement," said Sir Roland, "and I will settle with the other man. I am sure your master will feel very grateful."

"As to that, Sir Roland, it is not much," said Wilson, "indeed, if master was always to be as he is now, I should not mind staying on with him, if he lived ever so long.   Death makes a great difference in people, Sir Roland."

"It is not death—but the Spirit of God which has made the difference in your master, Wilson. Many people get worse and worse in their ways and tempers, through long illnesses, till death cuts short their power of tormenting here, and delivers them over to a terrible eternity.   But God has shewn your master the evil of his heart, and His own willingness to pardon him for Christ's sake ; and that it is, which has produced the change in him.   But we will try and find some future opportunity for talking this matter over together; for remember, Wilson, on its being rightly understood and received depends your salvation as well as your master's: we are all alike in God's sight ; there is no distinction of persons with Him !   Shall I tell your master of your wish to stay with him, or would you rather do so yourself?"

"If it is not too much trouble, Sir Roland, I had much rather you should speak ; I don't feel very free yet with my master, though I am not afraid of him, as I used to be."

When Sir Roland had finished his letters, and had returned from a short ride, he went up to Mr. Anstruther, whom he found somewhat recovered from his agitating interview with Lord N——, and informed him of his servant's wish to remain with him.   Mr. Anstruther was much gratified ; and the next time that Wilson entered the room, after Sir Roland had left it, he thanked him with such a kindness of manner, as brought tears into the poor man's eyes.

"I have been a bad master to you, Wilson," he

said, " and have much to reproach myself with on that account."

" Indeed no sir," said Wilson ; " no gentleman has less to accuse himself of on that score — unless indeed it be Sir Roland, or Mr. Scott, or that kind of gentleman. I never saw you do a wrong thing, sir, in all my days ;—but to hear the account other servants give of what their masters do at times, dear sir! it would almost make your hair stand on end. There's Lord——"

" Never mind, Wilson," said Mr. Anstruther, stopping him. " I have no business with other people's faults ; I have enough to do with my own just now."

" Certainly, sir," said Wilson ; " but I only meant to shew that you had never done any thing at all, as it were, compared to others."

" We must see about it, Wilson, not as compared to others, but as compared to the word of God," said Mr. Anstruther, " for that is what we must be judged by."

Wilson stared at this announcement, so extraordinary as coming from his master ; and was still more astonished when Mr. Anstruther taking the Scriptures from his ;pillow, and turning to the parable of the talents, said —

" You can read well I think, Wilson ? just read that parable to me."

When it was finished, he said, " Now do you not see that it is not only those who abuse but those who fail to use properly the powers that God gives them, who will be condemned eternally ?"

Poor Wilson was quite at a loss what to say or think, these subjects being entirely new to him.

" I ought," continued Mr. Anstruther, " to have
used the influence which a master should have over
his servants, to lead you to what is good—to make you
a fellow-walker with myself in the paths of peace and
godliness; therefore if judged by my own deeds, you
see from the Bible itself, what a fearful doom I deserve
to have pronounced against me.   But, Wilson, Sir Roland, whose kindness I can never repay, has shewn me
not only my own sinfulness, but the way by which my
sins can obtain forgiveness—even through the merits
and sufferings of our Lord and Saviour Jesus Christ.
—I cannot talk much with you now, I so soon get exhausted; but I am glad to have been able, so far to
tell you, what it is which makes me resigned and happy
now, while in the days of health and strength I was
morose, and miserable—and unkind too, I am afraid,
my poor fellow," he added, holding out his hand.

Wilson was much moved, and respectfully kissing
his master's extended hand, burst into tears.   Mr. Anstruther was exceedingly touched by this unexpected
proof of feeling in one whom he had supposed so wholly
indifferent to him ; but after a few minutes, he continued in a kind voice —

" You will read the Scriptures constantly, Wilson,
and pray to the Almighty Father to send His Holy
Spirit to teach you to understand them?   You probably
have a Bible? "

Wilson was silent.

" Well! you are no worse than your master," added
Mr. Anstruther, with a deep sigh; "I had none till
Sir Roland gave me this!   There is my purse—go
now and get yourself one, and never let a day pass
without reading some of its holy and blessed words."

Wilson, with many thanks and promises, left the room, and proceeded to do as his master desired.

"How the Lord smooths my path," thought the dying man. "Oh! that I had known Him as I might have done, all the days of my life. Oh God!" he exclaimed aloud, clasping his hands and raising his earnest eyes to heaven, "that I should have been so long within hearing of Thy voice, yet never have listened! Surely it is because 'Thou art God, and not man,' that Thou hast patience so long with Thy rebellious servants: and now 'Thou crownest me with loving-kindness, because thy compassions fail not.'"

Long did his mind continue to dwell on this delightful theme; for this fresh mercy of God—this new proof of his Heavenly Father's watchful tenderness in continuing about him one whose services long use had made so essential to his comfort—drew his heart out towards Him with a degree of fervour and devotion that he had seldom before experienced.

And it is often thus! for great mercies, and great deliverances, are scarcely so touching to the heart, as the wonderful sympathy of the Almighty, often manifested in the smallest, and apparently most insignificant occurrences in life. The rescue from imminent peril, either temporal or eternal, or the fruition of exalted happiness, is a work which, at a glance, might appear such as a deity would delight in! But that "the High and Holy One, who inhabiteth eternity," should not only

> "Stay His car
> For every sigh a contrite spirit brings,"

but — even where the soul's interests seem not concerned — should deign to consider what will please and
gratify the passing moments of life — is a sweetness of
mercy so great, as to fill the Christian's heart with
overpowering love and gratitude.

CHAPTER XIV.

> " In sleep
> The soul hath a capacity of horror
> Unknown to waking hours."—*City of the Plague.*

> " The morning dawns on *his* unpillowed head
> Who keeps *his* vigils by the sufferer's bed."—MS.

> " But now, mine enemy, the strife is past,
> And thou may'st lay thy victim low at last.
> Strike, and I will not fear thee ; for a light
> Flashes around me from the depth of night—
> Not with an earthly hope's uncertain ray,
> Nor pride's fell fire, nor passion's blinding ray :
> A light that dazzles not the aching eye,
> But pure and soothing, tranquil, holy, high !"
> *Unknown.*

Mr. Anstruther's strength now diminished hourly, but his hope seemed to grow brighter and brighter. A deep regret for his past ungracious life was, indeed, often felt ; but the nearer he drew to his heavenly home the more did its glory and blessedness fill his soul. He suffered intensely from difficulty in breathing, and Sir Roland was in continual anxiety about him.

This devoted friend passed every night in his room, and never left him during the day, unless when business absolutely required him to do so, or when he went out for a few moments to revive his oppressed, yet thankful spirit in the summer air, at such times as Mr. Anstruther fell into his short, flushed, and unrefreshing slumbers.

One night, while resting on the sofa, Sir Roland was aroused from his watchful sleep by sounds of distress and anguish proceeding from the bed of death. He arose in much alarm, and approaching Mr. Anstruther, found him apparently awake, but wholly unconscious of the objects around him. His countenance exhibited the utmost agony and agitation, and he moved his arms violently about, as if endeavouring to keep off some invisible enemy, while he murmured broken sentences of despair, and of earnest supplication. Sir Roland endeavoured to rouse him by taking his hand and speaking to him; but this seemed only to increase the wildness and terror of his looks. At length, finding all other efforts vain, he knelt down by his side, and implored that the Lord would send relief to the troubled spirit of his servant, and pour peace into his agitated mind. His prayer was answered, and Mr. Anstruther soon recovered his full recollection. He sighed heavily.

"What is it, Anstruther? What oppresses you?" asked Sir Roland, bending over him.

"Oh! I have had such dreams, Ashton! if things so vivid, so actually before me, could be dreams—so fearful—so terrific! Oh, if my hope should at last prove but a delusion!"

"Do not let such thoughts arise in your mind, Anstruther," said Sir Roland; " you know in whom you have believed, and that He is a faithful Saviour, who will never cast out any who come to God through

Him, 'No man can pluck you out of your Father's hand.' And what makes you fear it?"

"Oh, I have been in such dreadful straits! I seemed on a rock rising out of the burning abyss of hell. Demons rose on every side, and drowned my prayers in curses and revilings. They taunted my hope—'as if one like me could go to heaven!' They brought before my shrinking mind unremembered sins, and, howling, pointed to the deep forgetfulness of God which has marked my life. Each fiery wave bore on its crest, fiends who strove to reach me; some failed, but others seized me, and, with horrible rejoicings, tried to drag me down to their own terrible torments. I battled with them in vain, till, amid the horrors of that combat, a voice of comfort reached my heart— it was yours, dear Ashton, raised in prayer for my afflicted soul. But oh! am I indeed safe? have I not been staying myself up with false hopes? Can sins like mine be really pardoned? or were the terrors of that dreadful moment only foretastes of my awful, inevitable, eternal doom? No sufferings I ever underwent could be compared to the terrors of that confused, affrighting vision. Ah! Ashton, surely the power of Satan was there, to torture—to agonise; and would he have been permitted to do so if I were indeed a redeemed child of God?"

He spoke with the utmost difficulty, continually labouring for breath, and the impress of death was on his fine but agonised brow. Sir Roland much agitated, answered—

"Satan doubtless desires, and will endeavour to the last, to drive you from your hold of Christ; but do not let this effort of his malice dishearten you, my dear

Anstruther.   Remember that even in your dream you
were not given up to the powers of evil,—your feet
were still kept upon the ' Rock.'   And you must not
judge of your real state by impressions made on your
mind in the irresponsible hours of slumber, when the
soul, like a ship without compass or rudder, is driven
about to distraction.   No ; let this dreadful trial only
serve as an additional reason for thankfulness that you
are delivered from Satan's fell dominion through a
dreary, God-forsaken eternity !"

"But am I delivered, Ashton?   Oh, my soul is
tortured by this scaring vision !"

"My dear Anstruther, are you not trusting to
Christ for all your salvation ?"

"I did trust to him most truly."

"Then, do you think He *cannot* save? or that He
will not ?"

"Oh ! He is both willing and able," exclaimed Mr.
Anstruther ; faith and hope again beaming from his
animated eyes.   "Yes; and I shall be saved !   It is
past, Ashton—thank God! quite passed—that dark
cloud ; and God's favour again shines in my soul,
making all light—all joyful there."

"Thank God !" said Sir Roland, greatly relieved.
"But you seem much exhausted, Anstruther ?"

"I feel so, and long to sleep again ; but I dread
a renewal of these horrors."

"I will be by your side," said Sir Roland, "and
wake you if I see you become at all agitated."

In utter weakness Mr. Anstruther again closed his
eyes, and Sir Roland, taking his station by his side,
watched him with the utmost solicitude.   If he saw
him become at all restless and uneasy, he gently roused

him, and in his low, penetrating voice, whispered to him words of hope, and peace, and comfort. At times Mr. Anstruther would unclose his languid eyes, and gaze on Sir Roland with a look of unutterable love; but at other moments he could only express, by a faint smile, or quiet pressure of the hand, the gratitude he felt for his devoted kindness, and the comfort which his words conveyed. At length, notwithstanding his difficulty in breathing, he fell into a deep and tranquil sleep, while an expression of heavenly calm rested on his features.

The morning twilight stole into the room; and after a time, seeing that the sleeper continued tranquil and undisturbed, Sir Roland rose, and going to the window, gazed from it, though often turning towards the bed, to watch if all remained quiet there. The crimson flush in the sky became deeper and deeper, till at length, the tops of the mountains caught the blaze of the sun's unclouded rising. Peak after peak shone out in the beam, which stole down the mountain's side, till its streams of light stretched far along, and flooded all the plain. A cloud of silvery vapour marked the course of the river, and rose steadily for a time, obscuring the base of the mountains by a veil of prismatic colouring; till a light morning breeze, rolling it all away, left the whole scene glowing "in bright tranquillity."

Long did Sir Roland stand, and look out upon the newly awakened world, though scarcely conscious of what his eye rested upon.

There is something very strange in the sensation experienced in looking out at the calm, clear, morning light, after a night of watching in the room of sickness.

It is seldom, perhaps, excepting on such occasions, that
the high-born of the earth witness the beauty of that
delightful hour, with all its bright accompaniments,—
its "charm of earliest birds," its dewy meadows, and
fresh "untasted air;" and then the unrested spirit has
such a dreamy feeling! and all without—the gay and
laughing light, and bright life-like look — seems in
strange contrast with the scene *within*—where pain, or
danger, or perhaps even death itself, reigns in gloomy
quiet!

When anxiety has been exchanged for the delighted feeling that danger is over — that every passing
hour brings the loved object of our cares nearer to
health and strength — then, indeed, there is happiness
in the night-watch! — then sensations of exquisite, unspeakable joy thrilling through the breast, make us
meet the cheerful morning light with an answering
gleam within.

But far different from these were Sir Roland's
feelings, as he turned from the splendid glow which
was flooding all the landscape, to gaze on the pale
deathlike countenance of him, over whom he was
watching with more than a brother's love, and who
now seemed on the very threshold of the grave. He
left the window, and again took his silent station by
the bed of death. The oppression on the lungs, from
which Mr. Anstruther had suffered so much for many
days, was increasing fearfully, and his respiration
became so difficult, that at last Sir Roland, alarmed,
endeavoured to raise him up. The action roused him,
yet his breathing was one continued spasm: he grasped
Sir Roland's hand, and murmured,—

"This cannot last; but, oh!"—and a bright smile

played over his face—"the glory of the prospect—
the blessedness of feeling—that I am near my Father's
kingdom. But open the window, Ashton, I would
see you once more — once more before — my eyes —
close for ever."

"The window is open," said Sir Roland; "and the
sun streaming in."

"Is it so?" said the dying man, as a shudder passed
through his frame: "then this is death!—I can see
nothing — all is dark. I hear your voice, Ashton—and
would fain have looked on you — again looked on that
countenance"—He stopped, and a deep sob heaved
his breast; "Oh! it is a pang to part!"

Sir Roland could scarcely repress his emotion.

"We shall meet again," he said; "soon meet again,
in perfect happiness, where we shall never part."

"Oh! yes; oh! yes," said Mr. Anstruther;
"time will soon be passed, and you—will be with us.
A little while ago—how could I have met—this hour—
with all its terrors—so great? but now the brightness—
of Heaven is around me! The Almighty God—bless
you, Ashton," he continued, straining Sir Roland's
hand with dying energy to his lips; "the blessing of
him—who was ready to perish—fall on you! Raise
me — oh! raise me; give me more air!"

Sir Roland raised him, and, ringing the bell, desired Wilson to throw up all the windows, and to go
instantly and call Mr. Scott. Mr. Anstruther gasped
agonizingly for breath; but at intervals spoke words
descriptive of his firm trust in Christ—his happiness
and peace. When he heard Mr. Scott enter the room,
he held out his hand to him, and also to his servant;
then leaning his head on Sir Roland's breast, and

raising his hand to mark his high hope (for speech
was gone) after a few long-drawn sighs, he lay tranquil, as in sleep.

> "Oh! change; oh! wondrous change;
>   Burst are the prison-bars!
>   This moment there—so low,
>   So agonised; and now,—
>   Beyond the stars!"

Sir Roland gazed long with struggling emotion on
the countenance, so fine in death! — then pressing his
lips on the cold brow, and laying the inanimate form
he had been supporting, back on the pillow, he covered
his face with his hands, and leaning his head on the
bed, gave way to a burst of irrepressible sorrow.   He
continued for a time lost in a maze of confused feeling;
but his heart, at length, arose from this troubled state,
and poured itself forth in silent thankfulness to God,
for His mercy to the soul of him who was gone.

To those who know not the strength of the Christian
tie, his deep feeling may seem surprising; but they
who have experienced the blessedness of being employed to bring a soul to salvation, know full well the
gift of love which accompanies the work.   In this
particular case too, there was something more than
usual — an earthly as well as a heavenly cause — for
the strong affection felt; for that fascination which, as
has been observed, was so remarkable in Mr. Anstruther, even during the unamiableness of his former
conduct, rendered him, when it was joined to the
graces of the Spirit of God, perfectly irresistible.
Attendance on him had been, therefore, a most delightful duty, and Sir Roland, during his illness, had
become attached to him in the warmest manner.

Mr. Scott had motioned to Wilson, after the first moment, to leave the room for a time, and had retired himself into the window, that Sir Roland might not be checked in the expression of his first grief-ful feelings. After a time, the latter joined him, and they gazed together on the fine scene before them. The room they were in was one of the highest in the house, having been selected for Mr. Anstruther purposely on that account, as it looked over the walls, while the lower apartments looked on them, thus obtaining a fresher and freer circulation of air, which it had been hoped (unavailing care!) would have benefited him; and it was in consequence of being situated so high, that it commanded the beautiful view we have before described. As the two friends stood gazing upon it together, Mr. Scott, laying his hand on Sir Roland's shoulder, said, in a voice of the deepest sympathy,—

"*His* prospect is far more glorious now!"

A smile of heavenly expression lighted up Sir Roland's face, though his lips quivered convulsively, as he replied—

"Yes, his 'mortal has put on immortality,' and he dwells with his King and his God for ever."

He shaded his face with his hand as he leaned against the window, and remained for some time silent. At length, rousing himself, he said—

"I will not give way to selfish regret: it was for this that I prayed, and now—why should I repine? If I had no other mercy to be thankful for in life, this one is enough to bind me to God for ever; and I trust I may henceforth be more devoted to his service than I have ever yet been. Oh! my dear Scott, whilst we

rejoice over this one soul that is saved, let us remember the thousands who are around us perishing —
perishing with the riches of redeeming love within
their grasp!—I will go now to my own room, and try
to rest. I shall then be more fit for the business of the
day; for irksome and distasteful as it is, it is still the
work that God sets me to do, and it must be done.
Will you—if it is not painful to you" (and a shade
passed over his countenance) — "will you see to all
this for me?"— an inclination of his head towards the
bed shewing what he meant.

Mr. Scott signified that he would, and grasping his
friend's hand, Sir Roland left the room without again
looking towards the dead.

How dreadful is every thing connected with death,
to those who are left behind! And doubtless it is intended so to be, for death is the manifestation of God's
wrath against sin; and it should never be regarded
lightly. To the true Christian indeed, "death is the
gate of life:" yet still it is a gate which divides what
has been, from what shall be; and though the future
on which we enter may be bright beyond conception,
yet the parting with the past, and all its dear remembrances, must ever be a pang to nature. "Death," as
the good and noble—though visionary—Sir Harry Vane
well says, "instead of taking any thing from us, gives
us all, even the perfection of our nature. It doth not
bring us into darkness, but takes darkness out of us—
us out of darkness, and puts us into marvellous light."
Yet still the thought of death, and all its sad accompaniments, as regards the body, must ever be shocking
to human nature.

Sir Roland felt this peculiarly; and it was not till

after he was informed that Mr. Anstruther's body was
placed in the coffin, that he again visited the chamber
of death. He then remembered his friend's dying wish
respecting the little faded flower; and overcoming his
reluctance, he went to fulfil that—his last desire, though
he shuddered as he entered the chamber, and beheld
the still open coffin. Before he approached it, he
went to the desk Mr. Anstruther had named, and
opening it, took out a small sealed packet, which he
concluded to be the one which had been mentioned.
It was some minutes before he could prevail on himself
to break the seal—which the hand of such love had
placed upon it; and, when he did so with a sinking
heart—the countenance that met his view almost overcame him. There was, perhaps, in Mrs. Anstruther's
picture no resemblance to the features of her son;
but the expression was most perfectly his, in its
brightest, finest moments. This then was his mother—
the mother he had so much loved, so deeply, sadly
mourned! As Sir Roland gazed upon the picture, he
recalled to mind the sufferings which Mr. Anstruther
had so feelingly described, and which he and his
mother had had to endure; and tears started at the
remembrance of their griefs, though he knew that they
were now, where "pain and sorrow had vanished
before them." He put the picture back, and then
sought for the little faded flower that had been preserved and cherished with such deep affection. He
found it; and, after regarding it for a moment with an
aching heart, he laid it for the *second* time within the
gloomy place of death. He had not meant to look
again upon the dead; but, when he was by the side of

the coffin, his eyes involuntarily sought the features
they had so often dwelt upon of late. He was struck
by their still unchanged expression, and, after gazing
for a long, long time upon the face which lay so calm
in death, he stooped—and once more pressed his lips
upon the marble brow.

CHAPTER XV.

" That hour of parting o'er,
When shall the pang it leaves be felt no more ? "
MRS. HEMANS.

" It draws me on—I know not what to name it,
Resistless does it draw me to his grave."
Death of Wallenstein. COLERIDGE'S TRANSLATION.

THE funeral was fixed for the next day ; and many of the foreign ministers, and of the English, staying at ——, expressed their desire of paying the last tribute of respect to the deceased, by following him to the grave. As Mr. Roberts was absent (having again accompanied Lord N——,) it was arranged for Mr. Singleton to perform the service, which, he said, he had no objection to doing, over one for whom he really had " a sure and certain hope of a joyful resurrection."

The evening before the ceremony was to take place, Mr. Singleton received a message from the officiating Roman Catholic priest, to inquire whether it would be displeasing if the procession which usually accompanied interments amongst themselves were to attend the body to the grave, as, if so, it should go no farther than to the entrance of the burial-ground; but that it was necessary that it should accompany it

till it arrived there. Mr. Singleton thanked him for
his kind consideration, and confessed that it would be
more agreeable for the procession not to accompany
them the whole way; for, in fact, he did not know
what Roman Catholics usually did on those occasions,
and whether their ritual might not oblige them to use
ceremonies that it might be painful for a Protestant to
witness. It was arranged, therefore, according to his
wish ; and, when the time arrived for the funeral to set
forth on the following day, the friends of the deceased
found the Romish priests and their attendants ready to
join them, bearing with them all that was usual on
such occasions.

When the funeral train arrived at the entrance of
the burial-ground, the Romish procession, as it had
been agreed, paused, while the body and the accompanying friends passed in; but the priests, divesting
themselves of their sacerdotal robes—as a mark of
attention—followed within the enclosure, as private individuals, and remained during the whole ceremony in
the most respectful silence.* When the procession
reached the spot selected for the interment, the coffin
was placed on high tressels, and the ceremony commenced. But when they came to the moment when
the body was to be lowered into the grave, the pang
of parting was so great, that Sir Roland, who acted as
chief mourner, involuntarily laid a restraining hand
upon the pall, and leaned his head for a moment on

---

* This account of the conduct of the Romish priests was given to
the author by an English clergyman, who was called upon, some few
years ago, to bury an English Protestant in part of the Austrian do-
minions, and exhibits a degree of liberality and courtesy scarcely to
have been expected.

the coffin. There was a pause—for all felt affected! The great change that had taken place latterly in the deceased was very generally known amongst the English at ——, and they were all acquainted with the devoted attention and regard that Sir Roland had shewn towards him. When therefore, after a moment, the latter recovered his self-possession, and raising his head, motioned for the body to be removed—there was not one in all the assembly that did not look on his pale and expressive countenance, with feelings of the strongest sympathy and admiration. He was, however, wholly unconscious of it, for his eyes were bent on the ground; and he remained composed and collected during the rest of the ceremony, though a shudder passed over him as the heavy, dull, fall of the earth, sounded on the coffin-lid.

When all was concluded, Mr. Singleton addressed a few words to those assembled. He spoke of the deceased—of his great abilities, and high attainments; but reminded them how these qualities had failed in making him either happy in himself, or beloved by others, until that " wisdom which is from above," and which is " peaceable, gentle, and easy to be entreated," had shone on his mind, and made him a new creature. He recalled to them how, a few short months before, they had seen him whose body they had just consigned to the earth, amongst them, in all the strength of youth and health—and besought them " to watch and pray," lest their summons should come when they looked not for it. He paused a moment—then raising his hand, and speaking in the fulness of his heart—his powerful voice gaining energy from the high feeling which possessed him, he exclaimed—

"Oh! Lord God, suffer not these—the work of Thine hands, to perish! let not their souls sink in the darkness of sin and destruction; but redeem them unto Thyself, through Christ's most precious blood."

A murmured "Amen," rose from every lip.

Before the assemblage left the burial-ground, Sir Roland and Mr. Singleton passed over to the side where the Romish priests were standing, and thanked them for the kindness and courtesy they had shewn; they added, that they should be happy in any way to shew their gratitude for a token of respect so little to have been looked for. "And if," added Mr. Singleton, "in the course of our acquaintance, any discussion ever arises concerning the differences in our faith and feelings, let us pray for the power of the Holy Spirit to lead us into all truth."

Sir Roland, Mr. Singleton, and Mr. Scott, lingered till all the others had left the burial-ground, and remained for a time in the quiet of its seclusion, conversing on the themes ever most interesting to them, and examining many of the monuments around—where affection had, as usual, striven in various ways to commemorate the virtues of the deceased, and to express its own deep regrets.

As they were considering one high and handsome tomb, Sir Roland was surprised at seeing a man enter the enclosure, and, after looking suspiciously around, advance straight to the spot where the body of Mr. Anstruther had been laid. He stood regarding it for some time, with his arms folded across his breast; but it would have been difficult to have defined the emotions that clouded his countenance. The expression was altogether most repellent, though the features were strikingly handsome. As his appearance excited no particular interest either in Mr. Scott or his cousin, they walked slowly away together, not wishing to be interrupted in their own thoughts and conversation; but such was not the case with Sir Roland—one glance had sufficed to tell him who the stranger was: and his heart sickened at the conviction, that the wretched father of Mr. Anstruther stood before him! The likeness was so strong that he could not be mistaken. There was the same outline of feature—the same harsh expression, which used in former times to be seen in his friend—the same tall figure—and the same peculiarly gentlemanlike appearance, which shone conspicuous, even through the almost threadbare garments in which he was attired.

Sir Roland was so much concealed by the monuments, amongst which he was standing, that he was at first unperceived by the stranger; but after a few minutes, the latter, uttering a bitter groan, raised his head, and his eye then encountered that of Sir Roland, who had remained, as it were, spell-bound at the sight of him. He started—and it seemed as if a momentary faintness came over him; but recovering himself, he instantly advanced to Sir Roland, and addressing him in a haughty manner, said—

"I am speaking to Sir Roland Ashton?" Sir Roland bowed in reply; and the other continued in an excited manner—"You, then, I have to thank for doing what it was my place to have done—watching over *him*"—and he pointed to the grave.

"I was with him, certainly, during his illness," answered Sir Roland.

" And it was you then, doubtless, whom he charged with his dying curse for his father ! "

" Far from it," replied Sir Roland, greatly shocked, " his last feelings for you were those of strong interest."

" They must have been his last then, indeed," returned the other, with a taunting laugh.

" I had seen but little of him for many years," continued Sir Roland, endeavouring to soothe the evidently excited state of the stranger's mind, " but when he mentioned you to me during his last illness, it was with much feeling; and at his request, I wrote off to every city in Europe, where I had any friends, to endeavour to discover where you were."

" In Paris ! " said Mr. Anstruther, gloomily. " I have been there for years."

" No less than three letters of inquiry have I directed there, within the last month," rejoined Sir Roland, " but I could gain no tidings of you."

" Tidings ! no ! " exclaimed Mr. Anstruther, with a shout of derision—" How could you hope to discover any *one* devil (and he ground his teeth as he spoke) from out of the legions, that infest that accursed, infernal place? What did he want of me?" he continued, furiously; " he who was pampered with all life's luxuries, whilst I gambled, robbed, plundered, for my daily bread—and failed to get it."

Sir Roland could scarcely restrain his horror and indignation at this extraordinary avowal; but perceiving that the stranger was evidently almost unconscious of what he said, and pitying the destitution which could have led to such a course—remembering too, the dying request of his friend, he controlled himself, and answered calmly,—

"He wished much to know where you were, in order, if possible, to be of use to you; he thought indeed, that if you knew of his dying state, you might come to see him, perhaps, once again; but if not, he begged me, if ever I met you, to endeavour—to speak —to say—what joy and happiness he had found at last, in the knowledge and love of God."

"There is no God—there can be—there shall be no God!" ejaculated Mr. Anstruther frantically, raising his clenched hands to heaven, as if he defied the Omnipotent!

Sir Roland was horrified beyond measure, and scarcely knew what course to pursue with the distracted being before him. He was thankful however, that his two companions were at a distance; for though, under other circumstances, he might have been glad of their presence and assistance, yet as it was, he was happy that they were not witnesses of the conversation he was holding with the stranger; as tenderness towards the memory of his late friend made him averse to his father's state and circumstances becoming known to any but himself. He therefore endeavoured to soothe the wretched man, and asked him, in a kind voice, how he happened to be in —— just at that time.

"I have been here above a week," answered Mr. Anstruther, sullenly. "I knew he was ill" (and he glanced at the fresh-turned earth close to which he again stood) "so came—I know not for what—but yet I came. It was near a month ago that I heard he was dying; I heard it in one of the hells (fitly named!) of Paris!—heard it from one of high name, who honours those abodes with his presence—one whose asso-

ciate I used to be, though now, of course, he does not
know me.   However, I heard it there!   I heard too,
from him, there—there in that devilish place, that you—
Sir Roland Ashton, were tending him like a brother.
He said too—while a fiendish laugh echoed around
from his companions as he spoke—that you were
making a saint of him!   I could have murdered him
as he stood!—But it was there I heard it.   I had reasons for wishing to leave Paris—so thought to turn my
steps here, though I hardly know why, for I never loved
him, and he!—he hated me with the deadliest hatred!
and well he might—well he might!" and the wretched
man raised his eyes with a bitter look to heaven.
"Still he was mine," he continued, "and the only
thing I had on earth; so I sought to be near him—
and so I was—Yes! as near as Lazarus was to Dives!"
—and he laughed scornfully.—"I lingered unobserved
near his house—*his* house—the Embassy-house—the
great man's house—the resort of princes, and nobles,
and crowned heads!   I was there—a starved and outcast being, where he was revelling in life's luxuries—
and—and—dying."

He paused, and Sir Roland, much moved, inquired
why he had not made it known that he was there?

"Did I not know," exclaimed Mr. Anstruther, his
eye again kindling with fury, "that he hated me?—
and yet I thought I would try, at least, to ask how he
was—and, had my courage not failed me, I might perhaps, at last—have sent for you."

"Would to God you had!" exclaimed Sir Roland,
much agitated.

"Yes," continued Mr. Anstruther, with a softened
expression, "stranger as you were, I felt I could sooner

trust to you than to my own—only child!" A convulsive burst of agony stopped his utterance; and Sir
Roland, pained beyond measure, would have approached
him; but, perceiving his intention, Mr. Anstruther,
resuming his stern and haughty manner, exclaimed,—

"I want no pity—will have none!"

After a pause, he continued, "I thought, as I
was saying, that I would try and inquire how he
was, and I approached the gate of the court-yard;
but at the instant, one, in the royal livery, must
needs brush by, and in a loud and authoritative
tone, ask after 'the secretary.' I waited for the answer with shaking limbs;—'No better.' Another
time I lurked near, though unseen, and again had to
listen for the reply given to a—stranger! At last,
having rested all one dreary night under the gateway,
I watched in the morning for signs of stir and life in
the house, and—for the first time, ventured myself to
ask for him.—It was well—it was right—that to me
first should be spoken the word of death;—that on my
ear first should fall that chill, dull, fearful sound!
Yes—he was dead!" and the unhappy man covered
his face with his hands, and shuddered. "I know not
what I felt," he continued; "all was blank and cold
within, and around. I have scarcely tasted food since
that hour, nor did I once lose sight of the house till I
saw the funeral come forth this morning. I saw the
coffin that held him," (and he looked for a moment
down on the ground) "and I saw you—for I knew it
must be you—again holding the place I should have
held—chief mourner! I followed at a distance, for,"
he continued, with a bitter smile, holding out his arm,
"what had garments like these to do, by the side of

peers and princes? I watched till, as I thought, all had
left the burial-ground, and then came here—to die!"

"You are exhausted, Mr. Anstruther," said Sir
Roland kindly, "food and rest will restore you to, I
trust, happier thoughts; come home with me."

"I have no home!—nor will I go with you," he
answered, with despairing violence. "You have already
heaped coals of fire on my head by what you have done
for *him*. Go—go *you* to your home, for you deserve
a home," and his features quivered convulsively, "but
no power on earth moves me from this place alive!"

"It was your son's earnest request," said Sir Roland,
with strong emotion, "that if ever I met with you, I
should try to speak to you the words of pardon and of
peace."

"Peace!" exclaimed Mr. Anstruther, "what is
peace? I know enough of your Scriptures to know
that they say—and truly—'there is no peace for the
wicked.' Pardon!—pardon for me—me—who murdered my wife, and sought to murder *his* soul!" and
he stamped his foot with fury on the side of the grave,
shrieking, with a shout of derision, "Pardon for
me!"

Mr. Scott and Mr. Singleton had wandered away a
short distance, before they discovered that Sir Roland
was not with them; and when at length they turned,
and saw him in deep conversation with the stranger,
they thought it possible that it might be some one with
whom he was acquainted, though he was unknown to
them, and they therefore, continued their walk, and
kept aloof for some time; till at length, Mr. Anstruther's loud tone catching their ear, they became surprised, and even alarmed, at his vehement gestures, and

hastened forward to join Sir Roland. Seeing them
advance rapidly from amongst the graves and monuments, and nervously apprehensive lest they should
discover who the stranger was—Sir Roland, by an
almost imperceptible gesture and glance of the eye,
endeavoured to keep them back ; and Mr. Anstruther,
continuing to speak in a loud, excited manner, he said
to him, in a low tone, " We will talk together of these
things another time ; these gentlemen are strangers to
you."

But Mr. Anstruther, in whose eye the fury of madness burned, exclaimed aloud, throwing his arms wildly
above his head, —

" What are strangers to me !—all are strangers. I
fear no one ! —let those who have hope—have fear—
I have neither ! This will set all at rest," and he drew
forth a pistol, which he held high in the air.

Sir Roland sprung forward to wrest it, if possible,
from his hand; but quick as lightning, the maniac
dropped it to the level of his breast, exclaiming—

"Advance another step, and I send this ball through
your heart."

Sir Roland's cheek became white as ashes, and his
pulse for a moment ceased to beat !

Mr. Scott, in an agony of terror, rushed forward to
place himself before his friend ; but the latter held
him back with the grasp of a giant, and by a motion of
his hand on his arm, directed him to go round the tomb
near which he was standing ; wishing him, if possible,
to get behind Mr. Anstruther, which Mr. Singleton
had done at the first moment of alarm. Sir Roland
kept his unblenching eye full on that of the madman,
while, in the deep tone of his persuasive voice, he said—

but so low that only Mr. Anstruther could hear—
" You would not injure *his* friend," pointing to the
grave.

" No ! no, no, no," hurriedly replied the wretched
man, in quivering accents, as he gradually lowered the
pistol—" but no one shall tear me from this spot alive."
He raised the pistol to his head, as the glare of madness again lighted up his countenance, but his arm was
caught from behind by Mr. Singleton ; and Mr. Scott
coming up at the same moment, they succeeded in
wresting the deadly instrument from his hand.

Thinking all danger past, they relaxed their hold ;
but the instant Mr. Anstruther felt his arm at liberty
again, he drew forth another pistol, and before a hand
could be raised to prevent him, he placed it to his
breast—and fired !

The body sprung into the air ; then fell forward on
the fresh-made grave !

Sir Roland covered his face with his hands, and
groaned in the agony of his spirit. His friends hastened
to raise the body of the suicide, but life was extinct :
the ball had passed through the heart, and the life-blood
of the miserable man was welling forth in torrents—
sinking deep into the light-strewn earth that covered
the body of his son !

Perceiving that all aid was vain, they laid the corpse
again on the ground, and hastened to Sir Roland's
assistance, for he was completely overcome, and had
leant his head on the tomb that was near him, in almost
a state of insensibility.

" Take my arm, Sir Roland," said Mr. Singleton,
" and let us leave this dreary place."

Sir Roland made an effort to recover from the

dreadful shock he had received; and taking the arm of his friend, he turned in silence to leave the burial-ground. But before they had gone far, he perceived that a crowd of persons, attracted by the report of the pistol, were rushing in at the gate; and the thought struck him, that if the deceased had any papers about him, they might lead to the discovery of his name, which was what he so anxiously desired to prevent. This fear gave him strength in a moment, and with sudden energy he withdrew his arm from that of Mr. Singleton, and begging him to wait for him, returned with rapid steps to the place where the murdered body lay.

"What would you do?" said Mr. Scott, who hastened after him.

"I must see if he had any papers," replied Sir Roland, hurriedly.

"Why? what can it signify? Let others find them; why harass yourself?"

"I must have them," answered Sir Roland, with a gesture of impatience.

"Let me search, then, for you," said Mr. Scott, as they arrived at the fatal spot; and resting one knee on the ground, he proceeded to examine the garments of the deceased. In doing so, his eye rested on the fine features, and the likeness instantly struck him. He started; and, looking up to Sir Roland with an expression of surprise and horror, was about to make an exclamation, when the latter earnestly silenced him, for by this time some of the crowd approached.

"There is not the vestige of a paper," he said.

"Thank God," murmured Sir Roland; "tell them so."

Mr. Scott informed the people around of the fact, and the two friends then passed on.

"Forgive me, Scott, for being so impatient with you," said Sir Roland.

"Don't think about it," answered Mr. Scott, kindly pressing the arm that held his; "I should have been dead, I think, if I had been in your place."

"It has been terrible indeed," replied Sir Roland, "having all along had the knowledge which you have but just acquired. But as you love me, Scott, mention it to no one—not even to Singleton. I feel for Anstruther as he would have felt for himself, had he been alive, poor fellow!"

They then rejoined Mr. Singleton, who had, during their absence, been accosted by one of the guard, with inquiries concerning the disastrous occurrence which had taken place. He related all the circumstances, as far as he was acquainted with them, and begged that, if possible, Sir Roland might be spared any interrogations for the present, as he had been so much overcome by the frightful event. Sir Roland, coming up with Mr. Scott at that moment, thanked him for his consideration, and informed the guard that no papers of any kind had been found on the person of the deceased; and fervently did he trust that no clue would ever be afforded which could lead to the discovery of the unhappy man's identity.

When he arrived at home, he threw himself on his sofa, thoroughly exhausted.

"I shall leave you, Sir Roland," said Mr. Singleton, "to Scott's care; he is, I know, an excellent and silent nurse (rare perfection!), and you must need rest both for mind and body.   You have gone through very much to-day."

Sir Roland thanked him for all his kindness, and begged he would come to him soon again.

" I shall go to my own room, too," said Mr. Scott, " for there is nothing like perfect quiet ; so let your man come for orders, then pray rest; and may God be with you, my dear Ashton — as He assuredly will."

Sir Roland confessed that he should like to be alone, for that he felt as if his head would burst.

When he had given orders for what he wanted, he told his man to ask Mr. Anstruther's servant to go and see what had been done respecting the unhappy suicide ; (the news of whose miserable end had reached the Embassy-house long before Sir Roland had returned there) " or no," he continued, " I should prefer your going yourself, Thompson — and tell Wilson I would thank him to wait on me, instead of you.   Make arrangements, if you can," and a shudder passed over him, " for having this unfortunate man buried respectably, and I will be answerable. — But do not let him lie near — Mr. Anstruther."

Sir Roland made this arrangement respecting the servants in the fear that, if Wilson saw the body, he might observe the likeness to his late master, which was so very striking in death ; whereas his own man, not having seen Mr. Anstruther since his last fatal attack, would not so readily be struck with the resemblance ; and Wilson was well satisfied with the change, for he had felt a sincere regret at his master's death, and was better pleased, after the funeral, to be employed about the living than the dead.

Sir Roland, the next day, gave Mr. Scott an outline of the elder Mr. Anstruther's history, as far as he was acquainted with it, renewing his request that he would be silent on the subject to every one. It was a recital calculated to excite the greatest horror in a Christian breast, and Mr. Scott was greatly shocked at hearing it.

"I wish I had known earlier," he said, "who it was you were talking to, so as to have taken part of the burthen off from you; for it must have been dreadful, knowing who he was, to see him in that state of excitement, and to have to bear it alone."

"It was terrible," replied Sir Roland; "and I should have been very glad to have had you and Singleton by me, only I dreaded your discovering who he was. That apprehension was as trying—or more so—than the sight of him; though it is frightful to witness the workings of insanity in any one—and in this case the whole circumstances were so harrowing!"

"Tell me, Ashton," asked Mr. Scott, "what did you feel when he levelled the pistol at your breast?"

"What did I feel? Why, deadly fear, to be sure! What could you have expected me to feel?"

"Why, 'deadly fear,' certainly—at least I think I should have felt it; but not having ever been put in that situation, I could not tell from experience, so I wanted to know your sensations—for I knew you would tell me the truth."

"My deliberate opinion," said Sir Roland, "is, that death, to a Christian, is better than life in its best estate; for to him 'to be absent from the body, is indeed to be present with the Lord.' But when a violent death is suddenly presented to one, I could scarcely believe —judging from my own sensations—that any man could

remain wholly unmoved and fearless. Human nature
shrinks from the act of death, under all circumstances;
and the sudden, forcible rending asunder of soul and body
in cold blood especially, must always be a thing harrowing to every nerve. I remember a very spirited officer
saying, 'it was useless to pretend that soldiers felt no fear
in danger—unless perhaps, in the heat of battle—but
that he was the bravest man who could best conceal,
and control his fear.'"

" Well, you certainly concealed and controlled
yours yesterday, Ashton, for not a step did you move."

" Standing still was my best chance, you will remember. But it is a painful subject to me, Scott, fresh
as it now is in my mind; for the fearful end of that
unhappy man—his end—no, rather the fearful beginning of his immortal state—fills me with horror! How
unlike the feelings that accompany the thoughts of
his son's death!—*they* are all joy, as far as he was
concerned—though it is inconceivable how much I feel
his loss. But the two events are at present so mixed
together in my mind, that the one poisons my enjoyment of the other! How remarkably, in this case,
have the ways of the Almighty borne out His words:—
the wife's unfaithful marriage so fearfully visited!—
the mother's faithful prayers so fully answered!"

An officer of justice called in the course of the day
to take Sir Roland's deposition, and that of his friends,
concerning the unhappy occurrence which had taken
place the day before; but there seemed not the
slightest suspicion as to who the stranger was; and the
questions which were put were, happily, not such as to
oblige Sir Roland or Mr. Scott to betray the know-

ledge they possessed, which was a great relief to the mind of the former.

A plain but handsome monument was soon after erected by Sir Roland over the spot where George Anstruther's remains rested; it bore a simple inscription, stating his name and age, and that he died "trusting in the merits of the Lord Jesus Christ;" and at the conclusion there was carved that encouraging text, so peculiarly applicable in his case—"Cast thy bread upon the waters, for thou shalt find it after many days."*

* This text is supposed to advert to the practice of scattering rice on the surface of the waters during the artificial irrigation of the land, by which means the grain, sinking deep into the softened earth, brought forth an abundant increase, when the temporary inundation had subsided.

CHAPTER XVI.

" Oh, shame beyond the bitterest thought
    That evil spirit ever fram'd,
That sinners know what Jesus wrought,
    Yet feel their haughty hearts untam'd—
That souls in refuge, holding by the cross,
Should wince and fret at this world's little loss."

KEBLE.

" Vien dietro a me, e lascia dir le genti ;
    Sta come torre ferma, che non crolla
    Giammai la cima per soffiar de' venti."

DANTE : *Purgatorio*, Canto V.

" And compassed with the world's too tempting blazonry."

KEBLE.

" Il n'y a que le cœur fixé sur Dieu, qui ne ségare pas sur la
terre."

" Séparez vous de ce qui vous sépare de Dieu."

Lettres Chrétiennes.

" There's nothing here, there's nothing in all this
    To satisfy the heart, the gasping heart !
  *   *   *   *   *
These cannot be man's best, and only pleasures !"

COLERIDGE.

A DAY or two after the events had taken place
which we have recorded in our last chapter, Lord
N—— returned from ——, but only to announce a
still longer absence, which he was about to make. He
had business which called him to England, and which

might possibly detain him there for some months, and
Sir Roland, during that time, was to act as "chargé
d'affaires."

It required all Sir Roland's patience to keep him
from murmuring under this arrangement, and indeed
more than all—for he did murmur—and bitterly too,
in his own mind, for he had fully purposed, as soon
as Lord N—— should return from his short absence,
to request to be allowed to go to England himself for a
few weeks.　He had staid willingly at —— as long as
Mr. Anstruther required his society, but now that that
friend was laid in his quiet and happy grave, he felt a
double desire to depart, and the thought of staying was
more irksome to him a thousand times than it had been
before.　He missed Mr. Anstruther so exceedingly—
and the constant delightful occupation of tending and
watching over him—that his heart yearned more than
ever for those he loved—far away.　He unbosomed
his troubles to Mr. Scott; but when he had poured
them all forth, he said laughing—

"Now, how I hate myself for what I have been
saying!　One has no idea how horrid one is, till one's
thoughts break out into words; then, when one's ear
hears—what one's tongue speaks—of what one's heart
feels—one begins to understand somewhat of the blackness of said heart.　How short-lived are its memories!
A little while ago, when poor Anstruther was dying, I
felt as if I could forego cheerfully—so full did I seem of
love and gratitude—all that God might ever call upon
me to give up; or do willingly any thing which He might
set before me to do: but now, the moment my wishes
are thwarted, up springs the old, thankless, detestable

nature again! And I felt so desperately cross too, with my kind uncle, who I know would not intentionally vex me for worlds! He tries me certainly — but it is, not knowing what he does. But God tries me, knowing full well what *He* does; and what folly and madness it is to repine at His dispensations—merciful and kind as they invariably are. Pray take a sponge, Scott, and wash out from the 'tablets of your memory' all that has passed within the last quarter of an hour, and you will see how wonderfully well I shall behave all the rest of the time."

Lord N—— had indeed, no idea of the sacrifice he was exacting of his nephew, in obliging him to remain at ——, for he was totally innocent of having ever even suspected his attachment to Lady Constance Templeton. A conscious feeling had always made Sir Roland enclose his letters to her, in those he sent to his mother, or to Lord St. Ervan; and Lord N—— had been so little in England of late years, that Lady Constance's existence was scarcely remembered by him. As it was however there was no help for it—and Lord N—— must needs go, and Sir Roland must needs stay; and the latter kept his word most conscientiously to Mr. Scott, and behaved " wonderfully well," during all the preparations for the journey. But when the carriage which was to convey Lord N—— to England, actually came to the door—and what was worse, actually drove off on its homeward destination with, " decidedly," as Sir Roland thought, " the wrong person in it"—a violent irruption of splenetic combustion seemed about to take place. He tried to laugh himself out of it, but that utterly failed (it was no laughing matter to him, poor fellow!) and reasoning was just as bad; so he told Mr. Scott, with a smile, "that he must go and take the matter seriously up, for that it would never do to be so beaten, and by such a trifle."

He did go, and "took the matter seriously up," for he felt almost alarmed at the power which so slight a thing as the postponement of his wishes for a few months, exercised over him. He went to Mr. Anstruther's apartment, which was now his favourite sitting-room, and there looked into his own heart with shame and fear.

"Is it possible," he thought, "that I have forgotten all the lessons I so lately learnt in this spot? Can I so soon sin against Him who then shewed me such mercy? What if God, justly displeased at my wayward folly— my deep ingratitude, should, in very faithfulness, afflict me more sorely, even as regards *her*, and shew my weak and wilful heart that it must learn to bear — and to resign? How could I hope then, to possess my soul in patience, if I cannot now brook this light disappointment?" And leaning his face on his hands, he prayed earnestly that faith and temper might not give way before this, so slight a trial.

"Why should we not go to religion for the loss of our temper, as well as for the loss of our child?" asks that mistress of the human heart, Hannah More. Ah! if all would but do so, what a smiling face would this world wear, compared with its present fretful and frowning look! Evil passions destroyed in their birth, would then never live to "set the course of the world on fire;"—man, ceasing to "hate his brother without a cause," would never become a murderer; and godliness and peace would again reign in the earth!

" Ah bella pace!
Ah, de' mortali universal sospiro!
Se l'uom ti conoscesse, e piu geloso
Fosse di te! riprenderìa suoi dritti
Allor natura: vi sarìa nel mondo
Una sola famiglia, arbitro Amore
Reggerebbe le cose, nè coperta
Più di delitti si vedrìa la terra."—Monti.

That "trifles form the sum of human things" (another of
Hannah More's excellent sayings) all will acknowledge;
yet how few act as if they believed it! For one hour
which is agonised by fearful griefs, or torn by afflictive
bereavements, how many thousands do we spend in oppressive and stinging bitterness, owing to the tempers—
selfish, malignant, unfeeling—of ourselves or others!

" Ah! ma'am," said an unfortunate servant to his
late mistress (he having in evil hour been induced to
marry a violent and quarrelsome wife) "in former
times, if there was any disturbance in the house, I
could go into my own room, and shut the noise *out*;
now, I shut it *in* !" A bad case, certainly; yet not so
bad as when the noise is—not only in our room, but in
our heart! If "a contentious woman is," as Solomon says,
" like a continual dropping"—of water, a contentious
heart is like a continual dropping—of fire, wasting,
blackening, desolating, all within; and consuming, in
misery, all the goodly fuel which a gracious God has so
richly provided, to keep alive the cheerful blaze of
kindly smiles, and of bright and warm affections!

Sir Roland was wise therefore, and faithful to himself and to his God, to check with a strong hand, the
first beginnings of evil; and when, having implored the
washing of Christ's blood, and the strength of His
Spirit, he was again enabled to commit himself and his

every interest to the care of his heavenly Father, he
felt once more, tranquil and at peace!

> " Lord! what a change within us one short hour,
>   Spent in thy presence, will avail to make;
>   What burdens lighten, what temptations slake,
>   What parched ground refresh as with a shower!
> We kneel, and all around us seems to lower —
>   We rise, and all the distant and the near
>   Stand forth in sunny outline, brave and clear;
> We kneel, how weak! we rise, how full of power!
> Why, therefore, should we do ourselves this wrong,
> Or others, that we are not always strong!
>   That we are ever overborne with care,
> That we should ever weak or heartless be,
>   Anxious or troubled, when with us is prayer,
> And joy, and strength, and courage, are with Thee?" *

New trials however, awaited Sir Roland, arising
from the situation which he now occupied at ——.
As a subordinate, he had been allowed to take his own
way with tolerable impunity; but now that he was left
' en chef,' he was, of course, much more under observation. He had always, as in duty bound, attended at
court, and when invited, at the dinners and occasional
small evening parties of the sovereign at whose capital
he was residing; and those who were unacquainted
with his character and principles, imagined that it was
only shyness at first, and then his continual attendance
on Mr. Anstruther, which had prevented his joining in
all their gay amusements. Great therefore, were the
expectations formed of what was to take place, when
one so young, and so rich, should hold the reins in his
own hands! Many an anxious mother, and gay, joyous
daughter, looked forward with delight to the brilliant
' fêtes' which it was thought ' le beau ministre Anglais,'
would of course give for their amusement, and ' bals

* Rev. R. C. Trench.

costumés'—' courses à cheval'—' théâtres de société'—
' fêtes champêtres,' &c. glanced in bright and rapid
succession through the enchanted brain of many a fair,
but thoughtless being, who seemed unconscious that
she was formed for nobler purposes, than just to flutter
—and to fade !

But Sir Roland resolutely refused, either to attend
the large parties given by others, or to swell the number
of them himself. He gave frequent dinners, and small
early evening parties, which were always exceedingly
agreeable ; but beyond that rational mode of enjoying
society, he would not go. He had to encounter argument upon argument, remonstrance upon remonstrance,
but nothing shook him ; and the amiability of temper
with which he bore all the frequently irritating things
that were said to him, generally, in the end, disarmed
his assailants, and turned their wrath into admiration.

At length, all other efforts having failed, a young,
married English lady, of high rank and great beauty,
volunteered, as a " forlorn hope," for one final assault.
Lady Stanmore reigned as a sort of queen over the
society in which she moved ; and, being accustomed to
see all around submitting to her sway, she had acquired
some faint idea, that no one could resist her wishes.
From natural kindness of heart—for she was most
sweet and amiable in manners and disposition—she had
been very attentive to Mr. Anstruther during his last
illness—continually calling to inquire after him, and
sending him any thing which she thought likely to promote his ease or amusement. The object of these kind
attentions had, indeed, many a time turned with a sickening mind, from the volumes of new publications she
had sent for his perusal, though he felt the kindness

and amiability of her thoughtful attentions; and often did he breathe a prayer for her; asking of God to enlist her warm and sympathetic heart in His own blessed service.

This attention on her part towards Mr. Anstruther, had established a sort of amicable feeling between her and Sir Roland, even before they had become personally acquainted with each other; and she now trusted that the little claim it formed, might give her additional influence over him, and induce him the more readily to comply with her requests; and certainly her entreaties were (partly perhaps for that reason) those which he found it the most difficult to withstand. She was confident of success, and boasted in anticipation, to the band of discomfited champions who had gone before her, that she was certain of reducing this " Timon," as she called him, to perfect subjection to her will; and that they would see that in less than a week, cards would be issued for a fancy ball at the Embassy-house, she herself, after " unexampled solicitations," being induced, with Lord Stanmore as aide-de-camp (for she was wise enough to feel that a husband's side was the only safe place for a young married woman, and never went into public without him) to accept the station and duties of mistress of the ceremonies !

The evening after this bold declaration, she was to meet Sir Roland at dinner at the —— ambassador's; and then and there, did she determine to " carry" the hitherto impregnable fortress. She informed Lord Stanmore beforehand, that she had most important business to transact with Sir Roland, with which he should be made acquainted *en tems et lieu ;* and that, in the meantime, he must favour her having

a long discourse with him, by preventing any one's
approaching to interrupt her proceedings.

The plan of operations being thus arranged, and
dinner concluded, Lady Stanmore wiled Sir Roland
away to a distant part of the room, by strolling from
picture to picture, making observations, and asking his
opinion—so that, even had he wished it, he could not
have declined accompanying her—and then when they
reached a deep-niched window, through which, spite of
the blaze of lamps within, the last faint streaks of sunset were still discernible—whence they could

> " Gaze on the twilight's tender gray,
>   Escaping unobserved away ;"

she seated herself; and said playfully, to Sir Roland,
that she had much to say to him—matters of gravest
import to discuss.

" I am all attention," he said courteously; whilst
leaning against the open window he looked out on the
quiet of the evening hour.—His thoughts flew for a
moment to England, and a sigh arose.—He waited for
Lady Stanmore to proceed, but she too, was silent !
The themes she was about to enter upon, seemed so
uncongenial to the spirit of that gentle hour, that she
felt she had been an unskilful general in arraying her
forces to such disadvantage.   There was also something
in Sir Roland's countenance and manner which, young
as he was, bore great command ; and the dignity of his
mind, which, though lively and animated, yet never
verged towards levity, acted as a restraint upon the
follies of others.   Lady Stanmore herself too, felt the
influence of that silent scene ; for hers was a heart
formed by nature for all good and wise emotions,

though circumstances and education had placed her in
a situation which, with her great attractions, she found
too fascinating to withstand.

Perceiving at length that she did not speak, Sir
Roland turned to her, saying—

" Is the subject you were about to introduce, of so
overwhelming a nature, that it deprives you of the
power of speech, Lady Stanmore? or are you ma-
liciously collecting all your powers together, to destroy
me at once by a coup de main ?"

" No," she replied, " my arguments seem rather to
have faded away with that last ray of light.—In short,"
she added, rallying her spirits to the onset, " I must
resolutely turn away from ' twilight's sober livery,'
and from that imploring moon which I see just rising
through the trees, and return to the glare and blaze of
these lamps, if I hope for victory in the cause I am
about to plead :" and she smilingly seated herself with
her back to the window, having the brilliant room and
its gay groups just before her, and motioned for Sir
Roland also to sit down. He obeyed; and she began—

" I wished very much — I wanted to say—I meant
to ask——" She could not get on, so laughing, though
with some embarrassment, she exclaimed—

" I shall never succeed in pleading my cause if I
begin in this set, formal manner ; so let us introduce
the subject with a little preliminary nonsense ; though
I am afraid, *qu'il me faudrait faire tous les frais moi-
même*, in that case also; for you are never guilty of
talking nonsense, are you ?"

" You underrate my powers cruelly," replied Sir
Roland. " It is not my hourly study certainly ; but
there are, I assure you, some fine specimens of that

kind of oratory on record, of my production. But perhaps you would better like to have some grave, deep, philosophical subject started, from which your lighter fabric might rise with all the charm of graceful airiness. Shall I begin—as a peculiar-minded friend of mine did once to a young lady, whom he met for the first time at a dinner-table—and ask you ' What your opinion is concerning the mode in which oysters derive their nourishment ? ' "

" Yes ! I think that will do beautifully," replied Lady Stanmore, smiling ; " any subject will shine after that ! But we will go on by gentle degrees, and I shall parry your friend's awful question, by asking in my turn, how people in this country can like to derive *their* nourishment from those lively animals, so very long after the creatures themselves have been ' dead to all sense of propriety ;' it is horrible — dreadful ! It must be at least a quarter of a century since those we had to-day, have ' mourned' (though, alas ! not ' sweetly ') ' their parted sea !' Well, that may lead on to other dinner contemplations ; and dinners lead to conversation, and conversation to society, and society to company, and company to amusements, and amusements to ——"

" The point of attack," interrupted Sir Roland, laughingly. " I half suspected what the 'grave subject of discussion' was to be, from the very first ; and I was fully convinced of it," he added, in a quieter tone, " when I saw that you were forced to turn your contemplative eyes and softened feelings, from God's beautiful works out there, to this hot room and well-dressed company ;—though perhaps, I am too free in reading what passes before me."

"Oh! one is weak and sentimental sometimes," said Lady Stanmore, fearing that her arguments would again melt away from her grasp; "the 'witching hour' of eve is all very charming, when it is arrayed in loveliness like that we looked upon just now; but those are things we cannot command; black, stormy nights will come, as well as bright and stilly ones; and when the moon, which now, 'apparent queen, asserts her matchless reign,' is 'hid in her vacant inter-lunar cave,' (one must be poetical of course in talking of her) — why then the 'sable-stoled' night is a dismal thing to look out upon. Now the bright gleam of lamps and smiles we can always command within; and it is surely wise to apply ourselves to what is in our power at all times, and not to depend for pleasure on what we cannot control!"

She waited for Sir Roland's answer, and he replied—

"I think indeed, it is wise—and the only wisdom—to look for happiness to that which we have it in our power always to command. But perhaps I may be allowed to demur to part of your description as to what we can always command. Lamps, I will concede—but cannot smiles; I mean what you, of course, intend I should mean — smiles of happiness. That smiles of some kind, may always be commanded in the scenes you speak of, we will not dispute — smiles of gaiety, of vanity, of excitement—and may be some-times of real pleasure; but are they always smiles of happiness? I need not ask you to believe me, when I venture to assert that they are not; a mind like yours, Lady Stanmore, will answer the question for itself, or I am mistaken — will tell you whether the smiles you meet are not unfrequently those of absent, heart-sickness!"

"I do not say," replied Lady Stanmore, not quite at her ease, "that one is always positively, substantially happy at those places; but still you must confess that a well-lighted, brilliant ball-room, filled with — out of compliment to you I will say only *apparently* — gay and happy beings — is an animating and exhilarating sight. You will concede me *that*, at least?"

"I must draw largely on my imagination if I do," said Sir Roland; "for I am afraid you will really think me the 'Timon' I know you call me, if I venture to confess, that I have never yet trusted myself within that magic circle."

"Never been to a ball! — really, *never* been to a ball!" exclaimed Lady Stanmore, in the greatest astonishment. "You don't mean to say that? I knew that your estates lay in Cornwall; but I was not in the least aware that you had been brought up in its mines! Do you really mean that you have never, positively *never*, entered a ball-room?"

Sir Roland confirmed the terrible fact by a bow of profound humility, looking at the same time with a smiling eye to Lady Stanmore.

"Well! I suppose I am bound to believe that bow," she said, "though I am happy to find you have grace enough not to put the shocking confession again into words. The case is really far worse than I had suspected; the evil is deep-seated—firmly rooted, I fear. I thought I might have been able to have called back some fond remembrance — to have reanimated some smothered embers in your cold heart; but alas! your mind is like Australia: 'a land of no recollections.' What shall I do? I have nothing in common with you!"

"Oh, yes! you have — much — much;

> 'The common air, the earth, the skies,
>   To me are opening Paradise;'

and so they are to you — I know they are: let us think of them, and then advocate your ball-room, if you can!"

"Yes! I can, and will," said Lady Stanmore, gaily, "notwithstanding that you think to flatter me into your opinion, by attributing to me all sorts of vulgar tastes. I will assert, and without fear of contradiction, that the 'common air' is often uncommonly cold and disagreeable—that the 'earth' is often dirty and dreary—and the 'skies' often cross and gloomy; and so, with many thanks for fresh argument supplied, I say again,

> 'Turn from such joys away,
>   To those which ne'er decay,'

—but which can be renewed at pleasure."

"You are a sad perverter of reason and poetry, I see," said Sir Roland; "but may I ask Lady Stanmore, what it is this discussion is meant to lead to? Are you so very complimentary as to make it any point for me to appear at the fête which I believe you are going to give next week? or do you only wish to humble and disappoint me, by making me full of anxiety for the invitation you intend to withhold?"

"Oh, no! I assure you I fly at nobler game — at least, not nobler, for you are the quarry that I seek — but though I should be delighted to see you at our house on Wednesday, yet I want a more enlarged field of action than one 'fête' can supply. In short I want

you to do, what you ought to do — contribute to the
'general joy' of the whole society here. I want you
to open your fine apartments, and fill them with all
that is enchanting in life. Now *do*. Will you give
one party? Begin with the quietest kind: a concert —
and then you will see how pleasant it is; and you will
go on to balls; and — oh! you have no idea how delightful you will find it — and every body will be so
enchanted with you! — 'vous vous tuerez à force de
plaire?' Now *will* you?" and she turned her animated
eyes beseechingly on him.

Sir Roland could not but return her look with a
smile; but it was a sad one, for he grieved to see that
young and kindly heart given up to such follies;
(though across that shade of regret there shone for a
moment the image of one still younger, and still
lovelier, than the beautiful creature at his side — whose
soul was raised far above these things;—and he blessed
God that it was so.) He answered—though not till a
sigh of mingled feelings had forced its way—

" You have heard music at my house, Lady
Stanmore? "

" Oh, yes! instrumental — some of these bands —
and magnificent they are. But I want a real concert,
with all the finest opera-singers, and 'five hundred
invitations.' "

" I cannot do that," he said, gravely.

" Why not?"

" There are many reasons — some which I cannot
discuss with you," he added, with a slight embarrassment.

" Well then, let it be a ball!" exclaimed Lady
Stanmore (who seemed to think with Sir Archy Mac-

sycophant, that " every refusal was a step ;") " do the
thing handsomely at once—let it be a fancy ball!
You should do something to atone for your past life
of neglect! Your court-dress would do perfectly for
you; so you need have no care about that; and I,
and Lord Stanmore, would take the whole trouble off
your hands, if you liked it; you should just keep out
of your great apartments for a day or two, and then
return—and find yourself in the palace of the fairies!
You cannot, I am sure refuse, when I am kind enough
to make such an offer?"

" It is hard indeed," said Sir Roland, " to refuse
you any thing; but nevertheless, I am afraid it must
be done."

" But why? What reason can you have? I will
listen to every thing you have to say, sure of being
able to answer all your ' unanswerable arguments.' "

" But what if I will not yield to reason, and determine to have my own way, simply on the old regal
plea — ' Le roi le veut?'" said Sir Roland.

" Why then I shall give you up for ever, and, as the
German lady said, ' Leave you die in your hole.' But
that will not be the case I am sure, so now—do tell me
what are your reasons."

" Mentioning them would involve a graver discussion than might probably be agreeable to you,"
urged Sir Roland.

Lady Stanmore certainly shrunk from the idea of
any really serious subject being started, so sought to
parry it by saying—

" You do not really mean that you think, because
one likes the cheerful pleasures of life, that one must
therefore be dead to nature and all her charms?"

"Oh! no, did I not say that I knew you were alive to them all? But the love of nature, though a more refined and ennobling taste than the delight in the —forgive me if I call them—frivolous pleasures of dissipation, yet is not a whit more spiritual, unless we look 'through nature up to nature's God.' Poor Rousseau fondly thought he 'worshipped God on the mountains,' because his sensitive, but unprincipled mind, was melted by the lovely things around him in those lovely places; but what God did he worship? Surely not the God of the Christian! surely not the God who said, 'blessed are the pure in heart!' And I have a friend who says he can 'worship God in the fields,' but cannot 'worship Him by Act of Parliament'—as he calls going to Church. I confess, I have never been able to discover his God in the fields! I am more inclined to agree with Lord Bacon, when he says, 'I have sought Thee in courts, fields, and gardens, but I have found Thee in Thy temple;" though still more perhaps, with Augustine, who says, 'I sought Thee long in surrounding things, but when I looked within myself, then I found Thee.' Yes, Lady Stanmore, I know that you are alive to all these things, and also—to all generous and kind affections. I knew you by the latter character, you will remember, before I had the pleasure of being personally acquainted with you."

"It was very little I did for him, poor fellow!" said Lady Stanmore, answering Sir Roland's meaning, for she knew that he adverted to her attention to Mr. Anstruther; "but I always felt more interested in him than others did—there always seemed heart in him, if one could but get at it. And then, when one is

very prosperous and happy oneself, one feels so much
for those who are not so; and there was something so
sad in his early death—pining away—whilst we were
dancing and singing around him—all but you;—you
never left him!"

The colour of emotion rose in Sir Roland's cheek.

" He would not have exchanged his painful death-
bed," he said, " for all the pleasures this world could
have given him."

" Why?" asked Lady Stanmore in astonishment.

" Because he felt it was the path-way to his Father's
kingdom—he had learnt to estimate life—and eternity."

Lady Stanmore looked down in silence.

" He offered up many a prayer for you, Lady
Stanmore," continued Sir Roland, withdrawing his eye
from her softened countenance, " that your steps might
early be led into the only path of peace and true
happiness."

Lady Stanmore turned to the open casement and
leant out, but not before a starting tear had marked
her emotion. She was silent for a few minutes; but
soon recovering—though still looking from the window,
she said—

" But you know, Sir Roland, Solomon says, 'there
is a time for all things;' and amongst those 'all things,'
he names dancing."

" But does he name the time for it?" asked Sir
Roland.

" No," replied Lady Stanmore, returning again to
her seat, and continuing with renewed gaiety, " therefore we are at liberty to fix that for ourselves; and I
say, that the time to dance 'par excellence' is—at my
house next Wednesday—and at yours the Wednesday

after! So will you engage me for the first set of quadrilles on both of those occasions?"

" I will—if you will in conscience and honesty tell me that I am wrong in settling the 'time for dancing' to be, when we have nothing better to do."

" When I offer my hand, I expect it to be accepted unconditionally and thankfully," said Lady Stanmore good-humouredly, though with somewhat of pique in her tone.

" My dear Lady Stanmore," said Sir Roland, " could I have accepted it, your offer would have been felt—nay, it is felt, as most flattering, and would have been most gratefully received; but you must remember, that to avail myself of it, I must outrage all the main principles of my life."

" Oh! Sir Roland, what must your principles be worth, if they can be overthrown by such a trifle? They must be more out of the perpendicular already than the leaning towers of Saragossa or Pisa—literally tottering to their fall!"

" What would our great Duke have said," rejoined Sir Roland, " if in the heat of the battle of Waterloo, he had perceived Lord Hill dressed in the French uniform? what would he—and all the *two* armies have thought?"

" Ah! j'aperçois le piège qu'on me tend," said Lady Stanmore, laughing and shaking her head; " so spread my wings and fly off, but only to settle down in some other place; though I must say you are very modest," she added, looking archly at Sir Roland, " to compare yourself to one of the most distinguished officers in the army."

" I did not think of that," said Sir Roland smiling,

M

"it was merely that his was the first name that occurred to me; and if I had gone into the ranks, I might have stumbled on the name of Shaw, so that might not have saved me from your sarcastic reproof either."

"Ah! but you good people always do think so very much of yourselves, you think 'surely we are the men, and wisdom shall die with us.'"

"Are you acquainted with many of our 'profession,' Lady Stanmore?"

"No, you are the only one I know to speak to; I bow to a few others here, but do not know them."

"Then even if you think me so vain and self-conceited, you should not include all in your censure. One whom you condemn to 'the ranks' ought not to be taken as a fair specimen of his army."

"Oh! but I know you are all alike in that, all of you fancy yourselves like Atlas, bearing the whole world on your shoulders."

"One often feels the weight of it certainly," said Sir Roland.

"How?"

"It is oppressive to the spirit, when one thinks 'how,' in the words of Scripture, 'the whole world lieth in wickedness;' and when one sees how the love of it beguiles the best and loveliest; and one feels its weight too in oneself, when it so often clogs the soul in its endeavours to rise above its ensnaring pursuits."

The solemnity of his tone checked Lady Stanmore for a moment, but then she said—

"But you all think every thing depends on yourselves."

"No, Lady Stanmore, forgive me, we do not think that; for every hour teaches us we can do nothing of ourselves, but we ought to *act* as if we thought it; as I read somewhere the other day, 'every man should feel as if the battle depended entirely on himself.' Not *that* it depended, but *as if* it depended—there is a wide difference between the two."

" You are a subtle reasoner, Sir Roland. But why talk of battles at all? above all, of Waterloo, that prince of battles? We are now in the 'silvery times of peace,' and instead of the martyr's stake and wheel, I only offer you sweet sounds and pleasant sights."

" The warfare of the Christian, you must remember, is chiefly within," said Sir Roland; "and are you not, Lady Stanmore, at this moment, a very Napoleon ranging all your forces against me?"

" To give me so high a rank is rather a questionable compliment—coming from you," she answered smiling; "it avows me certainly great in power, but that is but to prove me pre-eminent in evil, according to your view; for you rank me as belonging to the terrible armies of the world."

" I have not ranked you among them," said Sir Roland, " you have yourself claimed your station there. Would," he added earnestly, " that I could 'transplant you out of the kingdom of this world into the kingdom of God;' but it requires a stronger arm than mine to effect that."

There was a pause. Lady Stanmore would gladly have given up the object she had originally in view; for she felt now but faint hopes of success, and her better feelings were awakened by what Sir Roland said, in a way that was painful to her, because she could not make up her mind to follow where they led; but the thought of the mortification she would feel if

she had to own to her friends that she had been defeated, made her determine to leave no effort untried
which might at last give her the victory. She therefore soon began again in a gay tone—

" But now, Sir Roland, do tell me when it is you
think it possible that there may be ' nothing better to
do than dance.' "

" I thought so yesterday evening ; and so I danced."

" You danced yesterday evening ! You actually
danced ! Where? Oh ! I know ! It must have been
at the Opera—in disguise—as one of the ' corps de
ballet !' Your feet asserting their indisputable right
to dance, you could refrain no longer ! I see it all
now—your ' besoin de sauter' not being allowed to
evaporate by the well-regulated safety-valves of private
balls, becomes condensed, till, when at high pressure,
it explodes on the stage, in spangled muslin and
chaplets of roses !"

" Ah ! you have at length discovered my incognito !" said Sir Roland. " What now remains for
me ?"

" But now, do really tell me," said Lady Stanmore,
" where did you dance ? or are you only imposing on
my weak mind ?"

" No, I assure you I did dance. I danced two
quadrilles."

" And where ?"

" At Lady Wentworth's."

" Oh ! now I know you are leading me over ' bog
and fell,' and I will follow you no farther."

" No really, I did dance there. There was a set of
children there, but not enough to make up a quadrille
by one, so I filled up the vacant space, and we danced

most perseveringly to an old country dance which was all that Lady Wentworth, who was orchestre, could bring out of the stores of her memory.   There is nothing very dreadful now the marvel is out, is there?"

" No, but you are very provoking."

" Why?"

" Because you are reasonable, and there is nothing so tormenting in existence as having to do with a reasonable person; one must either submit to be considered *un*-reasonable oneself, and that is bad enough, or one must, perforce, become reasonable oneself, and that is worse.   Nothing is so intolerable as reason; it is like the railroad, running all on one level—no awful heights, no frightful precipices, to vary and enliven the scene— one flat dreary plain, with your object always in view, never lost in the dim, exquisite haze of uncertainty, so exciting and delightful, but always *perché là*, vulgarly visible to all the world, as well as to yourself.   So now, that I have, I hope, reasoned you out of being reasonable, I will make one more effort to render you agreeable."

Sir Roland smiled and bowed.

" Are you content to leave the fashioning of your ball entirely in my hands, or do you wish to have *une voix en chapitre?*"

" Dear Lady Stanmore, let us drop this subject, and turn to some other on which we might agree."

" No, no—not yet! that beating of a retreat of yours sounds most inviting for a pursuit; I am sure you feel your courage fast melting away."

" On the contrary, it is to save the misery of a triumph that I wish to pursue the subject no further," said Sir Roland, smiling; "unless," he added more gravely, "you will really talk of it in sober seriousness, then I have no objection to saying what I feel; otherwise, we waste words to no purpose."

"Are you going to claim the right of eldership, and lecture me?" said Lady Stanmore, with a hesitating smile.

"I may do so, you know," replied Sir Roland; "for I have, I know not how many years over my head more than you have. I am indeed, quite old enough to take orders," he added smiling.

"And I am old enough only to give them, I suppose."

"Well then, give them now; and say whether we shall drop this subject, or treat it as reasonable creatures."

"As we have gone so far, I may as well hear all you have to say, and then you shall listen to me; and if I fail to convince you, we will then let the subject rest for ever."

"Will you open the case then?"

"Why, no—I think not—no, you shall begin, and tell me all your weighty objections to these things."

"In the first place then, there is great expense attending them; an expense of means that might be much more profitably employed."

"I grant you that, perhaps, as regards a humble private individual like myself," said Lady Stanmore; "but you are the representative, for the time being, of the greatest nation in the world, and in your case therefore, such considerations savour of illiberality."

"If the money saved were expended on selfish pleasures, I might perhaps, deserve to incur that suspicion, but scarcely I think, when —— But however, if you think me illiberal, Lady Stanmore, I must perforce, submit."

Sir Roland spoke with rather a pained feeling, and a glow of pride stained his cheek, for his munificence was known to be unbounded. Besides the large sums he spent in private ways, there were many public works of charity and utility to which he had subscribed largely, and to which subscriptions he had thought it right to affix his name, in order that it might not be said, that he lived in a quiet way for the purpose of avoiding expense; for he felt that his country, as well as his religion, was in some degree implicated in his conduct.

Lady Stanmore was shocked at the expression she had used, for she knew how little Sir Roland deserved the imputation she had apparently cast upon him. She hastened to say—

" Oh, no ! you know I cannot think you illiberal, no one can do that; your name is known too well, and seen too often, for any one to do that. Pray forgive my seeming, but most unintentional rudeness."

" It is easy to forgive you any thing, Lady Stanmore," replied Sir Roland, touched by her manner, " particularly when I feel the pride of my own heart requires so much forgiveness. It is painful to feel how soon a word spoken against self, causes that smouldering fire to blaze."

" I was very unjust," she replied sweetly, " but what I said was meant for foreign ministers in general, not for you."

" Well, taking it for them then," replied Sir Roland good-humouredly, " I think they might do more good to the places in which they reside than by giving

fêtes and balls, for even if there were no objection
whatever to such parties of dissipation, surely it would
redound more to the high estimation in which we all
desire our country to be held by other nations, if each
successive minister were to leave behind him some
lasting memorial, according to his means, of good done
to the country in which he had resided.   Do you think
I am wrong in so viewing the subject as far as expense
is concerned ?"

   " No, certainly not," said Lady Stanmore.   " And
yet, alas!" she exclaimed, lifting up her hands in
pretended dismay, " what does that most indiscreet
admission involve?   My poor fabric is dispersed by it
to the four winds."

   " Touched by Ithuriel's spear, so may every thing
that hides the light of truth from your heart, dissolve
and vanish away," said Sir Roland, with a bright
smile.

   " Thank you," said Lady Stanmore, gratefully; " I
know you wish all for my good.   And now," she added,
with a pretended sigh, " as I am reduced to the awful
quiet of despair, I may as well listen to all you have to
say, and get my lecture over at one sitting.   I only
wish I had given my *fête*, for I do not want my pleasure in it to be disturbed."

   " You will think me very hard-hearted then, I am
afraid," said Sir Roland, smiling demurely, " if I say that
I hope it may be disturbed."

   " Yes, I do think you very hard-hearted, for, as you
know you think we ball-goers will have no happiness
hereafter, you should in common charity wish us to
have as much as we can here."

   " Oh, do not speak lightly on those subjects, dear

Lady Stanmore," said Sir Roland, earnestly ; " think
what is involved in an ' hereafter without happiness.'"

" You are so very solemn, Sir Roland," said Lady
Stanmore, rather startled ; " you talk as if you thought
I were on the brink of the grave."

" And who shall say that you are not on the brink
of the grave ?   I would truly have you ever remember
that you may be so."

" Then I should be for ever gloomy and miserable."

" No, you would not—when you knew and felt
that your treasure lay on the other side of that grave."

" But I cannot help having many treasures here,
too.   I have my mother — my husband—my child "—
and the tears started into her eyes.

" Enjoy them to the utmost," said Sir Roland ;
" they are Heaven's gifts, meant to be loved and cherished ; and God grant that they may form part of
your treasure hereafter !   But will your enjoyment
here be lessened by the certainty of possessing those
pure and sweet affections in heaven ?   Here, you may
be called upon to part; there—partings are unknown."
After a moment's silence he resumed, " Another strong
objection to dissipated parties is the great temptations
into which they throw our servants.   When we consider how much we are answerable for them whilst in
our service, it is a fearful thing to expose them night
after night to the force of almost every evil.   I need
not dwell on this objection ; I am sure it must commend itself to every conscience not wholly dead to its
great responsibilities.   Then for ourselves—these things
come as mists and clouds between our souls and God.
It is difficult enough to be sober-minded at any time—
how much more so when we are surrounded by all

most calculated to intoxicate the brain ! We naturally acquire the tone of feeling of those with whom we associate, and you perhaps, know better than I do, Lady Stanmore, whether the conversation at those places is calculated to lead the heart to God, or whether it is not rather likely to deaden all spiritual feeling."

" But," said Lady Stanmore, " the society at dinner-parties is just the same. I am sure I never heard a word at any one of them which could do me any good—except perhaps, to-night," she added, looking kindly at Sir Roland.

" You could not even have heard that little in a ball-room," he replied.

" Why not ? "

" Because those who love to speak of the things of God do not frequent ball-rooms."

" But why should they not just as well as dinners?"

" The nature of the two meetings is very different," answered Sir Roland. " I cannot but think that dissipation is injurious, yet I feel that society is highly advantageous to all men ; it rubs off the angles of their tempers, and teaches them to look kindly on their fellows, and prevents their hugging themselves up, and ' nursing their own dignity' too much. A dinner is a rational mode of meeting, and sanctioned too, we must remember, by the highest authority. It takes place at a reasonable hour, and affords reasonable people, an opportunity for reasonable conversation—as we can fully testify at this moment—can we not? But even to dinner-parties amongst worldly people, I should scarcely feel myself justified in going, exeepting as obliged by my situation here, if I did not go with the

earnest desire and indeed continual prayer that I might
be enabled to speak to my great Master's glory."

"You have indeed done so to-night," said Lady
Stanmore with some emotion; "but you have never
done so before to me."

"No, Lady Stanmore, I have generally seen you
surrounded by those who would not have welcomed
such intrusion, and I am not fond of public disputa-
tions. I wish indeed, that all men could enjoy the
things of God as I do, but I think I should do harm
by forcing the subject in general society. The Almighty almost always gives me the great happiness of
being able to say something for Him, and to-night He
has seemed to make my way with you so easy, by your
patient kindness, that I could not but enter on the
path opened before me. It has been with true pleasure that I have done so, and may the blessing of God
rest on what is passed, as far as it has been according
to His will and word. But at a ball, how should I
have dared to have talked as I have done? how could
I have said, 'Love not the world, neither the things
that are in the world?'"

"But why should we not love the world—to a
certain extent, at least?"

"I cannot better answer you, than by finishing the
passage which I began from the word of God," replied
Sir Roland: "'If any man love the world, the love of
the Father is not in him.'"

"But what would you have me to do?—if I did
not go out at all, I should only sit at home wishing to
go."

"What I would have you do, Lady Stanmore—as
you ask me," said Sir Roland, "would be to pray ear-

nestly — continually, that a new heart, new affections, new desires, might be given you; then you would seek and enjoy new pleasures, and new occupations, and, above all, you would learn to know and love that Being, of whom truly it has been said, ' None who find Him seek further.'—Have I been too severe a lecturer ?"

"No! a most kind and faithful one; but I know not what sort of a disciple I shall make. I feel there is a great deal of truth in what you have said, but what can I do? I cannot all of a sudden leave off these things we have been speaking of, and it might not be liked, even if I were willing."

"I was not urging you, Lady Stanmore, to give these things up suddenly," said Sir Roland, "I was only stating why I could not take them up suddenly. No, it is far better to 'count the cost before you begin the warfare,' and not to enter in haste on a course which you might not have strength to pursue. Besides, though religion will certainly, I think, lead to our giving up these worldly dissipations, yet it is a terrible mistake to fancy that merely giving them up makes one religious, or even proves one to be so. A hermit may carry the world in his breast though he dwell in ' untrodden solitudes,' and so may we in the morose seclusion of our own chambers. But if really and truly you are inclined to believe that the service of God is better, and more satisfying than that of the world, let me entreat of you to begin at the right end—by prayer: that golden key which will open to you all the treasury of heaven, all the riches of Christ; and then, as truth enters and fills your heart, error must give way."

"But if," said Lady Stanmore, hesitating and colouring deeply —" if I thought it wrong to go to these things, and it was wished that I should what ought I to do?"

"You have always with you the two best guides a woman can have, dear Lady Stanmore—your God and your husband! Keep them ever near you in their legitimate places—God ever first, your husband ever next, and you cannot go wrong. Prayerful study of the Bible will help you through every difficulty, for all Scripture, we are told, is given by inspiration of God, 'that the man of God may be perfect, thoroughly furnished unto all good works.'"

"Well, Mary," said Lord Stanmore, when Lady Stanmore and Sir Roland rejoined him, "have you been successful? You look very little elated for a conqueror."

"No, my forces are all routed and dispersed, and I do not know whether I shall ever be able to muster them again."

"Lady Stanmore has imposed a severe task on me," said Sir Roland, "or rather, has forced me on a dreadful service, the difficulty of which you, Lord Stanmore, can best appreciate—that of refusing a request of hers."

"No, he is not capable of appreciating that difficulty," said Lady Stanmore, taking her husband's arm and looking at him with the utmost affection, "for he has never refused me any thing in his life."

"Has Ashton refused you any thing?" said Lord Stanmore, shaking his head at Sir Roland;—"then let him look to himself."

"I must leave my cause in Lady Stanmore's hands," said Sir Roland, "and I have no doubt she will do me justice; and may I beg, if you can forgive me, and if you are not better engaged, that you will both honour me with your company at dinner to-morrow?"

This was agreed to, and with the kindest feelings, the parties then separated.

Lady Stanmore gave her *fête* the following week, but Sir Roland's arguments and words often recurred to her mind, and her pleasure was not undisturbed.

CHAPTER XVII.

"A web of a different colour, but wrought by the same subtle hand."
CHARLOTTE ELIZABETH.

" And what is home, and where ? but with the loving."
MRS. HEMANS.

No sooner is our great enemy baffled on one side, than
he commences the attack on another. Having failed
in forcing Sir Roland to act contrary to his principles,
as respected those dissipations which he thought uncongenial to the spirit of Christianity, his wily adversary changed his mode of warfare, and raised up temptations in the course of duty. Sir Roland's large fortune and many worldly advantages, made him a person
of importance and consideration every where; but the
high station he temporarily filled at ――――, of course
added very much to his consequence there, and his peculiar character, aided by the charm of his countenance and manner, caused him to be an object of great
attraction, especially, as was natural, to the younger
portion of his female acquaintance, with many of whom
it became, for his sake, quite a fashion to profess
seriousness and religion.

Some there were in ―――― who, sincerely agreeing
with Sir Roland in principle, were thankful to find
that one so young and admired, could also be so strong
and steady in his uprightness; and some who had before been utterly careless on the subject, really were

aroused, and led by the force of his example, to search
and see whether his way was not the way of godliness and peace. But many others, either from excited
feelings, or from pure affectation, in order to please
him, adopted for the moment a tone of conversation
and a line of conduct, wholly at variance with their usual
habits and dispositions. But whatever was the cause,
to be so courted and admired as he was, was a great
trial to one over whose head scarce five-and-twenty
summers had shed their brightness; and Sir Roland
felt the evil; the more so, because it was one which
was calculated to draw his heart from God, rather
than make him fly to Him for strength and refuge.
That he was not one who could close his eyes to
his own defects, or be content to slumber in the
midst of danger, was an inestimable blessing; but his
watchfulness of conscience, invaluable as it was, made
his mind, under his present circumstances, a scene
of perpetual warfare; for he could not endure quietly
to give way to the feelings of vanity which, spite of
himself, were roused perpetually within him, when he
saw the evident and flattering admiration which he
excited, and the marked attentions which were shewn
him on every side.

None however, of the fair, and in many instances,
amiable beings who surrounded him, had power to
withdraw his thoughts for one moment from Lady
Constance. Her image dwelt unceasingly with him,
dressed in all the bright hues with which the heart so
fondly delights to deck the distant objects of its love;
and the remembrance of her sweetness and cheerful
piety, warm and quick affections, and exceeding
beauty, came across his soul continually, with ever-

soothing, yet ever-animating influence. The appointment he had made to meet her every night in prayer had never been forgotten or neglected. It had been a source of the greatest pleasure and comfort to him, riveting the image of her he loved ever closer and closer to his heart. In society the most uncongenial to him, or when watching in stillness by Mr. Anstruther's death-bed, he had ever found rest and peace in joining his spirit with hers before the throne of God; the silent midnight hour was rich to him in feelings of heart-felt love and pure devotion; for happily those two delightful sentiments were ever united in his breast.

Home thus ever shone before him in all its brightest colours, and ardently did he desire to be again within its happy precincts, and with her who formed the dearest portion of its charm—free from the glare of public life, and from all the thronging temptations of the world.

Inexpressible therefore, was his delight, when he received a letter from his uncle, saying, that he expected to be able to return to his post in the course of the following month; and that the new secretary whom the government had appointed would accompany him. The joy of his heart was unbounded; yet never did time seem to move with such leaden feet, as during the interval that elapsed between the receipt of his uncle's letter, and the time when he could set out on his much-longed-for journey. At last his uncle arrived, and with him the new secretary; and gladly did Sir Roland relinquish into the hands of the latter, all the papers and letters, &c. which had tormented him so long, and given him so many weary hours. His extreme rapture was, however, rather damped by a claim which his uncle made upon him for future services. There was some important business which he had commenced, for the completion of which, the concurrence of several of the different courts was indispensable; but some hindrances having occurred in the course of the affair, it could not be carried forward at that time; and Sir Roland having commenced it, and fully understanding all its bearings, Lord N—— had, whilst in England, obtained a promise that he should be appointed on a special mission for the purpose of carrying it through, when the proper time arrived. Sir Roland could not well refuse to undertake this business, as his uncle made so great a point of his doing so; but the very idea of it was most irksome to him, desirous as he was, of remaining at home. He determined however, not to think of the evil day till it arrived, so set himself with all diligence to speed his joyful preparations for returning to England.

At last all was concluded; and, having taken leave of his uncle, and the many friends he had made in ——, he stood in the court of the Embassy-house, waiting for his servant to put the finishing stroke to the packing of his carriage, and conversing with Mr. Scott, who was going to stay some time longer on the continent with Mr. Singleton.

" You will come soon to Llanaven, Scott," he said.

" Not I !" answered the other—" not for these six years at least. I will never sing second to any one."

" Then, stay away for ever!" said Sir Roland laughingly, shaking his friend's hand; and springing into the carriage, he threw himself back in the corner, exclaiming, "Home!"

CHAPTER XVIII.

"Oh! dear, dear England! how my longing eye
Turned westward, shaping in the steady clouds
Thy sands and high white cliffs!"

COLERIDGE.

"The form that stands before me falsifies
No feature of the image that hath lived
So long within me."

COLERIDGE.

SIR ROLAND passed through much beautiful country
on his way from —— ; but the picture of home in
his mind was so far more enchanting to him, that he
scarcely saw what passed before his outward eye. He
had received letters from Lady Constance, and from
his mother, just before he started, full of delight at his
anticipated return. All was well with them; "but all
would be better when he was there again, to share
their happiness." How often, and in how many ways
did he fancy to himself his return home—his meeting
with Lady Constance—his quiet evening with his
mother—his early morning walk over his own delightful grounds, with his own sea sparkling, and dancing in
the light. Love was with him, certainly the first, and
most arresting object, in the blissful scenes which
imagination spread out before him; but it could not
exclude other objects of interest and affection from his
breast. It did not stand forth in the landscape like

some splendid but overpowering mountain, shining in the sun's rich rays itself, but casting all into shadow around; but it stood rather as in itself a source of light ("whose fountain who shall tell?") gilding every other object, and bringing to view all the beauty and loveliness of surrounding things. His affection for his mother, ever deep and lively, gained fresh strength from his heightened feelings, and his full heart seemed so fraught with love and happiness, that it expanded to embrace the whole world!

Those who would underrate true love, would underrate the Almighty's *first* gift to the affections! With some indeed, this feeling is ephemeral as the morning dew, and the character raised by it perhaps, a moment, above its ordinary level, sinks again when the cause which elevated it is past; but with others, true love endures through long, long years of married life!— when peace, and joy, and affection, gild the decline of life with rays as bright as were its morning beams! Happy are they!

The evening was perfectly calm on which Sir Roland crossed the sea on his return to England, and the ripple of the waters as he looked into their clear depths from the vessel's side, soothed his thoughts into the most delightful state of enjoyable happiness. The moon was not visible; but still, as night came on, the ruffled waters in the wake of the vessel reflected light from the innumerable stars that lit the sky, and from the never wholly-dying summer twilight. It was just such a time as quiets down the thrilling agitation, and flutter of both mind and body, which so often destroy the enjoyment of expected, and longed-for meetings; and the absence of the moon, which Sir Roland had at first regretted, was in fact, a blessing to him; for there is certainly a most exciting power in her peculiar light. Even if the heart is at rest, and there is nothing to disturb its tranquillity, yet the moon herself with all her soft and pure accompaniments, produces strong though undefined sensations, akin to melancholy, which depress the spirit, while they elevate the soul; but when real cause exists for anxiety, and sorrow mixes with this feeling—then the blue and silvery gleaming of the star of night, draws forth all the deep sad-heartedness, which perhaps, had slumbered in the glare of sunshine. "Daylight is the flesh and blood—moonlight is the spirit." Perhaps it was this feeling, which in former days, induced the idea of melancholy persons being moon-struck—of "moon-struck madness," which we find in our older poets; but be that as it may, poets, old and young, have ever paid tribute to the charm and power of the queen of night; and not all the nonsense-verses which have been perpetrated to her dishonour, can dim one ray of her real beauty, or take one charm from her softening influence. Indeed, Sir Walter Scott's declaration, "that never was there lover who had not got, at least, as far as 'Oh! Thou,'" in a sonnet to her praise—far from detracting from her glory, proves only, how loveliest things will flow together.

Sir Roland continued on deck enjoying the stillness of the darkening hours, till midnight brought again the welcome time for meeting her he loved, in the presence of God. All was quiet in the vessel, excepting the occasional voice of the sailors; and unobserved, and uninterrupted, he poured forth his soul to the Lord of earth, and air, and seas. Long did he pray—for his heart was filled with deep, though tranquil feelings; and it was ever a delight to his pure spirit, to pour forth its hopes, its wants, its thankfulness, to Him who hears and answers the prayers of those who love Him! He thought with delight, that but one more night would elapse before he should again, in very life and form, meet her whose image had been to him through long absence, the last waking thought at night, as well as the "morning-star of memory;" and wrapping his cloak around him, he laid himself down on the deck, and slept in the soft, still, summer air.

The sun's bright beams early awoke him the next morning, making him exchange his undefined but pleasant dreams, for the reality of enjoyment, which the beautiful scene before him afforded; where the lightest of all possible breezes springing up with the dawn of day, just agitated the waters sufficiently to make them, towards the east, one sheet of trembling, sparkling, "shimmering," light.

The vessel impelling itself onwards through the smooth waters, at length entered the forest of masts, which lines the Thames as it flows through the suburbs of London.—The wheels stopped!—and once again Sir Roland trod his native land.

Certainly the disembarking from a steamer at London Bridge, is not the most sentimental or romantic of landings! The pebbly shore of the ocean might inspire enthusiasm—but not *that!*—and never surely, could the most devoted lover of his country, returning

from the longest exile, on stepping forth at that spot,
be inclined to exclaim, "Oh! cara terra degli avi
miei—ti bacio," still less to "suit the action to the
word."

Overlooking, however, all these minor considerations, Sir Roland was enchanted to find himself again
in England, and only wished that the next instant
could have transported him to Claverton; but having,
unfortunately, business to transact at the Foreign
Office, he was obliged to remain some hours in London;
though as soon as that was despatched, he joyfully
—how joyfully!—turned his face towards the west.
The railroad, that friend of the impatient, did not at
that time run its level course in that direction, but
four horses and a light calèche, bore him on with tolerable speed, and brought him rapidly on his way; till
at length, he began to recognise old accustomed
scenes, and points of view familiar to him; and
thicker, and thicker still, grew the delightful evidences
that he was near his home, till at last, the woods of
Claverton appeared in sight. As that had been the
last place he had visited before his departure from
England, so, naturally, was it the first to which he
directed his steps on his return; and his happiness
was unbounded when the carriage passed through the
park-gate, and he found himself once again in a spot
so inexpressibly dear to him.

It was a lovely evening towards the end of July,
without a breath to ruffle the lake which calmly spread
"its lucid mirror to the light," skirted in some parts
by hanging woods, and in others, by miniature cliffs,
whose bright and clear reflections were pictured to
the life on the silvery waters. The deer and sheep

had sought the woods and far-stretching trees for shelter from the still fervid heat; and all nature seemed to repose in luxury and enjoyment.

When he was within a short distance of the house, Sir Roland fancied he descried some one walking in the garden; he thought it must be Lady Constance, and stopping the carriage (which he ordered round to the stable) he jumped out, and flying down the green slope which divided the road from the shrubbery, he bounded over the iron railings, and found himself once more—there. He paused a moment to recover breath, and to still the throbbing of his heart, which, what with excitement, happiness, and exertion, beat almost to suffocation. While standing concealed among the trees, he again caught the flutter of the white dress which had before attracted him, and he now saw that it was Lady Constance, who just then entered the very summerhouse where he had last parted from her. If he could himself have chosen the time and place of their meeting, thus it would have been; there—in the same spot where he had last seen her, and where he had so often pictured her to his imagination, in her great beauty, and in her—to him still more precious—tearful regret. She was standing within the walls of the summerhouse when he advanced, so that she was not aware of his approach till he was almost close to her, when hearing a step, she came forward.

"Roland! dear Roland!" she exclaimed, in the joyful surprise of the first moment; then turning deadly pale, and staggering backwards, she would have fallen, had not Sir Roland sprung forward and caught her.

"My dearest Constance," he said, in alarm, "what is this? are you not well?"

"Oh!" she exclaimed, in a voice of the deepest anguish; and leaning her head on his shoulder, she burst into an agony of tears.

"Constance! Constance!" cried Sir Roland, terrified at her emotion, "has any thing happened? tell me I beseech you—my mother—Henry?"

Lady Constance shook her head, but could not speak.

"Your father?" at length he asked, in a voice almost inaudible from agitation.

A renewed burst of sorrow in Lady Constance proved but too truly, that he had now touched on the cause of her overwhelming affliction.

"He is not——" he could not finish.

"No," answered Lady Constance, understanding him, and struggling for words, "but they think he cannot live."

"My God!" exclaimed Sir Roland, looking up, in the anguish of his mind. "Oh, Constance!" he said, after a pause, "is this the meeting I have so longed for—in tears of such affliction?" and his own burst forth as he spoke.

Yet still she was there—he was with her; and there was a strange mingling of extremest joy, and bitterest sorrow in his heart, as he seated himself in silence by her side. He longed to know what had caused this sudden danger to one for whom he felt so much regard, yet he could not bear to ask Lady Constance, knowing that the subject must be so painful to her; but she, becoming more composed, was about to speak to him, when a step on the terrace made her rise hastily.

"It is your mother," she said to Sir Roland.

"My mother here!" he exclaimed; and flying along the gravel walk, the next moment he found himself folded in her fond embrace.

The servants had informed her of his arrival, and she had come out immediately to meet a son who was the delight of her heart. The joy of meeting for an instant banished all trouble from their minds— but only for an instant; and Lady Constance joining them, her pale face and tearful eyes brought back sadder, and more painful feelings.

"I will go in," she said, to Lady Ashton; "I have taken my walk as you wished, and now you must stay out and enjoy the air, and dear Roland's welcome company;" and smiling through her tears, she held out her hand to him, and kissing Lady Ashton, passed on to the house.

Sir Roland looked after her in silence till she had disappeared.

"How ill she looks!" he said, with a heavy sigh. "Oh! my dear mother, how little can we reckon on this world's happiness! If you could but know how I have looked forward to this hour! with what sinful impatience I have longed for it; and now—to meet with such bitter feelings!"

He begged his mother to tell him how the event had occurred, which had thrown this sudden blight on prospects which had seemed so full of happiness when last he had heard from home; and Lady Ashton informed him, that two days previously, Lord St. Ervan

had been examining, with his steward, some buildings
which were out of repair, and on which his carpenters
were at work, when a beam, which had been loosened
from its place, unexpectedly fell, and struck him with
such violence that he was taken up senseless.   For
many hours he had lain without speech or motion,
but, after a while, he gradually regained the powers of
his mind; but the injuries he had received were of so
fatal a nature, that not the least hope could be entertained of his recovery; and indeed, it became but too
evident that his last hour rapidly approached.   Lady
Ashton said that she had come over on the first
intelligence of the dreadful event, and had remained
at Claverton ever since; and she expressed her wish
that Sir Roland should continue there with them.
To this, of course, he readily acceded, for all pleasure
in the thoughts of his own place was for the moment
lost; and his only desire was to remain with the
afflicted objects of his tenderest regards.

   " And Constance," he said, " how has she borne
it? tell me, my dear mother, how has she been? "

   " Poor child ! " answered Lady Ashton, "she and
Florence have both suffered terribly, the blow was
so sudden.   I was not here at the first dreadful
moment, but I believe Constance was nearly frantic
when her father was brought home; and one cannot
wonder, for you know how devotedly fond they were
of each other, and how constantly he made her his
companion.   Such an event would have been afflicting
had it occurred to a stranger, but to see one's father,
the being one loved most in the world—who had left
one in health, cheerful and happy but a short time
before—brought home bleeding, wounded, and ap-

parently lifeless, it must have been dreadful! Since
I have been here she has been quite calm — too much
so indeed — I had rather see more frequent tears, they
might relieve her."

"She shed many when with me," said Sir Roland,
his own starting at the remembrance.

"I am glad of it," replied Lady Ashton. "She
has scarcely left her father's side since the fatal accident took place, nor has she once closed her eyes.
It was with difficulty I had persuaded her to come
into the air for a short time just now, when he was
asleep."

"But she will kill herself," exclaimed Sir Roland,
"she must have rest."

"I cannot persuade her to lie down; she says she
cannot bear to lose one of the few moments that
remain of his loved presence, and I cannot wonder;
indeed, it is the same with myself; and I fear the time
fast approaches when she will have leisure enough for
sleep — and tears too, poor girl!" and Lady Ashton
covered her face and sobbed aloud.

Sir Roland pressed his mother to his heart, and
would have spoken of comfort, but could not. At
length Lady Ashton became more calm.

"He has begged me to be guardian to his children," she said, "and I have of course consented."

A joy indescribable rushed through Sir Roland's
whole being as he received this communication from
his mother — so trembling a joy, that he could not trust
his voice to speak in reply.

"He has, you know," continued Lady Ashton,
"no near relations but his two cousins, Captain
Templeton (on whom this property is entailed) and

his sister, Mrs. Mordaunt. The latter, the moment she had heard of the fatal accident which had taken place, wrote by express, in the kindest manner, to entreat that the two girls might be consigned to her care; and she urged her considerate offer so strongly, that it was most painful to Lord St. Ervan to refuse. But she is one of the last persons with whom he would wish to leave them, for she is a most thoroughly worldly character and has besides, several sons, not considered very steady, who have their home with her in London. I have heard Lord St. Ervan say that he has frequently asked her to visit him here, but that she always refused, saying, though with the utmost good-humour, that she could not endure his 'puritanical ways.' He had left his children wards in chancery, by a deed he executed the moment his senses recovered from the effects of the stunning blow he had received, but he directed that they should live with their excellent governess, Miss Gower, for he never dreamed that Mrs. Mordaunt would wish to take the charge of them; but when he received her letter, which was couched in the strongest, as well as the kindest terms, he felt a terror lest, when he was gone, she might, through good intention, petition the chancellor to let her have the charge of them; and the plea that she was the only near female relation, and that otherwise they would be left alone with a governess, was one which, he feared, might very naturally meet with success. This idea filled him with such apprehension that he asked me if, under these circumstances, I would consent to being named their guardian, to which of course I agreed: as I should be most happy to render them any service in my power, and be to them of what little comfort I could."

" And they will live with us, then?" said Sir Roland; at the moment forgetting, in that joyful thought, the dreadful circumstance which would be the occasion of their change of abode.

" No; I begged him earnestly to let them do so," said Lady Ashton; " telling him what a happiness it would be to me, but he declined it positively, and with so much warmth and agitation—entreating me to name it no more—that I dared not repeat my request. They are to live with Miss Gower, at Westley, which is only ten miles distant, and is the only house he possesses in the county that is unentailed."

" Westley ! Westley is no place for them to live in," exclaimed Sir Roland—" not for a day ! and close too, to that odious town of X——, with its barracks and idle lounging officers—they will be harassed to death : I cannot consent to their living there,—I cannot endure the thoughts of it."

" My dear Roland," said Lady Ashton, smiling at his vehemence, " you forget that your consent has not been asked."

Sir Roland coloured deeply, for he felt that he had spoken more in accordance with his wishes, than with the realities of the case. He laughed faintly and said, " Oh ! yes, I spoke foolishly—I did not mean that, of course ; I only meant that my will would not consent to their living at that place. But my dear mother," he continued, laying his cheek to hers and kissing her fondly, " will you not try, once more, to move him ? try—implore of him to let them live with you."

"I would gladly do it, if I thought it would be of any avail, dear Roland," replied Lady Ashton, returning his warm caresses ; "you cannot be more anxious about it than I am;" (Sir Roland, however, felt that he was far more anxious even than his kind mother) "but he so resolutely forbade the subject being mentioned again, that I really dare not renew it. He is in so weak a state that any agitation might destroy him at once."

"Did he give no reason?"

"None—but he entreated me to urge it no further."

Sir Roland was lost in thought, and they walked on for some time in silence.

"I trust I may see him," at length he said, with much emotion, "if only once to clasp his hand; it would be painful indeed, never again ——"

"Oh! yes," replied Lady Ashton; "he knew of your arrival, and was delighted, though the news threw him for a time into great agitation; but he said he must see you, and would send when he felt equal to the exertion."

"Dear, kind friend," exclaimed Sir Roland. "Oh! my dear mother, how much shall we miss him! and those poor girls!" He dashed the starting tear from his eye. "What a blow! How soon is happiness destroyed! This hour is the one I have had ever before me—ever!—from the first moment when I left this country! but I had arrayed it in all the glowing colours of happiness—how mournful is the difference! But, oh! my God, keep me from murmuring.—And now, dear mother, tell me of Henry; it is longer than usual since I have heard of him. Happy fellow! he knows nothing of our present griefs. When did you hear from him last, and where was he?"

" He was still on the South American station, but he said they were soon to leave it, so that he feared he might lose many of our letters. He begged, however, that we would continue to write, and that we would direct to different places, as his ship was moving about, and he did not know its exact destination; by which means, he hoped that at least some of our letters might reach him. I wrote about this sad event, and of your expected return, and directed my letter both to Rio and to Valparaiso."

" Did he talk of coming home?"

" No."

" Shall we go towards the house now? I feel so very anxious to see Lord St. Ervan. There is no fear of any thing sudden, is there?"

" The doctor says he cannot tell; a state like his is beyond the usual calculations of art. He thinks it possible a sudden stroke might come, and deprive him of sense, if not of life; but he rather expects that nature will gradually give way under his excessive weakness and exhaustion. We have but to wait—and thankful may we be, that his trust has long rested on Him who never fails His people. His mind is in perfect peace; and it is wonderful how he is sustained in cheerful hope, even when looking on his—so soon to be orphaned children. Poor Florence, child-like, grieves him most, with her loving expressions and unrestrained tears; but Constance's mind seems to strengthen his, she is so very bright in faith for one so young; and God's everlasting arms are indeed ' underneath her and

around.' But I almost fear for her when all is over.
These afflictions must be felt, though we may submit
with fulness of heart to God. Trials would not be
trials were they not sufferings."

As they approached the house they saw Lady Constance coming towards them. Sir Roland hastened to
meet her, and she informed him that her father wished
to see him. He gave her his arm, and they returned together to the house. Before he parted from her to go to
Lord St. Ervan, he took her hand, and looking at her
with the deepest affection, he said—

"Constance, you know not how full my heart is of
you."

"Dear Roland," she replied, "you were always so
kind!—and your travels have not spoilt you, or made
you forgetful of those whom you loved at home."

"I must have forgotten myself ere I could have
forgotten them," he replied. "Constance, our appointed meetings before God have been most precious
to me; have they been so to you?"

"They have indeed," said she, looking up affectionately at Sir Roland's anxious countenance; "I
have never once failed in praying for, and with you."

"You are looking so ill, dear Constance," said Sir
Roland; "will you not take care of yourself for our
sakes?"

Lady Constance's countenance became agitated, as
she answered, "I am well—quite well; but do not
think of me now, dear Roland, go to *him*, he wants
you."

"Will you not come with me?"

"No, he wishes to see you alone."

"Yes," answered Sir Roland, "and I wish to speak to him alone;" and the hand that held Lady Constance's trembled, as the thought of what he wished to say to Lord St. Ervan, darted through his mind.

"Go, then, now," said Lady Constance, "he is quite composed, and his mind is peaceful and happy."

CHAPTER XIX.

Sir Roland left Lady Constance and mounted the stairs to Lord St. Ervan's room. He paused an instant before he entered it, for a faint sickness came over him at the thought of the scene he was about to witness. The stillness of the chamber of death struck a chill to his heart; but soon summoning his courage he entered.

"My dear Roland," said Lord St. Ervan, in a low voice, as he approached, his accents seeming to come painfully forth, "I rejoice so much to see you once again."

Sir Roland kissed the hand held out to him in silence.

"You find pain and sorrow where you left all smiling," resumed Lord St. Ervan; "but you know who guides and directs. At first it seemed dreadful to leave *them*," he stopped, and closed his eyes a moment, "but God has taken away that sting, too. And you, Roland, you are well, God be praised—it is a joy to see you once more; you were ever the best"—he stopped, and grasped Sir Roland's hand with convulsive emotion.

"My dear sir," said Sir Roland, deeply touched, "words cannot express the sorrow of this hour. Oh!

is there any thing I can do; any charge you can leave
with me?—it will be my joy to fulfil it."

"Serve your God, my dear boy, ever more and
more faithfully, that is my best wish for you; and put
all your trust in Him who alone can support in an
hour like this. Yes, he can support!—my Saviour's
feet have trod the rugged path of death for me, and
made it all smooth and easy to my feeble steps. Trust
Him, Roland—trust Him!"

"God grant me grace to live wholly for Him,"
replied Sir Roland; adding, after a pause, in a hesitating voice, "But is there nothing, as regards this world,
that I can do? have you nothing to commit to my
care—my attention?"

"Nothing," sighed Lord St. Ervan. "No; all my
earthly concerns are settled."

Sir Roland knelt on one knee by the side of Lord
St. Ervan's bed, still holding his cold and feeble hand
in his. They were both silent—the same subject at
that moment filled the heart of each, yet neither could
speak of it to the other. Lord St. Ervan well remembered Sir Roland's former proposal concerning Lady
Constance, and earnestly desired that he should renew
it now; but he could not be the first to mention the
subject, ignorant as he was of the present state of his
affections; for absence he thought, and the charms of
other, newer friends, might have displaced the first love
of his "boyhood's waxen heart," and he could not endure the idea that his beautiful and precious child
should be trusted to the compassion, or cast on the
faded affection, of any man. Sir Roland was equally embarrassed, and could not summon courage to pronounce
the name which seemed the sum of existence to him.

At length Lord St. Ervan, opening his eyes, on which the heaviness of death began already almost to settle, turned to Sir Roland, and said—

" Your mother will have told you our arrangements for my children. She is indeed most kind."

Sir Roland's heart fluttered when he found this opening made ; and he answered, hurriedly—

" She has informed me that she is to have the charge of your children. But will you not, my dear Lord St. Ervan, let them also reside with her, it would make her so happy ? And surely—forgive me—but surely it would be far better—far pleasanter for them, too."

" It cannot be," said Lord St. Ervan, hastily.

Sir Roland felt convinced that Lord St. Ervan would gladly have acceded to the proposal, had Lady Ashton had a home of her own ; but Llanaven was, in fact, *his* home, though his mother resided there ; and he could fully appreciate the delicacy which made it impossible for a father to throw his daughters on the society of men like himself and his brother. He now, more than ever, desired that he should consent to his union with Lady Constance, in the event of his being able to obtain her affection, as in that case he thought he could not object to her living with Lady Ashton. His anxious feelings were ever on his lips, but for a time he could find no words to express them. Fearing however, from Lord St. Ervan's extreme weakness, that life might ebb away before he had spoken the wish of his heart, with a strong effort he began at length—

" You will remember, my dear lord, a conversation I had with you before I left England ? "

Lord St. Ervan, roused to animation, fixed his eyes eagerly on Sir Roland, who continued—

"You cannot suppose that my heart is changed; that one, who had from childhood loved Constance, could ever cease to do so. No, her happiness is more than ever my care, and her love—that which alone can make me happy. Will you not now—now after above a year of exile—will you not let me seek a place in her heart?"

"Oh! if you had one," replied Lord St. Ervan, "I should indeed be but too happy; the only sadness of my heart would be removed. But, Roland, my poor boy! have you indeed thought of her—her only— through all your wanderings? I grieve for the pain I must have given you; but you were both young, and I thought it best you both should know your own hearts. You have given me great happiness, for now that I am convinced of your constancy, there is no one on earth to whom I could give her with such perfect peace and confidence. Truly grateful, indeed, to God should I be, could I see your faith plighted before I died."

"Thank you a thousand, thousand times," said Sir Roland, repeatedly pressing the hand he held to his lips, "you cannot know the joy your words give me! But now, dear Lord St. Ervan, as you are willing to give Constance to my care—to trust her to my love— you will surely not object to giving my mother her heart's desire, by letting her and Florence reside with us at Llanaven?"

He looked earnestly at Lord St. Ervan, who replied—

"I can say nothing till I have spoken to my child, and I feel that life fast fails;—send her to me, will you?"

Sir Roland left the room with a spirit much
lightened; yet he was very unwilling that his wishes
should be so abruptly mentioned to Lady Constance.
He had earnestly desired Lord St. Ervan's consent to
his final union with her, but he would fain have had
time allowed him, in which he might have sought to
awaken in her heart a feeling, corresponding to that
which had so long dwelt in his own; for to offer her
his hand without having first endeavoured to win her
heart, was, he thought, a step that well might startle
her, even though she had ever, he knew, regarded him
him with the kindest feelings. He had so honourably
fulfilled Lord St. Ervan's wishes, that he had never
sought to excite in her mind—however much he desired to do so—an exclusive feeling towards himself;
and he could form no idea how this sudden proposal
would be received. The glow of dawning hope and
confidence which had arisen within him, when with
Lord St. Ervan, faded gradually away as he descended
the stairs, and walked along the terrace to the summerhouse, where he expected to find Lady Constance;
and a timidity he had never experienced before, made
him pause ere he approached her. He even thought
of returning to Lord St. Ervan, and entreating him
not to speak for the present to his daughter; but
recollecting the desire he had expressed of seeing
the engagement formed before his death—and fearing
to agitate and distress his mind—he gave up that
idea; and "casting all his care upon God," he advanced
towards the summer-house, where he found Lady Constance, and informed her of her father's wish to see her.
He walked by her in silence to the house; but when
they had reached it, he felt it was impossible to part

from her, without speaking some, of the many words which crowded to his lips. His heart seemed bursting to open itself to her, but broken, incoherent sentences were all that could find utterance. He dared not in that hurried moment enter on the subject that caused him so much anxiety; but Lady Constance could not have failed to have observed the earnest tenderness of his manner, had not her heart been filled, to the exclusion of every other feeling, with the thought of her father. Her love for him was so intense, that though she knew that she and her sister must soon be orphans—that they would have nothing they could call a home—no relation with whom to live—yet she never thought of that. Her whole sum of feeling seemed centred in the one overwhelming thought of her father's death, the moment of which, she could not conceal from herself, was fast and fearfully approaching. Without him, the world seemed one universal blank, and no thought of her future comfortless life intruded to mix with the pure current of her filial regret. The tension of her mind on that subject made all things else pass as dreams before her; and not all Sir Roland's warm expressions of love and devotion could rouse her mind to a consciousness of what he was saying. The sound of his words reached indeed her ear, but their meaning was lost to her mind, further than that she felt they were words of kindness and affection—sounds familiar from him.

"Dear Roland," she said in reply, "I know that you feel for us—that you love us."

"As my own life! Constance," he replied.

She smiled kindly, but her mind was evidently wandering far away, and Sir Roland fearful of de-taining her any longer, reluctantly suffered her to leave him.

When she entered her father's room, she was surprised, and for an instant delighted, at seeing him apparently so much better; for the excitement and joy he felt at the hope of her happiness had lent an unwonted glow to his cheek, and lighted his eye with an unusual lustre.   But she knew by sad and bitter experience how delusive were such appearances; and the hope which for a moment glanced through her mind, gave way to a darker sense of desolation than before.

"My dear child," said Lord St. Ervan, as she approached him, and knelt down by his side, "I wish much to speak to you, and have many things to say. Your kind friend Lady Ashton, has urged me to let you reside with her, instead of living at Westley; but considering that her sons were often with her, that arrangement did not at first seem desirable. A conversation I have since had with Roland has, however, opened new prospects for you, Constance, and you must decide whether or not they shall be accepted."

"My dear father," said Lady Constance, "you have always arranged every thing for me, and I feel incapable — especially now — of forming any judgment for myself. Tell me what you think best, and it must be right."

"In a case like that which I am going to mention— you, my dear Constance, and you alone, must decide.— Have you ever suspected that Roland was attached to you?"

Lady Constance started, and instantly replied, "Never." — The next moment, however, his manner and last words at the ante-room door, and several other little circumstances, flashed across her mind, though at the time they had not apparently made the slightest impression ; but before she could speak again, her father continued—

"He has however confided to me his ardent desire to obtain your love; and if you were favourable towards him — and felt you could form an engagement ——"

Lord St. Ervan stopped — for he saw that his daughter looked in his face with an almost bewildered expression.

"My dear Constance," he added after a moment, "do not agitate yourself. If this subject is painful to you, let it be dropped for ever."

"Oh no!—not—painful," she answered hurriedly— leaning her head down upon the bed — "but so unexpected!" Her mind was now thoroughly roused, and she saw in an instant that Sir Roland's proposal had given her father satisfaction; and so earnest was she to please him, that had the prospect been one in which her happiness was to have been wrecked for ever, she would have consented to it without a shadow of reluctance. But such was not the case; Sir Roland, with his mother and brother, had been the only objects of real affection she had ever known beyond those of her own family; she had other acquaintances and friends — but none like these. Still she had never thought of Sir Roland in the light of a husband, and it is difficult to say, what would have been her decision at that moment, had she had nothing but her own feelings to consult; but she saw at a glance, that by engaging herself to him, she would not only insure a

kind and happy home for her sister, but would also
cheer the dying hours of her father. These thoughts
—which passed like lightning through her mind—
reconciled her instantly to the idea of forming an engagement, which otherwise she might have hesitated to
have undertaken.

Her father laid his hand fondly on her head, and
soothingly said—

"You shall defer your answer, dear Constance, till
your mind is accustomed to the thought, which is now
so suddenly brought before it, and till your heart is
sure of the decision it would wish to make. I knew
not what your feelings might be, and I would not have
tried to penetrate them—only time with me is almost
at an end—and on your determination, my darling,
must depend ——"

"My dearest father," interrupted Lady Constance
hurriedly, "your wishes must be mine. Tell me only
what you think, what you feel, and I——" she paused.

"Think not of me, my dearest child," replied Lord
St. Ervan, "but ask your own heart its wishes, and be
ruled by them. I do not say that it would be otherwise than joy to me, to confide you to one, who of all
the human beings I ever met with, appears to me the
brightest image of his Maker — but still the heart will
not at all times follow the lead of reason, and if you
could not be happy——"

"Oh! yes," exclaimed Lady Constance, "I will—
I will be his."

She rose from her knees, and threw her arms round
her father's neck, who pressed her with all a dying
parent's love, to his heart.

"My God, I thank thee," he murmured, and closing

his eyes, sunk into an almost deathlike state of exhaustion. Lady Constance, in terror, called the nurse, and they administered a reviving draught, which after a time partially restored him.

He opened his eyes, and seeing the nurse near him, he whispered something to her, and she instantly withdrew; and, in a few moments after, Lady Constance was startled by finding Sir Roland by her side. His countenance betrayed the greatest anxiety; but that expression was in an instant changed to a deep flush of joy, as Lord St. Ervan—placing Lady Constance's hand in his, said faintly, "She will be yours."

Sir Roland put his arm round the being he so long had loved, and she, with perfect confidence laying her head upon his breast, gave way to a burst of tears.

Lord St. Ervan's strength sunk under the great excitement of his feelings, and now that all motive for exertion was over, his powers seemed almost suddenly to fail. Feeling himself dying, he whispered to Sir Roland—after a pause of deep emotion, "I would see Florence—your mother."

Sir Roland, roused from the fulness of his mingled feelings, observed with terror, the great alteration which had taken place, and in much alarm was about to speak, when Lord St. Ervan, bending his fading eye upon the still weeping girl by his side, seemed to warn him not to alarm her; he therefore gently disengaged himself, and placing Lady Constance on a chair by her father's bed, hastened to summon his mother and Lady Florence to the chamber, intimating in a low tone to the former that the last sad scene drew near. When Lord St. Ervan saw them enter the room, he extended his arms to take a last embrace of Lady Florence, who, with the unrestrained grief of childhood, wept aloud upon his breast. Tears streamed from his eyes, as he tenderly soothed her, and whispered to her of that happy land, whither he was hastening, and where she would soon follow him, through that Redeemer, whom her young heart had already learned to love. He then turned to Sir Roland and begged him to pray with him, adding, "My soul is in perfect peace." His request was instantly complied with, and all knelt round the bed of suffering, so soon to be exchanged for the glories of a heavenly home.

When Sir Roland had ended a prayer, in which his full heart poured forth all its holy feelings, he raised his head, and became instantly and painfully aware, that a change had taken place in Lord St. Ervan's appearance. He still breathed, but that was all the sign of life he gave. They watched by him for some hours, but he gave no proof of consciousness, nor did a single sigh mark the moment when his soul departed. He — "passed away in sleep, in the deep quiet of the night!"

CHAPTER XX.

" And yet we mourn thee !   Yes ! thy place is void
Within our hearts,   *   *   *
*   *   And o'er that tie destroyed,
Though faith rejoice, fond nature still must melt."

MRS. HEMANS.

THE funeral was over, and the first shock which
death leaves on the mind, was beginning to subside ;
but Lady Constance's spirits seemed not to revive, so
incalculable to her was the loss of one, whose eye had
never looked upon her but in love and kindness. Ever
since her mother's death, which took place when she
was of too early an age to retain any thing but a faint
remembrance of it, she had been her father's almost
constant companion ; and he had delighted to train her
young mind, not only in the purest spirit of religion,
but also in the paths of learning and science.   All her
occupations, therefore, reminded her of his care and
affection ; and the notes with which he had enriched
her books of study, were continually before her eyes,
reminding her of the time when she had read them
with him.   How much did she miss the wisdom
of that mind, which she formerly could consult on
every subject ! The earth, the sky, the ocean,—all

brought him to her remembrance, who had taught her
the knowledge of their treasures, and the love of their
Creator; and the cheerfulness of whose mind had added
a charm to all his instruction. Yet the thought of his
happiness was joy to her heart, and she loved to be
away from others, that she might, uninterruptedly,
indulge her thoughts of him. "She awoke each day
to the stupendous thought, that her father was in
heaven, but she felt the more, that she was not there;
that a veil of separation hung between them, which
nothing but death could raise."

But after a time she saw that she was acting selfishly
and unkindly, in absenting herself so much from those,
who strove with every attention which love could suggest, to soothe her sorrow, and win her back to cheerfulness; and soon as she felt her fault, she resolutely
denied its indulgence.

The engagement between her and Sir Roland was
known only to themselves, Lady Ashton, and Miss
Gower; for Lady Ashton thought that it would be
painful to Lady Constance to have it made subject of
comment and conversation, so immediately after her
father's death. To Henry Ashton they would of course
have immediately communicated it, had they been certain where he was; but they did not like the idea of a
letter containing intelligence of such a nature, to be
passing from hand to hand, and finally perhaps, to be
opened by a stranger. It was Lady Constance's wish
that the marriage should not take place for some time;
and finally it was decided, that it should be deferred till
Sir Roland returned from the continent, after fulfilling
his engagement with Lord N ——.

It had been a great trial to Lady Constance having

to leave Claverton and all its haunts — endeared by so many ties — so many recollections ! And soon a new source of grief arose, in the bad state of health into which Miss Gower had fallen, and which, very soon after Lord St. Ervan's death, obliged her to quit the pupils to whom she was so much attached. This separation was a most painful one on both sides, and to Lady Constance, the loss was irreparable ; for Miss Gower had lived with her from the time of her mother's death, and was in every way qualified to lead her young mind in the healthful paths, of solid piety, and self-denying exertion. Kind as were her other friends, none could so well enter into her feelings as regarded her father, for none had known him so well as Miss Gower ; and the loss therefore, of this valued companion, renewed in some degree the acute regret she felt for him.

Sir Roland was unremitting in his devotion to Lady Constance ; and the strength of his attachment, which daily increased, shewed itself in nothing more than in the self-denial which he exercised, in never intruding on her solitude, or pressing her in any way, to be with him more than she herself desired. She was deeply touched by his tender and considerate affection ; but the very circumstance of their engagement, which should have brought her heart into closest union with his, seemed to have a totally contrary effect. In her childish years, when she had been so much with him and his brother, though Henry, who was nearer her own age, was more frequently her companion, yet Sir Roland was ever the one she looked up to, for help in her griefs and troubles, and to him she would now — had their relative circumstances remained unchanged —

have freely poured forth all her sorrows—looking to him for comfort, counsel, and love. But her hurried engagement had arrested and altered the whole current of her feelings. The new tie that was formed between them, had arisen before her heart was prepared to receive and sanction it; and though she revered and admired him beyond any living creature, yet she now felt a 'gêne' and discomfort in his presence, which was most painful to her. She was in fact doubly bereaved.—In her father she had lost the being whom most she loved on earth, and Sir Roland—to whom she would once have gone in all the fulness of her grieving heart—she now felt an insurmountable difficulty in approaching. She felt as if more would be required of her than she could give, and that feeling restrained the expression of the sentiments which really did exist in her heart.

How often do the sweetest and tenderest ties of life—if unaccompanied by corresponding feelings—instead of drawing hearts into closer union, erect a barrier between them, causing the sense of distance to increase, as the nearness of the bond presses upon the reluctant spirit! It was this feeling which stole over Lady Constance as she became calm enough, after her father's death, to join again in the usual routine of life at Llanaven, and which shut up her whole heart—even to her sister—for she found it impossible to talk of Sir Roland as she used to do; and where there is one point, which we feel we must avoid in conversing with those most intimate with us, it throws a restraint on all communication. A coldness and abstraction of feeling, seemed to usurp dominion over one, who was by nature, so open and so free; whose mind had seemed to dwell

upon her lips, and whose every word had expressed
the feelings of her guileless, loving, and expansive
heart.

This change was unperceived by Lady Ashton, who
thought Lady Constance's depression was only the
natural state of a mind, unrecovered as yet from its
terrible bereavement. For a time Sir Roland strove to
believe so too; for he knew that the effect of grief, ever
lies most heavily on the young and untried spirit; but
he could not long blind himself to the truth — the
quickened eye of love, saw deeper into the secret of
her heart. He knew it could not be grief for her
father, which made her so cold to him—for previous to
her engagement, she had freely told her sorrows, and
sought his sympathy. But now, if her eye caught
his—instead of lighting up in smiling brightness as in
former times, or returning his looks of tender concern,
with her usual sweet and grateful expression — she
hurriedly withdrew her glance, and with busy idleness,
would appear to occupy herself in some way apart from
him.—If at any time, she was alone with him, in the
room or garden, she would suddenly seem to recollect
something which she had to fetch — something to do
elsewhere—as an excuse for leaving him. He felt her
alienation in a thousand ways; and things to which he
could not have given a name—wounded him to his
inmost soul!

She was never unkind, nor had she any feeling but
that of love for him, who loved her with so full a heart;
but she dreaded that he might speak —and she not be
able to answer as he might wish; or that he
might think her ungrateful for not fully responding
to his feelings of devoted attachment. At length

the suffering of Sir Roland's mind became so intolerable, that he resolved to speak to her, and either restore the former freedom of their intercourse, or break for ever the tie that bound them together. He had tried every means which affection and devoted love could devise, to win her back to confidence and peace, but all seemed in vain; and had he not known that — if their engagement were once at an end—Llanaven could not continue a home to the orphan sisters, he would at once — whatever it might have cost him — have restored her her plighted troth, and have entreated her to break a bond which seemed so great a burden on her spirit. But situated as she was, he could not do this—and indeed the bare idea of it was agony to him— but he determined at least to speak openly to her upon the subject, and then leave her free to act as her heart dictated.

He had much occupation, connected with the care of his own property, and with the public business of the county, but when he could find time, he often accompanied Lady Constance in her rides and walks about the beautiful country in which they resided. On the smooth sands, or amongst the picturesque cliffs of that lovely region, Lady Constance and her friends, had delighted in former happy days, to roam for hours together, searching for the many objects which the facile mind of childhood considers as treasures, or climbing up the rocks by unaccustomed ways, whose danger made them all the more enjoyable. Amongst these well-known places, again would she and Sir Roland often ramble together; but the unchanged scenes without, made the change within, but the more strongly and painfully felt. Lady Constance continually strug-

gled against her feelings, and strove to be all that Sir
Roland could wish, but the very effort produced the
constraint which she was so anxious to throw off.

They were strolling along beneath the cliffs, on
one of those still, soft, genial days we sometimes have
in the month of February, "when Spring's first gale
comes forth to whisper where the violets lie," and
overcome by the lassitude occasioned by the unusual
warmth of the air, they seated themselves on a grass-
covered ledge of the rock, whilst Lady Florence, at
some distance, regardless of the heat, was climbing
about in search of the little flowers, which bloom the
first, or playing with a Newfoundland dog, which belonged to Henry, and which was a universal favourite,
for the absent sailor's sake.

Sir Roland generally had with him a volume of
poetry, or of some pleasant instruction, such as suited
the light studies of the open air, and now he read for
some time to Lady Constance, as they sat together;
but even while thus employed, he could not but feel
miserable, as he observed the coldness and abstraction
of the manner in which she listened. He ceased after
a while, but the pause in his voice seemed unobserved
by her.

He spoke to her at length, and she started as one
awakened from sleep; but turning to him with a kind
smile, though with a heightened colour, she said—

"I beg your pardon, I have been very rude and
inattentive; the heavy air and the rolling of the waves
sent my mind, I think, to sleep; but I liked what you
were reading, though my thoughts had wandered from
it for a moment."

"Constance," said Sir Roland, "I cannot bear that

sad and patient look. I had rather a thousand times
see you occasionally overwhelmed with grief, than for
you to appear as if all feeling—all power of enjoyment
were gone."

He paused; then with earnest energy he continued—for he had, after silently committing his way
to God, nerved himself to speak upon the subject that
was to decide all his earthly fate—

"I have long observed the sorrow and oppression
of your mind, and I was but too willing for a while to
believe that it was the natural effect of the griefs you
had had to endure; but time as it passes brings no
change to you, and the reserve and embarrassment
you always shew when in my society, presses the painful conviction upon me, that I—who would do all to
make you happy—am the miserable cause of your
unhappiness."

"Oh! no, no," said Lady Constance, interrupting
him, "dear Roland, do not say that, indeed it is not
so; I am not—you do not make me unhappy, but I
cannot so soon forget"—and she burst into tears.

Sir Roland with difficulty repressed his own emotion, but waiting till he could command his voice, he
said—

"Dear Constance, would that you could always let
those tears of natural feeling flow freely before me.
Oh! that it were as in old times, when every trouble
of your heart was brought to me; when I was your
comforter, and your support. I know indeed, that
you have now a better and holier refuge to fly to;
One who 'in all your affliction is afflicted'—but still,
if your heart were with me as it used to be, you would
love to claim the sympathy, which is yours now, a

thousand times more than ever. Yes, I cannot disguise it from myself—it were worse than madness to
endeavour to do so—you do not love me—the fatal
tie, which should have bound us together, heart and
soul, is felt as a galling chain by you. I will not ask
you to break it—I cannot ask you to do that—not
yet—my selfish heart refuses to do that yet—but I
would entreat—beseech you to believe, that worlds
could not induce me to urge the fulfilment of your
engagement, unless I saw and felt it was your heart's
desire it should continue. You have been—perhaps
unwisely, precipitately—offered an affection—wholly
yours—but which, I now feel, does not meet with an
answering feeling in your breast. It were vain to offer
me liberty! it would be like opening the cage to the
pinioned bird—I have no power to fly; but I set you
free—perfectly free—though my own faith I shall
ever keep plighted to you till—your will shall perforce break the bond."

He spoke hurriedly, as fearing his resolution should
fail, and Lady Constance was too much agitated to interrupt him. When he paused however, she instantly
besought him to believe she had no wish to end their
engagement—no desire but to make herself worthy of
his affection.

"Do not speak so," replied Sir Roland, "if I am
in any way worthy of you, it is only in the devoted
love I bear you. But, Constance, are you speaking
your whole mind, in saying you wish our engagement,
to continue? Remember, dearest, it were better—oh!
many, many times—to break it off now, than to find
too late, that you have mistaken the feelings within
you. I have no wish," he added with a sad smile, "to

persuade you that you do not love me, but I do most
earnestly desire that you should hold yourself as free
from any restraint.—I have sometimes thought—you
will let me say all I feel, Constance," he continued,
looking at her for a moment, then withdrawing his
eyes from her countenance, while his own was crossed
by strong and contending emotions, "I have sometimes
thought, that—amongst the many persons with whom
you are acquainted, there might perhaps be some one
whom—whose good qualities—who might——" He
stopped—then continued with a desperate effort—
"who might have left a favourable impression on
your mind. Forgive me for venturing on such a
subject—but I would not for worlds—were such the
case—stand in the way of your happiness. Could
you confide in me sufficiently—to tell me—for I do
not love you selfishly—whether——" He raised his
eyes for a moment, and Lady Constance met their
gaze unshrinkingly, though her colour had mounted to
her temples.

"No, Roland," she answered, "I have never given
a thought to any being, and I feel sure that I could not
intrust my happiness with greater security to any one
than to you, whom I have known from childhood—
who have ever been the kindest and best of friends.
But I have feared you would not be satisfied with me;
I mean," she added, as she raised her troubled eyes to
his, "I thought my cold heart might not content you—
I feared——"

"Dearest Constance," said Sir Roland, "do not
distress yourself; do not say another word; tell me
only that you wish no change—and let me now as for
the first time begin and try to make you like me."

Lady Constance was much moved by his generosity, and with a glowing smile she held out her
hand to him, saying—

" That would be impossible, for you have ever been
one of the dearest of my friends."

" Thank you, dear Constance, for your kindness,"
he replied—though a sigh arose as he felt how in-
adequately her feelings answered to his—" let us then
be at least true friends. Should I succeed in obtaining
your full affection, then we shall indeed be happy—
but if not—better, far better it will be, that I alone
should suffer."

After this conversation Lady Constance felt much
of her reserve wear off, and her intercourse with Sir
Roland became more like what it had been before their
engagement. Sir Roland was careful not to disturb
this tranquil state of things, by shewing any anxiety to
engage a more exclusive feeling—though he would
fain have done so—and their days flowed on in works
of piety and usefulness, and in pleasant study and
recreation.

Sir Roland had not expected to be called away from
home till late in the spring. Great therefore, was his
disappointment, at hearing from his uncle, that circumstances having brought their foreign plans more
forward than was expected, his presence was desired
immediately, and that he trusted he would be able to
join him without delay. This was a severe trial to
him, coming too, just at the time when a feeling of
returning confidence had begun to dawn in Lady Constance's heart towards him, and her mind had seemed
to shake off somewhat of its oppression and unhappi-

ness. His habitual submission to the will of God, restrained him however from murmuring, though a sigh of deep regret would often escape from his bosom. Lady Constance endeavoured by every thoughtful attention to speak her regard for him, and to render him perfectly happy in his feelings respecting her. He felt all her kindness—and her sweetness of manner towards him, would have made him indeed but too happy, had there not been in all her looks and actions, a something—undefined, but not the less felt—which continually brought to his heart, the chilling conviction—that all she did for him, proceeded more from a desire to give him pleasure than from the spring of love within. Still he hoped that the time would come, when her heart would be wholly his—when he could feel that she sought his side—not because she knew that then only was he happy—but because that then only would she be happy herself. The oppression on his spirits increased hourly however, during the few days that intervened between the receipt of his uncle's letter, and the time fixed for him to go, and he felt utterly miserable.

"Come with me, Constance," he said on the morning of his departure; "come with me once more upon the shore. My kind mother's preparations will not be finished yet, and we shall have time for a walk."

Lady Constance hastened to prepare herself, and was with him again in a few moments. She took his arm and they walked on slowly, sadly, and in silence, till they reached the little turfy bank where they had sat a few weeks before, during that conversation which had served at the time to restore somewhat of peace and hope to Sir Roland's bosom. But how was that peace now again troubled! that hope where was it flown!

"Let us rest here," said Sir Roland.—"Oh! Constance, how miserable I feel! my heart seems to droop within me! It is weak thus to give way;—but there are times in which one's soul seems crushed by a weight it cannot resist."

"Dear Roland," replied Lady Constance, "you will soon return to us; will you not?"

"I know not, Constance; it seems to me as if I were going for ever! But I must not—must not give way to this despondency. I am a great professor, but I fear a poor doer of my heavenly Father's will, for my heart is terribly rebellious. But now, dear, I will try and shake off this unmanly folly, and enjoy the few moments that yet remain to me, of being with you. But yet there is one thing I must say.—On this very spot, Constance, some weeks ago, you assured me you did not wish to break our engagement.—I would not renew this subject," he added, seeing Lady Constance looked distressed—"only that I do so earnestly desire your happiness! and I wish that if ever we are united, it should be with the full consent of your whole heart, —unbiassed by any thing but its own inclinations. When I am away, my mother's home might still be yours and Florence's, even if—" he stopped abruptly, for a throb of such agony passed through his heart, as for the moment completely overcame him; recovering, however, he continued—"even if our engagement were at an end.—I have spoken of Florence, because I fear that that child's happiness may be dearer to you than your own—I have at least sometimes fancied that —you sacrifice yourself for her."

He fixed his dark eyes with intense anxiety upon
Lady Constance, whose countenance could ill bear his
scrutiny, for she felt conscious that a desire that Lady
Florence should continue under Lady Ashton's protection, had mingled with her other feelings, in determining her to continue her engagement with Sir Roland.
Still she knew that her high regard for him, and her
desire for his happiness, had had by far the greater
share in her decision, and this reflection enabled her—
when the first moment of discomfort which his words
had produced, had passed—to meet his searching glance
with openness.   She replied—

" Roland, I will not deny that one of the charms of
my engagement to you, has been the thought of my
sister's happiness, but I can truly say, that never would
I, even for her sake, have renewed my engagement,
had not you yourself been one, whom I loved, and who
I knew would make me happy.   Have I not known
you," she said—kindly desirous of setting his heart at
rest—"since my earliest days? and when have I ever
heard an unkind word from your lips?   And do you
think I cannot trust you now—when, as you tell me,
all your heart is mine?"

" As I *tell* you, Constance," repeated Sir Roland
reproachfully, " you know that all my heart *is* yours—
at least all I dare give to mortal being."

" I do know it, in truth," replied Lady Constance,
" but I did not like," she added playfully, "to presume upon my knowledge."

" Dear Constance," replied Sir Roland, enchanted
at this return of ease and confidence, "you have taken
a load from my heart; and strange to say, the last—the
parting hour, seems the happiest and the best to me.

God is very merciful —who in the bitter cup of separation infuses so sweet a draught! and in His deep compassion, sends earthly comfort to temper earthly sorrow. Constance, you will write to me, in my sad exile?   You do not know the weary life I am about to lead.   You will write to me?'"

"Surely I will," replied Lady Constance; "and tell you all I do, so you will not escape the task of Mentor, but will have to fulfil that, in addition to all your other burthens."

"That will be rather the charm, that will compensate for all the rest," said Sir Roland. "What a joy and delight will it be, to leave all the wearisome work, and bustling scenes I shall be engaged in, to meet you in quiet and solitude — you and God, dear Constance. Yes! thanks be to Him! the thought of you, is ever accompanied with His gracious presence, for I know that you love Him as well I do. But oh! this hateful journey! Now when all smiles upon me, I must depart, and leave what alone makes life pleasant, to mix in scenes which I detest. I would give worlds to stay with you! it seems impossible—impossible for me to go. Dear Constance, if you knew what an agony it is for me to part from you—you whom I have loved beyond the time to which memory goes back!—and yet, perhaps," he added, sadly, "it is best for me to go—when I am away, you may perhaps think of me with greater tenderness than you do now," and he covered his face with his hands to hide his struggling emotion. After a few moments he started up, exclaiming, "But this is useless folly, and we must part; yet I am cruel, and selfish enough to feel, that were this parting the same anguish to you, that it is to me

—I should be happy! Do not hate me, Constance, for I am very miserable."

Lady Constance whose tears flowed fast, replied—

" You are unjust, Roland—indeed you are—to doubt that I love you. Oh! do believe me, when I say I do—and when I tell you how sad this parting is to me. If only I could feel that you were satisfied with me—that you did not doubt me—then I too should be happy. Surely my tears must shew that this is no joyful moment?"

Sir Roland pressed her hand to his heart, and felt somewhat of consolation at the sight of her distress; but his were mingled—confused emotions, and he could not speak. He knew she loved him, but he felt that her love was not like his, and his mind was still troubled. He struggled long for composure—and prayed earnestly for strength and comfort—and they were sent; his heart was lifted up to Him whose unfailing love is ever-satisfying! and he rejoiced, with calmed feeling, that this world was not ' his all.'

" Constance," he said at length, " I do not doubt your love, and you will forgive the waywardness of my unreasonable heart. Oh! you are dear to me—dearer than any thing on earth should be—for you make me forget every thing almost, but yourself. I suffer sorely for my idolatry! When my heart gives God again His proper place within me—then I shall again be happy — not till then! But all must be well, and we shall perhaps soon wander on this shore again with more joyful spirits. But now," he added in a constrained manner, " I must be going. You will come back with me?"

Lady Constance had still continued sitting on the

bank, but now she sprung up, and with a faltering voice
exclaimed, "Oh! Roland, do not speak so coldly to
me!" and she burst into tears.

"Coldly! Constance," said Sir Roland, as every
nerve trembled—"coldly! I cold to you!"

He felt the injustice of the accusation, yet it
brought with it a joy inexpressible.   That reproof
was dearer to him than all the protestations of love
which language could have supplied, for it shewed
him that she valued his affection—that she felt pained
at any apparent diminution in it! He was at that
moment happier than he had ever been through all his
life—a new existence seemed given him; and as he
looked on her he was about to leave, he felt how far
better it was to be absent—and beloved, than present
—and an object of indifference! He could not express what passed within him, but he spoke hurried
words of deep affection, and when Lady Constance
again looked at him, she saw in his countenance a joy
it had never beamed with before.

Arm in arm they returned to the house; Sir Roland's heart too full of happiness almost for speech,
and Lady Constance happy too in the consciousness of
the peace and joy she had given him. They joined
Lady Ashton, and after a few minutes Lady Constance
left the room that Sir Roland might be with his mother
alone; but when the grating sound of the carriage-
wheels was heard on the gravel before the house, she
again joined them. Sir Roland's spirit sunk anew
under the prospect of separation, and it was not without a painful effort that he spoke composedly.

At last the servant announced that the carriage
was ready, and feeling that delay only prolonged the

suffering, and increased the difficulty of parting, he rose, and embraced his mother, kissed the blooming child who hung in tears about his neck, and pressing Lady Constance for a moment to his heart, threw himself into the carriage, which soon bore him far away from the dearest objects of his earthly affections.

CHAPTER XXI.

"I do not think his bright blue eyes, are like his brother's, keen,
Nor his brow so full of childish thought, as his hath ever been;
But his youthful heart's a fountain clear, of mind and tender feeling,
And his very look's a dream of light, rich depths of love revealing."

MOULTRIE.

"His very heart athirst
To gaze at nature in her green array,
Upon the ship's tall side he stands possessed
With visions prompted by intense desire."—COWPER.

SIR ROLAND was one whose society was most delightful, for to the most pleasing manners, he added all
the charm of a cultivated mind, and of a lively, bright,
poetical imagination. Lady Constance felt his .loss
exceedingly; yet, when her first feelings of regret were
past, she experienced a repose of nerves and of mind to
which she had long been a stranger. It was however,
deeply painful to her to feel that Sir Roland's absence was
a relief—painful, as regarded her own future prospects
—painful, doubly, as it made her seem in her own
eyes, ungrateful to one whose heart was so wholly
given up to her. When she thought of his almost
faultless character, of his ardent piety, and above all,
of the deep, devoted love he bore to her, she wondered
that she could feel any thing but the liveliest attachment to him; and often, bitterly, did she weep over the
coldness, and waywardness of her heart, and tremble

with self-reproach, as she could not but be conscious that now, in his absence, she felt a peace, his presence had never imparted. And yet her feelings were not unnatural ; for when with Sir Roland, she was perpetually watching over herself in order to be kind and attentive to him ; she was fearful of paining him, anxious to be pleased with all he did, and to shew him that he made her happy ; and thus, unconsciously, she was ever acting a part, though influenced by the purest feelings, and the kindest motives ; and it was an inexpressible rest to her mind and spirits, when she could again speak and act, without having to think how she spoke and acted. Now that he was absent she breathed more freely, and her step regained its elastic spring ; the liveliness of her girlish spirits again began to animate her countenance, and her voice was once more heard in tones of joyous cheerfulness which had long been silenced.

It was a happy thing for her in some respects, that Lady Ashton was of a most confiding, unsuspicious disposition ; singularly amiable herself, she was willing to think all the world the same, and glaring indeed must have been the defect she could ever have perceived in those she loved. The beautiful simplicity of her character, and the singleness of her mind, though they assisted greatly in making her an upright, uncompromising follower of her Saviour's, yet unfitted her exceedingly for any deep insight into the characters of her fellow-creatures, and made her but little versed in reading their feelings and sentiments. What they ought to feel—that, she supposed they did feel ; and no questioning doubt on such subjects ever entered her mind. Her own uneventful life had served much

to increase this peculiarity of disposition. Married
early, to the only man she had ever loved, she lived
with him in continually-increasing confidence and
affection, till death's heavy hand severed the perfect
tie which existed between them; and then, the dutiful
love, and amiable consideration of her sons, conspired
to keep distrust and anxiety far from her breast.

From the moment that she found Lady Constance
had promised her hand to Sir Roland, no doubt had
ever crossed her mind, as to the whole of her young
friend's heart having been given with her faith; and
all the many things which had brought such bitter conviction of the contrary to Sir Roland's love-quickened
eye, had passed beneath hers, without awakening one
mistrustful feeling. It would in truth have been difficult for any one—especially a mother—to have looked
on Sir Roland, and to have imagined it possible that
the unshackled heart of any girl, could have refused
itself to his love !

Lady Ashton's unquestioning confidence was a great
relief to Lady Constance, freeing her as it did from
scrutinising observation, and making her feel perfectly
at her ease. Yet it often also made her feel uncomfortable; for in speaking of Sir Roland, Lady Ashton
always seemed to infer her devoted attachment to him,
and would express with every kindness her heart could
dictate, her sympathy for the sorrow which she thought
his absence must occasion her; and Lady Constance,
whose whole soul was truth itself, was forced to keep
silence, when she would otherwise gladly have opened
her heart, and all its feelings to one whom she loved
as a mother. She hoped indeed that the time would
come, in which her feelings for her future husband,

would be all he could desire, and all that his mother
now fondly imagined them to be; yet it was painful to
her to see Lady Ashton give her credit for sentiments,
which she was conscious she did not possess.

Sir Roland had left England but a few days, when
Lady Ashton received a letter from Henry, dated from
Rio, saying that he was coming home directly, and
that he hoped to obtain leave of absence for a few
weeks, or perhaps even months, before he was obliged
to join the new ship to which he had been appointed.
This unexpected news spread universal joy among the
inmates of Llanaven, for they had not seen the young
seaman for above three years, and he was always the
life and delight of the house when at home.

There is something singularly captivating in the
profession of a sailor—something so chivalrous, so full
of daring, and of danger!   In early youth, the being,
who under all circumstances would be beloved, becomes, when absent on his storm-rocked home, the
object of intensest interest and affection; and a halo of
bright, but tenderest feeling, ever shines around him,
and the sublime element on which he moves!

Henry Ashton was indeed, in every respect worthy
of the great affection that was bestowed upon him.
He was wholly unlike Sir Roland in countenance,
though in their tall slight figures, and in the fine outline of their heads, there was much resemblance.   Sir
Roland's was a high, intellectual style of beauty, very
rarely to be met with; and on his pale brow there was
a pensive dignity unusual at his age—heightening the
expression of extreme sensibility which filled his dark
stedfast eye.

Henry's countenance on the contrary was a con-

tinual alternation of light and shade. His full blue
eyes had a languor and gentleness in their expression
when at rest, which was most touching; while when
animated, they lit up with a lustre which seemed
almost to emit living sparks. His naturally fair complexion was bronzed by the sea-air, and by the burning
suns of southern climes, yet his forehead, shaded by
his gold-brown hair, was pure and white as in childhood. He had not the fine features which Sir Roland
possessed, but his countenance—varying with every
thought and feeling—was irresistible in its changeful
beauty.

The character of the two brothers had many things
in common, for they were both generous, both affectionate, both warm-hearted, and both warm-tempered;
but the developement of these qualities in the one,
differed so much, from what it was in the other, that
at first sight they might have been pronounced totally
dissimilar. There was a difference of four years in
their ages, yet their attachment was unbounded, and
it would have been difficult to say, which—of the fair-
haired sunny child, whose countenance "like spring
time smiled," or the dark-eyed boy, whose very soul
beamed from his face—had the more devoted love for
the other. Yet it was curious to trace the different
ways in which the same feeling would shew itself!
When quite a little child, if any thing were given to
Henry, he would invariably ask the same for his
brother; and if denied it, he would often dash his
own gift down on the ground, and with bitter words,
and streaming tears refuse to take it; while Sir Roland
—equally thoughtful for the little one—if refused the
boon he asked for him, would carry off his own pos-

session, and give that to the child—nor feel he made a sacrifice.

Henry's temper though quick was thoroughly amiable, and his naturally careless, joyous, disposition, would carry away in its bounding flood, many a grievance, and sense of wrong, which would have wounded another to the very soul; and though his mood would chafe and fret at any opposition that he met with, yet so much of playfulness and of sweet temper mingled itself with his flashing fits of anger, that it were hard to say whether they did not bring out more of beauty than they hid; as water when thrown high in the air by opposing rocks, shines in the sunbeam, with a sparkling, beauteous light, the tranquil stream can never shew. His faults—casting scarcely more of shade over his character than the summer cloud leaves on the ocean—were forgiven almost before felt; and he had therefore never fully set himself to correct them, for never had he fully learnt to know them. His religious feelings were strong and enlightened, and vice he could not tolerate; but his mind was not in perfect training and subjection, and the power of self-government was almost, to him, unknown.

With Sir Roland it was different; his temper was naturally far more quick and fiery than that of his brother, but the violence of his feelings could not be misunderstood by a heart early awakened to a sense of its responsibilities before God; and happy was it for him, that the undaunted energy of his mind, equalled its force and vehemence. He early learnt to know the depth and power of the passions against which he had to contend; and strenuously did he determine to have the mastery over them. When at school, Henry would fight a hundred battles, and laugh as he fought; but Sir Roland's sense of right, and nobility of character made him abhor such debasing, unchristian, and un-gentlemanlike scenes. Never but once—and that when quite a boy—did he allow his passion to triumph over his better principle, and then he suffered bitterly for so doing; for in the battle which ensued—and which did not take place till after he had endured unnumbered pro-vocations—he struck his adversary with such violence, that the blow, falling on the temple, dashed him to the ground. The boy was taken up senseless, and it was at first thought—dead; but though he afterwards reco-vered, yet the shock which the circumstance gave to Sir Roland was so dreadful, that it acted as a most salutary check against any further outbreaks of passionate feel-ing. It could not, however, still the power of the tempest within; a mightier force than unassisted human energy was required to effect that; and happily, such force was in time given; the force of a living—loving faith, which slaked the inward fire, and imparted so continual a sense of God's presence to his soul, as hushed the tumult of passion, and gave him a self-subdued — or rather, heaven-subdued — spirit, such as few are enabled to boast.

The exact time of Henry Ashton's arrival could not be calculated; and as he would land at Falmouth—which was not very far from Llanaven—there would be no time for the post to reach the latter place before he could do so himself. This kept his friends in a state of continual excitement and expectation; and every sound —especially the noise of the receding waves, drawing the pebbly shingle with them in their retreat, which from time to time reached them from the shore—seemed

the welcome approach of his carriage-wheels. Lady
Florence, incapable of settling to any thing, passed
most of the day on the heights, watching for his ship,
which would probably pass in sight, and then she would
return home when the light failed, and tell of all the successive objects she had seen, and which she had felt
sure were his ship, but which, as they neared her ex-
pectant eyes, transformed themselves into fishing-boats,
or sea-gulls, or some such light gear.   At length one
morning, the vehement barking of his old Newfoundland, aroused their attention, and Lady Florence, half
doubting—having so often been deceived—began repeating those pleasant lines :—

> " The gladsome bounding of his ancient hound,
> Says he in truth is here—our long, long lost, is found,"

and had hardly finished—when the sound of the tramp-
ling of horses and the whirring of wheels was really
heard before the house, too distinctly to be mistaken.

All flew out of the room — and Lady Florence
reached the house-door, long before the bell could be
rung, or any servant could appear.   Henry, for it was
indeed he, sprung from the carriage, and caught the
child in his arms, nearly squeezing her to death ; then
rushing to his mother and Lady Constance — in an
ecstasy of happiness, pressed them both together to
his joyful heart.

"And am I really here again ?" he said, " really
here ?—it is too delightful !   But where is Roland ?"

" He is gone," answered his mother, when she
could find words to speak; " his business with his
uncle took him away just before we knew you were
coming."

"How intolerable!" said Henry, impatiently, as his brow contracted to a sudden frown. "I had so reckoned on finding him here—and did so long to see him!—However it is something, is it not (and the cloud cleared from his joyous countenance) to find oneself once more amongst so many that one loves? You cannot think," he added, as he seated himself on the drawing-room sofa, holding his mother's and Lady Constance's hand in his, whilst Lady Florence knelt before him,—"what a relief it is to look at your lovely, blooming faces, after having, for weeks, had nothing but the tough, weather-beaten visages of our old tars to refresh one's eyes with. And Constance—dear lovely Constance! how you are grown—and more beautiful than ever! And my dearest mother, looking so well, and ten years younger! And you—you little torment, (to Lady Florence) twice as black and frightful as you ever were before, and I have no doubt, seven times as mischievous! I have kept a monkey on board ever since I went to America, on purpose to remind me of you; and now I have brought him home in order that an improving system of 'enseignement mutuel' may go on between you."

"Have you?" said Lady Florence,—"where is it?" and away she flew.

"How beautiful she is," said Henry, when she was out of hearing; "I don't mind telling you that, to your face, Constance, for nothing can make you vain—but I am not so sure about that little fairy."

"Do not be too sure about me," replied Lady Constance; "how can you tell what evils may have grown up since I have been deprived of—what you used to call—your 'paternal admonitions?'"

"Did I call them so?" asked Henry. "Well! I don't feel very paternal just now, so I may perhaps let your vices escape for a time. I feel very filial, I know," he added; and putting his arm suddenly round his mother's neck, much to the discomfiture of cap and cape, he pressed his rough lip vehemently to her cheek.

"My dear Henry," she exclaimed, shrinking from him, but laughing, "when did you shave last? not since you took your monkey on board, I should think! You have carried off at least a square inch of my cheek."

"Not quite so bad as that, I hope, my beautiful mother," he replied, kissing her again with the utmost gentleness and affection, "but I confess I have not shaved to-day, for I left the ship before I had light to discern my chin from the captain's, and cleared out, and got off as fast as possible, to come here; and I have had no breakfast either, for tea-cups as well as razors have shared the plenitude of my neglect to-day, and I am regularly starving; shall I ring?" and he jumped up—stormed at the bell—and then threw himself down in his place again, with such force, as made his two companions start.

"I have ordered breakfast for you," said Lady Ashton, quietly, "and here it comes;" and the door opened, and a man appeared, bearing all the requisites for his repast.

"What is so pleasant-looking as an English breakfast? Its white damask, white bread, white cream, white sugar, clear china, and bright silver — all so delicate, so refined, so pure, so clean!" So thought Henry as he seated himself at the table, and ate many satisfactory, wedge-shaped pieces of the loaf, and drank sundry cups of tea.

His mother and Lady Constance sat silently by, with that unconscious smile of pleasure on the lip, with which we often watch the enjoyment of those we love. Henry frequently looked at them — as he satisfied his really craving hunger, with a laughing eye, and a nod or shake of his head, as much as to say, he was far too busy to talk; till at length, pausing in his operations, —

" This is what I call enjoyment!" he said, throwing himself back in his chair, and contemplating the 'wreck of matter' before him, and the bright, happy faces on each side — " this is what I call real enjoyment! it only wants Roland's dear old face there opposite me, to make it perfect. I wish my uncle and all his politics were in the depths of the Black Sea rather than have taken him away at this moment ! — But still this is very delightful ! — When did I last see butter ?" he continued, in a soliloquising tone, " or cream — or a white cloth — or white bread — or white hands? You land ladies have no idea of the effect of these things on us 'rude and boisterous captains of the sea,' (including lieutenants.) Yet it is not all the mere love of the good things of this world, but it is a little — just a little — because they are part and parcel of a system of humanised life, which is most enchanting — perfectly ecstatic ! after knocking about for years at sea, as I have done, seeing scarcely even a mermaid combing her hair, and being fed on nothing but 'toasts of ammunition bread.' Oh! it is glorious! But now, my dear mother, 'mamma mia, tutta graziosa è buona,' let me go to my room (the old room I suppose) and make

myself respectable, and fit to appear again in your
delicate presence—and to kiss your delicate cheek."

"Wait till I ring, and know that every thing is
ready, and a good fire burning," said Lady Ashton.

The bell was promptly answered by an old servant
who had not appeared before, and who now came in with
coals, for which he supposed he had been summoned.

"Heave on the coals, old fellow," exclaimed Henry,
"and then give me your hand;" and he shook it, and
not only it, but with it the whole person of the unfortunate man, with such vehemence as nearly deprived
him of breath and senses.

"How are you, James? and the old lady at the
lodge, and all of you? Your face is the pleasantest I
have seen for many a year. I think I must take you
to sea with me, next time I go; you'll come of course?"

"Thank you, sir—quite well—glad to see you
home again—grown so tall—not a bit like Sir Roland
—quite well," said the poor man by snatches, as he
regained breath and power of speech.

"And now, James," said Henry, releasing him,
"come with me to my berth, and see that all is made
snug there."

CHAPTER XXII.

A wond'rous and mysterious thing
    Is hidden in the breast;
A sea of tears, a ceaseless spring
    Of waters ill at rest.
*   *   *   *   *

Oh! many are the founts through which
    This mystic water flows,
And many are the things whose touch
    Disturbs its dim repose.

For joy hath its own flood-gate meet,
    A tear-spring all its own;
And pleasant are its waters sweet,—
    But they rarely flow alone.

For near, too near, the fount of woe
    Opens its portal wide;
And seldom do *those* waters flow
    But *these* flow at their side.

                                        MS.

"I REALLY think Henry is rather mad," said Lady Constance, laughing, when he had left the room.

"He does seem so, certainly," said Lady Ashton; "but he will get reasonable enough in time, I dare say. A sailor returning home is like a prisoner set free; and Henry's spirits, at the best, are almost overpoweringly joyous."

"Oh! I delighted in him as he was," said Lady

Constance, "he used to be like moving sunshine, and made all bright around him. But now, he is like a storm of thunder and lightning."

"He is always so, at first, when he returns from sea," said Lady Ashton; "but you have never before seen him at the first moment. He used to have time to part with a little of his nonsense to the winds before he reached Claverton; and there, of course, he was under a little more restraint."

Henry's spirits were certainly always high, especially when returning home after any absence; but his violent outbreaks on the present occasion, did not all proceed from pure joy. The mind, when excited, chooses any excess that may seem easiest—laughter, or tears—rather than tranquillity; that state, difficult at all times to be attained by a warm, animated temper, is impossible then. Henry's rapture, indeed, at returning home was unbounded; but the sight of the mourning dresses of the two sisters, gave his heart such a revulsion, that the moment his first joyful greeting was over, he was on the point of bursting into violent tears. Desirous of restraining this natural impulse, he made a desperate effort over his sorrowful emotion, and the exertion sent him to the opposite extreme, of obstreperous gaiety. When however, old James had finished all his operations, and had left his room, he locked the door, and throwing himself into a chair—tears, though of a calmer nature than those he would have shed at first, streamed from his eyes. The sight of the two young things whom he loved so much, in the black weeds, so unsuited to their years, had brought more vividly to his mind, than ever before,

what they must have suffered and gone through; and
it was some time before he could regain his composure.
This burst, however, relieved him; and taking up a
pen, he poured forth in a letter to his brother, all his
griefs, and his joys; his regrets for his absence, his
delight at being again at home, and his unbounded
admiration of Lady Constance! and having finished,
he applied himself to repairing the neglects of his
early toilet, and then descending, went to rejoin the
party in the drawing-room.

"And do I really see that 'blessed uniform' again?"
exclaimed Lady Florence, who had re-entered whilst
Henry was away, having first seen the monkey installed in comfort by a warm fire;—"it certainly is
the most delightful dress that ever was invented."

"I am glad I am so charming an object in your
eyes, Flory; we will certainly have a middy's uniform
made for the monkey, and then you shall carry him
about on your shoulder.—When did you get my letter,
dear mother, saying I was coming home?"

"About a week ago.—What letters of mine have
you received? and when did they reach you?"

"I have only had one for these six months—dated
July, which followed me about from place to place for
an age—for our ship was always in motion."

He sighed as he looked at Lady Constance, for it
was that letter which had announced to him, the tidings
of her father's death. He saw that she remembered it
too, for the tears started into her eyes, and she turned
away. He strove to divert the current of her thoughts,
and began speaking of Sir Roland.

"When did he go?" he asked, "and how long will
he be gone? Are you quite sure that it was solely to

please *mon respectable oncle*, that he has returned to the continent? Gossip has wide wings, you know, and from what I heard, even out in the 'far west,' I suspect there may have been 'metal more attractive,' than mere old men's politics, to draw him back again."

Lady Constance felt most thankful that she had turned away, before Henry began talking of his brother, for the subject was to her always embarrassing; and Lady Ashton's open nature would have prompted her instantly to undeceive Henry, by telling him of Sir Roland's engagement; but being rather of a timid disposition, and not liking to act without being quite sure that what she did would be agreeable to Sir Roland, she determined to keep silence, till she had written, and ascertained his wishes on the subject.

Sir Roland had indeed, just before his departure from England, particularly requested that his brother—who it was expected, would have continued abroad for some time longer—might not be informed of the situation in which he stood as regarded Lady Constance; for determining that his union with her should depend entirely on her own free choice—and not feeling certain at that time, of what that choice might ultimately be— he thought, with considerate kindness, that if she should at last wish to break off their marriage, it would be less unpleasant to her to do so, if the knowledge of their engagement were confined to the few who were already acquainted with it, than if it were more widely known. Yet most certainly, if he had anticipated his brother's return, he would have desired him instantly to have been informed of it— for he loved him too much to wish to shew him any want of confidence. But at the time of his own departure, there appeared no chance of Henry's coming home; for the ship he was in, had still a considerable time to remain abroad; and it was only in consequence of obtaining his promotion as lieutenant much earlier than was expected, that he returned so soon, having been appointed to another ship.

Lady Ashton, after a moment, replied to Henry's observations about his brother, by asking,—

"Why, what have you heard of him?"

"Oh! I heard that all the Continent was at his disposal—every man wanting him for his sister or daughter, and every sister and daughter wanting him for herself; and I thought it just possible that he might have found, amongst the many offered, some one, worth accepting."

A smile played over Lady Constance's countenance, and a feeling of gratification stole across her mind, at hearing Henry's account of Sir Roland; for it is pleasant to find that others value that which we possess, even though we may be conscious that we do not sufficiently appreciate it ourselves. Our vanity, as well as our affection is often gratified at feeling that what others covet, is devoted solely to ourselves.

Yet a sigh involuntarily arose in her breast, as she said, "He is indeed worthy of all the love that can be bestowed upon him."

"Yes," said Henry, "I know of no one who deserves to be loved, if he does not. There is nothing like him! He is the perfect Bayard of our day—the 'chevalier,' par excellence, 'sans peur et sans reproche.' Nevertheless, if I had been him, I would have tried my fortune in this cloudy little island of our own, before I sailed across the sea to seek it. I had rather marry you, Constance, a thousand times — though that," he said with a smile, "would be no great exertion ; or I would rather, even have the reversion of that sun-burnt gipsy there, when she has got tired of her monkey — than espouse all the 'Pogalubofs,' 'Tibofs,' 'Bulcacofs,' 'Timidofs,' in existence — with their impossible names."

"Do not work yourself up to such a frenzy," said Lady Florence, "perhaps he will never marry at all !"

"Well, who knows but you may be right, Flory ; so go, and put on your bonnet, and come out with me and my 'blessed uniform,' and you, Constance — come along — and mother dear — come too ; I long to see each 'dingle and bosky dell,' and every nook 'by flood and fell,' and all the dear old child-remembered haunts. Come with me, all three — witches — graces — whatever you are ! Fly, you two young ones.— Mother, can I fetch your things ? or shall they ?"

"Florence will, she knows where to find them."

Shawls, bonnets, all were soon on, and the happiest quartet in the world sallied forth on a fine bright March day, with a wind just fresh enough to make exercise delightful. Henry Ashton walked between his mother and Lady Constance, and Lady Florence spun about, first on one side, then on the other, but more frequently in front, walking backwards before them, in the way in which children are wont to do, to the infinite torment of their seniors ; till Henry Ashton, threatening to "capsize her if she came across his bows again," made her sober her glee for awhile, and she walked quietly by Lady Ashton's side ; but finding such inaction irksome, she devoted herself exclusively to the society of the old Newfoundland, who seemed never tired of fetching the sticks and stones, she seemed never tired of throwing.

"Let us go and see the old lady at the lodge," said Henry, "she was not visible this morning as I passed."

They called accordingly, and the sailor's frank cordial greeting, accompanied by a shake of the hand, rather less distressing than the one he had afflicted her old partner with in the morning, enchanted the poor old dame, who declared, "he was Mr. Henry all over; though," she added in true west country dialect, "he was grown up so long."

When they had taken leave of her — Henry Ashton having first insisted that she should come up that evening, and drink his health in a bowl of punch — he said, "Constance, do you remember, years ago, our all climbing up to the top of that old woman's house? you, and Roland, and I? and I wanted to help you, but you said you could manage quite as cleverly as we did, so you tumbled down, and beat your bonnet into the shape of a cocked-hat, and hurt your arm, and were so cross!"

"You might be a little more civil in your recollections," said Lady Constance, laughing; "however, I utterly refuse to recollect any thing about it, and I believe the whole to be a figment of your own invention."

"True, I assure you; — you were dreadfully cross sometimes, and used to scratch awfully."

"You had better not bring such things too vividly to my recollection, lest I should be tempted to renew that pleasing exercise," said Lady Constance.

"I have a good thick coat-sleeve now, happily, and

not the poor little bare arms, you used to tear so un-
mercifully, I have the marks now—the surgeon when
bleeding me, thought I must have fallen into the hands
of the Chippewa Indians in tender youth, and have
been tattooed."

"What could you be blooded for?" asked Lady
Florence.

"To cool my temper, my dearly beloved; I grew
so fierce in those hot climates, that I became a terror
to all beholders, especially to small girls, with blue eyes
and rosy cheeks. It was dreadful the deaths I put
them to! I hove some into the sea—impaled others
on Cactuses—bobbed for sharks with others!—but I
have kept one particularly dreadful mode of extinction,
solely for the benefit of small English girls, which
tortures them horribly—especially if their hair curls,
or their names begin with an F;" and he cast a terrific glance at the curly-haired "F." by his side. "But
now let us go down to the shore."

Lady Ashton said she was tired, so told them to go
without her; but they accompanied her home first, and
then descended the cliffs, by a *corniche* path, which led
down from the shrubbery.

"How exactly every thing is as it was," said Henry,
"the trees, to be sure, and you children—are grown;
but the sea does not seem to me an hour older! Do
you really mean to say that it has been splashing away
on this shore ever since I went? Do you remember,
Constance——"

"No—I do not mean to remember any thing," she
replied; "your memory is such an ill-taught thing, I
desire to have nothing in common with it."

"Oh! do not be so cross with me," he said beseechingly, "I was going to remember something very pretty of you: how you cried and bemoaned yourself one day when I fell down this cliff, and did not hurt myself at all; you were so sweet, so very sweet as a child, spite of your scratchings — which to do you justice, was only your baby-work. But, oh! the many hours we have been here together!— the many holes we have dug in the sand, and watched to see filled with water — the many times we have stood with our backs to the sea, purposely, when the tide was coming in, and then been so wonderfully surprised, when the waves came over our feet! Those were delightful days!" and he walked on with a smile on his cheek, as if he were going over in his mind, the charms of those happy hours.

"But," he continued, after half a minute's silence, "if there is one pleasure in existence more delightful than all others, it is — to be, as I am now, with those one loves, and to whom one can say 'Do you remember?'—The friends of after days may be and often are, dear, but not like these—the first."

"Well, dear Henry," said Lady Constance, "I will not check another of your recollections. I shall like to hear them, though they will often perhaps sadden me."

"Dear Constance," he said with much feeling, "do not fancy me a heartless wretch, because I seem in spirits, and talk nonsense. I cannot help being happy, for I am at home again with those I do so dearly love! but still I grieve so very much for your affliction!"— He kissed her hand affectionately, and added, "But you know how much we all love you, and that we would do any thing to make you, and poor Flory happy."

" I am much happier than I was," replied Lady Constance, " but still I cannot help feeling *his* loss, and shedding many, many tears; even your return has saddened me, thinking how fond he used to be of you, and how much he would have rejoiced to see you again." And with renewed tears, she entered on some of the particulars of her father's death, and of her own sad feelings, to which Henry Ashton listened with the deepest interest; answering with kind, heart-soothing words; and leading her thoughts back to cheerfulness, by his animated affection, and bright views of life and of eternity.

" And my dear brother," he said, " how did he like going back again? He used to tell me, when he was abroad that he longed so much to return home ? "

" It was no wish of his to go back," answered Lady Constance, thankful that the trembling of her voice was concealed by the lingering sobs, which she could not yet quite overcome.

" If he were here, my happiness would be complete," said Henry; "only that there is ever the undying sensation which accompanies extreme happiness— the something which whispers amidst it all — ' How fleeting!' ' Why are the joys that will not last, so perishingly sweet ?' It is a very good thing, though, Constance, that it is so ! Joy on the one side—sorrow on the other — lift the soul towards God. And after all it is ' unwise to cast away sweet flowers, because they are not amaranth.' "

"I am glad you have those contented yet serious feelings, Henry," said Lady Constance; "that is the only frame of mind which turns all to good."

"I cannot imagine how people get through life without them," he answered; "the commonest little squalls of trouble one would think were enough to set people on the look-out for a sure anchorage, and quiet haven; and yet one sees thousands — women too, who seem as if a breath would blow them into nothing — bearing on through weights of woe, heavy enough to crush the earth — without one bright or hopeful look to the 'land of pure delight'— without one moment's sense of the love of God, or one craving for His sympathy! I have known little of trouble or sorrow, myself, certainly, but I know this—that with God I could be happy, were I alone in the world; but that without Him — not all the heights of my glorious profession — not all the riches of the world — its best riches, home-love — not you, nor my dear mother, nor — almost dearer than all—Roland himself, could make me happy without Him. I am as sure of that as if I had lived all the years, and gone through all the troubles of the wandering Jew."

"Yes, it is true," answered Lady Constance, "that without Him, there can be no abiding peace on earth; but my weak heart has often been very sorrowful even with Him. And yet, perhaps I should say, it was when forgetting Him, and thinking too much of my earthly father, that I missed the comfort which my heavenly One alone could bestow! I should think the sea, Henry, must be a place peculiarly fitted to awaken thoughts of God in the heart."

"It is in the power of no place to do that," replied

Henry, "it is the Spirit of God alone, as you well
know, Constance, that can ever awaken our dead souls,
or put one ray of light into their darkness. The sea
may perhaps, as well as the starry heavens, and other
works of God, furnish an argument for the Deist
against the Atheist;— as Napoleon, when going to
Egypt, hearing some of his generals talking infidel
trash, pointed up to the star-lit heavens, and said,
' Messieurs, qui est-ce qui a fait tout celà ?' but
never, dear Constance, will such things make a man a
Christian. I remember indeed on one of those — oh!
heavenly nights, which we have in the south, where
the sky is literally paved with stars — that we were
talking on the subject of Christianity on board of ship,
and one man said in a tone of the greatest contempt —
pointing upwards: ' Yes, you turn from such a glorious sight as this, and set up a rush-light in its
stead'—meaning revelation. Enormous noodle! as if
revelation did away with the God of nature, and did
not rather exalt Him a thousand-fold. But these *ir-
religionists* are so intensely silly! I do not wonder
at Scripture always calling them ' fools!' Their
arguments are such as Balaam's ass might blow
away."

" Yet they are not so easily got rid of either," said
Lady Constance.

" No, because they have struck deep in the un-
fathomable mire of the unregenerate human heart, and
their roots are nurtured from beneath by the fosterer
of all ill things. I can make allowances for all mistakes in religion, but I cannot tolerate those who scoff
at it."

" But there are some who though unbelievers

themselves, yet do not scoff at Christianity,",said Lady
Constance.

"Yes, and I have a true, though painful friendship
for several persons of that kind ; painful—because the
more I like them, the more of course do I feel, for
what I know from Scripture, must be their hopeless
case, as long as they reject the only hope of sinners."

"Yet how strange it is," said Lady Constance,
"that many who deny Christianity are remarkably
amiable, upright, benevolent and moral people — often
more so apparently than really pious Christians."

"More shame then for the pious Christians," said
Henry smiling. "Yet it is to be accounted for this
way: Satan cares not one jot, whether we sleep away,
or violently sin away our souls; therefore, those whom
he secures by opiates, he is judicious enough not to
arouse, by making them commit alarming crimes; while
the very faulty dispositions of others may be the
means, in God's hands, of making them feel they were
not fit for heaven on their own account, and so of
leading them to Him, who alone can take them there.
Whitfield said, he never had so much success in
preaching as among the colliers ; who having evidently
no righteousness of their own, were most thankful to
hear of, and most ready to accept, the imputed righteousness of another. Those amiable, good sort of
honourable unbelievers, and worldlings, remind me of a
story I have heard my mother tell of an old ·man,
whom she knew when a girl, and who was once suffering dreadfully from gout, or something — and was
complaining accordingly, when a friend said, ' You do
not look ill in the face.' ' I'm *not* ill in the face,' he
answered in a rage. Now these people are ' not ill in

the face,' the outward man is well enough to look upon, whilst within exists the deadly disease of unpardoned sins, and an undevoted heart."

"I think," said Lady Constance, "that Erskine says so admirably, 'God is not obeyed by our doing what He desires, but by our doing it out of love to Him.'"

"Yes, that is the only acceptable motive—the only one of God's own planting," replied Henry; "'Love is the fulfilment of the law,' both to God and man,

> 'Love is life's only sign!
> The spring of the regenerate heart,
> The pulse, the glow of every part
> Is the true love of Christ our Lord,
> As man embrac'd, as God ador'd.'

But how delightful it is to hear you talk in this way, Constance, and yet so strange! You were quite a little girl when last we parted, not much older than Florence — skipping and flying about as she does now, and talking any thing but sense — though very dear nonsense. Now, you are grown sober, and tall, and ——" he stopped, and looked at her with an expression which shewed he did not disapprove the change which time had made. She laughed, and coloured as she said,—

"You must not forget that time is as awake and busy on the deck of a man-of-war, as he is on 'terra firma;' you, too, are very different in some ways, to what you were, though not in all."

"What am I changed in?"

"You are much taller, and——"

"Much handsomer," interrupted Henry, "am I

not? say so, dear Constance, do flatter me a little, it is so pleasant to hear oneself praised."

"I do not know that you are handsomer," said Lady Constance.

"Oh! your eye has been spoilt by having my Adonis brother so long before it," he said smiling. "Well, if I must yield, let it be to him, and welcome."

"You are too different to admit of a comparison."

"That does not satisfy me at all," said Henry, "I want something positive said in my favour. If you go on provoking me, I will not yield even to my peerless brother, and I will make you this evening sing, 'Les yeux noirs, et les yeux bleux,' and take all said in praise of the latter to myself. How often by the bye have I thought of that silly song, when I saw the dark-eyed, but really beautiful women of the south. The *remembrance* of my *anticipations* of what you would be, 'Signorina mia,' made their magnificent gazelle-like orbs shrink into shrivelled sloes in my estimation. But I am grievously disappointed after all!"

"I think you are talking great nonsense, my dear Henry," said Lady Constance quietly; "if you wish me to understand that you think me celestially beauti-ful, say so at once, and waste no more time; and I in return will say that I think you quite good-looking enough for any man; so let that matter be considered as 'signed, sealed, and delivered,' and settled for life."

"Not for life, alas! Constance, unless we mean for the future to subsist solely on Hebe's fare—determined to 'flourish in immortal youth;' but ——"

"Well then for the present at least; so now be rational again."

" But why should you return my civilities with such asperity? art thou incensed at being reckoned beautiful?"

" Not in the least—but I hate," added Lady Constance with a provoked smile, " having inuendoes made on the subject. It seems so much as if one was considered ' la bête' as well as ' la belle.' "

" You know, Constance, I could not——"

" Oh! spare me compliments to my understanding now," she cried; " pray let it be inserted at once in the agreement, that I am besides all other good things, ' wisest, virtuousest, discreetest, best——' "

" Yes, if you add also, ' provokingest, hard-heartedest,' " said Henry laughing, though half angry.

" Agreed," she replied.

" But tell me, Constance, do you really suppose every woman likes to be thought beautiful?"

" If she is so, of course; why not?"

" Aye, if she is so;—but who is to decide that question?"

" A sensible woman will decide it for herself."

" But I thought it was reckoned the proper thing for a young lady to be wholly unconscious of her beauty, and to start like a timid fawn, if zephyrs whispered it in flitting by, or flowers bowed their fragrant heads as she passed, in acknowledgment of her surpassing loveliness!"

" Any one might well start, under those circumstances," said Lady Constance, laughing with her gleeful voice, " but I imagine that that race of young ladies is past—evanished with the whispering zephyrs and bowing flowers. These railroad days cherish not such unconscious lovelinesses. No, my dear Henry, it is the part of all sensible bodies, men or women, to find out what they are, and to appreciate themselves accordingly."

"Well, that will do, as far as people's sense concerning themselves goes," answered Henry; "but how are they to shew their sense in their estimate of others?"

"Oh! that is equally simple," answered Lady Constance gaily, "we should reckon all as sensible people, who are sensible of our merits, of course."

"Then," said Henry, pausing in his walk, and turning to her with a bright smile, "you must write me down in our agreement—'most sensiblest'—for no words can express what I think of you."

There was something in Henry Ashton's manner as he said this, which startled Lady Constance, and an undefined sensation of dread took possession of her. She considered herself already as Sir Roland's wife; and words like these, even if spoken in jest, she could not like. She coloured deeply; but a slight feeling of displeasure enabled her to meet her companion's eye calmly, though gravely, as she said after a moment's pause,—

"Now a truce, dear Henry, to all this nonsense; I hate this foolish style of conversation, though I have given way to it myself. It is so different to what we had been having before—so different to our former habits! Do let us be as in the dear old times, or I shall have no comfort in you, and shall feel for you quite as a stranger."

"Do not do that, Constance," said Henry, completely checked, and his bright look giving way to one of pained embarrassment, "I would not offend you for the world."

"I know you would not," she replied, "and you have not offended me; but I want to consider you as my old companion — the brother of my childish days; and if you are to be making absurd speeches every moment, you will tire me to death; and then I must take refuge with my mother (for so she always called Lady Ashton) and give you quite up — and you might as well be at sea again."

Henry Ashton took her hand, and kissing it with deep, affectionate respect, said,—

"Forgive me, Constance, I will not be so foolish again."

"I have nothing to forgive, Henry," said Lady Constance, much touched, "I was talking nonsense as well as you; and after all I am making a great deal, perhaps, of nothing; only—I do not like——"

"I perfectly understand you, my darling sister," said Henry, comprehending her meaning, and with intuitive delicacy, resuming his old, natural, unconstrained manner again, "you like that I should be the 'Henry' of your scratching days, and not the conceited, presumptuous coxcomb I was just now."

"Yes," said Lady Constance, quite at her ease again, and breathing freely, "we cannot be better than we were when digging holes in the sand, and letting the sea wash over our feet."

Lady Constance was truly wise in thus early putting an end to Henry Ashton's demonstrations of regard. She was young both in years and in experience, yet she could not misunderstand his manner to her; and though she did not suppose that what he felt for her on this, the first day of his return — was

love—yet she felt that it was what would—if allowed
to continue and increase—render her intercourse with
him extremely unpleasant, and completely destroy all
the happiness and freedom of their former days. She
wished earnestly to tell him of her engagement to Sir
Roland, as that she thought, would immediately settle
their relative positions, and prevent his ever having
a feeling for her, beyond what he might freely have for
his childhood's companion, and the betrothed of his
brother. But as Lady Ashton had told her of Sir
Roland's wish that it should not be known, she did not
like to do what she thought he might disapprove.
What she had said however, seemed to have entirely
the desired effect, for Henry Ashton, from that time,
treated her with the same free cordiality he used
towards her sister—making no difference in his manner
between the two; and this set her quite at rest,
and enabled her to enjoy his society again without
fear or scruple. And true enjoyment it was; for
he was full of information, and anecdote; having seen
much, observed much, and read much; and having
withal an internal laboratory which converted all into
profit.

CHAPTER XXIII.

"Our best affections here,
They are not like the toys of infancy,
The soul outgrows them not,
We do not cast them off."—*Unknown.*

"There are noble things which pass over thy powerful mind."
Ivanhoe.

THE time passed happily at Llanaven, while Sir
Roland was in all the turmoil of business, and of
almost incessant travelling abroad. The transaction
he was carrying on, was happily, one in which he felt
great interest; for unlike many diplomatic matters it
was of such a nature as, if well conducted, would
conduce to the happiness of thousands. But his own
happiness was sorely disturbed by receiving no letters
from home. He knew of course that many were
written; but he was so constantly in motion, that
he did not know where to tell his uncle to forward
them to him; so that after the first few days, he
was above two months without beholding the handwriting of either Lady Constance or his mother; and
consequently, all that time had elapsed, before he
knew of his brother's arrival at home.

On his return to his uncle's, he found a pile of

letters awaiting his perusal.   They had been arranged
for him by Lord N——'s thoughtful order, according
to the date of their arrivals, and with eager haste
he began to examine their contents.   The first which
met his hand was from Lady Constance, written with a
kindness and affectionate cheerfulness, that gladdened
his very heart; and long did he gaze on the characters, which so beloved a hand had traced, ere he
felt inclined to open any other letter.   The kindly
style in which she had written, was not in the least
assumed, for the relief which, as it has been observed,
her spirits experienced from Sir Roland's absence, had
communicated itself to her whole being; and her
regard for him again flowed forth, almost as freely as
in the former pleasant days of their unclouded affection.

The next letter he opened was one from Lady
Ashton, containing the unlooked-for news of Henry's
expected arrival, but saying that the time of his coming
was uncertain.

Another kind letter then presented itself from Lady
Constance, full of pleased anticipations of Henry's
return, and more than ever satisfactory in its tone of
feeling towards himself.   He pressed it to his lips, and
felt a glow of joy and of confidence in the love of her
who wrote it, which had never before warmed his
heart.

Alas! how slight a veil may hang between the ex-
tremes of pleasure and of pain!   A seal broken — a
little sheet of paper unfolded—a word—written or
spoken !—and the whole hue and tenor of our lives may
be for ever changed !

With an almost listless hand (so full was he of

happiness) did Sir Roland open the next letter. It was from Lady Ashton, telling him of Henry's actual arrival, and giving an account of his looks, &c. He read the beginning with excessive pleasure, and paused a moment, as a flow of deep affection came over him, at the thought of his brother, and of the joy and happiness which all at home must have experienced, at this delightful meeting. How ardently did he desire to be at Llanaven at that moment!—The yearning of his heart, to his brother especially, was inexpressible; and the thought of his being at home made him, with impatience, sigh for the weary time of his own exile to expire. How did he long again to be amongst those so dear to him! to enjoy with them their rambles through the woods, their rides over the breezy downs, their moonlight walks by the side of the restless sea. But he strove to subdue the murmurs that involuntarily arose, and one upward glance brought down peace and strength. Again he took up the letter.—What was there in the few short words that followed, that could so completely unhinge his soul? They were: " Shall I not tell Henry, now he is come home, of your engagement to Constance?"—Simple words!—yet they brought with them a hurricane of feeling to Sir Roland. He glanced impatiently at the date, and saw that the letter had been written full two months before! An idea new and horrible seized his imagination—tremors shook him from head to foot—the paper rustled in his shaking hand, and the characters flitted and faded from before his eyes!—Unable to still his painful trembling, he leaned his head upon his hand.

" With what an agony," he thought, at length, when the confusion had cleared a little from his mind, " have

I thirsted for these letters! and now with what agony do I receive them! Two months! And Henry has been two long months with Constance, in all the freedom of early friendship—unknowing of her engagement! He must love her!—he must love her—it is impossible—but he must love her!—and she—?" He shrunk as if a gulf had opened before his feet. His mind rapidly reviewed the scenes of their early youth, recalling how Henry had ever been Lady Constance's chosen companion—the partner of all her occupations—the participator in all her pleasures!—The thoughts which these recollections awakened within him now for the first time, seemed to scorch his very brain as they crossed it.—He started up with the insupportable suffering, and walked to and fro with hurried steps. "Oh! God!" he exclaimed aloud, "save me from this—save me from this.—Why did I not tell him at once of our engagement, and put him on his guard?—And yet," he continued, as he paused in his agitated walk, "I did it for her sake! But to lose her!—now, when my happiness was at its height; her—whose image never leaves me—to see her love another!—Oh! my Father! avert this intolerable anguish from me!" and again he agitatedly paced the apartment. "But," he said, with sudden hope, "I may be tormenting myself, with that which has existence only in my own wild brain;" and he again took up his mother's letter. It contained nothing to alarm him, save that the reality—so terrible to his imagination — remained unchanged: "Henry was there with Constance, believing her unshackled!" His impulse, when he had finished reading the letter, was instantly to write, and desire that his brother should be told of his engagement, and he seized a pen, and wrote to that effect. He then with a trembling hand took up another of the letters: it was from Henry himself — the one he had written in the height of his feelings, on the first morning of his arrival. He spoke with ecstasy of being again at home, again with those he loved;—but though at another time, Sir Roland would have delighted in dwelling on all the particulars of that which interested his brother, yet now he had but one thought in life, and his eye ran feverishly over the lines, till it rested on the name of "Constance." His head swam, and his heart beat audibly, as he read the expressions of extreme admiration with which his brother spoke of her — and crushing the paper in his hand, he burst into tears.

"If such," he thought, when he grew more composed—"if such were his feelings, on the first day of their meeting, what must they be now?—And will she not—does she not return them?"

He dared not answer that question to himself—he knew she had never loved *him*, as his love to her deserved, "and now," he thought, "will all her heart be filled with him — her childhood's favourite — whose blighting love has come between me and happiness." His mind was too confused for prayer, and he sat as if paralysed. A flush of indignation for a moment darkened his brow—but then a milder feeling softened the expression of his eye, as he reflected, "And if he does love her, is he to be blamed, is he not rather 'sinned against than sinning?' Oh! that I had known he was coming home! or that my dear mother had not attended to what she thought were my wishes. He ought to have known all instantly, and not have risked his happiness—or mine."

He dwelt on the thought of his brother, of that young, gay, joyous being—and a tide of noble tenderness rushed over him.

" He shall not be told it now," he exclaimed aloud, in the fervour of his generous feeling ; and he took the note he had written, and tore it into fragments. "I may be—Oh! God grant that I am premature in my fears—a self-tormentor! and yet can he be so long with her—so intimately—and remain indifferent?" He thought of her loveliness, her gentleness and piety, and all the attractions which had bound his heart so completely to her; and a smile, though a sad one, rested on his lips, as the vision passed before him. Slowly he took up the pen and began to write—the effort was great ;—he paused, "I will at least," he thought, "read all these killing letters before I decide."

He read them in the order in which they had come. Those from Lady Ashton contained not a word to influence him either way, though she frequently renewed the question contained in her first.   Those which Lady Constance had written immediately after Henry's arrival, were short, but joyous and affectionate ; often saying that his own presence was all that was wanting to make their happiness complete.   In reading these, Sir Roland's fears vanished, and he upbraided himself for his faithless folly, and for his doubts of her truth. Then again, her letters became more sober, and more full ; and yet they seemed he thought—but it might be only fancy—less free than before ; she seemed more studious of pleasing him, more full of inquiries as to what he was engaged in—but she dwelt more, he thought, on what she read, and what she did—less, on what she felt.   At the moment of reading them, he

was satisfied with their contents, but when he had
closed them, it seemed as if something were wanting.—
Again he read them, and again he was satisfied ;— he
closed them—and again the nameless want pressed on
his heart.   Henry's letters were frank, affectionate, and
full of happiness ; and though he often mentioned Lady
Constance, yet it was never again with the vehement,
enthusiastic admiration which had at first, so startled
and alarmed Sir Roland — and again the latter smiled
at the folly of his fears.

But these letters must be answered, and what should
he say ?   After a second perusal of them, he felt so
tranquil, that he thought his first design, of informing
his brother of his engagement, could involve no risk of
that brother's happiness, and would be but a just mark
of confidence and affection on his part; and he determined to write both to Lady Ashton and to Henry
himself to that effect.   Yet still he felt dissatisfied—he
paused, and passed his hand often across his troubled
brow.   He could not determine what it was best to do.
A decision would have been difficult, had he been a
dispassioned judge in the case of another ; but here
where all his hopes of earthly happiness were involved
—where an affection that seemed his very self, was
henceforth to form his sum of human joy or misery—
can it be wondered at that he found it almost impossible
to decide?   If Henry and Lady Constance remained
in their feelings towards each other, as they had been
in former days, all would be well either way, but if not—
would it not be crushing the hearts of the two beings
he loved best on earth, if he suffered his claim to interfere between them ? — Hard thoughts were these ! — a
bitter sentence to pronounce against himself ! — Should

he write to Lady Ashton, and ask in confidence, whether she had perceived any particular attachment between Lady Constance and his brother? But no; this course displeased his open nature; it seemed as if he were placing a spy upon their actions; and it might also be needlessly disturbing his mother's peace. Should he endeavour to obtain his brother's confidence? but then it seemed as if the bare suggestion of the thing, might awaken in Henry's breast, feelings which else might never have existed. Again he thought (and this course seemed to offer most of peace) that he would write at once to Lady Constance herself, and ask — without naming his brother—if, in his absence, she still wished — as she had said she did, when they were last together—that their engagement should continue. He would entreat her to remember what he had before told her —"that worlds should not induce him to urge the fulfilment of her vow, unless her whole heart could ratify it." He would beg of her, to consider herself entirely, and to let him feel at least, that she thought him worthy of her fullest confidence.

Yes! this he would do!—But ere he had got through many lines, "No"—he thought, "this might seem like distrust of her, and might be felt as throwing myself on her generosity! What shall I do? oh! my God, undertake for me."

He pushed the writing materials from him, and started up. "I cannot write to-day," he said; "I cannot sufficiently command my thoughts. To-morrow may bring calmer feelings. I must," he added, with a faint smile, "like Hezekiah, 'spread my letter before the Lord,' and doubtless I shall be directed aright."

He locked up the papers that had such power to

trouble him, and went to gaze once again from the old accustomed window. He was in the room where he had so long watched over Mr. Anstruther, in days when his own prospects had been brighter, than now they seemed. He recalled to mind, the elevated state of feeling he had often enjoyed in that spot, where he had felt at times as if nothing could shake the happiness which rested on God alone—which had Him for its source, and satisfying portion;—and again somewhat of peace stole into his heart.

" A few short years," he thought, " and I shall be even as that being, who here once suffered so much, but who is now beyond the reach of evil!

> ' How shall I then look back and smile,
> On thoughts that bitterest seemed erewhile,
> And bless the pangs that made me see
> This was no world of rest for me.' "

It was just a year since Mr. Anstruther's death; and the world without was so unchanged ! There were the same bright lights, the same length and breadth of shadow—the same bright vivid colourings; and Sir Roland, after looking forth for a time, could have almost fancied that, if he turned, he should again behold before him Mr. Anstruther's pale, and suffering, yet spiritual countenance. He remembered his words—that " if ever he was in trouble he should think of him, and be comforted"—and he was comforted. A blessed conviction filled his mind that the same God who had sustained the dying spirit of his friend, would be with him also, and would strengthen him under every trial.

CHAPTER XXIV.

" How often is our path
Crossed by some being, whose bright spirit sheds
A passing gladness o'er it; but whose course
Leads down another current, never more
To blend with ours! yet far within our souls,
Amidst the rushing of the busy world,
Dwells many a secret thought, which lingers still
Around that image."— MRS. HEMANS.

WHEN ready for dinner, Sir Roland descended the stairs, and found Lord N—— in the drawing-room, who informed him that they were to dine at the —— ambassador's, to whose house they accordingly proceeded.

When first Sir Roland had returned to —— from England, he had stayed but a short time at Lord N——'s, and had had so much business that he had scarcely had time to see any one. His appearance, therefore, on the present occasion was hailed with the greatest delight; for though some were strangers, yet many in that large party had been in —— when he was formerly there; and by them he was warmly greeted. One indeed, there was, to whom his presence brought a mixture of pain and pleasure, difficult to be concealed;—from whose eye, no power could keep the springing tear, when she again so unexpectedly beheld

before her, one, whose image she could not banish—
though she knew he thought not of her.

Isabella Harcourt was a pale but lovely - looking
creature, who had become acquainted with Sir Roland
when he was at —— the year before. She belonged
to a gay, worldly family ; but of delicate health, and
shrinking mind, she at that time wearied of the fashion and dissipation which could not give her peace,
and craved for something to rest upon—something to
satisfy the void within. Her only brother—younger
than herself—was then fast sinking before the fell power
of consumption, to which fatal disease he had since
fallen a victim. To him she was devotedly attached,
and gladly would she have exchanged each gay scene,
and cheerful meeting, to have stayed by his sick couch,
and soothed his suffering moments.

At a little evening party, the year before, while
sitting alone in silent abstraction, she suddenly
caught words of heavenly wisdom, which were accidentally uttered in her hearing; and turning, met a
countenance that had never since left her memory !
Her young and romantic heart became irresistibly
attracted by Sir Roland's character, and (too timid to
speak much herself) she would often sit by, and listen,
when he spoke of religion to others, till her whole soul
seemed filled with the subject. Never, till then, had
the words of truth reached her ears, and they fell like
dew upon her heart, which, though so young, was tired
of all the glare of life. She gradually obtained clearer
and clearer views of religion ; but she also began fearfully to understand the nature of her feelings towards
Sir Roland, and bitterly did she mourn over the in-
caution with which she had suffered her heart's best

earthly love, to fix itself where she felt it was not returned.

Sir Roland was indeed to her both " bane and
antidote," for while he was the cause of much earthly
sorrow, his words and bright example, were the means
of leading her to Him, who never fails or disappoints
His people, and who alone could heal the wounds so
unwittingly inflicted.   There was also a feeling within
her, which told her, that whether for happiness or sorrow, this world could not be long for her; and her
affectionate heart would at times rejoice, even through
tears, that one she loved so much, had not placed his
hopes of happiness on a being, so soon to have been
lost to him.

It had been impossible for Sir Roland, during his
former stay at Lord N——'s, not to perceive the effect
which his presence always had upon Isabella Harcourt.
Her mind, though diffident and retiring to the utmost degree, was like a shrine of crystal, too transparent to
conceal what it contained ; and her ever-varying countenance revealed but too faithfully every emotion which
agitated her.   Often when Sir Roland was conversing
with others (for she seldom spoke to him herself) would
her attention be rivetted on him and his words, to the
total forgetfulness of all around her, till suddenly perhaps, catching his eye, she would shrink back into
concealment.   She repeated to her brother (often
without knowing its meaning) all that she could recall
of Sir Roland's conversations on religious subjects; and
the boy eagerly listened to things so new, and so delightful to him.   His parents and eldest sisters were
always kind, and would try to cheer his drooping, and
often fretful mind, with accounts of their pursuits and

pleasures; but in these he could feel no interest; and though Isabella, in her fond love, was ever striving to soothe and please him, yet her naturally pensive mind dejected, rather than enlivened him. She loved the poetical, and sentimental, and fanciful style of German literature, and was but little acquainted with Scripture truth; her thoughts of death were rather as of a release of the spirit from the burthen of the flesh, that it might with freer love hover around the objects of its earthly affections, than as that which must fix man's doom for ever. She endeavoured to feed her dying brother's mind, with the fancies which filled her own, and would tell him "that the sighing of the summer winds in the high branches of the trees—' The *Psithurisma* of the dark-blue pine'—was the voice of those of other days, calling them to join their happy throng!"

Such fanciful imaginations were ill calculated to supply the invalid with strength to bear up under the depressing influence of sickness and confinement, or to support and guide a spirit already on the confines of eternity. But when Isabella Harcourt had heard the words of sober, though exalted piety which Sir Roland spoke—these unsubstantial fictions rolled away before their influence, like the vapours of night, before the morning beam; and as she repeated to her brother the words which had had such power to arrest her own attention, then indeed he too began to feel, that there was something, which at last, could suit and satisfy the wants of his soul. He urged his sister to go as much as possible where she could meet Sir Roland, and to listen, for his sake, to all he said; and Isabella, thus stimulated, watched with almost breathless eagerness, to catch the faintest sounds of a voice already too dear to her;—drinking in at the same moment—poison to her heart, and health to her soul. The latter however, was all she communicated to her brother, keeping her unhappiness concealed; and some months after, when Sir Roland had departed for England, and her brother died, it was with a mixture of joy and sorrow not to be described, that she felt that the latter had owed his salvation almost entirely, as far as human means were concerned, to one thus doubly endeared to her grateful heart.

Her close attendance upon her brother greatly injured her health, which had never been strong, and in fact the same disease which had laid him in his early grave, was evidently stealing with insidious power, into the very springs of her life. The loss of the brother so deeply loved, and her other griefs, preyed continually on her spirits, and though in gentle acquiescence with her parents' wishes she still went out into society, it was evident to all, (but those most immediately about her) that the grave just closed on the only son, must soon be unclosed again to receive her—his nurse—his comforter—the guide of his young steps to the throne of grace and mercy.

Sir Roland could not be insensible to the devotion of this sweet and beautiful creature, yet he was far above the sinful weakness of doing aught to increase a sentiment, of which he knew too well the force.

It has been said that the feeling entertained for those who love us, but whose love we cannot return, is, "ni amour—ni amitié; mais une classe apart." No truer saying! It may be vanity—it may be kindliness (probably a mixture of the two)—but give it what name we will, we may observe, that a sentiment of

interest ever dwells in the breast of those who have
been beloved, for those who have wasted on them the
treasures of a vain affection ; even though the measure
of that interest, amount not to reciprocity !

Painfully did Sir Roland feel this towards Isabella
Harcourt, and when he met her so unexpectedly at
the —— ambassador's on the occasion we are speaking
of, nothing could still the pang that darted through him
at witnessing her uncontrollable emotion. She looked
so ill too ! and when the sudden suffusion of colour
which had arisen for a moment, faded away from her
cheek, it " left its domain as wan as clay." The sight
of her—clad too in her mourning garments—for an
instant completely unmanned him, for he was in no
mood to deem lightly of the pain of unrequited love ;
that seemed to him at the moment, the one only grief
of life — the single, all-poisoning drop of gall, which
could embitter the whole cup of existence. He did not
approach Isabella Harcourt directly, but lingered long
in his greetings with other friends, in order to give
her, as well as himself, time to recover their composure. In the meanwhile, dinner was announced,
and it was only in the little confusion incident on
taking their places at table, that they again caught
each other's eye and exchanged salutations ; and being
finally seated on the same side of the table, but not
next to each other, they had no further intercourse at
that time, though the sound of Sir Roland's voice
would at intervals reach the poor girl's ear, and send
a sickness to her very heart.

After dinner, when all were again assembled in the
drawing-room, Sir Roland felt that he ought, in common
civility, to go and speak to her, but he could not

bear to approach her, and remained for some time near
the door, in conversation with others; till perceiving
that Lord N—— was talking to her, in his kindly,
cheerful manner — bringing every now and then a
smile on her countenance — he thought it a favourable
opportunity, so crossed the room, and joined their
party. Her manner was fluttered for a moment as he
addressed her; but as he immediately afterwards, joined
in his uncle's jesting conversation, her embarrassment
soon passed, though a deeper shade of depression
seemed to succeed to every smile, which Lord N——'s
observations produced. She had never in her life
sought to speak to Sir Roland, though she had frequently been a party in conversations he had had with
others, but now she earnestly desired to address him,
and to tell him of the blessing he had been to her and
to her brother. Since Frederic Harcourt's death, she
had had no one to whom she could speak on the subject of religion — no human being even to whom she
could talk with pleasure of him; for no one about her,
could have understood her feelings, of tearful happiness as regarded his immortal state. Her family
though kind, were thoroughly given up to the world,
and the language of spirituality would have been as
Arabic to them. Having (with some reason certainly)
laughed at her former fanciful ideas, they treated her
new feelings with no more respect; but, jokingly calling them, " les dernières fantasies d'Isabelle," expected
soon to see them depart as the others had done, and
be replaced by something perhaps more visionary still.
Isabella's candid mind made her sensible that she had
laid herself open to these suspicions, and she bore them
therefore with the greatest sweetness and patience; but

she deplored that those she loved, could not discern
between the rovings of a childish, untaught imagination, and the breathings of that religion, which is
beyond all others, a "reasonable service."

With these feelings, it would have been the greatest
delight to have been able to speak to Sir Roland—to
have talked to him of her brother—and to have heard
again from his lips, words of truth, and strength, and
comfort.

But how could she speak to him? with his uncle
by, it was impossible; and even had they been alone,
how would she have summoned courage to have addressed him?   While these thoughts were passing
through her mind (rendering her so abstracted, that
though she mechanically smiled when they smiled, yet
in fact she heard scarcely any thing of the lively raillery
Lord N—— was bestowing upon his nephew) another
gentleman joined their circle, and Sir Roland availing
himself of the interruption, moved away, glad of ending
a scene so painful to him. Isabella Harcourt's eyes
followed him as he departed, and there are few perhaps of the energetic actions of life, which equal in
difficulty and exertion, the powerful effort she made at
that moment, to preserve her composure. She had
heard Sir Roland say, that in a few days he should
again quit ——; it was not probable they could meet
again before that time, and she was confident, that if
many months elapsed before his return, the grave would
first have closed above her head. She so longed to
hear from him one word at least of heavenly truth, on
which her memory might dwell! and to tell him of the
change his former words had been the means of effect-
ing. But no! he had left her—and her heart seemed

turned to stone; its fluttering action ceased, and a slow, heavy, throbbing pulsation succeeded, which seemed to paralyse her very life, and to deprive her of all power and feeling.

There was music, and she was asked to sing, for her voice was beautiful. She rose immediately, and without embarrassment sat down to the piano. Generally on such occasions, her voice and hands would shake with nervous timidity, but what was all the world to her at that moment! They placed before her Beethoven's harrowing song, "In questa tomba oscura," and she went through it without pause or fault. How many times had she sung that music to herself, while her voice had failed, and her heart sunk at its sad despairing words! but now!—not the vocal miracle of Egypt itself could have been more insensible to its own thrilling strains, than was this sad musician, to the power of the harmony she was producing in such perfection. Had she caught Sir Roland's eye at that moment, probably the whole barrier of cold insensibility would have given way, and some terrible outbursting of feeling have ensued; but the tones which failed to arouse her, were too trying for him to endure in the presence of others; and at the very commencement of her singing, he had retreated into a deep window apart.— It was the same in which he had the year before held his long conversation with Lady Stanmore, and he could not but painfully feel the contrast between the bright and tranquil hope which had animated his bosom at that time, and the agitating suspense, and heavy despondency which now oppressed him.— Often had he heard the music which Isabella Harcourt was now singing, from Lady Constance, and that remembrance alone was sufficient at the moment to trouble him; but mingled with it was the agonising pity he felt for her who was then before him, whose feelings he could too well interpret, and whose present unnatural calm could not deceive him. He remained in his concealment after her voice had ceased, intending if possible to escape from the room unperceived, and walk home by himself, leaving word for Lord N—— that he was gone; but before he had effected his purpose, he was painfully embarrassed, by seeing Isabella Harcourt, with some other lady whom he did not know, enter the recess: he himself being nearly hid, by the voluminous curtain, which, though looped back, yet hung so as to throw a deep shadow where he stood.

" You look ill to-night, Isabella ? " said her friend.

" Do I ? " she replied. " I am not very well."

" Did the singing tire you ? "

" No—not much."

They were silent, and stood looking out at the summer night.

" Miss Aubrey," said a young man, joining them, " there is a general petition for your 'Ombra Adorata.' "

" Suppose I were perverse," replied the young lady who was thus solicited, " and refused to sing more than the third word—'aspetta.' "

" If you were," he replied gaily, " I should go on and say, ' Teco sarò indiviso,' for I will positively not return without you. I shall be torn in pieces of the multitude, instead of enjoying the 'fortunato Eliso which I was anticipating in hearing you."

" Sing to them then, 'Deh! frena i turbidi,' yourself. But I must say, I think the presiding genius o the revels to-night seems in a most lugubrious mood

he first makes one mournful ghost speak for itself,"
and she laid her hand lightly on her companion's
shoulder, "and then he invokes another. You do really
look sadly like a ghost to-night, Isabella," she said
kindly.

"I am tired; and the room is so hot."

"But is not heat now, the best thing in the world
for the voice, Miss Harcourt? will it not make
Miss Aubrey sing so that we shall be constrained to
exclaim,

> 'It were the Bulbul—but her throat
> Though tuneful, pours not such a note?'"

"Ah! 'Una voce poco fa,'" replied the obdurate
songstress.

"I tremble for your next quotation!" said the
delegate, with affected terror.

"What! do you really suspect me of intending to
follow in the wake of the three hundred and sixty-five
young ladies, who yearly perpetrate wretched puns on
that unfortunate song? No—from this moment it
shall be nameless for me."

"Well then, if you are too fastidious, and too
veracious to say, 'Mi manca la voce,' will you not
come and exert it in our behalf? You really must.
Hark! the populace are raging horribly, I shall be
rent piecemeal. Come, 'Ombra Adorata,'" he said,
entreatingly offering his arm. "Miss Harcourt," he
added, in a more subdued manner, and turning back
for her, "will you not come with us?"

"Thank you, no," replied Isabella, "I will wait
here, if Miss Aubrey will return. To follow your song-
quoting example," and she smiled faintly, "I will

repeat from my own of to-night, 'In questa tomba oscura lascia mi riposar.' "

"I will return to you, dear Isabella," said Miss Aubrey, looking kindly back.

" 'Lascia mi riposar,' " repeated Isabella, murmuringly to herself, when the others were gone. "Oh! yes, ' imploro pace.' "

She was silent, and leaned her head against the side of the open window, while every breath she drew was an oppressive sigh. Sir Roland knew not what to do, his distress was extreme. In her present position, if Isabella Harcourt turned, she could not but perceive him, and to leave the recess without being observed was now impossible. And yet he could not bear to speak to her—the very sight of her was grief to him. For several minutes she remained without moving; but at length she rose, and leaned out of the window, and Sir Roland, taking advantage of the slight noise she made in moving, left his shadowed spot, so quickly that she could not perceive whence he came, and approaching her, said, in as steady and cheerful a voice as he could command,—

"Miss Harcourt, are you prudent in going to the open window, after being in that hot room?"

She started at the sound—so unexpected, of his voice, but she could not answer him; the blood so long apparently stagnated at her heart, rushed in torrents to her head, and she could hardly prevent herself from falling. Sir Roland spoke again,—

"Are you not cold, Miss Harcourt?" he asked.

"What is it?" she said confusedly, "who spoke?"

"It was I," said Sir Roland. "Are you not well?"

"I was dizzy for a moment," she answered, sinking into a chair but perfectly composed again, "but it is past."

"Are you often so?" he asked.

"Sometimes.   No—not often."

He stood in painful silence. She made an effort to speak—her lips moved, but no sound issued from them.—Again she tried, but the effort was vain.

"You are not well," said Sir Roland, "shall I call Mrs. Harcourt?"

"No—no," she replied; but added, after a pause, "I have suffered much, since last we met, and——" a convulsive sob rose, and for a moment she was nearly overcome.

"I know you have," replied Sir Roland, much moved; "but there is One, Miss Harcourt, of whom we used to speak, who is ever with His people in their trials."

"Yes," she said, raising her calm, tearless eye to his; "God is with us in our sorrows."

Sir Roland remembering the touching petition he had overheard from her, "imploro pace," said, "Our gracious Lord's words are ever verified to those whose faith is strong: 'Peace I leave with you, my peace I give unto you, not as the world giveth, give I unto you.'"

"Not as the world giveth—no—not as the world giveth," said Isabella, with almost a wild expression.

"No, Miss Harcourt," said Sir Roland, "His is that peace of God, which the world cannot give—and neither can it take away."

Gay voices were heard again approaching, and

Miss Aubrey, and her former companion, with several others, entered the little retreat. A light, animated conversation ensued, during which Sir Roland once more addressing Isabella, said,—

"I must wish you good-night now, this has been a busy and a wearying day to me, so I shall escape amidst this gay 'tintamar.'"

They shook hands — and they parted.

Sir Roland stole out of the room unobserved, and returning home, retired to his own apartment. His mind felt shattered and disturbed; his own anxieties pressed heavily on him, and heightened a thousand fold, the sentiment of painful, heart-felt regret with which he thought of Isabella Harcourt. There was something so touching in every thing connected with her, (for he had heard much of her from some who knew her well) and he saw so clearly that the feeling of preference she had for him, had originated at first from a higher source — that it was heavenly truth which had first attracted her — that the deepest respect, mingled with all his other feelings respecting her.

"Oh!" he exclaimed vehemently, clasping his hands, "what would I give — what would I give to see Constance strive to hide her feelings towards me, as this poor, poor girl does? But *she* has no love to hide," and a bitter smile passed his lips. "It is the full heart that is the 'sealed fountain.' Yet why should I reproach her? ungrateful that I am! is she not all kindness and affection? and if she does not— cannot love me, why should I blame her? And am I sure indeed that she does not?"

A hope full of happiness rose within him, as he

thought of her letters, and the many expressions in them that breathed affection. But then might she not have said the same things to a brother? He felt uneasy and dissatisfied with himself and with all things. "Oh vain, unquiet heart," he said, " be still —be still."

It was absolutely necessary that he should answer his letters from home, the next day, and having finished all his business with Lord N—— he applied himself to the heavy task. He earnestly implored direction that he might be led to the conclusion that would be best; and also that he might be kept upright in his desire of seeking above all things, that 'favour of God which is better than life itself.'

He determined to reply to his brother's and Lady Constance's letters first, and then bring the full scope of his feelings to bear upon the answer he should make to Lady Ashton. When he had finished writing to them he felt such a flood of affection in his heart, and such an elevation of mind, as raised him above all selfish feeling; he determined that, let it cost even his life's happiness, he would do nothing that should in any way disturb the peace of those, so inexpressibly dear to him; and resolutely taking his pen he told his mother that it was his wish that his brother should not be informed of his engagement to Lady Constance. When done—he sealed the letter and put it with the others, and his heart felt lightened of its load. He looked at the little scroll—and though he felt, that possibly it bore in its thin folds, the joy or sorrow of his life, yet he could not wish one word unsaid—one line untraced.

He felt the joy of a hard-bought victory—the glow of "pure self-sacrificing love."

"Now," he said, "conscience is clear; if I suffer —the stings of selfish guilt will not mix their poison in the cup; if I am happy—then indeed I shall feel it to be a God-given, God-preserved happiness!"

CHAPTER XXV.

" Yet mourn ye not as they
Whose spirit's light is quenched!—for him the past
Is sealed.   He may not fall, he may not cast
          His birthright's hope away !
All is not here of our belov'd and bless'd—
Leave ye the sleeper with his God to rest! "

MRS. HEMANS.

" But their hearts wounded, like the wounded air,
    Soon close ; where past the shaft, no trace is found.
As from the wing, no scar the sky retains ;
The parted wave no furrow from the keel ;
So dies in human hearts the thought of death.
E'en with the tender tear which nature sheds
O'er those we love, we drop it in their grave."

YOUNG.

" What griefs that make no sign,
    That ask no aid but thine,
Father of mercies ! here before thee swell !
    As to the open sky,
    All their dark waters lie
To Thee reveal'd, in each close bosom-cell."

MRS. HEMANS.

WHEN Sir Roland had sent his letters to the post
he went out to enjoy the beauty of the weather and of
the country. He felt the want exceedingly, of his
former companions, for Mr. Scott and Mr. Singleton
were still travelling together in other countries ; and

his mind dwelt with deep regret on the thoughts of Mr. Anstruther. He wandered towards the burying-ground, desirous of once more visiting the spot where his remains reposed. What a crowd of emotions did the sight of it produce! how many recollections did it recall! The frightful catastrophe which had occurred there, again brought a shudder over his mind; while the remembrance of his friend—of his glorious hope of salvation, and of his strong affection for himself, served to soften and elevate his feelings. He rejoiced in the conviction that one more redeemed soul was added to the innumerable multitude that surrounds the throne of God, and he read the passage—which, as has been mentioned, he had had inscribed on Mr. Anstruther's monument: 'Cast thy bread upon the waters, and thou shalt find it after many days'—with an earnest determination, more than ever to 'spend and be spent,' in the service of that God, who can reward his people with such deep and soul-felt happiness.

There was another grave in that silent place, over which he heaved many a sigh. Young Harcourt was buried there! Attracted by a new and splendid monument erected since he last visited the place, Sir Roland turned to examine it; and found inscribed, the name of Frederic Harcourt. Much there was besides, of 'blighted hopes,' and 'crushed affections,' and of 'afflicted parents heart-broken for an only son.' In reading it, Sir Roland recalled to mind the ultra-fashionable mourning, and vain, gay, trifling conversation of her he had met the night before; and he sighed to think how soon the 'world' can swallow up the deepest well of human affections, even a mother's love. But where was the sister's grief recorded? the

B

grief of her, who was her brother's comforter in life, and who would soon, alas! be his companion in the grave! Where was her grief recorded? Not on the monumental stone!—nowhere on earth! But in the presence of Him who alone knew the strength of the tie which He had formed and severed.

> " The sorrow for the dead
>   Mantling its lonely head
> From the world's glare, is, in thy sight, set free ;
>   And the fond aching love,
>   Thy minister to move
> All the wrung spirit, softening it for Thee." *

On leaving the burial-ground Sir Roland met Mr. Roberts, and they strolled together conversing on various subjects for some time.

"I must go and inquire after this poor girl again, before I go home," at length said Mr. Roberts.

"What poor girl?"

"Miss Harcourt—Isabella Harcourt."

"Inquire after her," said Sir Roland, astonished, "why she dined at the —— ambassador's last night."

"I know she did, but dining one day, does not prevent people's dying the next you know, if they like it," replied the other.

"Roberts, how can you bear to speak in such a way; tell me what has happened?"

"She was taken ill last night, and is, I understand, in a very precarious state to-day."

"How was she taken ill?" said Sir Roland greatly shocked.

"Something of a fit I heard. Poor girl! I thought

* Mrs. Hemans.

she looked desperately ill last night; that odious
mother of hers, for whom I cherish a pet aversion, will
drag her about, I believe, till she is actually a corpse,
because she is the beauty of the family; protesting too
all the time that she ' outrages her own feelings for
the sake of her remaining children,' by going out at
all. I really believe there is many a quiet, gentle girl,
who is made a stalking-horse to a fantastical mother's
vagrant absurdities, till she drops in the field — the
hard-run field of nightly dissipation."

" I believe you," replied Sir Roland, " and am
afraid it is the case in this instance. That poor girl
has never recovered her brother's death, and will, I
fear, soon follow him."

"I am really afraid she will," answered Mr. Roberts; " as I looked at her beautiful face last night,
and her shadowy figure, she seemed scarcely a creature of this earth. I should have taken to crying if I
had looked at her long, though it would have been
almost like ' iron tears, down Pluto's rugged cheek.'
I have called there twice already to-day, so you see I
am not quite a brute, though I confess I spoke like
one just now. Had you not heard of her illness
before ? "

" No."

" Will you go with me then now, and inquire ? "

" No — do you go now, and just write down the
answer, and send it up to me, when you get home, and
I will call there after dinner."

Sir Roland declined accompanying Mr. Roberts,
because he could not bear to be under observation
when he went to make an inquiry, the answer to which
might be so distressing. He was not much surprised,

though shocked and deeply pained, by what he had
heard ; he had seen that Isabella Harcourt's general
health was very weak, and the unnatural calmness of
her manner the preceding evening after dinner, contrasted with the strong agitation she had betrayed on
their first meeting, convinced him that she had made
an effort over herself most difficult—and as he feared
most fatal.   He felt miserable at the thoughts of her
death, and accused himself, as if he were in part guilty
of it ; though in fact he was wholly free from blame.

Mr. Roberts, on his return home, sent up a written
message, saying that Miss Harcourt was rather better ;
and after dinner Sir Roland called at the house himself, and was happy to hear that she continued to
amend.   He felt indescribably relieved; " And yet,"
he thought, " why should I rejoice that her trials are
to be prolonged ?   ' The sooner death, the earlier immortality ; ' " and to her he well knew the future state
must be an immortality of glory.   He left —— the
next day, but before he set out, he again called at Mr.
Harcourt's, and hearing that Isabella was considered
out of danger, he departed with a lightened heart, in
prosecution of the business in which he was engaged.

Mr. Roberts's report that Isabella Harcourt had
' had something of a fit,' was not so great an exaggera-
tion as such reports usually prove to be.   On returning
home from the dinner party the night before, after
having parted from Sir Roland in the manner before
described, she continued to maintain the appearance of
perfect composure.   On wishing her good-night, her
father pressed her fondly to his breast for a moment,
and said,—

" You look sadly ill, my darling child, you really

must give up going out for a little while; these hot rooms and late hours do not suit you."

She answered her father only by a prolonged kiss of affection; she could not trust herself to speak, for the voice of kindness had begun to stir the tide of feeling within. She retired to her own room, and began to prepare herself for rest; she took off her rings and bracelets, and laid them on the table, and then proceeded to take a gold chain off her neck, to which hung a small miniature which she always wore, though concealed from sight. She held it a moment in her hand; and as she gazed on the features of her brother, and thought of his loving affection—now lost to her for ever on earth! and remembered too, all her unhappiness! her forced composure gave way, a flood of self-pity, rushed over her, and uttering a cry of irrepressible anguish, she fell on the floor. The sound of her fall, and of her grief-full cry, aroused her youngest sister who slept in the same apartment, and who springing towards her, found her senseless, and in strong convulsions. She spread the alarm, and assistance being procured, Isabella Harcourt was laid on her bed; and when the physician arrived, he bled her, and used every means his art could devise; yet it was long before she became tranquil, or recovered the slightest degree of consciousness. After a time, however, she slept; the nervous action of the muscles ceased, and when after many hours she awoke again, her mind was perfectly clear, though her weakness was so great she could scarcely utter a sound. Immediate danger seemed then past, and it was at that stage of her illness that Sir Roland received the account which so much relieved him on the morning of his departure

R 2

from ——; but her enfeebled constitution had received a shock she was never destined to recover.

When all anxiety as to her life was, for the moment, at an end, Mrs. Harcourt and her elder daughters resumed their usual habits of gaiety; and Isabella was left almost entirely to the companionship of her youngest sister Sophia, an amiable and sensible girl, between whom and her sister there existed a strong affection. Having no pretensions to beauty, Sophia was treated rather slightingly by the rest of the family; and Isabella, who was kind to every one, was on that account perhaps, more particularly so to her.

A few days after her seizure Isabella was lying on the sofa in her room, and Sophia was sitting with her, when the latter said—

"You must be very much the fashion here, Isabella, for so many people have called to inquire after you."

"It is very kind of them," she replied.

"There are cards of all sorts and sizes, with every type under the sun I believe," continued Sophia; "would you like to see the names of your 'anxious inquirers?'"

"Yes," said Isabella—for she thought Sir Roland might have called, and that his card might be amongst the number. Sophia went to fetch them, and soon returned, with a packet of cards in her hand. Isabella looked over them, and after a time she found the one she sought. It was that which Sir Roland had sent up on the morning of his departure, and over the name there was written in pencil, "I leave —— to-day." A deadly pang crossed Isabella's heart, as she thus learnt that he was actually gone; but a moment's consideration served to convince her that it was best that it should be so, as it would tend to the recovery of her composure, sooner than if she fancied he might still be calling at the house, or that she might be likely to meet him, should she ever again be able to leave the house.

" Here are cards enough to make trays for all your minerals, Sophia," she observed, as she kindly began fashioning some of them. " It will be pleasant idle work for me."

She shaped them with neat-handed care ;—but she could not so use Sir Roland's ! She looked at it for a time, till fast-coming recollections grew too strong for her.

" Give me the Bible, will you, dear Sophia," she said, " there is a passage I wish to write out; one that suits such a poor weak thing as I am—weak both in body and in soul."

" What passage is it ? "

" It is where our Lord Christ leaves ' His peace for His people. I know the sense but do not exactly remember the words."

She then took a pen and wrote on the back of Sir Roland's card the passage he had repeated to her on the last evening of their meeting : " Peace I leave with you, my peace I give unto you, not as the world giveth, give I unto you;" and she added underneath, his own words : " His is a peace which the world cannot give, neither can it take away." She placed the card in the Bible, and it was used by her, as her mark when reading that sacred book, to the hour of her death.

Mrs. Harcourt—with that wonderful blindness which so often prevents those who live with invalids,

from seeing the danger which every one else perceives—would not acknowledge, even to herself, that
she was uneasy about her daughter's health; being
swayed partly, though she knew it not, by a disinclination to leave off her usual habits of gaiety and
dissipation, as well as being naturally averse, to the
admission of melancholy and desponding thoughts,
concerning a child of whom she was really very fond.
She had been advised to remove her to a warmer
climate, though the physician who gave the counsel
was fully aware, that the prolongation, for a few
months, of a flickering existence, was all that could
possibly be hoped. But Mrs. Harcourt had no wish
to follow this course; as some attention having been
paid to one of her elder daughters by a wealthy, but
not particularly reputable peer, she was anxious not to
throw any difficulties in the way of a match she
desired, by leaving —— at that moment.

Isabella Harcourt had lingered for two months, in
all the variations of the flattering and delusive illness,
which was destroying her, when Mr. Scott returned
to ——. She had been acquainted with him during
his former stay in that city; and though she had never
heard him speak on the subject of religion, yet she
knew that his principles were the same as Sir Roland's,
and that they were particular friends. For these reasons
she wished much to meet him again; and she longed also
to hear once more the sound of any voice which could
speak to her of God; for kind and devoted as her
sister Sophia was, she knew but little of spiritual religion;
and her other friends and acquaintances were not of a
class, from whom she could derive any benefit in that

way. She wished moreover most earnestly to be enabled through Mr. Scott to convey to Sir Roland that, which she had been incapable of telling him herself, namely: the happy effects of his words on herself and on her brother. She therefore begged of her mother, if he should call, to be allowed to see him in the sitting-room, where she usually·received her friends, and Mrs. Harcourt, who was naturally of an easy and good-natured disposition, promised to grant her request; though she laughed at her for her "methodism," saying, she supposed she wanted to see Mr. Scott in quality of a "father confessor."

When the latter, therefore, called a few days after, Mrs. Harcourt said, that she had "a foolish sick child, who had taken a fancy to seeing him, if he would not mind going into another room." Mr. Scott though rather surprised, was not at all displeased, for he remembered Isabella Harcourt well; and having heard that her health was declining, but not knowing the state of her mind, he gladly went, where he thought perhaps a few words might be made of service and comfort to a dying fellow-creature. He followed Mrs. Harcourt into Isabella's little sitting-room, where they found her reclining on the sofa—for she was far too ill to sit up—with Sophia, who had been reading to her. The sight of the former shocked Mr. Scott greatly, for she seemed in the very last stage of consumption, and her thin white hand seemed, when she held it out to him, scarcely to belong to a living creature. But the disease which was destroying her, had lost none of its usual beautifying effects in her case, and he thought he had never before seen any thing so lovely. Her complexion, when in comparative health, had been very

pale, but now a bright flush lighted up her eyes, and
gave an animation to her countenance which it had
never before possessed.

" Decked for the tomb," he thought, " may she be
also prepared for heaven."

" Isabella, my love," said Mrs. Harcourt on entering, " you said that you would like to see Mr. Scott, as
an old friend, if he called, and he is therefore come to
pay you a visit. Now, Mr. Scott," she added, gaily
turning to him, " you must not make her melancholy—
you must cheer her spirits. We are thinking of going
soon to Italy, and then she will get quite well, and
strong again."

Isabella involuntarily shook her head, as the tears
started into her eyes; and a feeling of disgust rose in
Mr. Scott's mind, for he knew that they had been
advised to go to a warmer climate long before, and he
knew also what report said, was the motive of Mrs.
Harcourt's prolonged stay at —— ; and he felt indignant that the health, and indeed the life of one
child, should be sacrificed to ambitious projects for
another. He answered Mrs. Harcourt's injunction by
saying, " He hoped he should not be so unfortunate
as to bring gloom, where he wished all might be
happiness."

" Thank you," replied Mrs. Harcourt, " I really
believe I may trust her to you, for I know in former
days, you have often made me laugh with your amusing
observations; so as the carriage is waiting perhaps you
will excuse me."

" Gladly," thought Mr. Scott; but as he was not
in the " Palais de la verité," all that transpired was:
" I beg I may not detain you;" and with great *em-*

pressement, he advanced to open the door for her to pass.

Sophia Harcourt remained in the room with her sister some little time, and then wandered into the next, and placed herself out of hearing, for she knew Isabella wished to speak to Mr. Scott alone. When she was gone, Isabella began with some embarrassment,

" I thought I should like to see you again, Mr. Scott, partly because I know you feel, as I hope I do, on the subject of religion, and it is a great comfort to be able to speak to those who can understand one."

Mr. Scott with much surprise replied,

" I am most happy, Miss Harcourt, to have this opportunity of seeing you, and most happy am I also to find you feeling an interest in the only subject which can bring peace to the tried spirit. But have you no other friend — no acquaintance from whom you can receive benefit on these subjects ? "

" No," she replied; " many kindly call to see me, but none speak of other than wearisome subjects—subjects which sadden instead of enlivening me; they mean it all amiably, to keep up my spirits, but they know not how they depress me, and make me long for the quiet of the grave for this poor weary head, and the peace of heaven for my soul."

She spoke with many pauses, but Mr. Scott could not interrupt her. He felt astonished at her words, and was deeply touched, and delighted, at seeing one — so beautiful — so calculated to feel, and inspire earth's best affections, yet thus cut off in the midst of youth's hopes and joys — so supported by a spirit, evidently not of this world — so raised above all that perishes, to the Imperishable Himself ! — and he mar-

velled how the light of truth, could have penetrated
into that dark house. He knew indeed, that, as Augustine said, "God can speak without the noise of
words," but he also knew that it was seldom that the
work of salvation was commenced in the soul, without
some visible means being made use of, by the Great
Giver of the Spirit. At length he said,—

"When—if I may ask—did you first begin to
think seriously of religion ?"

"Only last year."

"Last year! not when I was here, surely?"

"Yes, it was," she replied, raising her handkerchief
to her face, to hide the colour which rose as she recalled the circumstances under which she first felt an
awakening on the subject; "but though I was acquainted with you, you never spoke to me concerning it."

"No," replied Mr. Scott, "I thought you would
not listen. I remember hearing then—you will not
mind my saying so now—that you were very *roman-
esque,* and indulged in many fanciful ideas."

"And you were willing I should perish in them,"
said Isabella, with somewhat of stern sadness in her
deep, feeling tone, as she turned her eyes on Mr.
Scott.

He felt the rebuke, and colouring high, he answered,
"I did not know—I could not be aware Miss Harcourt, that you would be anxious or willing to hear
any thing on these subjects."

"Oh!" said Isabella, "it is pleasant to speak to
the willing, but the unwilling need it most, Mr. Scott;
and perhaps many a one whom we fancy averse to
these things, may be only waiting for the electric

spark of the word of truth, to fire the whole train of
holy affections in their hearts. God will, doubtless,
always, if He see fit, apply it in His own best time;
but if we are backward in speaking, we lose the
crown."

"I confess," said Mr. Scott, with that genuine
humility which Mr. Singleton had truly said was so
beautiful a part of his character, "that I have deserved
your rebuke, Miss Harcourt, and may God pardon me,
and quicken me in His most delightful service.—You
will forgive me?"

"Oh! willingly; and I am sure you will now be
glad to 'water,' what another has 'planted;' though
we both know that God alone can 'give the increase.'"

"It is so indeed," replied Mr. Scott; "but you
seem to have found some one—have you not? more
faithful and kind than me, Miss Harcourt, to arouse
your mind?"

Isabella did not answer; for she shrank from entering on the subject, which yet she so much wished to
speak about.

"May I know—if it is not too much to ask—who
it was who was so much more faithful than me?"
again asked Mr. Scott, smiling, and slightly colouring.

"He was only an acquaintance of mine; though a
friend of yours," answered Isabella, mastering the difficulty she felt in speaking of Sir Roland, "and he knew
not at first, that I was a listener to his words."

"Ashton?" asked Mr. Scott, surprised.

Isabella Harcourt answered by an inclination of
the head.

"I never knew that he had talked to you on religious subjects," continued Mr. Scott; "I wonder he

never mentioned it, for he generally told me of any one for whom he felt a hope."

"Perhaps he did not feel one for me, last year; and yet I remember, that latterly, he would speak as if he thought I understood him."

"And was it solely by his means that your mind became enlightened? Did you never hear religious truth from any other?"

"I heard Mr. Singleton several times in the pulpit, and he was indeed delightful; but in conversation I never heard any one but *him;*—at dinners, or early evening parties."

"Your trials, perhaps," said Mr. Scott, in a feeling tone, "have helped to make the love of God precious to you."

"They have done much, indeed," she answered with a starting tear, "to hasten on the work; but oh! how our estimate of things changes as death draws near! What was once so terrible to me—the loss of my dear brother—is now all joy; excepting that I miss his sweet voice and looks so much."

"You have then comfort, Miss Harcourt, in thinking of his present state?"

"Comfort!" she exclaimed, her whole countenance lighting up, and her eyes beaming with the loftiest expression, as they were raised for an instant to heaven; —"Comfort is a cold word, Mr. Scott; I have all happiness in thinking of him."

"Was it his illness which inclined him to heavenly things?"

"Oh! no, not that alone; his health was always delicate; but it was not that; for formerly he would be impatient at his weakness, and murmur that he was cut off from the usual exercises and enjoyments of his age, and would think his a hard and cruel fate; and often then, though I felt it was not right, I knew not what to say to him. But last year, I heard words unlike what I had ever heard before, and I repeated them all to him, though I scarcely understood more than their general tendency myself; and then it was, that grace and love grew up in his heart; and often, very often, would he teach me the meaning of those things, of which the words alone, were all that I could teach him."

"Well, Miss Harcourt," said Mr. Scott, "you were kind enough to say that you hoped for good from me to-day, but you have taught me a lesson, which I trust I may never again forget—or neglect."

"I cannot wish you to forget any Heaven-taught lesson, Mr. Scott," replied Isabella kindly; "but you owe nothing to me; I was indeed to blame just now, in speaking to you, I fear harshly; but at the moment, such a horror seized me of what must have been my eternal state, had I been left to die with no brighter hope—no clearer faith, than the foolish fancies you alluded to, that I felt indignant—you will forgive me now"—and a look and smile of the utmost kindness glowed on her features, "that you who knew the way of life should have withheld the knowledge of it from me—and I, so evidently sinking."

"I would almost ask you," said Mr. Scott, with a pained look, "not to mention that subject again, though it is perhaps as well that we should be made to shrink under the sense of sin. The Lord often sees fit to humble us, and shew us our deficiencies on those very points, on which perhaps we have piqued ourselves as excelling; at least I know I have often thought, with great complacency, how very zealous I was in speaking, and now I am justly reproved for my want of zeal."

" You cannot I dare say, always speak as you would wish," said Isabella, "but try, oh! try; think of me—dying—and try."

Mr. Scott felt a sudden emotion which prevented him from answering immediately; but after a moment he replied,

" With the help of God, I will." He then added— " I cannot however grudge Ashton this 'crown of rejoicing'—for such I am confident it will be to him hereafter."

Isabella was infinitely relieved by Mr. Scott's thus making a way by which she might naturally, as it would seem, enter on the subject she wished so much to have communicated to Sir Roland; it was still however with great difficulty that she summoned up courage to say,

" I much wish that you should tell him how great a blessing he has been, not only to me, but also to my brother. His faith and love were indeed far higher and clearer, and more joyous than mine."

" He had less to bear," replied Mr. Scott. " It was, doubtless, hard for him to leave this world, especially so young; but that was his only source of trouble. You have had to bear the bitterer lot, of seeing him languish and depart; and this perhaps tends to sink and sadden your spirts, even though your faith may not be dimmed by it. He had not the trials you have had."

" Oh, no, no," she replied, pressing her hand on

her eyes, to stem back the tears which still would have
a way. " Yet," she continued, when she could command her voice—unconsciously adverting to the cause
of grief which she felt had helped to accelerate her fate
—" nothing would have saved my life—nothing could
have saved my life, and all is well ordered. I must be
happy soon, and though these foolish tears will come
sometimes, yet in general my mind is in perfect peace.
You will tell him that, will you? and of my brother,
that he may be encouraged to go on and speak for God
—always—every where. If the injunction is to be accepted concerning this world's wealth, ' Freely ye have
received, freely give;' how much more of the heavenly
treasure—the knowledge of Christ as our Saviour!
That inestimable gift we have indeed most freely received, and we should be ever ' ready to distribute,
willing to communicate,' of that which can make all
rich for eternity."

" Ashton will, I am sure, be most rejoiced to know
that his words have been the means of sustaining you,
not only under sickness and sorrow, but in the view
even, of——"

" Do not stop," said Isabella, faintly smiling, " I
can bear the word ' death,' for my mind is familiar with
the thought of it ; and, thank God, it brings no terrors.
You have been very good in coming to me, and I am
very, very glad to have seen you again."

" I deserve any thing but your thanks, Miss Harcourt," replied Mr. Scott, " but I am sure I owe much
to you; and shall I trust never again be forgetful of
the best interests of my fellow-creatures."

" No more of that," said Isabella, again smiling,
" that thought must now give place to the remem-

brance that you have been of comfort—great comfort
to me ; my heart feels much relieved and lightened by
having spoken to you, for the kindest and dearest
sometimes, cannot understand one.   But true Christians
must understand each other, they are taught the same
lesson, in the same school, by the same heavenly
Teacher.   Is not that what you understand by the
communion of saints ? that they, as true believers are
one body, of which Christ is the Head ?   That they
have one *commonality* in the Spirit of God, 'one Lord,
one Faith, one Baptism' of the Holy Ghost ? "

" Surely," replied Mr. Scott; " how else can it be
understood ?   Yes, that it is which spite of all errors in
unessential points—spite of all remaining infirmity,
binds the hearts of true Christians together, with a
chain whose links will be even more closely riveted in
heaven than they are upon earth ; for there—all dissen-
tient opinions, all erroneous feelings, will be done away
with for ever, and we shall all be 'made perfect in
Christ Jesus.'   The 'church triumphant' in heaven,
and the 'church militant still on earth,' are thus continually One, though its members occupy for a time
different chambers in God's universe.   Death cannot
separate those who are Christ's,

' Flesh it may sever, but not souls divide.' "

" It is a blessed and delightful view to me," said
Isabella, " especially when I think of Frederic ; and
raises the heart far above the things of this life, which
are but for a season—and so unsatisfying !   Yet I feel
very inconsistent; at times I seem so far above the
earth, that all its bustle, and jarring interests, cannot
touch, or trouble me, whilst at other times the least

thing will depress me.   But still God surrounds me
with blessings, with kind and loving friends, and every
comfort, and makes my passage to the tomb so smooth,
it seems all pleasure to slide gently down.   But I must
not detain you longer, Mr. Scott, your visit has been
very pleasant to me, and we know," she added, with a
happy smile, " that this will not be our last meeting —
nor our parting here—a parting for ever.   God bless
you."

" God ever bless you, Miss Harcourt," he replied,
with much emotion, " we shall indeed meet again."

A few days after this interview, Isabella Harcourt
was driving slowly in the carriage, in a retired part of
the environs of ——, with her mother, who had at last
become really alarmed about her, when Mr. Scott rode
by.   He reined back his horse, and she started up, intending to stop the carriage ; but her weakness was so
great that she sunk back again exhausted, and merely
smiled and shook her head, as if to say that she could
not speak ; and he passed on with a heavy heart.   She
never left the house again.   Mr. Scott went from ——
the next day, and in about a fortnight afterwards, he
read, recorded among the deaths in Galignani's paper,
" Isabella, third daughter of Henry Harcourt, Esq., in
her nineteenth year."

When dying, Isabella gave her Bible to her sister
Sophia, with earnest entreaty never to neglect its happy
truths ;   and when—after she was gone—her sister
opened the book, and found Sir Roland's card in it,
well did she remember the day in which Isabella wrote
the peace-giving text upon it, and took it for her Bible's
mark.   This little incident served to confirm an

idea she had long entertained; she had a quick observant mind, and young as she was, she had long suspected—having been so much with Isabella—that there was some grief, which preyed upon the mind of the latter, independent of the regret she felt for her brother—a grief which had fearfully increased from the night of her sudden illness. She had not noticed at the time, whose card it was, that Isabella had taken to write that passage on from the Scriptures, but when she found it was Sir Roland's, she instantly recollected his name as having frequently been mentioned between her brother and sister, and from that, and several other circumstances which now recurred to her, she felt convinced that Isabella had been attached to him, and that her attachment was not a happy one. She kept this secret, however, close in her own breast; whilst bitterly, with renewed grief, did she weep for the sorrow and suffering, which she had so often witnessed, without being fully aware of its cause.

Isabella Harcourt was buried in the same tomb with her brother; and at her earnest request, their names were united by an encircling line; and beneath them was written, "One Lord, one Faith!"

END OF VOL. I.

London : Printed by Moyes and Barclay, Castle Street, Leicester Square.

SIR ROLAND ASHTON.

LONDON:

PRINTED BY MOYES AND BARCLAY, CASTLE STREET,

LEICESTER SQUARE.

SIR ROLAND ASHTON.

A Tale of the Times.

BY

LADY CATHARINE LONG.

"He deemed it incumbent upon every individual, however humble, to offer the tribute of his influence and example, if they amounted but to a mite, on the altar of his God."—*Private Life.*

IN TWO VOLUMES.

VOL. II.

LONDON:

JAMES NISBET AND CO., BERNERS STREET.

MDCCCXLIV.

SIR ROLAND ASHTON:

𝔄 𝔗𝔞𝔩𝔢 𝔬𝔣 𝔱𝔥𝔢 𝔗𝔦𝔪𝔢𝔰.

CHAPTER I.

" My soul is full of words—my voice finds none ! "

Anon.

" The game of life
Looks cheerful, when one carries in one's heart
The unalienable treasure ! "—COLERIDGE.

WHEN Lady Ashton received the letter which it
had cost Sir Roland so much to write—containing his
request that Henry might not be made acquainted with
his engagement—she immediately informed Lady
Constance of it; and though they both felt surprised,
yet supposing that he had some good reason for his
determination, they of course acquiesced in it. Had
Lady Ashton been asked at that time, whether any
greater attachment than was desirable had sprung up
between Henry and Lady Constance, she would unhesitatingly have answered " No;" and had Lady Constance herself been applied to, she would have returned
the same answer. But if Henry had been asked, he
would at once have declared, that he loved Lady Constance more than his life, and that he fully believed his
love was returned by her. In each of these cases the
answers would have been made in all sincerity of

heart; for Lady Ashton had no suspicion of the truth, nor was Lady Constance in the least aware that Henry was attached to her, or that she felt for him otherwise than she had always done before. But Henry — thoroughly aware of the state of his own heart — had perceived with equal clearness what passed in Lady Constance's, and he was but too correct in thinking that she returned, in some measure at least, the unbounded affection which he felt for her.

It has been said that Lady Constance was wise, and right, in repressing Henry's expressions of regard for her on the first day of his arrival; and so she undoubtedly was; and yet unfortunately the effect was exactly contrary to that which she wished and intended; for from the very moment of her speaking, a change — the least to be desired — took place in the nature of his feeling for her, and rendered it one of devoted attachment. The enthusiastic admiration, which he had described in the letter which had so much troubled Sir Roland, was a most natural feeling for a sailor to have on his first emancipation from his watery prison, towards one, so charming as Lady Constance, and whom he had known and loved from a child; but it was a sentiment of so slight a nature, that had it been allowed a free expression, it might perhaps have remained merely on the surface of his mind, and have been soon effaced by absence; but the instant its outward demonstrations were repressed, it sunk deep into his heart, taking root there, and flourishing but too luxuriantly. He felt however from that moment, a restraint which prevented his ever again saying a syllable which could make Lady Constance imagine that he cherished for her any exclusive feeling, or aspired to

any greater degree of favour than he had ever before
possessed; and thus she was deluded into a perfect security of feeling as regarded both him and herself.
She had been accustomed from early years to have
him as her almost inseparable companion, whenever
he was at home, so that it was no new, or marvellous
thing now, that he should be constantly at her side.
He had ever lavished on her all the tender and affectionate attentions which a devoted brother could bestow on a favourite sister, and she was not surprised
therefore, at now again receiving them; and his fear
was so great lest he should say any thing which might
offend her, that it placed a check on all expressions
which could have given her an insight into his feelings;
and if at times he had unwittingly paid her any attention
which might have seemed particular, he instantly did
something of the same kind also for Lady Florence, so
as to take away all appearance of preference.

He could not account to himself for the spell which
thus seemed laid upon him, but he was not the less
conscious of it; and it not only affected his manner to
Lady Constance herself, but it had an influence also on
his way of speaking of her to others.   Even in writing to
his brother, he felt such a restraint in mentioning her, that
he could not open his heart to him, as he had been ever
used to do, and this made all his later letters differ so
much in tone and feeling, from the animated avowal
of his delighted admiration, which he had written on
the morning of his return to Llanaven.   It was not
however, Lady Constance's first check on his conversation alone, which produced this effect; but that judicious and proper step on her part was so consist-
ently followed up by the quiet, and almost dignified con-

duct which she maintained, that he felt a respect for her, and almost an awe, which he could not overcome, and which made him love her all the more; for the heart which if lightly won, might have been lightly prized, appeared to him worth every sacrifice. He controlled even his very looks therefore, lest they should offend, and though he could not understand why he might not love, and tell her that he did so, yet he felt that though he did love, he could not tell her so. This feeling was the more unaccountable to him, because he could not but think that he perceived that she liked him—that she was ever happy to be with him, as he was ever enchanted to be with her. Her manner to him in other respects too was as free and intimate as in their earliest days; and lively-spirited as they both were, they amused themselves in their light-hearted conversations, or in their rambles about the cliffs, with as much zest and pleasure as did their young companion Lady Florence herself.

Totally unsuspicious, Lady Ashton rejoiced to see Lady Constance's recovered gaiety, and Henry's happiness; and she encouraged as much as possible every thing which could contribute to their cheerful pleasures, often joining in their walks and expeditions, and seeming to grow young again herself, amidst their animated smiles. Throughout all, however, Henry Ashton felt the subduing power of Lady Constance's manner, and never could he go beyond the limits it imposed.

It was not that Lady Constance purposely acted in that way, for she had no idea of any thing existing in Henry's mind, which required repression. Had she dreamed that he liked her, she would instantly — notwithstanding Sir Roland's express wish to the contrary

—have informed him of the position in which she stood, and have ended his hopes for ever; but she saw nothing that could awaken the slightest suspicion, and her conduct resulted merely from the sense of what she owed to herself, and to Sir Roland, which a pure high-principled feeling instinctively taught her. Her deep regard for the latter indeed, continually increased, for it was impossible to be allowed an insight into his noble mind, without loving and admiring him; and, unaware of any preference for Henry, she wrote in answer to his letters, with all the warmth of old affection; expressing continually a regret—which was most sincere and genuine—that he was not with them to share, and increase their pleasures. Henry too, continually wrote to the same effect, for he knew no reason why he should dread his brother's presence; on the contrary, he often longed to have him there, that he might speak to him of the sentiments, of which nevertheless he could not write. These letters so unintentionally deluding, completely lulled all those fears in Sir Roland's breast, which had been so terribly excited at —— ; and an undoubting confidence sprang up, which increased his love and happiness a thousand-fold.

It being summer time, the party at Llanaven dined early, and then enjoyed the whole of the delightful evenings out in the air; often indeed prolonging their rambles, till the stars were the only lights to guide them home. This style of living brought Henry and Lady Constance continually together, and indeed they were seldom separated; for Henry having no public business and no superintendance of the property to occupy him, as Sir Roland had, was able to devote all his time to his mother and to his *sisters.* With his feelings, this life was of course most delightful, and it is not to be supposed that it was without its charm for Lady Constance, who thus unconsciously learnt to find Henry's society indispensable to her happiness. Had Sir Roland enjoyed equal advantages in these respects with his brother, he would in all probability have been equally, if not even more beloved; for there was much more in fact in his character that suited Lady Constance, than in Henry's : there were far higher attainments, a deeper tone of feeling, and a purer and more exalted sense of religion. The graces of the Spirit in him seemed indeed, scarcely to derive any assistance from the things of earth, but to be entirely maintained from above; and might be, not unaptly, compared to the flowers which grow in the loftier regions of the Alps, with scarcely a grain of soil to nourish their growth; but which, ' rooted in the rifted rock,' and blooming with a splendour and brilliancy of colour unknown to others of their kind, ' disdain,' as Rogers charmingly says,

> " To grow in lower climes,
> And delighted drink the clouds before they fall."

But Henry's feelings were more like the flowers of the lower ranges of the mountains, which having a greater depth of earthy soil between them and the ' rock,' expand in wilder profusion, though with hues far less pure and bright; and which, unable to support themselves alone, seek to twine about the plants of congenial growth which flourish around. Much indeed, of the love of God dwelt in his heart, but there was more admixture of earthly feeling in him, than in his brother;

and his piety, though true and warm, was more tinctured with the inconsistency, so often to be found in persons of light and joyous tempers. Nevertheless there was a frankness and warmth in his disposition and manners, which made him a universal favourite— one whom every one felt it was impossible not to love· He was the very perfection of a sailor! full of the fire and enthusiasm—the romance, poetry, wild gaiety, and sentiment, which so often unite their incongruous materials in the formation of those restless beings— the most delightful perhaps to think of—the least satisfactory perhaps in general to live with, (naval reader of course excepted) of all mortals in existence!

The evenings at Llanaven generally ended with music, for Henry Ashton had a fine voice, and often joined the sisters in their songs; Lady Ashton also occasionally assisting in their concerts. Lady Florence, though in most things remarkably childish for her age, shewed uncommon talents both for playing and singing; and was, in those accomplishments, quite equal to her sister.

"I never can go to sea again," said Henry, flourishing about the room, after they had been singing one of his favourite songs, "never! Fancy, after all this divine harmony, going where the whole of one's music is ' Piping to dinner,' or heaving your anchor up to the strains of a two-stringed fiddle? I shall die no other death!"

"Oh! yes, you will have the winds whistling through the shrouds, to enliven you," said Lady Constance.

"Delightful prospect, certainly!" answered Henry.
" No—

'I'll go no more to the roaring seas,'

I'll work for my bread no longer.   Ambition's torch is quenched within me."

"Did it ever burn very fiercely?"

"Often; once indeed I was nearly destroyed by its spontaneous combustion.   We were in a boat, and wanted to land from the ship; but a heavy surf beating us continually back, in a fit of desperation I jumped overboard, and swam to shore with a rope, and by that means we all got in at last.   Like a blockhead as I was, I went in with all my clothes on, which, by a natural process, became saturated with salt water.   Hearing I was drenched, the captain of a man-of-war near, sent for me on board, and kindly rigged me out in one of his own uniforms: a post-captain's uniform!—Ye powers! what I felt! laughing gas was desperation—despondency to it!—Two epaulettes!—one on each shoulder!—None of the 'single blessedness' of your lieutenant's rig.   No—the perfect—the right thing!   I looked from shoulder to shoulder till they seemed to expand into wings of gigantic dimensions, bearing up my soaring genius beyond the extremest Ararat of all fame and glory!   My breast swelled with things too big for earth or seas!—I was very near ordering the captain off his own quarter-deck—but I stopped just short of that insanity; and an unlucky fire having dried my own garments—which at that moment appeared to me the most despicable things on earth—I was forced to put them on again—constrained to

'Forget the captain, and resume the mid.'

The change was disgusting!—nauseous in the extreme. But now, I have given ambition to the winds, and only long to be allowed to vegetate in this spot all my life. This 'dolce far niente' life is so very charming!"

"'Dolce' it is," said Lady Constance, "but I refuse to call it 'far niente;' I think we are very busy, and well employed."

"I am sure," exclaimed Lady Florence, "I am always 'stowing away' some piece of knowledge or other, as you would say."

"I cry you mercy, fair dames," said Henry, "I did not mean to despise your doings—nor indeed my own. I think we are mightily active, hard-working people. But when one has been used to the rough life of a sailor, battling it with the elements, turning out for night-watches with the thermometer below zero, &c., this inexpressibly delectable existence seems all like a delightful stream of self-indulgence; it is like passing through the soft summer air, where one is unconscious of any resistance.—'How shall I hence depart?'"

"We will not think about it till the time comes," said Lady Ashton, with a sigh; "that will be quite soon enough."

"But when 'self' is good, Henry, to indulge it is good also," observed Lady Constance.

"That is a very pleasant piece of philosophy of yours," he replied, "but rather of the Epicurean school, is it not?"

"No," she answered: "the Epicurean would follow 'self' without making any very minute inquiries as to the character it bore; but malign it as you will, if rightly understood, mine is true Christian philosophy. It is that, we must remember," she added more gravely, "which constitutes the happiness of the angels in heaven, and which will will form ours there too some day I hope; for there our will will be God's, and God's ours. When our 'will' or our 'self' becomes perfectly in unison with God's will, then our holiness is, as Erskine says, 'purified from self-denial.' I delight in that idea, it is so original, and so true! I like all that passage of his," and rising she fetched the book, and read from one of Erskine's delightful introductions: "'There is no self-denial in the character of God, it is His delight to do that which is good. Neither would there be any self-denial in our virtue, if we perfectly loved God, because that love would find its highest gratification in a conformity to the will of God. But how are we to grow in this love? How is our holiness to be purified from self-denial? No otherwise, than by abiding in the love of God, as revealed in Jesus Christ.' "

"I have nothing to advance against that, certainly," said Henry Ashton, "only that it makes me out to be very rebellious, I am afraid; for it costs me sometimes an immense deal of self-denial to do even the least little bit of good; which I fear proves that 'self' with me is intrinsically bad."

"It is so with us all, dear Henry," said Lady Ashton, "it was only Christ who could say, 'the prince of this world cometh, and hath *nothing in me.*' I am afraid he possesses large territories in all of our hearts; but still in the main, our way of life may, if we are God's children, be good, and pleasant too."

"I grant it—I know my life is very pleasant now;

and I am quite willing to believe, on your assurances, kind friends, that it is very good also. But now, Constance, let us come a little to particulars as to this ' dolce far molto' life of ours. To begin.—What good is it to keep pricking the air through loops of silk, with that species of small harpoon which you are using there ? "

" My 'crochet' work, do you mean ? "

" Yes, if that's what you call it. But to proceed— after the manner of the old hen in ' Water my chickens,' (how I should like to play at that game once more in my life) I ask, what is the ' crochet' work for ? "

" To make a purse."

" What is the purse for ? "

" To hold money."

" Whose money ? "

" Yours—if you can get any."

" I have done," he answered, looking up from the drawing he was finishing, with a pleased smile, " I am a perfect convert to the truth of all your positions."

" You liked the one I did for Roland the other day," said Lady Constance, " so I thought in the fulness of my generosity, that I would do one for you too."

" Did *you* do that purse for Roland ? " said Henry, looking down again at his drawing, while his colour heightened a little—for he would have preferred having had the first done for himself —" I thought it had been my mother."

" No," replied Lady Ashton, " I sent him one some time ago."

" Ah ! he needs more of them than I do," said Henry.

He felt at that moment what he had scarcely ever

felt in his life before: an inclination to be irritated with his brother; and the question arose in his mind: why Sir Roland should have so very large a fortune, whilst he had, as he called it, 'to work for his bread.' But this mood was too intolerable to last, so, "Pshaw," he thought, "it is much better for me to have something to do, and not be an idle fellow all my life; and he can never have more than he knows how to use well;" and the momentary cloud passed away.

It was in truth a matter of surprise to many that Sir Roland's property being so very large, his brother should have been left with a mere younger son's fortune of a few thousand pounds. But their father had purposely so disposed it, for he was thoroughly acquainted with the dispositions of his two sons, though they were but boys at the time of his death; and he felt convinced, that to leave an independent fortune, to one of Henry Ashton's volatile temperament, and reckless disposition, would be the thing in the world most likely to injure, and perhaps even, completely ruin him. He also well knew the noble and generous temper of his eldest son, and he was confident that he could with perfect security leave all Henry's interests in his keeping; and therefore, with the exception of ten thousand pounds to the latter, he left the whole of his vast property to him.

"Well, Henry," said Lady Constance, after an unusually long pause in their conversation, "have you laid by the character of inquisitor?"

"No, I am going to put Florence to the 'question' next — What are you doing there, Giovinetta, with that many-coloured piece of silk, which looks like all the signals in the navy sewn together?"

"I am making a case with many divisions."

"What is the case for?"

"Needles, and other implements for working."

"Who for?"

"You, if you know how to use it."

"Ah! I see I ought to have examined my witnesses separately; you are too cunning—you landswomen —for us simple mariners; but nevertheless, I mean to be an incorruptible judge, spite of all your 'sops for Cerberus.' What makes you fancy I ever used needles and thread, or such unseemly, and womanly trumpery, Signora Firenze?"

"I have heard that sailors like to mend their clothes instead of going in rags and tatters, so I thought I would supply you with the means of making a decent appearance."

"But there is no 'true blue' after all, amongst the rainbow colours you have got together there."

"I keep that for the last; when you are going away it will be time enough to 'hoist the blue Peter.'"

"You are getting a great deal too nautical for me, young lady, and very unfeeling to boot, to mention such a thing. That detested signal ought to be expunged out of the books of the Admiralty;" and he sung low in his 'moonlight voice'—

> "Parte la nave, spiéga le vele
> Vento crudele, mi fa partir."

But instead of the "Addio," &c. with which the verse concludes, a heavy sigh burst forth, at the thought of the bitter hour of parting that must come so soon.

CHAPTER II.

"They know th' Almighty's power,
　Who, waken'd by the rushing midnight shower,
　Watch for the fitful breeze
　To howl and chafe amid the bending trees,
　Watch for the still white gleam
　To bathe the landscape in a fiery stream,
　Touching the tremulous eye with sense of light
　Too rapid and too pure for all but angel sight.

"They know th' Almighty's love,
　Who, when the whirlwinds rock the topmost grove,
　Stand in the shade, and hear
　The tumult with a deep exulting fear,
　How, in their fiercest sway,
　Curb'd by some power unseen, they die away,
　Like a bold steed that owns his rider's arm,
　Proud to be check'd and sooth'd by that o'ermastering charm.

"But there are storms within
　That heave the struggling heart with wilder din."
　　*　　　　*　　　　*　　　　*　　　　*　　　　*

　　　　　　　　　　　　　　　　　　　KEBLE.

　　" A grief without a pang, void, dark and drear,
　　　　A stifled, drowsy, unimpassioned grief,
　　　　Which finds no natural outlet, no relief
　　In word, or sigh, or tear."
　　　　　　　　　　　　　　　　COLERIDGE.

A PARTY of friends and neighbours were invited to
stay a few days at Llanaven, which was an intolerable
annoyance to Henry Ashton, who could ill brook to

have his present happy mode of life broken in upon, by persons in whom he felt no interest. A few mornings before they were to arrive, he was walking with his mother and the two sisters on the shore; the wind was rising, and a dark line in the distance of the ocean, shewed that the rough waves of the Atlantic were pouring in.

"There will be a gale before night," he said. — "It is strange, that I never care for a storm when I am at sea, but hate to hear the wind howl and rave when I am on shore. I never could enter into that somewhat selfish feeling of Lucretius :

'Suave, mari magno turbantibus æquora ventis
E terra magnum alterius spectare laborem.'

You understand my beautiful Latin of course, good people?"

"I do just understand that," said Lady Ashton smiling, "because I have heard it before from one, whose heart is kind and feeling, as your own. Roland often edifies us by his quotations; considerately translating them for the benefit of the unlearned."

"I rather think, Henry," said Lady Florence, "that you must have been the sailor, who when the slates and tiles were *skirrying* about his head in a high wind, wished himself 'snug at sea.'"

"No bad wish either, Flory; but however, it is not quite that; the slates and tiles do not frighten me; but you see all hands are employed on board ship in a stiff gale, and one has no time to be afraid, however much one may have the inclination."

"It must be very fearful though," said Lady

Ashton, whose heart sickened at the thought of Henry's frequent exposures, "to feel at such times that there is 'nothing but a plank between us and eternity.'"

"There is really no danger, dear mother, in a man-of-war, unless indeed one gets on a lee shore. But now, when I hear the winds roaring and storming, I have time to sit and think how many brave fellows may be sinking and drowning; — in how many places perhaps in 'the dead of night,' the 'seaman's cry is heard along the deep.' Then I call to mind all the thrilling magnificence of a sea-storm, till I find myself trembling at the thought of things which have no power to shake a nerve when I am actually in the midst of them. Dear mother! I dare say you often lie awake and think of me till your poor heart sinks, as you hear the waves thunder on the shore, and the winds blow as if they would tear the old house to pieces! but remember, the wind seldom blows with you, and me, at the same time; —and then, as I said before, there really is scarcely ever any danger for a man-of-war."

Lady Ashton pressed the arm of her son while he stooped down to kiss her tearful cheek. "I will try and remember your words, dear," she said, "I shall need comfort from them now, more than ever, for I shall more than ever dread evil to you."

"Why more than ever?"

"Because you are dearer to me than ever."

Henry's heart swelled for a moment—then in his gayest tone he said, "I see I must begin to make my-self detestable that you may all be glad when I go away. I am too irresistible now, am I not, Florence?

But, Constance, you were asking me the other day
about storms in the Atlantic. In former days I used
to fancy that a vessel went up and down the waves like
a horse galloping over a hilly country ; (though I had
no idea then of the hills into which the waters piled
themselves,) but that is not at all the case. When
there is is a furious wind, of course, one moves rapidly,
but not nearly so much so even then, as the waves ;
but when there is no wind, only the terrible swell after
a storm, then the ship lies supine on the waters, which
rise and fall horribly under her ; bearing her up one
moment as if she was going to scale the heavens, and
then sinking away from under her till she seems buried
in an abyss, with huge mountains of water on every
side. At such times one can observe the dread magnificence of the thing ; for there is comparatively but
little to do ; but when the wind blows a hurricane, one
has no time for observation, for every nerve and muscle
is on the stretch. It is as much as one can do to prevent going overboard ; and the straining and groaning
of the vessel is awful ; and sometimes she hangs on the
summit of a mountainous wave — for the waves at such
times, are of course much higher and sharper than in
the mere swell — and quivers as if she recoiled from the
fearful descent before her ; just as a horse might rear,
and back, and tremble, refusing to leap into a chasm.
That is horrible, appalling ! and if one had but the
time, one might then be terrified to one's heart's content ; but as I told you, one is happily too busy to
suffer much. But the swell is perfectly sickening till
one gets accustomed to the motion ; you can imagine
it — as nearly as the creeping of a flea can give you an
idea of the actions of an elephant — from the sensation

in the descent of a swing, which was always intolerable
to me. Do you remember, Constance, our once watching an unlucky turnip which had got into the sea, by
means best known to itself? It was a stormy day,
and every wave as it came curling onwards to break
on the shore, bore turnip on its foaming crest, and we
always expected to see it thrown up at our feet, and
determined to wait till we had got it; but when the
wave rolled over and dashed itself to pieces—turnip
slid down its back;—then again rode in triumph on
the ridge of the next wave—then again slid down the
back of that one; and so on with every one in succession, till at last we gave up the hopeless vegetable, and
came home to dinner without it."

"I remember it perfectly," said Lady Constance,
"and recollect the provocation I felt at seeing it continually disappear, and afterwards beholding it swimming
with the utmost tranquillity, amidst the coating of white
bubbles which covered the water after the wave had
broken on the shore."

"Well, that is exactly the way one is carried up
and down at the will of the mighty waves in those
great seas, after the violence of the storm is over.
There one lies like a log on the immensity of the waters
submitting in passive helplessness to its caprices; now
aloft, now below. I often thought of what this dear
mother of mine would have likened it to; that she
would have said: 'Thus we ought to repose on God's
providence, and in acquiescing faith, and unquestioning dependence, resign ourselves to all the variations of
fate, which the great and good Ruler of storm and
calm might deem it best to send us.'

'That on his guiding arm unseen
  Our undivided hearts might lean;
  And this our frail and foundering bark
  Glide in the narrow wake of his beloved ark.'

Have I guessed right, my dearest, best, and wisest
mother?"

"It might have so occurred to me, Henry, but I
delight in having it as your own thought; and I trust
the remembrance of your words may often be allowed
to bring down quieting balm to my faithless, and
trembling heart, when I hear the storms rage—and
think of you."

Henry felt much affected, and was silent for a
time. At length he exclaimed, "How the wind rises!
it will blow 'great guns' to-night, Flory; I hate these
on-shore winds; there is sure to be mischief somewhere or other on this coast."

Henry Ashton was right; it blew a hurricane all
that night, and all the next day. The ocean was
covered with breakers as far as the eye could reach;
and the foam and spray from the waves below, as they
dashed against the rocks, flew over the very tops of the
cliffs. In the afternoon of the next day the wind having
lulled a little, Lady Constance ventured forth with
Henry, to view the magnificence of the scene. A few
hours before, he had "swept the horizon" with his glass,
and not a ship was to be seen; but now one vessel was
just discernible, though what she was they could not
make out; but proceeding along the cliff they found
one of the preventive men on his stormy look-out.

"What is she?" asked Henry, as they came up,

for the old man was attentively examining the vessel
with his telescope.

"Can't say rightly, sir; the spray dashes over her
so, she's all in a haze."

"Give me a look with your glass," said Henry;
and he took it out of the sailor's hand. "Your focus
does not quite suit me," he added, altering it.

"May be, sir," replied the man, while a good-
humoured smile lighted up his tanned and seamed
visage, "old and young seldom see alike, Mr. Henry."

"Except through one glass, old shipmate," answered the other. "Good John Bunyan's glass of
faith—all see alike through that—old and young—
rich and poor.—Isn't it so?"

"Aye, aye, sir," said the old man, shaking his head,
"an' we look steady enough—all see alike there; no
doubt of that."

"I can't make her out yet," said Henry, still examining the vessel through the glass, "she seems to
labour prodigiously. What is she likely to be? Is
there any steamer due?"

"No, sir; none of the great ones any how."

"Let me look at it," said Lady Constance; and she
watched it for a few minutes.

"It is not a steamer," she said, "I see it distinctly now—it is no steamer, but I do not know
what kind of vessel it is."

"It would puzzle a much more experienced eye
than yours, Constance, to make her out now," replied
Henry; "but we will take another turn, for it must be
shivering work for you to be standing here, and we
will ask Dickson to give us another look by-and-bye."

"It is not cold," said Lady Constance, "though it is blustering; it is like billows of cotton in one's face—the wind is so very soft."

"Have you often such gales in England at this time of year?" asked Henry; "I have been so long away, that I almost forget the behaviour of the elements in this remote corner of the globe."

"Do not speak slightingly of us," replied Lady Constance; "remote we may be, but like the spider who sits in a corner, we spread our dominion far and wide."

"And do you think I've touched my hat to the royal colours so many, many hundreds of times," asked Henry, "without fully appreciating the value and power of the flag which 'has braved a thousand years, the battle and the breeze?'"

"No, I dare say you are very proud of it as it floats over your head; but why do you touch your hat to it?"

"It is the ensign of the sovereignty we serve, and no sailor in a man-of-war ever mounts the ship's side without touching his hat to it, as he puts his foot upon the deck. Majesty is always supposed to be present there."

"I like that," said Lady Constance, "for I am sure those external things keep up the inward feeling very much. I wouldn't have been born in a republic for any thing, the feeling of loyalty is so ennobling and delightful. I am sure I could die for the queen."

"Well, dearest Constance," replied Henry, looking delightedly at her animated, and beautiful countenance, "I trust for both your sakes you will never be put to the trial—though I feel sure you would not fail."

"I do so delight," said Lady Constance, "in the juxtaposition of those two apostolic injunctions: 'Fear God, honour the king.'"

"So do I," replied Henry, "and nothing is wanting when one is sure, that in following one's own feelings one is also obeying the Lord; 'duty and delight going hand in hand.'"

"How bright then," observed Lady Constance, "will be the time when in obeying the Lord, we shall be invariably following our own feelings—our will, as we were saying the other day, being lost in God's. Now it is a perpetual warfare, the old nature against the new; and the heart is often so sluggish too, in its endeavours for others! No one knows the exertion it is to me sometimes to go to the school, or the cottages, to read to the people, or teach the children. On hot indolent summer days, how often I long to sit on the cliffs and do nothing but enjoy my existence, listening to the booming waters, watching the woods just stirring in the air, or fixing my eye listlessly for ages on the ceaseless waves which roll on and on, till they 'die upon the shore.' And then what trouble it is to make myself go and do what I ought! And yet I love the poor children, and my heart quite yearns over them, when I am amongst them; and if I see any good doing in any one of their souls, oh! it is worth all the landscapes upon earth! But it would fare ill with me if I lived amongst those who did not keep up the warmth of heavenly love in my heart. Here you all help me; my mother with her most persuasive way, entices me on—you animate me, and make all cheerful with your high spirits; and Roland," and a sigh composed of mingled feelings rose to her lips—"with him I am convinced I could go to the stake; his standard is so high, his zeal so unflagging, his love so perfect!—one is ashamed to be left so far behind!"

Henry's brow was knit for a moment; he loved his brother almost, if not to the full, as intensely as he did Lady Constance, but any thing which seemed to bring the hearts of those two beloved beings too near to each other, gave him a pang which made him inwardly start, and which ruffled for the instant, the deep, pure stream of his brotherly love. To a superstitious fancy it might have seemed that he intuitively dreaded evil from that quarter—though there was then no appearance of any thing to trouble him. His brow however soon relaxed, as the secret conviction (which he certainly had) that he was the most beloved of the two, stole over his mind, and a glow of repentant love towards his brother warmed his heart as he answered,—

"Yes, one could not only go to the stake *with* him, but *for* him."

"Dear Henry!" exclaimed Lady Constance, her heart full of affection for both the brothers.

Again the cloud passed over Henry's mind and brow, and he could not return her bright look with an untroubled smile; for he knew not whether it was the sense of what his brother deserved, or his own devotion to him, which had brought forth her approving exclamation. But hating himself for the feelings which came thus, like the glances of a demon's eye, across his breast, he drew himself hastily up with a sort of shudder, and unconsciously quickened his pace, as if to escape from some haunting evil.

"Are you cold?" said Lady Constance wondering

at his shivering, and at his rapid movements, "this blustering gale is I think, so warm ; it is such an exertion to 'make head against it' as you would say."

"Yes," replied Henry, as his mind resumed its quiet, "and you miserable women carry so much sail, I wonder you can make any way at all."

"I think I should have been blown down several times to-day," answered Lady Constance, "if it had not been for your strong arm."

They drew near again to the old seaman, with whom they found Lady Ashton talking, she having been tempted forth by Lady Florence.

"Well, Dickson, can you make her out yet?"

"Yes, Mr. Henry, plain enough now ; she is some merchant-vessel, and seems terribly crippled by the storm. She has got up signals of distress, and I doubt whether she will hold out long."

"Long enough to get into Falmouth I hope," said Henry ; "the wind blows a hurricane again now, and she ought to fly like the scud before it."

"She will never get there, sir ;. she is water-logged, I'm thinking," replied the man.

"Give me your glass. She is indeed," said Henry, after carefully examining the vessel, which was now about a mile to the westward of them, with scarcely a sail set, and the waves continually breaking over her. "If she ships many more seas she will go down. We must get out to her, Dickson, or all hands may perish."

"Bless you ! Mr. Henry—what boat could live in such a sea, amongst these rocks and breakers ? it would be a sheer tempting of Providence."

"It must be tried though, Master Dickson," replied Henry coolly, "you don't think I shall let those poor fellows go down before my eyes without an effort to save them?"

He again raised the glass. "There's a woman on board," he exclaimed, "I am sure I made one out. Do you look, Dickson."

"There are two," said the old man quietly, as he kept the glass steady to his eye, "and a child too, or I'm mistaken."

"Dickson," said Henry hurriedly, "you cannot leave your post I know, but your walk extends nearly to the house; do you go back with the ladies, in case the wind proves too strong for them. I must go and get help down at the village."

"It's madness—and can't be thought of," said the sailor, grasping Henry Ashton's arm like a vice; "we must let matters take their course, for we can't mend 'em."

"You talk like a hard-hearted wretch," exclaimed Henry, his eyes flashing as he shook off the old man's grasp.

Dickson touched his hat in quaint acknowledgment of the compliment paid him, and quietly answered, "Not a bit, sir, I'm as sorry as can be, both for the women and the young 'un; but nothing will save them, and there's no use throwing away good lives after bad."

Henry Ashton turned from him not choosing to argue further when his mind was made up.

"My dear mother," he said, "you will go home, will you not, with Constance and Florence? it will only make you nervous watching my cockle-shell as it tosses about; but I assure you there will be but little danger when we have once passed the surf and rocks near the shore."

"Ay, *when!*" said Dickson, doggedly—shaking his head.

Henry Ashton felt infinitely provoked at the old man's pertinacious doubts, especially as by expressing them, he was likely to alarm Lady Ashton as to the result of his venturous experiment. With a somewhat quivering smile he continued, "Do not mind him, dear mother, his blood is old and cold, but a stout heart and strong arm will do much, with the blessing of God, in such a cause."

"But if it is so hopeless," said Lady Ashton in terror—evidently divided between her natural affection and her warm benevolence,—and clinging to her son's arm.

"It is not so hopeless, dearest mother," replied Henry soothingly ; "and how could you endure for me to go home and sit quietly, whilst the ocean was swallowing up my fellow-creatures—I, almost within hearing of their cries. Look at that vessel, and remember it contains human beings, who to all appearance must soon meet with a watery grave unless we can help them. Think of all their terror, their agony —the loss in many cases perhaps of soul as well as body—think of women like yourself, and of that little child!"

He paused, and Lady Ashton burying her face on his arm, murmured, " Go—go, I cannot keep you— their blood would be upon my soul."

She threw her arm around his neck, and kissed him—as if perhaps for the last time ; but her heart was

strong, though her tears burst forth. He pressed her
to his breast, and then motioned to Dickson to follow
her, as she resolutely turned to. go home. Lady
Florence went with her, but Lady Constance who had
watched with fixed look, and bloodless cheek, the result of Henry's conference with his mother, stood like
a statue—utterly incapable of moving.

"Constance," said Henry, with a tremor in his
voice—for he was fully aware of the danger of the
venturous attempt he was about to make—"you will
wish me 'God speed,' will you not?   You will pray for
me?—My best—my dearest—my most beloved!" he
continued vehemently, as he pressed her hand to his
lips, and burst into tears—for he thought that this
might be their last meeting, and all restraint gave way
before his strong emotion,—"you will pray for me?"

Lady Constance could not speak, nor did a tear
wet her eye; all she seemed to have of life was the
power of breathing, and of suffering.

"Speak to me, Constance," continued Henry,
"time must not be lost, but even now, if you tell me
to stay—but no, you could not do it—you could not
desire it—but oh! if you knew what I feel at leaving
you—you to whom now for the first time—it may be
for the last—I dare to say how much—how completely
you are all the world to me—my hope—my joy—my
first—my only love! Oh! forgive me," he added,—
"you will forgive me at such a time as this, and if I
perish—you will at least know how you were every
thing—every thing to me!—My dearest! you will bid
me go, will you not?"

He listened for her answer, and at last caught the
scarcely audible word by which she sent him from her.

He stood, for a moment, as if he could not part—then flew down the path that led to the village, nor once turned to look on her, whom he felt he might be leaving for ever.

Lady Constance sat down on the cliff, where Henry Ashton had parted from her, with her hands clasped on her knee. She seemed perfectly torpid ; as if a sleep had come over every thought. Her eye followed the waves as they rolled in towards the shore, as if her only motive for staying there was to watch their ceaseless motion; at times she looked at the unfortunate vessel, but regarded it without the smallest emotion, nor remembered that there were perishing souls on board, whose fate at another time would have awakened the utmost anxiety in her breast. She did not even think of Henry; for in fact her mind was for the time incapable of framing, or retaining any one defined idea. " Feeling itself seemed almost unfelt ;" for the terrible emotion which for an instant had swept across her soul had benumbed her by its very intensity. She felt no pain of body or of mind, only a sense of suffocation seemed to rest on both. The spray, continually dashing up from the thundering waves below, almost drenched her, and the wind blew her hair across her face and eyes, but she was scarcely aware of it, though sometimes she raised her hand and mechanically threw it back.

It was not the sense of Henry's danger which thus oppressed her ; had that been her grief, her spirit wakened to double life, would, as it were, have lived in the presence of God, for him, and for his safety— but it was his love which stunned her—a love so fatal —so unlooked for—so fraught with every evil and

every misery. Yet even that was scarcely so overwhelming to her, as the conviction, which the last short
hour had brought with it, that she returned his feelings—that he was indeed all to her, as she was every
thing to him! She might have lived in his presence
for ever, without being aware of the nature of her
feelings; but parting!—that it was which rent the
veil from her eyes—and by shewing her her own heart,
brought with it, an anguish so intolerable!—that had
its impression remained on her mind in all its first
vividness, life or reason must have given way under its
dreadful force. She remained on that bleak point till
old Dickson, having seen Lady Ashton and her young
companion safe under the shelter of the trees at Llanaven, returned to her.

"You'd best let me see you home, my lady," said
the old man, as he stood sorrowfully by the poor girl;
"it's bad walking against such a storm for one like
you, by yourself. You'll scarcely keep your feet a
minute; and may be might be blown over the cliff
when the wind takes one of its slants. Shall I help you
up?" he continued, taking her arm with rough kindness;
for he saw the utter sorrow of her face.

She rose, and walked by the sailor's side, who often
stayed her with his arm, when the wind was too strong
against her, and who strove with homely feeling to
cheer her evident dejection.

"It was hard," he said, "to see fellow-creatures
in such jeopardy; but many had been saved in worse
straits than that, and Mr. Henry had a cool head as
well as a stout heart and arm; and as he *would* go, it
was to be hoped God would take care of him, and send
him safe ashore again."

These and many other topics of consolation passed
Lady Constance's ear, but one word chased another
from her mind. At the entrance to the shrubbery
however, she turned to thank the kind old man, whose
features worked with strong feeling as he answered,

" You thank me for nothing, young lady,—but
you will pray, no doubt for Mr. Henry, that it may
please the Lord to prosper him, and send him back; it
is no common job he has got in hand," and he turned
to resume his watchful walk.

Lady Constance paused when she had closed the
shrubbery gate:

" Pray for him," she thought, as her powers of
mind began to rouse a little from their sleep; " Pray
for his return!—oh! no—better for him to sink into
the ocean, than return to hear—what he must hear."

She walked on, and her thoughts became gradually
clearer and clearer, though her feelings still continued
unmoved. When she had passed the thick shrubbery,
she came upon the open lawn which stretched quite to
the cliffs' edge; and there she found her sister who, as
the view was intercepted from the house by trees, had
had a table brought out, and set under the shelter of
the shrubbery on the opposite side, in order to support
a standing telescope, through which she was intently
gazing on the vessel, which was by that time almost
opposite the house.

" It seems lower in the water than it was, Constance," she said, when she saw her sister approach,
" Oh! if it should go down before any help comes!
and I see nothing of the boat yet!"

CHAPTER III.

"Why should I fear because the surges roll?
I have one life!—God gave it me—one life
To use for Him and man—I will not fear!"—MS.

THE spot where Henry Ashton had left Lady Constance, was a bluff, high point in Llanaven Park, from which the ground gradually descending on both sides, formed two coves, beyond which the high cliffs immediately rose again.   Sir Roland's house was situated about midway down the descent to the west, the ground continuing to slope from it, quite to the level of the shore.   The woods, feathering in some parts almost to the water's edge, and in others, waving over the cliffs, were interspersed with glades of the greenest turf; and with dells, where the deer crouched down amid high fern, and glowing heather; and where the delicate heath peculiar to Cornwall grew in rich profusion; the scene altogether contrasting beautifully in its calm and quiet, with the full swell and bright, restless, sparkling, of the ever-sounding sea.

In the cove to the east of the high point (which bore the name of Tower's cliff), was situated the little village of Carncombe, about a mile from Llanaven, and thither had Henry Ashton flown, with all the

speed which his high motive could lend him, to endeavour to procure assistance in his bold and generous
enterprise.

He found most of the sailors and fishermen belonging to the place, collected together on the shore, looking at the vessel, which seemed fast settling, and
which was drifting on to the east in utter helplessness.

" We must do something to help her," he exclaimed,
as he arrived almost breathless with the rapidity with
which he had descended the hill.

The men all touched their hats to him, but answered as with one voice, " Nothing to be done, sir."

" Something we must try, however," said the young
officer indignantly ; " unless we would wish to pass, as
Cornish men too often do, for wreckers ;" and he sent
a searching glance from his fearless eye through the
little crowd assembled ; a glance which some could but
ill stand ; " though I hope," he added more cheerfully,
" that we shall be able now to redeem a little the
honour of our coast."

" I am afraid, sir," said a respectable-looking man,
" that no help can be given these poor fellows, we have
unluckily no means of getting a rope out to them,
which would be the only chance."

" I think, and I believe," replied Henry, " that by
good care and management, Terry, we might get a boat
out to them with ropes ; they are not near a quarter of
a mile off. If not—I'll swim."

" You'll be dashed to pieces on these rocks, sir,"
observed the other.

" Not a bit of it," said Henry gaily, " at any rate
I'll try. But we will make an attempt the other way
first. Here who will lend a hand to get my boat down

to the shore, as you preventive men daren't lend yours I suppose, as your officer happens to be absent."

Several men volunteered for this safe piece of service, and the light boat was soon at the brink of the waves. Henry jumped into it.

" Give me all the ropes you can muster," he said, and coil after coil of rope and cable was laid on board. " I'll tie one end of this round me," he continued laughing, " and then perhaps you will be able to haul my empty jacket ashore when my body is all gone to bits, that will be better than nothing. Now who will go with me?"

Not a voice answered his appeal.

" Cowards! he exclaimed, with a glance which literally shot fire.

Then shouting between his hands, his sonorous voice rising above the roar of the tempest, while laughter danced in his clear blue eye, he exclaimed—

" Holloa! are there no women astir there? Is there no Grace Darling on the Cornish coast? Must Northumberland carry away all the honours?" Then lowering his voice again, and speaking to the men around, he added, " Grace Darling—a woman!— risked her life to save men;—here men leave women and children to perish before their eyes!"

" Are there women on board?" asked Terry in an altered tone.

" Yes, and a child," answered Henry Ashton. " Could not you make them out with your glasses? Perhaps not though down here, but on the point, old Dickson and I made them out plain enough; two women and a child, and there may be more for aught I know."

" If I thought there could be a chance——" said Terry hesitatingly.

" There can be no chance," replied Henry, in a kind but earnest voice, " if we do nothing; but God may bless our endeavours, if, in dependence on Him, and in accordance with His command, we 'do as we would be done by.'"

" I'll go with you, sir," said the man, stripping off his heavy jacket, preparatory to setting out; " God's blessing is the best inheritance, and though my wife and children depend wholly on me ——"

" You all remember," cried Henry aloud to those on shore, " and bear my words to my brother, that if we perish, Terry's wife and family are to be provided for."

A loud cheer answered this injunction, while a voice from the crowd exclaimed—

" He wouldn't want the telling."

Tears started into Henry's eyes at this tribute of confidence in his brother's generosity, and Terry, quite overcome, stooped to arrange some of the ropes at the bottom of the boat.

" I want another hand still," said Henry, looking round, " come, you have strong voices among you, have ye all weak hearts?"

" If you'll give me a hundred pounds, I don't care if I go with you," said a bold, reprobate-looking young man, whom Henry knew bore but a bad character.

" I'll have no such Jonah on board," he answered, " unless to heave out to the fishes, if the boat wants lightening."

A loud laugh followed this reply, and the unfortunate object against whom it was directed, got pushed

about from one to another in a most unmerciful
manner.

" Well, Terry," continued Henry, " you and I must
brunt the waves alone I am afraid ; but never mind, one
volunteer is better than twenty pressed men.   Now
mark, you men on shore—for I suppose some of you
will wait to see what becomes of us—above all things
take care that the hawser does not chafe against the
rocks, for if it breaks, we may all go down with one
foot almost on the shore ;" and he threw them the end
of the rope he had fastened to the stern of his boat.

" I'll ask them once more," he said in a low tone to
Terry, " for three would be far better than two—that
is, three that could be depended on."

Then raising his voice, he called out, " Now, men,
I give you one chance more—will any of you come ? "

" I will," said a pale-looking lad, who had but lately
joined the group.

" You ! " exclaimed Henry, as a buzz and murmur
of discontent rose amongst the men, " you look, my
poor lad, as if the weight of an oar would crush you."

" I am strong," said the youth, holding out his
muscular hands, " though I look so thin ; I don't mind
going a bit ; I have no one to leave behind."

" Have you any one to go to ?" asked Henry kindly,
pointing upwards.

" Yes, the same God as you have, Mr. Henry,"
replied the boy, his pale cheek flushing up.

" In with you then," said Henry, " and sit down
there.—But stay, can you swim ? "

" Yes, sir."

" And you, Terry ? "

" No fear of that, sir."

"Now, my men," exclaimed Henry to those on shore, "be sure you have an eye to the rope, and watch as I told you, that it doesn't chafe against the rocks."

All was now ready.

"Trim the boat well, Terry," said Henry, "and sit still both of you. Now, boys, be ready to shove off, but don't stir a finger till I give the word."

Wave after wave dashed up, but yet Henry Ashton sat mute at the helm. At last—"Now," he cried,— "the moment the next wave has broken—off with us.—Now,—yo—ho——y."

The boat grated on the shingle, then, partly rising over, partly going through a heavy wave which came thundering to the shore, it soon rode safely behind a ledge of rocks which at a short distance from the land, rose some feet out of the sea. Henry and his men were drenched from head to foot, but that was a matter not the least regarded.

The danger of swamping at the first outset was happily passed, but a far greater difficulty remained to be overcome. On each side of the little reef, behind which they now lay in comparative quiet, the sea was pouring in furiously; and the waves—dashing against the seaward side of the rocks, which to the left were little more than a wall—came over into their boat, threatening to fill, and sink her. To remain therefore, was impossible, as well as wholly useless; but how to stand against the rush of waters on either side, was a question not so easily decided. To the left the opening was tolerably wide between the reef and a neighbouring range of rocks, and the waters therefore had less power; but there was a shoal at that point, so near the surface in places, that the boat might have been stove

in an instant had she been dashed on it.   To the
right, on the contrary, the sea was deep, but the opening
was narrow—high rocks rising near—and a continuous
torrent of conflicting waters came in during a storm,
with such fury—forming innumerable eddies and whirl-
pools—that it seemed impossible that any boat could be
got through against such a stream, in safety.   On this
side however, Henry Ashton was compelled to attempt
his passage into the open sea, and after a brief but
energetic commendation of their souls to God—in
which his two companions joined most sincerely—and
a blessing implored on their exertions, he ordered his
men to pull for the opening.   They did so;—but the
force of the current seizing the boat, she turned round
like a shuttlecock, and was only saved from destruction
by a wave of tremendous force coming in from the right,
which overpowering the rest of the waters, whirled her
back to the quiet spot from which she had made so in-
effectual an attempt to escape.

"It will never do, sir, I am afraid," said Terry,
drawing a long breath.

"We won't give it up yet, my friend," answered
Henry, "we must think of the women and children.
How would it be for us to get out upon the rock at this
right side where the reef is deepest, and taking every
thing out of the boat, draw her by a rope at her bows
through the passage?   She might graze a little, but if
we could get the rope over that jutting rock we could
surely pull her round, and she might spin like a minnow
if she liked it, when we were out of her; and come the
worst, should the rope break, or the boat be beat to
pieces, we should be pretty safe on the reef till the
storm abated."

This idea was instantly acted upon, though not

without much difficulty, for the rocks were slippery
with sea-weed, and offered but little on which either
hand or foot could take firm hold.   However with perseverance they at last succeeded, and having taken
every thing that was loose out of the boat, they proceeded to pass the strong rope which they had attached
to her bows, over a mass of the rock which projected
some feet across the narrow passage. Having done
this, they endeavoured to obtain footing on the other
side firm enough to enable them to resist the force of the
current against which they would have to haul the boat ;
for if by a sudden jerk they should be precipitated into
the sea at that point, death would be almost inevitable.
They therefore scraped away the slippery sea-weed,
and fixed their feet firmly in niches, and broken parts
of the rock ; and having achieved this important point,
they put forth all their strength to make the boat
turn the point, and to drag her through the tumult of
the opposing waters.   To add to their other difficulties,
the waves—though their force just there was much
diminished by the depth of the reef on which they stood,
and also by the shelter of the rocks which ran out, on
the right, a considerable way into the sea—continually
broke over them, blinding them with the spray, and
rendering their hold of the rope almost hopelessly slippery. However their stout hearts did not give way,
and with desperate energy they put forth all their
strength for the final effort.   They felt the boat yield to
their strenuous pull—but they knew that the first part
of her passage was by far the easiest, as she had then
but little current to contend with—and after a few
moments they saw her head appear round the point,
under the projecting rock.

"I almost wish we had thought of hoisting her over

the reef," said Henry Ashton, "she is but a light thing;
or if we could even now drop the rope with the hook,
from the end of that rock, so as to grapple her, and
keep her head out of the water, we might be able to get
her through; but this way we shall never succeed; the
rope will never stand the strain. She's tearing at it
now like a dog at its chain."

Terry mounted the rock with the rope and hook,
and after many failures, succeeded at last in making
it take fast hold of the fore part of the boat. He then
with little difficulty raised the head above the waters, and
Henry and his feeble-looking, but stout-hearted companion, hauled away manfully; and when it had passed
the point of rock where Terry stood, he also descended
to where the others were standing; and—the main
force of the current being now passed—their united
efforts soon brought the little boat along side of them.

" Stow away all the things, and jump in, my men,"
said Henry; and following them, he seized the rudder.
"God has been very merciful to us, and we will trust
Him yet a little further. We must watch our opportunity though, or we shall get swamped at last.—Now
for it—strike with your oars," and they rose buoyantly
on the crest of an advancing wave.

" Well!" he cried, " we've 'hoped almost against
hope;' but we've been brought well through, thank God,
and I can never sufficiently praise you, my men, for
your steadiness and courage. Now then pull away as
fast as you can. I would take your oar, Warner, and
let you steer," he added, " but you have not knowledge
enough to manage the helm in such a sea as this; and
if the wave once took us on the broadside, we should
be capsized in a moment."

" I can hold on, sir," said the boy, " never fear."

They proceeded now in silence, for it was hard work for the rowers, and Henry Ashton's attention, and strength too, were fully occupied in keeping the boat's head right against the waves.

CHAPTER IV.

"Thou hast paid the penalty of thoughtless love
Dearer than most."—SULLIVAN.

"How affection grew
To this, I know not; day succeeded day,
Each fraught with the same innocent delights,
Without one shock to ruffle the disguise
Of sisterly regard which veiled it well,
Till *his* changed mien revealed it to my soul."

TALFOURD.

THE manœuvres of the little boat and its crew, had
been watched with intense interest by the assemblage
on shore; and when they were seen dancing over the
waves, after the perilous passage through the rocks had
been passed, the spectators sent up a shout of exulta-
tion, and waved their hats in the air to cheer on the
intrepid little party. They however, needed no such
stimulus to their exertions; and the acclamations of the
people — which sounded to them scarcely louder than
the 'wailing sea-bird's' cry,—added but little to the
enthusiasm with which they had undertaken and carried
on their noble enterprise.

Lady Ashton on reaching home had retired to
her own room to pray for the safety of her son, and
for the rescue of the poor creatures in the vessel who

were in such awful peril. She resisted the inclination
she felt to watch the progress of the wreck, for she
knew the only help she could afford would be by
offering up her earnest supplications to Heaven; and
she also knew that by that means only could she obtain
for herself the strength and composure, which she so
much needed.

The projecting point of Tower's cliff prevented any
of Henry Ashton's operations from being visible from
Llanaven, till his boat had got some little way out
from the rocks. But when it was at last seen riding
safely on the waves, Lady Florence in an extasy of
joy, called to her sister to inform her of it; and Lady
Constance, then first roused to any thing like feeling,
threw herself on her knees and burst into a passionate
flood of tears.

"Do not, dear Constance," said Lady Florence, her
tears starting in sympathy with her sister's, "do not
cry; they seem to go on so safely—and the people in
the ship appear so animated by seeing them. Henry
has a rope tied to the back of his boat, so you see, dear
Constance, he has taken every care. I can see his
dear face every now and then as he turns—this glass
makes things so very clear. I see that little child,
too, quite well now—one of the women is holding it in
her arms. Poor little thing! how wet it must be, for
the waves go over the deck continually, though I
dare say it is not half so frightened as its mother.
The boat is very near now, and the ship does not drift
away as it did. I see Henry making signs to them
about something. Do come and look, Constance, you
would not feel half so anxious if you saw better what
was going on. Do come."

"No thank you, dear," replied Lady Constance, who had resumed her calm composure; "I could not look steadily through the glass now — I am sure I could not; and you can tell me what happens. Besides I can see the vessels very well, though not what goes on in them."

"I do think they must have struck on a rock," continued Lady Florence, " all the people seem in such a ferment! There—Henry has reached the ship at last—quite close—and they are trying to get a rope to him, but the wind blows it away.—He has got it now, and is fastening it to a cable he has in the boat. Ah!" she screamed suddenly, " he is over! — he is over; he is gone down!"—and she threw herself on the ground, and in her frantic terror tore up the very grass with her hands.

"Florence, my dear Florence," said Lady Constance, with stony coldness, " do not be so frightened; remember how well he swims, there is no danger for him;" and stooping over her sister she raised her up.

"No, I am sure he's dead — drowned," replied Lady Florence, "I saw him go down;—I saw something strike him when he went over;" and again she threw herself upon the ground.

Lady Constance was horrified; yet still retaining her unnatural calmness, she knelt down and looked through the glass. It was some moments before she could sufficiently make out the scene—now brought so near to her view—as to understand what was going on; but when she did — sinking back, she covered her face with her hands, and passionate tears again burst forth. She seemed capable of enduring with a cold —

almost stern resolution, the idea of Henry's danger—of his death !—but now again she saw that he was safe—and her heart melted within her.

" I knew it," cried Lady Florence, mistaking very naturally the cause of her sister's tears, " I told you he was gone ! "

" Oh ! no, dear Florence," sobbed Lady Constance, " he is not gone, he has reached the boat again. I was selfish, and forgot you. — Do you watch again, dear," she continued, rising and giving her place to her sister, " you will see better than I shall what happens."

Lady Florence had joyfully sprung from the ground at hearing of Henry's safety, and she now, wiping away her tears, resumed her attentive watch.

Lady Constance sat down again on the grass by her side. Her thoughts were still in a whirl of confusion ; yet across the deep gloom which hung like a cloud over her faculties, there shot at times a gleam of joy, indescribable ! at the recollection of Henry's words—but these short moments of unallowed happiness, were ever followed by a deeper sense of horror, and misery, and benumbing dread.

" They have lowered one woman into the boat," said Lady Florence, " and now the other is safe ; but it seemed as if they must have missed it, it is so tossed about ; and now a man is swinging down the rope with the child in his arms, and Henry is holding his out to receive it ; and one of the poor women too, got up for a moment, but seemed thrown down again by the rocking of the boat. Henry has given her the child, and she is holding it to her, and wrapping it up ; I suppose she is its mother. Poor thing !—oh ! poor

thing!" and the blinding tears prevented her for a
few moments from seeing what was going on.

She soon however continued,

"Henry is waving something white as if to the
people on shore; for his face is turned that way.
Yes—he has moved the rope from the back to the
front of the boat, and I suppose they are going to
draw them back, and they have a rope fastened to
the ship too, which makes it so much safer! I must
go and tell my mother; or will you, Constance?"

"No, do you go, Florence."

She accordingly went, and announced to Lady
Ashton the joyful news of Henry's success, in bringing
off the women and the child. Lady Ashton's tears
flowed fast, for her heart was thankful;—and it also
yearned painfully over the son whose bold intrepidity
had been so much blessed.

"Well, now, dear Florence," she said rising, "our
part comes; we must go down to the village, and see
what can be done for these poor sufferers."

"I am almost sure," said Lady Florence, "that
one of the women in the boat is a lady; she did not
look the least like a common person;—the captain's
wife perhaps—and the child seemed to be hers."

"Do you think so?" asked Lady Ashton, "then we
will have the carriage, and send some better things for
her to put on. I have already sent some common
ones with other comforts down to the village, but if
you are right in your conjecture we will bring the
poor thing up here."

"And the child?" exclaimed Lady Florence,
"that will be delightful! Put on your bonnet, dear

mother, and let us go; or do you mean to wait for the carriage?"

"No, that will detain us, for it is not yet ordered; and it will have to go round by the road; but with the wind at our backs we shall be at the village in a very short time."

They sallied forth full of joy, and buoyant with the hope of usefulness, and Lady Ashton invited Lady Constance to join them as they passed near where she was sitting on the lawn; but she declined, saying she would attend to having comfortable arrangements made in the house in case Lady Ashton brought any one back with her from the village.

The two happy ones then proceeded on their joyful way, leaving the wretched Lady Constance behind;— she whose kindly spirit would at another time have been the first in all acts of benevolence, but whose powers both of body and mind seemed now almost gone—broken down by the weight of her oppressive misery. When she was again alone she quite forgot what she had undertaken to do, and for a long time remained with torpid mind, seated on the grass without the slightest motion, till at length recollecting herself, she started up, and entered the house.

When she had finished all the arrangements necessary for the accommodation of any guest who might come, she went into her own room, and throwing herself on her knees, implored of God guidance and strength. The little affairs in which she had been occupied, had brought back her wandering senses to the realities of life, and she now with a clear mind, and determined will, began to consider what she must do.

There seemed indeed but one course pointed out by
duty, and that she resolutely determined to follow.
She sat down instantly, and wrote to Henry, informing
him of her engagement to Sir Roland, and telling him
why it had not been made known to him before; entreating him also to leave Llanaven as soon as possible.
She expressed her deep sorrow for the unhappy error
into which he had been led, assuring him that never
till that day had she had the slightest suspicion of his
sentiments — and beseeching him to think of her no
more. Of her own feelings she said nothing; she
could not say the truth — and she would not say that
which was not true.

When she had finished this trying letter, she concealed it in her dress, intending to put it into Henry's
hand when she should take leave of him at night;
and having fulfilled her hard task towards him, she sat
down to look into her own heart. She saw — she felt,
how much, much more tenderly she loved the one she
must part from, than the one to whom her faith belonged, — and her soul was overwhelmed with shame
and grief. She comforted herself in some degree by
the hope that neither by word nor look had she ever
betrayed feelings — whose existence, indeed, had been
unknown even to herself but a few short hours before;
and she determined never to reveal to living soul the
weakness of her heart.

It was not her intention, most certainly, to marry
Sir Roland whilst her heart remained full of his brother; but considering herself bound to him by every
tie : — by her own reiterated promise — by her father's
wish — and by his own deep love, and true devotion —
she determined in the strength of God, to subdue the

faithless preference she felt for Henry; nothing doubting but that her heavenly Father would in answer to
continual prayer, and in furtherance of conscientious
exertion, do for her, in her heart, what she despaired
of ever doing for herself. Fortified by these thoughts
she determined to give way — no, not for an instant —
to vain — and as she could not help feeling them — sinful regrets. She resolved to shut out all tenderness of
recollection; and not even to dwell with pity on the
thoughts of Henry's wounded heart, lest her own should
continue to feel for him too much.

Miserable, wretched, indeed she could not help
being; but she murmured not, nor blamed any but herself; and in her deep sorrow, resigned herself entirely
to the will of God.

CHAPTER V.

" The pause of anxious fear, awaiting soon
    The dimly-visioned object of its dread ;
  When the hushed bosom fears to pant or sob,
  And the heart dares not throb."

ANON.

" My noble boy,—whom every tongue
Blest at that hour."

SOUTHEY.

LADY Ashton and her young companion arrived at
the village just as the party in the boat reached the
reef of rocks which it had given Henry so much trouble to pass, in his way out ; and where fresh difficulties
now arose. His prompt and energetic mind, however,
soon determined what course to pursue, and the moment the boat neared the reef, he made a signal to the
men on shore to leave off hauling in the rope. It
might have been possible to have shot the boat through
the opening in the rocks without its being upset, bu.
the risk was very great ; besides which, he reflected
that there were many more, still to be brought from
the sinking vessel, and he determined, therefore, to
leave his boat on the seaward side, and endeavour to
induce some of the people on shore to come out that
little way to their assistance. He made all the party

get out on the reef, sheltering the women and child as
well as he could from the soaking spray; after which,
he clambered to the other side himself, and endeavoured to speak loud enough to make his voice heard
by some of the spectators on shore; but his attempts
were wholly unavailing, the tumult of the storm being so
great; nor could he make any one understand his signals;
so, in despair of otherwise obtaining assistance, he threw
himself into the sea where it was calmest, and after buf-
feting for a time with the waves—which, when no longer
sheltered by the reef, rolled with tremendous power—he
was thrown with stunning violence upon the shore. He
lay senseless for a few minutes, to the agonising alarm
of his mother and Lady Florence, who had witnessed
his bold leap into the sea with dismay; but soon recovering—after a few words of deepest love to his mother
—he entreated some of the men to go with him out to
the reef with another boat. This request was more
readily complied with than his former one had been,
for, besides that it was attended with much less risk
and difficulty, the hearts of the men were warmed with
the enthusiasm and bravery which Henry and his companions had displayed; and the success of their enterprise had animated them all. The sight too, of the
women and the child, so near, yet divided from them
by the boiling surge, seemed to kindle every kindly
feeling in their natures; and now, instead of a general
refusal, Henry had many more offers of service than he
could possibly accept. He selected, however, two men
whom he knew to be among the boldest and strongest
of them, to go with him; and obtained their promise, not
only to take the boat to the reef, but afterwards to go
on with him to the wreck in the place of Terry and

Warner, who were both much fatigued with the great
exertions they had already made.

The boat was soon ready, and a rope attached to
the stern; and Henry Ashton committed himself once
more to the mercy of the waves. He was not, however, so happy in his outset this time as on the former
occasion, for the men, being over-full of zeal and animation, did not wait for him to give the signal for
launching, but pushing off immediately after a huge
wave had broken on the shore—without perceiving
that another was following fast upon it—the boat was
struck, and immediately swamped. The danger, which is
always great in these cases, was much increased now by
the tremendous weight of the billows; but the two men,
who were active swimmers, soon regained the boat,
which was at no very great distance; and clinging
to it, though it was bottom upwards, were quickly
drawn to shore. But with Henry it fared less well; he
received a blow on the head as the boat went over,
which confused his senses; and before he could recover from its effects, the waters had drawn him a considerable way out. He was exceedingly exhausted
with his previous efforts, and having missed the ropes
which were thrown out to him at first, he was left
wholly dependent on his own powers for regaining a
place of safety. He felt his strength almost fail him,
and for a moment the torpor of despair—added to the
effect of the stunning blow he had received—made
him almost cease from exertion; and casting an imploring glance to Heaven, he was nearly sinking unre-
sistingly in the foaming waves, when he caught a fleeting
glance of his mother, standing on the shore, with the

most agonised terror depicted on her countenance,
and with her arms stretched out towards him. That
sight roused his almost dormant faculties, and fresh-
strung his weakened arms, and he determined to
make one more effort for his life. He dreaded, however, being again dashed on the shore, having suffered
so much from the rude shock he had sustained on the
former occasion, so he determined, if possible, to reach
the comparatively calm shelter of the reef; feeling certain, that if once he were seen on the rocks—should
he have strength enough left to mount them—the
men on land, whose spirit and courage he knew were
now completely roused, would not fail to risk every
danger to reach him. He was happy enough to be
able to succeed in this attempt, and it may well be
imagined with what emotions of transport Lady Ashton
heard one of the fishermen exclaim, " That he saw Mr.
Henry on the reef." He had been lost sight of for
some minutes, the height of the waves intercepting
the view of him from those on shore ; who also, imagin-
ing that he would certainly endeavour to regain the
land, had fixed all their attention in that quarter. No
time was now lost in launching another boat for the
rescue of the gallant young sailor,—for whom at that
instant every one would gladly have risked his own
life—and as the men proceeded this time with more
caution, it was happily and safely sent on its venturous
way, with Henry's two former companions in it,—who,
nothing daunted by their first failure, were eager to set
out again—and another volunteer, who took the helm.

The first danger at starting being over, there was now
no great difficulty in reaching the little haven under

the lee of the reef, and Henry, cheered by seeing the
strenuous efforts made to join him, crawled over the
rock, as well as his weakness would allow, and directed
the party there to come over to the side nearest the
shore, whence they could be easily let down into the
boat. As this would be comparatively a safe business —
when he had seen Terry in the boat, he desired the new
reinforcement of rowers to come with him in order to
set out on a second expedition to the wreck. They all
endeavoured to persuade him to let the other sailor go
in his place, seeing how suffering and exhausted he was;
but he well knew that the presence of an officer was
invaluable on occasions like the present, where order
was as essential as courage; and that unless he were
there to direct and control both his own men, and those
on board the wreck, there would be in all probability
such a rush for the boat, as would inevitably sink her.
He therefore persisted in going, though he felt at
times almost as if he should die — so extremely spent
was he, as well as suffering from the effects of the
stunning blow on his head, and of the violent contusions
he had received on his chest and side when thrown with
such force on the shore. He felt, however, a trust in
God which was most refreshing to his soul, and which
kept him in perfect peace as he sped forward on his
dangerous way.

In the meantime the party on the reef having safely
descended into the boat were all, after tremendous
tossing in the surf, safely landed; and every one was
anxious to be of service to those who had so narrowly
escaped a watery grave. The women and the little
child were of course objects of especial interest, and
Lady Ashton accompanied them to a respectable cot-

tage, where she had provided fresh clothing for them,
and induced them to take some refreshment; and perceiving that Lady Florence was right in her conjecture
that one of them was a person of superior situation in
life (the other—a foreigner—being evidently her servant) she expressed her hope that she would go to
Llanaven; which offer being gratefully accepted, Lady
Ashton, after seeing the party safely deposited in the
carriage under Lady Florence's care, returned herself
to the shore; being now by far too anxious and uneasy
about her son's fate, to think of going home till she had
seen him again return from his dangerous expedition.

Henry Ashton's strength was happily not so much
taxed with having to manage the helm on his second
expedition, as it had been on the first, as the ropes at
the bow and stern served much to steady his boat.
He succeeded in bringing off six more of the men and
landing them on the reef; and he then set out a third
time for the captain and four other sailors who were all
that now remained on the wreck. The vessel had—
as Lady Florence had conjectured when watching it
through the telescope—struck on a rock, which though
an advantage as preventing its drifting away from
those who were going to its relief, yet made it inevitable that it must soon be dashed to pieces, by the
violence of the waves which broke incessantly over it.
That it had stood so long the fury of the shocks it every
instant received, had been matter of joyful surprise to
Henry; and he trusted that it would hold together, till
he had made this last expedition to it; but to his horror,
when he had now got about half way, he saw the ill-
fated vessel suddenly part, and in a moment as it were,
dissolve in the waters. He instantly cut away the rope

which attached his boat to it, and in great agitation, exhorted his men to redouble their exertions to reach the spot. They rowed gallantly forward—though the difficulty was again much increased by having lost all assistance from the ship—and in a short time they saw two men floating on a spar, and farther on still, another; and having with great difficulty got them into the boat, they learned from them, that having expected the ship to go to pieces from one moment to another, they had all secured something with which to keep themselves afloat, till the boat should reach them. This account greatly encouraged Henry and his men, and after a short time they were happy enough to rescue also the captain and the only other remaining sailor.

Completely exhausted, Henry now gave up the management of the helm to the captain of the merchant-vessel, and threw himself at the bottom of the boat, for his life seemed almost gone. When they drew near to the reef he endeavoured to speak, but could not make one audible sound; and the men not being aware of what he wished to say—(which was to desire them to climb over the reef, and get a boat from the shore to take them off as the others had done) went on unhesitatingly to the dangerous opening between the rocks. Henry who saw their fearful mistake, and knew that it was then too late to remedy it, thought all hope of being saved was gone; yet in his extreme weakness he could scarcely keep his mind sufficiently alive to watch the event. And when contrary to all rational expectation, the boat was hauled, by the exertions of the excited men on shore, safe through the awful torrent, and was borne by a tremendous wave high up on the shore—amid shouts that rent the air—the gallant spirit which had infused its high energy into so many hearts, seemed flown for ever.

" He would go!" exclaimed Dickson (who had been relieved from his watch)—clasping his hands above his head, while tears gushed from his eyes as he saw Henry Ashton's lifeless body lifted from the boat, " He would go!"

Lady Ashton whose soul seemed at the moment raised above her mighty grief, laid her hand on the old man's arm, and said,

" If he has perished—he has perished as a servant of God should do."

" Aye! he has perished nobly," replied Dickson, " but he was so over-venturesome!"

Henry was carried into the nearest cottage, and every effort was used to recall animation; but though it was, happily, soon evident that life was not extinct, yet it was long before any thing like consciousness could be restored. Lady Ashton begged the men to procure something on which they could convey him to Llanaven, as the carriage was not then at the village; and a litter of hurdles and a mattrass being soon procured, his exhausted frame was laid on it, and carefully covered with cloaks that the wind might not chill him in his wet garments. There was not a man there who was not forward in offering to be one of the bearers of his rude couch, for his frank, generous character, and cordial manners, had always made him a favourite; and at that moment the remembrance of his brave daring, united to the deathlike appearance of his fine countenance, awoke in their rude breasts a sympathy and admiration seldom called forth. Almost all the inhabitants of the village, excepting those who were busy in attending to the sufferers from the wreck, accompanied him and Lady Ashton over the cliff, in token of their deep interest and respect; and then, after having seen him safe home, they took their leave with expressions of so much kind feeling and admiration as moved Lady Ashton to tears. She said she could not then thank them as she wished, but would soon visit them all at their own homes.

Thoughtful at all times, and for every one, she had previously sent a messenger to warn the sisters of Henry's state, lest they should be too much shocked at the sight of him; all was therefore ready for his reception and comfort when he arrived, and he was immediately conveyed to his bed, and laid there in peace and tranquillity.

Then, and not till then did Lady Ashton's strength and spirits give way, and she sunk fainting, on the floor by his bedside. After a time however she recovered, and a few hours rest enabled her to be again unweariedly watching over the son whose late noble and generous conduct had endeared him a thousand-fold to her heart.

To Lady Constance the trial was dreadful of seeing Henry brought home in the deathlike state, in which he reached Llanaven; and it was impossible for her at the first moment to repress the floods of unspeakable tenderness and grief, which would burst forth. The anxiety of every one on his account too—his praises on every lip—conspired to heighten her feelings for him, and to add to the trials of her heart, left alone, as she

was, to combat the worst, and most powerful of spiritual enemies—those that steal into the breast under the
guise of the gentle, sweet, and delightful affections of
life. Alone indeed, she was not, for God was with
her, and on His strong arm she leant — and was
supported.

CHAPTER VI.

THE doctor who was called in to Henry Ashton blooded him immediately; and having watched him for some time with great attention, was able at last to cheer Lady Ashton with the hope that no material injury had been sustained; although the blow on the head, he said, would make it necessary for him to be kept quiet and free from excitement for some time, lest inflammation should take place. This, though not wholly satisfactory, was yet a great relief to Lady Ashton's mind, and enabled her to devote some of her attention to the stranger who had been cast by Providence on her care and kindness.

This young creature, though a mother, seemed scarcely beyond girlhood; while her quiet, distressed countenance spoke of early sorrow. Lady Ashton learnt from her that her husband was with his regiment at Gibraltar, and that circumstances rendering it advisable for her to return to England without delay, she had embarked with her little son a fortnight before, in the merchant-vessel which had met with so disastrous a fate. Her name was Montague, and she had purposed proceeding, she said, directly to the house of an uncle who resided in London.

This was all that Lady Ashton learnt from herself, and she had too much delicacy to intrude any further into the secrets of this evidently sorrowful heart. The child's nurse however, (a Maltese woman) more communicative than her mistress, occasionally mentioned circumstances, from which Lady Ashton gathered, that the husband of this poor girl had been most unkind, and neglectful of her ; and that having been left in almost perfect destitution, and abandoned by her lawful protector, she had at length determined to accept the repeated invitations of her uncle, Mr. Stanhope, and return to England, to take refuge with him in her distress.

This account filled Lady Ashton's kind heart with pity for a young creature, so early tried with such severe afflictions ; and her compassion was still further, and most painfully excited by the fear which she could not help entertaining, that she might soon be called to endure another sorrow in the loss of her little boy, who seemed her only joy and comfort. The poor child, she was informed, had not been strong for some time before he left Gibraltar, and a feverish restlessness, and irritating cough, had much alarmed his mother, and made her fear for his lungs. The continued exposure for many hours on the wreck, while the sea was breaking over them, had fearfully aggravated his illness, and Lady Ashton felt extremely anxious and uneasy about him. He was a pretty child of two years old, and seemed to know no rest or happiness but in his mother's arms.

Mrs. Montague, unwilling to intrude on Lady Ashton's hospitality, had been desirous of setting off directly for London ; but Lady Ashton would not per-

mit that, and was glad in any way to be of service or
comfort to her. With her usual unfailed kindness,
having obtained Mr. Stanhope's direction, she wrote to
invite him to Llanaven; and in a few days she had the
pleasure of announcing his arrival to his niece, and of
seeing the comfort his presence afforded her.

All were most assiduous in their attentions to her
and her child; and it was with a pleasure, second only
to that of the poor mother herself, that after a few days
they saw the severe illness of the patient infant give
way, and heard the doctor pronounce him out of
danger.

Lady Ashton was exceedingly pleased with Mr.
Stanhope, whom she found a most gentlemanlike and
agreeable person, as well as an enlightened Christian.
He told her many circumstances in the history of
his niece which much interested her, and which made
her feel more than ever for the desolate state of this
poor young creature. She was, it seemed, the only
child of his sister, and had been brought up by her
mother in the indulgence of every wish and fancy.
Mr. Lindsay, her father, was a man of ordinary mind
and thoroughly worldly character; but some years after
their marriage, Mrs. Lindsay had become decidedly
pious, and very earnest in her desires to serve God.
She had however unfortunately adopted high Calvin-
istic views, which preventing her, as those extreme
opinions invariably do, from "rightly dividing the
word of truth," had led her to look, in all events, solely
to the sovereign decrees of God, instead of using—in
dependence on his grace—her own exertions in the
path of duty. Forgetting the distinction (which is so

admirably set forth in Wilberforce's "Practical Christianity") between spiritual life and moral power, she
imagined that—because it is impossible for any one to
understand the things of God unless taught by the
Spirit of God—that therefore all human instructions
and exhortations were useless.

"My sister would often tell me," said Mr. Stanhope, "that she could not make general invitations,
when she knew that Christ died only for 'His people.'
I used in vain to shew her that by refusing to do so,
she was refusing to do, what God Himself had done
throughout the whole of the Scriptures: those sacred
books being not only full of exhortations, and promises,
but also of reproaches, that men 'would not come to
Him that they might have life.' I urged on her the
passages in which God repeatedly announced that he
had 'no pleasure in the death of the wicked'—that it
was not his will 'that any should perish, but that all
should come to everlasting life;' and I reminded her
how St. John after speaking to the Christian converts
on the subject of Christ having died for their sins,
adds, 'and not for ours only, but also for the sins of
the whole world.' I endeavoured to shew her how
these passages, and many others equally strong, proved
that, though we cannot even think a good thought of
ourselves, yet that we must necessarily possess a *moral*
power by which we are enabled to go to God for
spiritual power; otherwise that all God's promises and
reproaches, would be but awful mockery of the unhappy beings whom He in fearful power had created,
only to destroy—only to consign helplessly to everlasting condemnation; a thought horrible as untrue!
But she was blinded. I would urge at other times

that the ungodly were said to be condemned because
they rejected the blood of Christ! and I asked her,
how—if, as she said 'Christ died only for his elect'—
these ungodly ones could be said to reject that which
had never been offered to them? She could not explain—but her awful delusion still continued; and the
effect was: that though she delighted in the society of
real Christians, and did all in her power to forward
them in a life of holiness, yet unless she saw that God
had visibly drawn any particular heart to Himself, she
never used the slightest endeavour to awaken the dead-
ness of that heart, to shew it the way of life, or even
to restrain it from outward evil. To her husband she
never spoke on the subject of religion, and Mary—
Mrs. Montague, of whom she was doatingly fond, she
suffered to go on in every way exactly as her fancy
dictated. To my earnest entreaties on this subject
she would reply, 'that when the converting grace of
God came to the soul of her child all evil would be
subdued by it; but that if it was decreed that she
was never to be one of Christ's redeemed, all her endeavours to improve her would only add to her final
condemnation.' I asked her one day, what course she
had pursued the year before, when the child had had the
scarlet fever? whether she had sent for any physician to her? Unsuspicious of the deduction I meant
to draw from her words, she answered, that 'of course
she had had a physician, and had followed all his pre-
scriptions.' 'And yet,' I said, ' you knew that without
the blessing of God, that man's advice and prescrip-
tions could be of no avail.' She admitted it. ' Then
why,' I urged, ' will you not do for the child's soul
what you did for her body? Why not guide her to

the great Physician, and follow all His spiritual pre-
scriptions for her, looking to Him for His blessing on
your work?' She was silent—but still unconvinced;
for Satan, who delights in stirring up the activity of
the wicked, rejoices equally in keeping the godly idle."

"I was afraid at first," said Lady Ashton, "that
you were going to say that all the power is in man
himself."

" Oh! no," replied Mr. Stanhope, " I am convinced that that is not the case, for it is God alone
who can make us either ' to will or to do of His good
pleasure;' but though I know full well that we have
no power of ourselves to turn to Him, yet the power is
surely promised, if sought. In the parable of the mar-
riage-feast, it is, I think, plainly shewn that all are
invited—all may come in ; those who did so, were certainly compelled, but the others were freely and honestly invited, and the guilt of the refusal was distinctly laid at their door ; for it says, ' those that were
bidden were not worthy to come in.' Some being
forced to enter, does not prove that others are forced
to stay out !—These things, I feel, are far beyond our
comprehension, and it is, I think, in the endeavour to
be ' wise above that which is written,' that we make so
many mistakes. I believe that man must have power
of some kind, or God would not entreat and invite
him, neither could he be considered a responsible agent.
Again, I receive as perfect truth our Saviour's words,
' No man can come unto me except my Father draw
him.' These two things I cordially believe, though I
cannot understand how the seeming contradictions they
involve are reconciled ; but feeling with adoring gratitude that it is God alone, who has drawn me to the

knowledge and love of His Son, I accept with, I trust,
a sincere heart, all my salvation from Him. When
we have cast off the dulness of these mortal bodies,
then, and not till then, shall we comprehend these
things. But in the meantime much evil arises from
taking up either side of this question, to the deter-
minate exclusion of the other."

"I fully agree in what you say," said Lady Ashton,
"and feel that indeed much evil is done by endeavouring
to explain infinite things according to our finite ideas.
When we can understand how, in ourselves, mind acts
on body, and body on mind : or when we can even find
out how one blade of grass grows — then we may with
some shadow of reason reject what we find in the Bible,
because we cannot comprehend it in all its bearings.
Will you tell me further about your poor niece ?"

"Her disposition," replied Mr. Stanhope, "was
always remarkably gentle and amiable, and therefore
the evil effects of her mother's injudicious treatment were
not for a length of time so visible in her, as they would
have been in most others. But when she was about
fifteen, she took a great fancy to one of her cousins, a
niece of Mr. Lindsay's, and her mother allowed her to
have her continually at the house. I never liked this
girl ; she was vain and foolish, and affected, and full of
fantastical romance ; and was always filling poor
Mary's head with nonsense. There are barracks at
the town near Mr. Lindsay's estate, in Lancashire, and
among other young officers, in an evil hour, appeared
Mr. Montague. He was good-looking and agreeable,
but as wild and unprincipled as possible. Mary, it
was supposed, would naturally inherit all the property
belonging to her parents, which was very considerable,

and Mr. Montague, really I believe liking her, and
certainly liking the idea of her ' broad acres,' contrived
to make himself particularly acceptable to her, though
he was far from being a favourite with her parents.
Indeed I have understood that he rather endeavoured
to displease them, for the purpose of making them
refuse his offer; trusting that poor Mary's love would
overcome her sense of duty, and that he might persuade her to run away with him; for he thought that
if he married her without settlements, he should obtain
unshackled power over the fortune which he fancied
was irrevocably settled on her. He therefore, when
forbidden the house, induced this foolish cousin of
hers to contrive meetings between them, and to
convey letters to and fro, which the unprincipled girl
was but too ready to do; thinking it very fine and interesting to lead her young but indiscreet companion,
into a sentimental and clandestine correspondence.
She filled her ears, too, with continued invectives
against the cruelty and tyranny of her parents, whom
she represented as sordid and unfeeling, objecting to
her marriage only because it would oblige them to
part with some of their fortune. At any other time
Mary's affectionate feelings would have made her
resent such language, but then, she was blinded by
her own wishes, and could see nothing clearly; and
being contradicted now, for the first time in her
life, and on the point on which naturally she felt the
strongest, she gave way to great irritation, and was
finally induced by her two worthless advisers to leave
her home and set off for Gretna Green. Her father,
who was of the most harsh and irascible nature, took
no steps to follow or reclaim her, and when after a

short time she wrote to him, asking his forgiveness, he returned her letter unopened, desiring her cousin — the author of all the mischief — to inform her, that as she had chosen to act in defiance of her parents' commands, she must thenceforth consider herself an alien from their hearts, and home; and moreover, that as his fortune was not entailed, he should most decidedly leave it away from her. From her mother she heard nothing, for though that kind parent's heart was broken with grief, she dared not venture to oppose her husband, who had forbidden all intercourse. Things were in this miserable state when Montague's regiment was ordered abroad, and poor Mary had of course to accompany him, though he would gladly, I believe, have dispensed with her society; for thoroughly disappointed in the main object which had induced him to marry, he seemed to consider his wife merely as an expensive incumbrance. However, as she had no other home, he could not refuse her going out with him, so she accompanied him to Gibraltar, to which place his regiment was ordered. I went to see what I could do for her before she set off, for I always loved her very much, and I never saw a creature so altered — so thoroughly miserable. It was dreadful to her to leave England without again seeing her parents, especially her mother, of whom she was excessively fond; but her father was inexorable, and would not allow even a letter to pass between them. My poor sister sunk under this cruelty, and the first letter her unhappy child received after arriving at Gibraltar, was to announce the death of this most tender but mistaken parent; and no message of love or forgiveness was forwarded to soften the terrible blow, or soothe the

wretchedness of this early victim of sorrow and folly.
A few posts after, she received the news of the death
of her father also, which had taken place very suddenly; and this intelligence was followed by the account that all his property had been left to his brother,
and that her mother's fortune—about five thousand
pounds—was all that she was ever to expect. From
that time Montague, I have understood, ceased even
the outward appearance of kindness and respect towards
her, spending his time and money in the worst ways.
At Gibraltar her little boy was born, and there for
nearly two years after his birth did she endure privations and neglect of every kind, till nearly starved,
and her child's health as well as her own declining—
her worthless husband having ceased even to live in
the same house with her—she at last acceded to my
often-expressed wish, that she should return and live
with me.   Montague was most willing that she should
do so, as he was by that means relieved from the
charge of both her, and her child; and, anxious to
escape from him, she set out in that unfortunate vessel,
in which, had it not been for your son's bravery she
must inevitably have perished."

After this sad account of the unhappiness of her
guest, Lady Ashton felt more than ever interested in
her fate; and was very desirous of finding out whether
she had any comfort in looking to God for pardon and
consolation.   In conversing with her soon after however, she discovered that the same mistaken views
which had acted so injuriously on her mother's mind,
were working much mischief also in hers.   She fancied
herself to be one who was by an irrevocable decree,

condemned for ever; she knew that her conduct had not been such as was in accordance with the will of God, and never having been taught the willingness of her heavenly Father to pardon and accept all who came to Him in Christ's name, she thought her doom already fixed: her eternal portion appointed with the lost. There was something in her gentle and meek resignation which was most touching to Lady Ashton's feeling heart; she acknowledged the justice of God in all the bitter trials that had been sent her, blaming herself alone for all her sufferings, and her gratitude at the improvement in her child's health was unbounded; yet still the chill sense of God's anger and of her own hopeless state, as she imagined it, prevented her enjoying peace of mind; and for a length of time she seemed incapable of receiving any spiritual consolation.

CHAPTER VII.

" What a lot is mine !
I who would rather perish than requite
Long years of kindness with one throb of pain,
Must make that soul a wreck ! "

TALFOURD.

As soon as Lady Ashton's uneasiness on account of
her son had been allayed sufficiently to enable her with
comfort to leave the house, she was very anxious to
reward the men who had so bravely assisted him on the
day of the wreck. She took measures for establishing
Terry in a small farm close to the village which had
long been the object of his ambition, but which hitherto
he had not had sufficient capital to undertake; and as
she had liberty from Sir Roland always to do what she
thought right and kind, she desired the steward to provide for him every thing which was necessary, and to
have the lease of the farm made out for him directly.
When this was settled, she requested him to take the
lad Warner, who was an orphan, into his service; she
herself, also bestowing upon the brave boy a handsome
reward, as well as on all the other villagers and sailors
who had exerted themselves on the late occasion. The
vessel which had been lost having been insured, the
captain, who was also the owner, was not a loser to any

great amount; and the sailors who had formed his crew, after being liberally supplied with clothes, &c. by Lady Ashton's generosity, were provided by her also, with the means of immediately reaching their homes, or wherever else they had intended going.

Henry Ashton very willingly submitted, for the first few days after his fatiguing exploit, to the confinement and quiet which had been prescribed for him, for he felt almost incapable of speaking, or of making the least exertion; but when the effects of his fatigues and injuries began to wear off a little, he became most impatient to rejoin the party down stairs, being naturally, exceedingly anxious to see Lady Constance again. He half however, dreaded their meeting, for he had no idea how she would receive him after the avowal which his excited feelings, at the moment of their parting on the cliff, had drawn from him; for though he was fully persuaded that he was not an object of indifference to her, yet her former manner had given him no encouragement to speak as he had done. When constantly in the habit of being with her, he had not thought deeply on the subject — giving himself up simply to the enjoyment of her society; but now, when alone in his chamber, where his weakness kept him still reclining, he thought over each circumstance which had occurred during their late intercourse together; and when he recalled her rebuke on the first day of his arrival, and the restraint he had always felt since that time as to the expression of his feelings, he began to be terrified at the idea that he might perhaps have deeply offended her by his vehement declarations of attachment at their late interview. Then again, the conviction of her affection came to cheer him, and he thought, "Why should I not love her?" He knew no reason indeed, why he should not,—and yet he was anxious, and uneasy ; and the uncertainty began to prey upon his mind.

"I must go down stairs again," he said to his mother one morning; "I am much better, and this confinement gets intolerable."

"I shall be delighted to see you again among us," she replied, "if you feel equal to it."

"I am quite equal to enjoying my life again among you all, dear mother," he answered with a smile, "but I am not equal to staying up here any longer."

He accordingly went down that evening, though it was with difficulty that he was able to move his stiffened limbs.   When he entered, leaning on his mother's arm, Lady Florence joyfully went to meet him; but Lady Constance remained at the window, where she had been conversing with Mr. Stanhope.   She was fully aware of his entrance, but she continued looking out, as if watching the pale light fading from the sea ; though sight, hearing, every thing was for the moment gone ! But when at length Lady Florence called to her, saying, that "Henry was come down again," she was obliged to shew that she knew he was there, and to come forward and meet him.   Speak to him she could not—and they shook hands in silence ; Lady Florence happily by her gaiety preventing any one besides themselves, being aware of the restraint which lay so coldly on them both.   The twilight hid the expression of their countenances—and they were thankful that it did so.— Henry's heart swelled almost to bursting ; he saw that it was not the melting of affection, at meeting again what it loves, after perils and dangers past, which was working in Lady Constance's mind—had it been that, her silence would have been more eloquent to him than thousands of gentlest words; but it was coldness, and, as it seemed to him, displeasure, which marked her manner, and the instant her passive hand had quitted his, she left him to return again to the window.

Mr. Stanhope, begging Lady Ashton to introduce him to Henry, began directly to offer his grateful thanks to the preserver of his niece, and to express the high admiration which he felt for his gallant and noble conduct.

Henry could not be insensible to the warmth of his commendations, or to the kindness of his expressions, but assured him that far greater exertions than he had made, would have been overpaid, by the happiness he had felt in being the means of rescuing his fellow-creatures— especially Mrs. Montague and her child—from such a dreadful death. But conversation was irksome, and painful to him, in the present excitement of his mind, and he soon became silent; while Lady Ashton and Mr. Stanhope continued to talk together with great interest.

Lady Constance still remained at the window; and after a time Henry's desire to go and speak to her became so strong, that he could no longer resist it. He with difficulty rose, and was endeavouring to make his way quietly along by the help of chairs and tables, when Lady Florence perceiving him, ran to offer her assistance.

He was annoyed, and said quickly,

"I am not a baby, Florence; I can manage very well for myself."

But seeing the colour rise in the little girl's cheek,

and the tears fill her eyes, his heart reproached him; and smiling down with 'good-humoured crossness' on her sweet face, he added—

"However, as you are here, you tormenting little animal, I may as well make use of this strong shoulder of yours;" and he playfully leant on her, till her slight form bent beneath his ponderous hand.

"There," he said, when they got to the window, "I think you have had enough of playing the crutch to such a 'gouty old commodore' as I am," and he put his arm round her and kissed her affectionately; "but you," he continued, with a bitterness which reached— as it was intended—Lady Constance's very soul, "you have a heart within your breast, and that makes you kind and strong, to love and help.—But now go," he continued, "and bring Monsieur Jacko to pay his respects to me, and mind he is in his best trim, combed and brushed to a nicety—not a hair out of its place— or I shall have a terrible word to say to his young mistress;" and having despatched his little helper on this— as he hoped, lengthy business,—he sat down near where Lady Constance was standing. For a long time both were silent; at length Henry, whose mind was in a complete turmoil of anxiety, and sorrow, and indignation, and affection, said in a low voice,

"And is this the way we meet, Constance, after a week's absence — after such a parting? Is this your first greeting, after all my pain and danger?"

Lady Constance was moved even to tears, but endeavouring to repress them, she said in a calm voice,

"You are better now, are you not?"

"Yes, I am better; I thank God—for my mother's sake—not for yours;—you care not how I am; and for myself — I could almost say, would God I had perished in the ocean rather than have lived to see this hour," and he leant his head down on the window.

"Constance," he said again, "why are you thus? My dearest, speak to me—I cannot bear my existence if this is to go on. Why this bitter unkindness? Have I offended you by the words that were forced from me when I felt that we might be parting for ever? I thought not of offence, and would rather have sunk fathoms deep into the raging sea, than have spoken of the feelings that had so long dwelt in me, could I have thought they would have been so displeasing to you. Think them unexpressed, dear Constance, if they offended you—forget my folly—my madness—be again to me only as you were before, and I will never——"

He stopped, for he felt he could not thus bind himself to silence. "Can you not forgive me?" he added.

"I have nothing to forgive, Henry," replied Lady Constance sadly, "only do not again"—and her voice trembled—"repeat words like those—and then all may be well again in time."

"But, Constance, my dear Constance, why may I not speak those words again?"

"Because it would be vain—useless—worse than useless!" she answered hurriedly—endeavouring to pass him.

He caught her muslin dress to detain her—it rent in his rough grasp! Lady Constance burst into tears.

"Oh! forgive me," he exclaimed, "rude ruffian that I am! I did not mean it, Constance, you know I could not mean to hurt a thing of yours."

"Oh! I am not weeping for my dress," she answered with a half-smile struggling through her tears, "I care not if it were torn to atoms; but a bird flying across one sometimes would overset one's foolish spirits; and I am not quite well. Do not look so ruefully at that work of ruin," she added (for Henry sat with the torn dress still in his hand, as if mourning over it, though in fact his thoughts were far otherwise occupied) "there,"—and she playfully tore it still more—"you see the destruction of that slight thing does not cost me a sigh." Yet one rose to her lips.

"But there are things," replied Henry looking up at her, though the faint light scarcely enabled him to read her countenance, "which you would rend with a light and careless hand, but whose destruction is—my destruction."

"Henry," said Lady Constance firmly, "there must be no more of this,—will you be again my friend, and brother, or must you be to me as a stranger?"

"Let me be your friend again, then, if I may not be any thing more. But oh! Constance, think how long we have known—how long we have loved each other—though not perhaps as now I love."

Lady Constance did think of it—and the thought choked her utterance. At length she said almost inaudibly,

"Henry, you do not know how much it costs me to grieve one I have loved so long, but it must—must be done—you must forget me—you can never be to me more than you have been from childhood."

"But why may I not hope that in time I may be more, Constance?" urged Henry vehemently;—"I would wait years—my life almost!   Why must I be silent?"

Lady Constance dared not tell him why, for she dreaded its being too much for him to bear.   She paused a moment, endeavouring to quell her over-powering emotion, then spoke almost haughtily—for she had wound herself up to end this cruel strife,—

" It should be enough for you, Henry, that the subject does not please me—that I request—nay, de-sire—it may never be renewed.   Now," she continued in a kinder and more cheerful tone—for she was in terror lest he should be over-excited—" let this subject rest for ever, and let us talk of other things—that is," she added smiling, " when I come down again in re-spectable apparel, for I must change this poor dress before the lamps come in, to betray my misfortunes;" and disengaging herself, with a kind look, she left the room.

Henry remained sunk in thought; he was some-what happier than at first, for Lady Constance was kinder, and that removed a load of ice from his heart; but yet, on further thought, he almost wished that she had retained her cold repellent manner.

" It would soon," he told himself, " have made me cease to love her; or else I might still have hoped that there was something misunderstood—something— which if removed—our hearts might have been drawn together again.   But this cold command ' not to speak because she does not like it,' seems as if there were no cause of displeasure, except the love which she forbids —as if she really did not care for me!   And yet,"— and he dwelt fondly on the many things which had brought " confirmation strong" to his mind that he was more to her than all others in existence. He mused, and mused, till his heart grew dark within him.

" Can she be ambitious ? " he thought, " and can she be willing to sacrifice her love for me, because I am not rich, and great ?   I cannot think it — I cannot believe it — she was ever so noble ! and Roland would surely help me if I wanted it."

The thought of his brother brought with it a sudden dart of anguish.   " Did she love Roland ?   He had been long with her, and she admired his character so much, and so continually wrote to him !   But no," he thought again, " I know — I feel her love is mine, and she used to write often to me too.   No — her heart is with me, and there must be some dreadful — some fatal reason for her conduct, unknown to me. Any how it makes me miserable — miserable ! "

Lady Florence and her monkey — and lamps and tea, came in — and lastly, Lady Constance.   She had not before been able to see Henry's countenance, and she was now greatly shocked at the change in his appearance.   Not less so was he, at that which had taken place in her, and which was wholly unaccountable to him.   " For," he thought, " she has had no illness — no fatigue — no stunning blow ! "   Alas ! she had had the sickness of the heart — the weariness of the labouring and perplexed spirit — the stunning force of agonising sorrow ! — worse — a thousand times worse than all he had suffered !

She seated herself at a distance out of his sight ; and weary, depressed, and miserable, Henry soon pleaded a fatigue he truly felt, and retired to his own room.

CHAPTER VIII.

" But absence—absence !—any thing but this !
  I cannot bear
  This present agony ! this nearness of despair."

MS.

WHEN Mrs. Montague's little boy was quite out of
danger, she felt very anxious to leave Llanaven, fearful
of being burthensome to her kind hostess, though Lady
Ashton wished her much to stay ; but as the country
air was considered best for the child at that time, it
was determined, that instead of accompanying her
uncle to town, Mrs. Montague should take a cottage
which was pleasantly situated near the village of Carncombe ; and stay there for some months, or till the
child's health should be quite re-established.

Lady Constance was most anxious to be able to
tell Henry Ashton of the reason of her late conduct
towards him, but it was some time before he was sufficiently recovered to make it safe for him to have any
great excitement ; therefore all she could do, was
kindly, but firmly to repress any thing like a renewal
of his former expressions, and to keep as much as possible, out of his society. The party of friends who

had been invited to Llanaven had been requested by
Lady Ashton to defer their visit in consequence of
Henry's illness, and of the precarious state of Mrs.
Montague's little boy; but when both the invalids
were convalescent, another day was named for them to
come, and they accordingly soon arrived.

This was perhaps the most trying time of all for
Lady Constance, as far as regarded the steadfastness of
her resolutions; for it being impossible whilst other
company was in the house, to keep away from Henry,
she found it most difficult to resist shewing him more
kindness and cordiality than she wished.   Every thing,
indeed, conspired to try her unhappy heart to the very
utmost; for his late brave action, forming a continual
subject of conversation, kept her feelings for ever on
the stretch.   She could not enter a cottage but the
first person inquired after was "Mr. Henry;"—and
loud praises, and long discourses always followed the
mention of his name, which she had to listen to and
bear as best she might; so that even in the very path
of her duties, trial and temptation rose up before her.

The first day that he was thought equal to it,
Henry drove down with Lady Ashton to the village,
to visit Terry and some of the other people, and thank
them for the assistance they had rendered him on the
day of the wreck.   Lady Constance had gone there
previously not knowing of their intention, and was in
Terry's cottage when they entered it.   The remembrance of Henry's gallant behaviour, together with his
changed looks and unexpected appearance, so overcame poor Terry and his wife, that they burst into
tears; and some of the other villagers also, hearing
that he was come, crowded in, making it altogether a

touching scene. Lady Ashton's mother's heart was quite overcome, and Henry himself was much moved. To poor Lady Constance it was terrible, especially as Henry's eyes continually sought her, as the people poured forth in the best manner they could their delight at seeing him again. But her eyes were dry, and though every nerve within her trembled, she endeavoured to subdue all outward appearance of emotion. She made her escape as soon as possible, and when alone again on the wild shore, she sat down behind a rock, concealed from every eye but His who "knows our bitterness!"—and her full heart bursting forth,— long, long did she weep.

After a time she heard the carriage pass, on its way home, and secure then from the chance of being seen, she rose and pursued her sad, and solitary way back over the cliffs. She hastened along, for every step was fraught with remembrance, and though in general she had much command over her thoughts, and never suffered them to rest on the forbidden ground, yet just then, her feelings were so much excited, and her spirits so shaken, that it seemed almost as if nature must give up the unequal contest.

In the evening Henry Ashton was gloomy and silent; to Lady Constance his manner was abrupt and cold; he would not speak to her, or remain near her; and once when his mother asked him to sing a particular duet with her, he answered aloud that "he would sing it — but with Florence;" casting on Lady Constance as he passed her, a withering glance of disdain and indignation. She endeavoured to be calm, and occupied herself in promoting the pleasure of her guests, but her heart bled within her, for she knew

what must be the force of the feelings which could
make Henry act towards her in such a way; and
though at moments, perhaps, she felt her pride roused
by his manner, yet she grieved more for him than for
herself; and she could not long feel angry with one
whom she was—how unwillingly! making so unhappy.
Though Henry was now quite able to bear the fatal
intelligence she had to communicate, yet amidst the
bustle of a large party she could not find an opportunity of being with him alone a sufficient time to
inform him of it; and seeing the impetuosity of his
character—which was so much greater than she had
imagined—she dared not give him the letter she had
written, lest some violent and uncontrolled outbreak of
feeling should reveal to others what she was so anxious
to keep concealed from every eye. She longed to be
separated from him—to be any where rather than with
him; for his dispirited countenance, and eyes for ever
fixed on her in sorrow or reproach—or in affection,
still more trying—kept up a never-sleeping strife
within her. Lady Ashton, too, added frequently to
the difficulty and misery of her situation, by begging
her to watch over him, and prevent his over-exerting
himself, when the younger portion of the party were
out together;—entreating him also to keep quietly by
her.   At times he would obey this injunction, and
giving Lady Constance his arm, would endeavour to
win from her kind and encouraging words; then—
failing to do so—in anger and despair, he would
almost violently cast her off, and go and join, with
mad and reckless mirth, in the conversation and amusements of the others.

How, often in the bitterness of her heart would

Lady Constance contrast the conduct of this wayward child of impulse, with Sir Roland's feeling and devoted tenderness; and wonder why she could not tear her affections from Henry, and bestow them on one, who loved her so perfectly, and so nobly, and who would not, she felt sure, even could he at that moment have looked into the depths of her faithless heart, have treated her otherwise than with generous kindness. She trusted, indeed, that she might in time do him full justice; that she might truly give her heart, where her vows were paid, and be enabled to look back to this harrowing period, merely as to a fevered, distracting dream. She omitted nothing in her power to effect this; she banished Henry as much as possible from her mind, and continued unremittingly to correspond with Sir Roland. She constantly carried his picture about her, that she might remind herself of his claims upon her, and often did his full dark eye seem to reproach her for her want of love, and to remind her of the noble, devoted spirit which animated the original. But above all, she looked to God for strength; and if He did not as yet give her power over her wayward feelings, He at least enabled her to escape the guilt of ever willingly yielding to them.

Mrs. Montague was at length established in her new home; the other friends who had been staying at Llanaven all by degrees departed, and the little party there, were again alone. Lady Constance had wished it so to be, yet now, how did she shrink from what lay before her! Just at that time she received a letter most unexpectedly from her cousin, Mrs. Mordaunt, regretting that Lady Constance's absence from town

that year had prevented their meeting; and saying,
that her sons having engaged a moor in the Highlands,
she purposed going there with them, and taking a little
tour in Scotland. She invited Lady Constance most
kindly and cordially to accompany her in her expedition, assuring her of the extreme pleasure it would
give her, and begging her to join her in London as
soon as she possibly could.

At any other time, Lady Constance would instantly,
for many reasons, have declined this proposal; but at
that moment all she seemed to desire in existence, was
absence from Henry. In the letter she had written to
him, she had entreated him to leave Llanaven as soon
as possible, knowing of no other means by which they
could be separated, but now she felt that her departure would be by far the most desirable step, as besides
depriving Lady Ashton of her son's society, his sudden
absence would have looked most unaccountable and
suspicious. She remembered also that her father,
though he did not wish her to reside with Mrs. Mordaunt, yet had expressed his particular desire that she
should in every possible way, shew gratitude for her
cousin's kindness, in offering to take charge of her and
her sister; and this, joined to the other consideration,
at last made her determine to request leave to accompany her to the Highlands.

Lady Ashton did not like the proposal at all, and was
much astonished at Lady Constance's wish to leave
friends whom she loved so much, to go with those of
whom she had hitherto known so little; and she said
moreover that she thought Sir Roland would not be
pleased at her doing so. Lady Constance however replied that she was sure Sir Roland would approve of her

motives, and urged that the change would do her good.
Lady Ashton looked at her pale countenance, and saw
indeed that she seemed ill; and not liking to oppose
her further, she yielded a reluctant consent to her wish.
Lady Constance thanked her with an aching heart;
and anxious that she should not have time to retract,
instantly wrote and sent off a letter, gratefully accepting Mrs. Mordaunt's invitation.

She felt now that deliverance was at hand, yet
how did her spirit sink at the thought of separation !
She determined no longer to delay the terrible task
she had in hand, but resolutely and at once to perform
it; and more aware now than she had been before of
the irritability of Henry's temper, she thought it would
be best to speak to him, and endeavour to soothe the
violence of his first feelings, rather than to leave him to
sustain alone the unmitigated severity of the blow.
She therefore asked him to accompany her on a walk
by the sea-shore ; and he, though much surprised, instantly complied with her request. He gave her his
arm, and once more, but in silence, they descended
together the *corniche* path down the cliffs. They
reached the shore — yet still they were silent, for
Henry was in a state of torturing expectation, and
Lady Constance knew not how to speak ; such an
anguish seized her heart at the thought of what she
had to say as almost paralysed her. At length with a
trembling voice,

"Henry," she said, "you have been angry lately
at my conduct ?"

"Have I not had reason, Constance?" he exclaimed
vehemently, "have you not been cruel—unjust ?"

"If you will only listen calmly I will try and explain——"

"Hear me first, I implore you," interrupted Henry, "and oh! forgive me for the impatience, and unmanly temper I am conscious of having shewn. But you are so changed, so cold, so heartless towards me, when formerly you were so affectionate, so——. I have felt almost mad, for you would not speak, you would not tell me why I should not love you. Constance, who can love you better than I do?—Oh! let me speak," he added, for she had endeavoured to interrupt him, "I know I am not rich, but I feel certain that Roland would do every thing to make me happy and then—will you not be be mine?"

Lady Constance turned from him, for her very heart sickened.

"Say at least," continued Henry, "that I need not despair — that you are not angry with me?"

"I am not angry with you, Henry," she replied, as her tears flowed, "but I cannot ——"

They heard voices at a little distance, and looking back they saw Lady Ashton and Lady Florence walking towards them.

"Come with me this way," said Henry, impatiently. "Constance, I must have your answer?"

"You have had it, Henry," she replied sadly, "I have told you that you must not love me, for I never can be yours. But, I beseech of you restrain yourself; for the sake of all you love, do not let Lady Ashton see your feelings.—Oh! I entreat of you, be calm when they come up;" and she looked at him imploringly, for she dreaded lest his vehemence should be observed.

" I cannot wait for them," replied Henry, in gloomy agitation, " will you not come with me ?"

" I dare not ; Lady Ashton will think it so strange if we go when she is coming to join us. Henry, dear Henry, will you not stay, and be tranquil? Walk for a moment towards the sea, and then return to us, and I will go and meet them. Pray — pray do," and she clasped her hands in agony.

Henry looked at her, and his countenance softened.

" I will do any thing you wish," he sighed ; and he walked slowly away, while Lady Constance went to meet her sister and Lady Ashton.

" I am glad to find you," said the latter ; " it is such a relief to be without strangers again, and able to enjoy each other's society."

" I am very glad the house is quiet again," said Lady Constance, " visitors with whom one has not much in common, soon weary one."

" We are all out early to-day," observed Lady Ashton, " we will sit here a little while, and get Henry to read to us. I dare say he has some book with him ; he is like Roland in that."

" I had strolled down here for a little while," said Lady Constance with some embarrassment, for it was most distressing to her to remain with Henry, " but I think I must now occupy myself at home."

" Oh ! not for this one morning ; it is so charming to feel oneself so free again ; stay and enjoy this delightful air with us."

Lady Constance complied, fearful of attracting attention if she persisted in a refusal.

" We will sit down on the shingles," said Lady

Ashton, " and, Florence, go and ask Henry to come and read to us if he has a book."

Lady Florence went, and taking hold of Henry's reluctant arm, drew him back to where the others were sitting. There was a languor and dejection in his manner which terrified Lady Constance, who dreaded lest it should be observed. She was seated a little behind Lady Ashton, and she looked at him with a beseeching countenance. He was touched by her distress, and exerted himself to appear cheerful.

" Will you read to us, Henry?" asked his mother, " have you a book?"

" I have nothing but my pocket Testament."

" Well, read us something out of that. I am sure when one looks on this ocean, which had so nearly taken you from us the other day, we cannot enough think of God, or thank God sufficiently for His mercy. But who that sees it to-day—its little sunny waves chasing each other as in sport, would think that it could ever be roused to the force and fury that we witnessed then?"

"It was like the human mind," said Henry, as his brow lowered; "calm till roused by the winds of passion; and then the storm is terrible."

He looked towards Lady Constance, but she had placed herself so that he could not see her countenance.

" How soothing the plashing of the water sounds," said Lady Ashton, "as it rolls so gently over on the beach; and yet its bright smiling look, and soft whisperings, seem but like the blandishments of a murderer, when we remember how many it ' has roughly cradled to their last long sleep.' "

" Does it not seem rather like penitence?" said Henry,

> " Mourning with low regretful murmur, for the deeds
> Its fury and its wrath so ruthlessly have done ?"

"Did you ever see any one lost?" asked Lady Florence, "it must be so dreadful."

"It is dreadful," replied Henry, "I never saw but one. They say a field of battle is less trying to the feelings than one solitary death, and I suppose it is the same with the wide fields of the ocean, for I am sure the destruction of a whole fleet could scarcely have shocked me as that one thing did. It was a little lad, a nice little fellow, who fell overboard when reefing one of the topsails in a tremendous gale of wind. It was impossible to stop the ship, for we were running at eleven knots an hour, and I believe I should have madly gone after him, without knowing what I did, had I not been held back by a brother officer who knew I must inevitably have been lost too. But I saw his face a little way off as he rose the first time on a great wave, and oh! the expression of it! The remembrance is terrible even now. We had soon left him far behind, but for a length of time we knew whereabouts he was, by the flock of vile sea-birds which hovered about him."

"Horrible!" exclaimed Lady Ashton.

"Yes, this life is full of misery."

"Yet you, dear Henry, can know 'of misery but the name,' excepting as your kind heart makes you feel for others," said his mother.

Henry was silent. Then, "Shall I read?" he said, and he drew forth his book.

His mind was full of a strange mixture of tenderness and wayward anger towards Lady Constance, and he threw himself back on the shingle so as to be able to see her, while he said,

"Life saved, is sometimes only suffering prolonged!"

Lady Constance, startled by his sudden action, looked towards him for a moment, but when she caught his eye, and saw the terrible expression of his countenance—almost alarmed, she shook her head, and turned away—her own emotion being almost uncontrollable. She would gladly have risen and left them all, but she dared not stir; and Henry, now feeling for her distress, opened his book, and read out of it some of the sublime chapters of the Revelations. The subject, as he proceeded, took full possession of his mind, and raised it to the contemplation of the magnificent, splendid, and eternal things of heaven. Earth, and its sorrows for a moment faded from before his eyes, and the love of God seemed all in all to him; and when once more he looked at Lady Constance, it was with a calm elevation of expression, far different from that which before had marred the character of his beautiful countenance. They soon after rose, and Henry, giving his arm to Lady Ashton, assisted her up the cliff, and when they reached the house he retired into his own room.

CHAPTER IX.

" There are hidden but marvellous inspirations through which the tempted but pure spirit receives strength to triumph over even that which is dearest to it."—F. BREMER.

" Will he not pity ?—He whose searching eye
  Reads all the secrets of thine agony ?—
      Oh ! pray to be forgiven
  Thy fond idolatry—thy blind excess."
                            MRS. HEMANS.

" Help me to raise these yearnings from the dust
  And fix on Thee, th' Undying One, my heart."
                            MRS. HEMANS.

HENRY ASHTON felt thoroughly miserable; not only because his hopes seemed all dashed to the ground, but because he was conscious that his conduct towards Lady Constance was not what it should be. He was shocked when he reflected on his violence, contrasted with her gentleness, and forbearing patience, and he felt himself utterly unworthy of her love. His soul was humbled before God, and earnestly did he implore strength to subdue his hasty temper, and to bear his great trial.

Instead of the harsh, indignant feeling he had so often given way to, he now felt full of devoted tenderness towards Lady Constance, and willingly would he have endured any sorrow rather than have seen her suffer. He wrote on a slip of paper, " Can you forgive me? and will you come out with me again this evening?" and then, it being near the time of their early dinner, he went down into the drawing-room.   Lady Constance was arranging some music, and going up to her he silently put the little paper into her hand.   She read it and wrote underneath his words, " I do forgive, and will go out with you."   He was looking over her, and felt overjoyed as she traced these words, but when he saw her add, " but hope nothing,"—his impatient indignation again returned, and he was about to leave her in his former abrupt manner, when checking himself, he quietly took the pencil from her hand and wrote, " Then may God have mercy on me."

Dinner was announced, and they proceeded to the dining-room, where, in pursuance of his kind desire to spare Lady Constance all uneasiness, he exerted himself so much to be gay and pleasant, that his spirits really were relieved, and at moments he felt almost cheerful.   His mother remarking the difference said,

" You are more like yourself to-day, Henry, than you have been since your illness.   I like to see that your spirits are better when we are alone than when there is company; I always pity those who need excitement."

" I require none," he answered, " I have too much already within myself, of one kind or another."

After dinner while they were yet sitting round the table, a servant came in with a letter for Henry, saying that a man had just brought it over express.   He opened it when the servant had left the room, and having read it with a quivering look and heightened colour, he threw it over to his mother, and leaned his forehead on his hand so as to shade his face as she read it.

" To-morrow, oh! that is cruel," she exclaimed.

" To-morrow!" cried Lady Florence, "what of to-morrow? you are not going to-morrow, Henry? Oh! you cannot go," and she threw herself on her knees by his side, and leaned her head against him, sobbing violently.

He glanced for a moment at Lady Constance, who sat pale and tearless, then bending over the little girl he stroked her hair and caressed her, to hide the tears he was ashamed to shew. At last finding he could not repress his emotion, he started up and gently removing her, said,

" Get you gone, you little witch, why do you come, and wile these great tears from a sailor's eyes?" and going to his mother he sat down by her, and leant his head on her shoulder. She embraced him with a full heart.

" This is, indeed, short notice," she said; " what can be the cause of this sudden summons?"

" I do not know," he replied, " you see it only says that orders have been received for sailing without delay. I must be off to-night, I fear, but will speak to the man who brought the letter."

" Shall I send for him here?"

" No," he replied, " I will go to him, when I am fit to be seen; but it won't do," he added, forcing a smile, " to shew these woman's eyes to all the world. Let us go into the drawing-room, and after a turn on the lawn I shall be more of a man again; but this is a cruel wrench."

As he entered the room with his mother he turned

to look for Lady Constance, but she had taken the opportunity of escaping to her own room. When there she sat down in silent sorrow, for her heart sunk within her.

" Yet why," she thought, "should I grieve? it is what I have been desiring. Absence! how far better than being together—yet so divided."

She had indeed determined to go away herself, but then she would have left Henry at home in quiet and safety. But for him to go—to enter again on his perilous duties, was terrible to her! Yet still after the first shock she felt it was best for him; his mind would be occupied, and when far away from all the scenes which could recall his ill-fated affection, he would sooner be likely to overcome it. She again thought of writing to him, and of giving him the letter at the last moment, as then all fear of his betraying his emotion to his mother would be over. But she dreaded for him the effect of such a stroke, coming on the pain of parting ; and determined again, that cost her what it might, she would speak to him, and try to soothe his lacerated feelings. She prayed earnestly that strength and comfort might be imparted to them both ; and besought that nothing might escape her which might serve to betray the state of her own heart.

She was yet on her knees when Lady Ashton came to the door, to ask her to come out, and take a last walk with them before Henry's departure. She started up on hearing herself called, and though she would infinitely have preferred staying at home, till she could take the promised lonely walk with Henry, yet she could not refuse the invitation ; and in the confusion of the moment was glad indeed to busy herself by putting on her bonnet, and making other little preparations, so as to hide her agitation.

Henry had spoken to the man who brought over his letter, and found that it would only be necessary for him to join his ship early on the morrow; therefore, he declared he would not go that evening, but would start very early the ensuing morning.

They then all set off for the village that Henry might take leave of Mrs. Montague, and of some of his poor neighbours there; and they afterwards walked home by the shore. When they came to the little cove to the west in Llanaven Park, Lady Ashton proposed that they should sit and rest there a little, before she went in to make her final preparations for Henry's departure. The sun had set behind the woods and the full moon rose from the ocean.

" Repeat me something," said Lady Ashton to Henry, who sat between her and Lady Constance; " something that I may remember when you are gone."

" I will repeat then that beautiful entreaty to be ' thought of,' which you like so much, and which is suited but too well to this sad and lovely hour;" and he spoke in a low, and often broken voice, those exquisite lines:

> " Go where the water glideth gently ever—
>   Glideth thro' meadows that yet greenest be;
> Go listen to our own beloved river,
>   And think of me !
>
> Wander thro' forests where the small flower layeth
>   Its fairy gem beneath the giant tree ;
> Listen the dim brook pining as it playeth,
>   And think of me !

Go when the sky is silver pale at even
    And the wind moaneth on the lonely tree;
Go forth beneath the solitary heaven,
      And think of me!

And when the moon riseth as she were dreaming,
    And treadeth with white feet the lulled sea,
Go silent as a star beneath her beaming,
      And think of me!

Yes! think of me in joy's most blessed hour,
    And when affliction draweth tears from thee;
In the world's crowd—and in thy lonely bower,
      Oh! think of me!"

He took his mother's hand as he finished, and Lady Ashton pressed his to her lips with a mother's painful love. He looked at Lady Constance; her head was turned away, but the moonbeams shone on the tears which fell abundantly on her hands and dress; and he sadly felt, " At least she loves me."

" I could linger here with you till midnight, Henry," said his mother, " but I must go now, I have so much to do."

" You need not all go," he answered, " and I shall be of no use. Constance, stay with me, and let us enjoy this scene a little longer."

She remained by him.—He waited till the others were out of hearing then turning to her he said,

" Now at this last moment, Constance, will you not bid me hope? Do not be cold and heartless, when we must part to-night, never more, perhaps, to meet."

He waited for her to speak; but she was silent, while in her bent brow and agitated countenance he saw evidences of the deepest emotion, and most agonized distress.

" You terrify me," he exclaimed—" I entreat you for my sake—for our early love's sake, tell me why you look so wretched ?"

" What can I say ?" she replied in broken accents, " how can I tell you, that you must not think of me— must not love me, but—as—engaged to Roland;" and her head sunk upon her clasped hands.

Henry started to his feet, as if a scorpion had stung him—and recoiled from her in horror.

" Engaged to Roland ?" he almost shrieked. Then in a low voice, and slowly, as if endeavouring to understand the meaning of the words, he repeated, " Engaged to Roland !"

" Oh ! yes," said Lady Constance, " I am—have long been engaged to him."

Henry rushed from her. He walked up and down the beach in a state of distraction; his wild actions and frantic exclamations spoke the intensity of the anguish which tore his heart—his senses were bewildered under this dreadful shock. Though Lady Constance had forbidden him to hope, still he had hoped, but this—this was worse than death. " Engaged to Roland !"—had it been to any one else it would have been less torturing, but his own brother ! . . . . .

And then the thought of that brother rushed over him; that generous, devoted brother, to whom he had been looking with full confidence to smoothe his path to happiness ! His whole soul melted with agonizing remorse as he felt that he was the destroyer of that brother's happiness; for he knew that he was the one loved; and delightful as that conviction was, it brought with it pangs unspeakable. The next moment fury flashed over his mind as he thought of this tyrant claim standing between him and Lady Constance; and raising his arms a moment as if in supplication to heaven, he dashed himself on the ground.

By degrees he became more calm, and rising, he sat for some time almost in a state of torpor. Lady Constance, from whom he still kept aloof, was even more severely tried than he was. She had not indeed the first force of the stunning blow to sustain, but she had to witness the expression of Henry's anguish, and to resist the strong temptation of saying what would have turned that anguish into joy. Sir Roland's often-repeated entreaty, that she would never let his claim interfere with her happiness, rushed across her mind, and at times she could scarcely control the impulse which prompted her to fly to Henry, and speak words of peace and happiness; but she could not so abuse the generosity which made her free, and in agony of spirit she implored of God to direct her path aright, and to heal these tearing wounds. She fancied her love for Henry had been wholly unperceived by him, and she resolved to conquer it; yet the sight of his misery distracted her, and unable to bear it any longer she covered her face with her hands and wept convulsively.

Henry arose at length, and walking slowly towards her, sat down by her side. He knew that she loved him—he saw her grief—yet for her, at that moment, he felt no pity; he looked upon her as the betrayer of both himself and his brother, and his soul was filled with bitterness.

"Why," he said, addressing her in a voice of stern coldness, "was not this told me before? why was my happiness to be thus cruelly, thus wantonly destroyed?"

Lady Constance felt his injustice, and was terrified at his words and manner. With a trembling voice she told him it had been Sir Roland's wish that their engagement should not be known.

" And was it his wish too that his brother's love should be permitted—and then crushed ? "

" Oh ! Henry," said Lady Constance, distressed beyond endurance, "do not speak so. I take God, who knows my heart, to witness, that I never knew you loved me—never dreamed of your feelings towards me, till that day on the cliff; and surely I have not since encouraged them."

He looked in her troubled, yet ingenuous countenance and he felt her truth and his own harshness.

" No," he replied in a faltering voice, "no, you have been kindly, kindly cruel. But you, Constance —has it been no effort to you—— ? "

" I am bound, Henry," she replied with dignity, " by every tie to Roland."

Henry's heart sunk within him ; he sighed bitterly. " Tell me," he said, " how this miserable engagement was formed ? "

Lady Constance gave him the outline of the case, and he then clearly saw that her heart had never had a part in it. This conviction relieved him greatly as removing the painful impression which had at first rested on his mind—that hers were fickle and light affections, easily won and as soon lost ; but as his value for her love increased, so did the intense wish to claim it as his own, increase also. He thought if he could but once hear her confess that it was his—that he could go and live on that remembrance for ever ; but he saw that she strove to hide her feelings, that she seemed to

think they were unperceived by him; and respecting
her the more for the high principle which guided her,
he restrained his earnest desire; and determined, with
an effort worthy of true love, not to let her see that he
had read her heart.

" You are sure," said he at length, " that Roland
loves you ? "

" Yes," she replied, her heart torn with the remembrance of his devotion.

" But can he love you as I do?—impossible !"—

" He does—oh! yes—he does," cried Lady Constance with terrible emotion.

" Dreadful ! — dreadful — every way miserable !"
exclaimed Henry ; and as he reflected that he had stolen
from Sir Roland the treasure of Lady Constance's love,
he ejaculated with heartfelt anguish, and the deepest
affection, " My brother — my brother !" while burst
after burst of grief broke from his labouring breast.

When he grew calmer Lady Constance rose, and
said, " And now, Henry, we must part — and you ——"

" Not yet, oh! not yet," he cried, " think, Constance, it is a parting for ever. Never can I see you
again, never — never."

" Try, dear Henry," she said, terribly shaken, " try
to look to God for comfort, and then in time ——"

" Oh! never," he said despairingly, " never!—No! I
am an exile from my home, an outcast—a heart-broken,
miserable wretch. You — lost to me !—Roland ! Oh!
my God! my God, have mercy !—Him to whom I was
going with hopeful heart—now—worse than a stranger !
—And to see him no more! the dearest, the noblest,
the best !—Oh !" he exclaimed, again throwing himself on the earth, " I cannot live through this — this

agony is insupportable. Pray for me, pray for me, Constance, that my heart may break, and life cease at once."

The struggle in Lady Constance's mind was dreadful as she looked on Henry as he lay on the ground before her in his extreme agony. She would have given worlds to have been able to say that which would have raised him to life and hope, and again she thought of Sir Roland's entreaty that she would consider herself as perfectly free — that she would forget her engagement to him, should it ever interfere with her wishes.—For a moment her heart throbbed wildly in indecision; and the fatal words had almost passed her lips, which would have made her guilty and miserable for ever. But there was a merciful restraining power over her; and though she could frame no prayer, yet her heart was drawn to God, and she continued mentally to exclaim, " My Father! my Father! my Father!" — till the mighty force of the temptation was subdued, and strength and clear thought were again restored. Then were rapidly brought to her mind her solemn and often-renewed vows—the love so deep, so disinterested, so long cherished, of him whose nobleness had set her free—and with renewed power she fought, and conquered.

" Henry," she said, in gentle yet firm accents, " you must not give way to these feelings, and I — must not again witness them. In time, do not doubt it, God will give you comfort if you seek it from Him; but now I must leave you — I cannot stay."

Henry continued lying on the ground as if wholly insensible to her words, till the ringing sound of the pebbles beneath her retreating steps roused him. He sprung up, exclaiming—

"Constance, you cannot leave me thus. Oh! do not go from me when I am so wretched. I would not—I will not offend you; but still at least say, Farewell!—tell me you forgive me—all my waywardness—my intemperance—all my folly and madness. Say Farewell."

"Farewell, Henry—and may our God bless you!"

She turned, and took the homeward path alone. He longed to follow her; to support her steps once more along the way they had so often trod together; but a feeling of deep respect checked him, and he remained immovable, gazing on her retreating form, till it was wholly lost to sight.

"Now I am indeed alone," he thought. "Home! blessed home! is lost to me for ever. All gone! My mother! from you too I must part. Oh that I could but feel resigned! that I could but lift my heart to God. But such a blight! so sudden, so terrible—and on every thing. My very life seems gone. But oh! my God," he exclaimed, raising his sad eyes to heaven, "Thou wilt have mercy, though I cannot ask Thee as I should."

He lingered yet for some time on the beach, for he could not endure the thought of returning home. How could he again see Lady Constance? how meet —how part with her?

At length the great clock struck ten, and fearful that his mother might remark his prolonged absence, he slowly took the road towards the house. The moon, now high up in the skies, was bathing every thing in her silver light, as he turned to gaze on the well-known scene; and mentally he took leave of every endeared object.

"Never," he exclaimed, "will these weary feet
tread this path again; never more shall I dare, even
in heart, to visit this loved place! The sea must
henceforth be my only earthly home—I am severed
from every tie. Oh! that I dared lay my head upon
my mother's breast, and tell her of my grief!—but I
must not harrow her dear heart with my regrets! All
earthly comfort is denied me;—my God lead me to
rest on Thee!"

When he entered the house he found Lady Ashton
in the hall; and hurriedly saying that he had staid out
later than he intended, and had still some little things
to arrange, he retired to his room. When there, he
locked the door, and seating himself, he opened his
desk, and proceeded to take from it the many little
things which he had treasured up for Lady Constance's
sake. There was a little sketch of her, which he had
taken but a few weeks before—the purse which she
had worked for him—a seal—a pencil-case;—and several other little tokens of remembrance which she had
given him from time to time. All must be parted
with—he dared not take with him one thing that had
come from her. But oh! what an agony it was to put
each cherished trifle aside, and feel it must be his no
longer! Each fresh thing, in succession, seemed to tear
away a portion of his existence; and when at last he
came to the most valued of all—the golden lock of hair
—his powers of endurance seemed completely to give
way, and his head sunk upon the table amidst out-
burstings of heart-broken anguish. Recovering a little, he looked up, and felt that it must be done—that
this too must be put away from him; and with a feeling
of despair he opened the case, where the bright lock

had so long lain, mingled with the scarcely less beautiful hair of his mother and of Lady Florence, and contrasting well with a jet-black curl from Sir Roland's forehead, which lay immediately within it. He took it up to separate it from the rest, and as its slender length unfolded before him, how well did he remember the day—just before he went last to sea— when Lady Constance had let him choose it from among her girlish curls, and his mother had cut it off and arranged it with the others—cherished remembrances all, of those so dear to him! whose thought had then, brought with it nought but peace and joy. He coiled it again in his hand, and felt as if it could not be given up!

Glancing, however, at the vacant space it had left in the case, he felt a gloomy satisfaction at having separated it from Sir Roland's; and in a bitter mood he cast away his brother's also, as bringing with it now none but hateful thoughts; but a sense of proud, disdainful indignation, succeeding, he again took it up, and replacing it within the folds of Lady Constance's pale-gold tress, he determined to send them both so united, to her. Hatred and wrath however, were such strange guests within his heart, that they could not long maintain a place there, and gradually his breast begun to heave with mingled emotions of regret and brotherly love; and pressing both the beloved locks he held in his hand together to his lips, he rested his head again upon the table as gentler tears flowed forth. They remained undried upon his cheek, for nature was exhausted—and he slept!

After some hours of uneasy rest, he was awakened by the servant coming to tell him that the carriage

would soon be round. He started, and felt bewildered
at finding himself up, and his things strewed all around
him, and at first he could not recollect what had happened. But at last the sad reality returned to his
mind, and he had again to take up the load of misery,
which he had forgotten for a while. He exerted himself however to shake it off, and having added the
lock of Lady Constance's hair to his other treasured
tokens of her affection, he folded them all together,
and merely writing within, " Pray for me," he sealed
the packet, and left it directed to her. Then, with revived love, he put his brother's curl back into its case,
and locked it in his desk; and proceeding to change
his dress, he descended to the breakfast-room, where
he found his mother and Lady Florence, ready and
waiting for him.

CHAPTER X.

> " I bid adieu
> To every recollection which might touch
> My duty to him. I shall never muse
> On childhood's pleasures, innocent no more
> For me   *   *   *   *
> *   *   *   nor repeat
> One name—O never !—I am very weak,
> I did not know how weak."—TALFOURD.

LADY Ashton had been too much occupied on the previous evening to remark the pallor and agitation in Lady Constance's countenance when she returned home ; and saying she was tired, the latter soon went to her own room. She was more tranquil than she had been for a length of time, for the dreaded hour was over, and she had been enabled to act as she felt duty required. Yet the remembrance of Henry's agony was terrible to her, and absorbed in miserable thoughts, she let the hours pass unheeded by, till the sun rising warned her that the time of his departure was near. She had not thought of rest, for the trying scenes she had gone through had left her too feverish and excited for sleep. But now she dreaded lest a summons might come for her to go and take a last leave of Henry; for she knew that her sister and Lady Ashton purposed being up to see him, and they might naturally suppose that she would wish to do the same.

Terribly indeed did her heart yearn to see him once again — and she would have given worlds to have watched even the vessel which was soon to put leagues of ocean waste between them, till its lessening sails had disappeared from the horizon; but she dared not meet him. Fearful, however, lest her resolution might fail, she hastily threw off her dress, and laid down on her bed; and had scarcely taken this wise precaution, before Lady Florence's light step was heard at the door, and her young face looked in, bright and glowing as the morning, though a tear was on her cheek. She approached her sister's bed and told her that Henry was down, and that Lady Ashton had sent her to say he would soon be gone.

"I cannot go down," said Lady Constance, "I do not feel well; you must wish him good-bye for me;" and she turned her face to the pillow to hide her tears.

Lady Florence returned to the breakfast-room, and Henry was relieved by knowing that he should not have the struggle of a parting before witnesses, though his heart sunk at finding that he should no more see her whom he felt he was leaving for ever.

The entrance door was on the north side of the house, and therefore at a distance from Lady Constance's room, which faced the sea; but in the stillness of the morning, when nothing was astir but the wakeful birds, the sound of the carriage was distinctly heard; and when it drove up to the door, and the rushing of the wheels reached Lady Constance's ear, the desire of seeing Henry once more was so irresistible, that springing from off her bed, and hastily throwing a cloak around her, she opened the door, and ran down a passage, at the end of which was a window looking out on the entrance.

There, was the carriage which was to convey him away, and footsteps moved to and fro beneath in the hall—and there were all the busy sounds—the "dreadful notes of preparation;" and then—his voice was heard. That loved sound in a moment recalled Lady Constance to a sense of her duty. Though it was impossible she could be seen by any one inside the house, yet if Henry looked up as he got into the carriage, or looked back—as he was sure to do—when driving away, she would then be distinctly visible to him; and her secret stand there would speak more of encouragement to his love, than her open appearance down-stairs, amongst the others, would have done; and might indeed too clearly mark the nature of the feelings which made her so urgently crave for yet one more look. She felt that this was wrong, and she knew that she had no right to make even this small concession to her own heart; and flying back with greater speed than she had come, she happily reached her own apartment unobserved. She felt strengthened by the self-denial she had exercised, and though when she heard the carriage drive off, her heart seemed to die within her, yet her conscience was at ease, and she was able wholly to give herself up to the will and guidance of God. She threw herself again upon her bed, and worn-out both in body and mind, she fell asleep, and remained in that happy state of forgetfulness, till the day was far advanced.

The evening which followed was a melancholy one to all the party, and the beauty of the weather, and the glorious moon, instead of being enjoyed by them as usual, seemed only to add to their depression. Lady Constance proposed returning home early, and strove to occupy herself so as to distract her thoughts from the subject which yet would ever present itself to her mind. The pang of parting was too recent for Lady Ashton to bear to talk of it, and Lady Constance was thankful to be spared the burden of conversation ; and they therefore both took up their books.

But Lady Florence—whose regret for her late playfellow and companion, though perfectly sincere, was by no means the deep feeling that oppressed her two companions—rather enjoyed indulging her sorrows by feeding them with melancholy thoughts (as many young and unwise spirits love to do) and sitting down at the pianoforte, she begun singing that saddest song, the " Treasures of the Deep." Her voice was rich and beautiful, and her powers in the delightful art of music were, as has been said, far beyond her years.

Lady Constance longed from the first to stop her, but a conscious feeling restrained her from doing so ; and Lady Ashton, who never liked to interfere with the pleasures of others, bore the harrowing sounds in silence, though they were the last she would willingly have listened to at that moment. Both of them sat tranquil even during those sad and beautiful lines—

> " But more—thy billows and thy depths have more !
> High hearts, and brave are gathered to thy breast ;

> They hear not now the booming waters roar,
> The battle-thunders cannot break their rest ;"

but at the next verse it seemed as if Lady Constance's
nature could sustain no more. She was never one
whose emotions could readily express themselves in
tears, but the quivering of her countenance, and her
sob-like breathings became so uncontrollable as her
sister, continuing to sing, came to the words—

> " Dark roll thy tides o'er manhood's noble head ; "

that, fearful she must be betraying her intolerable
suffering, she instinctively looked up, to see if she were
observed. But Lady Ashton's affectionate heart was at
that moment wholly absorbed in its own regretful feelings, and she was stealthily wiping away the quiet tears
of love and sorrow which had flowed down her cheek.
At sight of her emotion, Lady Constance's endurance completely gave way, and in an agitated voice,
she called to her sister—

" Oh ! Florence, do not sing that song."

" Dear Constance," said Lady Ashton, turning her
tearful eyes towards the poor girl, and holding out her
hand, " you are ever so thoughtful ! "

Lady Constance kissed the kind hand which was
pressed in hers, and completely overcome sunk upon
her knees at Lady Ashton's side, and burying her face
in her lap, burst into an almost hysterical flood of tears.
Lady Ashton bent over her with the fondest affection,
saying,

" Do not, my dearest child, do not grieve yourself
or mind me ; he will soon perhaps return, and I ought
not to give way ; but he is so dear—so very dear."

Lady Constance knew that too well ; and she longed

to pour forth all her feelings to Lady Ashton, and not to be forced to keep silence, while that kind friend attributed to sympathy in *her* sorrows, the tears and sighs of anguish, which burst forth for her own.

Poor Lady Florence was in consternation at the effects of her song, and added her tears to those of the others, as she stood with her arm round Lady Ashton's neck; till the latter, smilingly said, "We are really all very silly; we must not let such trifles overset us."

" Trifles!" thought Lady Constance.

She was still further tried, when on going to her room that night, she found lying on her table, the packet which Henry Ashton had left for her; and which the servants, having but just found, had placed there. Recognising his writing, she opened it with a trembling hand, and how was she overcome at the sight of its contents! Not all the most agonized expressions of grief could have touched her, as did those mute evidences of his uncomplaining misery—of the complete separation which had taken place between them, and which must thenceforth, for ever exist. She knew what it must have cost him even to let his eye rest upon the little tokens which lay before her, fraught as they were with such sweet, yet bitter recollections; but what must have been the struggle to part with them—to cast away all that could link his memory with the happiness, now gone for ever! She wept for hours, for she could not restrain her tears. Perpetually did Henry's image appear before her; first as the bright, joy-giving creature which he had ever hitherto been; then as the miserable wanderer he now was from his home—and all for her! She was the unhappy cause of all his misery—herself most miserable! At length her eye caught the words which Henry had written within the cover of his packet, and which she had not observed before :—" Pray for me." She instantly sunk upon her knees, though fresh tears burst forth, and earnestly did she pray for him, and for herself. She rose calmed and strengthened, and then went to seek the rest she so much needed.

The next morning she arose with an animated desire to do her duty in every way. She determined that the example which Henry had set her, should not be lost, but that she would also put away from her all that might recall softening impressions, or lead her thoughts to dwell on that, from which she ought so carefully to withdraw them. She could not indeed, as he had done, cast away all that might remind her of her unfortunate love, for the whole atmosphere was filled with his remembrance; but she determined on the more difficult task of denying him a place in her memory; and strengthened by renewed supplications at the throne of grace, she went down full of the wise, and pious resolutions which had been given her from above.

Mrs. Montague's society proved a great resource to her just at that time, for she felt a strong regard for her, and really loved the little child; but even there, the name she most wished to avoid, ever sounded in her ears; for Mrs. Montague, naturally grateful for what Henry Ashton had done for her, was continually speaking of him. The two friends, however, often conversed on other, higher subjects ; and though Lady Constance was very humble in her estimate of her own powers, yet she was encouraged to believe that her words were not entirely unblest. Lady Ashton's unremitting kindness towards Mrs. Montague in endeavouring to lead her to " the Holy Spirit—the Comforter," seemed after a time, by the aid of Almighty power, gradually to melt the seal from her heart, and open it to receive the joyful intelligence, that there was mercy and pardon for her, through the blood of Christ, as well as for all who would accept it; and as this conviction began to enter her mind, she seemed to gain a new existence. Joy and love sprung up out of the former darkness, and in the transporting hope that the gates of Heaven were indeed open to receive her, she seemed for a time to lose all sense of earthly sorrow. When she was in this happy state of mind, it was a great comfort to Lady Constance to be with her ; and many a time did she reproach herself for her own unhappiness, when she saw Mrs. Montague's cheerful resignation to the many sorrows of her lot; and her faith too was often invigorated and refreshed by the conversation of one, to whom the pure truth of God was so new and so delightful.

As the cause which had made Lady Constance wish to leave Llanaven was now removed, she was very anxious to give up her engagement with Mrs. Mordaunt; but Lady Ashton would on no account allow of her doing so, for she thought that she had enjoyed the idea of it, and that she now only wished to relinquish it on her account. It was determined therefore that she should go on the ensuing week, and after staying a few days with Mrs. Mordaunt in London, proceed with her to the Highlands; and Lady Ashton decided on going up with her herself, wishing to see her safe in her cousin's charge.

Lady Constance had seen but little society beyond that which she had had at her father's, or in Lady Ashton's house; and she would have shrunk from the idea of going thus among strangers, had not the harassed state of her mind made her feel as if "any change must better her condition." She longed to be taken away from her own thoughts, and to be forced into conversation which had no reference to the object, whose remembrance she wished so much to banish. She indeed most conscientiously fought against the indulgence of her feelings, at all times, but every thing at home tended to encourage them; she had not only herself, but every one else to struggle against, for it was so natural to talk of Henry ! She never intentionally suffered herself to be unemployed; yet often would the open page remain unturned for ages, or the needle rest idle in her hand, while her thoughts were following one solitary vessel tossing about on the stormy sea. She would rouse herself when she found her mind thus wandering, and renew her efforts to fix her attention on what was before her ; and by degrees she began to obtain some command over her fancy and recollection.

Never from the very first had she permitted herself to dwell on Henry's name—excepting in prayer; but she would sometimes be for hours supplicating God for him; and the faint light of early dawn would often creep into her chamber, while she was yet on her knees. She was young and had still much to learn of the deceitfulness of her own heart, and of the wily strength of her great spiritual enemy. We may be, perhaps, in a general way, "not ignorant of his devices," as St. Paul expresses it; but the last moment of our lives will probably the first, which shall free us from his

attacks, or deliver us from his delusions. Lady
Constance soon found that this seemingly pious exercise, was only a snare to bind her to that, which she
should strive to forget; and unutterably bitter was the
moment when she felt that this indulgence, too, must
be resigned. She continued indeed, in heartfelt terms
to commend him she loved to his heavenly Father;
but from that time she did so in brief words; nor ever
suffered his cherished name to linger on her lips.

When the day came for her departure from home,
her spirits drooped anew. She had never been separated from her sister for even a day, and she felt as if
driven away from all she loved. At parting she threw
her arms round the child, and all the sorrow of her
heart seemed to burst forth in the continued floods of
tears which she shed. The little girl had gathered for
her a nosegay of the sweetest flowers in the garden,
but she would not take a bud or leaf away with her
from Llanaven; for all there breathed of him whom
she was determined to forget. Not liking, however,
to pain her sister by refusing her little present, she
took it; but before she had got many miles on her
journey she threw it away. She held it long, it is true,
in her hand on the carriage window before she could
resolve to give it up, for trifles are at times so precious! but she did let it drop at last, and then her
heart was lightened.

CHAPTER XI.

"Why, what a motley thing is this same life!
    Laughter and sighs commingling! Scarcely ends
    The smile, but tear-drops stray adown the cheek
    From grief's full anguish pressed ;—unequal war!
    The smile may gleam upon the lip, but bring
    No message from the heart.—But who that weeps
    Knows not the bitter fount from whence those waters flow?"
                                                                            MS.

WHEN the travellers arrived in London they drove
directly to Mrs. Mordaunt's; and Lady Ashton having consigned her charge safely to that lady's care,
returned herself the next day into Cornwall.

If Lady Constance had been under the influence of
a fairy's wand, she could scarcely have undergone a
greater change than she experienced in going from
Lady Ashton's at Llanaven, to Mrs. Mordaunt's, in
Lower Grosvenor Street. The house was large and
handsomely furnished, and Mrs. Mordaunt herself was
a clever and lady-like person, and lived in the high
society in which she had been born. But there was
an air of refinement about every thing at Llanaven
which Lady Constance looked for in vain in her new
abode. Even in Henry Ashton's exuberant spirits there
was never the slightest approach to any thing but what
was gentlemanlike, and Sir Roland's manners as well as

his mother's were particularly pleasing and delightful. But at Mrs. Mordaunt's, there was frequently a something in the conversation which seemed to require repressing, lest it should verge on what was disagreeable; so that the really refined and Christian mind felt no repose; whilst a word on the subject of religion threw a chill on every one around. It was, perhaps, an air of spirituality diffused over every thing at Llanaven, which made the society there so peculiarly delightful; for though its inmates by no means thought it necessary to force religious observations into all their social intercourse, yet amongst themselves they felt that such topics, when occurring naturally, were ever welcome; and falling in with the accustomed tenor of their minds, seemed never out of place. Indeed the pure, invigorating sea-breeze does not differ more from the murky atmosphere of the great Emporium of the world, than did this healthy tone of feeling from that of the society into which Lady Constance was now thrown; and spite of all her unhappiness at Llanaven, she would often gladly have returned to the seclusion and quiet of that dear, and delightful place. That was, however, out of the question now, and amidst her many unpleasant feelings she was forced to acknowledge that the change really had a good effect upon her spirits.

Only two of Mrs. Mordaunt's sons were staying with her at that time: Robert the eldest, and the youngest—Augustus. The other—Philip—who was evidently the mother's favourite, was just then absent, but was to join them, it was said, in Scotland. He was in the law, and by no means one of those who are said "to follow that profession without overtaking it," for he was very clever, and was getting on exceedingly well.

The eldest son, however, had attained even a greater degree of excellence than his brother in his particular profession, which was that of perfect idleness; while the youngest, a youth of most moderate abilities, was in one of the public offices.

Mrs. Mordaunt pursued the ordinary routine of a London life; and though it was late in the season, there were still dinner-parties going on, while a few lingering balls and concerts served occasionally to diversify the scene.

A short time after Lady Constance's arrival in town, there was a large dinner-party in Grosvenor street; but all there were strangers to her, excepting Mrs. Mordaunt and her two sons. At dinner she found herself between Augustus Mordaunt and another young man of singular manners, whose name she did not know, but who had evidently determined to place himself next to her, and who, as soon as they were seated, without the slightest preface or introduction, began,

" You are quite well I hope, Lady Constance, and enjoy your visit to London ? "

She was rather surprised at this abrupt and familiar commencement of acquaintance, and answered his inquiries with cold civility. He then proceeded in the same tone to ask after Sir Roland Ashton and the other members of that family, speaking of them as if he had lived all his life in their society. Lady Constance looked at him with astonishment, and asked if he were well acquainted with them.

" Not particularly," he replied, " I once saw a man's back half way down Grafton street, and I was told it was Sir Roland Ashton; and I think, yes I am sure, that a few months ago I read the name of Henry

William Ashton as promoted to the rank of lieutenant
in her Majesty's navy. That is all the personal acquaintance I have with them."

Lady Constance was alarmed; she supposed of
course that her neighbour was mad, and she sat with
fear and trepidation by his side. She endeavoured to
give her attention to the low-toned observations of her
other companion, but that did not improve the state of
things at all, for the stranger seemed seized with the
rage of persecution towards the unhappy Augustus,
though he appeared to be as perfect a stranger to him
as he was to Sir Roland. All his timid insinuations
were caught up and repeated in a loud tone, and an
inquisitorial examination entered into, as to the motive
and whole bearing of what he said, even when he only
observed that, "August was often a very hot month."
The unhappy youth suffered dreadfully under this process, being evidently in extreme terror of his tormentor,
and he at length took refuge in total silence, his face
having become purple from the continual coatings of
colour which had overspread it during his many confu-
sions.

Lady Constance was exceedingly embarrassed, and
longed for the moment of retiring to arrive. But the
crowning stroke to her dismay was put at last by the
stranger's asking her in a loud tone, "How she liked
the Mordaunt family?" adding, "I am scarcely acquainted with any of them myself, but they are generally considered, I believe, a very odd set."

Lady Constance gazed at him now in utter consternation, thinking the next step must inevitably be the
smashing of all the glass on the table, or perhaps the
presenting the point of a knife to her own throat; but

a curiously suppressed smile lurking in the corner of
the maniac's mouth, caused a new light to flash upon
her, and her lip curling in sympathy she replied,
" that she liked them all very much, excepting one.'"

" And that is the youngest of course ! I have
heard he is a very —— I do not know what sort of
person."

The unfortunate Augustus coloured deeper than
ever, and seemed ready to sink into the earth, but
his dismay changed into an expression of extreme,
and almost childish delight, when Lady Constance
replied,

" No, not the youngest."

" The eldest then ? "

" No—the second."

" Well now you really are a cousin worth having—
one after my own heart ! " exclaimed Philip Mordaunt,
(for such the lunatic proved to be) his quick black eye
shining with delight. " Enchanting ! after passing eight
and twenty years upon this dull earth, to meet at last
with a kindred spirit, one who can discover one's
devices. Lady Constance, how is it possible that two
souls, cast so evidently in the same mould, should not
have been drawn together by strong attraction long
ere this ? "

" It is just possible that there may be some antago-
nist principle which has counteracted the force of the
attraction, " answered Lady Constance, with somewhat of gravity tempering her smile ; for though all
fears for her life had ceased, she did not yet feel quite
satisfied with her cousin's manner.

" Oh ! aye ! " he replied, pretending to muse deeply,
" like the contracting and expanding power of the metal

in the pendulum, keeping it always in its proper place. Well, it may be so!" Then turning round with a really pleasing smile, he added in a lower voice,

" But my fair cousin need not contract her kindly good-nature for fear of my presumption expanding too much, I shall ever keep my proper place as respects her, I trust."

Lady Constance smiled and inquired, if the mode of introduction he had used towards her was that which he usually adopted in such cases. He answered, " No, but that he knew he was not expected, having been absent on business, which it was supposed would have detained him much longer than it did; and the fancy having seized him of preserving a brilliant incognito, he had threatened Augustus with extinction if he revealed his secret." He then asked her how she had found him out.

" I perceived by your ill-suppressed mirth," said Lady Constance, " that there was some mystery, and catching a likeness to your mother, I felt sure it must be you."

Philip Mordaunt then entered on many amusing subjects of conversation, and made himself so agreeable that Lady Constance grew quite at her ease with him ; and now instead of wishing for it, was rather sorry when the signal for retiring was given.

When Mrs. Mordaunt had been a few minutes in the drawing-room, she went up to Lady Constance, and said she hoped Philip had made himself very agreeable. Lady Constance in reply informed her of his proceedings, at which she was much amused, and said it was exactly like him, for he delighted in distracting and mystifying people; but that he was, never-theless, a dear, good-natured, clever creature.

As they were talking together a singularly lovely person came up to them, and in the pleasantest manner possible begged of Mrs. Mordaunt to introduce her to Lady Constance, as she said she believed they had a mutual friend, of whom it would give her much pleasure to hear some account. Mrs. Mordaunt performed the requisite ceremony, and then leaving them, went to devote her attentions to her other guests.

The moment Lady Constance had heard her new acquaintance named as Lady Stanmore, she recollected Sir Roland's having often mentioned her with great interest; and she felt sure that he was the mutual friend who had been alluded to. The thought of him, and the dread of what might be said, made her feel ready to sink, but as she was one who possessed *par excellence* the painful, but beautiful habit of blushing, her heightened colour passed very well for the little embarrassment of introduction. Lady Stanmore instantly began on the dreaded subject, and spoke of Sir Roland in terms of such excessive praise, that Lady Constance's mind was filled with a painful mixture of gratification, remorse, and pride. The conversation was most trying to her, and yet after the first minute she felt it a joy, in such a land of strangers, to speak of any member of the family she loved so much, and she listened with delight to the high character given of Sir Roland.

Lady Stanmore said that he was admired and esteemed by every one, and that there were many she believed, who would gladly have had nearer ties than those of mere acquaintance with him; but that he was a perfect disciple of Plato's, and seemed to bear a charmed life about him, walking unscathed through all the "dread artillery" which was directed against him. She then adverted to his "peculiar opinions," as she called them, and playfully, though not without some emotion, spoke of what she called his attempt "to convert her." "And I am angry with myself," she added, "for not being angry with him about it, for it has often made me very uncomfortable."

"Roland's opinions if rightly received could not create discomfort I should think in any heart," said Lady Constance.

"Then I suppose you would insinuate that I am uncomfortable because I have not rightly received them?"

Lady Constance smiled.

"Then are you one of the advocates of those dreadful opinions?"

"I am an advocate of the opinions Roland holds, but I do not find them dreadful."

"Ah! I see you have held, one the right side, and the other the left, of the same book, and learnt together what he would call 'its happy lessons.'"

"They are happy lessons!" said Lady Constance. "The only happy ones," she added abstractedly.

"That is a bold word," observed Lady Stanmore; "and a sad one too, from one so young. I begin to suspect that Sir Roland's study of the philosophers was not so very profound, as we abroad innocently supposed it to be. But however," she continued, for she saw trouble on Lady Constance's countenance, "study what he might, and whom he might, he did his masters no discredit. But it is astonishing how his pro-

voking words continually ring in my ears, and drop their
bitterness into every pleasure.   I perpetually see visions
of my servants coming to untimely ends because of the
temptations which he says I throw them into; and the
lightest of ball-dresses hangs heavy on me, because he
terrifies me with having to answer for the use of every
thing I have."

"But did he press on you merely the evil of *these*
things? that is not like him; he usually goes much
deeper, and shews that the change must lie in the
heart."

"Oh! yes, he did do that; but I believe I brought
the lecture concerning these things rather upon myself,
by asking him to do something, which he was ungracious enough to refuse."

"I am sure he felt he ought not to do what you
wished, or he would never have refused," replied Lady
Constance warmly, "for he hates saying 'no' to any
one."

"You need not be afraid that his refusal made us
hate each other very bitterly," said Lady Stanmore; "for
he has the art of making his 'no' almost as pleasant
as 'yes;' and that is a great thing for *me* to say, who
hate being contradicted above all things in existence.
But do you never go out in the world?"

"Not to late parties."

"And do you not long to do so?"

"Not very much," replied Lady Constance smiling.
"I should not think dissipation could be very improving in any way."

"Perhaps not—particularly, but then what is one to
do?   Are you not very dull at home?"

"Dull!" exclaimed Lady Constance, "no! the

happiest and the merriest people in the world." (She forgot all her sorrows at that moment.)

"I wish I could decide one way or the other," sighed Lady Stanmore, "for now I enjoy nothing."

Lady Constance looked at her till the tear almost swelled in her eye, and she longed to speak; but ever diffident, she shrunk from the idea of seeming to teach one older than herself, especially after so short an acquaintance.

Lady Stanmore read her expressive countenance, however, and answered,—

"Say what you like, for I see you are restraining something; and you cannot make me more uncomfortable than I am. Yet I do not know what makes me talk so freely to you, unless it is that I take up your friendship where I left off Sir Roland's, and choose to fancy I have known you a long time; though he declined being much of a counsellor to me, and referred me rather cavalierly to my husband."

"Is Lord Stanmore then a religious person?" asked Lady Constance with pleased surprise.

"N—o, perhaps not exactly what you would call a religious person; but he is the best husband, and the best every thing in the world."

"But why then should Roland refer you to him on these subjects?"

"Because he was my husband I suppose! he probably wisely thought that as such he was the best counsellor I could have — better at least than any other man."

Lady Constance was silent, for she felt puzzled.

"I should however add," continued Lady Stanmore rather reluctantly, "that he named another counsellor before even him; but I scarcely like speaking of so awful a being in this place."

"Why not? we are saying no harm," said Lady Constance, in the simplicity of a heart to which the thought of God was as the breath of life—though His name never lightly passed her lips.

"I do not know, but it seems out of place in common, every-day life."

"But we are talking of the things of God, and why should we not, with all reverence, mention His name? for it must have been Him to whom Roland referred you."

"I will not deny that it was—but I hate all appearance of parade in these things."

"I think I should do so too," said Lady Constance gently, "but no one can hear us now."

Lady Stanmore looked round to ascertain if that were really the case, then said—

"I remember his words as if I had heard them but yesterday, 'Keep God ever first, your husband ever next, and you cannot go wrong.'"

The tears sprung to Lady Constance's eyes, and rolled in an instant down her cheek, as she heard words, which so completely brought before her him whose wisdom and piety had dictated them; and she felt a love for him at that moment which banished every other feeling.

"I am very foolish," she said; "but what you repeated was the only word of religion I have heard ever since Lady Ashton left me; and you do not know how it has refreshed me; it was quite a spring in the desert. I have never in all my life before, been separated from those who had the love of God in them, and you cannot conceive how I thirst after their con-

versation, now, after being deprived of it for three
whole days."

Lady Stanmore smiled.

" There certainly must be something very fascinating," she said, "in that which makes its absence so
bitterly felt. Do you talk of religion for ever at home,
and of nothing else ?"

" Oh ! no, of a thousand other things ; but still—
it is there—we always feel that."

" Well I dare say you good people are very good,
but you seem to me to be always in the clouds."

" You have a little boy I know, Lady Stanmore,
and when he is old enough to go to school, will you
not often talk of him with Lord Stanmore, and find
pleasure in doing so because you know he loves him as
well as you do ; and even though you often talk of
other things, will it not be a delight to know that
whenever you are inclined to speak of him, it will be a
welcome subject ? And do you not think it would be
an irksome restraint to live only with those who were
strangers to him, and did not care for him ? to find
that if you spoke of him your companions thought the
subject disagreeable, and changed it as soon as possible ?
I am sure you would. Well then only," and she
lowered her voice, "put the name of God in the room
of that of your child, and you have before you the
feeling of those who truly love Him. Would you
mind my quoting something from Malachi ?"

" Oh ! no."

" He says, ' Then they that feared the Lord spake
often one to another, and the Lord hearkened and
heard it, and a book of remembrance was written before him, for them that feared the Lord and that

thought upon his name. And they shall be mine, saith the Lord of Hosts, in that day when I shall make up my jewels; and I will spare them as a man spareth his own son that serveth him. Then shall ye return and discern between the righteous and the wicked, between him that serveth God and him that serveth him not.' "

" His jewels," said Lady Stanmore thoughtfully, " what a beautiful idea! To be one of the jewels of the Lord! What high praise!"

" High privilege rather," observed Lady Constance; " the earthly jewel is without lustre till the light shines on it, so are we till the Spirit shines on us."

" Ah, you—what shall I call you, for I hate cant names?—you thorough-going Christians are dreadful persons to argue with, you have something ready to say at all times."

" I do not often like to argue, I feel afraid; but what we have been talking of now seems very plain."

" Yes, just as plain to you perhaps as French is to a Frenchman, but difficult to those who are not accustomed to the language. I understood however what you meant just now about the love of God; but do you really so love Him as to feel unhappy when not talking of Him?"

" No; but I do feel uncomfortable when I am with those to whom I can never speak of Him with satisfaction. This little conversation to-night has been very pleasant to me, for at least you do not seem to dislike the subject."

" I do not dislike it as you represent it, or as Sir Roland Ashton did; but I have some cousins who provoke me infinitely. They are always talking at me, or finding fault with me, and weary me to death. They look like—any thing but ladies, and say ' they cannot afford to dress well, and subscribe to Missionary Societies also;' they fly from meeting to meeting, and talk of dear Mr. this, and sweet Mr. that, and then come and are as cross to their servants, and as easily put out as any one else, and talk of Christian tempers in a most unchristian manner. But you dress yourself as well as possible and look so nice! And do not seem to repent of every smile you give. And he too—Sir Roland I mean—looked always so very gentlemanlike, and as if he thought it worth while to be agreeable; so that he gained ' golden opinions from all sorts of men.' Your looks, poor things," she added with a smile, " you cannot help, but you do your best to compensate to society, for the want of beauty, and that is all that can be expected. However, not to talk nonsense, I confess I like clean religion—not dirty; I like civil religion— not rude; I like quiet religion—and not a perpetual flutter of spiritual dissipation; and I like warm, loving religion—and not a spirit of detraction, and of cold harshness."

" I remember," said Lady Constance, "that Roland used to say, ' if ever you were led to God, it would be through the affections;—by love and not by fear.'"

" Did he say so?" exclaimed Lady Stanmore, a tear swelling in her soft dark eye, and a lovely expression of pleasure overspreading her countenance, " he judged of me too well; for it is more fear that I feel, than love, at this moment. I am afraid of being condemned — afraid of losing heaven — afraid of — every thing I believe. But I find no love to God in this cold heart; though sometimes I think I should love Him, if I were more worthy of Him; but when I begin to look into myself I see so much to alter—so much to give up—that I am in despair, and do nothing."

"I cannot judge of course," said Lady Constance, "but still it does appear to me, that you scarcely as yet see, or feel what Christ has done for you."

"What do you mean?"

"That He has saved you."

"Saved me. Oh no! Oh no!" she said in some agitation.

"Why do you say so?"

"Because I know I am not fit to go to heaven."

"Can you tell me of one who is fit to go there?"

"You seem to be so, and I am sure Sir Roland Ashton was."

"But, dear Lady Stanmore, if we are fit, how have we become so?"

"By being virtuous and good, and loving God."

"Oh! no, that is not it. It is by believing in and trusting to Him who is 'able and willing to save to the uttermost all who come to God through Him!' Christ has borne the punishment of our sins, and of yours too; for His, was an all-sufficient sacrifice. If we are saved, it is by believing that He has suffered in our stead, and that we are pardoned for His sake. Then we appear before God as clothed in His righteousness— as He appeared before God on the cross clothed in our sins. It is Christ who must open God's gates to us, and then as His redeemed—the purchased of His blood, we shall be allowed to enter in, unquestioned."

She spoke rapidly, for her energy quite for the moment overcame her diffidence. Lady Stanmore was much moved.

" I cannot think this can apply to me," she said.

" To whom then?" asked Lady Constance.

" To people who love God."

" Christ came to save those which were lost, not those who could go to heaven without Him."

" I do not say that any can do that exactly."

" Christ will be an *entire* Saviour, or none. If we look to any thing but Him, His Spirit is not leading us."

" But we may do our best, and then He will have mercy on us."

" Had the thief on the cross done his best?"

" No, that always puzzled me."

" He was saved in the only way which is open for us; he believed that Christ suffered, in order that he might be pardoned, and therefore he went to God and sought the pardon, which had been so dearly purchased, and so freely given. Roland has done the same, I have done the same; you will—oh! I trust you will be able also to do so in time. Remember what Isaiah says of Christ: ' He was wounded for *our* transgressions, He was bruised for *our* iniquities; the chastisement of *our* peace was upon Him, and with HIS stripes WE are healed. .... The Lord hath laid upon *Him* the iniquity of *us all.*' You see, there is no mention made of our righteousness, only of Christ's meritorious, vicarial sacrifice."

" Oh! you must speak plainer to me," said Lady Stanmore, smiling and colouring.

" I mean that His death had such value in God's eyes, that for the sake of it, He grants Him the pardon of all who seek for it through Him; and by calling it a vicarial sacrifice, I mean of course that it is a sacrifice of one person for another—instead of that other—of Christ instead of us."

" Yet you, who say you are saved so entirely without any merit of your own, seem to desire so much to do what is right."

" Not half so much as we ought," answered Lady Constance, quickly. " Besides we love Him who has loved us, and He said, ' if ye love me keep my commandments.' And when we give ourselves up to Him, He puts His Spirit into our hearts—His pure Spirit, and that makes us love holiness. As some old writer said, ' We work *from* life and not *for* life.' But still if you knew all, you would see we had nothing to boast of; and it is that which makes us feel so thankful not to have to depend for gaining heaven, on our own merits. It is such an unspeakable comfort also, to be able for His sake to go to God at all times; when we have done wrong—for new pardon; when we are unhappy—for comfort; and we always find it, because He ' ever liveth in heaven to make intercession for us.' "

" Your words are so new to me," said Lady Stanmore, " they really almost seem like another language ! But there breathes such an exalted spirit over these things as almost overpowers me. There must be a great reality in them, of which I, and those I associate with, have certainly no idea. Every thing with you and Sir Roland seems to go up, and up — to God; and at times I seem almost, to go with you a little way. I cannot say what I feel at moments, it seems as if a curtain were lifted, shewing something indescribable, and bright, and awful ! I almost seem as if on the verge of an invisible world."

"We are so undoubtedly," said Lady Constance; "nothing but the dulness of——But here is Mrs. Mordaunt coming to us."

"The discussion concerning your ' mutual friend' seems to have been very animated and interesting," said that lady as she approached; "shall I be very unwelcome if I interrupt it? I long for some music, and your powers are too well known, Lady Stanmore, for me not to appeal to you to take compassion on me."

"I shall be very happy," replied Lady Stanmore. "Lady Constance do you not sing?"

"Sometimes."

"Will you sing with me?"

"Oh! yes, if you wish it, and if there is any thing we both know."

They went to the pianoforte, and soon found something which suited them. Whilst Lady Stanmore was playing the introductory symphony she said in a low voice to Lady Constance, "I should like to see you again; could you drive out with me to-morrow?"

"Call here, and I will, if I can; I should like it very much."

The sound of their beautiful voices soon brought up the party from below, which was in fact Mrs. Mordaunt's hope and intention: for conversation had begun sorely to flag between her and her lady-guests. The moment the gentlemen entered the drawing-room, Lord Stanmore took his favourite station by the side of his lovely wife, who was ever glad to have him by her; and Augustus Mordaunt also took that which was his favourite—by Lady Constance's side; or rather, as his brother Philip afterwards designated it, "to the north-

east of her." He kept on murmuring small, inane
praises of her singing, during the bars of symphony
which occasionally occurred; and small sighs sounded
every now and then in her ear, which altogether excited Lady Constance's risible faculties to so trying a
degree, that she had difficulty sometimes, when she
opened her lips, to prevent a burst of merriment from
coming forth, instead of the pathetic notes of Beethoven
or Rossini.

Philip Mordaunt perceiving what was going on,
and ever bent on mischief, took his station in sight of
Lady Constance, though concealed from others, and
contrived to attract her eye from time to time, imitating
in large all his brother's small performances; till at
length, having succeeded in making it impossible for
her to trust her voice at all, during one very important
passage, he felt satisfied with his success, and left her
in peace.

Robert Mordaunt in the meantime stood by, and
with the air of a connoisseur propounded his admiration
of both Lady Stanmore's and Lady Constance's powers.
But when the latter retired from the pianoforte, and
gave way to other performers, his attentions were
ostentatiously, and pompously devoted to her. He
stood before her making speeches, and taking up
her whole attention; and stooping, would frequently
say a few words in a low tone, in order that his intimacy with his noble and beautiful cousin might be
observed by the rest of the company; determined evidently that they should imagine there was something
very particular between them.

Lady Constance disliked him at all times, and now

more than ever. She would fain have risen from the sofa, and have left him, but he stood so immediately before her, that she could not do so without asking him to move, which she was far too shy to do; and though colouring with vexation at his absurd and obtrusive attentions, she was forced to resign herself to her fate, and sit still.

Lady Stanmore who knew Mr. Mordaunt's old habit of devoting himself pointedly to whosoever was the " bright particular star" of any party, and had often herself suffered from his persecutions, felt for Lady Constance, though she could not refrain occasionally from giving her a look which made it most difficult for her to keep her countenance; but at length seeing her look really uncomfortable, she begged Philip to go and " get Lady Constance out of quarantine." He proceeded immediately on his mission, and delighting in tormenting every body, went up to his brother, and whispered that Lady Stanmore seemed much hurt at his neglect of her, and that in fact he believed she had something very particular to say to him. Highly gratified, Mr. Mordaunt went off to Lady Stanmore, who soon, bored to death by him, formed secret, strong resolutions never again to succour the unfortunate.

Philip meanwhile seated himself by Lady Constance.

" I beg you will observe that I do not stand before you," he said; " for I can afford to give you freedom, certain that you will not wish to exercise it by leaving me. Are you not infinitely obliged to me for delivering you from the ' Giant Despair' who was imprisoning you ? "

" I think you might leave it to others to laugh at
your brothers, and not do so yourself," replied Lady
Constance half joking, but half gravely.   " I am used
to see brothers love each other."

" Ah! when one has left people behind, they seem
so very perfect!"

Lady Constance felt that they did.

" But now what would you have me do with such
a couple brothers as I have?" continued Philip, " the
one such a 'Pomposo furioso,' the other always full of
his 'sentimentalibus lachrymirorum.' What can happen? I must either laugh at them to shew the world
I am wise enough to see their follies—or cry over them
to shew how much I feel for them. Your gentle
nature might perhaps make you take the latter course;
I confess the former better suits the temper of my
genius. But I wish particularly to ask you one question. Are you in the habit of making every one in
love with you?"

Lady Constance laughed and coloured; " I do not
call that love," she said.

" The 'sieur' Robert means his to be taken for
such, I can assure you, and if you manage well, I think
you really might become Lady Constance Mordaunt!
which would not sound so ill after all, would it? But
as for the wretched Augustus, his really is love—I can
see that."

" Then why do you laugh at him?"

" Because the love of a simpleton is always laugh-
able."

" I do not think it is ever a subject for laughter,
when it is genuine, let it be in whom it may. But as

for your brother Augustus, I think he would like any one who is good-natured to him, and did not laugh at him."

" That is a very sweeping piece of insinuated censure, Lady Constance," exclaimed Philip, " including a mother and both her eldest hopes."

" *You* seem to me by far the worst."

" Oh! no, I assure you, I am sometimes very kind to him, and take him out a walk with me, or shew him the exhibition, or the Zoological Gardens. But there he stood at your north-east shoulder—(whispering by the bye as if he had been the ' cooling western breeze') and it was irresistibly ludicrous! But again I ask—are you in the habit of making every one in love with you? I only want to know—as you will be with us some time I hope—what we have to expect—what will be the average of suicides, &c., which may be looked for. I have something to do with a life insurance office, and it may materially affect the funds of that company, should you have the habit alluded to, and stay long in a place like this, where population is dense."

" Oh no, I have no such habit; you may be quite easy about your friends. I think however that nothing is so absurd as to fancy, because people like to talk to each other, that therefore they must necessarily be in love. There are pleasant men in the world, why should not one be allowed to talk to them in peace?"

" We were not, I believe, talking of *pleasant* men at that moment," replied Philip. " But even then, though it may perhaps be play to you, it may be death to the pleasant men, and is always, believe me, a dangerous experiment. Cease to try it, I pray! and leave people to die of natural deaths. It is very difficult to define the exact line of demarcation between 'liking' and something stronger (a pang went through Lady Constance's heart, for she felt that indeed it was so) and when once that imperceptible line is past, retreat is impossible — recovery hopeless. Therefore, my dear cousin, take the advice of an old and experienced man, and tread not these precipices; for with all your pretended tenderness of heart, you of the flowing robes, always put us nearest the edge. However I must now take myself off and leave you, lest I should be set down as one of the slain; which I am not, mark you," he added, shaking his head defyingly, " and never mean to be; which fact I think it best to state at once, in order that you really may be able to enjoy my agreeable conversation, and sweet society without scruple or remorse."

The moment Philip Mordaunt had vacated his seat, Augustus took up his station again near Lady Constance. He had not dared to do so as long as his brothers were there, but he lost not a moment when they had departed. He did not venture to sit down by her, but leant on the back of her sofa, and said—as nearly nothing for some time as possible.

Lady Constance was too shy to get up and cross the room alone (for she was sitting rather apart from all the others) and encouraged by her remaining near him, Augustus began at last to speak in intelligible language, which was highly distasteful and embarrassing to her; while Philip from a distance looked repeatedly at her, glancing also at Augustus, and shaking his head in a solemn reproving manner; till at last in desperation she rose, and joined Mrs. Mordaunt, who was the nearest person with whom she could take refuge. She longed to escape and go up stairs, but feared being thought rude; and soon after the party, to her great relief, broke up, when immediately wishing her cousins good night, and thoroughly wearied, she retreated to her own room. When there she sat for some time enjoying the relief of solitude, yet sad in spirit. Her arms hung listlessly by her side, and it was long before she could rouse herself sufficiently to begin the task of *untoiletting*.

"And is this the life that people lead?" she thought. "Oh! dear Llanaven!"

Starting tears warned her that she must not pursue this subject, and with a sigh as if of parting with those she loved, she resolutely closed that page of fond recollection.

CHAPTER XII.

" There is companionship in Nature's voice,
  And her bright look makes e'en the sorrowing glad.
  But in the crush of man—the tumult's noise,
  The heart's sad solitude—how doubly sad!"—MS.

            " O thou rich world unseen !
  Thou curtain'd realms of spirits   *   *
  *   *   *   *   *   dost thou lie
  Spread all around, yet by some filmy screen
  Shut from us ever ?"—MRS. HEMANS.

THE breakfast-table the next morning was not quite
so wearisome a scene as usual, for Philip Mordaunt
made himself very agreeable ; refraining moreover, from
laughing at his brothers so audaciously as he had done
the previous evening.

Before they had separated, a note came from Lady
Stanmore to Lady Constance inviting her to dine early
with her that day, and as the weather was very hot, to
take a drive afterwards into the country. This proposal
arrived just in time to save Lady Constance much embarrassment, for Mrs. Mordaunt had the moment before
asked her if she would like to go to the opera with her
that evening ; and though she would on no account have
gone there, yet she would have found it very difficult

to have declined doing so; for few things are so unpleasant as having to refuse that which another offers
from a good-natured wish to please.   There is something apparently so ungracious in the rejection of
proffered kindness! and it almost invariably gives
offence ; particularly when, as in a case like the present, the refusal necessarily implies a censure of that,
in which the kind proposer sees no harm.

From this difficulty Lady Stanmore's note happily
relieved poor Lady Constance, who had been sitting in
nervous trepidation—her cheeks growing hotter, and
her hands becoming colder every instant—thinking how
she could, with most gratitude, and least offence, decline going with Mrs. Mordaunt.   She immediately
expressed so strong a desire to accept the invitation to
dine with Lady Stanmore that her cousin, who was
thoroughly good-natured, instantly agreed to her doing
so ; telling her "not to consider her, for that she would
find some one else to go with her to the opera."

Lady Constance joyfully wrote her answer, and at
three o'clock she went to Lady Stanmore's.   Lord
Stanmore was going to a parliamentary dinner, so they
were sure of the whole evening to themselves, and at
about five o'clock they set out on their drive.   They
went to Hampstead, and enjoyed exceedingly the pure
air of the heath, and the appearance of real country
which now and then presents itself on that beautiful
side of London; and then returning by Primrose Hill
they drove all down Oxford Street to Lady Stanmore's
house in Park Lane ; that particular line of return being
chosen at Lady Constance's express desire, as during
her former visits to London she had always delighted in
seeing the evening sky from that point.

Certainly there are few scenes which equal Oxford
Street at the time when the sun is sinking in the far
west.   The gloomy avenue of houses — the murky atmosphere, all on fire with the lurid splendour of the
setting sun — the massive clouds, indistinct in their
rugged outlines, but reflecting every shade of swarthy
colouring — altogether form a scene of heavy, oppressive grandeur seldom to be surpassed.

When the spirit within one is disturbed and unhappy, these scenes assume a character peculiarly impressive and striking.   The country with its clear lovely
sunsets, its green fields, its murmuring rivers and
shining lakes, seems in unison with the quiet griefs,
and gentle sorrows of the heart; or even if wilder
passions are abroad, nature rather soothes than irritates
the wretchedness of man.   But in London the unhappy
spirit has to battle against every thing !   There is
gaiety to mock it—there is misery to harrow it—there
is activity to keep it alive to its sufferings ;—every thing
in short but what it craves—peace !

We pass, perhaps, in all the outward splendour of
equipage and attendants—sorrowing, solitary creatures
—amidst throngs of human beings who know us not,
nor care for us.   " Rivers of human faces" pass by us,
but not one turns to look on us ; or if it did, could it
read the deadly agony which perhaps lurks within !

And they too have their feelings !—Each one of
those thousands, who pass us in the crowded " stony-
hearted" streets, is a world to himself: a world of love,
and hate, and griping want, and torturing anxiety—of
joyful anticipation — or of misery-worn, dull, dead-
heartedness !

Then night !—night, when all the vast canopy of

smoke which the busy day kept pouring forth, has sunk and left the sky at last clear and bright—how solemn is night over the sleeping streets! The moon-beams lying so white on the houses, and the shadows so doubly black; the rolling of the wheels heard at immeasurable distances through the empty squares; and the church-clocks taking up the tolling hour from each other, and repeating it all around, till the last faint chime scarcely fall upon the ear! all so sullen—so mournfully silent. And the cold moon which goes so noiselessly along, over the heads of the hushed multitude—as if she thought that hush were peace! Oh! would she look with intelligent eye, on that over which she glides so gently and unmoved, what scenes would be revealed to her watching glance! Unroof but one single street of all the miles of habitations which compose the largest capital of the world, and what vicissitudes of life would be unveiled! Here, death with all its grim and fell accompaniments — there, the first child's welcome birth! Here avarice and hatred—there love and peace! Poverty—sin—luxury—desperation — joy—madness—grief! all mingled together—yet all so separate!

Thoughts like these make London a scene of deep and harrowing interest for those who sympathise with their fellow-creatures—who feel for human woe and suffering. And amid the thousand causes of sorrow and regret which fill the labouring mind, the only source of real comfort flows from the knowledge that all must be right! That though the moon—herself but a creature of God's hand—knows nought of all the things over which she spreads the mantle of her light, yet that the Lord—the universal Father, knows, and sees,

and permits all this; and that when " The wrath of man
has worked the glory of God—the remainder of wrath
will He restrain."

When the drive was over and the carriage stopped
at Lord Stanmore's door, the evening twilight was still
so bright, and the young moon was shining so in-
vitingly, that Lady Stanmore proposed to her companion to take a little walk in the Park before they went
in; and dismissing the carriage, and taking the footman with them they strolled along the crisped and
parched grass, down to the springs near the Magazine.
The fine trees looked beautiful in the moonlight, for
that white tint served to conceal the blackened hue of
the foliage, and their walk altogether was delightful.

" These are the hours I love the best of all the
time I spend in London," said Lady Stanmore—
" these little odd hours, stolen as it were from the
world.   Dearly as I love my husband, I sometimes
enjoy his dining out alone at these great dinners (for
he never leaves me for other dinners) that I may
get a little quiet evening either quite alone, or with
some one who is really comfortable to me, as you are.
Sometimes I remain at home, and open my windows
to listen to the dear street organs which I love so much !
and sometimes I drive into the country, or take a walk
like this.   I always think London the most romantic
place in the world !   Many people do not know what
I mean when I say so, and I cannot define it myself,
though I feel it.   How solemn and grand that sunset
was just now, and how quietly the moon shines now amid
such thousands of human beings; and we perhaps
almost alone, of all those thousands, enjoying it !

I never know what it is I feel at these times; a mournful, tearful sensation fills my heart as if I had once been happy, and were so now no longer; and yet I never was so happy in all my life as I am now. How strange it is that so many things should pass within us, which we can neither control, nor comprehend; which seem something beyond earth,—and yet are not of heaven— for they are sorrowful."

"I have often wondered, too, whence these sensations come," said Lady Constance, "and what they are; for as you say, they are too sorrowful to be feelings which can exist in heaven, and yet they soften, and refine the heart. I think they must be aspirations of our higher nature, pent up in souls which are too narrow for them. There are some things which we know we shall enjoy hereafter, but the foretaste of which even, is too much for our poor spirits here. Music is one—that we know we shall have in perfection, from the golden harps of the angels, and the songs of the redeemed; yet music here—how sad it sounds! amidst brightest happiness often making one's heart appear 'a fountain of tears!' Beautiful scenery, too, how oppressive that is! but *there* the everlasting hills and clear fountains of God's paradise, will form a part of our perfect happiness."

"Yes, and love," said Lady Stanmore, "that too, is painful here—that too, will be perfect there. I do not mean only what is usually called—love—but affection of all kinds; doating love of relations—especially of children—how painful it is! Sometimes when I look at my baby, and press its soft cheek to mine, I feel as if my heart must burst. One may truly say of love like that, ' 'Tis bliss but to a certain point—beyond 'tis agony !' Of all kinds of love *that* certainly appears to me the most perfect, for it is unmixed with any thing else. My husband loves me, or I should soon cease to love him; but besides that, he is pleasant to me in a thousand ways; and all my friends I love for something in themselves. But my baby—what can it do for me? at first it does not even know me—and yet upon that little thing I bestow love enough to fill the world."

" I cannot, I dare say, judge of that," said Lady Constance, " yet I can believe all you say about it. Oh! it is happy that this world is not our last—or best."

Lady Stanmore sighed.

" I wish," continued Lady Constance, " that you felt a clear hope of salvation; a heart like yours cannot even here, I am sure, be satisfied with earthly things."

" It is not.—But last night, when we were interrupted, we were speaking of being on the verge of an invisible world. What were you going to say about it?"

" That we always are so; we walk surrounded by beings invisible to us."

" Why should you think so?" asked Lady Stanmore; "it is a most uncomfortable idea."

" It is certainly uncomfortable when we reflect on the evil beings that are ever at our side, seeking to tempt, and to destroy; but it is delightful when we think of the angels of God who are sent ' to minister to those who shall be heirs of salvation.'"

" How do you know that they are so sent?"

" The Scriptures tell us of it."

" Where?"

" In the first of Hebrews."

"I must, I see, read the Scriptures more attentively."

"Do," said Lady Constance; "you will find them so beautiful! as well as comforting and strengthening."

"But do you really suppose," asked Lady Stanmore, "that there are spirits before my eyes at this moment, and yet invisible to me? the thought is a trembling one."

"Probably there are. Scripture gives us reason to believe that there are evil spirits ever by us; and encourages us to hope that there are also good ones ever ready to succour the tried and tempted people of God."

"Where? does Scripture speak of it, besides the passage you mentioned?"

"Yes; you remember when the King of Syria sent horses and chariots, and a great host to compass the city of Dothan about, in order to take Elisha prisoner, that his servant was afraid; and the prophet told him not to fear, for there were more with them than against them, and then he prayed that the servant's eyes might be opened, and it says, 'And the Lord opened the eyes of the young man, and he saw: and behold the mountain was full of horses and chariots of fire, round about Elisha.'"

"Can it really be? Can there be dreadful, and glorious spirits close to us, and we unconscious of their presence?"

"No doubt. Indeed we know by our own experience, that disembodied spirits must at times, be in the very room with us without our seeing them."

"What do you mean? Ghosts?"

"Oh! no, I do not believe they exist. But have you ever been in the room when any one has died?"

"Once—only once. It was a little brother of mine, sweet little creature! he died leaning on me, with his dear arm round my neck. It was many years ago."

"His spirit when it left the body must then have been in the room, and close to you, for an instant at least—and yet you could not see it."

"That is true! though it never struck me before. But what a fearful feeling this is;—it seems to connect us so intimately with another world."

"It is, I think, very awful! In all probability also, sounds pass close to our ears, and are yet unheard. We are given to understand in Scripture, that the moment the soul departs from the body, it is either 'present with the Lord,' or else consigned to Satan's kingdom. And can we suppose that when the painful moment of death is past, and all the glories of heaven burst on the redeemed soul, that it utters no sounds of joy and praise? Or can we believe that when the careless, ungodly, unbelieving sinner, is seized by the dreadful beings who are in waiting for their prey, and is dragged down—where it is grief to think of!—can we believe that no shriek of horror or despair bursts forth? Yet no sound reaches our ear—and men will often call it 'a happy release!' Such thoughts as these always make me tremble for those who have not gone to Christ, and made 'their calling and election sure,' through Him; and I would never willingly be with any one at the hour of death, by whose side I did not hope to stand in the day of judgment."

They walked on in silence for a length of time, but

Lady Constance felt the arm that held hers, tremble violently.

"These things are horrible—overpowering!" said Lady Stanmore at length.

Lady Constance pressed her arm affectionately.

"Better," she said, "to feel them so now, dear Lady Stanmore, than then—first—when escape is impossible! But I like rather to dwell on the bright side of the subject; for 'it is better,' as some one said 'to be drawn, than driven to heaven!' Think of the extasy of joy when all trouble is past, and we exchange perhaps a suffering death-bed for all the glories of heaven." Her voice trembled, for she thought of her father.

"Do you remember," she continued, after a little pause, "the beautiful words in the Revelation?"

"Which do you mean?"

"'They shall hunger no more, neither thirst any more; neither shall the sun light on them, nor any heat. For the Lamb which is in the midst of the throne shall feed them, and shall lead them unto living fountains of waters: and God shall wipe away all tears from their eyes.'"

The tears swelled into Lady Stanmore's eyes, as she heard these words.

"How new all these thoughts seem to me," she said; "while your heart and memory are full of God's word."

"It is a letter written to us by our best Friend," replied Lady Constance. "Dear Lady Stanmore, will you not read it, till the Spirit which it promises fills your heart with the love of God and of Christ? Then, then only, will you be really happy!"

CHAPTER XIII.

"Cette infatigable persévérance de la sottise qui ne manque jamais une occasion d'être sotte."

When Lady Constance returned home from Lady Stanmore's, she found the attentive Augustus ready to hand her out of the carriage, he having resigned the charms of the "ballet" in order to secure that privilege, hoping afterwards to enjoy a little conversation with her. She however retired immediately to her room; and he was obliged, much to his mortification, to content himself with lighting her candle, wishing her good night, and watching her with a pathetic look, as she went up the first flight of stairs from the drawing-room.

Lady Constance went to rest that night, happier than she had been for a long time: she felt a great interest in Lady Stanmore, and trusted that the hours they had spent together had not been wholly unprofitable; and the God whom she had tried to serve, left her not comfortless.

The next day being Sunday, the whole party walked together to St. George's church, and then returned home to luncheon. While that essential occupation was going on, Mr. Mordaunt's groom brought round his horses, and walked them up and down before the house.

"You are going out early to-day, Robert," said his mother, "how does that happen?"

"I promised to go to Roehampton, Murray has got a new horse, and wants me to look at it; and if it goes well, he is to drive me over to Hampton Court to dine with the T——'s; so perhaps I shall not be at home till late."

"What will the Park do without you," said Philip, "now, when there are so few stars left? The 'Gog,' will be all agog!"

"Your language is elegant!" replied his brother contemptuously; "why cannot you call things by their right names, and say 'the statue of Achilles?' It sounds much better, I assure you. I wish I could polish you a little."

"Many thanks; but I was always particularly obliged to 'John Bull' for supplying me with the very appropriate name of 'Gog,' for that unpleasant man in the green skin, and uneasy attitude, opposite our Duke's house. Don't you think 'Gog' is a delightful name for him, mother? Lady Constance, does not 'Gog' sound remarkably well? so aristocratic! something so decided and authoritative in it. 'Gog!' what can one want more? Augustus, you have often told me that you knew nothing like it in the Greek of Homer or the Latin of Virgil. 'Gog!'"

"There, Philip," said his mother, "you have convinced us all I dare say, by this time, even Robert, so we will let the 'Gog' alone for the present."

"I am never to be convinced by Philip's rhetoric," said Mr. Mordaunt, with an indignant glance.

Philip shrugged his shoulders in token of resignation.

"Where are you going, Philip?" said Augustus in a timid voice.

"My steps are free and unconfined as the wind, and the dust in this weather. I go unquestioned, and unquestioned come."

"You can drive with us in the carriage, Augustus," said Mrs. Mordaunt, "if you like it."

Augustus' countenance grew very bright.

"Constance, the carriage will be at the door at three."

"Thank you," said Lady Constance, colouring highly, "but I shall be going to church."

"What again?"

"Yes, I am used to going twice."

"You can go in the evening to some other church, if you like it, for at St. George's the service is at such an inconvenient hour;" said Mrs. Mordaunt, "and then you need not lose your drive; or perhaps (for she was thoroughly good-natured and desirous of pleasing her young guest) you would rather go now, and then we will dine early, and go to the Zoological Gardens afterwards; it is quite the fashion to do so now. I will put the carriage off if you would like it best."

"Thank you very much," said Lady Constance, "but I had rather be quiet to-day; do not think of me."

"Are you not well, my dear?" asked Mrs. Mordaunt anxiously; "or is it," she added, looking sideways at Lady Constance with a smiling eye, and a mouth jokingly puckered up, "because it is Sunday?"

Lady Constance coloured higher than before, and said, "I certainly do like being quiet on Sunday."

"Well, my dear, I am for letting every body go to heaven their own way," said Mrs. Mordaunt; "and I dare say yours is a very good one: but I am afraid I should find it rather dull."

Lady Constance made no answer.

Mr. Mordaunt rose, and ringing the bell, ordered his horses to be called; he then took his leave with somewhat of less parade than usual, and the remaining quartet sat silent, doing nothing.

"Shall we go up stairs, Constance?" said Mrs. Mordaunt.

Lady Constance rose.

"You, of course, are going out, Philip," said his mother, in a low voice, and with a peculiar smile, as she passed him. He murmured an assent; then turning to Lady Constance, he whispered,

"I am not quite a heathen; I am going to church again, though I am sorry I cannot go with you."

"Augustus, at three I shall be ready," said Mrs. Mordaunt.

"Thank you," he answered, consequentially, "but I am going to church;" and he gave a triumphant, and appropriating look at Lady Constance.

His mother cast up her eyes with an air of resignation at his folly; and knowing that he wished to be persecuted, merely said, "Oh! by all means," and passed up stairs with Lady Constance.

The latter fondly hoped to escape Augustus' unwelcome companionship when she went to church; and in order to do so, she sent her maid down stairs when she was ready, to summon the footman who was to walk with her; and then descended quietly herself, without going into any of the rooms. But her watch-

ful cousin, intent on his prey, was sitting with the
dining-room door open, on purpose that she should
not escape him; and the moment her light step fell on
the pavement of the hall, he issued forth with his hat
on, and his gloves in his hand. She was very much annoyed, but could not prevent his walking along the
pavement at her side, or going into his own mother's
pew; though she determinately and coldly refused his
repeated entreaties that she would take his arm, and
sat as far from him in the pew as possible. On their
return he still accompanied her, making solemn observations on many parts of the sermon, (all of which he
misunderstood) and asserting that "this was the only
way to spend the sabbath."

"Must we part?" he asked, as he saw her preparing to go up to her room when they got home.

"Certainly," she said; and disappeared. After
she had been in her room some little time, her maid
brought her a sealed note from him, entreating her to
come down into the drawing-room, as he had something of importance to say to her. She went down
accordingly, and Augustus, enchanted beyond measure, gave her a chair with somewhat of his eldest
brother's pomp, added to his own *niaiserie*. This, however, she declined.

"Lady Constance," he began, "I feel happy in being
able, as I hope, to render some trifling service to one,
whom it will ever be my happiness to make happy."

Lady Constance made a slight inclination. "Painful duties arise in life sometimes, and this is one. (A
pause.) Even the duty of a child must sometimes
give way to higher calls, though the struggle is great—
to deeper sentiments. (Another pause, during which,

'l'air martyr,' was plainly visible.) "These are the the things, Lady Constance, which make life a battle-field, (Lady Constance wondered *what* things!) but come what may we must do our duty. I can no longer conceal from you, Lady Constance——"

He paused again, and Lady Constance, who had felt several times dreadfully inclined to laugh, now on the contrary, became alarmed; and vague ideas of some bad news having arrived from Llanaven, took possession of her.

"What is it?," she said, "pray tell me at once. There has been no news from home, has there? Tell me directly, Augustus."

"Oh! dear, no," he answered deliberately, and with a look which seemed to say how trifling he considered all from thence, compared with his own deep responsibilities. "No, Lady Constance, but it is the having to betray a mother's secrets—I had almost said confidence—but happily she did not confide in me, I found all out by providential accident.—It is the having to betray a mother's secrets, which is so hard to flesh and blood."

"Why need you do so?" asked Lady Constance, coldly.

"To save one, who is—I will not at this moment," he added, with an air of proud self-denial, "say all that she is—to save her from great distress and per-plexity, to save her from being drawn into a vortex!" —he stopped, for expressions seemed to fail, and he drew a deep breath.

"Pray, Augustus," said Lady Constance, "if you have any thing to say—say it, for I wish to go up stairs again."

"Cruel!" he exclaimed, "when I am outraging every feeling to serve you."

"I can scarcely believe that any thing very dreadful awaits me in this house," she replied, (excepting, she might have added, having to listen to your exceeding nonsense) "but whatever it is, if you wish to tell it me, I shall be obliged to you to speak."

"I will," he said, "and yet nothing but the sense of virtue, and the earnest desire I have to render myself valuable——"

"This is intolerable," said Lady Constance, "will you tell me at once what you wish to say, or must I go without hearing it?"

"I dare say it is embarrassing for you to be here," continued Augustus, with a protecting air, "but I am happy in conversing with you, and perhaps forget, what it may be natural you should feel."

Lady Constance walked towards the door.

"I will speak then to the point at once, Lady Constance," cried Augustus, in consternation, for he had no idea she would have wished to leave him, "I will say—will tell you, then—that unknown to you, my mother is making preparations—for giving a ball on Thursday next. There!" and he seemed overpowered with the importance of the intelligence he had communicated.

"Is that all?" said Lady Constance, much relieved.

"That all!" exclaimed Augustus, with surprise and indignation. "I thought I had understood that you abominated those things — that they were repugnant to every feeling of your nature—that you abhorred——"

"Thank you, Augustus," said Lady Constance, kindly, "I am really much obliged to you for having taken so much trouble about me, and for having told me about this, as it will perhaps spare me a great deal of difficulty; for though the terms you use are rather strong, yet I certainly do not like those late-houred dissipations."

Augustus' joy was beyond bounds. He was really kind-hearted, and was rejoiced to have been of use, and Lady Constance's manner, so cordial to what it had been before, perfectly enchanted him. He was beginning to pour forth rhapsodies, but Lady Constance resuming her cold, and distant manner, said,

"I feel sure that you are glad to have been of service to me, Augustus, in this affair, but you would also much oblige me, if you would cease that foolish and useless way of addressing me. We are cousins, and as such, I should wish always to have a friendly feeling towards you; but that is all—and must ever be all, between us."

Augustus was daunted for a moment; but his excessive vanity soon recovered from the blow it had received; and feeling sure that Lady Constance was only concealing her preference for him, from an idea that it was right to do so for a time, he followed her as she went to the door, and opening it for her, slowly, so as to detain her an instant, he said,

"Lady Constance, you will not, I trust, always think it—necessary—to conceal——"

"I have nothing to conceal," she replied, in great indignation.

"In time I will hope——"

"Never."

"Oh!" he said smilingly, shaking his head, "we do not always know ourselves!"

Lady Constance thought that was perfectly true, but disdaining to answer, she passed through the half-opened door, and ran up stairs.

Augustus Mordaunt's manner to her was so exceedingly disagreeable, that she felt inclined to write directly to Lady Ashton, and say that she must return home; but she felt after a few minutes, that she could not do this without giving great offence to Mrs. Mordaunt; and remembering also, that her coming at all had been against Lady Ashton's wish, she felt averse to take such a step; so she gave up the idea of writing, and hoped by continual repression, to get rid in time of his distasteful and presumptuous assiduities.

What had been said about the ball brought with it also much perplexing thought to one so young, and so disinclined to oppose the will, and wishes of others. Though she had said, "Is that all?" at the moment when her mind was relieved by finding that that "was all," yet now, on thinking over the subject, she found it placed her in a very disagreeable situation as regarded Mrs. Mordaunt; but knowing that the plainest path is ever the smoothest, she determined to speak to her about it as soon as she could possibly find an opportunity. She determined not to attend the ball, for she knew Lady Ashton would not like it, and she also well remembered her father's disapprobation of those things, which would have been quite sufficient for her, even if she had not disliked the thoughts of it herself. She felt also for a moment displeased at the idea of being deceived into doing a thing which she did not approve; but being sure that Mrs. Mordaunt had been actuated entirely by a wish to please —however mistaken, that slight shade of anger soon passed from her mind.

Mrs. Mordaunt had indeed imagined that by surprising Lady Constance, into a scene of that kind, she would be giving her a great pleasure. She had often seen girls who—though forbidden certain things—yet were very glad when circumstances seemed to offer a sort of apology for their doing them; (those for instance, who not being allowed to waltz, delighted in those dances where waltzing was introduced under another name) and supposing that Lady Constance possessed the same lax principles, she thought she would be but too glad to find herself obliged to go to so gay and pleasant a thing as a ball; and therefore, with really kind intention had arranged this little surprise for her.

The next morning Lady Constance spoke at once and openly to her, on the subject, thanking her so sincerely, and cordially, for her kind wish to please her, and expressing such pained concern at seeming ungrateful, (the tears springing into her eyes as she spoke) that Mrs. Mordaunt, after the first moment of displeasure, kissed her affectionately, saying, she was "a dear creature, though a sad little Puritan;" and a greater degree of kindly feeling and intimacy was established between them, from that moment, than had ever before existed.

They spent the rest of the morning in "unavoidably postponing" the unhappy ball, and much pleasant conversation passed between them whilst so employed.

CHAPTER XIV.

"Il avoit cette suprême confiance des sots, qui en fait les enfans privilégiés de la nature ; et qui ne lui permettoit pas de croire, qu'une femme à laquelle il avait adressés ses hommages, pût penser à un autre homme que lui.

      *   *   *   *   *

"Oh ! cette une exécrable puissance que celle de la sottise qui marche à son but !"

On the 8th of August, Lady Constance and her friends set off for Scotland ; and their journey having been happily accomplished, the party found themselves in a small but tolerably comfortable house in the neighbourhood of Loch Lomond. Mr. Mordaunt had engaged a moor in that neighbourhood, and whilst he and his brothers were shooting, Mrs. Mordaunt and Lady Constance wandered about the beautiful scenery that surrounded the Loch.

When the first ardour of the *chasse* was over, it was proposed taking a little tour ; but Mr. Mordaunt, who had some little discernment—though not much—had found out by that time, that his devotions were any thing but acceptable to Lady Constance ; and though marvelling that so handsome a person as himself, and with so good a fortune, should fail in creating an interest where he desired it, yet finding that such unfortunately was the case in the present instance, he accepted an invitation from a friend in the neighbourhood, and went to stay some weeks with him at his house, instead of accompanying the tourists in their journey. With many pompous speeches he took leave of his 'fair cousin' and of his mother, and left them to the care and guardianship of Philip and Augustus.

Augustus was enchanted at seeing one rival off the field, and his assiduities towards Lady Constance became greater than ever. He was far more insufferable to her than even his eldest brother had been, for to the weakest intellect, he joined the most egregious vanity. He was good-looking—all the family were so—and thought himself particularly irresistible. He was exceedingly afraid of his mother, and of his brothers also, because they laughed at him without his ever being able to discover why; and Lady Constance having at first pitied his embarrassment, and spoken kindly to him, (as she would have done to a frightened child,) he set it down immèdiately in his mind that she must be in love with him. This fancy never left his head, and believing that the coldness which she soon found it absolutely necessary to shew, was only timidity on her part, he sought to reassure her, by patronising speeches and encouraging looks; and though she told him perhaps six times a-day, that his attentions displeased her, he considered it merely as the proper thing to say, and was in nowise discouraged.

Her provocation was extreme, and she would often sit for hours in her own room in order to avoid him. She wished herself at Llanaven a thousand times a-day; and yet again a thousand times felt it was best to be away; for the petty annoyances of her present life,

were far less trying she knew than the heart-struggles
she would have to endure there.

Mrs. Mordaunt and Philip were excessively amused
at Augustus' proceedings, and encouraged him by being
unusually gracious, and cordial ; but at last Philip perceiving that it annoyed Lady Constance, determined to
put an end to the joke.

They were going out one day in a boat to one of
the islands in the Loch, when Mrs. Mordaunt having forgotten something in the house, after Lady Constance
and Augustus were in the boat, returned with Philip to
fetch it.   Lady Constance was going to follow them,
when Augustus thinking it would be a very acceptable
piece of pleasantry, pushed off from the shore, and
declared he would row her to the island, and leave the
others to follow in another boat.   She requested him
to return, and insisted indeed on his doing so, but he
only laughed, and said, "he knew she wished to be
disobeyed ;" till finding all argument useless, she was
so extremely displeased that she sat perfectly silent, and
refused even to answer a word that he said.

He was not used to the water, and rowed very ill,
and the boat rocked from side to side so violently that
at times Lady Constance was really alarmed for her
life ; but having made an exclamation of fear at one
particularly dreadful lurch, and receiving the assurance
—by no means consolatory—from him, that "she need
not fear, for if she went down, he was determined to
perish with her" — accompanied by a smile which was
meant to be particularly "fin et malicieux," she
determined for the future to repress her terror, and sit
as quiet as the existing circumstances would allow.

Philip meanwhile having perceived what was going

on, abruptly left his mother; and calling to a lad to
help him to push off another boat, he jumped in, and
seizing the oars was soon in hot pursuit. Augustus
saw him from a distance, and exerted himself more
vigorously than ever, but Philip's more stalwart arm
made his little skiff soon gain upon the other. Lady
Constance was truly thankful for this prospect of
deliverance, whilst Augustus continued to cheer her, as
he fondly imagined, with hopes of escaping from their
pursuer.

" Don't be afraid, Lady Constance, we shall beat
him yet."   "We shall have a pleasant stroll together on
the shore still before he can come to disturb us."   " We
shall enjoy our row a quarter of an hour yet, before he
interferes with us," &c.

Seeing his brother however gaining on him much
more than he liked, he turned the head of the boat
away from the island which they had nearly reached,
and rowed out again into the open loch. Lady Constance now grew desperate, and though not much
versed in such matters, she got up and taking hold of
the rudder, suddenly turned it so as to point the boat's
head again towards the shore of the island.

Augustus was exceedingly vexed; but he tried to
laugh it off, saying, " It was astonishing how people
would sometimes disappoint themselves rather than shew
what they liked ;" and Philip having by this time come
up with them—in a voice of thunder, and with flashing
eyes, ordered his brother instantly to row to the shore,
and let Lady Constance land.   All Augustus' old fear
of Philip returned when he received this fierce injunction, and he began to fear he had gone too far in his
sportive wit.   He obeyed therefore, and Lady Con-

stance, to her great relief, in a few moments found herself again safe on solid ground.

As soon as they had all three landed, Philip, knowing that Lady Constance was then beyond the reach of
annoyance from Augustus, felt his love of tormenting
return strong upon him.   Still keeping up the appearance of violent anger, which had at first been perfectly
natural, he drew Lady Constance's arm through his,
and placing himself between her, and his brother, exclaimed with a menacing air,

"Augustus, your aim is perceived; and though
doubtless had Lady Constance's heart been disengaged,
your talents and abilities could not have failed to make
her completely devoted to you, yet learn to your confusion that her heart is no longer hers—nor yours—but
mine!   I claim her as my own!   We are engaged to
each other by mutual vows, and promises innumerable!
Speak to her again therefore—at your peril!"

Augustus was rendered furious by this announcement; he had felt convinced that Lady Constance had
but one feeling in life, and that that one, was devotion
to himself; and he would not tamely submit to have
this bright castle of vanity thus crumbled to the earth.
His fear of his brother vanished for the instant, before
the violence of his excitement; and he insisted that
Lady Constance was his, and his alone.

"Ask her!" said Philip coolly.

Augustus appealed to Lady Constance in vehement
terms; but before she could utter a word, Philip exclaimed, "There you heard what she said."

"I did not hear her voice," replied Augustus.

"Then you should have listened! she said, 'she
was mine, and mine only;' and she will prove it to

you by going where I lead her, while you must instantly return, and bring my mother here. Now, begone!"

Augustus still hesitated; but Philip taking hold of Lady Constance gently but firmly by the wrist, commenced scrambling up a ledge of rocks — supporting her with such strength, that her feet scarcely needed the slight hold they could take of the rugged pathway—till the unhappy Augustus seeing all further remonstrance useless, proceeded slowly towards the boats.

Lady Constance was really terrified by Philip's words and manners. Her first fear of him returned to her mind, and she thought she had only escaped from an idiot, to fall into the hands of a madman. When they had reached a smooth spot however he released her arm, and gave way to an overpowering burst of laughter. She still feared for his senses, and her terrified look adding to his uncontrollable merriment, only prolonged the term of her fears; for he could make no intelligible sound; and it was long ere he could cease wiping away the tears his immoderate mirth caused to flow.

" I beg your pardon," at last he said, " I will speak in a minute."

Lady Constance then saw that her fears were vain, and relieved from her anxiety she could not help laughing with him; and Augustus was gone some little distance before they were become composed, and rational again.

In a few minutes however, a new fear seemed to seize upon Lady Constance, and she exclaimed earnestly,

" Oh ! call him back pray, Philip, call him back, and tell him it was but a joke about our being engaged," and she called him herself at the height of her voice.

" If you choose to have him back," said Philip, " I declare I will leave him here, and go back myself, and will never help you again."

But Lady Constance's mind was too much excited, and again she called to Augustus, and signed for him to return. Too happy to obey her, he instantly turned the boat's head and rowed back again towards the island.

" Why have you brought him back ? " said Philip indignantly, " Lady Constance must I believe that you like that intolerable *sillyton ?* "

" Like him ! oh ! no, I cannot bear him ! I beg your pardon for saying so—but he torments me to death. But I am so afraid—as he becomes sullen sometimes—that he may refuse to return with Mrs. Mordaunt, and may employ himself in writing to that fellow-clerk of his in the Foreign office, to whom he sends such volumes every day ; and if he should mention your ridiculous account, and it was repeated, it might reach Llanaven. Oh ! Philip, he is near, if yóu have really any friendship for me, tell him it was only a joke."

" I devour my own words ! never ! "

But seeing distress evidently painted on Lady Constance's face ; and having himself moreover some little private reasons for not wishing a report like the one in question to reach England, he promised quickly to arrange the matter with his brother.

When Augustus had landed, he came up to Lady Constance with a look of such imbecile triumph on his countenance, that Philip felt tempted to throw him into the loch. He did not do so however, but addressing him in a low, solemn voice, he told him " that if a syllable of what had passed was repeated by him, either by letter or word of mouth, to any living soul, excepting his mother, his prospects in life would be ruined for ever. Instant expulsion from the Foreign office, and all future hopes in that quarter, would be the first step, and it was impossible to say what would be the second !

"And now," he added, "having warned you, I bid you again depart. As you row our mother here, you may freely pour forth all your griefs and wrongs to her; but a syllable to any one else, and you know—or rather," he added impressively, "you do *not* know— what will happen !"

"Why did you not make him promise ?" said Lady Constance, when she saw Augustus again in his boat rowing away ; for she felt but half satisfied.

"Make him promise, my dear cousin!" replied Philip, "certainly not. That would have made him suppose that I depended upon him;—whereas I mean him to feel that he depends upon me ! and happily he believes every word I say. Let me advise you never to give orders in such a way as to allow people to fancy you can be disobeyed if you do, you may be sure you will be."

"But why did you say he might tell his mother ?"

"Because I know he dare not for his life; besides which I should not mind if he did tell her. If he does not, I shall."

"Tell her what ?"

"That we are engaged," answered Philip very solemnly. "The words which I spoke, and which you did not contradict, in this Scotland you know, are sufficient of themselves in a court of law, to constitute us man and wife; so you cannot retract, even if you wished it. But I have no fear of that being the case."

Philip Mordaunt was so incomparable an actor, that his mother even, who knew him best, was continually taken in by him; and Lady Constance, who was unused to this species of joking, at that moment really felt an actual terror take possession of her; for though Philip had always been on the pleasantest terms with her, and had never shewn her any thing but a brother's kindness; yet in his vain and extraordinary family, she felt as if she could be secure of nothing. Her persecutor however not wishing really to terrify her, and seeing she was uncomfortable, hastened to relieve her in part by saying,

"But do not fear; I will promise never to claim you, till you claim me! so unless Augustus bears witness against us, your fate lies in your own hands. No, my dear cousin," he continued, in his cordial pleasant way, "there is happily nothing of that sort between us, though I feel a wonderful drawing of heart towards you. I never had a sister, and have often longed for one, and you seem more like it, than any body I ever met. You do not mind my always calling you 'cousin,' do you? I am so tired of Robert's formal '*Lady* Constance,' and Augustus' sentimental 'Lady *C-o-n-stance*,' that I hate the very sound. My mother's 'Constance' sounds charming; but I should not perhaps quite like that from my lips; but may I always call you 'dear cousin,' or 'fair cousin,' or even '*plain* cousin' sometimes?"

Lady Constance smiled. "Take care," she replied, "lest we should quarrel irreconcilably in the latter case. Do you not remember that when Horace Walpole was asked to make up a quarrel between two ladies, he said, 'Did they call each other ugly?' 'No.' 'Then,' he said, 'perhaps I may succeed.' However you may call me by whatever name makes you feel me the most of a friend, and relation."

" You are truly kind," said Philip, "I often long to talk to you as if we had known each other all our lives. " I have no one who is quite comfortable to me here. My dear mother listens to me with exemplary patience; but then I feel that it is patience, and I want sympathy. Now you I am sure would sympathise with me — if you knew I was in trouble."

" My dear Philip, I am sure I should," said Lady Constance with energy, for her heart melted at the idea of any one being in trouble.

" Now you are really my own delightful cousin," he answered, taking her hand and kissing it with the utmost affection, "and I will talk to you, and tell you all my misery. You see — I *am* engaged! but I can't marry; and that troubles me."

" You are engaged?" said Lady Constance, surprised, " then marry. You are not very poor, are you?"

" Oh! no, I am getting on very well; but my 'love' is a minor, and rich; and her guardian will not hear of me, and forbids me the house, wanting her, I am sure, for his own son — like all old guardians in plays and farces; so for the next two years I cannot marry, and can only see her indeed occasionally, and at other people's houses; for since my unfortunate proposal, he keeps her entirely in the country, and seldom allows her even to go to his sister, who is in town. She was there however the last Sunday we were in London, and it was with her that I went to church that evening, for she is a good girl, and as lovely as she is good ; much too good indeed for me ! I wish you knew her, Constance.—There ! now that I am talking of Clara all reserve seems gone with you, and I can and may call you Constance, may I not ? it seems so natural and comfortable. But do you not pity me ? "

" I do truly ; but still you know that she loves you, and you know that you love her ; is not that joy enough ? and after two years, if all goes on well, you will be happy—how happy !" and a cloud rested on her beautiful brow. " But tell me about her, and about yourself," she continued, " for I am sure it must be a relief to speak, Clara—what is she ? "

" Clara Leslie, she is very lovely,—not perhaps so strictly so as you are, but ——"

" Never mind comparisons," said Lady Constance laughing, " she is beautiful in your eyes, for she has the best beauties, goodness and love for you, and that is enough to make you happy. Now, go on till you are tired."

" Ah ! when will that be ? "

He went on however, and relieved his heart by pouring it forth into Lady Constance's kind ear. She grieved over his troubles, but as she listened to them, her own sadder ones, disturbed by his words from the depths in which she endeavoured in general to bury them, rose up in such overwhelming force, that, leaning her face on her hands, she gave way to uncontrollable tears.

" I did not mean to distress you, my dear cousin," said Philip Mordaunt, with much emotion ; " I will not say another word of my foolish love."

"Oh, yes!" said Lady Constance, "go on, and do not mind me; it is a relief to cry sometimes — even for nothing;" and her tears flowed afresh at thinking how much she had to weep for.

After a time Augustus and his mother arrived at the little island; the former being evidently very sullen and very unhappy; and after a rather dull walk (for Lady Constance and Philip were both saddened by their late conversation), they all returned to the mainland.

Lady Constance was now much more at her ease than she had been before with her relations. She felt a great regard for Mrs. Mordaunt, who was an amiable person and full of agreeable conversation, and who was indefatigable in the endeavour to make the time pass pleasantly to her; Augustus was subdued — and for Philip she really felt a great affection. She saw much in him that was solidly good, and amiable, though mixed with a good deal of worldliness and vanity. He would often talk with her on serious subjects, which he promised to think more of, than he had hitherto done; and he said he should like her to know and talk with Clara Leslie and help her to clearer views than she then had. She could not however always persuade him to behave to Augustus as she wished; for he would often encourage him in his folly; and then at other times, when really he might, by accident, have spoken a sensible word, he scared his few senses from him, by his contemptuous, dogmatical manner.

Augustus Mordaunt was certainly a person whom it was almost impossible to improve. The least rebuff

seemed to annihilate him — excepting when his vanity
was concerned — and the smallest meed of praise made
him think himself Solon *redivivus*. He was not able
for a length of time perfectly to fathom the affair of
the engagement, for he saw evidently that though
Philip and Lady Constance were much more together
than they had hitherto been, yet that there was no love
between them; and his own hopes would flicker up, if
Lady Constance for a moment forgot the cold caution
which she found so necessary, though it was so uncongenial to her nature. Once indeed when she felt
pained at something Philip had said to him, and spoke
kindly when the former had left the room, he, recovering
the whole of his presumption in an instant, turned to
her saying,

" Ah ! Lady Constance, I knew the truth would
come out at last !" and was about to pour forth a
volume of absurdity, when she stopped him by saying,

" Augustus, I shall speak to you no more, since I
find you are weak enough to imagine I can have any
motive in being kind to you, beyond that of the commonest compassion."

This severe rebuke had happily the desired effect,
and nothing more was heard of his hopes or pretensions ; and during the remainder of their stay in Scotland, he contented himself by being silent, and very
cross, and by pointedly avoiding Lady Constance on
all occasions.

After having made several little tours, the party,
joined again by Mr. Mordaunt, returned to London,
and at last the sad yet joyful day was fixed for Lady
Constance's return to Llanaven. Lady Ashton wrote

a pressing invitation to Mrs. Mordaunt to accompany her charge back into Cornwall, and give her the pleasure of a visit; and, Mrs. Mordaunt, who was much softened in her dislike of Methodists, and felt a real affection for her young cousin, whose extreme amiability and unaffected piety had greatly won upon her, acceded with pleasure to the proposal and accompanied by Philip Mordaunt set out with Lady Constance for Llanaven.

CHAPTER XV.

" Hours came for me in which no consolation would appease my
heart, in which I in vain combated myself, and said, ' Now I will
read, and then pray, and then sleep ; ' but yet anguish would not
leave me, but followed me still when I read, prevented me from
prayer, and chased away sleep ;—yes, many such hours have been."

                                        F. BREMER.

LIFE had gone on most smoothly with Lady Ashton during Lady Constance's absence. She had heard
repeatedly from both Sir Roland and Henry, and received good accounts of both. Sir Roland, who had
also written continually to Lady Constance, was still
fully employed in the business of his mission; he
deeply regretted his prolonged absence, and added
that it was impossible for him yet to name a time for
his return.   He spoke to Lady Constance in unabated terms of his deep attachment, and of the happiness with which he looked forward to the time when
they should meet again, never he hoped more to part.
These letters filled her with sadness, though they no
longer rent her heart as once they had done. She felt
her regard for him grew even stronger and stronger;
for his was a character whose beauty was the more
valued, the more it was known; and her efforts to

bring her affections into their legitimate channel seemed
not wholly without a blessing. It had been a great
relief to her having so much new matter to communicate to him during her stay in town, and her tour in
Scotland, as it enabled her to fill her letters without
alluding much to herself or home concerns, and also
gave a tone of cheerfulness to her communications,
which she could not otherwise have commanded.

Henry's letters to his mother were written in apparently the highest spirits—for he could not bear
her to be troubled by his unhappiness—yet at times a
few words of the deepest melancholy would reveal the
grief that never left him.

When he had driven from the door on the sad day
of his departure from Llanaven, he looked back at
the dear home—where his boyish pleasures had been
so perfect, and where he had lately enjoyed, both such
excess of happiness, and such racking misery—and examined over and over again each window, in the hope, yet
dread, of seeing Lady Constance; and though he felt the
blank of disappointment at finding she was not there, yet
he loved her the more for the resolution and principle
which he felt sure alone had prevented her from taking
one last farewell. He looked on every object as he
passed rapidly along, as knowing he should look on
it no more, and his heart seemed almost to break as
he heard the park-gate swing to and fro on its hinges
after he had passed it for ever. Amidst all his griefs,
however, his kindly heart did not forget the feelings of
others ; and knowing that the old woman at the lodge
would be waiting for him, he mastered himself sufficiently to look out for a moment as he passed, and

waving his hand, he threw out a little sum of money as a farewell remembrance.

When every thing of home was passed, he dropped on his knees in the carriage, and leaning his head on the seat, gave vent to his great grief. His spirit was young and unsubdued, and for a time bitter murmurs rose in his heart against the cruelty of a fate, which not only separated him from all whom he loved, but made even the thought and remembrance of them misery to him! On her, the dearest of all, he dared not let his thoughts dwell for a moment; principle as well as feeling shut her loved image for ever from his mind; and he could not, at that distracted moment, form even the wish, or hope, that the time might come in which he could think of her and not be miserable.

It was too much wretchedness however for him to be at enmity with God, as well as cut off from all earthly affections; and his heart soon softened towards the powerful yet gracious Being whose compassions fail not, and who drew his soul to Himself for comfort and peace, giving him that, which He bids him seek. After deeper and more fervent prayer than he had been able to offer up for many days, he felt his spirit much relieved, and his heart calmed. He would, he thought, try to live for others more than he had hitherto done —he would look more to the end for which he was created: namely, the glory of God; and would strive to be more like his blessed Lord, in patience and exertion—and in these great and heaven-guided resolutions, he obtained somewhat of tranquillity.

When he joined his ship, he found it was to sail with sealed orders, but he cared not for that; there was but one spot in the world for him—the rest was a vacant wilderness, and when at the proper time, the orders were examined, and it was found that the ship's destination was the Mediterranean; it seemed almost surprising to him that others should rejoice so much, at being sent to that always favourite station, when it was a matter of such total indifference to him. He felt that this was wrong, but such a coldness had again crept over his heart, that he walked the deck, almost like one in sleep. He strove to animate himself, and tried to talk, and listen to the conversation of others; but before half a sentence had reached his ear, his mind was again far away.

The ship had a fine passage out, and soon reached Gibraltar; and the officers had leave to go on shore, and examine the peculiarities of that curious place. Henry Ashton landed amongst the others, and while wandering with listless steps over the rock, he suddenly remembered that Mrs. Montague's husband was stationed there. He determined instantly to find him out, and leaving the others, he directed his steps back towards the town, inquiring for the military quarters. Having been directed to them, he soon discovered Captain Montague amidst a group of officers; and going up to him, with a sailor's frankness, he introduced himself, saying that, " as he had had the pleasure of seeing Mrs. Montague very lately, he thought he would be glad to hear a good account of her."

The young man coloured up painfully, and instantly taking Henry Ashton's arm, walked away with him. One or two of the more thoughtless of his companions called after him, saying,

" You'll let us have the interesting news, Mon-

tague," and "When may we have the happiness of
expecting her back?" &c.; but he took no notice,
and continued on his way in silence, till he was out of
sight and hearing of them.

"You saw her lately?—in Cornwall?" he asked,
in a low voice, "and the child, how was it?"

"Much better."

"Thank God!" he exclaimed, "they said it was
dying."

"Yes," said Henry, "my mother feared at one
time that it could not live."

"Your mother! You are not?—can you be—
Mr. Ashton?"

"That is my name," said Henry, smiling.

His companion grasped his hand without speaking
a word, while every feature quivered; then quitting
him abruptly, he walked up and down in great agitation. In a few minutes he returned, and again taking
Henry Ashton's hand, said,

"How can I ever thank you for what you have
done?—for saving me from being a murderer."

Henry Ashton, who knew nothing of Captain Montague's history, (though from several little things
which had reached his ear, he had judged him not a
very attentive husband) was rather startled by this
address; but taking no notice of the latter part of it,
he answered that he had merely done what any naval
officer would have done in his place, adding good-
humouredly,

"You land-fighters think a great deal more of
these things than we do. The water is nothing to
such fish as we are."

"But Mr. Stanhope informed me that it had been a most desperate risk for you, and that you had been severely injured by your exertions."

"Ah! that was only by my own folly. I need not have been hurt, had I taken care."

"I cannot express to you what I feel, Mr. Ashton," again exclaimed Captain Montague, "for I am the greatest wretch on earth; and my cruelty and neglect had nearly consigned those I should have watched over, and loved best on earth, to a watery grave."

"Of that," said Henry, with an embarrassed countenance, "I know nothing; but if you have formerly, as you say, been unkind, you are happy in having it now in your power to make the future a different scene."

"I will leave nothing undone to atone for my past conduct."

"Atonement is out of our power, Captain Montague, either to God or man," said Henry, gravely, "nothing we can do can affect the past."

Captain Montague's eye sunk under the remonstrance of his young companion—whose senior he was by several years—but feeling that his intentions were sincere, he soon answered,

"True, nothing can undo the past, but I trust the future will be very different."

"Be it so!" said Henry, kindly, "and I shall be much mistaken if you find it hard to obtain forgiveness. Mrs. Montague seems to be one of the sweetest persons possible; and it is a dear little child."

Captain Montague sighed, and was silent a moment, then said,

"I had written to you, Mr. Ashton, to try and express my thanks; but probably the letter had not reached you before you sailed from England."

"It had not," replied Henry, "but thanks were not needed. I came off without knowing where I was bound, or I should have been happy to have brought out any thing for you which Mrs. Montague might have wished to send."

Captain Montague thanked him, but looked confused, for he knew that his wife would not have thought of writing to him at that time; though when he despatched Henry Ashton's letter, he had written a most kind and affectionate letter to her, full of remorse for his past conduct, and of loving promises for the future.

The report of the loss of the vessel in which Mrs. Montague had sailed, had reached Gibraltar, unaccompanied by any particulars several days before Mr. Stanhope's letter arrived, mentioning her safety, and that of the child; and during that fearful interval, he had had the weight of their blood upon his conscience, which dreadful feeling had left so strong an impression on him, that, when he was relieved from it, it seemed as if all other sensations were absorbed in joy and gratitude; and his affections, now, turned back into their natural channel, seemed to flow in a fuller tide than they had ever done before. After a few minutes' silence he continued,

"I have applied for leave of absence, for I long to return to England; but I fear I shall not be able to get it for some weeks yet, and perhaps I may see you again before that time. I shall be most happy if I go to take home any thing you may have to send, or to do any thing in my power to serve you. Will you dine with us this evening at the mess?"

Henry accepted the invitation, and Captain Montague then walked with him about the place, pointing out all that was most worthy of observation—glad indeed to shew any civility to one to whom he felt so deeply indebted. Henry was much pleased with his new companion, and with several of the officers whom he met at table, and taking leave kindly of them all, when dinner was over, he returned to his vessel.

This meeting with Captain Montague, seemed for the time to relieve his spirits a little, for it drew his thoughts away from himself; but when again on board and following the routine of a sailor's life, his sense of misery seemed almost deepened upon him.

He had never before been in the Mediterranean; and had his heart been at ease, how would he have enjoyed its lovely climate, and its beautiful shores! but now, as he looked into the clear depths of its blue waters, he only seemed to long for repose within its bosom. He seemed incapable of peace, and to be driven from every subject on which his thoughts could rest, for every avenue to feeling was filled with the objects that should be avoided. His very prayers had been so full of her! for he was one whose spirit had hitherto sought rather to bring the blessing of God down on his earthly treasures, than to raise itself up to God.

Yet it was not the feeling merely of disappointed affections, or of separation from what he loved, which brought this deadly blight on every thing; it was the fear of sin, the cloud of guilt upon his soul, which made every thought of home so terrible to him. His young, romantic heart, would rather have delighted in the former case in nourishing up its regrets, and in dwelling upon the recollections of former happiness; but his awakened conscience, and high principle would not allow of his doing so now; and not having strength to cope with the evil, and subdue it, he found his only refuge was in endeavouring to shut out memory altogether. The life which he led unhappily presented nothing to fill the space thus left so vacant, and all that he felt therefore in general, was a cold, almost unendurable sense of utter desolation!

There were none on board with whom he had ever sailed before, and if any of his former shipmates had seen him then, they would scarcely have recognised in his pale, melancholy countenance the features of him whose once buoyant mind, and bounding heart, had made all bright around, and often infused its gladness even into the weary night-watch.

Among all his new companions, there was but one who excited any interest in him, and that was Mr. St. Clair, the first-lieutenant. He was a middle-aged man, with a grave but pleasant countenance; and though he was one who spoke but little, yet that little was invariably kind, and conciliating. A laugh or joke seldom indeed passed his lips, but no officer on board was more tolerant of the laughter and jokes of others. Even when the "sky-larking" of the half-crazy 'mids,' passed almost all bounds of endurance, and called forth hard words and severe looks from others in the ship, his indulgent smile and kind excuse were ever ready.

"There's a great noise below there, Mr. St. Clair," the captain would exclaim.

"Young spirits, sir, young spirits; all the better when work comes," would be the kind-hearted answer.

Yet when in passing along decks, his " Have a care, young gentlemen," was heard, it was invariably treated with respect, and the " Aye, aye, sir," was never more cheerfully returned than to him; while quiet would be for a moment restored.

The light-hearted beings over whom he exercised this 'mild control,' used among themselves to call him St. John St. Clair—John being his christian name; but the application was given in all kindliness, for he was greatly beloved, and the strong religious opinions which suggested the name bringing with them no harshness, were tolerated for his sake, and in many instances indeed, they became, through him, reverenced for their own.

Under circumstances of less intolerable suffering, Henry Ashton would often have gladly conversed with him; but it was impossible for him to talk much on indifferent subjects, and the source of his affliction was one which he could lay open to no human eye; nor could he seek comfort under it from any human voice. Scarcely indeed, to Heaven could he, at that distressful time, look for consolation, " il étoit triste de la tristesse, qui étoit alors le fond de sa vie," and all his energies seemed gone.

After cruising about for some time, the ship touched at Malta; and when there, Mr. St. Clair received a letter from a friend of his who had formerly sailed with Henry Ashton, and who made particular inquiries after him; asking if he were still the life of the crew, as he had formerly been. Surprised at receiving a character of him so unlike what his present appearance warranted, Mr. St. Clair watched him more closely; and he soon became convinced that it was trouble of heart which had converted the once gay and high-spirited young sailor, into the silent, melancholy being who then trod the decks with so abstracted an air. This conviction roused all his kindly feelings, and made him anxious if possible to assuage the sorrow of so young a heart.

When Henry's turn therefore came for keeping the night-watch, he lingered some time on deck, watching for an opportunity of quiet conversation with him. Henry, unaware of his object, took no notice of him, but continued his monotonous walk up and down in silence; till at length, full of his own sad thoughts, he stopt and leant over the gangway, his face buried on his arm. A rough but kind hand laid on his shoulder, soon roused him from his reverie. He started, and was rather surprised at finding it was Mr. St. Clair's; for he had scarcely exchanged a syllable with him, excepting on matters of duty, since he had been on board.

"These night scenes waken melancholy thoughts, Mr. Ashton," said the first-lieutenant.

"Not more so than sunshine," replied Henry, gloomily.

"Not if we like holding silent communion with the Father of our spirits," said Mr. St. Clair; "but otherwise darkness is generally felt to be a dreary thing."

"All times are much alike, I think," replied Henry.

"To me, I confess," said Mr. St. Clair, "these tranquil hours, when most of the poor fellows are below in their hammocks, are particularly delightful;

the unusual quiet makes one more mindful of ' Him,
ne'er seen but ever nigh.' "

Henry was silent and again leant down his head.

" Has the thought of Him no charm for you, Mr.
Ashton ?" continued his kind companion.

" It used to have," answered Henry, without raising his head.

" You have not the look of one whom sin has separated from his God !" said Mr. St. Clair, in a tone
which would have unlocked the closest heart.

" No," said Henry. " I have sins enough certainly,
but I have no fears of God's anger, though I cannot
just now enjoy His love."

His young heart was touched by Mr. St. Clair's
manner, and with that yearning for commiseration, so
natural to all, especially to the young when affliction is
new and bewildering to them, he longed to pour forth
all his miseries. But that was impossible. His
troubles did not belong to himself alone—the most
sacred feelings of others were involved in them ; and
those he could not betray.

" Prayer will bring God's light back into your
heart, young man," replied Mr. St. Clair, in a softened
voice ; " no sorrow can withstand His gracious promise there. You have found that I dare say at times."

" I have never known sorrow till now," replied
Henry.

" Then you must have had the life of one of a mil-
lion," sighed his companion ; "but nevertheless the
burthen is not the lighter because our shoulders are
unaccustomed to bearing it. I don't seek your confidence as to your earthly trials ; you can tell them to
your God ; and it is but poor pleasure to hear the

record of sufferings which make one's heart bleed, while one cannot raise a finger in help. But a little word of God's peace will sometimes cheer a drooping spirit, if Satan's power is not too hard upon it. You seem, I am happy to see, to have some hope beyond this world."

" I had—but every thing now seems gone !"

" Oh ! that must not be," said Mr. St. Clair with cheerful warmth, " you must rouse yourself, and not let the evil one gain so much advantage over you. Remember, doubting of God's mercy is a sore sin ; and so is, rejecting His consolations."

" I used to think," said Henry, " that sorrow would always raise the heart to God, but I find it far otherwise."

The recollection of his conversation with Lady Constance when he was walking with her on the shore, on the first day of his arrival at Llanaven, rushed over his mind at that moment, and completely overwhelmed him. He remembered so well his own words, . " Joy on the one side, sorrow on the other, lift the soul to God," and as he felt how little that was now his own experience, and the memory of that delightful hour flashed across him, his spirits completely gave way, and a deep burst of grief broke for an instant the silence of the night.

Mr. St. Clair felt a painful compassion for this young and sorrowing heart, and spoke words of kindest sympathy. After a few moments Henry became more composed.

" I am very weak," he said, " but I trust I shall be able to look more to God than I have done lately, and then I shall be strengthened."

Mr. St. Clair remained with him during the whole of his watch; they walked up and down the deck together for some time, and then sat down leaning against a coil of rope. In the course of their conversation Mr. St. Clair adverted to circumstances in his own life which had shewn forth the power of God to sustain under trial and affliction, and as Henry Ashton expressed a wish to know what they were, Mr. St. Clair gratified his curiosity and gave him the outline of a life which did indeed shew that God is " a very present help in time of trouble."* Henry as he listened felt grieved and shocked at the rebellion of his own heart, and fervently, though secretly, imploring the pardon and strength of his Heavenly Father, he found a peace of mind to which he had long been a stranger.

From that time he took great delight in the society of his new friend, and though the source of his sorrow was one which he could not even touch upon to others, yet he felt his faith so animated by Mr. St. Clair's example and conversation, that he was enabled with some success to combat its terrible power in his own heart.

His ship was stationed for some time at Beyrout, and Henry obtained leave to go on shore and visit some of those places in Syria which must ever afford intense interest to the truly Christ-loving heart; for though

> " —— fast as evening sunbeams from the sea
> Thy footsteps all in Sion's deep decay
> Were blotted from the holy ground: yet dear
> Is every stone of hers; for Thou wast surely here."

When he saw the dreadful degradation of the ancient

---

* The first-lieutenant's story was found too long an episode to introduce in this work.

people of God, ground down as they were under a second Egyptian bondage, and tyrannised over in every way—his heart burnt within him! Devoutly did he pray that the Lord would soon arise, and appear in behalf of His afflicted people, and his ardent spirit recovering somewhat of its old enthusiasm, made him earnestly desire, that if human means were in any way to be instrumental in the promised restoration of Israel, his arm might be amongst those permitted to uplift itself in the cause. Vain wish! Yet doubtless not forgotten by that God, who has said, as regards this beloved nation: "Blessed is he that blesseth thee!"

CHAPTER XVI.

"The almost infinite power to suffer which is bound up in our
mysterious being."—*Christian Ladies' Magazine.*

"Cherchez auprès de Dieu la force que vous ne trouverez en
nul autre."—MADAME DE GUYON.

HENRY ASHTON continued to write frequently to
his mother, though it was ever a task to him to do so.
To Lady Constance of course he wrote no more, nor
could he master himself sufficiently to continue his
correspondence with his brother, but he sent many
kind messages to them both, in his letters to Lady
Ashton, and endeavoured in every way, as far as truth
would allow, to prevent her from suspecting the real
cause of his unusual silence.

After remaining for a few months at Beyrout his
ship was to return to Malta, and she was on her way
back, when a frightful accident occurred, spreading
sudden death and anguish around. Henry and Mr.
St. Clair had been conversing together for some time
on deck one day, while the men were practising at
the guns, when a violent shock was felt from the
explosion of a cartridge-box near them, which tore

away and scattered in all directions, a considerable part of the bulk-head by which it stood, killing two unfortunate men on the spot, and severely wounding several others. Mr. St. Clair providentially escaped with a slight graze, but Henry Ashton, who had been standing quite close to the spot, was instantly struck backwards — fragments both of metal and of wood having entered his side and chest, carrying portions of his clothes also with them into the fearful wounds. It was thought indeed at first that he was dead, for he lay motionless on the deck with a ghastly pallor on his cheek, and the surgeon under that impression passed him by, and naturally gave his attention where he thought it would be of more avail. Mr. St. Clair also thought that all was over, but restraining his feelings with seamanly self-command, he likewise went to render assistance to the unfortunate men who were wounded. When every thing had been done for them however, and the bodies of those who were dead were about to be removed, a slight contraction on Henry Ashton's brow, as they were bearing him away, proved that life in him was not quite extinct. The surgeon therefore instantly attended to him, and entered into a minute examination of his wounds, and while he was doing so, Mr. St. Clair watched his countenance with the most intense anxiety; and his heart sunk within him when, after a time, the other shook his head saying,

"There is life certainly, but I see no hope; it is impossible he can recover; feeling is almost gone, or he never would have endured what I have been doing, without having betrayed evidences of extreme pain—his side is full of splinters."

He was carried carefully to his berth where every attention was paid him, and from time to time the surgeon was able to extract from some of his many wounds splinters of wood or metal, and portions of his dress, but it was some days before any thing like consciousness returned.   Mr. St. Clair was unwearied in his kindness, nursing him with the utmost tenderness, and devoting all the time he could spare from his duties to watching over him; and great was his delight, when, after days of almost hopeless anxiety, Henry at last opened his eyes and endeavoured to utter articulate sounds.   His weakness however still continued almost like death, and the utmost he could do was to whisper occasionally one word at a time. The surgeon still gave no hopes of his life, for he said it was impossible that his constitution could stand what he must have to undergo before all extraneous matter was extracted from his wounds.

By the time he reached Malta his consciousness had quite returned, and with it also returned the most exquisite sense of pain, and the noise and bustle became intolerable to him.   " Home," was ever on his lips, and he implored that he might be sent there.   He felt that he could not live, and the trials that had formerly seemed so great, faded away before the near view of eternity.   He could now think of Lady Constance and his brother with deep but calm affection, and longed only to see them once again, and then to lay his head on his mother's breast — his mother, towards whom his heart yearned so painfully—and die.

The " Oriental" was not at Malta when his vessel

arrived, but as there was a ship of war just sailing homewards, it was thought best for him to go by that, as he would then have the advantage of the surgical attendance on board. His mind was much relieved when he found he was to return home, and he often expressed to Mr. St. Clair his deep sense of God's goodness in arranging all so much in accordance with his wishes.

"Ah!" he exclaimed, "how eternity changes one's view of things! Sin now seems the only evil."

"But sin is washed away from your soul, is it not? asked the other."

"I trust so," he replied, "but I regret its existence all the more, and my late rebellion has been terrible."

"You seemed to have much to bear," said Mr. St. Clair.

"I had," replied Henry, sighing deeply; "at least I thought so then, but now I am thankful for it. It has loosened my tie on life, and I have now no wish but to go to Him whose love and mercy has pardoned, and will receive, me."

"But mere disappointment in the things of life is not the best frame of mind in which to die, Mr. Ashton," said his friend, who felt most anxious that his ground of hope should be clear, and that love to Him who had died for his sake, should be the acting principle of his mind.

"I know that," said Henry, "and it is not so with me; but had all been bright on earth, the pain of parting would have been greater."

"You are at peace with God, are you not?"

A smile, the first Mr. St. Clair had ever seen pass

Henry's sad and suffering countenance, lighted up his full blue eyes, and was his only answer.

"Trusting only to the merits of Christ?" continued his friend.

"Only," murmured Henry, raising his hand involuntarily in the fervour of his feelings, though the next moment an expression of extreme pain convulsed his features, for the slightest motion agonised him.

His removal from his own ship to the frigate in which he was to return home, was attended by the most excruciating torture, and the surgeon scarcely thought he would live through it. Mr. St. Clair supported him the whole time, and not a single murmur escaped his lips, though the unbending contraction of his brow, and the frequent irrepressible sounds of anguish which burst from him, shewed how much he had to endure. When lowered into the boat on his hammock he put out his hand as if to search for something.

"What is it?" asked Mr. St. Clair.

"My desk," he said.

It was the one in which he had been used to keep Lady Constance's picture, and his other treasures—remembrances of her—and he had forgotten for the moment that all had been removed; but recollecting it the next instant, he added, "It does not signify, I care not for it."

"Every thing is in the boat with you," said Mr. St. Clair.

"I shall need nothing long," replied Henry.

Mr. St. Clair turned away to hide the tear that filled his eye, at the thought that indeed, in all probability, the fine and noble-looking being before him would soon be beyond the reach of human comforts, or of human sorrows.

He accompanied Henry on board the frigate and made every thing as easy about him as he could, and earnestly did he wish he were able to return home with him, but that could not be, and as the vessel was getting under weigh he was forced to go. He bent over the poor sufferer and in solemn, afflicting words commended him to God, though Henry could only answer by a kindling glance of gratitude and a slight pressure of the hand, for his strength was almost exhausted.

The vessel had to touch at Gibraltar on its way home, and, as it lay there, Captain Montague who had just obtained his desired leave of absence, and had intended returning to England by the next steamer, hearing that Henry Ashton was on board and in a dying state, entreated the captain of the frigate to give him a passage home with him in order that he might, if possible, be of comfort and service to one to whom he owed so much. His request having been granted, he went immediately on board, and took his station by Henry's side; and it was impossible for any thing to exceed the devotion with which he watched and tended him.

Henry soon felt the comfort of his kind cares, but he greatly missed the sustaining power of Mr. St. Clair's fervent piety, and was thus left wholly to the resources of his own mind. God however did not desert him, but poured strength and light into his soul, shewing him his sins in the strongest colours, but supporting him at the same time with His own gracious promises of pardon ; so that in fact the time so apparently

destitute of spiritual comfort, was to him richer in
heavenly joys than any former period of his life had
ever been. He learned to depend simply upon God,
and found strength every moment in close communion
with Him, and happy as his former years had been, he
experienced now, when tortured in body, and separated
in heart from all the earthly objects of his affection, a
peace and " rest which belongeth only to the people of
God." He longed continually to be able to speak of
these things to his attentive but thoughtless companion,
who though full at that time of all kindly feelings
towards him, seemed wholly indifferent to the love of
God. But it was such pain to him to speak, or to
make the slightest exertion, that he was forced to
remain silent, and could only pray therefore for him,
who seemed so little to feel the value of prayer for
himself, but whose unceasing kindness, night and day,
filled him with a deep concern for his welfare.

Life indeed seemed at times almost ebbing away
from Henry's enfeebled frame. Many splinters had,
from time to time, been extracted from his wounds,
but each succeeding operation seemed to leave him
weaker than the last, so that the surgeon dreaded
any further attempts, lest the exhausted sufferer
should die under his hands. Yet in this weak and
almost lifeless state Henry Ashton was permitted
greatly to glorify God, for the few words he ever
voluntarily spoke were those of bright and heavenly
joy, and of perfect acquiescence in his Heavenly
Father's will.

Patience and resignation are indeed often shewn
by those who have no solid ground for hope as regards

the next world ; natural gentleness and amiability often preserving the mind from murmuring under pain and sorrow ; but it belongs to the true Christian alone, to feel the brightness of assured hope at such times, and to be enabled to justify by his clear, full testimony, the unfading truth of the " Rock of his Salvation."

CHAPTER XVII.

" It is not that which is apparent, not that which may be known
and told, which makes up the bitterest portion of human suffering—
which plants the deepest furrow in the brow and sprinkles the hair
with the earliest grey, it is the grief which lies fathom deep in the
soul and never passes the lip—that which devours the heart in secret
* * * that which springs from crushed affections and annihilated
hopes."—*Phantasmagoria.*

" So be it, Lord ! I know it best,
Though not as yet this wayward breast
Beat quite in answer to thy voice,
Yet surely I have made my choice.
* * * *
So * * rather let me die
Than close with aught beside to last eternally."—KEBLE.

LADY CONSTANCE had found her return to Llanaven
extremely trying, and for a time every wound in her
heart seemed opened afresh; but she determined to
gain the mastery over her feelings, and not to give
way to wandering thoughts. She therefore resolutely
set herself much active employment, attending her
schools with diligence and perseverance, and she soon
found that in this path the peace of God, and His
great consolations, were still open to her. She was
glad to see that Lady Ashton and Mrs. Mordaunt
appeared pleased with each other, and her hopeful

spirit made her look forward to the day when her kind cousin would be of one mind and one spirit with them. In Philip Mordaunt she felt great interest, and there really did seem in him some awakening of the heart, so that she began to hope that the visit which had in some respects been so irksome to her, might prove in the end of much good.

The captain of the ship in which Henry Ashton had gone out, knowing that the Oriental steamer, though later in its departure from Malta than the frigate, would yet reach England first, had written to Lady Ashton by that conveyance, informing her, in the gentlest manner possible, of the dreadful event which had taken place, and saying that her son was returning home at his own earnest request, and would probably arrive within a few days of the time when she would receive that letter, beseeching her to be prepared for the worst, as the surgeon had expressed it as his opinion, that his life hung by the slenderest thread.

This terrible announcement reached Lady Ashton just as all her guests had departed from Llanaven, and it may well be conceived with what feelings it was received. She was walking in the garden with Lady Constance when the letter was given her, and after reading a few lines—without cry or groan, she sunk upon the earth. Lady Constance in great alarm hastened to raise her, and called for help, but they were too far from the house for her to be heard; and Lady Ashton after a few minutes opening her eyes again, and fixing them on her with a piercing look, as if she thought to read in her countenance a confirmation of all her hopes or fears, faintly murmured,

" Is he still alive ? " and sunk again upon the ground.

Lady Constance whose whole thoughts and attention had been solely devoted to her, asked in the utmost terror, " Alive ? Who ? "

" Henry ! " exclaimed the almost distracted mother; " Oh, Constance ! read the letter, and tell me at once —oh, tell me at once ! " and she buried her face in her hands.

Lady Constance took the letter, but for a moment she could discern no distinct word; though feeling even through her dreadful agony the necessity of self-command she exerted herself to be calm, and passing her eye rapidly over the page till she came to the assurance of Henry's not having been killed, she threw her arm round Lady Ashton as she lay by her side, exclaiming,

" He may still be alive ! " and then mingled her burning tears with those of her afflicted friend.

" Constance," said the latter after a time, raising herself up, " what has happened ? for I scarcely know."

Lady Constance struggling again for composure, endeavoured to read the letter, but every word came forth almost singly, and was uttered as with a spasm, till at last when she read of Henry's extreme danger, she threw herself into Lady Ashton's arms, and wept in uncontrolled, uncontrollable anguish. Yet her sufferings at that moment were almost entirely for Lady Ashton; she knew how doatingly she loved her sons—how every feeling was bound up in their loved idea ; and this dreadful stroke seemed almost insupportable. At length Lady Ashton exclaimed—suddenly disengaging herself,

"We must be going, my dear Constance, we must not leave him, if—oh, my God!"—and she clasped her hands in extreme anguish—"if he is still alive! we must not leave him alone, with no one to receive him or attend to him. Order the carriage instantly. You will come with me? he may be even now at Falmouth. Oh! how could I lose a moment?"

These words brought Lady Constance's thoughts back upon herself, and a torrent of conflicting emotions rushed over her mind. Was she to meet Henry? Was she to go to *him*, from whom if living, she ought to fly to the ends of the world? What would he think? What would he feel?

Yet how could she bid Lady Ashton go alone to meet her dying—her perhaps dead son? How bid her sustain the anguish of the shock, the torture of suspense, alone, with no one to speak to her, none to comfort her? How could she say, "I will not go with you to the scene of trial?" What excuse could she frame for such apparently unnatural conduct? What she should do—what she ought to do—she knew not, and she felt almost on the verge of losing her senses, for in her extremity she forgot to apply to the Fountain of Wisdom. Her course was, however, soon decided by Lady Ashton's returning to her and saying,

"Would you like your maid to go as well as mine, Constance? I thought perhaps she might be useful; she is putting up your things, but you had better see that all is right. The length of our stay must be uncertain, so take all you want. You have ordered the carriage, my dear, have you not?"

"Oh!" said Lady Constance, exceedingly pained at having in her distress forgotten to do so, and

blushing deeply " how could I be so cruel — so forgetful !" and flying to the house, she hastened to repair
her neglect.

The servants, however, knowing the state of the
case, had prepared the carriage, and were only waiting
for orders to come round, so no time happily was
lost.

When Lady Constance next met Lady Ashton, she
threw her arms round her neck, and said,

" Can you forgive me ? "

" For what, my dear child ? "

" For forgetting what you wished me to do."

" I am sure you would not have done so, had not
your heart been too full of us and our troubles,"
replied Lady Ashton, with that gentle kindness which
never deserted her ; " but you will come with me, my
child, and help me at this cruel, cruel moment."

Lady Constance could not refuse, but unable to consent she drooped her head on Lady Ashton's shoulder
almost in a state of insensibility. Her silence surprised
and pained Lady Ashton, who said in a disturbed and
somewhat reproachful voice,

" Do you shrink from the sad task, Constance ?
Ah ! if it is hard to you to see him suffer, think, my
dear, think what it must be to me !" Her voice failed
and she burst into tears.

" Oh ! no," said Lady Constance almost distracted,
" I shrink from no pain. My God knows how willingly
at this moment I would die to give you happiness."

" I know all your affection, dear Constance," said
Lady Ashton, " but the young heart dreads witnessing
pain and sorrow, and I will not ask you to go with me,
if you feel averse to it."

" There is nothing I would not do for you," replied Lady Constance.

" Thank you, my dear," said Lady Ashton, kissing her with renewed love, " and my poor boy too — your brother I might almost say — he has also a great claim on your affection, and you will, I am sure, gladly be of use and comfort to him."

She again kissed the miserable girl who was incapable of speaking, and telling her to hasten her preparations, she left her in a state of misery not to be described.

Indecision was however at an end; Lady Constance had no choice, and she must go. Mrs. Montague having heard of the affliction which had occurred, had instantly offered to come and stay with Lady Florence, and her kind proposal having been gladly accepted, the unhappy mother, and her still more unhappy companion, set off on their journey to Falmouth, there to wait for news of Henry.

They had not long to be in suspense, for after one night of restless anxiety the early dawn shewed them a frigate which had arrived during the darkness lying in the Falmouth Roads. Lady Ashton instantly rung and sent her servant down to inquire what vessel it was, and the man soon returned, saying that it was the —— which had just arrived from the Mediterranean, and which was lying to in order to land an invalid officer. This news filled Lady Ashton with overpowering joy; it was the frigate in which Henry was to return, and she could not doubt but that he was the officer mentioned. She went directly to inform Lady Constance of the happy intelligence, and to beg her to dress quickly and go down with her to the shore.

Lady Constance would gladly have been spared the latter trial, but her heart was filled with a joy which for a moment overbore all other feelings, and she was soon ready to join Lady Ashton. When about to set out however a sickness came over her which made it seem impossible for her to proceed; she paused, and asked if it would not be better for her to stay behind and make any preparations which might be necessary; but Lady Ashton expressing a wish to have her support, she could say no more.

When arrived on the shore, they saw a man-of-war's boat approaching, and as it drew near they plainly distinguished that some person was in it lying down and supported by some one else; and their hearts felt convinced it must be Henry. Lady Constance could not bear to stay amongst the group of idlers who were beginning to collect about the spot, and begged Lady Ashton to go to some little distance; but the latter who saw no crowd—or any thing in existence excepting Henry—could not move; till Lady Constance in an agony, suggesting that the sight of her at the first moment might overpower him, and be too much for his strength during the exhaustion and fatigue of landing, at length induced her to remove a little way off, and leave her servants to receive him at the first moment.

The boat neared the shore, and at length Henry's form became plainly visible to those who watched his return with such intense anxiety; but the gentleness with which the men rowed, and with which they finally let the boat just float to the shore, on the surface of the—happily calm—sea, told a tale of the sufferings they were so careful not to increase, which sent de-

spondency and anguish again into their hearts. Lady
Ashton could scarcely restrain herself from rushing
back to meet her son as she saw him lifted on his
mattrass from the boat, but Lady Constance longed
rather to fly and hide herself from every eye. She felt
as if all the world were watching her, and reading the
agony which struggled in her heart.

When Lady Ashton had seen Henry safely taken
out of the boat and being carried to the hotel—for he
could not bear the motion of a common carriage—she
turned, in order to go and receive him there herself,
and Lady Constance mechanically gave her the support
of her arm. They walked on quickly but in silence,
and having reached the hotel, they prepared a couch
for Henry to be laid on as soon as he arrived: but
when Lady Constance heard the sound of the men's
steps who were carrying him, she could endure to
remain no longer; but telling Lady Ashton she would
leave her alone for a time with him, she quitted the room;
and had scarcely escaped by one door before he was
brought in at another.

When Henry was laid on the sofa he remained perfectly without motion, and as his face was covered with
the handkerchief which had been put over it to save
him from the prying curiosity of the crowd, terror
seized Lady Ashton lest he should at last have died—
even at the very moment of their meeting. She stood
breathless and without power to move or speak; and
never would she have had courage herself to have
uncovered the features which might even now she
thought be rigid in death. But Captain Montague,
who had accompanied Henry, gently removed the handkerchief, and Lady Ashton then relieved from her

terrible fear by seeing life still in his countenance, though agonised at heart by witnessing the ravages which suffering had made on his appearance, sunk on her knees by his side, and pressed her lips to his death-like cheek. He opened his eyes, and seeing who it was a deep sob rose from his breast, and every feature became convulsed with emotion.

" My mother !" he exclaimed with difficulty. "Oh! how I have longed for you, longed once more to see that dear, dear face !"

Lady Ashton could scarcely answer—the mixture of joy and sorrow in her heart was so great; but she spoke broken words of tenderest love, and over and over again kissed the pale and faded cheek which had so lately bloomed with health and happiness. Henry held her hand, and seemed as if he could not bear for a moment to take his eyes from her loved countenance; but weariness and pain soon forced him again to close them. He entreated if possible to be removed to Llanaven directly; and Lady Ashton, who had already ordered arrangements to be made to enable him to lie down in the carriage, rose to see if all was ready. On opening the door she again observed Captain Montague, and returned for a moment to ask Henry who he was. On being informed, her kind heart rejoiced at the thought of the happiness his return would afford his poor wife; and hearing of all his attention to Henry during the voyage, she went immediately, and in her own peculiarly gracious manner, expressed the gratitude she so truly felt for his kindness. Captain Montague, knowing that in all probability Lady Ashton must have heard from Mr. Stanhope of his conduct to Mrs. Mon-

tague, was excessively confused at seeing her, and
would gladly have escaped from her thanks; but having
said something about his contrition for his past conduct,
Lady Ashton, who knew of the affectionate letter he had
written, smiling kindly said, " that all was forgotten, and
that she was sure he would never again so act, as to
bring back the remembrance of former troubles." She
then gladly availed herself of his offer to go and see
that every thing was ready, and begging that the carriage might be brought round as soon as possible, she
returned to Henry. After having sat by him for a
little while, she said,—

" I must go though and tell Constance to get ready,
for she is here with me."

" Constance here!" exclaimed Henry, with a start
which brought spasms of pain over him from head
to foot, and forced from him sounds of extremest
anguish.

" Yes," replied Lady Ashton, after she had done
what she could to relieve him, " she came to be a comfort to me, though I think she would gladly have been
spared the trial; she is always so feeling, as you well
know."

Henry remained silent, for his spirits were overpowered; and he groaned within himself to find what
power the things of earth still had to trouble him.

Lady Ashton left the room, and went to tell Lady
Constance that they were to return immediately, and
begged her to come down and see Henry. Lady Constance instantly complied; for she had fortified her
mind by prayer, and was determined not to give
way to her feelings. It required, however, her

utmost self-control not to sink to the earth when, on entering the room, she saw how fearfully he was changed ; but being mercifully enabled to retain somewhat of the exalted frame of mind which her late communion with God had inspired, she proceeded with scarcely a pause of hesitation, up to the sofa where he lay.   He, however, could not so command his feelings —the knowledge that she was acquainted with them adding greatly to the difficulty of the task; but having caught sight of her for a moment, he shut his eyes, and averted his head, while great drops of weakness and agony poured from his closed lids.   She spoke to him, however, calmly; and he just gave her his hand, and withdrawing it again immediately, remained silent and exhausted ; and Lady Constance, soon making an excuse for returning up stairs, gladly left the room.

"Why," she thought, as in desolate misery she sat down in her own chamber, "is this world such a scene of suffering ? Why should not all be happy ?" But she soon subdued this questioning and faithless spirit, and with a heavy heart rose to make preparations for their departure.

CHAPTER XVIII.

" E dove
Sì può da Te sdegnato
Fuggir, che a Te pietoso ?"—METASTASIO.

" Each on his cross by Thee we hang awhile,
    Watching Thy patient smile
  Till we have learned to say, ' 'Tis justly done,
  Only in glory, Lord, Thy sinful servant own.' "

KEBLE.

WHEN all was ready, the melancholy party set off,
and Captain Montague, having procured a horse, rode
forward to Llanaven, to announce their approach;
being naturally, of course, most anxious also to see his
wife and child.   The journey to the others was trying
in every way, for though the carriage went at a foot's
pace, and Lady Ashton had caused the board which supported Henry's mattrass to be slung from the top, yet still
every jerk or motion brought on such violent pain that
they were obliged continually to stop.   When they had
passed through the park-gate, and Henry again heard
it swing to and fro after them, how distinctly did he
remember the feelings which he had experienced when
last he had heard that sound ! and amid all that he was
enduring at that moment, he was enabled to thank his

God that the severity of the blow under which he had then so nearly been crushed, was in some degree mitigated ; and that he could now almost look on the loved being before him, and yet remember that Heaven had greater happiness, even than her affection, to bestow.

It was now near the end of October, and the day was so calm that scarcely a solitary leaf floated to the ground, though the touch of an infant's hand would have brought a bright profusion showering down; a dull mist shrouded the half-despoiled trees, adding by its grey, shadowless hue, to the heavy oppression of the scene ; and a mournful silence hung over every thing, to which the stillness of melancholy thought which reigned in the bosoms of those who were returning so slowly and sadly to their once joyous home, responded but too well.

When they arrived, they found the servants waiting in the hall, and Lady Florence, with Captain and Mrs. Montague, there also. Through all her own griefs, Lady Ashton felt a sensation of extreme pleasure at seeing the happiness painted on the countenance of the latter, though that bright look soon gave place to tears of deep regret, as Henry's pale, weak form was borne into the house. Lady Ashton had given orders to have the library prepared for him, as it was on the ground-floor, and thither accordingly he was at once conveyed. It was some days before he was sufficiently recovered from the fatigue of his removal, to be able to leave his bed, and even when he could do so, he preferred remaining quietly in his own room, as that saved him from the pain of being obliged to see Lady Constance. He still believed that he should not live, and he was most anxious that the peace of mind he now enjoyed

should not be disturbed by earthly thoughts. Even
when, after a time, others began to indulge in faint
hopes of his recovery, he still endeavoured to shut out
the idea of such an event from his own mind — it
brought with it no comfort to him — for he felt the
weakness of his own resolutions, and dreaded a return
to the ungracious, rebelling frame of mind which had
formerly given him so much distress.

Several trifling operations took place soon after his
return home, which he bore better than could have
been expected, and as he then really seemed to rally a
little, Lady Ashton urged him to allow himself to be
carried into the adjoining drawing-room, thinking that
society would help to raise his spirits, which appeared
to her so greatly depressed, for calm and quiet in him
looked like melancholy ; but in that she was mistaken ;
his mind was not sad when he was left to his own
thoughts, or when he listened to her voice reading his
favourite books; and often would he lie for hours at
night, sleeplessly enjoying the comforts which his pardoning God poured into his heart. But the slightest
allusion to Lady Constance agitated his excitable mind,
and brought back for the time all the weight of his
former intolerable anguish, and he fain would have
kept for ever out of her presence ; for the more he
recovered his strength, the more did the thought of her
regain power over him. It was natural that it should
be so, for that which softened the pang of death to him,
made life burthensome and dreary ; but his conscience,
more alive than it had ever been before to the evil of
sin, and of ingratitude to God, made him fear that disgust of life rather than desire of the presence of his
Heavenly Father had induced his former resignation

under the stroke which seemed likely to consign him to an early grave, and had he had the smallest idea that he could have recovered, he would rather a thousand times have borne all his illness and suffering alone, and unsoothed by the voice of affection, than have again thrown himself into Lady Constance's company. But he thought that he had but to reach home and then die, and his young warm heart yearned to see those again whom he loved, and to have his mother's hand to smoothe his pillow, and to close his eyes.

Lady Ashton's desire for him to join the others in the drawing-room, troubled him greatly, and long did he resist complying with it; but at last he feared exciting suspicion, and thinking it selfish also to keep her so much in his room—for she could not bear to be long away from him—he yielded to her request; though could she have known the trial to which she was exposing him, she would have been the last to have inflicted it. He, therefore, one day desired his servant to wheel him in on his sofa whilst all the rest were at dinner, in order, by that means, to have time to recover the little fatigue of removal, and the excitement of going for the first time into a room so peculiarly fraught with remembrances of former happiness, before the others came in; and when they entered, the pleasure which most of them expressed at seeing him again among them, and his little agitation at receiving their congratulations (for Captain and Mrs. Montague were still at Llanaven), served to hide the trouble which he felt at first again seeing Lady Constance.

The evening which ensued passed heavily; for talking was in every way painful to Henry; and his being there in his present weak state, put a check upon the

conversation of the others, who spoke in a subdued
tone as if fearful of disturbing him. At last Lady
Ashton wishing to enliven the scene, begged Lady
Constance to sing, but that she could not do; the
remembrance of the many times she had sung with
Henry, made the sound of music oppressive to her at
all times, and now, before him, and in the room too in
which they had so often sung together, it would have
been impossible for her to have commanded her voice
to steadiness, or perhaps even to have repressed the
outward signs of a sorrow which was continually swelling in her heart. Besides she knew the effect which
her singing would have on Henry's feelings, which
were always so susceptible, and she was most anxious
to avoid any thing which would increase the force of
trials which she could estimate but too well; she therefore excused herself, though not without difficulty, and
after another half hour, the party separated for the
night.

When Henry had been conveyed back to his own
room and was left alone, his spirits wholly gave way;
his mind had been forced back to earth, and spite of
the many ejaculatory appeals to Heaven which he had
made during the time he was in the drawing-room, he
had been most miserable. He had indeed found relief
at the moment of prayer, but the next instant the
waves of trouble seemed to close in upon him again,
and overwhelmed his strength. It had been one never-
ceasing strife between duty and inclination, and never
having been accustomed to exercise much self-control, the effort, so new, was almost more than he could
sustain. During that night he scarcely closed his eyes;
and instead of the cheerful heavenly frame which he

had of late so often enjoyed in those quiet hours — so peculiarly delightful to the Christian — his pillow was wet with the ceaseless tears which in his state of weakness he could not repress, and his breast heaved with sobs, which tortured his wounded frame, yet which nothing could subdue. He felt inclined murmuringly to question the mercy of that Providence which had preserved in life one so torn both in heart and frame, and impatiently asked why suffering so terrible should be appointed for him. Yet throughout all, his heart clung to God, and he continually implored His forgiveness; and that He would not cast him off, but would again send peace and strength to his soul.

He was not so well the next day, but thinking that perhaps it was best after having gone through the first trial to endeavour to inure himself to being with Lady Constance, he did not decline that evening going again into the drawing-room, and when there he exerted himself more than he had been able to do before, to shake off the weight that oppressed him, and to join in the general conversation. Again Lady Ashton asked Lady Constance to sing, but again she excused herself, and engaged in chess with Captain Montague, taking her station out of Henry's sight, and another heavy evening passed.

A few days afterwards the Montagues went to their own cottage, and then additional trials commenced; for Lady Constance had no longer the resource of having others to attend to, and the little home party was drawn again more closely and intimately together. Captain Montague's society was also missed, for he was very agreeable and conversable, and his liveliness had often proved a great resource, when no one seemed inclined to speak; for even Lady Florence's spirits had been subdued by the sight of Henry's pale cheek and languid eye, and she spoke and moved as if afraid of her own voice and step.

Lady Ashton, knowing how fond Henry had ever been of the society of the two sisters, proposed that they should now all sit with him in the morning in her little boudoir, which being next to the library, she had given up to Henry's use, and as no one dared to object to this arrangement, they returned again apparently to their old intimate style of companionship.

Daily and hourly trials now arose, and seeing Henry's evident constraint, Lady Constance was in continual fear lest his feelings should at some unguarded moment burst forth before others, or he be tempted to speak of them alone. And her fears were not unnatural, for she judged of him only by what she had seen of him in former times, and did not know how much the power of affliction had been sanctified to him, nor how sincerely, in all great points, he was regulated by high and Christian principle. He would sooner have died than have renewed the subject of his love to her, now that he knew she was engaged to another; and that other being his brother, brought affection also in aid of godly feeling to subdue the strong temptation. He perceived her fears however, and determined by one painful effort to set them at rest, but he could not find an opportunity of speaking with her alone, so had determined to write, when one day as she was sitting in the boudoir with him and Lady Ashton, the latter rising, said,

"I am going out, Constance, but shall not ask you

to go with me this rainy day, for you have a little cough, and are better at home."

"Oh! no," replied Lady Constance, "I should like to go."

"No, stay and finish your drawings, it will be much better for you."

Lady Constance had risen notwithstanding to follow Lady Ashton out of the room, when Henry, determining to speak to her, made her a sign to stay. Her heart sunk with terror, but she could not refuse his mute appeal, so sat down again to her drawing.

"Constance," he said when his mother had left the room, "I wish to speak to you."

He stopped and remained silent for some minutes, at length with an effort he continued,

"I feel that you do not trust me—that you do not yet know me, and I wish to relieve your mind of the fear I see perpetually oppresses it, and for that reason it is that I have asked you this once to stay with me a moment. You need not fear me, Constance, or imagine that I would ever again speak as I did when I thought I might do so. We are together indeed in presence, but I may truly say that never for an instant do I forget the gulf that lies between us, and I should not have returned home had I imagined it possible I could have lived. But when dying, I thought I should like—to see—I could think of you all then calmly——

He was unable to proceed, till having conquered his agitation, he added,

"You will be glad I am sure to know that God has been most merciful to me, and given me more strength and comfort far than I deserved, and I trust that in time—— But I only now wished to assure you that

you need never fear my forgetting what is due to you
—and to my dearest brother, and indeed," he added,
as a glow of pride flushed his cheek, "I should say—
to myself. Were I with you for centuries, no word
would ever pass my lips, but what was fitting for me
to speak."

A feeling of bitterness unconsciously tinged his
manner as he uttered the last words; and Lady Constance felt in heart relieved by it, as it helped to subdue the emotions of tenderness which had arisen within her. With that strange inconsistency of the human
heart, which makes us desire at the same moment for
things most contrary, though she would have given
worlds that Henry had never loved her, or she him,
and though anxious beyond measure to overcome her
own feelings, and ceaselessly striving to do so—yet
when she heard him speak of becoming reconciled to
losing her—a pang not to be described shot through
her heart, and bitterness also crossed her spirit as she
thought, "Is it for one who can so lightly forget, that
I am suffering all this?" Yet, she felt she was unjust
to him, and deeply sinful towards God in harbouring
such feelings for a moment, and her soul, humbled to
the dust, poured itself forth silently, in supplications
for pardon and strength, so earnest, so engrossing,
that for a moment she entirely forgot where she was,
and with whom she was. Henry's voice soon however
roused her again, as he said in a tone from which all
bitterness was gone,

"I will not detain you now, Constance, or ever
again allude to this subject. It is best it should be
forgotten, and God who never tries us beyond what
He gives us strength to bear, will I feel sure, when

this trouble has done its work, remove it from me.
I have been very sinful, very murmuring, but I am
not so much so as I was, and that makes me feel sure
that God has not left me to myself, as I too well deserved. Forgive my having spoken to you this once,
it was merely that you should not live in fear because
of me—for I saw that you distrusted me, and——"

Lady Ashton at that moment re-entered the room,
ready for walking. She stopped for an instant at the
door, surprised at the expression in Henry's countenance, for the effort of speaking as he was doing had
imparted a sad sternness to his look, most unusual in
him; and his contracted and rather frowning brow,
told of a displeasure which seldom rested on his
features. She had however too much wisdom
and good feeling to make any observation, and
crossing the room to fetch what she wanted, she
merely made some indifferent remark, and again went
out.

Lady Constance rose as soon as she was gone, and
would gladly have left the room without speaking, but
she felt that by doing so she would be betraying her
own feelings too much; so she continued for some time
busied in putting by all her various drawing materials,
hoping to be able in a few minutes to acquire tranquillity of voice and manner; but she knew not what
to say, and the longer she put off speaking the more
impossible did it seem for her to begin. She arranged
and rearranged her paints and pencils, as Henry lay
with his hand shading his eyes, and she was about at
last to leave the room in silence when he looked up,
saying,

"You are not angry with me, Constance?"

" Oh, no !" she replied hurriedly, with her hand on the door.   But then, with sudden self-control, returning a few steps into the room, and resting her hands on the back of a chair, to prevent her trembling from being perceived, she continued with calm dignity,

" No, Henry, I am not angry ; I am much obliged to you for speaking as you have done ; it will give me much more ease than I have hitherto had, for I confess I did fear that perhaps you might not always control yourself.   I feel that I did you injustice, and I do sincerely trust that you may soon be able quite to forget every thing that is painful."

Henry could not answer, but again covered his eyes with his hand ; and Lady Constance, thinking it best not to prolong a needless intercourse, turned away and left the room.

CHAPTER XIX.

> "Why art thou thus ?
> Have the full chords of kindly love, which once
> Sent forth sweet music through thy heart, been hushed?
> Or has the world unstrung the lyre ? or struck
> Sad discord from its trembling strings ?"—MS.

> "Nature on us, her suffering children, showers
> The gift of tears—the impassion'd cry of grief,
> When man can bear no more ;   *   *
>   *   *   *   *   To me a God
> Hath given strong utterance for mine agony,
> When others, in their deep despair, are mute !"
>
> MRS. HEMANS.

> "Yes, 't will be over soon !   This sickly dream
>   Of life will vanish from my feverish brain ;
> And death my wearied spirit will redeem
>   From this wild region of unvaried pain."—KIRKE WHITE.

LADY ASHTON, while pursuing her solitary walk towards the village, whither she was bound on some charitable errand, pondered with feelings of great discomposure on the strange expression she had observed on Henry's countenance.   It has been said before that she was of a singularly unsuspicious temper, and was never in the habit of looking beyond the things which met the eye ; but she had for some little time past had vague ideas that all was not as it had formerly been, between Henry and Lady Constance. Henry's brusque manner before his departure for the sea—Lady Constance's coldness to him, and unaccountable desire at that time to leave Llanaven, where previously she had been so happy—her disinclination to go to Falmouth —and her subsequent reserve of manner—all had at different times struck her with surprise ; but the slight impression they had made at the time had quickly faded away, and she had nearly forgotten some of the circumstances when the scene she had just witnessed —where not only Henry's countenance, but Lady Constance's heightened colour as she bent over her drawing had caught her attention—brought them all back to her recollection, and seemed to afford a key to what had before been so mysterious. Not having the faintest idea that Henry was attached to Lady Constance, and believing that her heart was wholly given to Sir Roland, the only solution of the present difficulty which occurred to her mind was, that some serious disagreement had taken place between them, and cooled the affection of those who had formerly seemed to love each other with the fondness of brother and sister ; and knowing that the fault could scarcely rest with Lady Constance, she felt a dread lest she might have heard something to Henry's disadvantage, unknown to her—something which had caused him entirely to lose her esteem, and affection.

Harassed by this painful thought she hurried back as soon as she had performed her kind mission at the village, and with the single-minded fervour of her character, determined immediately to speak to Lady Constance on the subject. She could not brook the

idea of blame resting unjustly on Henry's hitherto
spotless name, and she resolved if that were the case
to clear him to Lady Constance and all the world;
while at the same time knowing his rather ungoverned
temper, she thought he might really in some way have
offended; and if so she felt it would be best to try
and shew him his fault at once, for "a word spoken in
due season, how good is it!" At any rate she wished,
if possible, to restore peace and good feeling between
the two beings whom she loved so much, and whose
mutual alienation was the first painful tone of discord
which had ever sounded in her tranquil and happy
home; and bent on this kind object she went directly
on her return to the house to Lady Constance's room,
and finding her there, entered immediately on the
subject.

"Constance," she said, "has anything unpleasant
occurred between you and Henry? for he looked so
exceedingly discomposed when I last went into the
drawing-room, and you also seemed so little at your
ease, that I could not help fearing you had had some
little quarrel—though it seems hardly possible. Tell
me, my dear, was it so?"

Lady Constance, in the most inconceivable terror,
scarcely heard a distinct word of what Lady Ashton
said, but making out sufficient to prove that she had
no suspicion of the real state of the case, she felt in
some degree relieved, and was just able to command
herself sufficiently to answer,

"Oh! no, there has been no quarrel between us."

"What is there, then, my dear?" asked Lady Ashton, "for I see plainly that there is something which
is not pleasant. Now, dear Lady Constance, tell me

truly, I beg of you—have you ever heard any thing against Henry? any report against him?"

"I? against Henry?" exclaimed Lady Constance, her cheek glowing with indignation, and forgetting at the moment, all her fears; "never! who ever spoke but in his praise?"

Tears of affection rose to Lady Ashton's eyes, as she answered,

"Then, why, my dear child, if there has been no quarrel, and nothing has occurred to change your opinion of him—why have you, for some time past, been so cold in your manners to him, so—though I do not wish to pain you, yet I must say—so almost unkind? When he was well, and able to occupy himself, you were ever ready to be with him, and to oblige him. Now—when he is suffering and languid—incapable of taking any exercise, or of moving from his sofa—scarcely able even to bear the exertion of reading to himself—you never offer to do any thing for him, or to amuse him in any way, but leave him often either quite alone, or—as at this moment—with only Florence; and will not ever play or sing to him, though you know how exceedingly fond he is of your doing so."

Lady Constance, in a tremulous voice, murmured that Lady Florence often sung to him, and that he always liked hearing her.

"But still," continued Lady Ashton, "there are many things you used to sing together; and even sometimes if I have asked you, Constance, to sing some particularly favourite song of his, you have refused. I do not like to say a word to you, my dear child, or to reproach you in any way, for I know that the young

cannot be expected to be as considerate as those who
are older, and who have seen more of the troubles
and afflictions of the world ; but still I have, I confess,
sometimes felt it hard, that you should have seemed to
enter so little into our feelings, that you should have
been so wholly unmoved, when my heart has been
torn with anguish ;" and the tears flowed fast as she
spoke.

Lady Constance took her hand, and pressed it to
her lips, while her tears — bitter, burning tears — fell
upon it. She could not speak, and her heart could
only, in silent agony, appeal to Him, who knew its
weakness, and who gave it strength, saying, " Thou
God knowest."

Lady Ashton embraced her affectionately, saying,
with a smile,—

" After all I believe I must carry my complaints to
Roland, though I much doubt whether I shall obtain
redress even from him, for I am afraid he will be but
too much inclined to forgive your forgetfulness of those
who are present, when it proceeds from the engrossing
thought of one who is absent, and that one — himself."

" I am sure," said Lady Constance, in a voice
broken by sobs, " I would not willingly neglect any
one ; I have never meant — never intended to be
unkind."

" Well, my dear love," said Lady Ashton, again
kissing her, " I have been myself, perhaps, unkind in
speaking so strongly, but Henry's agitated countenance
disturbed my mind so much, that I could not rest till I
had asked you about it ; for I really feared — knowing
you are not naturally capricious — that he might in
some way have given you cause for displeasure ; parti-

cularly as you never once wrote to him, or he to you,
during his last absence at sea, though you used to do
so frequently in former times. However, I trust that
this little cloud, whatever it may be, will quickly pass
away, and that Roland will be soon here, making all
bright again with his dear, delightful countenance."

Lady Constance felt really ill after this communication with Lady Ashton, and her spirits seemed completely to fail under the many and continual trials to
which they were subjected. At times she almost
doubted whether it would not be best to tell Lady
Ashton at once the state of her feelings, and seek her
counsel how to act; but the shame of the confession
overcame her, and the thought of Sir Roland and his
deep love determined her to strive again to subdue her
rebellious heart. But it was a hard struggle, with
Henry and his suffering countenance perpetually before
her; and she soon found that fresh sorrows were preparing to try her fortitude still further.

It was known that several splinters still remained in
Henry's side, though for some time they had given him
but slight uneasiness. Gradually, however, they had
changed their place, and some of them, pressing upon
the more sensitive and vital parts, not only gave him
the most excruciating agony, but placed his life in extreme danger. He was emaciated to the utmost degree,
and his once joyous countenance now wore the traces
of ceaseless pain. He bore up against it as long as it
was possible, but at length he found he could no longer
endure the fatigue of sitting up, and he nearly fainted
one evening from excess of suffering. While his mother
was making some arrangements with the servants, by

which he could be conveyed back to his room, in an easier manner than usual, he beckoned to Lady Constance and her sister to come to him. He took their hands, and thanked them both for all their kindness and affection to him. He felt, he said, that he should see them again no more, and implored of them both to pray for him, and to thank their Heavenly Father that he was so early to be taken from a world of sin and sorrow.

"Constance," he continued, "you know what reason I have to be glad that my life will not last long; but pray for me that my patience fail not, and that my faith may be strengthened. I am a great sinner, but I thank God that He leaves me not hopeless, or comfortless. I know in whom I have trusted, and unworthy as I am, He will, I cannot doubt, redeem my soul from death!—Constance, Florence, my dear, dear sisters," he added with deep emotion, "may the God of all mercy and love be with you."

His head drooped on the cushion as he spoke, and his mother and the servants at that moment approaching, he was carried, more dead than alive, to his chamber.

He continued all night in a most alarming state, and when the surgeon who had been summoned, and who sat up with him, was able to examine his wounds by the next morning's light, he found that unless one or two of the ragged portions of metal which were causing such agony were removed, death must speedily ensue; and though the operation of removing them would be attended with very great pain and risk, yet it would, he declared, be the only chance of his recovering.

Henry himself had no wish to live; he seemed to have parted tranquilly with life, and all its hopes and joys, and to be calmly waiting for the Lord's pleasure; but he offered no opposition to any thing which it was thought advisable should be done, and only desired that his mother's wishes should be attended to on every point. He was told at length, that as every effort ought to be made to preserve life, it was thought right for the operation to be attempted, but he was gently warned at the same time, that it was but too probable that his strength might sink under the trial, and that he might therefore not live to see another day.

"I am ready," he answered, "to go, and ready also I trust patiently to stay, if God sees that further trial is necessary for me."

He begged to speak to his mother alone before the operation took place, as he could not endure that she should be with him at the time; but she said that nothing should induce her to leave him, and that she would support and attend him through all his sufferings.

Seeing she was resolved he did not oppose her, but taking her hand in his, and pressing it fondly to his lips, he laid his head upon her shoulder and told the surgeon that he was ready for him; adding with a faint smile of inexpressible affection,—

" You see I have the best of all supports; a heavenly Father's, and an earthly mother's love!"

Lady Ashton did not write to Sir Roland when first she received the letter informing her of the dreadful accident which had befallen Henry, for she thought that if all was over, she ought not to derange the course of the important business he was transacting, merely for the selfish gratification of having him with her in her sorrow; but as soon as she found that Henry was alive, and, as it was then thought, in a hopeless state—she sent off an immediate express to Lord N——, informing him of the event, and begging him to forward the news of it instantly to Sir Roland wherever he might be. A messenger was accordingly despatched after him with all possible haste, but did not reach him till he had arrived at St. Petersburg, where he had gone to obtain the Emperor's final agreement to the business he had in hand. The news of his brother's danger completely overwhelmed him, and instantly entreating a private interview of Nicholas, he informed him of the event, saying that it was his earnest desire to return instantly to England, and beseeching him therefore graciously to waive all further ceremony, and without delay to sign the document in the completion of which he was engaged. This request was instantly complied with by the Emperor, who at the same time expressed, in the kindest terms, his regret that Sir Roland's visit at his capital should be so soon brought to a close, and his concern at the melancholy nature of the event which occasioned his departure; and Sir Roland having now finished all necessary business, immediately set out for ——, and delivering the documents about which he had been engaged, into his uncle's hands, begging him now, as no further difficulty remained, to conclude the affair without him, and to let him instantly proceed to England, and this being of course agreed to, he set off on his melancholy journey home.

The anxiety of his mind would not allow of his stopping a single hour for rest, either on his journey from St. Petersburg to ——, or from thence to England, and harassed and almost worn out as he had previously been by incessant travelling, and the anxiety of important business, nothing but the state of feverish excitement he was in on his brother's account, could have enabled him to undergo the excessive fatigue to which he now exposed himself. He scarcely ever closed his eyes even in the carriage, so racking was his state of suspense, and if he did so occasionally, it was only a restless and momentary sleep that he could obtain. The thought even of Lady Constance could not turn his mind from the one painfully absorbing subject which filled it, and he could see nothing before him, but the brother to whom he was so strongly attached, dying—perhaps dead!

When at length he arrived in England, and after many hours' travelling began to meet with the old familiar things which reminded him that he was near his home, his agitation became almost insupportable, and that deadly sickness of heart came over him, which those but too well know, who have had experience of such trying moments. He could almost have turned away from the entrance to his own park, and could scarcely prevent himself from stopping the postboys when he came within sight of the house, so much did he dread what he might have to hear. He felt as if he could not have survived hearing of his brother's death, and nothing but ceaseless, though almost unconscious, prayer, gave him power to remain in the least tranquil. He closed his eyes as he drove up to the door, lest he should see by closed shutters, or mourning garments about, the evidence that all was over; and, sinking back in the carriage, he had become nearly insensible from intense anxiety, when old James—who well knew his strong attachment to his brother, and who had for some days been continually looking out for him—catching the sound of his wheels, came to the carriage-door almost before it had stopped, and with a joyful voice exclaimed—though his starting tears seemed to bely his statement,

"He's better now, Sir Roland, better, sir, now."

CHAPTER XX.

" And now to thee *he* comes ; still, still the same,
  As in the hours gone unregarded by !
  To thee,—how changed,—comes as *he* ever came."

                                                    ROGERS.

" Oh ! hear me, look upon me ! how my heart,
  After long desolation, now unfolds
  Unto this new delight,   *   *   *
      *   *   *   *   Oh, give me way,
      *   *   *   The eternal fount
  Leaps not more brightly forth from cliff to cliff
  Of high Parnassus down the golden vale,
  Than the strong joy bursts gushing from my heart,
  And swells around me to a flood of bliss—
      *   *   *   *   My brother !"

       Mrs. HEMANS' *Translation of* GOETHE'S *Iphigenia.*

OLD James's account of Henry Ashton was perfectly true. His constitution had sustained the painful
operation which he had had to go through, better than
had been expected ; and though still extremely weak,
he had been able for some days past to rejoin Lady
Ashton and her wards in the boudoir when Sir Roland
returned home.

The latter, when he had heard his servant's joyful
intelligence, still remained in the carriage for several
minutes, being nearly as much overcome by the revulsion of feeling which joy had brought with it, as he

had been before by excess of anxiety. James however,
not equally inclined to silence, spoke to him again, and
Sir Roland then rousing himself, got out, and grasping the old man's hand, entered the hall, and passed
onwards towards the drawing-room door.

It was open, and Lady Constance was standing
there alone, arranging some flowers at the table. The
sound of the carriage had not reached her ear, and
when she turned and so unexpectedly saw Sir Roland —
who at the sight of her had for a moment stood still,
checked by strong emotion — the flowers fell from her
hand, and uttering an exclamation of joy, she found
herself pressed to the noblest heart that ever beat in
the breast of man ! The sight of Sir Roland's well-
known and long-loved countenance banished at the
first instant of surprise all the *present* from her
mind, and old-accustomed affection, flooding her heart,
swept before it for a moment the recollection of the
many reasons she now had for dreading his presence —
but only for a moment. The next breath she drew,
brought with it confused and horrible feelings of remorse, shame, dread, and anguish, and no defined idea
could she form, but the earnest wish that she might
die, before full consciousness returned upon her.

Sir Roland, finding that she could not support
herself, placed her on the sofa, and sat down by her;
but the sound of his voice — that voice so unlike all
others — murmuring rapid words of happiness and
deep affection, roused her, and in an instant all the
horrors of her situation rushed over her. What had
before seemed but as a fearful dream, was now a dread
reality, and her soul shrunk from the precipice on
which she stood. She could not endure Sir Roland's

expressions of confiding happiness, and longed to throw herself at his feet, and confess all her faithlessness — all her unworthiness of his love — and beseech him to hate, and to forget her. But she could not speak — could scarcely think; and though her eyes were tearless, yet covering her face with her handkerchief, she sat trembling in every limb, while he endeavoured by the kindest words to calm and cheer her.

"I know, dear Constance," he said, "how much you must have had to go through; but it is all, I trust, over now, and nothing but joy appears before us. Henry will, I fully trust, now be well, and think what happiness it will be then, to be all united."

Still Lady Constance could not speak, and Sir Roland would probably have felt suspicion rise in his mind, had it not been for her first joyful, animated, greeting which had set his heart completely at rest, and filled it with a happiness he had never known before; for delightful as may be the communications which the pen can convey, there is nothing like the speaking countenance—the radiant eye—the "soul-full voice"—to carry the conviction of affection from heart to heart. He had felt that no doubt had entered his mind; and he could only therefore attribute Lady Constance's present distress, to the excitement of over-wrought feelings. His mother's entrance at that moment prevented any further conversation between them, and his heart remained filled with the most blissful emotions.

Lady Ashton was much affected at seeing him, and it was some time before she could speak. Her distress called forth those tears from Lady Constance's eyes which her own misery could not cause to flow, but

which gave some relief to her oppressed spirits ; and
when she saw Lady Ashton more composed, she gladly
escaped from the room.

Sir Roland was most anxious to see his brother,
and after a few minutes' conversation with Lady Ashton,
he asked her if he might not do so. She said she
would go and see if he was then able to receive him, as
he still from time to time suffered excessive pain ; and
though all immediate danger was over, yet his life
could not even then be considered safe.   After a short
time she returned, and Sir Roland with a trembling
heart followed her into his brother's room.

" I will leave you together," she said, smiling,
" and shall hope to find Henry all the better for this
happiness."

Sir Roland could scarcely control his emotion at
the sight of his brother, and he advanced to the
couch where he lay, with the lightest possible tread,
for it seemed, as if any emotion, or noise, must destroy
the weak, emaciated, being before him.

" Could that be Henry ? " he asked himself ; " that,
the being whom he had left, the very image of health,
and strength, and happiness ? "

Scarcely a trace indeed remained of what he once
had been.   He was much grown since Sir Roland had
seen him ; and the change from boyhood to man's full
proportions is always great ; but it was suffering and
sorrow which had altered him the most, and destroyed
almost every vestige of his former self. With the
eagerness of strong affection he had looked towards
the door as his brother entered, but the sight of him
seemed to blast his very soul, and suddenly pressing
his hand upon his eyes he turned his head away.   He

did not speak or move, as Sir Roland with swelling
heart stooped to kiss his pale forehead, for the conflict
within him was terrible. Affection for his brother
struggled in his breast with wounded feeling, and with
a sense of wrong, which—though he felt it was unreasonable and unjust—yet he could not overcome;
but above all, the sense of the injury he himself had
inflicted on his brother, and his remorse for it, overwhelmed him; and he could not bear to raise his eyes
to one from whom he felt he had stolen earth's best
treasure. He longed to throw himself in his arms, and
tell him how he loved—how he had injured him, and
he strove repeatedly to speak,

> *   *   " but he felt
> A gushing from his heart, that took away
> The power of speech."

Sir Roland, pained by his silence, knelt down by
him, and said in a troubled voice,

"Speak to me, Henry, or at least—somehow—
shew me—that you are glad to see me once again.
Oh! I have suffered so much for you."

Henry's heart could not resist the appeal; he
turned, and throwing his arm round his brother, he
pressed him convulsively to him, while passionate,
scalding, tears burst from his eyes.

Both were silent for a time; but at length Sir
Roland, endeavouring to command his voice, said,

"This is a sad meeting, my dearest brother, but all
will soon be well again, I trust."

Henry shook his head, and exclaimed vehemently,

"Oh! no, never—never! No—I can never——"

He checked himself, fearful lest by some unguarded

word he might betray the secret of his feelings; but Sir Roland, who naturally attributed his expressions to doubts of his own recovery, replied in a cheerful tone,

"Oh! yes; there may still be uncertainty, but you are so young, and have borne your sufferings so well hitherto, that there is every ground for hope; and at this moment I cannot bear to admit a doubt into my mind; I seem sure that God will grant you to our ceaseless prayers."

"Pray not for me—at least not for my life," said Henry despairingly; "it is a burthen—a burthen to me—and to all," he added indistinctly.

"Do not speak so, Henry," replied Sir Roland, much pained; "do not sink under this trial? It is not like you to do so—not like the lion-heart you used to have."

"I am in nothing like what I used to be," murmured Henry; "but I am wretched, and there would be peace in the grave."

He felt possessed by a mad desire to pour out his sorrows to his brother, as if he forgot that of all persons in existence, he was the one from whom he ought most sedulously to conceal them; but he had in former times been so accustomed to go to him with every trouble of his heart, that now to see him by his side — to feel himself supported on his breast—and yet to hide all his thoughts from him, gave him a feeling of almost bewildering pain.

"Happier thoughts will come when strength returns," said Sir Roland, who—though grieved at his brother's want of patience, and submission, yet possessed too much of the spirit of Him, who 'breaketh not the

bruised reed,' to speak to him harshly or reproachfully.
" Do you not remember the lines we used both to be
so fond of?

> ' Oh! come that day, when in this restless heart
>   Earth shall resign her part;
> When in the grave with Thee my limbs shall rest,
>   My soul with Thee be blest!
> But stay, presumptuous—Christ with thee abides
>   In the rock's dreary sides;
> He from the stone will wring celestial dew
> If but the prisoner's heart be faithful found, and true.'

And will not you, Henry—the ' prisoner of the Lord,'
' be faithful found, and true?' "

" Oh! yes," replied Henry, his heart soothed by
his brother's voice, and by the words he so often heard
in former happier days. " Oh! yes, I am not always so
faithless, but the sight of you seems almost to—to—
destroy me."

" You are so weak, that I dare say emotion is most
painful," said Sir Roland; " but you will soon be
yourself again. To find you here at all, is such
excessive joy to me—such a relief after all the racking
anxiety I have had, that I can hardly, I am afraid, feel
enough for the sufferings you still have to endure. It
is a comfort to know however that you have been here
so long;—not left to the rough mercy of sailors, but
tended by most gentle nurses. It were a pain, worthy
to be called pleasure, to be sick, and nursed by my
mother, and Constance."

Henry started from his brother's arms, and threw
himself impatiently upon the pillow of the sofa, murmuring inaudibly,

" Such nursing was not for me."

" Do your wounds pain you much now?" said Sir
Roland, after a minute, rising from his kneeling posture,
and sitting down by his brother's side.

" Some do," replied Henry gloomily, — " But not
all," he added in a milder tone — for he saw that his
brother was hurt at his manner, and he felt ashamed of
yielding so much to the power of his wayward temper.
— " At one time I could not move without agony, but,
thank God, since the last terrible operation, I have
been much relieved. — Forgive me," he continued,
holding out his hand to his brother, though he could
not yet bear to look at him, " forgive me, dear Roland,
for my impatience. You will I fear, in that at least,
recognise my old disposition, and indeed I am afraid
you will not think me much improved in any way
since last we met; but I have had much to try me,
and — but I trust you will not again see me so childish
and petulant, I was not so a little while ago, and
I cannot tell you at times, what happiness I have
felt in thinking of God, and enjoying the comforts
He has poured into my heart! I have lain awake
some nights for hours and hours, separated in heart
from all earthly ties, but filled with peace and joy
in thinking of the Lord — in feeling Him present
with me, and in looking to that time — which I then
thought so near — when I should be with Him for
evermore. But now — to feel how earth again grapples
my weak heart — to see how impatient I am — how
forgetful of God — how unkind to the best and dearest
here ——" His voice failed, and Sir Roland much
affected, said,

" He who has once strengthened will strengthen

again, Henry ; He ' who is touched with the sense of
our infirmities,' will restore you all your lost peace —
if you seek it aright.   My poor, poor brother, would I
could take your place !"

"God forbid you should ever go through what I
have had to bear," exclaimed Henry with energy,
fixing his large expressive eyes for the first time on
his brother's countenance ; "God keep such sufferings
ever far from you, Roland," and at the moment he
would have given worlds to have known that Lady
Constance's affection was wholly given with her faith.
"But how pale you look," he continued, "have you
been ill ?"

"Oh ! no," replied Sir Roland, "but you have, and
anxiety about that, and the fatigue of rapid travelling,
may perhaps have made me look pale for the moment.
But one good night's rest, with a happy heart as mine
now is, will soon set all that to rights."

"Roland," said Lady Ashton, who just then came
into the room, "I think perhaps Henry had better be
quiet now ; he cannot bear much fatigue, and you can
come to him again in a little while."

"Must he go ?" said Henry, who now he had
got over the first emotion of meeting, seemed almost
to lose all pain and sorrow, while looking at his
brother. "I was just beginning to enjoy having him
with me."

"He can come again soon, but you must remember
he too wants refreshment."

"Return soon then," said Henry, reluctantly parting with his brother.

" I will," replied Sir Roland, looking kindly back when he got to the door. Henry's eyes had followed him, and all the old love of their boyhood beamed in their countenances.

It was many days however before they met again, and then—with what changed feelings !

CHAPTER XXI.

" Oh ! there are griefs for nature too intense,
   Whose first rude shock but stupifies the soul ;
   Nor hath the fragile and o'erlaboured sense
   Strength e'en to feel, at once, their dread control.
   But when 'tis past, that still and speechless hour
   Of the sealed bosom and the tearless eye,
   Then the roused mind awakes with tenfold power
   To grasp the fulness of its agony !"—MRS. HEMANS.

" I have known fearful heart-struggles ; but this
   Makes all seem nothing."—TALFOURD.

WHEN Lady Ashton and Sir Roland had left
Henry, they went into the dining-room to luncheon,
where they found Lady Florence, who was enchanted
to see Sir Roland again, but Lady Constance was not
there, Sir Roland felt disappointed, but said nothing ;
and luncheon being finished they left the room, and
Sir Roland going into the drawing-room, found Lady
Constance busily painting, and went immediately and
sat down by her.

" Have you painted many things since I left you,
Constance ?" he asked.

" Yes, a great many," she replied calmly ; " I took
many sketches in Scotland."

" You seemed to like your tour then very much,"
said Sir Roland, " though I rather wonder," he added
with a smile, " at your courage in undertaking it ; and
never could quite make out what was the charm which
drew you forth from this place, to go among strangers :
but I was delighted to find you enjoyed yourself so
much."

" It was very delightful," said Lady Constance.
" Would you like to see some of the drawings I made
there ? " and she gave him her portfolio, though in
doing so her eye evidently avoided his.

He perceived it—and a cloud dimmed the happiness that had been so bright before. He turned
over the drawings, but his mind wandered from them
to her whose hand had traced them, and often did he
look at her as she sat by him, with a cheek deadly
pale, and with a composure in her air, which was
wholly unnatural. Sir Roland felt a chilling, icy fear
creep over him ; but disdaining suspicion, he tried to
shake it off, telling himself it might only be the first
embarrassment of renewed intercourse which made her
so reserved, still it checked him, though he continued
to endeavour to draw her on to conversation.

" Your cousin, Philip Mordaunt," he said, " seems
an agreeable person by your account. I hope he will
come and pay you a visit again soon, that I may make
his acquaintance, and Mrs. Mordaunt also. You seem
to have been a great favourite with her, Constance,
though it must have required all your gentle, yet
earnest piety, to overcome so settled an aversion to
any thing serious as she formerly had."

" She was always very kind," replied Lady Constance, " and latterly particularly so."

" You did not much like her other sons I think, did you ? "

" Not so much as I did Philip.   He was by far the cleverest and most agreeable, and so very kind-hearted."

" When does he expect to be married ? "

" In about two years, I believe, when Miss Leslie comes of age."

" Were you glad to return home, or did you regret leaving the

> ‘ Land of brown heath and shaggy wood ?' ''

asked Sir Roland.

" Oh ! I was both glad and sorry," answered Lady Constance, rather more cheerfully, and for a moment lifting her eyes from her paper, though still unable to look towards Sir Roland.

" I do not think the keen air of the north has made you more blooming than you were, dear Constance," he said as he looked at her beautiful pale countenance, which he was now able to observe more distinctly than he had before done ; " you look so ill !—Have you not been well ? "

" Yes—no—that is," she said colouring and smiling faintly, " I do not think I am so strong as I was, but it is nothing."

Sir Roland watched her countenance with a troubled mind, for every instant served more and more to convince him that there was some secret source of discomfort within her which she strove to hide,—something which made her more embarrassed and reserved with him, even than she had been before his departure from England.   Remaining by her was painful to him, yet he could not bear to go, so again he spoke.

"Henry was gone, I think, before you went to Scotland," he said, "was he not?"

"Yes," replied Lady Constance.

"He seemed to have but short notice given him, poor fellow! it must have been a great disappointment to him to have to go off in such a hurry."

Lady Constance was silent.

"What did you think of him when he first came home?" asked Sir Roland. "It is impossible for me to judge of him now, he looks so dreadfully ill; but was he much grown and as handsome as he used to be? for his countenance was so fine and animated."

He waited for an answer, but for some time Lady Constance could give none. At length she said,

"He was very much grown I think."

"Is he as tall as I am?"

"I should think he is."

"When was it that his terrible accident took place? I did not clearly understand about it from my mother's letter, and have scarcely had time to speak to her about it since my arrival."

"It was in the Mediterranean," replied Lady Constance, endeavouring to speak calmly, "but I do not know exactly where."

"Dreadful it must have been!" exclaimed Sir Roland; "though it is an infinite mercy he was not killed as those other poor fellows were. I had known very little of his movements for some time previously, for he was grown very idle and had not once written to me since he left home; but I suppose some of you heard continually."

"Oh! yes," replied Lady Constance, though she

scarcely knew what she was saying, and she bent
lower than ever over her drawing.

Again the conversation flagged, and Sir Roland
wearied with his attempts at keeping it up, and pained
at heart by her coldness of manner, at length rose
saying,

"Well, Constance, I will not trouble you with
questions and observations any longer, for you seem
tired of answering them. I must, I see, go and read
one of your letters, if I would find her who was to be
glad of my return."

The blood rushed over Lady Constance's cheek,
to her temples as she heard these words, spoken in
a voice of deepest sadness, and for a moment she
could not speak; but her heart reproached her, and
feeling the necessity of overcoming herself, she said,
though not without much hesitation,

"Oh! no, Roland—stay here."

"Do you really wish me to stay, Constance?"

"Oh! yes—I do—I wish—"· She stopped.·

"Then why are you so cold, so reserved?" he
asked, "why wound me so to the very heart? Why—
when your letters breathed at least kindness and affection—when—when your first look and word of welcome was such as to animate every hope, and fill me
with joy—why should you now be colder a thousand
times than you ever were before? Remember, I beseech you," he continued in a voice which trembled
with strong emotion, "that mine are not feelings which
can endure—or which deserve, to be lightly trifled
with."

Lady Constance knew not what to answer, and

Lady Ashton at that moment entering the room and asking Sir Roland to come with her for a little while, as she wished much to speak to him, happily relieved her from the terrible necessity of doing so. He, of course, rose to go with his mother, but he stopped an instant just to say,

"I promised to go soon again to Henry; shall I then return to you—or not?"

"Oh! yes," replied Lady Constance again bending down her head, but not before the troubled expression of her countenance at the sound of Henry's name had caught Sir Roland's eye. He stood for an instant rooted to the spot, in utter astonishment at her agitation; for his mind had long banished all thought of Henry's attachment to her, and he had never suspected hers to him; and indeed he scarcely remembered at the moment that he had mentioned his name. His mother however again calling him, he was forced to go.

"I am sorry," said Lady Ashton when they were in another room, "to take you from Constance; it must be such a delight to you to be together again, after such a long absence; but you shall soon go back to her, only I wanted so much to know what you think of Henry. A fresh eye can often judge so much better than one accustomed constantly to see a sick person. Did you find him worse than you expected?"

"I scarcely know," replied Sir Roland, "I had feared so greatly to find that he was gone, that his being alive at all was an unspeakable relief to me. I cannot but hope that he may recover, for at his age the constitution is generally so very strong. But what troubles me most is the excessive depression of his spirits; so

wholly unlike what they used to be. It makes me
fear that there may be more internal mischief than we
are aware of."

"I do not think that," replied Lady Ashton, "for
if so, he would not have improved as he has done, and
he is certainly better than he was. I cannot at times
help fancying that he must have some grief which
preys upon his mind, for I have observed his depression as well as you. Often have I sat for hours with
him, without his speaking one word, and though he
would lie with his eyes closed, yet I know he did not
sleep, for heavy sighs would often break forth, and his
eyes would be suddenly perhaps—ardently lifted up to
heaven for a moment—then closed again. It has often
made me very unhappy to see him."

"But is it likely, my dear mother," said Sir Roland, "that he should have any deadly grief, and not
tell you of it? He would surely find it a comfort to
speak to you of any thing that made him unhappy.
Have you ever said any thing to him about it?"

"I have not liked to do so," replied Lady Ashton,
"for he must know his own feelings best, and if he is not
free, or willing to confide in me, I might only pain
him by speaking to him on the subject. He cannot
doubt my readiness to hear all he likes to say, but he
seems to have grown reserved with every one."

"His manner to me when first we met was wholly
inexplicable," said Sir Roland, "he neither looked at
me nor spoke to me; I thought it might be that
he was overcome for the minute; but when he did
speak it was with a gloom and despondency which
grieved my very heart. But perhaps after all it may
only be weakness and confinement to the house, which

affects him; and it has often been observed, I believe, that those whose animal spirits are in general the highest, are apt to sink most in times of sickness. I think I shall get a yacht for him, it will enable him when it is fine to get out a little, for I am sure he could not now bear the motion of a carriage. I will see about one directly."

"I am glad you have thought of it," said Lady Ashton, "for I know he would like to go out, but the carriage tortures him. But you are looking very ill, too, Roland! What makes you so pale? Are you not well?"

"I am as well as any one can be, who has not laid his head upon a pillow for days and days," answered Sir Roland, smiling; "and who has had, moreover, such anxiety as I have had; but rest will soon restore me. You are not looking well either, my dear mother, nor any of you, I think."

"Constance is not looking well, certainly," observed Lady Ashton; "nor has she been quite like herself of late. I cannot, to say the truth, help thinking that something has occurred between her and Henry, which has caused disunion and unpleasant feeling, for they seem entirely estranged from each other; and both seem uncomfortable. Constance will never, I see, be in the room even with him, if she can help it, and I imagined at one time that she must have heard something against him, and asked her if she had; but she said 'No,' and spoke very kindly of him; so then I said, I supposed I must blame you for taking up all her heart and affections, and leaving none for those who were about her. But I do not know why I should pour out all my little troubles to you, only that it is a relief

to have some one to whom one can speak openly; and
you may be able, better than I can, to find out what
causes this discomfort, and to make all smooth and
happy again. I do not though, I am sure, mean to
accuse Constance of unkindness; to me she has ever
been as the most attentive and affectionate of daughters; it is only towards Henry that she seems so cold."

These words of Lady Ashton's awakened feelings
in Roland's mind, which she little dreamed of; and lit
a fire within his breast which no earthly power could
have quenched or controlled. He scarcely breathed
as she spoke, and his very existence seemed to hang
upon her words, for he felt the sudden and deadly conviction enter his soul, that it was not hatred, or dislike,
which had arisen between Lady Constance and his
brother, but feelings of a totally different nature. It
might be indeed (and his mind eagerly caught at the
idea), that perceiving an unhappy attachment in Henry
towards her, Lady Constance had kindly and conscientiously done all in her power to repress it; and if so,
her heart might still be his; but every thing tended to
destroy even that faint hope, and despair began to lay
her numbing hand on all his faculties. It was well that
it did so at that moment, as it enabled him to sit with
apparent calmness while his mother spoke.

He was, however, thoroughly determined at once
to know the worst, even if it cost him his life; and
calmed by this desperate resolution, he proceeded to
ask Lady Ashton, in a quiet voice, "When it was that
she first perceived this alienation between Lady Constance and his brother?"

"I cannot exactly recollect," replied Lady Ashton;
"but it was before he went away."

"Do you think it influenced her at all in her wish to go to Scotland?" asked Sir Roland.

"I cannot say," replied Lady Ashton. "She certainly urged me very eagerly to let her go, when it seemed likely that he would be remaining here; but when he was gone, she said she should prefer staying at home; but I thought that was only from a kind wish not to leave me alone, so I insisted on her going; as she had really seemed to wish it. But it might certainly have been that she only desired to be away from him;—and yet why should she desire it?"

"That is what we are trying to discover," said Sir Roland, with deadly calmness. "You said you asked her about it, I think, but I have forgotten exactly what answer she made?"

"She said that there had been no quarrel, and that she had never heard any thing against Henry; and I remember that she spoke warmly, and said, 'No one ever mentioned him but with praise.'"

Sir Roland compressed his lips, which were white as death, and for a moment his brow contracted.

Lady Ashton continued, "I am afraid I was harsh to her, for she cried very much, poor child! and said she never meant to be unkind to any one."

"Oh no! oh no!" exclaimed Sir Roland, starting up, and walking up and down the room; "she could never be unkind to any living soul!"

"I know she would not willingly have been so," said Lady Ashton, gently; "but it seemed so strange, as I told her, that though ever ready to be with Henry when he was well, yet when he was ill, and wholly dependent on others for amusement, she would never sit with him, nor sing to him, or, indeed, speak to him,.

if she could possibly help it; she seemed, too, to take
so little part in our affliction! I could not understand
it — nor do I now ; for she was always so amiable and
considerate ; and was so even then to me — in all but
slighting Henry. But I dare say it will all come right
in time."

"Never!" thought Sir Roland, with a despair
which cannot be described.

"Now you are come," continued Lady Ashton, "I
feel as if every thing must go well, it is such a joy to
me to see you here again. But I will not now detain
you any longer from Constance, or from poor Henry,
who was so anxious to see you ; and I am sure you will
soon reconcile them to each other, if there has really
been any misunderstanding. Go now, dear Roland,
back to the drawing-room, and I will go to Henry, and
tell him you will be with him soon, and, if you can, get
Constance to go in with you."

"Reconcile them!" thought Sir Roland, when his
mother had left the room. "Yes —that will not be
difficult! And yet it may be only that Henry likes
her—not that she loves him! If so, she might have
shunned him—and rightly. But why then should she
be so cold and distant with me? If she were indifferent
to him—why cruel to me? And yet, how her countenance lit up when first she saw me! And her exclamation of joy — how true — how natural — it seemed!
Oh! this is a dreadful—dreadful hour! But it must
be borne—must be endured ;—and I must—will know
my fate!"

He left the room determined to seek Lady Constance, and to implore her instantly to clear up every

difficulty. His mind was on the rack, and the strong control he had placed upon his feelings in his mother's presence, began almost to give way.

He passed through one drawing-room, and was approaching the door of the other, which was partly open, when he saw Lady Constance standing with her head resting on the chimney-piece. He paused, for her attitude was one of sorrow and suffering, and his heart melted within him. All his own miseries—his wrongs—her coldness—all vanished before the thought of her distress; and, after a moment, he was about to enter hastily—to entreat her to confide in him—to let him have the joy of, any how, making her happy, when she suddenly raised her head, and the expression of anguish in her countenance, as it was reflected in the glass by which she stood, again arrested him. His very breathing stopped, as, looking upwards with tear-less eyes, and clasping her hands in agony, he heard her exclaim,

" Would he had never returned! "

He felt a sudden bewilderment, as in a dream. The very ground appeared to tremble beneath his feet, and it seemed as if his senses must give way!

"Constance to wish he had never returned! She— for whom he was ready to resign every happiness—to wish him exiled—dead! She, whom he had imaged to himself as the gentlest and sweetest of human beings— to wish him swept from the face of the earth, so that her will might but have free course!"

His first impulse was instantly to upbraid her for her cruelty—her falsehood! But he had sufficient power over himself, even at that fearful moment, to control so violent an outbreak of his passionate nature;

and hastily throwing up the window which opened to the ground, he rushed out upon the lawn, and with hurried steps pursued the pathway down towards the shore. Regardless of the chill and biting wind, and of the cold, sleety rain which fell on his uncovered head, he went on—on—as if only desirous of flying from home and its miseries, till at length reaching the grassy spot, where, twice in former times, he had sat with Lady Constance, and spoken of their engagement, he suddenly stopped. The remembrance of that time— of the hopes and fears—now all turned to despair— which had then agitated him—of his devoted love and desire for *her* happiness, who now requited his devotion by ingratitude so deadly—overcame him, and he fell almost lifeless on the turf. No burst of anguish came to relieve him—no tear flowed to ease his burning brain; but his soul, completely unhinged, became the unresisting prey to every terrible and tumultuous feeling. Usually so self-controlled, he lost all power over his thoughts; and, excited almost to madness, it seemed as if all the demons from the depths of hell had risen with fury to take possession of the soul from which they had so long been exiled. Grief was too gentle a feeling to find a place there at that terrible moment, and passions of whose very existence he had till then been ignorant, fought within him for the mastery. Jealousy, hatred, revenge—all in turn wakened him; till, writhing under their deadly influence, in the frenzy of despair he exclaimed, " My God! my God! why hast Thou forsaken me ? "

In an instant the storm within him ceased,

" The soul that seemed forsaken, felt its present God again," and calmed, though not comforted, he rose from the earth.

Slowly did he retrace his steps back to the house, and painfully, for his limbs had stiffened with the chill and damp of the cold earth, and drenching rain; and his whole frame, previously exhausted by long fatigue and anxiety, began to feel the shivering lassitude of approaching fever. With difficulty he got home, and when there, he immediately went to his own room, and sent word to his mother that, not feeling well, he should not go down to dinner. She went to him, and was much alarmed at his altered appearance, and the quickness of his pulse, and wished to send for the physician; but he refused to allow her to do so, and said that rest would do him good, if any thing could, but that he must be alone, and try what perfect quiet would do.

"Do not think me unkind, dearest mother," he said; "but I have pains so terrible in my head, that speaking, or even raising my eyes, is intolerable to me."

"But then, I beseech you, let me send for advice," she replied. "Oh! am I to be deprived of you both?" And she burst into tears.

Sir Roland strained her to his breast, and held her long there, for he felt she was now his only earthly comfort; but no word or tears escaped to give one moment's ease to the feelings which suffocated him.

At length Lady Ashton said that she would leave him for awhile that he might rest, and then she would return to him again. Refreshments were sent up to him, but they went down again untouched; and his fever increased so rapidly on him, that he wrote his mother a message begging her not to return to him

that night, as he felt he could not talk. He added a
few words of deep affection ; but they breathed so sad
a tone, that Lady Ashton's heart sank within her, for
they sounded to her affrighted fancy as the passing-bell
of every earthly hope and happiness.

Rest, indeed, Sir Roland required ; but rest he
could not get, nor even could he seek it. And for
long hours through the night Lady Ashton, whose room
was next to his, heard his ceaseless, though unequal
tread, as he paced up and down his chamber, while
sounds from time to time reached her ear, which seemed
poured forth in the bitterness of anguish. She was
much alarmed, and repeatedly went to his door, but did
not like to go in, as he had begged her not to do so ;
for though he had never in his life spoken a syllable to
her that was not most affectionate and respectful, yet
there was something in his manner and character, which
bore a power that could not be disobeyed, even by
her. At length, alarmed beyond endurance, she
knocked. The sound of Sir Roland's steps instantly
ceased, and all was still as death. Lady Ashton feared
to knock again, and she waited in silent terror at the
door. In a few minutes, however, the weary steps of
restless moving were again heard, and summoning
courage, she knocked a second time. Sir Roland
asked, "Who was there ?" and Lady Ashton answering, he instantly unlocked and opened his door.

"What do you want with me, dear mother ?" he
said. "Why are you up so early ?"

"My dearest Roland," she said, "why are you up ?
You who require rest so much ?"

"Rest !" he exclaimed, "rest ! Aye ! rest would be
indeed delightful."

" Then why will you not lie down, and try to sleep ? "

" I cannot — I cannot," he said, vehemently, resuming his agitated walk.

" My dear son," exclaimed Lady Ashton, in extreme distress, for the wild and restless expression of Sir Roland's eye and the hollowness of his voice terrified her, " what has happened ? — what is the matter with you ? "

Sir Roland made some incoherent answer, which instantly convinced her that the fever whose sustaining excitement could alone have enabled him to endure the wearying fatigue of his continual agitation, was beginning to affect his head, and perceiving the necessity of prompt and decisive measures, she left the room, saying she would return in a few minutes, and sent off instantly to D——, for the physician, whilst she desired Sir Roland's servant to go to him, and endeavour by all means to persuade him to go to bed.

Sir Roland, now the maddening train of thought, which had throughout the night been whirling through his brain, was interrupted, became calmer, and submitted quietly to all that was required of him. But though he consented to lie down, and his wearied limbs seemed to rest with almost deathlike weight upon the bed, yet he found no repose of mind. He could not sleep, and continued ceaselessly to talk to himself, though the words he uttered were not often intelligible. When the physician arrived, he pronounced it to be brain-fever, and ordered that he should be kept as quiet as possible ; and having blooded him and prescribed every thing which he thought necessary for the moment, he told Lady Ashton he would go home to make

some needful arrangements, and would then come
back and remain all night with Sir Roland, about
whom he was forced to confess that he felt extremely
uneasy.

In the evening he returned, and found, as he had
feared, that the fever had increased rapidly, and that
the danger was very great. He sat up all night with
Sir Roland, who never obtained an instant's repose;
his mind continuing to ramble wildly, from subject to
subject, without an instant's intermission, and his violence becoming so great that he was with difficulty at
times prevented from throwing himself out of his bed.
He continually started up and asked, "Where he was?
and why he was detained there?" saying, "He must
get on, or he should arrive too late," that, "he must
see him again;" with other such expressions, proving
that his brother, who had been so long the object of his
anxious thought, continued to be so still. He continually talked of him, sometimes as ill—then as at sea
—then as by his side; and would at other times go
back to the days of their boyhood, and speak of games
and pleasures they had had together.

Sometimes his mind seemed to catch a glimpse of
what had just occurred, and he would speak in heart-
rending tones of misery, and cruelty, and hopes destroyed, and happiness gone. Then all would seem
bright, and he spoke in light and joyful tones, as if
talking cheerfully to those he loved. Towards his brother he ever seemed to feel the kindest affection, un-
shaded by doubt or displeasure, but when he spoke of
Lady Constance, which he often did, it was with every
variety of feeling; and at times his mind seemed as if
it touched on some point respecting her, which was in-

supportable to him, and when that was the case he grew excited, and violent shudderings came over him.

" I cannot believe it," he would sometimes exclaim; " it was *not* her — it is false, she never wished it," with other words of horror, or dismaying grief. Lady Ashton sat by him all that night, and many other nights and days of hopeless watching, and throughout all that time no instant's rest, or sleep ever visited his eyes. He knew his mother sometimes, and would then press her hand to his lips, and speak in tones of love, which overcame the spirits which could bear up against all else. At other times he was wholly lost, and would gaze from face to face of those around him, with an air of total vacancy; but in general he continued talking wildly, and at times violently, and almost ceaselessly rolling his head from side to side upon his pillow in the restlessness of pain. As he grew weaker, the fever abated, but still he never slept, which was most alarming, as obtaining rest, the physician declared, was the only chance of his recovery. But the wretchedness of his mind seemed to preclude all possibility of it, for if he remained more than usually tranquil for any little time, such pauses were invariably followed by starts of horror and wild exclamations, as if some violent struggle were going on within.

Lady Ashton rarely left him, for she feared every moment might be his last; but occasionally she went down for a few instants to Henry, to tell him how his brother was, and to see how he himself went on, for he had again been suffering much pain, and his anxiety about his brother was intense ! On one occasion, indeed, when it had been thought that Sir Roland was on the point of death, he had insisted on being carried up

to him; but when in the room he was so overcome that
he fainted away; and the emotion, together with the
pain of moving, did him so much injury, that he was
never again permitted to try the dangerous experiment.
His eager mind suffered dreadfully under the suspense
he had to endure, and his feelings were excited to an
almost unendurable degree.   He accused himself of
being the destroyer of his brother's happiness, and perhaps of his life; for he could not divest himself of the
idea, that Sir Roland's illness had been produced by
some unhappy discovery of his feelings for Lady Constance, or of hers for him, working on a mind and body
already exhausted by anxiety and fatigue on his account.   He was miserable beyond expression, and he
implored of God to take him, and not his brother. The
thought of Lady Constance became dreadful to him,
and he was thankful that now, in his mother's absence,
she never came into the room where he was.   So completely had circumstances altered his estimate of things,
that could he at that moment have been offered the free
gift of her hand, he would have rejected it with horror,
feeling it almost as the price of blood; and earnestly
and with all the vehemence of his true heart, did he
implore of the Almighty, not only to spare his brother's
life, but to grant that Lady Constance's full affections
might be allowed to flow back into their rightful channel, and to bless, with all life's happiness, the heart that
so truly loved her, and that so well deserved her love.
He thought not of himself — or rather in the warm de-
votedness of his feelings, he imagined, that to see his
brother happy, would be happiness enough for him,
and that he could then go forth a wanderer — but not
desolate.

Day after day passed, and to all Lady Ashton's anxious inquiries of the several physicians who were then in attendance on Sir Roland, the only encouragement she could obtain, was the poor assurance that "where there was life there was hope;" but to her sad mind it seemed evident that both life and hope were fast departing.

Exhausted to the last degree, Sir Roland now scarcely spoke or moved, save that the restless motion of his head still continued, accompanied by low moaning sounds. But even these faint signs of life, and of suffering, gradually grew fainter and fainter, till they wholly ceased ; and he lay at length with the cold calm of death stamped on his rigid features.

Lady Ashton, and the physician from ——, who never left the house, were sitting by his bedside at the time. The former had her arm under Sir Roland's head, and feeling the breathing—to her so precious !— gradually becoming heavier and heavier, and finding all motion cease, she looked in alarm at the deathlike countenance, and overcome by her terrible apprehensions, was about to give way to the expression of her agony, when the physician, perceiving her fears, made her an earnest sign not to speak or move, whispering that it was sleep, not death, which had at last visited the weary eyes of the sufferer.

CHAPTER XXII.

" Oh ! gentle sleep, whose lenient power thus soothes
  Disease and pain, how sweet thy visit to me
  Who wanted thy soft aid."— ORESTES, *Translation.*

" So near—and yet so distant !   Oh, 't is worse
  Than leagues of exile o'er the stormy sea !
  On me the fabled Titan's penal curse
  Hath lighted.   From my lips insulting flee
  The draughts of bliss, which flow so full and free."— MS.

      " Pregar, pregar, pregar,
Ch' altro ponno' i mortali al pianger nati ?"— ALFIERI.

        " Am I resigned to die ?
It is not so ;—that cannot be the world
That speaks the Christian's feelings when he hears
The distant sound of his Redeemer's foot
Hasting to fetch him to his Father's throne ;
When the first beam from Heaven's unclosing gate
Falls on his path to light him to his home."
                 LADY POWERSCOURT.

I⊤ was some time before Lady Ashton could believe that the marble-like repose that rested on the
countenance of her son was other than the sleep of
death.   Not the slightest heaving of the breast could
be perceived, nor could she discern the throbbing of
a pulse.   Nature was so utterly spent, that if indeed
a spark of life were still left, it seemed that it must

have retreated to the very depths of the heart, doubtful whether to flicker up anew, or totally to sink in darkness. At length the physician, who had sat all the time with his finger on the pale arm, which lay so motionless on the coverlid, looked up with brightening eye, and nodded smilingly to Lady Ashton, intimating that all went on well, and soon the bent brow relaxed, the mouth assumed its natural beautiful expression, and the faint, but regular sound of childlike breathings were distinctly heard. Then first did Lady Ashton give herself up to the blessed power of hope: then first did her heart melt within her, at the joyful thought that her son might still be spared to her. For long hours she sat there — scarcely daring to breathe — supporting his head upon her arm, indifferent to the fatigue and uneasiness of her constrained position, and dreading only lest any thing should occur to disturb slumbers so life-giving.

How did her heart lift itself to God! "Bless the Lord, oh! my soul, and all that is within me bless His holy name," were words for ever rising to her lips. As she gazed on the features of him who now lay, quiet and weak as an infant, in her arms, her mind rapidly recalled the various stages of his existence. She pictured him to herself as he was brought — her first-born — to her longing arms, and felt, as it had been yesterday, the

> " Mother's prime of bliss
>   When to her eager lips is brought
>   Her infant's thrilling kiss."

Then early childhood, when every thing is so new, so delightful! How well did she remember it all, and

all the sweet unfoldings of existence, which make
'life's early dawn' so very lovely. Boyhood, youth,
manhood, all in turn, passed in bright succession
through her mind; and delightful it was to trace him
through them all, and feel that there was no circumstance of his life she could have wished blotted from her
remembrance. As she dwelt upon these things, and
looked on the pale, still countenance before her, the
tears, so long unwept, streamed from her eyes, and
she felt that were he indeed to die, she should be able
to exclaim, like the noble father of a noble son, " I
had rather have my dead son than any living son in
Christendom."

But of all the fond recollections with which her
memory was so happily, and sweetly stored, none were
to be compared, in her mind, with the remembrances,
that through all the long days, and nights of fever and
delirium, through which she had then been watching
over him — when his mind, freed from the restraints
of reason, and caution, and habit, was likely to have
opened all its stores of various feelings—not one
syllable had ever passed his lips, that could have
sullied an angel's, or wounded a mother's ear. In his
lightest moods he had spoken but in words of cheerfulness, and affection, and his deeper sentiments had
ever been the noble gushings of his heart, and the
emanations of the true and ardent piety which was
the habit of his soul. The wild and violent passions
which, during the first burst of his distracted feelings,
had rushed in and overwhelmed his whole being, had
been entirely cast forth by that mighty Power which
in former times

" Lashed the vexed fiends to the foaming deep,"

and his mind had been, during all the hours of irresponsible existence which he had passed, as pure, as holy, and as spiritual, as his own devoutest aspirations could have desired. God had, as it seemed, " given His angels charge concerning him," and they had kept from his mind every thought that could have sullied or injured his bright profession, and from his lips, every breath that could have done " despite unto that Holy Spirit, whereby he was sealed unto the day of redemption."

Nor let this be considered as a mere fancy of the brain. Imagination in its highest, happiest flights, would never have imaged forth a thought, so beautiful, so sublime ! — could never have borne up the mind of man to such soaring heights; nor have brought Heaven thus down, in aid of his necessities. No ! the winged words of truth alone could have suggested or sustained this high, and bright idea ! — could have taught us that the redeemed soul is the peculiar object of the watchful care of God : of Him whose eyes neither slumber nor take rest, but who, when His blessing has been sought for in waking hours, thus " giveth it His beloved sleeping." *

It has been the happy lot of many who have had to watch by the couch of pain, when those that were stretched on it have been the children of God, to witness this — to see that the Heavenly Master does indeed thus acknowledge and sustain his servants, even when the mental powers are wholly suspended : when outward consciousness, reflection, and memory—are entirely lost. His Spirit then testifies with the spirit of the sufferer, " that he is one of the sons of God," and speaks through him, to its own honour, and glory.

* German version.

Often, when the moanings of pain have come ceaselessly from the unconscious breast, the words of prayer
and holy truth, and they alone, have had power to still
them; and when the shrieks of bodily agony have rung
through the ears, and tortured the heart of every being,
within hearing of the fearful sound—these too have been
hushed by the same blessed powers; and in speaking
of these things, we have no hesitation or fear in ap-
pealing, for the truth of what is said, to the testimony
of those, who have had blessed opportunities of judging
of them from what has passed before their own eyes.

In Sir Roland's case resort was of course had
continually to the throne of grace, both for him, and
with him; and not only did Lady Ashton perpetually
drop "words of holy balm" into his wounded spirit,
but the minister of the parish, an excellent and kind
old man, who had been there for many years, and
had known Sir Roland from his birth, also continually
came and prayed by his side, and spoke delightfully,
and in more cheerful accents than the poor mother
could command, of heaven's brightness—of "that
flowery land, whose green turf hides no graves."

Sir Roland's wandering glance at such times would
become arrested, and his eye would dwell upon the
countenance of the good old man, though evidently
gathering no intelligence thereby, of who he was; and
he would drink in eagerly the words, that for a time
stilled the unhappiness, which, though borne with
deepest resignation, yet evidently oppressed his spirit.
When the voice ceased—then the restless glance would
roam around the chamber, and the signs of uneasiness
would return; but when the voice of prayer was heard
again—then all was peace once more.

Lady Ashton had ever drawn comfort from the "fountain of living waters," even when her earthly happiness had seemed the fullest. Where, therefore, should she fly, when her trials were so great but to the same source of heavenly comfort? Happily she had not now "her faith to seek," but had for long years known Him who was now sustaining her soul, and saying to her, "Fear thou not, for I am with thee; be not dismayed, for I am thy God; I will strengthen thee; yea, I will help thee; yea, I will uphold thee with the right hand of my righteousness."

This most delightful passage, and many others of equal comfort from the Scriptures, were continually realised, and brought to her aid; but God, who often blesses the smallest things to the best and kindest purposes, caused also one little line of earthly poetry to present itself perpetually unbidden to her memory. A worldly spirit might have discerned in this nothing perhaps but a happy accident, but Lady Ashton's Christian heart, which loved to trace every—even the slightest, 'good gift to the Father of lights,' felt that it was He, who kept in her thoughts continually the word of comfort which so much strengthened her.

She had lately been reading the " Sacred Melodies " of one for whom it had been well had he never written in a strain less pure and noble, nor polluted the world, as he has too often done, through the medium of his silvery numbers. One line of those melodies it was which presented itself thousands of times in a day, to Lady Ashton's sleepless mind. The beautiful words,

" Earth has no sorrow that Heaven cannot cure,"

sounded perpetually in her heart, and never failed to

bring with them comfort and joy.   She felt the truth of them, and experienced that Heaven was even at that trying moment sustaining her soul in peace.   Thus was a little word, flowing from a pen too frequently dipped in earth's worst colouring, made an instrument of blessing in the hands of Him, who "chooses one thing and rejects another."   Thus also does He often give lessons, in his marvellous long-suffering and patience, by which the worst may be encouraged to forsake the ways of his iniquity, and to turn, while yet there is time, to Him who "discerneth the evil from the good."

Oh! that men would but consider from whom they derive their powers!   Oh! that they would but remember that He who gives talents, says also, "Occupy till I come!"   That they could but know the blessedness of working—speaking—writing for Him, who alone at the last day can say, "Well done, good and faithful servant, enter thou into the joy of thy Lord;" which, having once known, never again would they be found ranked with the worst enemies of God and man.

There is a story somewhere recorded, of an occasion in which a sentence of equal rigour went forth against a man who had committed murder, and one who had written a work of evil tendency; both were condemned to be burned to death!   The writer of the work exclaimed against the injustice—the inequality of the sentence, but received this just reply; "That the sentence indeed was unequal, for that the one delinquent had merely destroyed the temporal life of a single human being, and also that with his existence would cease his power of doing like mischief again; but that he—the writer—had done that, which might destroy the ever-living souls of thousands; and that, moreover, his evil deeds, far from perishing with him, would continue to flourish and increase, when he was silent in the grave!" "Shall I not visit for these things? saith the Lord."

With what just horror should we not regard the man who could deliberately poison the springs and streams around a populous city, sending death into the heedless bosom of all who drank? "Of how much greater condemnation think you not he is worthy," who poisons the springs of virtue in the heart, and who taints the young mind with all that is hateful—all that is degrading—all that is contemptible; and nourishes the vice of age with that which is hurrying it to a fearful doom!

And do such writers think they are esteemed and honoured in the world? Do they suppose that because a public—careless of the food it devours—living on excitement—loathing the trouble of thinking for itself—and rejoicing in the rescue of one hour from the *ennui* of a *blaséd* existence—reads their works, and passes on the praise which others bestow, rather than pause to consider its own verdict—do they suppose that therefore, the public honours and esteems the beings who thus cater to their worst feelings, and speak to the most degraded part of their natures? Let them not deceive themselves, for such is *not* the case!

It is said of Cæsar that "he loved treason, but hated traitors;" and such, let us rest assured, is a most common feeling. Those who are truly Christians hate the sin, though they may feel for, if they cannot love the sinner—of them we are not speaking; but the

people of this world, how much soever they may be—
to use the words of our Church—" far gone from original righteousness," have yet enough of the image of
God left within them, to make them contemn those,
who are ready to prey, as well as play upon their vices;
and who are—unwittingly perhaps—risking all, to
serve them in their base and degrading pleasures!
Yet if the lingering struggles of their better nature
prompt them to despise those—who are indeed so
despicable—should they not consider, that the encouragement they give to such iniquity, ranks them
amongst the followers of him, who is, first the tempter
—then the accuser of mankind? Let them remember
that those who read, or circulate that which is evil,
partake of the guilt of him who first put it forth!—for
were there no readers—writers soon would fail.

It has been well said, that "the impression which a
book leaves on the mind, is the best criterion of its
tendency." By that then let those who read them,
judge of the works we have been considering. Again
I speak not to the true Christian—for works of this
nature, whether in prose or in poetry, form not their
chosen libraries—but I appeal to the consciences of all
promiscuous readers of modern—or indeed of any—
books, and entreat them to ask themselves—and to
make their souls answer to the inquiry—whether the
work—whatever it may be, from the perusal of which
they may have just arisen—has led their hearts *to* God,
or *from* Him—has lessened, or increased their horror
of sin—has cultivated the high, and pure, and ennobling emotions of their souls, or nourished the degrading views of an evil nature? Let them remember
the folly—to use no stronger term—of acting by one

rule, when they know—for they all do know—that
they must be judged by another! Let them remember that there is no neutral ground in this world
—no halting space between God and Satan; and let
them therefore with open eyes " choose whom they
will serve," remembering that our Lord has said, " He
that is not for me, is against me; and he that gather-
eth not with me, scattereth abroad."

Hour after hour did Sir Roland's deep, deathlike
sleep continue, and hope in Lady Ashton's bosom
began almost to be tinged with dread, lest his exhausted nature might not have power to rally, but
might gradually sink away from sleep to death. The
physician, however, from time to time whispered words
of encouragement; but though his assurances soothed
her anxiety for the moment, yet when again alone
watching the quiet slumberer, sickening fears would
come over her. At length a deep sigh heaved
his breast, and a few moments after, Sir Roland
opened his eyes. The weight of illness hung heavy
upon them, but they had lost their vacant, wild expression, and consciousness beamed from them once more.
He turned his head so as to relieve Lady Ashton's
arm, and seeing her, he smiled faintly—and again he
slept. His slumbers however did not this time last
long, for he grew restless, though he had scarcely
strength to move a hand. Seeing Lady Ashton still
by him, he looked at her with the deepest affection,
just murmuring " My dearest mother," then lay as
tranquil as before. He did not however sleep, but
his mind remained in a dreamy state, unable to think,

and conscious only of what passed immediately before
it at the moment.

Lady Ashton sat by him for a few moments in a
state of happiness too great for words; she then rose,
and busied herself in preparing for him a cooling
drink. He watched her as he lay quietly on his
pillow; his eyes following every motion of her hand,
though his mind was unable to bear even the slight
exertion of thinking of what she was doing. He
drank what she gave him, and again laid down his
head, and watched her motions,; and when she sat at
rest by him again his eye was caught by the slight
waving and fluttering of the window-curtain, as it was
agitated by the draft from a partially opened window;
he watched it long and the gentle motion seemed
to soothe his senses. Then again and for many
hours he slept — a quiet, tranquil, and refreshing
slumber.

Immediate danger, it was then hoped was over,
but the excessive weakness in which the violence of
the fever had left him, felt to Sir Roland like the
sinkings of death; and not aware of what had brought
him to that condition, he naturally imagined he was
in the last stage of existence. Yet this thought
brought with it no trouble to his soul; on the contrary, he dwelt on it with joy and delight. The late
painful circumstances which had occurred, seemed
completely obliterated from his mind, but all his old
and happy impressions remained unchanged. He
spoke of Lady Constance as his, both in heart and
faith—of his brother as in their happiest days; and

yet he was willing to die—willing to leave all, and go to his heavenly Father's home.

When Lady Ashton heard him speak in this manner her mind again misgave her; but the physician assured her, that though if any relapse took place, his strength would probably immediately give way, yet that, unless that occurred, there was much to hope. He confessed that, when Sir Roland had first slept, he had felt a fear that all might not be well, as in some cases, patients had been known after such repose, to regain their reason for a few transient moments, then instantly sink into the grave. But that danger was now past, and though life in Sir Roland's state must necessarily be exceedingly precarious yet he repeated that if nothing unforeseen occurred he felt confident that he would finally recover. He advised Lady Ashton however to leave Sir Roland's mind in its present happy, and spiritual state, as it was one much more favourable to his recovery, than the idea of returning life with all its freshly awakened and exciting feelings could possibly be. She therefore took no pains to make him believe he was recovering, but left it to the Almighty Father who brought him up from the gates of death, to strengthen his mind gradually to receive the conviction that he should live—that he was destined for a longer period than he then thought, to struggle with the mixed and wearying stream of this world's interests.

It was delightful to Sir Roland to contemplate his great change, and his thoughts seemed already more in heaven than on earth. He could not speak much for his weakness was very great, but he reposed for hours in blissful anticipation of his summons home.

He thought with deepest affection of Lady Constance, for his mind, but partially recovered, still arrayed her image in all its former bright and lovely colours, but he was enabled to give her up for higher joys, and he longed to depart and to be with God, yet he earnestly desired to see her once again, and he asked his mother if he might not do so. She consented, and brought her into the room.

At sight of her a burst of natural feeling swept across Sir Roland's breast, and he felt that life would still be worth preserving ; but turning his eyes towards heaven, he implored that his mind might be kept stead-fast, and fixed on things above.

" Constance," he said, taking her hand as she knelt down beside him, " I have wished to see you thus once more, to bless you for all your love—all your kindness to me. I have not been to you all that I could have wished, at least I was not once, though I had begun to hope that my long, long love had found some little answer in your heart. But all that is over now—and love cannot save from parting. You will not cease to pray for me, my dearest, whilst I am here, and you will praise God on my behalf when I am gone? You will do that, will you not?"

Lady Constance could answer only with her tears.

" Do not grieve for me, dearest Constance," he continued, " God has been very merciful in weaning me by this illness, and this deadly prostration of strength, from the fulness of my earthly affections, and by filling my heart with love to Himself. But still to see you near me—to feel what life might have been with you — but this is folly, weakness, unfaithfulness, and I must not let earth steal again into my heart. I dare not keep you with me, your tears trouble me. Oh! Constance, look to Him who will be with you in all your sorrow, as he is with me at this hour."

Lady Constance could not speak, and her tears still flowed beyond all power of repression. Sir Roland became agitated, and murmured,—

"My dearest—dearest—leave me—go from me before my weak heart begins to fail. I longed to see you once again, and thought—you would have strengthened me; but now go, go—oh! leave me."

Lady Constance rose from her knees; but it seemed impossible for her to leave the room. She could scarcely support the idea that she should see Sir Roland no more, and her great affection for him, added to the overwhelming sense of the wrong she had done him, made his words of love and trust strike like daggers to her heart. Again she longed to tell him of her faithlessness, to hear him pardon and forgive; nay, anger and reproaches would have been more tolerable than his undoubting confidence. Yet she could not disturb his dying hour with feelings so terrible as her confession would awaken; she could not do it—but lost in the anguish of the moment—her heart yearning with love for him who seemed dying before her eyes, she stood by his side without power to speak or move.

Sir Roland gazed on her with looks in which the pity of an angel blended with earth's natural affections, till the latter beginning fast to gain the mastery, he exclaimed,

"Oh! Constance, try me not too much; leave me. This is indeed a bitter hour, and yet, oh! my Father," he said, taking her hand in both of his, and lifting it up for a moment towards heaven, "Thou knowest how I have loved her, and Thou canst support me.   Bless her, my God — bless her!"

Lady Ashton fearing the effects of any lengthened emotion now drew near, and when Sir Roland saw her by him, he placed Lady Constance's hand in hers, saying,

"Take her from me, mother — take her from me — and be to her the same as if she had been ——"

He could not finish, and Lady Ashton gently drew Lady Constance away, Sir Roland's eyes followed her as she left the room. When she was at the door she turned, and seeing him still looking at her, she felt as if she could not leave him. She stopped irresolute, and was about to return, but he shook his head, and made her a sign to go; and Lady Ashton with gentle violence drew her from the room.

When the door had closed upon her, Sir Roland lifting his eyes to heaven, murmured forth,

"And now, 'Return unto thy rest, oh, my soul!'"

CHAPTER XXIII.

" Lull'd in the countless chambers of the brain,
    Our thoughts are link'd by many a hidden chain,
    Awake but one, and lo! what myriads rise!"—ROGERS.

IT would be impossible to describe what Lady
Constance went through, during all the events which
we have been recording. She was conscious how
much the affectionate kindliness of her letters, must
have tended to induce in Sir Roland's mind, an idea of
her attachment to him, and she felt therefore how
doubly severe must be the blow, if at last she were
constrained to tell him that she could not fulfil the
engagement she had formed. Yet she had done all
with the best intentions, and had long hoped to bring
her heart sincerely to return his love. But the sight
of Henry, in the midst of his danger and suffering, had
revived tenfold those sentiments in his favour which
she had striven so much to subdue; and though never
willingly yielding to them, yet she could not but be
conscious that they held a power over her, which was
wholly incompatible with the idea of forming other
ties. She naturally supposed that when Sir Roland
returned, he would claim her hand, and she felt how

much her first joyful welcome must have nourished the
idea that she would be willing to bestow it on him.
But she felt that she could not do it! — Yet how
should she tell him so? How tell him to go from
her, a miserable, broken-hearted man? How tell him
that she loved another? These were her first troubles,
but soon Sir Roland's illness brought on more distress.
Her heart melted towards him, and she felt as if she
could have given life and all it possessed to restore
him to health and happiness. Henry, she never approached, and the thought of him was as terrible to
her, as the idea of her was to him; but she was ever
at hand to assist Lady Ashton in any thing that could
conduce to Sir Roland's comfort; and during the time
of his fearful illness, she took her post in his dressing-
room, ready at all times to do what might be required.
Often, during his state of insensibility, did Lady Ashton
claim her help in his own apartment, and as at times
she gazed on his countenance and recalled the fine
feelings which had so continually animated it, she
asked herself, " if there was aught on earth she loved
as she did him." — One mental glance at the chamber
below however answered that question but too fatally.

She never expected to see Sir Roland again, after
their sad parting, and every shadow of happiness
seemed fled from her bosom. She was told indeed
that there was hope, but her spirit was depressed and
she could feel none. All earth appeared to her one
melancholy scene of darkness, and tears, and misery.
That once joyous house was indeed become a scene of
mourning, and suffering; but besides all that the world
could see and judge of, she had her own deep griefs

to bear in her lonely heart, and desolate indeed she felt.

Sir Roland was much shaken by his interview with her, but he soon recovered his tranquillity, and heaven-ward feelings; and a shade of disappointment even would sometimes cross his mind, as the light of a fresh morning stole into his chamber. "Still here!" he would sigh; "still, still here."

Gradually however he felt his strength increase, and the idea rose in his mind that he might live. That thought brought with it at first, restless and uncom-fortable feelings, for his mind seemed unhinged, and the bright and glorious region he had fancied almost his own, seemed to recede from his view, and to give place to things which troubled and agitated his heart. After a time however, he felt, as it was natural that one so young, so loving, should feel, at the thought of being restored to all that life so brightly promised him; and flattering dreams of earthly happiness, floated again before his ardent mind.

Lady Ashton had been careful always to follow, and never to attempt to lead the train of his thoughts, being fearful of overstraining his mind; and per-ceiving that his illness had swept before it all remem-brance of the anxiety he had previously felt on his brother's account, she never spoke to him on the subject. She gathered from his questions that he imagined him still well, and at sea, and he seemed to have lost all recollection, both of the fearful accident he had had, and of his being actually then in the house. This circumstance alarmed her anew, for the thought that his mind might have been seriously injured by his illness, but the physician told her not to be uneasy on the subject, for that it often occurred after such severe illnesses as Sir Roland had had, that the mind, though perfectly clear upon those subjects which it fully admitted, yet would remain a length of time before it regained its tone ; but that as strength returned, so would also the full powers of thought and memory.

It was well indeed for Sir Roland, as far as his recovery was concerned, that his mind remained for a time clouded, for had the recollection of all the circumstances which at first occasioned his illness, returned suddenly upon him, both life as well as happiness must have been destroyed.

When he asked his mother as to the possibility of his recovery, she gently encouraged him in the idea, and by degrees she became more communicative in the answers she made to his various inquiries. He had hitherto spoken but little, and had seemed anxious rather to keep his mind aloft, than to let it become entangled again, with earthly thoughts. But now his busy heart, prompted many a question, though he was still too weak for much discourse.

In speaking to his mother one day he asked her where his brother then was. Lady Ashton not being aware of any thing which could make the knowledge of his being at home painfully agitating to Sir Roland, told him with a smile, that his brother was not far off, and that he hoped he would soon see him. This answer led to other questions, and Sir Roland's mind began to open a little as to the real state of the case. At first however he could remember nothing clearly, but a vague feeling of uneasiness took possession of

him, and he wearied himself in the endeavour to discover what there was to trouble him.   Gradually the
truth broke upon his mind, and his thoughts became
every instant darker and darker.   Wave after wave of
terrible remembrance rolled over him, till his senses
sunk again under their overwhelming force.   A violent
accession of fever and delirium took place, and the
physician himself began to despair of his life.   Youth
and strength of constitution however surmounted the
danger, and again he began to rally; but his weakness
after this second attack was greater even than at first,
and the full conviction of his misery — which returned
on this occasion with renewed consciousness — served
greatly to retard his recovery.

How different were his feelings now to what they
had been on the former occasion.   Then, though all
seemed bright in life, yet the joys of Heaven appeared
still brighter, and he was willing to leave all below for
everlasting happiness above.   Now, all seemed dark,
and the troubles of earth instead of making Heaven
appear the more desirable, came rather like a heavy
cloud between him and God.   He implored for resignation—he besought for peace—for rest—for death;
but for a time all comfort seemed denied him.

When the mind is happy there is perhaps no period
of existence so enchanting, as the recovery from sickness.   The sense of danger past, the buoyancy of the
heart, the enjoyment of each recovered power, as day
after day restores us to something we had lost—all are
so delightful!   The air from which we have been long
debarred, feels so reviving, the flowers are so sweet,
the song of the birds so exquisite, every thing seems

endowed with a charm, and beauty it never possessed before, and the very weakness of the frame instead of diminishing our happiness, rather adds to it, by making us the object of peculiar care and love. But oh! how desolate was returning health to Sir Roland! How valueless the life that was again forced on his acceptance! True, he had the tenderest care and love about him, and earth's luxuries were spread on every side, and he tried to feel the thankfulness which he expressed to God; but the aspect of every thing seemed changed, and his heart was completely cast down. The loss of Lady Constance's affection, and of the bright happiness it seemed to offer him, would of itself have been sufficient in that hour of weakness, to have sunk his spirit entirely; but that now seemed to form but the slightest portion of his sorrow. It was the being compelled to dethrone her from the high place she had ever held in his estimation—the being forced to feel that she was no longer worthy of the empire she had so long maintained over him—that caused his bitterest sufferings. At times he would not—could not—believe it; and he determined, spite of all appearances, still to consider her blameless and true. But at other times the conviction forced itself upon him, that she had deceived and betrayed him: written to him in words of affection—received him with warmest tokens of love—then—wished him exiled—perhaps dead! Of her love for Henry he felt no doubt, and he could still honour her for the self-denial, which she seemed latterly to have exercised as regarded him. "But why had she permitted herself to love him?" Vain

question! often asked—ever left unanswered. "Oh why
had she not openly and at once told him of her wishes,
and given him the happiness of making her happy?"
Ah! it is easy for the generous heart thus to speak;
to tell another to destroy its peace, and teach it "bro-
kenly" to "live on;" but it is not so easy for that
other, if equally generous, to speak that which shall
annihilate the hopes of affection, and tell the loving
heart that it loves not in return.

It was most natural for Sir Roland, who had not
traced this unhappy affair throughout, to think that
Lady Constance had not acted well by him—that she
had deceived him; and the very effort that she had
made to force herself to love him, bore in his eyes but
too clearly the appearance of hypocrisy and untruth.
And what could she have meant by it? "Could she
intend to marry him, yet love his brother? Impossible! "No!" his heart exclaimed; "let appearances be what they might, he would not distrust
her; or doubt the purity of her intentions." But
still—that terrible sentence, "Would he had never
returned!" rung hollowly through his heart, and forbade its having one moment's peace. He determined
however if possible to chase away thought, till he was
strong enough to endure the excitement of speaking to
her, and of hearing from herself all her wishes. He
would then ask her of those things which now so perplexed his harassed spirit, for he felt *she* would ever
be true in word, even if her heart had strayed away
from him; and comforted by that conviction, he strove
to commit his way to God.

Oh! what a repose it is when the heart can really
go to Him with all its troubles!—pour out the fulness

of its sorrows and perplexities, and, receiving in their
place, comfort, and wisdom, and grace ! No earthly
friend can feel for us as God does, for none like Him
can see the griefs that lie shrouded in our inmost
souls :

> " Not even the tenderest heart, and next our own,
>   Knows half the reasons why we smile or sigh.
>   *   *   *   *   *
>   And well it is for us our God should feel
>   Alone our secret throbbings ; so our prayer
>   May readier spring to Heaven, nor spend its zeal
>   On cloud-born idols of this lower air."

When Sir Roland's recovery from immediate
danger had relieved Henry Ashton's mind on his account, his thoughts returned too much to their old
channel. He felt particularly desolate, for his mother
was continually with Sir Roland, and Lady Constance
never entered his room. Lady Florence, indeed, was
unremitting in her cheerful endeavours to amuse him,
and proved a most kind comforter. The late sad events
had drawn forth much of strength and energy from her
character, and, instead of being the childish, giddy
little creature who used to fly about all animation and
spirits, she was now grown thoughtful and quiet, and full
of affectionate attentions to every one. She was much
grown, and began to lose the appearance of childhood,
and to assume that gentle dignity of look and manner,
which is so peculiarly beautiful in early youth. She
had ever been lovely as a child, and her fine countenance did not now belie its early promise. Lady Ashton,
in the secret of her soul, had long hoped that when she
grew older, she and Henry would become attached to
each other, so that she might have assembled around

her all those whom most she loved on earth. But Henry's unfortunate love for Lady Constance shut his heart completely, for the present, from every one else; and Lady Florence, with all her beauty and affection, was to him but as a sister. He pined to see Lady Constance again, and often as he heard her light step pass his door, or as the sound of her voice reached him from the next room, he longed to send her sister to entreat her to come to him, if only for one moment; but he always resisted the temptation, and, true to himself and to her, he never even left his room, though he was occasionally able to do so, for fear of meeting her, of needlessly trying the hearts of both, or of renewing those feelings which he knew had best slumber for ever. Yet to feel her so near—with only a slender door between them, and not dare to withdraw that slight screen, was misery to him in the extreme, and he wished himself in the midst of deserts or oceans, rather than in such a state of continual trial.

Sir Roland's situation, though equally painful, was very different from that of his brother. He had to act —Henry had merely to suffer. Ordinarily the latter is the more painful position of the two, for the mind is left—unrelieved by active exertion— to prey upon itself; but in Sir Roland's present state, the having to act, and speak was most trying, and the bare thought of it, bringing on accelerated pulsation, affected his head so seriously, that he knew not how he should be able to encounter so great an exertion. He found, however, that it was impossible he should perfectly recover till his mind was more tranquil; and, therefore, he determined, let it cost him what it might, to put an end to his painful uncertainties, and to change a position which daily became more and more insupportable.

Lady Ashton, ever bent on the gratification of those around her, when Sir Roland was sufficiently recovered to go out of his own room, begged Lady Constance to come with her and with him for a short time ; and the latter, terrified at the idea of going, yet afraid to refuse, reluctantly complied. When she entered, her unexpected appearance startled Sir Roland, and his agitation was so great that he could not speak to her. She approached him timidly, and held out her hand ; he took it — at first coldly — but then feeling his heart melt within him, he put it from him with a shudder, and silently turned away his head. Lady Ashton, whose heart overflowed with kindly feeling at the thought of the happiness which she hoped Lady Constance's appearance would give Sir Roland, was surprised and distressed at witnessing the apparently different effect which had been produced. She took no notice, however, of what she had observed, but exerted herself for a little while to converse, and then left the room, thinking that the constraint which lay upon her two companions might, perhaps, arise from a wish not to shew their feelings before her.

When alone, Sir Roland and Lady Constance sat for a length of time in perfect silence. Each had much to say to the other, but it was of so terrible a nature, that neither of them could enter on it at that moment. Sir Roland had not been well enough hitherto to think on the over-exciting subject sufficiently to enable him to decide what would be the best plan to pursue ; but he felt it would be far best to speak to Henry first, and not to agitate Lady Constance's mind till he was positive as to his brother's wishes. Having hastily decided on that course, his mind became rather more tranquil, but still he could not speak.

Lady Constance was much surprised at his manner — so different from his earnest tenderness at their last interview; but conceiving it impossible that any thing should have occurred since then, to alter his real feelings, she thought it was weakness and debility alone which caused him to be so silent, and she, therefore, exerted herself to speak.

"Is your head quite free from pain now?" she asked.

"Not quite," he replied.

"There is too much light in this room for you, is there not?" she continued, as she rose and went to the window, to let down the blinds.

"Do not trouble yourself," said Sir Roland, looking at her for a moment, as she stood by the window.

She turned back to see if the shade fell properly on him, and caught his eye, but the expression of it was so sad, and troubled, and his whole countenance was so changed, that terror struck to her very heart. Sir Roland, in whose mind affection could scarcely be restrained, even by the sense of the bitter wrongs he had endured, turned away; yet in Lady Constance's timid glance there had dwelt a sweetness—a truth and simplicity, that made him feel it was impossible she could ever have harboured an unkindly thought towards him, even though she might not return his love.

"Will that do better?" she asked in a trembling voice.

"Oh, yes!" he answered; "any thing will do for me." Then, fearing he had spoken with irritation, he added, "I thank you, very much, that is a great relief."

He looked at her again for an instant, and his heart could scarcely resist pouring itself out before her. But he felt that he must be sure — beyond all possibility of doubt — of Henry's feelings, before he could speak to Lady Constance of her own, and, therefore, he again restrained himself, though with difficulty, and said hurriedly, while every limb shook, —

"It is an effort too great for me to talk to you now, Constance; but in a few days, perhaps, you will let me converse with you?"

Lady Constance sat down unable to sustain herself. There was a tone of displeasure in Sir Roland's voice which overcame her, and she was wholly at a loss to imagine what could have occasioned so sudden a change in his feelings. The thought of the conversation, too, demanded, as it was, in a manner so. cold, so formal, filled her with apprehension, and she could not speak in answer.

Displeasure was, however, far from Sir Roland's mind at that moment. It was the great effort he was making to suppress his feelings, and to keep back from his lips the words he so longed to speak, which alone gave the appearance of it to his manner. All hope for himself, indeed, was past, but it was impossible to look at Lady Constance and suspect her of feelings of hatred and cruelty; yet still her terrible words rung through his brain, and he felt that he must have an explanation and be at peace with her; must have her restored to her bright place in his esteem, or his heart would break.

They both remained in painful silence, till Lady Ashton's re-entrance in some measure relieved them. She was again struck with the embarrassment of their manner, and involuntarily looked from the one to the other in the greatest surprise. She said nothing, however, but sat down quietly to her work; yet her mind felt deeply distressed. It seemed to her as if a spell had fallen upon the house, and had converted it, from the house of peace and love it used to be, into an abode of discord and misery. She had long traced the expression of wretchedness on the once beaming countenances of Henry and Lady Constance, and now Sir Roland, too, seemed affected by the same blighting influence. But she did not like to probe the feelings which appeared so much to court concealment, so determined patiently to wait for the passing away of the discomfort, or at least for the voluntary explanation of it. Yet it made her miserable at that moment, and she could scarcely restrain the tears of grief which swelled to her eye, at the thought of the wretchedness of those she loved so much.

Anxious to divert the thoughts of all from the painful subjects which seemed to occupy them so exclusively, she begged Lady Constance to fetch her guitar and sing to them, but Sir Roland hastily exclaimed,—

"Oh, no, not that!"

"Will it be too much for your head?" she asked.

"I could not bear it," he answered, evasively.

Lady Ashton sighed, for Sir Roland's manner was so wholly unlike any thing she had ever seen in him before, and she felt perfectly miserable. Lady Constance, too, was oppressed by a dread of she knew not what, and she soon found some excuse for leaving the chamber.

CHAPTER XXIV.

" Do not crush me with more love
Than lies in the word ' pardon.' "— TALFOURD.

" 'T is sweet to stammer one letter
Of the Eternal's language ;—on earth it is called Forgiveness !"
LONGFELLOW, *from the Swedish of* TEGNER.

SIR ROLAND was possessed of property in several
parts of Cornwall; and at about sixteen miles from
Llanaven he had another beautiful residence, though
wanting the ineffable charm which Llanaven possessed, in having the ocean for its boundary. Lady
Ashton having some business to transact at that place
for Sir Roland, proposed driving over there early the
next day, and Lady Constance, glad to escape from
home, even for a single day, asked to accompany her.
The offer was of course accepted, and Lady Florence
also expressed a wish to go. Lady Ashton, however,
fancying her sons would feel lonely, said she thought
she had better remain at home, but Sir Roland,
begging he might not be considered, it was finally
determined that both the sisters should go.

Sir Roland felt that their absence would enable
him, without fear of interruption, to obtain his dreaded
interview with his brother; and he determined that he

would not weakly put off the trial, though he scarcely
knew how he should speak, or what he should say, for
he had nothing but his own strong internal conviction
to act upon. He knew not even whether Henry was
acquainted with his engagement to Lady Constance,
whether he had ever spoken to her on the subject of
his attachment, or whether his evident melancholy was
not produced merely by her having shewn that she
would not permit or encourage it.

"Yet," he thought, in the latter case, "why should
his manner have been so cold and constrained towards
me at our first meeting. If he had had no reason
for uncomfortable feeling towards me, would it not
have been more natural that in his grief he should
have rejoiced at the sight of one, whom he well knew
would sympathise with him in all his troubles?"

Still he would not admit the idea of Henry's
having acted in any way dishonourable, or of his having
pursued his own wishes, when aware of his claims. In
short, his mind was in a state of the most painful per-
plexity, and he could not close his eyes during the
whole of that distracting night. He knew but too
well that his every prospect of happiness was doomed
to extinction. Yet it was agonising to think of hearing the dreaded words which must end it for ever.
His mind at times began almost to wander, and he
feared lest the strong excitement he was under might
again bring on his fever. He prayed earnestly that
his senses might be preserved, at least till he had
spoken that which, if it destroyed his own hopes, would
secure the happiness of those to whom he was so much
attached; and he continued in ardent, importunate
prayer through much of that long, long, weary night,

till at last his soul found a peace which, even in the happiest days of life, had never been bestowed. God does indeed impart, "to the still wrestlings of the lonely heart," His own sovereign peace and strength; and when Sir Roland rose in the morning, it was with a calmed and tranquil feeling which he would have thought it impossible to have attained.

When Lady Ashton and her companions had set out on their expedition, he instantly sent down to know if his brother could see him, determining to give himself no more time for harassing thought, but to force himself at once to go through the dreaded trial which lay before him. He knew that, however great his sufferings, the Lord would impose nothing but what He would give him strength to endure, and that the longer he put off his painful duty, the more difficult its performance would become.

"It can but last a few years," he repeated to himself, to still the tremors of his mind, while he was waiting for his brother's answer; "life can last but a few, few wretched years, and then—there must be peace."

He lifted up his heart to Heaven in prayer for composure, yet he felt a dead faintness come over him (for he was still very weak) when his servant re-entered the room and said, that "Mr. Ashton would be very happy to see him;" but determining not to give way, he instantly rose, and, taking his man's arm, he slowly descended the stairs.

Knowing that Henry was still confined to his sofa, he entered the room, purposely, by a door which was behind him, that he might avoid being seen on his first entrance; and then leaning on the back of a

chair for an instant, he directed his servant, by a sign,
to place another for him near the end of the couch
against which Henry was leaning, in order that he
might be enabled still to keep out of his sight.

Neither of the brothers spoke till the servant had
left the room. When he was gone, Henry put out his
hand to Sir Roland, and the latter clasped it in silence,
for his breath came thick and short, and he could not
speak.

"Thank God! you are here once more," at length
exclaimed Henry; "I had feared never again to have
seen you."

"Yes, I am better," said Sir Roland kindly; "and
you?"

"Oh! I am well enough," replied Henry; "you
are now the one to be thought of. I little imagined
when last we parted how much we should have had to
endure before we met again."

"Nor I," said Sir Roland, in a voice so choked
by emotion, that Henry surprised turned round towards him, saying,—

"Roland, you are still, I am sure, very ill: why
did you venture down so soon?"

"I am, indeed, still ill," replied Sir Roland, "but
I knew I should never be well, till I had spoken to
you, Henry, and therefore I determined to come."

"Spoken to me!" said Henry, in sudden apprehension.

"Yes, I must speak to you," replied Sir Roland, becoming calmer, now that he had entered on the subject.

He paused a moment, Henry's agitation was extreme; he could not feel a doubt as to the subject
on which his brother was about to enter, and, imagin-

ing he was come as a successful rival, to speak
with blameful indignation, his proud heart rose up
against him,

" And what have you to say to me?" he asked
scornfully.

" Much," said Sir Roland in a stern voice, for
his brother's manner was not such as to conciliate
him.

It must ever be a hard struggle for any man to feel
kindly towards another who has obtained the place—
refused to him—in the heart of the being he loves
better than his own life! And Sir Roland was but
man—young—devoted—and about to part with hopes
which had been his for many a year, hopes—which had
seemed the sum of earthly existence to him—part
with them too, in favour of one, who at that moment
seemed to meet his noble and generous advances with
a harsh and repellent spirit. He was soon however
enabled to overcome the emotions of anger within
him, and reflecting that Henry could not know of his
intention towards him, animated and softened too by
his own generous feelings, he continued in a milder
tone,

" Yes, I have much to say to you, and you must
bear with me patiently, Henry, for mine is a tried and
wounded heart. However, I did not come to speak
about myself, but about you. . . . . . You love Constance, Henry !"

Henry was silent. His heart beat with desperate
emotion, and his breath came audibly.

" I do not *ask* you if you love her," continued
Sir Roland with increasing agitation, " I know—I feel

you do. But I *do* ask you as a man—a lover—a brother—does she love you?"

Henry still could utter no sound.

" Answer me," continued Sir Roland, endeavouring to speak calmly, though his features worked convulsively, for he felt as if the answer he expected to receive must kill him.

Henry at length replied, but almost inaudibly,

" I do not know. She never said she did."

" For God's sake, do not trifle with me," exclaimed Sir Roland, with a vehemence which terrified his brother. " Tell me at once—for you must know—does she love you?"

" I thought so once," replied Henry, in a voice which seemed to deprecate his brother's anger, " but she never said so, and I have no right therefore to say she does."

" Said so! no—" exclaimed Sir Roland, " how should she say so to you, when——"

He suddenly checked himself, for he did not know whether his brother was informed of his engagement or not, and excited as his own mind was, he could yet feel for him; and not therefore till after a deadly pause of several minutes had elapsed could he bring himself to say,

" Henry, I do not know whether you know it, but Constance is engaged to me."

" I know it," replied Henry, with a haughty look, fire flashing from his eyes; " I have long known it—else I had not brooked your questioning."

A storm of passionate feeling swept furiously through Sir Roland's breast, but its very violence

warned him not to speak till it was past. He dropped
his head upon his hand, and his better nature struggled
for the mastery; his heart was full to overflowing, and
he strove to pray, though his mind could form no
petition. At length he looked up, and said calmly, and
in a tone of such deep anguish, as struck his brother
to the heart,

"I did not come here to intrude needlessly into
your feelings, Henry, though now I find I had more
right to do so than I had thought. No tongue but
your own should have dared to tell me that you permitted yourself to love, and sought a return—when
you knew of my engagement; that blow Fate had reserved as the last and the severest."

Henry's whole soul repelled this accusation, and he
was about vehemently to exclaim, that his brother
wronged him—that he was guiltless of all meditated
wrong against him—but his proud heart would not
bend, and he maintained a determined silence.

"I came," continued Sir Roland, finding that
Henry would not speak, "though I confess with different feelings from those which harrow me at this
moment, to seek your confidence for your own happiness sake—to learn as much as you would tell me of
your own sentiments—and as far as you knew them,
or felt justified in speaking of them—of hers."

He was unable to proceed, and Henry torn by contending emotions still remained silent. His mind was
in a state of utter bewilderment; he could scarcely
believe in the existence of such noble intentions as his
brother's words seemed to imply; he could not believe
that he had come to sacrifice his own love—to destroy
his own happiness, in order if possible to secure his;

it seemed beyond the power of human nature so to act.

" No," he thought, " he only comes to warn me that I have no hope, to tell me not to waste my heart's affections, vainly.   He cannot intend to give Constance up !   No one could do that !"

" Will you not answer me, Henry ?" said Sir Roland after a time, hurt and displeased at his brother's apparently ungrateful silence.

" What boots it," said the other with sullen gloom, " to repeat what you know already ?   You tell me I love Constance ;—I can tell you no more !"

" You might at least tell me in a more gracious—a more feeling manner," said Sir Roland, in a voice of deep emotion, " you cannot suppose it to be a matter of indifference to me, either as regards your happiness or my own."

" What would you ?" exclaimed Henry, distract-edly, dashing his hand to his forehead, " Constance is yours—yours by promise—by engagement ; I know she is yours, and I have no wish, no right.—Oh !" he added, bursting into a passion of tears, " I need not change the word, for God knows, I *have* no *wish* to separate you !"

Sir Roland pressed his hand on his brother's shoulder with the earnestness of affection, and said,

" Henry, listen to me—listen to me quietly, and I beseech you answer to what I shall ask.   You seem to say, that you have allowed yourself to love Constance, though you knew of our engagement."

" No," exclaimed Henry vehemently interrupting his brother, and springing from the sofa, regardless of pain or weakness ; " Sir Roland, I deny it ; I never knew, or dreamed of your engagement till I had spoken of my love;—and then she told me. No," he continued in violent excitement, " I take God, the all-seeing—all-knowing—to witness for me, that I would sooner have torn my heart quivering from my breast— sooner have committed any other crime under heaven —yes, any other crime! than have wilfully—knowingly sought to gain Constance's love from you!"

Sir Roland was greatly affected.

" I believe you, Henry," he exclaimed, " I fully believe you—it is your nature. Forgive me for believing the contrary for a moment. But I have been so tortured of late, I scarcely know whom to credit, whom to doubt! Your own words alone could have shaken my own trust in you; but I understood you wrong. And now, my dearest brother — for such through all trial you must ever be!—tell me—as you value my peace and your own—have you reason to believe that Constance prefers you?"

" Roland," answered Henry, turning round, and leaning from the couch till one knee bent before his brother, as he seized his hand forcibly in his own, " you shall know all. But oh! how ill you look" (for he then first saw his brother's countenance), " and I have been the cause of it," and he leant his head down on his brother's hand.

" Nothing comes but by God's permission," said Sir Roland kindly, " but tell me all, then I shall be easier."

" I will,—and you will judge as kindly."

Sir Roland's lips quivered for an instant, with pangs too great for speech, and then became pale and motionless as death.

" I came home," continued Henry, " and found Constance—such as you know her to be.   On that first day, I spoke words, partly foolish, words of—of—what I felt, though it was but a light feeling then.   She checked me, and forbad such expressions again.   Never from that time did I say or do a thing to make her think I loved her, more than I did Florence.   There was something in her manner that made it impossible for me to pass the barrier she chose to place between us.   But still I knew of no reason why I should not let my feelings have their way, and I gave them full scope within me.   Roland, we were together from morn till night; walked together—read together—sung together—till it seemed impossible to live asunder.   I saw she did not observe my feelings, and that she was not aware either that she——"

He stopped, his feeling nature made it impossible for him to say what must be so torturing to his brother.

" Go on," said Sir Roland, leaning his face on his hand, " I know what you would say—go on."

Henry continued : " I should never I believe have spoken—but on the day of the wreck here—which you have heard of—I thought I might perish and see her no more, and then I could not help speaking.   She answered nothing.   I did not see her again for many days, for I had been much hurt; at last we met, and she was cold, and bade me never speak again as I had done ; but she looked pale, and so ill and miserable, that I saw — I fancied at least that——" again he stopped, but Sir Roland waived his hand for him to continue.

" I thought in fact," he said, " that it was not

anger, or indifference which made her speak as she did; but I was ill, and at first I believe she dared not tell me all; for I was violent and intemperate, and—maddened by her conduct. At last, the night before I went to sea, she told me that she could never be more to me, than she was then, for that she was—engaged to you. I appealed—yes, Roland, I confess—that at that distracted moment I appealed to her heart! She answered——"

" What? What?" exclaimed Sir Roland almost frantic, as his brother hesitated to proceed.

" She told me," continued Henry, his eye falling before his brother's searching glance, " that she was bound by every tie to you!"·

" My precious Constance!" ejaculated Sir Roland in a voice of the deepest tenderness, while covering his face with his hands, his tears for the first time gushed forth. His soul bent beneath the mighty grief that lay on it, and for a time all was silent, save the full heavings of his troubled breast. At length, becoming more calm, he exclaimed,

" Yes, bound to me by every tie, but the one—the only one I value. That gone—she is free as the unfettered winds !"

A throb of such ecstasy passed through Henry's heart as he heard these words, as sent the blood giddily through his brain; but the next instant he abhorred himself for the selfishness which could make him feel such joy at that which was worse than death to his brother; and he felt that he could never bear to profit by his unbounded generosity. A sickening fear also came over him, lest Constance now might really have learnt to prefer his brother. He himself had

been absent from her for some time, and the constant
endeavours he was convinced she would make to subdue her feelings, added to her ever strong regard for
Sir Roland, might, at last, he thought, have enabled
her affections to return to their allegiance. His heart
sunk within him at the bare idea. And " yet," he
thought, " how have I prayed, and wished it might be
so—but now !——"

He felt humbled to the soul, and silently, with
earnest heart did he implore that his brother's example
might not be lost upon him.

" Henry," said Sir Roland after a long silence, " you
have not told me all. Go on, let me know every thing,
that I may see my path clearly."

" I have little more to say," replied Henry, throwing himself back exhausted on the sofa. " I went to
sea the morning after *that* evening ; I sent her back all
I possessed of hers—I have nothing left—and I never
wrote to her again."

" Nor to me," interrupted Sir Roland, " I wondered at it then, but do so now no longer."

" No, I could not write to you," continued Henry,
" my heart was full of remorse and misery ; I could
not speak to you about it, and dreaded even thinking
of you. Never either, would I have returned home
had I not believed that I was dying, and then, I thought
that I could give her up, and desired so cravingly to
be with my mother, that I came. She went with her
to Falmouth to meet me ; and though for a moment I
confess my heart bounded at thinking it was a proof of
her strong interest in me, yet I soon saw it was no wish
of hers, that brought her there, for she was cold, and
distant, and rarely spoke to me. I have seen her alone

but once since my return, and then only for a few
moments."

"And what did she say then?" asked Sir Roland
in a voice which struggled vainly for calmness.

"I merely wished to tell her not to fear my ever
renewing the subject—as I saw she apprehended it—
for that worlds would not induce me to do so; and she
replied that she was glad I had given her that assurance as it greatly relieved her mind. We have had no
further intercourse together."

"You have acted nobly, Henry," said Sir Roland,
with a deep sigh, "and she has had feelings that were
but too natural, and has fought against them, it should
seem, in a way that unassisted nature could not have
done. I cannot blame you—either of you—and I
thank God for it. It now only remains for me to
ascertain her wishes, and then——they shall be fulfilled."

"You cannot mean," exclaimed Henry (still scarcely
believing that Sir Roland could intend to resign Lady
Constance to him), "you cannot mean that you can
give her up?"

"To you?" said Sir Roland calmly; "certainly if
she wishes it; and I feel no doubt about it."

"Oh! but there is a doubt," replied Henry, warmed
with generous feeling, "she ever loved you so much,
and has been so cold, and distant with me."

"She would not have been distant, had she not dreaded
being nearer, Henry. No, no, try not to deceive me
into a vain, and hopeless hope. She loves you, and
you know it .... so do I. But we must not quite
dispose of her," he added, with desperate calmness,

and endeavouring to smile, " without her own consent.
Must I ask her what she wishes? or will you?"

" Oh! not I—not I," said Henry shuddering,
" her answer either way would kill me."

" Oh! no," replied Sir Roland, " joy never kills!
And if grief could kill—I should not now be here.
No," he exclaimed—and his manner grew excited—
" if mortal agony could destroy—it would have been
done by this uprooting of a love which remembers no
beginning—and can know no end."

All Henry's feelings were roused by this generous
burst of passionate despair in his brother, and he earnestly addressed him :

" Roland," he said, " hear me, and I beseech you
weigh my words, and do not lightly throw away a happiness which may still be yours. It is long since Constance and I were together; the foolish feeling we might
for a moment have had, will soon have passed ; she
reveres and admires you beyond all earthly beings — I
know she does," he repeated, as Sir Roland shook his
head; " she has spoken of you as if you were almost
more than human! She must love you if she were
long with you, and you will remain here with her, when
I — for I shall be soon well enough — am gone again
to sea. I shall be happy in your happiness, and ―― "

" Do not so deceive yourself, Henry," said Sir
Roland, who was much affected by his brother's generous burst of feeling. " We may, indeed, be comforted
in the loss of our own happiness, by ministering to that
of those we love ; but in this world we must live in ourselves, we cannot wholly live in others."

" But when you were ill, Roland, the thought of

Constance was terrible to me," said Henry; "and I would have given worlds to have seen you well, and happy with her; and earnestly did I pray that it might be so; therefore it is possible you see that change of circumstances may bring change of feeling, and —— "

" But how did you feel when I was out of danger?" asked Sir Roland, again interrupting his brother; "Did you then feel so indifferent to your own happiness? Did you not then find that another change of circumstance could bring another change of feeling?"

Henry was silent.

" I know all your arguments, Henry," continued Sir Roland; "for I have used them all myself—but vainly. No, do not trust for comfort to any excitement of mere human feeling, it is too ephemeral; but there is comfort to be found, and I shall find it, I doubt not."

" But still I implore you," continued Henry, earnestly, "do not speak to Constance now—not yet. I do not—I say it in truth—I do not know her feelings now, even if I ever did, and I shall soon be gone. Do not speak of me to her, nor perhaps of your engagement yet, and I feel sure, that soon—very soon—you will see that she loves you, and then all will be well."

" I will not affect a vain generosity, Henry," replied Sir Roland, "or say, much as I love you, that under some circumstances, I might not perhaps make the trial you so nobly suggest; for I do think that viewed alone, my feelings deserve perhaps more consideration than yours. Yours—dating as you have said they do— only from last year, however strong, are but like a beautiful fabric erected on your mind; while mine are like the native rock rooted in the very depths of my

being. Yours are like a painting — beautiful, perhaps,
and lasting, but not like mine, woven into the very
" substance of my life !"   Our hasty engagement
was not the beginning of my love, Henry !   From the
time we were all so much together, before you went to
sea, I was conscious — child as she then was — that I
felt for her, what I felt for nothing else in life — that
she was to me as a thing apart from all the world."

"Why did you not let me know your feelings?"
said Henry, in great agitation.

"Yours would have been a young and giddy spirit
then to have confided such feelings to," replied Sir
Roland, kindly ; " and perhaps I was always over-
inclined to keep them to myself ; I spoke to her father
before I went abroad, but he thought her too young,
and bid me say nothing to her.   Fatal — fatal precaution ! at least for me."

"But why did you not let me know, at least when
you were engaged ?" asked Henry.   "I have often
wondered why that was kept from me."

"I will tell you," said Sir Roland :—" Our engagement was formed, as you know, under circumstances of
great distress ; formed hastily, against my wish ; for I
earnestly desired more time to be given me for being in
her society.   But, however, it was formed then ; and
my mother, with proper feeling, thought it best that it
should not then be talked of.   You, we should certainly
have told, but knew not where to direct to you at first,
and afterwards I did not like to have it mentioned to
any one, for I saw — and miserable it made me — that
our engagement seemed to check instead of increasing
her former love for me, and I determined she should be
free to act as she wished.   You see, therefore," he

added, kindly, anxious to reconcile his brother to himself, "that you have not taken her affection from me, Henry, for it never was mine. You have only filled that heart which I could not satisfy. and I feel, therefore, that it is the will of God that you, and not I, should ——"

" No," interrupted Henry, " I cannot think it; you are suited to her in every way. Oh! if you could but know how ill I acted towards her, when she refused me; how violent—how intemperate I was—you would know how totally unworthy I am of having her happiness committed to my care."

" And yet she loved you through all," said Sir Roland, and a thrill of anguish darted through his heart; " while she never looked but with coldness upon me, who would not have said one harsh word to her. The heart speaks but too plainly there, Henry; so cease this generous strife against yourself."

Henry was silent for a few moments, for his heart was filled with sweet yet bitter feelings. At length he said, " But why, Roland, would you not let me be told of your engagement when I returned home? that would have saved all our misery."

" It might have done so," replied Sir Roland; "and had I been here at the time, I should undoubtedly have informed you instantly of it; not from any apprehension, but because my regard for you would have made me desire to shew you all confidence. But for the reason I have told you, I begged my mother not to mention it to any one till my return, and not in the least expecting you home, I did not think of excluding you from that generally expressed wish, and so my dear mother did not like to tell you."

" But you knew that I was here long before I returned to sea," resumed Henry; " why did you not write me then ? "

" Oh ! it matters not," replied Sir Roland, his pale cheek flushing at the remembrance of the struggle he had had at ——, and the deep affection which had dictated his decision.

" I will not ask, if you do not wish to tell me," said Henry; " but it has perplexed me often when I have thought of it, and I wished to know."

" It was merely," answered Sir Roland, " that I knew you had been together for a long time, and I thought it possible—judging from your first letter especially — that, in short, I felt it best to leave all in the hands of God — and he has decided — as is doubtless best."

Henry for a time could make no answer. Generous as were the impulses of his own nature, he had never even imagined such self-denying devotion to the happiness of others, as he now met with in his brother; he felt an admiration for him beyond all bounds, and his heart throbbed with anguish as he reflected that he had been the means of destroying his happiness.

" God will be your reward, Roland," at length he said; " but your words have made me very miserable."

Sir Roland grasped his brother's hand, for he felt that their hearts understood each other.

" Yet once more," exclaimed Henry, " I must beseech — entreat — implore of you, if you do not consider me wholly unworthy to be called your brother — defer your — her decision, at least, till I am gone — till you have been long together ! I exact this of your regard, Roland. I shall soon be able to rejoin my ship, and then ——"

"I did tell you, my dear brother," said Sir Roland, "that under some circumstances I might possibly have been tempted to follow your generous wish, but I cannot now; I could not do it; and perhaps it were best at once to tell you why. In the active life which your fine profession affords, you might in time have found relief of mind; but, my poor fellow! they have told my mother, that though your health may be entirely restored, and your strength to a certain degree, yet that you never will be able with safety to undertake again the arduous exertions of a sailor's life."

Henry shaded his face with his hand, and strong emotion shook him; for fond as he was of his home, and enchanting as was the prospect, however uncertain, of being united to Lady Constance, yet he was devotedly attached to his profession; and the idea of being cut off from it for ever, struck like despair to his heart.

"I would not have told you of this now," said Sir Roland, who saw with regret the pain his words had given his brother; "had it not been to prove to you how impossible it would be, even if I wished it, to follow your most disinterested suggestion! and I also hope that the prospect of happiness at home, which I can now offer you, may reconcile you to your great privation. Do you think that I, crowned with every earthly blessing of situation, could bear to see you cut off from following the profession in which you have always so much delighted, and deprived of all happiness here also? Never!—no, if Constance really loves you, she shall undoubtedly be yours."

Henry pressed his brother's hand vehemently to his lips,

"This is too much," he cried; "too much — I cannot endure this, when all I could ever have hoped for, was forgiveness!"

"Let that rest now, Henry;" said Sir Roland, hurriedly: "to-morrow I will endeavour to settle every thing, and then you will be happy, I — think. I am afraid," he added, after a pause, "that I have been intemperate and unkind, but you will feel for me, and forgive me."

"If you would not make me utterly miserable," said Henry, "do not speak in that way, when you have been every thing — every thing that is excellent and noble, beyond all power of belief; while I have been ungrateful — violent — unjust! Yet, I am blest — and yet — Oh! Roland! I cannot endure to think of it!"

"Try to look at these things, Henry, as all guided by a Master Spirit," replied Sir Roland. "He it is, great and good, 'who giveth to every one his portion in due season,' and when trial has done its work with me, its heavy weight will be removed. Do not fear for me, Henry; my love for Constance can never indeed cease, for it is *myself*; but God will in mercy change the nature of it, and make it the tranquil, deep affection which I feel for you. He will be my portion, and He is the only satisfying one. It is the remembrance or the forgetfulness of that, Henry, which converts miseries into blessings, or blessings into miseries. And now, my dear brother, may God, the God of *our* Father, bless you. We have mutually, perhaps, had something to forgive, but the deep heart's love has never failed, and never must. Now I will leave you, for we both need rest, and I shall find it best, perhaps, alone. My mind is much relieved, for any thing is better than uncertainty, and thank God, all — yes, all unhappy displeasure of feeling towards you is gone, and I find you still the same warm, generous being you ever were, God bless you."

Henry wrung his brother's hand, for he could not speak ; and Sir Roland, rising slowly, left the room.

He passed into the adjoining drawing-room, and sat there for some time, in that quiescent state which so often succeeds violent emotions. His mind took a tranquil survey of all that had occurred, as if it had been the record of events long since past, and in which he had no concern. He could even bear to remember that it was in that very room that he had heard those words of Lady Constance's which had so distracted him at the time, and which still lay so chill upon his heart ; yet he felt no disturbance. A vague sense of uneasiness was all he was conscious of, and each acute sensation was lost in the dull, deadening torpor through which, though he could see events clearly, he could not feel them. After a time, ringing for his servant, he returned up-stairs into his own apartment.

When Lady Ashton came home she went directly to visit him, and he told her, without emotion, that he had been down to see Henry, which had much fatigued him ; and Lady Ashton having no idea that there could exist any cause of excitement between them, naturally supposed that his evident lassitude and exhaustion proceeded solely from the unusual exertion he had been making, and with a tranquil mind, therefore, she left him, begging him to go early to rest, as sleep would refresh him.

Sleep, however, was far from Sir Roland's eyes, and for hours he tossed upon his feverish bed; his mind wandered from object to object, yet though none tortured, none gave it repose, for his soul had not yet wholly pierced through the mists of earthly trouble to the unclouded presence of God. At length finding this state of mind intolerable, he involuntarily exclaimed,—

"Why art thou so heavy, Oh! my soul; and why art thou so disquieted within me?"

The answer was sent in the power of the Spirit:—

"Trust thou in God, for thou shalt yet give Him thanks, which is the help of thy countenance and thy God."

His mind waked up from its dreamy state, and he sunk into real repose.

CHAPTER XXV.

> " His bearing is so altered,
> That distant I scarce knew him for himself;
> But looking in his face, I felt his smile,
> Gracious as ever, though its sweetness wore
> Unwonted sorrow in it."—TALFOURD.

> " Vain, vain, the things we tell ourselves; all vain !
> Hope flutters on, on wounded pinion still,
> With a deep life we have no power to crush.
> The fatal blow must by another's hand
> Be dealt : the ruthless lip of those we love
> Alone can teach us that we are not loved,
> Alone can tear Hope's quivering grasp away,
> And bid us, hopeless, loveless, lifeless, to live on."—MS.

> " Thou hast taught
> My soul all grief, all bitterness of thought !
> 'Twill soon be past — I bow to Heaven's decree,
> Which bade each pang be ministered by thee."
> MRS. HEMANS.

NOTWITHSTANDING the great fatigue he had undergone, Sir Roland rose earlier than usual the next morning. His energetic mind could never endure weakly to postpone the duties which he knew must be fulfilled ; and in his present most trying and difficult situation, he felt that the sooner every thing was decided, the sooner should he be enabled to regain his peace of mind.

When he had finished his almost untasted breakfast, he sent his servant to request Lady Ashton to come to him. She accordingly came, and when he had answered all her kind and anxious inquiries, he told her that he wished much to speak to Lady Constance alone, and that he would go down for that purpose into the little drawing-room, and there wait till it suited her to join him, requesting at the same time that they might not be interrupted.

There was nothing extraordinary in this request, considering the position in which he stood, as regarded Lady Constance, but it was made in so troubled a voice, and there was so unsettled an expression in his countenance, that Lady Ashton felt convinced that something most painful had occurred. She would not ask, but her anxious look was read by Sir Roland, who kindly replied to it,—

" You shall know all, my dearest mother, but not now. Pray for me — pray for me, for I am most miserable ! "

Lady Ashton approached him, and putting her arm round him, stooped to kiss his pale brow. He leant his head against her for a moment, but though he felt her tears fall upon his cheek, yet no drop came to ease his own burning eyes. His spirit was wound up for endurance, and he dare not indulge one softening thought. After a few minutes, he said,—

"I must ask you to leave me now, dear mother, for I have need to strengthen, not to melt my heart."

Lady Ashton, full of dismay and anxiety, left the room, and going to Lady Constance's apartment, told her of Sir Roland's wish to see her. Lady Constance had expected soon to receive this dreaded message, but when it arrived, the sickness of a fainting fit came over her. Recovering herself, however, she got up, and was about to leave the room, when she caught Lady Ashton's eye fixed in sorrowful inquiry upon her face. She turned to her, and throwing her arms round her neck, exclaimed,—

"Oh! do not hate me, though I have brought such misery into your home."

Lady Ashton kissed her affectionately, though she felt more than ever perplexed; but she could not then detain her from Sir Roland, so said,—

"Go, my dear, go, and comfort Roland if you can; he seems so very wretched."

Lady Constance left the room, and descending the stairs, found herself at the door of the apartment where she was to meet Sir Roland. There she paused, trembling from head to foot. It seemed impossible to open the door, or go into the presence of him whose happiness she had so wholly destroyed. The apartment was next to the one in which Henry was, and as she stood in timorous indecision, she caught the sound of his hollow cough, followed by an exclamation of excessive pain. This nerved her at once, for it roused all her deep interest in him, and made her feel the stern necessity of ending her unhappy engagement to Sir Roland. Not that she dreamed of marrying Henry; that seemed as impossible to her as fulfilling her vows to his brother; but she felt that she must be free, and then she thought she would leave Llanaven, at least till she and those whose peace she had so much disturbed, should have regained somewhat of tranquillity of heart. She was greatly relieved on entering the room to find Sir Roland was not yet there, and she sat down on the sofa, and took up a book that lay on a table near, in the hope of quieting her agitation a little before he should come in. She was, however, scarcely seated, when the door opened, and he entered, slowly, though without assistance. Her eye rested on him for one instant, but was quickly withdrawn, for her heart sickened at seeing him changed as he was! His countenance was grave, but betokened neither anger nor unkindly feeling; on the contrary, the sweet expression which generally played round his mouth, was even heightened by the melancholy which pervaded his whole appearance.

He did not raise his eyes to Lady Constance as he entered, but a slight inclination as he approached the sofa, shewed that he was aware of her being there. He sat down by her side, and instantly began.

" I have asked you to meet me here, Constance, because I have much to say to you."

He paused a moment, but getting exceedingly agitated, he hurriedly continued.

" I cannot wait to find gentle words, for I must speak whilst I can, Constance, and say that I see — I know and feel that our engagement had best — must, indeed, end."

He stopped, but Lady Constance could make no reply.

Then fell in all its fearful weight, the deadly, riving force of hopeless misery upon Sir Roland's heart. Till that moment, unknown to himself, " hope, which comes to all," a desperate hope that would not be denied, had lingered in his breast; though it was the agonising pang of its final extinction, which alone made him aware that it had still survived within him.

Lady Constance's silence proved but too plainly that she also thought their ill-fated engagement had

better cease; and though he knew it must be so, yet
the moment of final decision was dreadful to him. Not
that he could now have had comfort in the idea of that
which would once have given him such unbounded
happiness! No! the thought of his brother would
have haunted him, and have embittered the sweetness
of every domestic tie. Yet still the last crushing blow
was horrible, and an almost frantic feeling of despair
rushed over him for a moment, but terrified by its violence, he instantly laid his cause before Heaven, mentally exclaiming, "Leave me not, neither forsake me,
O God of my salvation!" Peace returned into his
heart, and when he spoke again it was in a calmer
manner.

"I will not go over all the causes," he said, "which
have brought us mutually to this decision, Constance;
suffice it, that we both of us know and feel that they
are insurmountable. You will now, I trust, at least let
me resume the same place I formerly possessed in your
regard, and deal kindly and openly with me. Though
the claims of later days must be foregone, you will not
forget that from earliest years I have ever loved and
watched over you, with more than brother's love. *That*
love can never cease, though even that has had much to
try it of late."

He was silent, and Lady Constance could scarcely
command her voice to speak; but she murmured something of "regard and friendship;" when Sir Roland,
with one of those bursts of terrible feeling which at
times overcame him, exclaimed wildly and passionately,—

"Talk not of friendship, Constance. They know it
but by name who have never given up love for it!"

His whole frame shook with emotion; but after a time, drawing a deep breath, he added, as Lady Constance sat trembling by his side,—

" I entreat you to forgive me, Constance, and to bear with me a little, for I cannot always speak, or think, or feel as I could wish. My spirit has been so shaken by trial and illness, that I am no longer master of myself. You will forgive me. It is easy for the happy to forgive ! "

" Happy ! — Oh ! Roland," exclaimed Lady Constance, at last, bursting into tears, " I am most miserable."

" And I most guilty for speaking as I have done," said Sir Roland, all his own griefs vanishing at the sight of her distress. " Oh ! I had meant to hide my feelings from you — to tell you that my love was gone, or a light thing that would soon pass away, so that your heart should not be troubled; but now I have wounded you, by my frantic violence, and have shewn you that which I would fain have hid from every eye but God's. Most unreasonable, too, I have been, for I have asked your friendship and then rejected it; but still you will give it me, and your confidence, too, Constance ? and I will try to merit them."

Lady Constance's falling tears proved how much his words affected her. Her mind, too, was perplexed, for she could no way divine what had occurred to produce so great a change in Sir Roland, or to make him determine so suddenly to break off their engagement. She had expected him to inquire why she was cold and changed, but she had not anticipated his having formed any definite resolution himself. Her conscious mind made her feel sure that Henry must be in some way connected with these things, though how Sir Roland could have become acquainted with his sentiments she was wholly at a loss to conceive.

Sir Roland felt a great difficulty in mentioning his brother; he could not expect that Lady Constance would willingly acknowledge her feelings, or shew the interest which she felt in him; he was most anxious to end a state so fearfully trying to himself, and to bring her to consent to that which could alone restore happiness to Henry. At length, after a long mental struggle, he began:

"I am but a poor advocate, Constance, but I am most anxious to try my powers once more. Not for myself — do not fear that," he added, a flush of pride glowing on his features, as he saw Lady Constance look up with sudden terror to his face. I know myself too well to supplicate in my own cause; but I would try to move you towards another, who loves you with a deep, devoted love; one who would die to make you happy.— You know that Henry loves you, Constance, and it is for him that I would plead. —You do not answer.— Constance," he added, with a sudden burst of feeling, "I cannot treat you as a stranger; I must speak openly and freely to you, for this constraint is intolerable. *My* love is now, you must remember, a thing — forgotten! but it may perhaps give me some little claim to be heard for another. Henry loves you, Constance, and do you not love him? — Answer that question to yourself, not to me — not to me! but act on the reply your heart shall make, openly—generously. He has suffered long, and deeply, and has been wholly, wholly without blame. He has told me all, and I am come as from him to you, to beg you to feel for him; and I beseech you,

let me tell him you will, in time at least, be his. I feel
sure that I have read your feelings, Constance, and
Henry thinks that he has done so too."

"Oh! no, Roland," said Lady Constance, earnestly,
"he cannot — he cannot! From the moment he told
me what he felt, I have never spoken to him, if I could
help it, I have never written to him; he has been to me
as a stranger."

"I know it, Constance," said Sir Roland, in a voice
of the deepest tenderness and respect, while his heart
bled at seeing her continued tears. "My mother,
though ignorant of the cause, told me of your coldness and unwillingness to be with him; and that, which
to her appeared unkindness, told me all the history of
your heart. You have acted as regards him, as you
were sure to do. But still, Constance, there are some
things I fain would ask, and which I feel that I must
know, at least you will let me have the comfort of feeling that there is perfect trust and confidence between
us. Tell me, I beseech you, why, when you felt that
you—that you—yes, I will say it—that you loved
him, why did you write to me — why receive me as
you did? I cannot think you insincere, yet why could
you seek to lead me astray? Why not have told me
at once, you could not be mine, and have given me
proof of your confiding friendship, even though you
refused me your love? It had been better—oh! far
better!"

"I will try and tell you, Roland," said Lady Constance, endeavouring to be calm. "But first, I never
spoke one word to Henry that could make him think I
liked him."

"Words are not needful," said Sir Roland, sadly,

"to shew either that we love, or that we cannot love."

"But I never, Roland, never did a thing to make him think I forgot my vows to you. He does not, he cannot say I did ;" and again she burst into tears.

"No, my dearest Constance," said Sir Roland, soothingly, "he did not say so ; he said only that he thought he saw that you were not indifferent towards him but that he was convinced that you — I scarcely know how to render his words without making him appear presumptuous and over-confident — but he was not so ; you must believe me when I say so, Constance ; he spoke in every way what was right and generous, only it is I who am so wretched an interpreter. But you were to tell me why you received me so warmly, and continued to write to me with so much affection."

"At the first moment I forgot every thing but the joy of seeing you," said Lady Constance ; "and what I wrote, Roland, I truly felt; and, indeed, a thousand-fold more, because I knew how much I was wronging you, — and I feel the same affection now."

Sir Roland pressed her hand a moment to his lips, then let it fall again, as he leant back on the sofa, and shaded his face.

"I trust," she continued after a moment, "to feel every thing I ought, and my mind was getting much more tranquil and happy, when — he returned so ill."

"And then all your efforts were scattered in an instant," said Sir Roland, with a pang, which made his heart and brow contract. "I see it all, and I thank God I can feel for it all. Oh ! it is as vain to try to love, as to strive to forget, Constance !"

He paused, and became exceedingly agitated, but at length he said,—

"There is still one more thing I would ask, and then I have done for ever. Yet my whole soul quivers and trembles as I think of it, and remember how sense, and reason, and life itself, reeled under the blow!"

"What could it be?" asked Lady Constance, in terror, as Sir Roland sat for a moment incapable of speaking.

"It was this. My mother, in the open confidence of her heart, unsuspicious herself, and not thinking of creating suspicion in me, had spoken of your coldness and strange distance of behaviour to Henry, which she thought proceeded from aversion, but which I soon saw was any thing but that. My soul was miserable, and it seemed as if I had nothing more to suffer in life; but as I stood in this room — this very room — after leaving her, I saw you in the next, for the door was partly open; I saw you clasp your hands, as in agony, and looking up to Heaven, I heard you — you, Constance, who were all the world to me, for whose sake I could willingly have suffered all things! — I heard you exclaim, "Would he had never returned!" — My senses gave way under my terrible feelings; and—Oh! I was almost going impiously to say, would that my life had done so too!"

"Roland," said Lady Constance seizing his hand, and forcing him to turn to her, "you could not think it was of you I spoke? Of you—oh! no—oh! no;—it was of Henry. I wished, oh! how fervently at that moment, that he had never come back to blight your happiness. —Oh! not—not of you!"

Sir Roland raised the hand he held in his, a mo-

ment towards heaven, while a flash of such joy shone
on his countenance as made every feature resplendent.

"Now I am happy," he exclaimed; "now I can
freely give you up—for you are restored to me the
same—same being that you ever were—true, noble,
heavenly! Forgive me that for a moment I could
doubt you; forgive me that for a moment I could
think you unkind, ungenerous! But it was at the first
instant of my distraction at finding that you loved
Henry,—and it was *I* who had just returned! My
heart has long felt that you could not really wish me
evil, but I longed to have your image, as it has ever
been, clear and bright within me; and God has granted
me my earnest prayer. You will forgive me?"

"Oh! I have nothing to forgive," said Lady Constance, again melting into tears, "but all to be forgiven."

"Speak of that I pray no more," said Sir Roland,
his sadness again returning, yet glowing with generous feeling; "but if you think, Constance, that you
owe me any kindness, let me entreat you to shew it in
listening to this my earnest entreaty. Let me tell
Henry that you will be his."

"Oh! no, no," said Lady Constance; "no, I cannot do that, Roland."

"Constance," he replied, "you should be above
all false refinement. You know that you have been
the cause of much misery to two hearts that love you!
Will you refuse to make the only reparation in your
power? It were a false boast, to say that such an act
would make me happy, we both know that—that could
not be the case, but it would make me happier than
any thing else could. I have hitherto lived too much

for myself, God will teach me to live for others, and
your happiness is now my care—and Henry's. Constance, at least let me entreat you to go to him, and
let him plead his own cause; he will perhaps do it
best. His coming to you is impossible, for now again
you know he cannot leave the sofa, but you will not let
that keep you from him?"

"Roland, I cannot go," said Lady Constance, "I
do not say I doubt his feelings, for that would not be
true; but it is long since he spoke of them to me, and
I could not—could not go to him now."

"I understand you, Constance," replied Sir Roland,
"and love you for your feelings; but remember, he
spoke to me of what he felt, and through me you know
that he still loves you beyond his life."

"Lady Constance made no answer, but her distress
was extreme, for she could not endure the idea of going to Henry.

"I will say but this one thing more, Constance,
and surely," added Sir Roland reproachfully, "you
surely will not refuse me every thing? Think only
for one moment how much Henry has suffered; think
of him now—in the next room—cut off, for the moment at least, from all enjoyment. Remember that
you, and you only, can give him peace and happiness,
and will you refuse? Constance, I never entreated
for myself, but now I do implore of you—go to
Henry! If you will not, alone—come with me."

"With you! oh! no, that would be worse than
death," cried Lady Constance burying her face in her
hands.

"No, Constance," said Sir Roland, "you should not
say that! I cannot leave you till you have granted my

request; it is cruel, inhuman, to give pain where you can relieve it, and you should know Henry enough to feel that he could never mistake you. Will you not Constance, let me take you to him—at least as my gift?—my heart would be easier then."

"Then I will go," said Lady Constance, instantly rising.

Sir Roland thanked her with warmest expressions of gratitude, and also rising, took her hand, and they crossed the room to the door which led into the apartment where Henry was lying. Lady Constance involuntarily shrunk back as he opened it, but he whispered to her,

"For my sake, I beseech you, Constance," and she again advanced.

Henry was lying with his back to them, but he was fully aware of their entrance, for he had caught the sound of Sir Roland's voice, of Lady Constance's name; yet he dared not turn, or look towards them. Sir Roland went up to him—placed Lady Constance's hand in his, and silently left the room.

CHAPTER XXVI.

"Il n'y a que Dieu qui puisse ainsi mêler tant de biens à tant de maux."—MADAME DE GUYON.

> "My soul indeed is fixed,
>   Yet cannot I but feel
> E'en now the sadness of long days to come;
> The cold void left me by a lost delight!
> *   *   *   *   *   *
>   How blissful was the thought
> With *her* to share each golden evening's peace!
> How grew the longing hour by hour, to read
> *Her* spirit yet more deeply!
> *   *   *   *   *   *
> Now is the twilight's gloom around me fallen:
> The festal day, the sun's magnificence,
> All riches of this many-colour'd world,
> What are they now? Dim, soundless, desolate,
> Veiled in the cloud that sinks upon my heart."
>   MRS. HEMANS'S *Translation from* GOETHE'S *Tasso.*

WHEN Sir Roland had left Lady Constance with Henry, he went up instantly to his own room, and locking the door, he threw himself on the sofa.

"Now," he exclaimed, "the worst is over! now I shall find repose!"

Alas! those who imagine that the active zeal of self-renunciation—the stirring animation of self-sacrifice, where the noble deed follows up the daring resolution—are the worst features of trial, have as yet learned but little in that bitter school. The real suffering of such times, compared to which all else is as "childhood's dewy tears," is, when having given up all—there is nothing left for us to do; and when after the first moment of unbounded gratitude is past, we find ourselves overlooked, amidst the happiness we have almost died to give,—then indeed bitterness overspreads the heart, for the very love which helped to carry us through, is chilled within us, and we feel indeed deserted; and none but those who look to God, not man, can be sustained in patience through such soul-sinking, protracted misery.

Such however were not Sir Roland's feelings at the moment we are speaking of, for it was not the glow of merely human feelings which had animated his generous and exalted spirit! He had set God before him throughout all that he had done and suffered, and had shaped his whole course by His laws. To Him alone had he looked in all his trials, seeking His blessing, and resting on his strength; and He, who is well called "Faithful," now poured into his soul such strong consolations, as completely for the moment overcame all earthly sorrow and regret—filling him with unspeakable happiness. He felt raised above all griefs, secured from all the painfully changeable ties of life, but joined, spirit and soul, with God; realising the words of St. Paul:—"Who shall separate us from the love of Christ? shall tribulation, or distress, or persecution, or famine, or nakedness, or peril, or sword? Nay, in all these things we are more than conquerors through him that loved us."

He remained for some time in this happy state of

mind, but was at last roused by Lady Ashton's voice at the door, asking if she might come in. He instantly rose, and admitted her. When they were both seated she said,

" I find you have been successful in your kind mediation, my dear Roland, and that Constance has been to visit Henry; I met her just now coming from his room, but I did not like to speak to her; however, as I found she was no longer with you, I thought I would come and see you."

" I am glad you have done so," he replied, " for I wished much to speak to you. But first I must beg an indulgent hearing of what I have to say."

He then informed her of the events which had taken place, dwelling as little as possible on his own feelings, and bringing forward every circumstance which could tend to exonerate his brother, and Lady Constance from all blame. But the intelligence was so wholly unexpected by Lady Ashton that she was completely overwhelmed by it, and reproached herself in the bitterest terms for her want of caution and discernment. Sir Roland strove to comfort her, and reconcile her to herself; but she was for a length of time inconsolable at the thought of the unhappiness she had brought upon him.

" You must not think so much of me, my dearest mother," he said with a smile of sadness. " Nothing can come but by my heavenly Father's permission, and you cannot doubt but that He who has been with me so graciously hitherto, will be with me always. If you could but know the comforts He has sent me, since last I saw you, you would be fully reconciled to leaving me in his hands. I remember, years ago, reading the

account of some one whose only son was dying, and
who in great trouble of mind had gone into his own
chamber to pray. When he came out again, he saw
by the countenance of a servant whom he met, that
all was over, ' Do not be afraid,' he said, ' to tell me
that he is dead, for, for the revelations that God has
just made of Himself to my soul, I could endure to
lose a son each day of my life.'   I recollect at the time
I read this, that I marvelled at the degree of comfort
given; but I marvel now no longer, for I have experienced the same. You, my dear mother, must help
me to sustain this blessed frame of mind, and not to
sink under trials which without God's help must, I
think, destroy me. Of me—we will talk no more;
but we must now think of promoting the happiness of
those whom I have so long, and so involuntarily made
miserable. Henry, you must feel, is not only blameless, but his conduct has been beyond all praise. So
young — so impetuous! yet in this case so self-re-
strained, so high-principled, so thoughtful for me! She
too——"

Lady Ashton involuntarily shook her head, and,
through choking tears, spoke something of " change
and light feelings."

" My mother," exclaimed Sir Roland, becoming
greatly agitated, " if you would not add bitterness to
my great trials, and sink the heart which God has so
sustained, do not, I implore you, blame her, or shew
her coldness, or displeasure. Hers are not light
feelings—she has never changed—for she never loved
me."

" Roland," exclaimed Lady Ashton, " what can you
mean? She was engaged to you!"

" I know it," he replied, and for a moment his brain felt dizzy; but regaining his composure he continued, " but her engagement was formed I am convinced solely to please her father. She never loved me! I saw that almost directly after, though I would not harass you, or compromise her by saying so; but I spoke to her about it, and implored her to break it off if she wished it; but she loved no one else then, and would not pain me by doing so. And remember too how much she always loved Henry from a child; and then when she was so unavoidably thrown with him again, oh! my dear mother, how could it be other-wise?"

" Ah!" said Lady Ashton, " I see and feel it all now, and all my own folly too. It was indeed blind-ness! but I was so fully persuaded that she loved you, that had an angel told me otherwise then, I could scarcely have given the assertion an instant's belief. But still my heart bleeds."

" And does not mine?" said Sir Roland, turning away, with a despairing gesture. " Yet will anger against those we love heal the wounds of the heart? No! thankful, most thankful am I, that blame and displeasure mix not with my feelings towards either of them. I should have mourned the loss of my own happiness doubly had that been the case; nay, it would have been doubly lost."

" I cannot be thankful enough to God that such are your feelings, my ever dear Roland," said Lady Ashton, with an expression of the deepest affection; " but it is sometimes harder to forgive a wrong done to those we love, than one committed against oneself."

" Think of Constance as the being who makes

Henry happy, not as her who has made me—miserable,"
said Sir Roland, though dropping his voice, so that the
last words were inaudible.

"Oh! I love her too well to be unjust towards
her," replied Lady Ashton, "for she is most sweet and
gentle; and now too I can well understand all that
seemed at the time so inexplicable in her conduct, her
avoidance of poor Henry, and seeming displeasure towards him! Oh! yes, she has acted well, and I was
cruel and unreasonable with her, poor child, when she
had already enough to bear, in seeing him so suffering,
and in not daring to speak to him one word of comfort.
Do not fear me, Roland, she shall be to me what she
has ever been."

"My dear mother," said Sir Roland, "now indeed
you make me happy, for I could not have endured to
see her drooping under your displeasure, and for all
her new-formed happiness to be destroyed by coldness
on our part. Never shall she see a frown on my brow,
nor, if I can help it, hear a sigh from my lips. The
fatal subject is of course closed between her and me for
ever, but do you talk to her openly about her feelings,
and her happiness, and love; else discomfort and distrust will grow up between you. You will do this for
my sake?"

"I will," said Lady Ashton rising, "and will seek
her now, for I doubt not her poor heart trembles at the
thought of our meeting, and she will feel relieved when
the first words are over."

She went accordingly, and found Lady Constance
in her own room, who on seeing her enter burst into
tears. Lady Ashton took her hand and kissed her
with the utmost kindness.

"Can you forgive me?" exclaimed the poor girl, turning and burying her face on Lady Ashton's shoulder.

"Yes, my dear child, I can forgive you," she replied, "for I have been the most to blame through all that has happened. But we will talk of this quietly some other time when your spirits are less excited, and you will find me still, as ever, a loving mother to you."

Lady Constance's heart swelled with emotions painfully tender, as Lady Ashton spoke in accents of such kindness and affection, and she would at that moment have gladly relinquished every bright hope of her life, to have restored peace and happiness to those she had so deeply wounded.

When Lady Ashton returned to Sir Roland, she found him much exhausted, but still calm and sustained by heavenly comforts. She told him of her interview with Lady Constance, and cheerèd him much by the kindly feelings she expressed; then left him to endeavour to seek repose. He retired early to rest that night, and slept calmly; but the awakening next morning! Oh! it required the near prospect of Heaven indeed, to sustain through sufferings like those he then endured.

When he awoke, he looked out, on one of the brightest scenes which nature can present. It had frozen severely during the night, and every fibre, and leaf, and slender stalk, was set with crystals which sparkled with the brilliancy of diamonds, or shone with the softer gleams of silver in the sun's early beams, making the earth a palace of fairy frost-work; while

the ocean beyond, lay dark and trembling under the
morning air. For an instant his mind, arrested by the
beauty of the scene, enjoyed a sense of tranquil pleasure; but when remembrance returned, in all its desperate force, his very soul gave way under its power,
and he sunk back upon his pillow prostrate with utter
misery. He felt that no hope, no joy, no happiness,
could ever come to him again; that his life was aimless
—his heart, vacant. He closed his eyes, and groaned,
in very agony and desolation of spirit.

When once in the midst of the current of daily
occupations, though the burthen they may have to
bear be heavy, yet step after weary step, the miserable
are enabled to drag on their weight of unhappiness
through the mournful day, till night again comes, and
brings with it, a dull and temporary, relief. But the
restless, ever-flowing sorrows of our waking hours, do
not sleep as we do; they—ever restless, ever flowing,
seem to accumulate like a weight of waters, whilst we
are losing the inward power of sustaining them; and
when the temporary barrier which sleep has raised
against their tearing power, is removed, and we awake
again to the light of day, then comes the mighty
torrent down upon the soul with overwhelming, desolating force!

> " Thou hast been called, oh ! sleep, the friend of woe,
> But 'tis the happy, who have called thee so !"

Sir Roland indeed felt most miserable, and in spite
of his resignation to the will of God, his soul was completely benumbed. All call for immediate exertion
was over, and his spirit sunk for the time under the
oppressive hand of deadly sorrow. Yet there was no

murmuring in his feelings, but rather a willingness
that God should rule, and that He should dispose
of him in all ways; yet it was impossible but that
he should feel the sudden rending away of ties and
hopes which had been his so long; and though he
knew, and blessed God that this was not his home, yet
he had—for he was young, and his spirit had been
bright and buoyant—figured life to himself in sweet
and glowing colours.   Now all was changed, all one
universal blank—one deep, dark sea of desolation, over
which there brooded only that calm of utter hopelessness,

" Which leaves the heavy heart in darkness—but in peace !"

He could not endure this state of mind, however, so he
rose determined to shake off his despondency, and not
weakly to give way to it, as if he knew not where to
go for comfort and strength.   He prayed long and
earnestly, and though he could not feel the exaltation of
spirit which had been granted him the day before, yet
he was enabled to look joyfully beyond the " waves of
this troublesome world," and to feel that, compared
with eternity, life was but as a dream.

One thing only now remained for him to do as regarded Henry and Lady Constance, which was to arrange
things for their future happiness, and to make such a
settlement upon them as would secure them in the possession of every worldly comfort.   It has been before
stated that Henry Ashton's fortune was by no means
large, and Lady Constance's was not so either; but
Sir Roland was determined that they should never
know the want of any thing to which they had been
accustomed, and ever energetic in following up his

resolutions, he wrote by that morning's post to his solicitor in London requesting him to come down to him as soon as possible. The thought of contributing to their happiness sent a thrill of joy through his heart, and he still felt there was something to live for. When he had finished and despatched this letter, he went down-stairs, for he felt convinced that the sooner he could resume his active habits of life, the better it would be for him, and the sooner he should be enabled to overcome that lassitude of misery, which seemed to make the thought of every duty so irksome to him. He knew that the first meeting with Lady Constance after the trying scene which had taken place the day before, must be exceedingly painful; but he resolved not to defer it, knowing how much the fearful anticipation of things adds to their difficulty and pain, and anxious as soon as possible to set the minds of others at ease. He went therefore at once into the drawing-room, where he found her alone, reading; she had not thought he would have been down so soon, or her fearful heart would have sent her back to her own chamber. He advanced to her directly, and they shook hands, but neither at the first moment could speak, and Lady Constance, soon putting down her book, rose, murmuring something about Lady Ashton, evidently as an excuse for leaving the room; but Sir Roland begged her to stay with him one moment, adding,

" Constance, if I am ever to regain peace of mind, if I am not henceforth to be an exile and a miserable wanderer on the earth, unable to endure my own home, I must accustom myself to look on you, as what you are now—belonging to another, and must overcome the pain of thinking of you, of seeing you before me as such. If you have any true regard for me, you will help me to forget my feelings, and not bring them ever to my mind, by shewing that you remember them yourself. I must hope, from your friendship, assistance in conquering my weakness, and then in time—I may learn to be at ease in your presence. Do not, I beseech, at any time leave the room because I enter it, or I shall never bear to do so ; and shall feel an always increasing sense of misery, and dejection, instead of learning to bow to God's decision, and teaching my selfish heart to be happy in the happiness of others. Shew me this confidence, this kindness, will you, Constance? For I feel it will be far easier for me to begin the effort now while I am still sustained by the fever of the first exertion, than if I waited for a while, till languid nature left no strength within me. I know this will be an effort to you, I fear an unwelcome one, but I trust you will feel for my trials, and not increase them."

He spoke with great difficulty, and with many interruptions, but Lady Constance could not find power to answer for some time. At length she said in the sweetest manner " that there was nothing she would not do that he could wish of her," and taking up her book again, she resumed her seat.

He thanked her—but his manner was colder than before, for the sound of her voice overpowered him, and he dared not give way to the slightest feelings, even of gratitude. He could scarcely even maintain his resolution of continuing in the room, but he felt that if once he were conquered, the next effort would be doubly difficult. He asked strength of the " Strengthener," and was enabled to overcome himself, and walking to the window he made some observation on the scene before him, where every thing still retained the beautiful appearance that had so much struck him on his first awakening; for though the sun shone brightly, yet its frozen beams, had not had power to displace a single gem, of all the thousands which it lit up in such splendid radiance.

Lady Ashton then entering afforded him some relief, and he soon after left the apartment, saying he would go and see his brother.

Henry was excessively confused at his first entrance, but Sir Roland's kind and cordial manner soon relieved him, and after talking on indifferent subjects for a few moments, the latter began,

" Henry, we have always lived together in the most free and intimate way, and remember now, that no coldness or restraint must be allowed to creep in between us. We both know what must be uppermost in each other's thoughts, but it will depend greatly upon you, whether my feelings continue to be those of unmitigated pain, or whether they shall have much of comfort, or indeed of pleasure mixed with them.   I will not promise," he added with a rather forced smile, " to talk to you of all my feelings, but you would make me very happy if I felt you could talk to me of yours. Do not fear paining me, your constraint of manner will pain me much more, for it will make me feel I have lost a brother as well as—other ties; and the sooner you can forget me, the sooner I shall be able to forget myself."

" My dear Roland," replied Henry, warmly, " I will try if possible to forget the deep injury I have done you, as you wish it, and only to enjoy the happiness you have bestowed; and I will try also to overcome the pain I feel every time I see you, or think of you: for if I lose you as my brother, all other happiness would be, indeed, dearly purchased."

"Well, Henry," answered Sir Roland in a cheerful tone, "all you have now to do, is to get well as fast as possible. It seems happily that no more operations will be necessary, so all is in progress for recovery, and the doctor and lawyer must see which can get their work done first. I have sent for L—— to come down here, and the care of your future prospects must be left to me; whilst you and your doctor must exert yourselves to be ready by the time we are."

It is impossible to describe Henry Ashton's feelings as his brother spoke these words. In former times, and under different circumstances, he had indeed looked up to Sir Roland as he would have looked to a father for help and assistance; but now, to receive not only Lady Constance herself, but the means of being united to her, from his hand, was a burden of gratitude he hardly knew how to sustain.

Painful thoughts had obtruded themselves on his mind on this subject, immediately after the first emotions of happiness had subsided on being with Lady Constance the day before, for he had felt that he could never ask, or wish her to leave the comforts and luxuries, with which she had from infancy been surrounded, to share with him a sailor's home; and yet he could not of course bear for a moment to look to Sir Roland for any thing; and thus distress had mingled itself with his cup of happiness, and embittered it; while Sir Roland's painful lot had been sweetened by the greatness of God's mercy. Now however all anxiety on the subject of his marriage was removed, and his whole soul was filled with gratitude.

"I have no words, Roland," he answered when his brother had finished, "to express what I feel. Your own heart must judge for me what I would say, my dearest brother!"

"Let me see that you are happy," said Sir Roland, "and the gift of a little of this world's goods will be amply repaid. Remember what I have said, Henry, and let me see, by your free expression of happiness, that you wish to make me happy. I have said somewhat of the same kind to Constance," he added, determined to overcome the difficulty he had in speaking of her, "and she has promised to be every thing that is kind."

Henry's colour rose at hearing her named by his brother, and Sir Roland, finding the effort to sustain an appearance of cheerfulness very trying, soon after left him.

As he was going out of the room, he met Lady Ashton with a letter in her hand, which she held out to him.

"This relates to you," she said, "and I am not quite sure who it comes from. It is edged with black and is signed 'Wentworth,' but it is full of anxiety and regard for you, so very pleasant to me."

"It is from Scott," said Sir Roland, looking at the letter; "his uncle must then be dead. Poor excellent old man! he is gone to his rest. How happy! I will take this up to my room, mother," he added, "and will you come there to me? But first take Constance in there," he said, pointing back to Henry's room, "otherwise I feel sure she will not go. It is all new to them at present, and it is not as if he could go to her."

Lady Ashton turned to do as he wished, while her heart swelled with a love too painful for him who had sent her on her kind mission. Lady Constance was of course too happy to go to Henry, though she had not liked to do it unasked; and Lady Ashton then went to Sir Roland, who had by that time read his friend's letter.

It was written to Lady Ashton, and Mr. Scott, now Lord Wentworth, expressed in it his deep concern and anxiety at hearing of Sir Roland's illness and danger, the news of which, he said, had but just reached him, for he had only that day arrived in London from the Continent. He added, that he trusted he should be pardoned for not waiting for an answer before he set off for Cornwall, but that his uneasiness was so great that he felt it impossible to endure the delay of the post.

"He may then be here to-day," said Lady Ashton, "and I shall be most happy if he comes."

"Yes, I shall be glad to see him," replied Sir Roland; though his heart writhed under the remembrance of the bounding spirits with which he had last parted from him at ——, when all his anticipations had been so bright.

A few hours afterwards Lord Wentworth arrived, and was of course most thankful to find Sir Roland so much better than he had expected. He was however much affected at seeing his altered looks; and the great depression of his spirits could not long escape his penetrating eye, but he attributed it to the effect of his illness, and trusted that, with strength, his natural animation would return.

"I am very glad," he said, "now that my fright is over, that it was strong enough to make me come down here directly; else I should have been entangled by the cobwebs in lawyers' chambers, and never have got free; for I am threatened with a life's-worth of business."

Sir Roland spent that evening down-stairs in the drawing-room for the first time since his illness. He was anxious to do so before Lord Wentworth became acquainted with his altered hopes respecting Lady Constance, as he feared that his friend, whose feelings were warm and keen, might shew too much of his regret and sorrow. How often had he anticipated the day when he should introduce Lady Constance to this, his dearest friend, as his wife—when he should see gathered around him, in his happy home, all that was most delightful to him on earth! And they were then now—all collected, all united, but with other uninvited guests, sorrow, and blighted love!—whose dark looks chased peace and joy away, and made his heart, as regarded earth's happiness, a dreary desert. He retired early, telling Lord Wentworth that he might breakfast with him in the morning, if he liked it, for that he was not yet equal to joining the family party, so early. It was agreed that he should do so, and they then parted for the night.

CHAPTER XXVII.

" Come, Disappointment, come,
   Though from hope's summit hurled,
   Still, rugged nurse, thou art forgiven !
   For thou severe wert sent—
   To wean me from the world ;
       To turn my eye
       From vanity,
And point to scenes of bliss, that never, never die."
                         HENRY KIRKE WHITE.

" Ahi ! null' altro che pianto al mondo dura."—PETRARCH.

WHEN Lord Wentworth joined Sir Roland the next
morning at his quiet breakfast-table, he was again
struck by the air of deep depression which marked his
whole countenance and manner.   Sir Roland was himself aware of it, and was distressed by his inability to
overcome it, for he would fain have concealed and controlled every regretful feeling ; but his bodily weakness was so great, that happiness itself would have
been almost a burden, and sorrow completely crushed
him.   He inquired most kindly after Lord Wentworth's aunt, and concerning the death of his uncle.

   " He died about six weeks ago," replied his friend,
" in the happiest possible state of mind ; his intellect

perfectly clear, and his faith bright and joyful. It was a scene to strengthen one's weak heart, which is so apt to lose sight of the value of eternity, amidst the hurrying — pressing things of time. But, Ashton," he continued, " you are far from recovered, and there is a look of weakness about you that I do not like."

" If you had seen me when I was at the worst," returned Sir Roland, exerting himself to speak cheerfully, — "judging at least from what my mother tells me—you would wonder to see me here at all, instead of complaining that I do not eat a hundred loaves, and walk a thousand miles a-day."

" Oh ! I don't care about your want of appetite, or lack of bodily strength," said Lord Wentworth, " but I do care (for I like to be one of Job's comforters) about a certain sinking of the whole being which I observe continually oppresses you. It is unlike yourself; unlike the cheerful spirit you used to possess."

" Well, never mind it," replied Sir Roland, " it will all be well in time, I doubt not."

" One's spirits ought to be good here, if any where," continued Lord Wentworth, " with such creatures around, as one has here. It is very well that you warned me that one of them was private property, for I should certainly have entered the lists for the prize ; and I don't know that I shall not do it now, while you are too feeble to break a lance. But really, Ashton, Lady Constance is most lovely, and should be the more so in your eyes just now, that she seems as if she had gone through all your illness with you, and given you back ' sigh for sigh,'— she looks so very pale and ill."

Sir Roland intended, of course, in time to inform

Lord Wentworth of the destruction of all his hopes,
though as he had never known of his actual engagement he did not mean to mention that at all; but now,
he shrank from the idea of speaking on the subject,
and determined if possible to wave it till they were
again at a distance from each other, when he should be
able to inform him concerning it easier he thought by
letter. He therefore answered calmly, " that Lady
Constance did look pale certainly, but that she was
not, he believed, ill in any way."

" I should have been ill, I think," returned Lord
Wentworth, " if you had behaved to me as you did to
her last night, Ashton — that is if I liked you, for you
scarcely either spoke to her or looked at her, and
seemed, in fact, to take much more interest in her
equally beautiful and more blooming sister. Yet I do
not know any thing in the world which would so completely subdue me, as seeing one I loved suffering from
anxiety on my account, even if it robbed her of every
trace of beauty. Yours is not a fickle heart, Ashton,
you cannot have changed ?"

" My heart changed — my heart changed !" exclaimed Sir Roland, his agitation becoming too great
for expression, " no, every thing has changed but
that."

" My dear Ashton," cried Lord Wentworth, pained
and surprised at this burst of affliction in Sir Roland,
and rising in great emotion to go to him, " what has
happened ? Is she not ? — Are you not——"

" Oh ! no, all is over between us," said Sir Roland
more calmly, " and I had meant not to speak of it now,
but your words roused the whole ocean of suffering
within me for the moment. Oh ! it is wrong, very,

very wrong, thus to give way, but it is a new thing
to me as yet, and — you know how I loved her!"

"And she does not return it?" asked Lord Wentworth, "I thought that must have been impossible, or
I would never have spoken as I did."

"No," replied Sir Roland, who, now the subject
had been entered on, thought it would be best to get
over the pain of disclosure at once, and speaking in a
hurried voice, "yet she has not changed, she never
loved me,—and now—she is engaged to—my brother!"

"Great God!" exclaimed Lord Wentworth, clasping his hands before his eyes, "hast Thou permitted
this?"

He started from Sir Roland's side, and walked up
and down the room for some time in the greatest agitation, occasionally bursting forth into such exclamations of grief and dismay, as proved that, in his deep
distress for his friend, he even forgot his presence.

Sir Roland however had calmed his own mind by
prayer, and was soon able to speak again in a more
tranquil manner.

"You must not forget, Scott, who rules," he said.
"Perfect wisdom, perfect power, and perfect love,
cannot do wrong, nor would I take my cause out of
his hand. It would be useless and false perhaps to
say that this trial has not been one of the severest that
mortal heart could have had to endure; but we, remember, have a source of strength, and comfort in the
unwitnessed soul, which passes man's comprehension.
The Almighty has been infinitely good to me!"

"But when did all this happen?" asked Lord
Wentworth, for the moment apparently incapable of
reconciling his mind to what had occurred. "When

last you wrote to me, all seemed going on well; and, though you did not say that any thing was settled, yet you appeared full of happiness."

" I was so then!—full of hope and of happiness. What I state has but just been decided."

" But where then is your brother?"

" My brother? Henry? Here! down-stairs.— Did you not know it?"

" Here!" exclaimed Lord Wentworth, in great surprise, " I thought you told me when you wrote, that he was at sea. Why was he not with us last night?"

" He was in too suffering a condition, poor fellow!" replied Sir Roland.

" Suffering!" said Lord Wentworth, with an involuntary movement of anger in his heart towards Henry, " what has *he* to suffer?"

Sir Roland related to him the accident which had befallen his brother and all his subsequent sufferings, and then lightly touched on the cause of his own illness, as proceeding chiefly from over-fatigue and anxiety of mind.

" And not that alone, I am sure, Ashton," returned Lord Wentworth, when Sir Roland had finished. " A blow like that you have received, was enough to have extinguished both sense and life."

" 'Man is immortal till his work is done,' you know," said Sir Roland smiling, " and doubtless, there is much remaining for me to do. But you act but the part of a poor friend, Scott, in speaking as you do. You should help me to look on, beyond these things— to anticipate the eternal joy that shall be, and not to mind so much the passing griefs that have been—or indeed still are. It is a comfort, however, to feel that there are those still left, who feel for me so strongly," and for a moment a tear swelled into his eye. But brushing it off before it fell, he added; " I find no peace in letting my thoughts dwell on these things, and I endeavour to put them aside as much as the weak, clinging nature of human affections will let me. But to have had such prospects and then to have lost them !—Oh ! the bursting asunder of such ties—and the seeing them transferred to another—is worse than a thousand deaths !"

Lord Wentworth mused for some time in silence; and then said,

" Ashton, do you mind being perfectly open with me as to this affair ? If you do, I will ask no further; but I cannot but suspect that there was more than mere unacknowledged and unreturned affection between you and Lady Constance. You could scarcely have loved her so long and so devotedly, yet never have spoken to her on the subject ?"

" I have told you," replied Sir Roland, his whole frame becoming agitated, " that she never returned my love."

" Well, Ashton, I will ask no more," said Lord Wentworth.

Sir Roland saw that his companion was confident that there had been something more than he was willing to confess between him and Lady Constance, and not liking to appear unkind he at length answered,

" I know that what I say to you, Scott, is as if it were not said, for that you would never breathe a word upon the subject to any living soul, so I will overcome my reluctance to speak upon the subject, and at once tell you that we were engaged."

"And she deserted you!" cried Lord Wentworth, his whole countenance glowing with animated indignation. "I thank God, then, that you never married her!"

"Scott," said Sir Roland, as his eyes flashed equal indignation, "you must not make me repent my confidence in you by allowing yourself again to speak in that way; you must not even think an injurious thought of her—not as you value my friendship!"

"I did not mean to wound your feelings," said Lord Wentworth, gently.

"But it does wound them more than I can say," replied Sir Roland vehemently, "to hear her blamed. She has had no blame—no fault, she has acted like an angel!—I beg your pardon," he added, after a moment's pause, and holding out his hand to his friend, "for my ungrateful anger, for I should have remembered that you were not acquainted with the circumstances; but her clear and lovely image is all that is left me, and I cannot endure that a breath should dim its brightness."

"I was wrong I confess to speak as I did, without knowing all that had occurred," said Lord Wentworth.

"You would not, I well know, have spoken so, had you known what has passed," answered Sir Roland, kindly, "and you shall know it, that you may learn rightly to estimate her, who must ever be dearer to me than my life; and Henry also, whose conduct has been faultless—most noble!"

He then, though with some difficulty, informed Lord Wentworth of the outlines of the affair, and of his own terrible feelings at the first moment of time, and the latter was constrained, though evidently with great reluctance, to acknowledge that what had occurred was most natural.

"Natural in all," he said, "excepting in her preferring any one to you, and that certainly surprises me."

"Wait till you have seen Henry," said Sir Roland, "and then your surprise will cease. He is by far the most fascinating being I ever saw, so I can well understand his being irresistible to her."

"Yours is a blessed spirit, Ashton," observed Lord Wentworth, sighing, "to enable you so to feel and speak of a successful rival. I could never do so, I am sure, were he ten times my brother!"

"I could not at first feel as I do now," replied Sir Roland, "towards either of them; and that was my severest trial, for I seemed bereft of every thing. Now, if I feel much oppressed, I look back for an instant to that hour of unparalleled horror, when my mind — totally without power to control itself — was, as I have told you, a prey to every evil passion, and then I learn to be resigned to the simple bereavements of earth, and to feel them indeed as nothing when compared to the deliverance of my soul from the power of Satan. Oh! what must those men endure, even in this world, who are given up to his bondage. Never till that fearful time could I sufficiently appreciate the mercy which has delivered me from it, and brought me into the 'glorious liberty of the sons of God!' And it is well, perhaps, for once to have experienced what the lashing torment of evil passions is, that I may fully feel from what depths of misery and condemnation Christ has redeemed me. No, Scott, if you have, as I know you have, a true regard for me, you will endeavour to keep far from me all that can excite enmity of heart, either against God or against man."

"Affliction may well be called no misfortune if it brings such peace as you possess," said Lord Wentworth, "and God forbid I should ever again say a word to trouble it; but my heart is still very earthly, and though, as I once told you, and can truly tell you again, I really never did love any one, yet I can imagine what it must be, and that made me feel so much for you."

"It is undoubtedly the strongest of human affections," said Sir Roland, "purposely made so by a God of wisdom and of love; else how should it enable us willingly to forego all other ties for its sake? Yet still we should keep those feelings ever second to the love of God ! and perhaps, though I thought I was, I might not have been doing so. These ties are, indeed, when happy, most delightful !

> 'Yet in the world e'en these abide, and we
> Above the world our calling boast,'

and we must not suffer ourselves to be held down by any earthly bands. I have long professed (to myself at least) to have my chief hopes set on heavenly things, and God sees fit that the grounds of my profession shall be proved — bitterly indeed — but, doubtless, wisely and kindly. He wills that I should see and feel the weakness of my wavering heart, and be humbled. ' It is not a light thing,' as Lady Powerscourt in one of her letters truly says, ' to profess love to a jealous

God.' It belongs to Him alone to look thoroughly into the heart and see what it contains, and, doubtless, He must have seen much that required pruning in mine, or He would never have allowed the knife of excision to have cut so deeply as it has."

"If you have stood in need of this, Ashton, what must most others require?" said Lord Wentworth.

"Scott—for I cannot help calling you by the old accustomed name, especially when I am going to find an old fault with you," said Sir Roland, smiling, "I wish you would not say those things, they force one either to appear presumptuously to take to oneself praise that does not belong to one, or to have the appearance of affected humility, in disclaiming that which one longs to appropriate. But with regard to the general question, I am far from considering afflictions in the light of punishments; witness Job— though I think it is well, when they befall oneself, to look into one's heart and see if there is any thing particularly offensive to God there; and even if we cannot convict ourselves of any known allowed sin, to pray with more earnestness than before, ' Cleanse Thou me from my secret faults.' But I am much inclined to believe that no suffering, either of mind or of outward circumstances, comes, in fact, from the hand of God Himself, for from ' Him cometh every good gift,' not evil ones."

"But we are told that ' sanctified afflictions are amongst chief mercies.'"

"The sanctification is the mercy, not the afflictions," replied Sir Roland, "for we continually witness the miserable sight of unsanctified affliction. There we see Satan's unmitigated work; but I believe that all trouble comes direct from him, as all sin does, and that it is, like the latter, permitted by God — not commanded."

" I confess it never struck me so," replied Lord Wentworth, " and I think Scripture will scarcely bear you out in the idea, for it says ' God does not willingly afflict us ;' and many other passages, which infer that He may afflict, though it may be no pleasure for Him to do so, continually convey the same meaning."

" I grant it," returned Sir Roland ; " but we know that many expressions are made use of in the Bible which seem to make Him the author of that which, in fact, He only tolerates. He is said to have ' hardened people's hearts' against himself, and to have hid the truth from them, lest they should be ' converted and live ;' whereas, we well know, from the whole spirit of Scripture, as well as from direct passages in it, that ' it is not the will of God that any should perish, but that all should come to everlasting life.' In like manner, I am strongly inclined to believe, that when He is said to afflict and chastise, it is only meant that He permits the affliction or the chastisement — sanctifying it or not, according to rules dictated by His own wisdom, but hidden at present from us."

" But what Scripture-warrant have you for such an opinion," asked Lord Wentworth, " for I well know you would not lightly take up an opinion respecting these things on any other authority, yet I cannot recall any thing that could give that idea ? "

" Look at the history of the patriarch I just now mentioned — Job. Does not God say to Satan, ' Behold he is in thy hand, only touch not his life,' restraining his malignant power within that bound ? And does not our Lord, when he had healed the woman who was bound down, say, 'Shall not this woman, whom Satan hath bound, lo! these eighteen years, be loosed?' St. Paul also says, 'Such an one I delivered over to Satan for the correction of the flesh.' And I dare say I could find other passages which do not occur to me at this moment, though it may be considered almost as a sort of summary of this doctrine, where it says, of our great adversary, 'With him dwelleth confusion, and every evil work,' as it expressly affirms that God is not the author of confusion, but of peace."

"It never struck me before in this light, certainly," said Lord Wentworth; "but what you have said deserves consideration, though I confess that it brings rather a frightful feeling to my mind, for it is horrible to imagine oneself the sport of the demon."

"We know that our souls are so, unless God controls his power there," answered Sir Roland; "why should we then start so much at the idea of our bodies and worldly concerns being so too? Remember always, that 'greater is He who is for us, than he who is against us.'"

"Still it is pleasanter to me to think, when I am in pain and sorrow, that I am in God's hands, than it would be to imagine I was in the clutches of one who torments me for his own malicious pleasure."

"It is said that he 'desires to have us, that he may torment us;' and when we are told that he is to torture both body and soul in hell, unless we are amongst Christ's redeemed, and know also that he certainly has power to torture our souls even here, I do not see why we are to suppose that our perishable bodies and worldly concerns are the only things he cannot touch.

The only difference I apprehend is, that here his operations on us are limited — in hell they will- be uncontrolled.   Dread — horrifying thought ! ''

"You certainly seem to have some grounds for
your opinion," observed Lord Wentworth : " but still
it is an uncomfortable one."

"Not so to me," replied Sir Roland, " for I had
much rather view God as the source only of good, than
as the active dispenser of that which troubles and
afflicts the soul.   But still our pleasure or displeasure
at an idea is not what we must go by.   We must examine all things by the light of God's Holy Spirit, and
not allow our wish to be father to our thought.   But I
desire to speak with great diffidence upon this subject,
lest I should be wrong ; I was only speaking of it as
matter of feeling when I said it was pleasanter to me to
to think that no shadow could fall on us from God's
throne, but that the dark form of Satan alone can come
between us and the full light of His countenance.   I
think it is vain also, and, therefore, erroneous, to call
pain and sorrow, as viewed by themselves — good ; they
are manifest, tangible evils, and as we are told that
eternal suffering is carefully to be avoided, and eternal
happiness carefully to be sought, so I think we are
allowed to avoid earthly sufferings, and to seek earthly
happiness in their measure, though of course that is
small, compared with the importance and duration of
eternity."

"But do you think this view is likely to be of use
to mankind ? " asked Lord Wentworth.

"If it is truth, we must receive it without questioning, Scott ; but I think it is likely to be of exceeding
use, for it helps us to realise the dread nature of Satan's

dominion, and give some faint idea of what we may expect at his hands, when he obtains full power over us. If, when in pain of body, or distress of mind, we reflected, that ' This is a sample of the terrible things which await us hereafter in our enemy's fell kingdom,' it would surely, speaking according to common reasoning, make us careful to be delivered from his power. And on the other hand, if every pleasure, every sweet affection, every joyful feeling, were felt as foretastes of those joys which are above—those 'pleasures which are at God's right hand for evermore,' surely our love would be increased towards Him who has prepared 'such great things for those that love Him,' and our zeal would be animated by the blessed prospect set before us, while we should desire more earnestly than ever to obtain a place by the fountain-head of that ' river of life which proceeds from the throne of God.'"

" You make out a good case, certainly," said Lord Wentworth, "and I will examine the Scriptures more carefully as regards it, than I have done hitherto; indeed I never at all viewed it in this light before, and I think you never held this opinion formerly either; at least I never remember your mentioning it."

" No, I did not always think of these things according to this view; but by the continual study of the word of God, and consideration of His ways, fresh views and beauties and delights steal upon the mind."

" But I have said," replied Lord Wentworth, smiling, "that as yet this thought is not one of delight to me, for I had rather feel that all—even suffering—came from a compassionate Father's hand, than from the capricious power of a ruthless enemy.

I like to be able in all times of trouble or sorrow to
say with your old favourite, Keble,

> ' O Lord, my God! do Thou thy holy will—
>   I will lie still—
>   I will not stir, lest I forsake thine arm,
>   And break the charm,
>   Which lulls me, clinging to my Father's breast,
>   In perfect rest.'"

" And can you suppose," replied Sir Roland, "that
I would receive any thing which broke down that feeling? Who has need of it as I have? But my view
of the case does not in the least alter or weaken our
perfect trust in God. The only difference is, that you
would pray to Him for resignation under the sufferings
which He *sends*, I for resignation under those which He
permits; you would pray for deliverance from the weight
of His hand, I from the permitted weight of Satan's;
we both equally go to God for the mercy! All I
mean is, that it is pleasanter to me to feel that when
He is forced to allow me to be chastised for my good,
He delivers me over for that purpose to one whose
ways I may have been too ready to choose, rather
than take the scourge into His own gracious hand.
But, as I said before, it is truth, not pleasure, we must
seek in the Holy Scriptures, yet I would speak with
diffidence on this, and on every subject which is not revealed beyond the power of doubt."

" I feel inclined to agree with you in part," said
Lord Wentworth; " and yet it is strange—if this idea
is a true one—that it should not have been more generally pressed upon men's attention."

" We know that for years and years the most im-

portant truths were nearly lost sight of, even in our
own favoured church and country," replied Sir Roland.
" From the time of Charles II.—when so many pious
and excellent men were forced from the ministry till
almost within our own memory, the leading truths of
salvation were scarcely remembered, and a cold Ar-
minianism sent the whole church, with some few bright
exceptions, into the sleep of spiritual death; till your
friends—as poor Roberts used to call them—the Dissenters, roused up the dying embers of discipline and of
truth too. The Second Advent—the Millenium—and
many other delightful views, were regarded as wild
enthusiasm, or were wholly unknown; therefore, this
opinion which I cannot but think, from the passages I
have quoted, was taught in the Scriptures, may have
been lost amongst them. But I may be wrong about
it altogether. One thing certainly I think is clear
(to argue against myself), which is, that great judgments, and death for outrageous sins, are frequently
spoken of in the Scriptures as God's express work.
' I, even *I*, do bring a flood of waters on the earth,'
He says to Noah. ' *I* can do nothing till thou art come
thither,' He says to Lot, when he was escaping to
Zoar. And to Samuel respecting the death of Eli's two
sons, he says, ' Behold *I* will do a thing,' &c. Yet that
does not altogether militate against what I was saying,
for the act of death seems ever to be spoken of as
God's especial work; but the sting of death—sin—is
certainly Satan's, and suffering too—the fruit of sin—
I believe, as I tell you, his also. Without them death
would be only as Milton says,

" A gentle wafting to eternal life !"

However it is in vain to attempt perfectly to understand the whole of any—the smallest portion of God's dealings with us; yet we can at least say, ' The Lord reigneth, let the earth rejoice!' One thing greatly comforts me, which is, that the more any dispensation crosses my inclination, the more do I feel the conviction pressed upon me of the absolute necessity for it. It were enough for a God of Love, who is ' gentle as a nurse amongst her children,' to do a thing merely to please his creatures; but when He suffers pain and agony to reach us—then it must indeed be that we could not do without it."

" Well, Ashton, I can scarcely pity you for all your sorrows, for you seem so full of consolation," said Lord Wentworth.

" Oh! yes, I am so," replied Sir Roland, though the allusion to himself brought back pangs of regret, which the high and holy subjects of which he had been speaking had for a time erased from his heart. " Soon I doubt not," he added, " sorrow and I shall part." Yet he leant his head down on his arm with a sigh so deep—as proved that that parting had still to come.

Lord Wentworth observed his changed manner, and regretted having recalled his thoughts from themes so full of consolation, to the sorrows of his own breast; he was silent for a short time, but then with sudden recollection said,

" I have by the by, Ashton, a message to deliver to you, which will please you much, though sadness will be mixed with the feeling."

" A message to me! From whom?" said Sir

Roland, looking up with that listless half-interest which
seems to say, " What can any thing avail me ?"

" You remember—Miss Harcourt, Isabella Harcourt I mean."

" Remember her, oh ! yes," said Sir Roland, again
dropping his head, for he felt his colour rise.

" You knew, did you not," continued Lord
Wentworth in a softened tone, " that she died last year
at ———— ?"

" Yes," replied Sir Roland.

" About a fortnight before her death, I returned
there," continued Lord Wentworth, " and she expressed a wish to see me, chiefly I believe because she
knew I was a friend of yours. It seemed that what
you had said at different times on religious subjects
had awakened her mind to think about them, and that
she, and a young brother also whom she lost, had both
been greatly comforted and sustained, by the bright
hopes of eternity which you had been the means of
imparting to them; and she begged me, whenever I
saw you, to tell you of the comfort your words had
been, in order, she said, poor girl ! that you might be
encouraged to speak for God at all times—and every
where:—I promised I would bear her message to you,
and I am glad to do so, for I am sure you will rejoice
at the thought of having been the means of saving two
such young spirits from destruction."

" I do indeed rejoice," said Sir Roland; yet the
remembrance of Isabella Harcourt was most painful to
him, and his heart sunk at the thought of her sorrows,
though he knew they were now all hushed in heaven.

" Ah !" he said, " how truly may it be said that,

' Love among mortals is but an endless sigh, heaven is its only real home!' "

"I do not think I ever felt any thing in my life so much, as I did seeing that dying girl," said Lord Wentworth; "her hectic colour made her look so beautiful, and it was so touching and delightful to see her — so young — supported by such bright hopes, though leaving all earth's joys. I was so surprised too at her sentiments, for I fancied her so very different;— and she upbraided me, most justly, for having known the truth myself, yet never having spoken of it to her. But, she said, you had been more faithful, and her gratitude to you seemed unbounded. Why did you never tell me that you thought her feelings were changed?"

"We never had much conversation together," replied Sir Roland, still leaning his head on the table, and avoiding a direct answer to Lord Wentworth's question.

"But you did not think that she had become more spiritual than before?"

"I really never talked much with her," answered Sir Roland, rather annoyed, "but I thought she seemed to like listening to religious conversation between others."

Lord Wentworth said no more. A suspicion of the truth darted through his mind, and was quickly confirmed by his recollection of Isabella's embarrassment while speaking of Sir Roland, and also of the sorrow which had occasionally overcome her. He knew his friend too well, however, to mention such a subject to him, but his heart was filled with double pity

for the young and lovely creature, for whom he had
before felt so much interest.

" How strange," he said to himself, " that two
beings, each so formed to be loved and admired, should
both have loved in vain !"   His thoughts raised themselves to Him—the source of love—with the delightful
conviction, that none could love *there* in vain ; and that
the craving heart finds there alone, that which can
never disappoint.

CHAPTER XXVIII.

"There are sufferings, sufferings to the death, which are not
bitter, which possess their own great, their marvellous enjoyment."
F. BREMER.

"And who can stay the soaring might
Of spirits weaned from earthly joys?"—KEBLE.

"He has not suffered you to walk smoothly down the stream of
time; but by large and rough billows has dashed you on the promises."—*Lady Ravenscourt's Letters.*

IT has often been said that the lot of human beings
is more equal in point of happiness than would at first
appear to the mere outward observers, and perhaps as
a general rule it is true. Those who are most capable
of enjoying the happiness of life, are usually also most
alive to its griefs; while the apathetic, if they miss the
sorrows of the more sensitive, lose their raptures too.
The apparently tranquil lot of some is vexed by a
thousand small, joy-cankering cares, which effectually
eat out the heart of enjoyment, though they leave the
outward form untouched; while others, who seem overwhelmed with affliction, find that one great trial which,
like Aaron's rod, swallows up all the rest, — making
them too light to be felt, is in fact easier to bear than
the slighter sorrows of happier days.

No one looking at the inmates of Llanaven, at the time of which we are now speaking, would probably have hesitated in pronouncing Henry Ashton far happier than his brother. Though still suffering, yet the worst of even his bodily pain was over, and he had the delightful hope of recovering to the possession of all he most coveted on earth. His mind was relieved from the trying grief which had so long oppressed it, and his loving heart was surrounded by friends, all anxious to ease his sufferings, and promote his happiness. The being in whom all his earthly hopes centred was his own, and the feelings which had for months been torture unto him were turned into sources of the most delightful happiness. His heart, too, was at peace with God, for he could look up to him as a reconciled Father, and feel, that though through weakness he had often failed, yet that he had been enabled in all his great and — humanly speaking — unmerited — trial, to keep an honourable and upright course.

But Sir Roland seemed overwhelmed with trouble. She, whom he had loved from boyhood, and of late years, with all the intensity, which the human heart could feel, was torn from him for ever! And at such a moment too!—during the first joy of re-union after long absence, when all his feelings roused to the highest pitch of excited happiness, were almost dizzy with their own excess;—when his long-tried heart seemed at last to have met with the full return of its love, in the joyful greeting of that voice, which reached to the very depths of his soul!—then the blow fell! Then it was that he found the heart he so much coveted was not only not his own, but irrevocably given to another! Weakness and suffering of body too, lent their aid to depress and crush his spirits, and the inability of employing his time as he was wont to do—for he could not leave the house, and his head was not sufficiently recovered to allow of his reading—threw the whole unrelieved weight of anguish upon his mind. Until Lord Wentworth's arrival, he had no one to whom he could in the least unbosom himself, for though all those around him loved him with the truest hearts, yet how could he speak to them of his sufferings? How could he remind his mother that what made Henry happy was the source of undying pain to him? How tell Henry himself that he had destroyed his happiness? Or how—worst of all—trouble the peace of her for whom he had sacrificed his own? No; all the depths of his terrible heart-agony had been hidden as far as his utmost exertions could enable him to do so, from every eye, and he endeavoured in every way to make his affliction appear as light as possible. Every thing therefore seemed to combine to make him miserable, and yet when alone, and able to raise his soul to God, he experienced such peace, such joy, such elevating communion with Heaven as more, much more than compensated for all that earth could take away. His thoughts could dwell with true unaltered affection on every being around him, and the delightful sensation which proceeds from the consciousness of bestowing happiness, sweetened every tie of his life. That twice-blessed mercy, which is the heart's best inmate, shed a " peace supreme" throughout his whole being, which was never lost; while with Henry on the contrary the sense of his own happiness was continually darkened by the reflection that he had destroyed his brother's, and made him, whom he loved as himself, a soli-

tary and stricken being. Thus did an equal-handed
Providence, in mercy, pour its own unutterable consolations into the wounded breast, lest it should sink dismayed with its suffering, while it troubled the joy of
the happy heart, teaching it, amid all its blessedness,
that earthly bliss is not unsullied, and that the fulness
even of earthly affections cannot satisfy an immortal
spirit.

When Sir Roland went down-stairs, he proposed to
Lord Wentworth to introduce him to his brother. The
latter consented, but with a coldness and reluctance of
manner which shewed evidently that he felt no inclination to be acquainted with him; and though Sir
Roland was vexed for Henry's sake, yet he could not
but appreciate the devoted attachment which made his
friend feel so strongly in his cause. He took no notice however of what he observed, for he knew that no
one could see Henry and not like him, and so he left
the matter to take its natural course.

And he was right; for Lord Wentworth had not
been with Henry five minutes, before he felt all his
enmity against him vanish away, and after half-an-
hour's conversation alone with him—for Sir Roland
had left the room—he learnt almost to forgive Lady
Constance for her choice. Still his heart remained
firm to its old allegiance; though he was forced to confess to himself, that it would be a most difficult task to
decide between two brothers, who were each so delightful in their peculiar ways. He was particularly
pleased at Henry's warm energetic manner of speaking
of Sir Roland, and when the latter re-entered the room,
he observed that he watched his countenance with the

most earnest anxiety. Still it was evident that it was an effort to both of them to be together, for the very affection which animated them, made them too full of each other to be at ease. Sir Roland's endeavour was to appear cheerful, while Henry's was to subdue his own spirits out of regard for his brother; though an involuntary sadness would often cloud his countenance as his eye dwelt upon that brother's altered form.

When Sir Roland and Lord Wentworth left Henry's room, the former said,

" I will return up-stairs, but you should go into the drawing-room and make further acquaintance with its inmates: and mind you make yourself very agreeable, as my credit, as far as taste is concerned you know, is at stake. I have been there already."

Lord Wentworth accordingly went into the drawing-room and did make himself very agreeable. His manners were so easy and unconstrained, and his temper so cheerful, that he was always a favourite, and in a very short time he had given Lady Constance a lesson in drawing and Lady Florence one in singing, finding much fault; and declaring that he must take them regularly in hand, to save them from being utterly ruined as regarded the fine arts. His heart though was far from being really happy, for the thought of Sir Roland haunted him, and the more he saw of Lady Constance, the more he felt how dreadful a blow it must be to him to lose her. As she sat by him with her beautifully earnest countenance, and sweet smile, he looked at her with painful interest, and could scarcely express the inclination he felt to ask her how she could desert Sir Roland, and consign one so worthy of her love to such extreme unhappiness. Feeling anxious however not to betray his knowledge of the painful circumstances which had occurred, he continued his lively conversation, till having set each of his young companions a whole week's work in painting, which he insisted should be ready for his inspection in an hour, he returned to Sir Roland, whose sufferings he was anxious in any way to alleviate, for he was convinced, notwithstanding his perfect resignation, that they must be very great.

" You will soon be well enough, I trust, to go out again, Ashton ?" he said, "and then when I have freed myself from Chancery Lane, and Lincoln's Inn, and Doctors' Commons, &c. &c., will you come abroad with me ? It would be such a pleasure to me, and we have still so much to see."

"I should be but a poor companion just now," replied Sir Roland; "besides which, I have too much to do here to be able to go away again so soon; and you too will find that you have plenty of occupation on your hands. No, my dear Wentworth," he added, sighing heavily, "I feel your kindness deeply, and your regard is most pleasant to me; but I always find it best to meet, and not turn my face from an enemy. God is with me every where, and there is something in the strenuous effort to overcome self and the firm determination to conquer—which suits my mind better than retreat or flight. It might have been well for my poor brother to leave his home under his great trial, even if his profession had not called him away, because with him, a prolonged stay, was prolonged temptation, and he had no tie of duty which bound him here. But I am in no temptation, though God knows, in trial

enough. My lot is cast—my fate decided; I have but
to take up my cross in the strength of God, and to go
on my way without turning to the right or to the left.
My station is here; and the sooner I learn to endure
the trials of it, the better it will be. Were I weakly
to go away now, I should only have to renew my grief
when I returned, and perhaps not have so much support from above, as I have at present."

"You are the best judge, certainly," said Lord
Wentworth, "but besides the great pleasure it would
be to me, I should have thought it might have relieved
your spirits."

"I do not say that it might not do that to a certain degree, and for a time," replied Sir Roland, "and
I would not, I am sure, ungraciously reject any allevia-
tion of my heavy sorrow, which God would allow me;
but I do not feel that I should be right to leave home
again so soon. There are many things which have
gone wrong already owing to my absence; and many
new things which require being done. I am conscious
that in many ways I formerly neglected things in
which I ought to have engaged actively, because I was
happier staying at home with—Constance; but I must
do so now no longer. I ought to have done a thousand
times more good in my day than I have done, for it is
but a poor return for favours, to neglect the work of
the bestower of them; and I think God permits affliction often to fall upon us in order to wean us from self,
and to make us wider dispensers of his bounty. In
one thing especially, I think, I was wrong formerly,
and that is in refusing to go into parliament; but
when they wanted me last year to stand for ——, I
could not endure the idea of it, and tried to quiet my

mind by telling myself it was a situation of great
temptation, and that it was wisest and best to keep out
of the way of it. But I fear it was the charm of my
home, and not the fear of evil, which was the prevail-
ing argument in my mind. They have sent to me
again to stand at the next election, and I shall now
accept the invitation, for I think I ought to do so."

"Why do you think it so much of a duty," asked
Lord Wentworth; "there are plenty ready to stand at
all times?"

"It is not the standing, or the sitting which is the
duty," answered Sir Roland, "but the doing the best
we can for our country; and I think that when we
continually pray for the high court of parliament
—that all things may be ' ordered and settled by their
endeavours, upon the best and surest foundations—
that peace and happiness, truth and justice, religion
and piety, may be established among us'—we are un-
warrantable in not using our utmost endeavours to
promote what we pretend to ask God for. There may
be higher duties which prevent a person entering into
parliament, but I am speaking of merely preferring
one's own peace and quiet to doing so, which was
what I certainly did."

"But would not every member of parliament tell
you that the only object of his life was 'to immolate himself on the altars of his beloved country?' would he not
say that he outraged every natural feeling by suffering
himself reluctantly to be dragged from the bosom of
his family? that his 'retirement from private life,' was
most painful? and that all worldly advantages, all
hopes of advancement or emolument, were as an abomination to him? that he was ready to thrust his hand

in the flames like a Scævola—to leap into the gulf like
a Curtius—to stand alone on the bridge which separates us from destruction like Cocles!—in short,
modestly speaking, to unite in his own person all the
glorious deeds and qualities of the heroes of antiquity!
looking for repayment solely to a sinking fund of
national gratitude to be established—' en tems et
lieu?'"

"On the hustings they tell us something of that
kind, certainly," said Sir Roland, laughing, "but elec-
tions have been too frequent of late years for the most
amiable simplicity to remain among the number
of believers in such professions. No—we know
perfectly that though there are some who really do
seek the good of their country, yet that many members, indifferent as to the measures passed—excepting
as party questions—yet like belonging to the 'House,'
as the 'best club in London,' and seek in it merely
the advancement of their own prospects and interests.
The utmost efforts of pseudo charity cannot make one
view the thing differently. Now I am, by the great
bounty of Providence, in a situation not to require
any thing, and I confess the going into parliament
would be to me a very great sacrifice (not that I
should say so if I agreed to stand, but I say so to you
naturally, because it is the truth). What personal
pleasure on earth can it be to me, to be forced to leave
the country at the time when it is most charming—to
go for hours to hear people abuse each other in all
manner of ways, and if called to account for saying so,
deny having done it though the whole house has just
heard them—to hear them attribute all manner of evil
designs to those who oppose them, merely because they

do oppose them—and worst of all—and oh! even here at a distance, it makes my very blood boil with indignation—having come into parliament with words of liberality and humanity on their lips—by their acts and votes seal the misery of thousands—thousands too of the most guiltless, and most helpless of our fellow-creatures—children, who because their natural protectors are too poor to help them, or too vicious (which I fear is often the case) to forego willingly the gains which they derive from the destruction of their children's bodies and souls—are to be left without protection by the laws of their country; while those who advocate their cause are to be laughed at, as sentimental and visionary! 'When the poor crieth, I will up, saith the Lord,' and when I think of those things I feel that His judgments must be near 'even at the door.' I have never ceased to reproach myself since I saw the speech and vote which —— gave the last time on this subject, when I remember that, but for my selfish indolence, he never would have been in his place so to have spoken and voted. And yet he called himself a Liberal (or I should have opposed him, of course by my interest, even if not personally—being one myself), and indeed, his speech on the hustings was an outpouring of eloquence about 'suffering humanity,' —the 'best interests of society,' and so forth."

" One voice would have done very little against such a majority," observed Lord Wentworth.

" One voice is all that God gives to one man," replied Sir Roland; "therefore all he is answerable for. God would have spared the cities of the plain had he found ten righteous men in them, and that number, remember, must have been formed of units. I do not,

however, expect, that the torrent of any evil will be
stemmed now, for I fully believe that the judgments
of the Lord are abroad upon the land, and that he is
hastening the day of His coming, before which we know
that crying sins, and great 'tribulations' must come;
but still we are not to be idle at our posts; so if the
election does not come on before I am able to attend to
the duties it will bring upon me, I shall stand, and tell
the cause of my doing so. If God himself prevents my
coming forward by this illness, or otherwise, then I
shall feel comfortable in the reflection that,

> 'They also serve who stand and wait.'

But they do not 'serve' who 'stand and wait' when
they should be 'running in the day of God's commandments.'   That is a flattering unction I have not unfrequently heard indolent neglectors of their duties lay to
their souls, but it is a fearful error."

"Well, then, you and I must strengthen each
other," said Lord Wentworth, "for the battle is pretty
well divided between the two Houses now, and we of
the aristocracy," he added, laughing, and assuming a
pompous tone, "are grown as pugnacious as you of the
lower House. I shall read your speeches the day before 'you rise on the spur of the occasion'— take all
the good out of them — wreath them round with
'flowers of eloquence' all my own, and 'perfectly elec-
trify the House.' This will do very well for two or
three nights, by which time it will be discovered that
my beautiful vase was 'once Toby Philpot,' and then I
shall be extinguished for ever. But really, Ashton, I
wish you would not talk of your conscience, for it
rouses the dormant embers of mine, and I must, I fear,

follow its dictates, and return to town. My absence is, I know, a source of great inconvenience just now to many, and having saved myself from a brain fever by coming down here to see about you in yours, I must now go back. But I may consider myself as '*toujours prié*,' may I not? I mean to make myself always kindly welcome, as people say, and uncommonly agreeable."

"You will be both at all times to me," said Sir Roland; "and it does me good to converse on other subjects besides those which in general too much engross my mind. But must you go directly?"

"I think I ought — to-morrow, and then I shall sooner be able to return. I may come when I can, without waiting to send notice, may I not?"

"By all means, and the sooner the better."

Lord Wentworth departed the next day for London, and Sir Roland then, determining to overcome his own feelings in every way, proposed that they should all go, after Lady Ashton's dinner, into Henry's room, as the latter was still suffering too much to bear being removed. He could not do so while Lord Wentworth was there, for he knew that his sensitive mind would have been on the rack for him, and that his own embarrassment at being for the first time with Henry and Lady Constance together, would have been greatly increased by feeling that his eye was on him. His mother he could perfectly trust, for though she was never forward in suspecting any thing, yet when once acquainted with a circumstance, she always exhibited the most perfect 'tact' in avoiding every thing that could possibly distress the feelings of those around her.

Anxious to betray as little disturbance of manner as possible, Sir Roland went into his brother's room while Lady Ashton and her young companions were still at their dinner, and after talking to him for a little while, he said that he had begged his mother to spend the early part of the evening there, for that it was hard, he thought, that he should be left alone. He did not wait for Henry to answer, but proceeded immediately to talk on other subjects, so as to give him time to recover from the nervous excitement into which his words had thrown him. Conversation, however, flagged between them, and Sir Roland took up a pencil, glad of any employment which might serve to hide the trouble which he was conscious that he could not wholly banish from his countenance. The strong impulse of both the brothers, when at length they heard the dinner-party approach the door, was to start up and leave the room, but Sir Roland remained immovable, sketching some trifle that lay on the table before him, and Henry, though he half rose up, yet, controlling himself, rested back again on the sofa. It was of course a most embarrassing time for all concerned, and no one could talk ; even Lady Florence found her observations so ill seconded that she became silent as the rest.

"Shall we not have some music?" at length said Sir Roland, anxious to relieve the general painful embarrassment. "Florence, as there is no pianoforte in this room, would you mind going into the drawing-room a little while? with the door open, we should hear you delightfully."

"It is not lighted," she replied, "and alone, with one candle in that great room, I should imagine all

sorts of things were dancing about me.   If Constance
will come with me, I will go, but I cannot possibly do
so by myself."

"You ridiculous child!" said Lady Ashton, good-
humouredly.   "However you shall have two candles,
or a dozen if you like it."

"Two and Constance will do very well," said Lady
Florence, and getting up, she tried playfully to make
her sister rise from her chair.

"Perhaps you can persuade your sister to sing with
you," said Sir Roland; for he felt a sort of desperate
determination to endure every thing, though he knew
that at that moment, of all earthly things, perhaps hearing Lady Constance's voice would be the most trying
to him.   Yet he thought it must be done, and the sooner
the better.

Lady Constance's eyes turned for an instant to
Henry, towards whom she had not glanced before, but
he was looking another way, and Lady Ashton, thinking she had better not sing just then, said,—

"No, no, Florence, do not be such a little coward;
go and sing by yourself."

Lady Florence took up a candle, but Sir Roland,
knowing that she was very timid, said,—

"No, dear Flory, never mind to-night.   You shall
not go amongst the fairies alone to please me."

He would have offered to go with her, but felt that
at that moment he could not have stood.

"No," said Lady Florence, gaily, taking up another
candle, "thus armed, I will venture in."

"Well, I will go with you, then," said Lady Ashton,
"and Constance, too," she added the next moment,

remembering that the latter would not at all like being left behind alone; "so you will be quite safe."

"Sing a trio, will you?" said Sir Roland.

They accordingly selected one, and their voices, sounding from a distance, had a peculiar and beautiful effect.

It was long since either Sir Roland or Henry had heard Lady Constance sing, and they were both greatly affected by it, though naturally in different ways. Henry was at first much agitated, but gradually all pain fading away, a happiness inexplicable took possession of his whole being. Sir Roland, on the contrary, bore the first few notes unmoved, but as the music, that "sea of painful delight," swelled louder and fuller on his ear, his mind seemed quite to fail under it; his sight became dizzy, and a noise as of rushing waters sounded through his brain. He had taxed his strength too greatly, and nature for a moment gave way as his head sunk on the table. Consciousness, however, did not quite leave him, and after a few minutes, making a great exertion, he raised himself again; and recollecting where he was, he looked in alarm at Henry, fearful that he might have observed his temporary faintness. But Henry, lost in his own happiness, was lying with his hand shading his eyes, in perfect enjoyment; the smile that rested on his lips proving how blissful were his feelings. Sir Roland looked at his happy countenance for a moment with mingled emotions, till at length the blessed thought, "This is my work," swallowed up all painful feeling; his mind became tranquillised, and he felt most thankful that his brother had not observed an emotion which would have given him so much uneasiness.

The next day Mr. L——, the solicitor, arrived from London, and Sir Roland was engaged with him for a length of time, which much fatigued him; but nevertheless, when he had set out again on his return—for he was too hurried to accept Sir Roland's invitation to stay—and the latter joined the party in the evening, his spirits were far better than they had been before. The sense of the generous sacrifices he had determined to make in order to contribute to his brother's and Lady Constance's happiness, filled his heart with delightful sensations; and when once again he heard the latter singing the well-remembered music which had so often enchanted him in former happy times, he was thankful to be enabled to endure it better than he had done the night before, and to feel that some of the bitterness of his trial was softened.

The month of February brought with it fine, mild weather, and Sir Roland was glad to be able again to get out in the open air. He went about and visited his poor tenants, and found much that wanted doing and improving.

The yacht which he had ordered for Henry had been for some time lying in the little harbour at Carncombe, but the weather had been hitherto too severe for it to be used; now the temperature was so mild that it was thought the air would be of use to the invalid, and he was therefore carried on board, where he greatly enjoyed the fresh breezes, and the swelling motion of the element he so much delighted in. At times, indeed, a bitter feeling of regret shot across him at the thought, that he should never now be able to attain that which used to be the highest object of his ambi-

tion, namely, the command of one of those magnificent
ships, whose

> " ——— march is o'er the mountain waves,
>   Whose home is on the deep."

But when the thought of all that home on shore now
offered him, rose before his mind, sorrow vanished
away, and he felt that it would be misery to be forced
to leave it.

Lady Constance and her sister almost always sailed
with him, and Lady Ashton also frequently joined
their parties, but Sir Roland seemed too full of business to have time to accompany them. He found
much to do at Llanaven, but still more he said at Tregaron, his other residence ; and he was perpetually driving over to the latter, and spending the greatest part of
the day there, often carrying his mother with him.

His constant activity prevented his mind from prey-
ing upon itself, and greatly promoted the restoration of
his health ; Henry also became so invigorated by the
sea air, that he was soon able, though still requiring
assistance, to walk instead of being carried to the shore.
Lord Wentworth returned to them after a short time,
and happiness seemed once more to shed its light on
Llanaven. One solitary heart, indeed, still bled, still
felt its desolation ; but amid the energetic exercise of
benevolence and piety, and in self-denying exertion for
others, the sorrows of that deeply tried heart were often
soothed, and peace and joy at moments again took their
accustomed places there.

> " So is it still : to holy tears,
>   In lonely hours Christ risen appears :
>   In social hours, who Christ would see,
>   Must turn all tasks to charity."

CHAPTER XXIX.

" Can thy generous nature,
While thus it sheds felicity around it,
Remain itself unbless'd ?"—TALFOURD.

" So his life hath flow'd,
From its mysterious urn a sacred stream,
In whose calm depth the beautiful and pure
Alone are mirror'd ; which, though shapes of ill
May hover round its surface, glides in light,
And takes no shadow from them."—TALFOURD.

THE settlements went on rapidly, and Sir Roland
was very anxious that the marriage should take place
as soon as possible. Henry was greatly recovered,
though it would be long, the surgeon said, before he
regained his former vigour and activity. Still he was
perfectly able to walk, and the motion of a carriage no
longer distressed him, and therefore there was no
reason why he should not be able to travel all over the
world if he wished it with Lady Constance. Sir Roland therefore begged Lady Ashton to get the day
fixed as soon as it was convenient, and to let him know
when the time was settled. She did so, and the first
week of the next month—the changeful April month—
was fixed upon. Sir Roland still continued his long
drives over to Tregaron, generally accompanied either
by his mother, or Lord Wentworth. Lady Florence
often petitioned to be allowed to go there also, but was

continually put off, first with one excuse, then with another.

At length Sir Roland said to her one morning at breakfast,

"Well, Florence, you shall have your wish to-day of going to Tregaron, on condition that you persuade all your companions to go too."

This was quickly arranged. It was a lovely day without a breath of wind, and there was a general petition for the barouche, which was accordingly ordered, and at eleven o'clock it drove up to the door. Lady Ashton with the two sisters and Henry, were to go inside, and Lord Wentworth, who piqued himself, he said, "on a lineal descent from Ericthonius by the mother's side," was to drive the four beautiful greys, with Sir Roland by him on the box. As Henry handed Lady Constance in, he looked for a moment at his brother's plain but handsome equipage, which, with its outriders, &c., was all in the very best taste, and a sigh involuntarily arose at thinking how little he should have to offer, in comparison of the wealth of which his unfortunate love had deprived her. But she, reading his thoughts in the sudden cloud which flitted over his speaking countenance, said a few words as she gave him her hand which more than eased his heart— filling him with gratitude and joy.

The drive was delightful to all, even to Sir Roland, for his heart swelled with kindlier emotions as he forgot himself in the happiness he was about to confer on others. When they entered the park-gates at Tregaron, he desired Lord Wentworth to stop, and dismounting from the box, he said rather hurriedly to those in the carriage,—

"I am going to speak to some workmen I see out

there, and you my dear mother or Wentworth will shew all the improvements that have been made—and explain—you know—all about it."

He hurried off, but Lady Ashton could not utter a word ; her heart was so full that the slightest attempt at speech would have drowned her in tears, neither could Lord Wentworth at that time explain what Sir Roland wished said, but as he drove along, he continually made them observe new things that had been done, new views that had been opened, &c., &c., till at length coming in sight of the house which stood beautifully on some rising ground, backed by fine woods with a lake in front, and which had lately been done up in the handsomest manner, turning to the party in the carriage, he silently pointed to it with his whip, for at that moment he too seemed to have lost the power of speaking. His heart overflowed with that painful pleasure which generous actions so often produce—actions which are more touching to the mind, than scenes of extremest woe.

When all the party had dismounted, Lord Wentworth led the way into the drawing-room. It had been entirely new furnished, and was most beautiful. Lady Florence was delighted, and wondered naturally, why a place at which they so seldom resided should have had so much pains bestowed upon it, and have been improved and adorned too in such haste; for when last she was there with her sister and Lady Ashton, all was quietly remaining as she had ever remembered it, and not a workman was to be seen. She was the only one who could make any remarks on the subject, for misgivings began to steal across the minds of Lady Constance and Henry as to the object of all this sudden improvement. It could not escape the observation of the most careless amongst them that every thing in the room was done exactly in accordance with Lady Constance's taste. There was the favourite colour—pale silvery green—on the walls, arranged in the panelling she so much admired. The windows were cut down to the ground, which had not been so before—the green silk, and soft white curtains, all such as she would have chosen! And well they might be so! for they had all been ordered and arranged with devoted care expressly to please her, by one who had studied her tastes too long, and with two much interest, to be mistaken in them.

Lady Constance sat down on one of the sofas, for a violent trembling seized her, as her sister, suspecting nothing, continued to make remarks on the various new objects which struck her eye. Lord Wentworth, who joined a great degree of nervousness to the most feeling and generous heart, finding it totally in vain to attempt to command his voice, went to the window, and writing in pencil on the back of a letter, the words:—" This is all for you," put it into Henry Ashton's hand. Henry looked at it for a few moments, then giving it to Lady Constance, hastily left the room. Lady Constance on reading it burst into tears, and Lady Ashton, who had vainly endeavoured to repress hers, could only leave her to her natural emotion. Lord Wentworth meanwhile escaped unobserved, and went in search of Henry, whom he found pacing one of the walks in a state of the greatest agitation.

" Well," he said gaily, not appearing to notice the other's emotion, " do you not like the improvements here? I expect most of the credit of them to be given to me, for I have been the 'arbiter elegantiarum;' all the sublime and beautiful has emanated from me. But now," he added more quietly, "do not say much to your brother about it; merely say——. However I need not dictate to you; your own kind feelings will tell you what to say, and do."

"Oh! no," said Henry, "I feel so overwhelmed that I know not what to think or say. I knew that he would help us, but to let us live here, is what I never dreamed of, and to prepare it all so thoughtfully—so beautifully!"

"He does not 'let you live here,'" said Lord Wentworth, smiling, "he gives this place to you, and with it all the property belonging to this part of his estate, which amounts, I believe, to between eight and nine thousand a-year."

Henry covered his face with his hands, and threw himself down on a seat which was near.

"Come, come," said Lord Wentworth, "you—a sailor—must not give way in this manner. You have borne pain enough, you must learn to bear pleasure now."

"Oh! it is not pleasure," exclaimed Henry, "it is not pleasure! I could have borne anger—unkindness —any thing but this. Oh! Lord Wentworth, if you did but know all you would feel for me."

"I do know all, I do feel for you," replied Lord Wentworth, laying his hand kindly on Henry Ashton's shoulder, "and I can fully understand that what you experience at this moment is suffering—not pleasure. But you must remember also the feelings of him—who has not I fully believe, his equal upon earth—and try

to overcome your own emotion. Say nothing to him
further than to give him to understand that you accept
what he has done."

"I cannot accept it," interrupted Henry, still unable to recover himself; "impossible! I should be
miserable."

"Mr. Ashton," said Lord Wentworth, gravely,
"you must have more command over yourself, and
learn to look at these things calmly. I know you
could not have expected your brother to have done so
much for you—no one could; but you must remember that his pleasure now is in your happiness; his fortune is very large, and his heart very liberal, and you
will only pain him by expostulations, which I know
will prove useless."

"Lord Wentworth, it is impossible that I can accept gifts like these," repeated Henry.

"I do not see that at all," said Lord Wentworth,
"I would not hurt your feelings, but surely you have
received a much more valuable gift, and you must be
aware that the difference to Lady Constance even now
will be great; and do you think he could endure her
to have any privation? You know enough of true
affection, Mr. Ashton, or you are not worthy of the
name you bear, to be well aware that its chief delight
is in contributing to the happiness of those he loves;
and surely you would not deprive your brother of
that remaining pleasure."

"Oh! no, of none—none that I could give him,"
exclaimed Henry, passionately, "I would willingly die
for him."

"I do not think your dying is what would give him
most pleasure just now," observed Lord Wentworth

with a playful smile, "I rather think he would prefer seeing you alive and happy. People do not take such pains with things which they are indifferent about, and he has been too busy and thoughtful for you to make me suppose he can be pleased by any thing but your acceptance and enjoyment of what he has prepared for you."

"But much less would have done for me," insisted Henry.

"Probably—for you have been used to ship biscuits, and tarpauling, but Lady Constance has not, and as it is natural he should think a little of her, he wishes you to have something beyond mere ship allowance to live on. As I said at first, I can truly feel for you, but you must learn to be generous as well as your brother, and freely to bestow on him the great pleasure of contributing to your happiness."

"But in time he might," said Henry, "and I do trust he will——"

"Never," said Lord Wentworth; "I know what you mean, but I have no hesitation in saying I am convinced he never will. I have known him and seen him of late years much more than you have,—and when you last parted you could not have been any very experienced reader of characters, and I am as confident as that I see you before me, that he never will form any other tie, so that need not trouble you. He has been 'wax to receive,' but will be 'marble to retain.' But do not fear for him on that account, for his hope is not *here*, nor ever has been, and he is even happier now at times, by having had some of the strong cords that bound him to earth, severed. I

should not perhaps have said this to you, who are at
this moment naturally full of expectations of earthly
happiness, and value them perhaps just now beyond
their true estimate, only I wished you to feel no scruple in accepting this portion of your brother's fortune,
for he can have, and I feel sure never will have, any
better use for it.   Come, you will promise me to say
nothing to him to pain him, or make him think that
you feel it unpleasant to receive his kindness.   A free
acceptance of a gift shews that we have generosity and
feeling enough ourselves to make us understand the
pleasure of 'giving,' and that we do not grudge that
pleasure to another.   It is, I confess, the more difficult
part to act of the two.   But if you say one word more
on the subject I shall vote you an unfit guardian of
Lady Constance's happiness—order the four greys out
instantly—and carry her off to the north before your
astonished eyes.   So now choose silence or death."

"I must perforce then choose the former," said
Henry smiling, though his heart was still heavy.
"Yes, I see that it will be best to let him have his
own generous way; and well indeed might you say
that 'he has not his equal upon earth.'   I often wish I
had never been born!"

"Then you wish a very foolish and a very wicked
wish," replied Lord Wentworth.   "But do, Mr. Ashton, let me implore of you, endeavour to overcome that
unrestrained habit of feeling which you seem to have.
I say of feeling—because I know that in action you
can, and do restrain yourself, for your brother has
told me that your conduct throughout this trying affair
was beyond praise."

" Oh ! how could he say that," exclaimed Henry, excessively touched, " when my heart was full of evil of all kinds."

" The heart is God's province," answered Lord Wentworth, "and yours; he could only judge of the conduct, and that he told me was most noble. But I ought perhaps to say that I do not think he would have mentioned to me any of the circumstances, had I not almost extracted them from him; for knowing of his attachment formerly, I naturally spoke to him about it when I came here, not dreaming of what had occurred; and he told me, merely I think, because he saw I suspected a good deal, and that he was anxious that no blame should attach to any. But will you try and restrain that unsubdued way of thinking and feeling; for if you do not, it will, in the life you are about to enter on, produce much misery where you least wish it."

" Ah ! I have troubled her too often already," said Henry, with a sigh; " God grant I may do so no more."

" Then," said Lord Wentworth smiling, " you must learn not to wish yourself dead upon every occasion,—for that is a desperate remedy—or unborn,—for that is useless. ' Supportez vous, et supportez les autres,' is a very good maxim. I have seen what self-command can do in your brother, not only on late occasions, but formerly when temper, and patience used to be much more tried than now; for a great event is more tolerable to the irritable part of our composition, than continual smaller provocations are; yet I have seen him bear, what you and I and other men, would scarcely have endured without dangerous

outbreaks of wrath; yet he is by nature far more
violent and passionate than either of us."

"So I have heard him say, and my mother too,
but I cannot remember it to have been so; he was
always kind and considerate towards me, and now —
his patience has been beyond conception."

"Let us profit then, my good fellow, by his example," returned Lord Wentworth. "But now, come
back to the house, and shew Lady Constance that you
are glad to have some better place to put her in than
the 'Hard' at Portsmouth. However, I feel in a very
tolerable humour with you after all, for you have con-
ferred a special favour on me in giving me an opportunity of finding fault. It is such an unspeakable
comfort to meet with somebody worse than one's self.
I always find myself oppressed by such masses of excellence round about me, that I cannot get in a word
of advice edgeways, and I am generally *en proie* to all
sorts of lectures; but now, 'avec cet amour enraciné
d'être quelque chose' which pervades us all, I am
quite elevated at having you to lecture, and I shall
certainly take some delicate opportunity of informing
Lady Constance, that if she ever enjoys a moment's
peace with you, it will be entirely owing to me. Now
will you come back with me, or must I order out the
greys?"

Henry Ashton laughed, and taking Lord Wentworth's arm, they were both proceeding towards the
house, when they perceived Sir Roland at a little
distance.

"There," said Lord Wentworth, dropping Henry's
arm and giving him a slight push on the shoulder,
"now, off with you directly, before my good advice

is all carried away by the winds, and remember you
say anything but what is uppermost in your mind."

"I cannot go," said Henry stopping short after
having taken a few steps; "I could not meet his kind
look; I feel like a murderer."

"Nonsense," exclaimed Lord Wentworth half angry,
yet half laughing. "I shall vote you a fresh splinter
in your side, and have you carried about again. But
really," he added in a most earnest tone, "I do beseech you to try and get over these feelings, or they
will in time produce perfect alienation between you.
Too much delicacy, or rather—for I will not step
down from the pedestal I have mounted with you—
too much pride, is as much the bane of life, as too
much any thing else. 'De trop même dans le bien,
n'est plus un bien,' remember. So now, do not make
yourself 'de trop' any longer with me, but go off
where your presence will I am sure, give nothing but
pleasure. I will go and make the agreeable to Lady
Constance meanwhile, and I daresay you will not be
missed. *Au revoir.*"

So saying he hurried off and would not look back
till he got to the house-door, when turning he saw the
brothers together and felt perfectly happy.

It was certainly a trial to Henry Ashton to meet
Sir Roland, for whom he felt at that moment an
agonised love and a devotion which would have made
it easy for him to have confronted death or any evil
for his sake; and to Sir Roland too, it was no slight
effort, for his heart was filled with mixed emotions
to which he dreaded giving way. When they met,
neither of them could speak for many minutes and

they walked together arm in arm in perfect silence.
At length Sir Roland said in a low voice and as if
following what he knew must be the train of Henry's
thoughts,

" It will be very pleasant to me, you know, to have
you so near."

" Roland," said Henry pressing his brother's arm
convulsively, " how can I ever thank you ? "

" By enjoying it all, and being happy, and letting
me see that you are so," replied Sir Roland kindly
smiling, as he returned Henry's ardent pressure.
" The preparing it all has been a great pleasure to me,
as great as, or greater perhaps than, having it will be
to you. Yes, my dear brother, I wish you to feel
that though at times, regrets, natural regrets, cross my
mind, yet that God makes up my loss to me in many
ways ; and I can never be sufficiently grateful that
what has passed, has left no trace of bitterness or
division between us. For a moment my jealous soul
was tortured—but that has long since passed, and I
feel a happiness inexpressible in being the instrument
of happiness both to you and to—Constance. You
must let me continue to love her Henry, for remember
she bears a double character with me. The one—I
have almost learnt to forget, but she must ever remain
the being who was the companion of my chidhood,
and youth, and who is now—or will be soon—a real
sister to me. As to you," he continued, endeavouring
to speak cheerfully, " you must never wonder if I find
a pleasure in pleasing you, you were always ' l'enfant
gâté de la maison ' and must consent to remain so still.
But now, my boy, go back to the others, and be sure
and tell my mother, or Wentworth, of any thing you

would like done—either of you—for the workmen are still about. I have some things yet to attend to out here, but will join you in a little while;" and he escaped from his brother's softening affection.

As he watched him spring up the steps of the terrace, pursue his way with bounding tread towards the house, and at last enter to join those within whom he so much loved, his heart was filled with the most exquisite happiness. He looked around at the scene which presented itself; the day was lovely—the air was perfectly still, and the lake had not a single ripple to disturb the perfect reflection of the tall trees that were pictured on its breast, excepting where the water-hen or wild duck flew skimming along its surface, leaving behind a glittering train which sparkled like diamonds in the sun, or the swan swam forth from the high reeds, and, jutting its full breast against the waters, threw them from its snowy sides in waving lines, which diverged almost to the very shores of the lake. The trees had, in some places, already assumed a light tinge of green, while the alder and the long sweeping branches of the birch, glowed with that bloomy purple which marks the swelling of the buds before the leaves burst forth. The rooks were in the very midst of those busy cares, which their newly hatched young required, contrasting in the straight course of their heavy flight, with the singularly graceful and undulating motion of the Cornish chough, which had its more distant nest among the rocks. The singing of the birds, the early flowers, and all those lovely things which thrill the heart with an indefinable joy even but to think of, combined to make that day and hour most charming.

But outward things alone cannot impart pleasure, it is the feeling within, which ever arrays them in

" Hues of its own, fresh borrowed from the heart,"

and which either causes " the sunniest flowers, that glad with their pure smiles the gardens round " to bloom without colour or fragrance for us, or makes " the wilderness and desert-place to blossom like the rose."   It was the sense of deep gratitude to God, and of glowing love to man—the noble exercise of the " power divine of doing good," which made Sir Roland at that moment happier, even than those, for whose dear sakes he had so long and so well exerted himself.

CHAPTER XXX.

"Oh! si vous saviez ce qu'il y a de paix dans la douleur ac-
ceptée."—*Lettres Chrétiennes.*

"Out of the depths have I cried unto Thee, oh! Lord. Lord,
hear my voice!"—*Psalm* cxxx.

THE settlements could not be finished quite so soon
as was expected; but at length the twenty-third of
April was fixed upon for the marriage to take place.
The delay was trying to Sir Roland, for much as he
was enabled to overcome his natural feelings, and often
as he enjoyed the highest order of happiness, in communion with God, still it was a time of excitement for
him, and he thought he should be better when all was
over, and that he was enabled again to return to the
tranquillity of his usual occupations.

"Wentworth," he said to his friend one day, "I
thought it a great proof of your friendship coming
down here to me, but I am going to exact another—
and that is that you should leave me for a time."

"Why?" asked Lord Wentworth, surprised and
apparently not particularly pleased; "why am I to go
away now, just as I have got fitted into my room, and
have made myself at home with every body, and every
thing? I do not think it is at all fair to expect it."

" You shall return again soon if you like it," said Sir Roland smiling.

" ' Return soon,' does not suit me half so well as staying as long as I like now I am here," replied Lord Wentworth, " my mind will have to be aired again, and got in order—new swept, and dusted—and I hate all that. Why am I to go ? "

" I will not tell you now," said Sir Roland smiling, " you may stay a week longer before I turn you out, and you will be in a quieter mood some day before that I dare say, than you are now, and then "—and his colour changed—" I will tell you why I certainly do wish you to leave me before—before the twenty-third."

The moment Sir Roland mentioned that day a cloud dimmed the brightness of Lord Wentworth's half-laughing eye; for he knew that feelings of a painful nature must at that moment occupy Sir Roland's mind, and he regretted having answered so lightly.

" Oh! I am always in a quiet mood my dear Ashton," he replied feelingly, " when it is any thing that concerns your comfort that has to be discussed; tell me now, all you wish to say. I will go to-day if you like it, and come again whenever you please."

" No, no, do not go to-day," said Sir Roland; " but to say the truth, I feel I shall be able to go through *that* day better, if you are not here, than if I knew your kind eye was on me. Now that I have no particular exertion to make, I find it is a great comfort and relief at times to be able to speak to you openly; but in action, I must have God and God alone with me; even your kindness comes between my spirit and His power. Man's sympathy softens, but God's strengthens. Man can as it were, stand on the brink of the stream against which we are striving and battleing, and speak words of comfort and direction and encouragement; but God is with us in the flood—stems the torrent for us, and bears us up so that the waters should not overflow us. So you shall leave me before that time comes, it is not far distant, and it will be a trying hour to me, and I must abstract my mind as much as possible from earth, and keep it stedfast upon God, to enable me to get through it at all. That over, I shall be truly happy to have you with me, for come down to earth again my mind must; and when there—no one is so delightful to me as you," and he held out his hand to Lord Wentworth, who pressing it warmly said,

" I feel you are quite right, for nothing but losing the sense of earthly things can at times sustain the soul, and I know that a sympathising look will often trouble and overset one, instead of conveying comfort. I know I have often distressed you when I least wished it, for in the intensity of my anxiety I have often forgotten you, for whom I was anxious. I admire Lady Ashton so much in that. Many times when my eye has been feverishly, and thoughtlessly fixed on you, fearful of the effect of particular things, I have looked for a moment towards her, in a sort of agony, and have perceived that though her lip quivered and at times a tear forced its way, yet she never raised her eye to your countenance, or did the least thing to attract attention to you. Beautiful it has been to see how completely she has forgotten herself in you, and indeed in all, and with what wonderful delicacy, and good feeling she has acted in every way."

" Yes, my dear mother's task has been no easy one," replied Sir Roland, " for what makes her happy on the one hand, makes her miserable on the other ; yet never has she wounded me by a look or word, that might seem either negligent or over-pitying, though I know her gentle heart has bled for me perpetually ; and never either I feel sure, has she damped Henry's happiness by a melancholy look or expression, on my account. She is indeed most precious to me, and I am blessed in so many ways that I ought to be most thankful, even though the dearest tie of my life is broken."

" Aye, I cannot but wish it had never come to that with you," said Lord Wentworth, " the disappointment, however deep, of a simple unacknowledged feeling, could never have been so great a trial as the ending of an engagement must be."

" You are wrong there, Wentworth,—as far as I am concerned at least," replied Sir Roland ; " and my engagement is one of the things for which I feel thankful to God. For them, certainly, it would have been pleasant had no previous tie existed, for it might have saved them much pain, but selfishly speaking, it is far better for me as it is. Had I returned home, loving Constance as I did when abroad with you, and found her engaged to Henry ; what would there have been for me to do. I should of course have provided well for them, and in the secret of my heart I should have been happy in so doing ; but my unexpected emotions would have smouldered in my own heart ; and, unable to overcome

them, I should have been deemed morose, and have
been a blot upon their page of happiness. My feelings would have been perpetually wounded by things
innocently said, and I should have been a thing of no
account with them. Now I do not say that there is
not vanity and pride in my present feelings, but certainly there is pleasure in the firm conviction which I
have, that next to each other, they value me the most
perhaps, of anything in this world, and that my happiness is their great object. It is delightful to feel that
I have been the means of making them happy, and it
is soothing to know that they are aware of it. As to
giving Constance up!—I feel sure she would never
have married me while she liked another, but still if I
had not released her from her promise, I do not think
she would ever have held herself free as to forming
any other tie; and I do not think she would have
borne the thought, or at least not for a length of time,
of marrying Henry, had I not urged it. Now in exerting myself for them, I have been most happy; activity is the only worldly resource in trouble, and I do
assure you that often in working for them, when you
and I have been over at Tregaron, and I have been
busy laying out the grounds, and arranging the house,
and every thing for them, my feelings have been so
buoyant, that I have at times forgotten that it was at
the expense of my own very heart's-life that I was
making them happy."

"Yes, I often wondered when I saw your zeal and
energy," replied Lord Wentworth; "but resignation
to the will of God carries great comfort with it."

"I think the true Christian word is 'acquiescence,'
not 'resignation;' it is a much higher order of feeling,

and I think a different one. We 'resign' ourselves, when we cannot prevent what is done; we 'acquiesce,' when we would not prevent it. That, I trust is my feeling; I would not rule for myself, not for all the universe! nor would I, if I could, now take Constance away from Henry. God's ways must be best. There is a verse in the Psalms also, whose beauty is to me excessive—revealing as it does, so much in so few words: "Call upon Me in the time of trouble; I will deliver thee, and thou shalt glorify Me." Man's words would have been: "And I will glorify thee!" but God who knows what is our highest privilege, and perfection—that indeed for which we were born—holds out as a reward, 'Thou shalt glorify me!' I cannot tell you the sublime ideas with which that passage fills me! The majesty with which the Lord confers as a favour the power of glorifying Him, is most striking; and as He certainly knows the value of His own service, we must not regret any affliction which makes us go to him to learn it. I am not yet very old, but I have truly learnt that 'affliction' need not be 'misfortune,' for nothing can be called that, which brings us nearer to God—the source of happiness! When it is blest by Him, then

> " Sorrow teacheth us the truth of things
> Which have been hid beneath the crown of flowers
> That gladness wears,"

and we are the better and therefore the happier for it."

In a few days Lord Wentworth left Llanaven, promising to return when the marriage was over. It was the wish of all that it should be quite private, and no one but their near neighbours, and friends the Montagues, were invited, excepting Mrs. Mordaunt and Philip, whom it was thought right to ask as being Lady Constance's nearest relations. Lady Ashton also secretly wished that Philip should come in order to act the part of 'father' in giving Lady Constance away; which, as it must otherwise naturally fall to Sir Roland, she feared might bring with it most painful feelings to him. The thought had never even glanced through his mind, for those who know the reality—the stern, inward, reality—of suffering and sacrifice, are often wholly unmoved by the little outward trifles which fill the anxious minds of watchful friends with dismay for their sakes; and many a thing which has been anticipated with terror by others, passes over the deeply sorrowing heart for which they were in pain, like the idle wind!

Neither Mrs. Mordaunt nor Philip, however, could come, though they wrote the kindest letters of regret, and congratulations, and Sir Roland was therefore to act the " father's" part. He gave orders that a rural feast should be prepared for all the tenants, and the poor of the various parishes around, and provided every thing most liberally for it. Lady Ashton had endeavoured to dissuade him from this, thinking it would be too much for him, but he said he wished it, for that he considered Henry as his heir, and liked that his marriage should be celebrated accordingly.

The tears sprang from Lady Ashton's eyes as she received this answer, but Sir Roland entreated her not to be unhappy on his account.

" It is not, my dear mother," he said, " that I determine never to form fresh ties, but I feel I never

can do so—never! But I shall not be unhappy; the
busy never are so, and I shall find plenty to do."

The day of the marriage at length arrived, and
was ushered in by the ringing of bells from the old
church-tower. The church itself was at no great
distance, so the drive was a very short one; but Lady
Ashton wishing to prevent the necessity of Sir Roland
going in the same carriage with Lady Constance, proposed that she and Mrs. Montague, and the two sisters
should go in one carriage, and Sir Roland, his brother,
and Captain Montague in another, and it was accordingly so arranged. Henry Ashton was excessively
nervous and uncomfortable, but Sir Roland was generally calm and collected, though he looked deadly pale;
and the compression of his lips, and slight contraction
of his brow, proved that his nature was under strong
constraint. It would indeed have been an insupportable hour to him had he not been sustained by strength
from above; for though we may know that we are to
lose what we love, yet no previous moment can compare with that which actually tears it from us. As
long as he could remain silent, he was happy in the
inward communion which he ceaselessly maintained
with God, but if Captain Montague or any one else
spoke to him, his spirit seemed disturbed from its rest,
and his manner became agitated. When they arrived
at the gate of the churchyard, their carriage being
before the other, he descended from it, and was walking towards the church, when Captain Montague, called
to him gaily, saying,

" As you are to act the part of 'father,' Sir Roland,

I believe I ought to leave to you the privilege of hand-
ing Lady Constance out."

" Oh ! no—no," said Henry, hurriedly.

But Sir Roland, warned by his brother's agitation
to maintain his own self-command, turned back and
assisted Lady Constance from the carriage; and then
giving her his arm, they walked together along the
path to the church-door.   There were children and
young women strewing flowers in the way, according
to the custom in many country places, and the whole
churchyard was thronged with the tenantry and poor
people, anxious to shew their respects, and also wishing
to gratify their own natural curiosity.   Sir Roland
walked all the way with his hat in his hand, bowing to
the right and left, in acknowledgment of the continued
salutations of the people, while Lady Constance who felt
an agony of heart for him which made her wholly forget
herself, walked by his side incapable of taking notice
of any one, and trembling so as hardly to be able to
sustain herself.   Captain and Mrs. Montague and Lady
Florence came next, and the latter gaily smiled and
bowed to all around, who could not but admire the
lovely creature shining forth in all her bloom and animation, a perfect contrast to her pale and silent companions.   Thoughts painfully oppressive rose to poor
Mrs. Montague's mind as she remembered how different
was her own hasty and imprudent marriage, and how
great the anxiety which followed it, and recollections
somewhat similar also clouded her husband's brow.
Henry and his mother then followed.   She, with her
kind and courteous manner seemed to acknowledge
individually every creature in the crowded area, while

Henry, pale with agitation, walked like his brother
bareheaded, and bowed on all sides, yet his troubled
eye seemed to rest on no one. At length they all
stood in their places near the communion table and the
clergyman began the service. Sir Roland mechanically
took his station by Lady Constance as he was directed ; he felt for a few moments as in a dizzy dream,
and took hold of the railings by which he was standing
to support himself : but this soon past, and his mind
became completely absorbed in silent earnest prayer
to God. He lost all sense of where he was, saw no
one, nor heard a single word of the service. When the
minister came to the words—so accidentally and painfully appropriate—" Who giveth this woman to be
married to this man ?" all those who were there, excepting Lady Ashton, Lady Constance, and Henry,
naturally looked at Sir Roland, but he was unconscious
of every thing around him, his mind being at this moment lost in the contemplation of that region, where what
we love is never taken from us.' There was a slight
pause, and then even Henry, and his mother turned
their eyes to him—the latter with fearful apprehension.
The cessation of the voice however, and the slight
movement which was made roused Sir Roland, and
brought back his thoughts to present things. In returning to earth however, his soul still retained its
heavenly feelings, and when the kind old minister—
supposing merely that he was not exactly aware of
what he had to do—repeated the question, he looked
on Henry's agitated countenance, with a calm smile,
and taking Lady Constance's hand in his, placed it in
that of his brother's. Lady Constance then first burst
into tears, and Sir Roland for a moment became trou-

bled, but earnestly lifting up his heart again to God, the peace he sought, returned to him.

As Henry and Lady Constance were going no farther than to Tregaron, it was arranged that they should set off from the church-door, all being anxious to avoid any unnecessary trial to Sir Roland. When the ceremony therefore was over, and the business of signing, &c. was all done, they proceeded arm-in-arm together along the crowded churchyard towards the gate, where Henry's own carriage was waiting to convey them to their new home. When they had nearly reached it, Henry anxiously turned round and missing Sir Roland, his heart misgave him, and hastily begging the old clergyman, who was walking by him, to give Constance his arm, he flew back into the church filled with undefined alarm. His fears however were instantly relieved by finding his brother well, but his attitude of deep despondency as he stood resting his head against a monument which had been erected to his father's memory, struck him to the very heart. He paused a moment in the church porch, unwilling to disturb him, yet incapable of returning without speaking to him; but the sound of his step caused Sir Roland to look up, and on seeing him he started, exclaiming,

" Henry, why are you here ?"

" My dear brother !" cried Henry advancing and vehemently throwing his arms round Sir Roland, as he burst into passionate tears.

Sir Roland instantly calmed at sight of his brother's strong emotion, returned his warm embrace, and said,

" My dear, dear Henry, do not give way so much,

nor grieve yourself for me; I may truly say that I
have that peace which passeth understanding, that
comfort which God alone can give; and though at the
moment of parting I felt that faintness which at times
comes over me, and which made me unable to follow
you, yet that is past. The sight of our father's tomb
has reminded me of the troublesome life he has quitted,
and of the never-ending nature of that scene of bliss he
has entered. Do not be anxious for me, I am happy—
happy for you—and for myself."

"Oh! what can I ever do for you?" exclaimed
Henry.

"A great deal," said Sir Roland, with his ever-
winning smile; "you must keep, as far as depends on
you, every cloud from Constance's brow, and strive
continually to increase in the grace and love of God.
His blessing be with you both. Now go, dear Henry,"
he continued, for he began to be agitated by his brother's regretful affection; "she—they all will be waiting for you; go," he continued smiling, "and I will
follow you."

Henry strained his hand once more to his lips
and tore himself away, but turning at the door he
seemed irresolute; until Sir Roland lifting his hand,
said kindly and cheerfully, "Not another word," and
Henry at last left the church and hurried back again
to the carriage, anxious if possible to hide his agitation
from the eyes of those around. It was however quickly
observed, and being naturally ascribed to the pain of
separation from his brother (their mutual strong affection being well-known), it only served to heighten the
interest of the people, who were all much attached both
to him and Sir Roland. The sight too of his naval

uniform, and the presence of Mrs. Montague brought
back to their minds the remembrance of his gallant
conduct at the time of the wreck, and aided in exciting their feelings to the utmost pitch; still—amid
the tears of many—loud expressions of good-will, and
of kind leave-taking sounded on all sides, ending at
last in one simultaneous and universal cheer. Henry
turned round and acknowledged it with his usual open,
and frank manner, while the tear that started afresh in
his eye, was of a nature far different from that which
had last dimmed it.

Lady Ashton had been very uneasy during his
absence, but not liking to follow him, had endeavoured
to occupy the attention of those immediately around,
by kind inquiries and observations; and Lady Florence, broken-hearted at parting with her sister, had
entered the carriage after her, occupying the seat that
was waiting for Henry, and mingling tears and kisses,
with her last farewells. At length however she descended, and Henry after shaking hands with those
around him, and turning to acknowledge a fresh burst
of cheering, got into the carriage, which immediately
drove off.

Sir Roland then left the church, and at the sight
of one who had so long been to them all that master
and landlord could be, the already excited enthusiasm of the people burst forth tenfold, and cheer after
cheer rent the air, as he passed amongst them. He
acknowledged their friendly greeting, smiling kindly,
though at times with a quivering lip, and then followed
his mother and the rest of the party into the carriage;
but turning round on the step, he said, in his peculiarly
pleasing manner, that he hoped soon to see all who

were there, at Llanaven, and that not one of them
must be missing; and the carriage then drove off amid
the renewed cheers of the people.

When arrived at home, Sir Roland felt quite unequal to sustaining the burden of conversation, and
soon left the drawing-room, hoping to find that ease
when alone which he was unable to obtain while
with others. But peace seemed for a time to fly from
him. He had thought that when all was over, he
should be at rest; but he now found that of all the
hours of his life (excepting perhaps the very first of
his bitter affliction), this was by far the most overpowering. It is said that the moment of death is not
so trying to the survivors, as the day when all that
remains of that which has been so dear is finally shut
from their eyes; and so it was now with Sir Roland.
Lady Constance had been virtually lost to him for
months, and he had learnt to accustom himself to that
thought; but he had never realized what it would be
when she was actually gone; when he should wander
from room to room and never hear her voice—roam
over cliff and shore, through garden, woods and glades,
and never meet her, or see the trace of her foot!
Yet thus it must be through life for him. A visitor
indeed she might be, but an inmate, never more—
never while he lived would his home again be her
home!

He wandered about bewildered with a feeling, as
of something lost, for which he must look in vain—but
scarcely able to define the cause of the vacant dreari-
ness within him. He could not at that moment look
up to God, his heart was fixed earthward—and he was
most desolate! At length this deadly dreamy misery

seemed to pass, and the full sense of his loss rushed
overwhelmingly over him. His spirit sunk beneath it ;
but when that storm was past, he was relieved, and his
heart again lifted itself to God.

Henry too—he was gone ! gone from the home of
which he had so often been the life and joy, to form
a new home for himself! gone—to exchange the
thoughtless freedom of his boyish days, for the cares,
and deeper duties of maturer life.

" Yet still it is but for a time," thought Sir Roland,
" and then all is peace. Yes, all must be peace," he
exclaimed, looking up to Heaven, " if God is faithfully
followed. It is only when withdrawing our gaze from
Him and looking to the troubles around us, that our
faith fails, and we feel sinking in the bitter, bitter waves
of this stormy life."

The rural party, consisting of many hundreds, were
assembled by two o'clock in the park at Llanaven, and
Sir Roland went amongst them, exerting himself to the
utmost to be cheerful, lest he should damp the general
festivity by the appearance of gloom on his own countenance. He succeeded in a great degree, but was not
a little relieved when Lord Wentworth (who at his
own earnest entreaty was to return immediately after
the marriage was concluded), made his appearance.
He instantly resigned his chair at the head of the table,
where his principal tenants were assembled, to him,
and after addressing a few words to them, he introduced
Lord Wentworth as his particular friend, and one who
was much more fitted than he was to do the honours of
the feast to them, and then retired amid loud and reiterated cheers.

He felt it impossible to talk on ordinary subjects, and dreading lest his absence of mind should be observed, he would not return to the rest of the party, but strolled by himself for some time, and at length descended to the shore, but finding that this listless mood was not calculated to strengthen his powers of endurance, he walked on at a quicker pace towards Carncombe, determining to visit the old and infirm of the village who had not been able to come to the feast. It was a great effort to him to approach the spot where so many trials had been his, and where he had not been since the time when his mind was completely overwhelmed, under its first sudden stroke. He passed it, however, and was enabled to thank God for the comparative ease and support which he then enjoyed. He went to see all who remained in the village, and found subject of gratitude in every visit. The presents which he liberally bestowed on the occasion, cheered the hearts of all, and made him feel, while witnessing their pleasure, that it is "more blessed to give than to receive," while the words of faith and trust which he spoke, animated the flagging spirits of the suffering, and made them partakers of that "comfort wherewith he himself was comforted of God."

CHAPTER XXXI.

"Thou, O Spirit, that dost prefer,
Before all temples, th' upright heart and pure."
                              MILTON.

"Every day is dedicated to the service of the Lord, and bears
upon its golden hours this inscription, 'Holiness to the Lord.'"
                              REV. C. B. TAYLOR.

A FEW months after the marriage had taken place,
Sir Roland entered into Parliament, and his hands were
then full of business, though of a kind particularly
disagreeable to him; for it brought him in continual
contact with many whose actions, conversation, and
principles were wholly repugnant to him; and the business itself was often carried on in a manner and spirit
as revolting to him as his former experience of diplomatic proceedings had been. Still there were some
who had honesty, and a few, though very few, who had
religious feeling, and with those, whether of his own
party or not, he chiefly associated; avoiding the society
of the others as far as courtesy and public duty would
permit, and continually praying when forced to be with
them, that at least, if he could be of no use to them, he
might be preserved from the contamination of their
conversation, and the corruption of their principles.

Ever delighted to return to Llanaven, he frequently collected round him there, those whom he most valued in life. Visits were continually exchanged between the inmates of that place and Tregaron, from participating in which he never shrank, and the great efforts he made to master himself, enabled him to feel that the pain of such meetings gradually decreased, while Henry's happiness with Lady Constance was a never-failing source of joy to his heart. He was still, however, conscious that they themselves were not wholly at their ease with him, and that they did not like to shew the happiness they enjoyed with each other for fear of paining him. But he trusted that in time that restraint would wear off, and that they would learn rightly to understand his feelings.

Time sped on, but the leaves of another summer had not yet fully clothed the trees at Llanaven, when the bells of the church were again ringing out their cheerful peals; and this time, for the birth of one, whom Sir Roland felt was destined to be the heir of all his possessions.

Lady Ashton and Lady Florence had been staying some time at Tregaron; and Sir Roland, taking advantage of a time when there was but little to be done in the House, had run down to Llanaven, being too anxious to remain in London; and his happiness was unspeakable when he heard the joyful news. It was early in the morning that it reached him, and he instantly wrote to his brother in terms of the deepest feeling, and desiring every thing that was kind to be said from him to Lady Constance.

"And now, my dear Henry," he added, at the conclusion of his letter, " as you are blest with every thing which can make your heart happy, I entreat you to let me partake your happiness with you. I have ever seen that you and Constance have feared to shew your mutual affection, and to let your joyful spirits have their way before me, thinking in your kind hearts that it might pain me. But such would not be the case. I should be a thousand times happier, if I felt that I was no check upon you, and if you would let all the expression of your feelings flow out before me. Now, at this most joyful moment, I ask this of your friendship : think of me, not at all ; but let me be to you as one whose attachment you know to be strong and sincere, and do you be to me as affectionate friends. Let me see the full delight of your hearts in each other, and in this new claimant on your affections, and then I shall be happy."

He despatched this letter, and desired the servant to return as soon as possible, to let him know how all went on, and then proceeded to give orders to his steward for preparations for another great day of rejoicing amongst the people. As he was returning home after a long walk, he saw some one riding up to the house at full speed, and was alarmed lest any ill news might be arriving. But the next moment he perceived that it was Henry himself, who, on seeing him, threw himself off his horse, and giving the reins to the servant, bounded down the green slope to meet him. He had scarcely read Sir Roland's letter, before he ordered his horse to ride over to Llanaven ; and with that delicacy of feeling which was so singularly blended in him with habitual recklessness of action, he insisted upon his coming back with him directly to Tregaron ; and with-

out making the slightest allusion to the latter part of
his letter, he immediately adopted the spirit of it, and
spoke with the fullest and most open delight of all
his happiness. Sir Roland was easily persuaded to
accompany him back, and ordering the carriage,
they set off together, leaving the horses to follow.
Henry dilated ceaselessly during the drive on the excessive joy he felt, a joy which any one who has been
in his situation, and is blest with feelings like his, will
well understand; and Sir Roland entered with the
warmest sympathy into his enjoyment, asking a hundred
questions about the new comer, and about every thing
in which Henry was concerned.

Lady Ashton was surprised and delighted at seeing
Sir Roland arrive, with his brother; he himself felt
most happy that he had come.

After he had sat some time in the drawing-room,
Henry came in, saying, that he must go up with him to
see the baby. He rose and followed him, but it was
with a strange confusion of heart that he entered the
room where the infant lay asleep. In former days the
thoughts of having children of his own, to watch over,
and love, and bring up in the ways of God, had ever
been most delightful to him: now, that prospect he felt
was shut out for ever, and it was impossible but that
some natural regrets should struggle in his breast. But
when he saw this child of his brother, lying in its
peaceful slumber, he felt he was no longer childless, but
that this little one would be to him as his own.

He was forced in a short time to return to town,
but as soon as he could possibly escape, he came back
to Llanaven. His intercourse with Tregaron was now,
indeed, all he could have wished it. Lady Constance

was perfectly recovered, and determined as much as possible to follow Henry's example in the freedom of her intercourse with Sir Roland; and he soon found the difference of their manner towards him, which enabled him to enter into all their enjoyments; especially the unbounded affection they felt for their child.

When the little creature, who was named after him, was old enough to be trusted alone to his care, he would walk about with him in his arms for hours in the day; and when about a year and a half after, Lady Constance's happiness was further increased by the birth of a daughter, he often begged that her boy might be left at Llanaven, and delighted in having him with him almost all the day. He would fain have adopted him entirely; but he felt that even if the parents would have consented, it would be a great evil to separate the child from its natural protectors, and though perhaps Henry and Lady Constance might have yielded to his wish, out of their great consideration for him, yet he knew it would be a terrible sacrifice to them. He felt for the boy, however, completely as if he had been his own, and his heart once more expanded under the power of devoted love.

Many friends he had too, whose visits were very pleasant to him. His uncle, who, fatigued with the cares of business, had resigned his post at ——, often came to stay with him; and through all his raillery, Sir Roland was thankful to perceive that his mind opened more and more to the power of truth; and that nothing seemed to make him so happy as conversing with him or Lady Ashton on the subjects of everlasting life. The Montagues still remained at Carncombe, and were ever welcome. Philip Mordaunt was married, but he still retained his affection for Lady Constance, and frequently came down with his young and pleasing wife to see her; and Sir Roland found him a most agreeable companion; and one whose mind was much awakened to the importance of spiritual things. Mrs. Mordaunt, too, wholly cured of her horror of "Methodist," confessed that at Llanaven and Tregaron, at least, the service and love of God seemed "ways of happiness and paths of peace."

But of all the acquaintances and friends of their later years, no one was so welcome at both houses as Lady Stanmore. Her heart first aroused by Sir Roland, and afterwards further enlightened by Lady Constance, felt no rest till she was able fully to admit the light of divine truth; she long and fondly clung to the world, and resisted the convictions of her own conscience; but God's mercy was greater than her unfaithfulness, and finally triumphed over it. From the time of Lady Constance's marriage, she and Lord Stanmore had paid frequent visits both to her and to Sir Roland; but it was the sustaining power of heavenly grace, as shewn so wonderfully in the latter, that at last overcame the resistance of her heart.

She had suspected when first she met Lady Constance in London, that there was some attachment between her and Sir Roland; and in staying at Tregaron, soon after Lady Constance's marriage, she playfully spoke of the "mistake" under which she had laboured. The distress which this unexpected allusion gave Lady Constance, escaped her eye at first, and she continued,—

" But it is impossible that either you or he could love in vain, so I must give up considering myself a

' witch ' for the future; but I certainly thought I had discovered the clue to the secret of his indifference to the many who would gladly have received his attentions at ——. A certain expression of trouble on your countenance when first I mentioned the subject in town, made me fancy that you must have been the object for which he was willing to give up all the rest of the world, and certain tears also which started from your eyes when I repeated some words of his that same night, made me imagine that his image was not an unwelcome one to you."

Lady Constance had turned her head away, apparently to look out of a window by which she was sitting, but in fact to hide the emotion which Lady Stanmore's words produced. The thought of Sir Roland's attachment was ever most grievous to her, and though she saw with thankfulness how much he had been able to overcome his feelings, yet she knew him too well to imagine that an affection such as his had been for her, could so easily be overcome, or the sorrow of its disappointment so soon be made to pass away. She could not answer the observation which had been made, or stem back the tears which started into her eyes. Lady Stanmore saw them fall, and kindly said,—

" I am sorry I have grieved you, dear Lady Constance, by my thoughtlessness, for I now fear I was wrong again, and that there must have been something formerly, which it now gives you pain to think of. It could not have been you who were not loved, or you would not now be bearing his name, through another; but is it possible that he could have been unaccepted where he wished to please ? How could you not like him ?"

Lady Constance answered only by pointing with her hand out of the window to Henry, who had just come in sight, walking with Lord Stanmore.

" I understand you," said Lady Stanmore, smiling, but shaking her head ; " yet I cannot quite forgive you. Your husband is certainly very charming, but to refuse Sir Roland, it must have required the heart of a tigress ! "

Lady Constance was exceedingly distressed, for she would not willingly have had Sir Roland's feelings made known to any human being, and she felt that her own want of self-command had, though most unintentionally, revealed them. She sat silent for some time, uncertain what to say, but at length she reflected that Lady Stanmore was now aware of Sir Roland's affection, and she determined therefore that she should be made acquainted also with his nobleness. After a short struggle with herself she began :—

" My dear Lady Stanmore, I have foolishly, by my weakness, revealed that which I had wished should never have been known or suspected by any one ; but let me implore you, never to let this subject pass your lips—not even to Lord Stanmore. It would distress me beyond measure that Roland's feelings should be made known. But as you have guessed them, you shall know how he has borne and acted under all he has had to endure."

She then informed Lady Stanmore of the circumstances under which her hasty engagement had been formed and broken, and how incomparably Sir Roland had acted throughout the whole.

Lady Stanmore was much touched, and expressed her surprise at his being able to command, and subdue

himself sufficiently to appear to take pleasure in his
brother's happiness.

"Appear!" exclaimed Lady Constance, "he *does*
take pleasure in it, for it is his own work. He released
me, unasked, from my fatal promise; he urged—entreated me to marry Henry; and to him it is that I
owe the means of doing so, for we were both poor,
and it was Sir Roland who gave this place and almost
all the fortune we have to Henry," and she covered
her face with her hands and burst into tears.

Lady Stanmore was speechless—she seemed suffo-
cating. In addition to the touching sentiments of extreme admiration which she felt at Sir Roland's conduct, an overpowering sense of the nature and value of
godly principles, and spiritual feelings, oppressed her
heart. She felt there must be a reality in religion
which she would never fully admit before, and her soul
humbled, yet elevated, lifted itself up in silent prayer
that she too might become a redeemed and devoted
servant of God. After saying a few kind and grateful
words to Lady Constance in return for the confidence
she had shewn her, and which she assured her should
never be betrayed, and expressing, though but faintly,
her sense of the nobleness of Sir Roland's conduct, she
retired into her own room, and there did she fervently,
on her knees, implore the blessing and forgiveness of
God for the long rebellion of her heart; entreating
Him to put His Spirit within her, and to make her
wholly His.

From that time the change in her was evident to
all, her natural amiability, enlisted in the cause of
Christianity, made her indeed a delightful creature.
The void in her heart, which had so long made her

restless and uneasy, was filled; and loving and beloved, she was a blessing to all who knew her.

Mr. St. Clair, returning to England, gladly accepted an invitation to visit Henry Ashton at Tregaron, and was delighted to find him so different a being, both in health and spirits from what he was when last he parted from him. Henry's gratitude and attachment to him were very great, and Sir Roland was truly glad to form a friendship with one, to whom, for his brother's sake, he felt so much indebted. Mr. Singleton also paid frequent and ever-welcome visits to Llanaven, and Lord Wentworth was almost continually there.

Sir Roland, after a time began to suspect that it was not only for his sake, that his friend shewed so much indifference to his own fine property in Dorsetshire, but that there was some greater attraction which drew him so often to Llanaven. Lady Florence was now near eighteen, very lovely and very lively, and Sir Roland could not but perceive that Lord Wentworth was much attached to her. He did not feel equal confidence, however, in her feeling towards him, and anxious that his friend should avoid the fate that had been so harrowing to him, he determined to speak to him, and entreat him to be sure of the grounds of his hope, before he ventured all his happiness on so young a creature.

Lord Wentworth was not handsome, but his animated look, and bright quick eye, gave a most pleasing expression to his countenance; and the amiability of his disposition, and his high principle, made Sir Roland feel confident that if Lady Florence really liked him, he would omit nothing in his power to make her happy.

"Do you not think Florence very lovely?" he said to him one day.

"Very," answered Lord Wentworth.

"I rather wished to speak to you about her," said Sir Roland.

"About her? You!" exclaimed Lord Wentworth in great alarm, "Ashton, you do not mean—you are not——"

"Me? Oh! no," replied Sir Roland, with a sad smile. "No, Wentworth, my heart is shut to that sort of thing. But I have thought that I perceived that yours was not, and I would entreat you to be sure that you have good reason for hope, before you let your feelings get too much entangled. I have no right to ask your confidence, but only wish that my fate may be a warning to you. I do not say, 'Love not,' far from it; I would say, 'Love,' but take care that your love is returned."

"I have taken care of that," said Lord Wentworth, smiling, with a heightened colour, "and was wishing to speak to you on the subject, when your question came out and terrified me so much."

"Why 'terrified you,' if your heart was at rest?" asked Sir Roland.

"A deadly fear seized me, that you might, without my perceiving it—have——"

"Oh! no. I see that she is lovely, and know that she is good, but my heart can never, I feel, be roused to any thing of that kind again. But how have you ascertained that your feelings are returned?"

"By asking her," replied Lord Wentworth, quietly.

"That is good authority, certainly," said Sir Roland, laughing, "and I am truly happy that you have such to go upon. And have you really settled it all with her? I am so thankful! for my heart has often trembled for you lately."

"Mine has, I know, many a time trembled for itself," said Lord Wentworth, "till at last I thought it would be best to put an end to doubt, one way or another, and so I spoke to her to-day, and feel very happy now."

"I suppose you do," said Sir Roland, amused at the absurdly quiet manner which Lord Wentworth chose to assume. I dare say you preferred receiving a favorable answer to having a refusal. Well, I am very thankful,— very thankful!" he added, though a shade of sadness settled on his countenance as he spoke.

"Ashton, will you let me speak one word to you?" exclaimed Lord Wentworth, suddenly, dropping his affected simplicity and apathy, and resuming his natural, animated manner.

"A thousand, if you like it."

"But it is about yourself."

"About me!" said Sir Roland. "There is not much to be said about me; but say whatever you like."

"I hardly know how to speak; but what I want to say is, that I wish so much that you would give up the determination never to—form any new ties—never, in short—to marry. I cannot think it right, that one so young should make such a resolution. Your heart is formed for affection, and you should cultivate it. I know you will forgive me, but it makes me unhappy to think, that you should cut yourself off from the best joys of life, by a too clinging regard to what is past. I know you love many, and specially that thing," he added, pointing playfully to Henry Ashton's boy, who was, as usual, sitting on Sir Roland's knee; "but it is not like having things of your own."

Sir Roland unconsciously raised the child in his arms as Lord Wentworth spoke, with a love scarcely less thrilling than that of a parent.

"You are wrong, Wentworth," he said, "in thinking I have determined never to marry. It is not so; but I do not feel that I could. The strong efforts I have made to detach my thoughts from the world — for she was the world to me — seem to have rendered me incapable of ever loving devotedly again, and without that I could not marry. I did not think, indeed, that I could ever again have felt such love for any living being as I do for this tiny thing;" and he pressed his lip repeatedly to the child's soft velvet cheek. "So in time I may feel other affections steal upon me: but I doubt it. However, do not be troubled for me; I am happier than I can express; and with a far more stable happiness than I ever enjoyed before, because my hope now cannot fail, and the more the tempest blows the closer does the refuge seem to me. If it is a daily conflict, it is, through Christ, a daily victory. 'In the world ye shall have tribulation,' He says, 'but be of good cheer, I have overcome the world.' Both these truths I have experienced, and I know that they are truths. Earth is not the home of happiness, for Satan is the prince of this world.

> 'Grief
> Stands symbol of our faith, and it shall last
> As long as man is mortal, and unhappy.

> The gay at heart may wander to the skies,
> And harps may there be found them, and the branch
> Of palm be put into their hands :— on earth
> We know them not ;— no votary of our faith,
> Till he has dropped his tears into the stream,
> Tastes of its sweetness.' "

" Yet no one ever tasted the sweetness of that stream more than you did, even before your heavy trial came," said Lord Wentworth.

" Nothing like what I have done since — oh! nothing like it !" exclaimed Sir Roland; " then — it was the best of my blessings ; now — it seems the only one — so completely does it swallow up all others.   No, Wentworth, I can add my testimony to that of Hernett, where he says "— and reaching down the book from the shelf, he read —"' Man may be disappointed in his greatest hopes in life, without on that account becoming unhappy.   I have long suspected, and am daily more and more, by the course of the world, and through my own daily experience, convinced, that there is no other actual misfortune, except this only — not to have God for our Friend.' "

THE END.

London:— Moyes and Barclay, Castle Street, Leicester Square.

MARY SPENCER

Bibliographical note:

this facsimile has been made from a copy in the
British Museum
(1362.a.16)

"O.1! MARY, WE HAVE GOT THE IMAGES AT LAST!"

P. 199.

MARY SPENCER:

A TALE FOR THE TIMES.

BY A. HOWARD.

" Evil men and seducers shall' wax worse, and worse, deceiving,
and being deceived."—1 Tim. iii. 13.

SEELEY, BURNSIDE, AND SEELEY,
FLEET STREET, LONDON.
MDCCCXLIV.

L. Seeley, Thames Ditton, Surrey.

MARY SPENCER.

CHAPTER I.

'But he who knew what human hearts would prove,
  How slow to learn the dictates of his love;
  That, hard by nature and of stubborn will,
  A life of ease would make them harder still,
  In pity to the souls his grace designed
  To rescue from the ruins of mankind,
  Call'd for a cloud to darken all their years,
  And said, " Go spend them in the vale of tears." '—COWPER.

'HUSH! Edward, hush, Mamma is still sleeping
one quiet pleasant sleep; come and see how pale
and sad she looks; it is very long since she slept
so soundly before, and her own little Edward will
sit quietly by me, and not disturb her with his
noisy play.'

This gentle admonition was addressed to a little
boy about six years old, who, tired of the restraint

which his young and joyous spirits had endured
for nearly half-an-hour, had just mounted a superb
rocking-horse, and was beginning to enjoy his elevated position, and the rapid motion of his favourite toy, when his sister's voice arrested his course
and sliding gently from the saddle, he once more
placed his stool by her side, and sat quietly down
to look over for the third or fourth time, the pic-
ture-books with which she vainly tried to amuse
him. Again and again his lips would part, and
some question about to be asked in a loud whisper
would be checked by Mary's placing her finger on
her own lips, and pointing out the beauties of the
coloured pictures with redoubled zeal : but it
would not do—Edward had seen mysteries in
the house which his young brain could not solve,
and pushing the tiresome books from him, he
looked up in his sister's face, and said—' But
Mary, will that dark cross man take away all our
beautiful things, and this nice house, and give my
rocking-horse away to some other little boy—and
will he put my own dear papa into prison ? Bateman says he will.'

Mary's eyes filled with tears, and drawing Edward on her knee, she whispered, 'No, Edward, the cross dark man cannot hurt poor Papa, for God will soon take him away from this sad world, to his own bright happy home in heaven, where he will have no more cough—no more sharp pains, and restless nights, but " God will wipe away all tears from his eyes." But his body must rest in the grave, Edward, till the resurrection-morning—that beautiful resurrection-morning.' Mary repeated, as if the star of hope from that goal of all her young wishes shed such a light over her future paths, that she saw not the thorns, and the weariness of the way, but was gazing with a feeling of present possession into that ' city which hath foundations,' when Edward recalled her to earth by repeating the rest of his question. ' But Mary, must I give them all my nice playthings, and shall we leave this large house, and live in a little cottage like poor old William Dalton's ? '

' We must go away from our happy home, Edward, and be content to give up some of those good things, which God has lent us so long : but God will not leave us ; he can make us as happy in our little rooms with their poor furniture, as if we were still in our own comfortable house, and had carriages and gay clothes, and many servants to wait upon us : but do not cry, Edward, you must not be a foolish little child any longer, but learn a great many useful things, and then you will soon grow up to be a man, and take care of dear Mamma when Papa is in heaven.'

There was something in the latter part of Mary's speech, that checked the half-uttered sob, which betrayed the depth of poor Edward's childish grief. Perhaps it was the promised manhood—some budding idea of the self-importance contained in those words, ' when you are a man,' that buoyed up his infant mind with the same kind of excitement which the planning of a new game, or the expectation of a pretty toy would have occasioned. Perhaps it was even the novelty connected with the idea of small rooms, and other garniture. Whatever it might be, we know not—little Edward himself knew not, but his fancy was amused and his tears dried, before his mother awoke from her short but refreshing sleep.

The father of Mary and Edward Spencer, was the only son of a gentleman, who, after squandering away a large property, died suddenly, leaving his son to begin life with a very small capital. By the wise arrangements of his guardians he was brought up to a mercantile life; and diligence, aided by the blessing of an overruling Providence, fixed his station among the most substantial merchants of the land, before he had completed his thirtieth year.

At this time Charles Spencer attended the ministry of a deservedly popular preacher in the metropolis—one whose life was the echo of his pulpit discourses. The young merchant heard the word with gladness, and welcomed with joy the news of salvation through a Saviour, to whose service (while he listened to the heavenly oratory with which —— pleaded his master's cause) he felt he could gladly devote every faculty of his being. Nor were these feelings altogether transient; the busy world into which he plunged the next day, wore off the brightness of their fervour, while worldly, ambitious, and selfish motives of action too often won a temporary dominion in his bosom; but Spencer was convinced that he was a sinner, and in the seclusion of his closet sought Him whom

to " know is life eternal," while in public he upheld
the cause of truth by appearing at meetings con-
vened to send the Gospel to the heathen, and by
contributing largely to the funds set apart for that
purpose. But though sincere, Spencer's faith was
feeble, and consequently his victory over the world
was incomplete. Grains of precious metal there
were indeed, mixed with the sparkling ore of his
profession, and the furnace was heating which
should try and bring forth the gold.

He married a beautiful portionless girl, who had
been brought up among those that fear God ; she
pursued her humble duties in the home of her
widowed mother, and her useful ones among the
children of the poor, scarcely troubled by one wandering or ambitious thought, till she consented to
become the wife of Charles Spencer. Her union
with him raised her at once to rank and affluence,
and the prosperous pair drove in their new barouche up the long shaded avenue that led to the
porch of their country-seat, their hearts insensibly
swelling with emotions that threatened hard to
root out those principles of godliness and humility
which had been planted in the mind of each. The

costly decorations of Elton Hall; the thickly wooded demesne; the gardens laid out with exquisite taste; the hot-houses stocked with rare exotics, invited them to spend the summer months in luxurious repose, and when the anxious excitement of some new speculation called Spencer back to London, a princely mansion in B—— square threw open its doors for their reception, and the soft carpets, the luxurious couches, perhaps even the very motto on the ancient crest, contributed its quota of aliment to 'the pride of life,' which struggled hard for the mastery in Spencer's breast. A few years passed on in this manner, yet did not his efforts for promoting the kingdom of God cease. An excellent school was built and endowed near Elton Hall, and a Scripture reader engaged to read the word of life to the unlearned inhabitants of the neighbouring village: contributions to every sound religious society were doubled, but all the while Spencer was verifying the words of him who "knew what was in man," "How hardly shall a rich man enter into the kingdom of God!"— his heart fluctuated between two masters; till at length the chastisement came—long, heavy, and severe—ending not till it drove him to follow the Lord fully. The first warning stroke was gentle; some trifling speculations failed; then came the news that a ship laden with rich merchandize was wrecked, and the whole cargo lost. In this vessel Spencer had a stake of considerable value, and his spirits, weakened by the effects of a feverish cold from which he had for some time suffered, gave way for the first time. A dark foreboding of the future seemed already to press upon him. The cold attacked his lungs, and warned by a dry short cough, he prepared with his Ellen, and their two children, to seek a milder climate, and a clearer sky.

In order completely to divest his mind of every care that might render void the salutary purpose of his sojourn in a foreign land, Spencer committed the entire management of his present harassing concerns and important projects, to his partner Mr. Thornton, who, besides being a zealous and skilful colleague, appeared to possess the additional qualifications of a faithful friend; and the readiness with which he took the whole toil off Spencer's mind, seemed to the poor invalid the noblest proof of sincere and ardent affection.

Early in the summer of 18—, the travellers arrived at the village of D——. They preferred this secluded spot to the gay resorts frequented by those who have to seek health in a land not their own ; for here they could dwell under the influence of a sunny sky, and balmy atmosphere, and enjoy complete repose unbroken by the presence of worldliness and fashion.

Mary Spencer was about twelve years old when her parents brought her and their infant son to D——, and through the whole course of her future life, she looked back upon her residence in this lovely spot with holy thankfulness, and remembered the lessons learned there in many an hour of sorrow and temptation.

The house in which her parents resided, was only separated by a grove of olives from the humble dwelling of Pastor Le Brun. He was one of those devoted ministers of the Protestant faith so often to be found in the south of France, who live among their beloved flocks upon a pittance which will scarcely provide the necessaries of life, and seldom wish for its expensive comforts. When Mary was sufficiently accustomed to the language

fully to comprehend and appreciate the beautiful
lessons which he taught, it was her greatest delight to sit and listen while Le Brun told of those
whose holy lives and martyr's deaths made the
surrounding country appear like sacred ground to
her young and aspiring mind. Sometimes he
would point to the distant ridge of the High Alps,
scarcely visible to their earnest gaze, and tell
of the dark and gloomy valleys which lie em-
bosomed among those vast mountains, and which
afforded a hiding-place to the people of God
through successive generations. 'The inhabitants of the valleys,' he said, 'like their Vaudois
brethren in the faith, remained true witnesses
for God when all Christendom had gone after
idols : and when the cruelties practised by
Louis the Eighth drove the suffering Albigenses
from their own troubled towns and villages, they
too received a brother's welcome to the refuge
of those wild fastnesses.' He would then describe some among the mountain-villages with
which he was familiar, till the name of many a
hamlet built on the edge of the snow-covered
precipice, or hid in the deep and rocky glens, was

treasured up in Mary's memory, coupled with a
deep veneration for that beauty of holiness which
had adorned so many of the martyred peasants of
St. Louis and Freyssiniere. While Le Brun spoke
of those " of whom the world was not worthy,"
he did not fail to set before this little child the
errors of that system of religion still dominant in
his native land. Le Brun loved his Romish brethren with a love utterly unknown to those who
would flatter them to sleep in their errors, and
hide from their eyes the fearful mark of the Beast
till it is too late to remove it from their foreheads
with the all-cleansing blood of Immanuel. He
loved their souls, and had often risked health
and home—yea, even life itself, in the endeavour
to snatch one Roman Catholic from the fearful
gulf over which he was hanging; and he loved
Mary's soul and knew that it was safe and very
right that she should be warned of a creed, whose
corrupt doctrines are often rendered attractive to
the young by the veil of fiction and romance thrown
over them, while they renounce the foundation of
all true religion, " Thou shalt have none other
Gods but me." But he did not stop here; he

knew that Mary might number herself among
Protestants, might abhor the name of Popery,
and all the while her own heart be at enmity with
God, and he took earnest and persevering pains to
teach her the laborious duty of self-examination.
' Never rest satisfied, my child,' he would say,
' with learning to cry Lord, Lord, and to speak
the language of his people; the barren fig-tree
threw out enough of such leaves, and looked as
comely as his fellows, but the good tree must
produce good fruit."

His precepts sank deep into Mary's heart, and
though often saddened by finding a canker concealed in the motive of her best actions, she gradually learned the glorious lesson, to count all her
own doings " but loss, for the excellency of the
knowledge of Christ Jesus her Lord."　She clung
to his cross for all her salvation, and while her
thoughts continually communed with Immanuel,
she became a settled and consistent Christian;
soothing her dying father's sorrows; often whispering words of high and heavenly hope, that
met at first but a feeble response in Mr. Spencer's
backsliding heart; but soon he too was able to

call the gnawing pain and distressing weakness—
" Our light affliction which is but for a moment."

And Mary shared all her mother's cares; she
watched with her by the restless bed of their beloved invalid through the long midnight hours.
She chose also to become the sole attendant of
her little brother, that he might not be left to the
care of the servant whom they had hired in Paris;
and it was at this time that she began, young as
she was, to endeavour to train Edward up for future usefulness and for eternity.

After a residence of some months at the village
of D——, Mr. Spencer's physicians advised him
to leave the spot he had chosen, and visit Italy,
or some other part of the south of France more
celebrated for its salubrious climate; but strange
and perplexing rumours from England detained
him at D—— till the winter was too far advanced
to admit of his travelling to any distant part of
the continent: or, what he now most earnestly
wished, returning home to his native land.

Days and weeks passed on in painful suspense,
and still tidings would occasionally reach him that
his affairs were not in the prosperous state they

once were : that heavy debts were incurring, and losses sustained, which a little prudence and forethought might have prevented. But though painful doubts would sometimes force themselves in, in spite of Spencer's confidence in his partner's skill and good faith, he always ended by saying, ' Thornton, though not a religious man, is honour itself; my property is as safe with him as in my own hands. I know he would not deceive me.'

Thus the frequent warning of real friends were regarded as officious, and even calumnious, and returning spring found Spencer still at D——, a fearful cough daily wasting his life, and scarcely strength left to return to London, when suddenly all remittances from England stopped, his letters addressed M. Thornton, Esq. —— street, were returned to him, and he prepared with an aching heart to accomplish his journey by short stages, the money in his hands barely sufficing to cover the heavy expense.

The mournful party arrived at their mansion in London early in the month of May, and found that Mr. Thornton had by foolish and dangerous speculations involved the firm in immense debt; that after vainly endeavouring to extricate himself from embarrassment, he had at last absconded with a large sum, which was now wanting to satisfy the demands of impatient creditors.

The blow fell heavily upon poor Spencer, but his faith was clear enough now to see the Lord's hand working through the second cause, and he bowed meekly to the stroke which he could not turn aside.

He made indeed a faint effort to stay the total ruin, but in vain; his health and energies were gone, and four months after his return to London he was carried from the scene of distress to an obscure lodging, and on the morning when our story begins, large placards were posted in the windows of No. —, B—— Square, giving notice of a bankrupt's sale.

CHAPTER II.

' And you and I shall surely stand
With Christ, on Zion's hill.'—Anon.

WHEN Mrs. Spencer had accompanied her husband to the lodging which was now his only home, she returned for a few hours to make some necessary arrangements, and collect her own and her children's wearing apparel; but, wearied out with painful exertion, and intense grief, she sought for the last time her own boudoir, and throwing herself upon a couch, fell into a gentle slumber, from which she was roused by Mary's appeal to little Edward; 'You must take care of poor Mamma, when Papa is in heaven.'

The words fell heavily upon her heart, but she subdued her grief for the sake of her children, and rising hastily from the couch she said, 'We must go now to poor Papa, and we will all nurse

him, and take great care of him, and perhaps,'—
she could not go on, for the hope which should
have followed that 'perhaps' was utterly vain.
But she was now impatient to rejoin her husband,
and even reproached herself for the delay of that
short slumber which wearied nature had forced
from her self-devotion.

While she hurriedly prepared to set out, forgetting at once the sorrow that oppressed her,
and the comforts she was leaving behind, in the
almost joyful feeling of being again by his side,
administering again to his comfort, Mary found
one moment to steal into her father's library, and
take a mute farewell of books that had been her
favourite companions during many solitary hours
since their return from France.

Through the mournful course of those four
months, her privilege of watching and waiting
upon her sick parent had often been suspended,
while he was engrossed to a degree far beyond
his fast sinking strength, with the vain effort to
save the wreck of his fortune, or in sad consulta-
tion with her mother upon some plan for the sub-
sistence of herself and his children, when he

c

should be taken from them : and now she looked
wistfully at several half-finished volumes, and almost longed to take them with her. 'They are
now no longer ours,' she said, and turning resolutely away to overcome the feeling of covetous-
ness that was rising within, she walked towards
the hall-door, and followed her mother into the
hackney coach in which Edward was already seated.

They drove slowly through one long street after
another, till at length they turned into one in
which the houses were lower and meaner than
most of those they had previously passed.   At the
door of one of these the horses stopped ; it was
opened by faithful Bateman, whose affection for
his master would not suffer him to resign his
charge, until the arrival of Mrs. Spencer and her
children rendered his services no longer needful.

Edward, whose prattle had not ceased during
their drive, became suddenly silent, and walked
along the narrow passage, and up the dingy staircase without uttering a word.   Bateman led the
way into a room on the second floor, and there by
the light of a few coals, propped up in an old arm-
chair, sat poor Spencer ; his head was bowed on

his breast, and a terrible fit of coughing prevented his returning at once the tender salutations of the beloved ones who stood around him.

Mrs. Spencer's strength gave way, and she sat down and sobbed bitterly, while Edward hid his face in his mother's lap, afraid to look round the gloomy room. Mary alone retained energy sufficient to cope with the griefs of that mournful hour; she could not soothe her mother, but her heart arose in prayer, and recollecting that the flickering light which played upon the discoloured walls, and the confusion with which the little furniture they had was huddled together, must necessarily increase the depression of those she loved, she prepared with eager hands to give an air of cheerfulness and neatness to their humble abode. She chose a large log of wood from among the scanty fuel laid up for their use, and throwing it on the fire, soon kindled a pleasant blaze. A few cups and saucers were next carefully washed and placed upon the table. The boiling kettle and bright light soon gave a sense of comfort to the sufferers, and Mary had the satisfaction of seeing her mother and Edward seated at the table, par-

taking with thankfulness of the frugal repast she
had spread for them.

A small yearly sum that had been settled upon
Mrs. Spencer, for her own private expenses, now
served to keep them from actual want, but it was
not enough to provide any of those luxuries,
which become necessaries to a frame worn out
with the torture of disease ; and Mary wondered
that all those kind friends, who used to smile upon
her when she was a very little girl, and look so
loving and affectionate, did not come near them
now, or think of her poor father who was dying,
and wanted many of those good things which he
had freely shared with others, in what she just
then called brighter days. She did not know
that her father had himself carefully concealed
the adverse state of his circumstances from his
one or two real friends, until his removal to this
obscure lodging rendered their diligent search
for him unavailing ; and she did not know
that many who had smiled upon her in the days
of prosperity, would turn away their heads now,
if she was walking along the dirty pavement of
the narrow street when one of their carriages

passed by. But she soon learned to call even these
days of sorrow bright days, for she was awakened
the next morning by the low sound of some one
speaking in prayer. She listened and heard her
father say, " My soul doth magnify the Lord, and
my spirit hath rejoiced in God my Saviour." He
paused for a few moments and then said again,
" I have heard of thee with the hearing of the
ear, but now mine eye seeth thee; wherefore I
abhor myself, and repent in dust and ashes."

He was again silent, and Mary rose softly from
the little bed which she had spread for herself in
one corner of the apartment, and went into the
sitting-room to prepare for the duties and trials of
the day. Mary's preparation was a sweet and
holy one; she fell on her knees and worshipped
the God of her salvation, trying to thank him for
his mercy to her dying parent, though a burst of
almost joyful tears was the only expression she
could use for some time; but the calm of true
devotion returned, and after earnestly seeking
forgiveness for the past, and more grace for the
future, she opened her Bible and was eagerly
drinking in its consolation, when her mother came

into the room. Mary flung her arms about her
neck, but neither of them could say much, and
each to hide her tears from the other, began to
make some preparation for their breakfast.

Little Edward was still sleeping, and Mary
leaned tenderly over him, hesitating whether she
would disturb the pleasant dream, which the smile
upon his young countenance told her he was
enjoying, when her father softly pronounced her
name. She was at his bedside in a moment, and
she thought his countenance was changed since
she looked at him a few minutes before.

She trembled violently while obeying his request that she would call her mother, and Edward.
' I am going now, Ellen,' he said, as his poor wife
knelt down, and took his cold hand in hers—' but
do not weep, my beloved, or think of me as if the
grave held your Charles; this poor frame must
rest there for a little while—a very little while,
Ellen, waiting the glorious resurrection.' He
stopped, and Mary held her breath to hear if her
father still breathed; but in a few moments he
went on in broken sentences, not addressing either
of the beloved mourners around his bed, but speak-

ing as if the visions of prophecy were passing before his mind, and already excluding every terrestrial thought ;—" His feet shall stand upon the mount of Olives"—" This corruptible must put on incorruption"—" Caught up to meet the Lord in the air"—" The inhabitant shall no more say I am sick"—Then opening his eyes, he turned them with an expression full of love upon his children, and said : ' We shall meet in that glorious city, my darling : perhaps your journey may be a long and weary one, for you are very young, or perhaps the Lord will come in the clouds of heaven before many years roll by, for all things seem hastening to that happy day ; but whichever way he leads you, my beloved ones, we shall meet in the new Jerusalem—the city of our God. Bring your Bible, Mary, and read it once more while I can hear it with you ;—but haste—haste—I must not tarry long.'

Mary could scarcely summon strength to obey the precious command, but she found the twenty-first chapter of Revelation, and read as distinctly as her sobs would permit ;—" And I saw no temple therein : for the Lord God Almighty, and the

Lamb are the temple of it. And the city had no need of the sun, neither of the moon, to shine in it, for the glory of God did lighten it, and the Lamb is the light thereof. And the nations of them which are saved shall walk in the light of it; and the kings of the earth do bring their glory and honour into it. And the gates of it shall not be shut at all by day; for there shall be no night there. And they shall bring the glory and honour of the nations into it. And there shall in no wise enter into it anything that defileth, neither whatsoever worketh abomination, or maketh a lie; but they which are written in the Lamb's book of life."

Mary read on in the strength of the effort with which she had subdued her sobs to obey her father's wish, but when she looked up, she saw that his head had sunk back again upon his pillow, and kneeling down beside her mother, she drew the terrified little Edward close to her side, and continued in mental prayer with her eyes fixed on her father's changing features, till at length the dying man said, "Fight the good fight of faith; lay hold on eternal life." The latter part of the sentence became less audible, and when it was uttered, Charles Spencer had passed from this troubled scene to join " the spirits of just men made perfect."

We need not linger long over the mournful hours that intervened between the moment of death, and the day when that worn body was committed to its humble grave.

The grief of the poor widow was deep, and though in some measure sanctified, it wore a character of hopelessness that almost threatened at once to snap asunder the frail cord of her own life, and thus leave her children orphans indeed. Mary's sorrow was truly hallowed; for some days after her father's death, she felt and spoke as if she had already done with earth, though still keenly alive to everything, however minute, that affected the happiness or comfort of her dear fellow-mourners. She did not seem to feel her own privations, or to admit one care for the future. With the eye of faith she saw that holy city, as if her feet already touched its threshold ; and the person from whom they rented their lodgings, told her neighbours, that ' the dear child would soon follow her father;

she was not for this world, but was already ripe
for glory.'

But so it was not—Mary was destined for many
long years of trial and usefulness in this world;
and surely an early meetness for heaven must be
the best preparative for doing our Saviour's will
on the road thither.   It seemed as if her Father's
love had provided a miraculous feast of peculiar
communion with the Lord, and had given her a
more vivid sight of his glory during these few
days, saying to her as the Angel did to Elijah of
old—" Arise and eat, for the journey is too great
for thee."

Edward was too young to feel those deeper
pangs of grief that increasing years always bring,
even to the young and happy-hearted; but he understood that his dear Papa would not speak to
him any more, that he could not smile upon him
now, and that in a day or two he would be laid in
the cold earth.   Mary tried to teach him that the
happy spirit was with the Lord Jesus Christ, but he
did not seem fully to comprehend how that could
be, and he looked wistfully at the bed, and the
lifeless form, and laying down his head on his little

arms, he cried himself to sleep, and as Mary
gently laid him down on her own bed, and spread
a light covering over him, she prayed that her
Edward might be dedicated to the Lord from that
hour, and that she might be strengthened to aid
her mother in training him up for the service of
the Holy One.

Four days after the death of Mr. Spencer, a
mourning train issued from a humble door in ——
Street. Mrs. Spencer and Mary, attired in some
half-worn mourning which was left among the
remains of their once ample wardrobe, followed
the coffin, leading little Edward by the hand. The
expression of their grief was veiled from the public eye, by the friendly hood which custom has
provided for scenes like these, and they did not
see the equipage which drove past just as they
reached the gate of the churchyard ; but Edward's
eye was attracted by a lady who looked out of
the carriage-window, and calling her coachman to
stop, beckoned to a little boy who was following
the funeral at a distance, and after asking him
some question, desired her servant to drive on
again.

At this moment they were met by the minister of the Gospel of peace, and Mary's heart beat high when that holy greeting broke on her ear;—" I know that my Redeemer liveth, and that he shall stand at the latter day upon this earth ; and though after my skin worms destroy this body, yet in my flesh shall I see God."

CHAPTER III.

' To praise Him is to serve Him, and fulfil
  Doing, and suffering, His unquestion'd will—
  To learn in God's own school the Christian part,
  And bind the task assigned thee to thine heart.'

                            COWPER.

' I saw Lady Sophia Benson, this morning, mamma,' said Edward, the evening after the funeral had taken place, ' she looked at me very hard, and the tears came into her eyes ; then she made her coachman stop and called a little boy to her. I think it was to ask about us—perhaps she will come and take us out of this ugly house. Do you think she will, mamma ?'

Poor little fellow ! the expectation that cheered him that evening was not to be realized for years to come, and though for a while he watched every carriage that went past, in hopes the kind face of Lady Sophia Benson might once more be seen at the window, he soon gave up the fruitless hope, and sought amusement in something else.　A new play of Mary's devising, or a simple lesson rendered pleasant by her mode of conveying it, often kept his infant mind diverted for hours which otherwise would have passed wearily away.

Mary saw that her mother's health had received a severe shock, and she often trembled to think that they might lose her also, and all her little plans were laid out in the manner which she thought would render life most agreeable to this dear parent.

She rose every morning at a very early hour, that her privilege of communion with God might not be intruded upon by any other duty, however sacred ; and after thus gathering strength for each day's supply, she began at once cheerfully to fulfil every menial office that their necessities required. The clean-swept floor, and white hearth-stone were each evidences of her toil ; and when Mrs. Spencer came into the sitting-room to unite with her children in a morning prayer, she was sure to find the frugal breakfast spread on the table, and the kettle singing on the fire, while the gloomy room itself seemed to grow brighter from the presence of the devoted young creature who welcomed her with a fond and cheering smile.

But in spite of every exertion to soothe her cares, and improve her health, Mary knew that her mother grew weaker and weaker. What could she do? To change their lodging seemed the only way left, and this could not be done without some expense, which Mrs. Spencer was very unwilling to incur, for if a shilling could be saved at all from their deep poverty, her children's future good was the purpose for which she laid it by.

But Mary felt that her mother could not live in her present abode; and her earnest entreaty, ' only a little way out of town, Mamma, where you can feel the light and warmth of the sun, and sometimes see the green fields,'—prevailed at last, and they removed to a pleasanter dwelling on the outskirts of the metropolis. The house was as poor, and the furniture as scanty as in their former dwelling, but then the sun shone more brightly upon them, the streets looked cleaner, and more cheerful, and they could walk every day where

green fields, and blooming gardens gladdened
their hearts, and raised their drooping spirits.
Mrs. Spencer seemed to revive at once, and was
soon able to resume her share of those duties
which had pressed too heavily upon a girl so
young as Mary. Edward too found room to run,
and play, and the sickly look and fretful voice that
had often wrung the heart of his mother and sister, were now exchanged for the joyous laugh,
and the glow of health. Too young to know cares
for the future, he enjoyed the blessings of to-day,
as the Christian would enjoy them, if he were influenced by the spirit of his master's command ;
" Take no thought for the morrow, for the morrow shall take thought for the things of itself :
sufficient unto the day is the evil thereof."

This command had often chased away a sad foreboding out of Mary's heart, and the strength thus
saved from useless repinings, she devoted to the
active fulfilment of her present duties.

Her mother now superintended their few domestic arrangements, and also assisted in the daily
instruction of her little son ; but Mary before their
calamities overtook them had been receiving a su-

perior education, and though deprived of this advantage at a very early age, her native talents, and able instructors, had already laid up a store of knowledge which she turned to good account in after life. She was familiar with the French and German languages, and had made some progress in the study of Latin and Greek. These she afterwards imparted to Edward with so much success, that she laid a fair groundwork for his classical education, while yet their poverty seemed to exclude all hope of its ever being completed.

History had been the delight of her leisure hours during their long sojourn in France, and she studied with her father some branches of science which seemed almost beyond the reach of her tender years.

To make full use of these acquirements was now Mary's earnest desire : ' I am in my fifteenth year, she reasoned with herself, and as I can teach Edward, surely I might find some other little girls or boys whose parents would engage me to instruct them, and then I would lay by the money for mamma, lest sickness should come upon her again ; or it will help, when Edward grows up, to enable

D

him to enter college.' She sat musing for a moment, and then continued her train of thought aloud ;—' No, he will never be able to enter college ; how could he be educated for it, and then it would require so much money—no, Edward must be contented with a humble trade, he can serve God in it as well as at college.'

Mrs. Spencer sighed while she looked at Mary's thoughtful and abstracted countenance, but Edward whose ear was caught by the sound of his own name, came close to his mother, and leaning upon her lap, said in a low voice ; ' Mamma, what is a humble trade ?'

' By a humble trade, my dear,' said Mrs. Spencer, ' Mary means one that can be carried on by people who have very little money to begin with, and one that belongs entirely to those who move in a humble station of life ; such for instance is the trade of Mr. Hawkins, our baker, and also those of the haberdasher, and cabinet-maker, whose shops you see on the opposite side of the street.'

' I will never be a baker, or a haberdasher, or a cabinet-maker,' interrupted Edward with a glowing cheek, ' I will be a gentleman, I will be a'——

' Whatever God pleases, my boy,'—gently interposed his mother ; ' it has pleased him to make you a poor boy now, and if it be his will to keep you poor and lowly all your life, be sure, my Edward, it is the best life for you. When we reach our happy home in the New Jerusalem, it will not trouble us much that we journeyed thither in the company of poor and unlearned persons, rather than with those who live in splendid houses, and have much of the wisdom of this world.'

But Edward's irritated feelings were not to be pacified even by his mother's gentle words, and he kept repeating in a peevish tone, ' but I will not be a baker, or a haberdasher either,' till Mary's conscience began to rebuke her for being the unintentional cause of kindling those feelings of pride and ambition in his infant breast. ' It was my pride,' she said in her heart, ' that made me dream of colleges, and learned professions for my poor brother, and my foolish words have brought uneasy thoughts for the future into his little head, which time may only ripen into the evil fruit of discon-

tent with the lot my God has prepared for him.
And yet,' she went on as the sudden thought
flashed into her mind, ' perhaps by diligence, and
self-denial, I may be able to lay by enough to pay
his expenses through college. It would take a
very large sum, and I have no way as yet to gain
even a very little money; but Edward is only
seven years old now, surely in ten or eleven years
more it might be possible, and then Edward would
be a clergyman; that is, if his own heart be first
given to the Lord; and he would spend his days
in teaching the poor and ignorant the way of eternal life.'

Mary did not speak these thoughts aloud, but a
few days after when she was sitting alone with her
mother, she said, ' Mamma, now you are nearly
well, and able to do so many things that I used to
do for you, I have a great deal of spare time—
several hours every day.'

' And yet it is not idle time, my Mary, for I believe you have learned to find employment for every
moment; your own and Edward's clothes bear
witness to your industry; and now that we have so
few books, I am much pleased with the method you

have taken to retain the knowledge you once had the means of acquiring.'

'Do you mean my chronological chart, Mamma? Oh that is very imperfect, though I hope it will help me with my plan. And I have written out all the problems that I can remember—but my beautiful globes—no, I will not wish for them; it was God's will that I should lose them, and I think it would be something like coveting, to long for them back again; but don't you think it would be a good way to make one column on my chart for prophetical dates? I would write the beginning of the 1260 days opposite the reign of Justinian; date 533 (that was the year he passed his edict giving so much power to the Pope, you know, Mamma) and opposite the date of the reign of terror in France, I would write end of the 1260 days, and the pouring out of the vials on the kingdoms of the beast. I think this would help me greatly in my plan, for M. Le Brun used to say, that while little children are learning history and chronology, they should be taught to see the fulfilling of God's word through it all.'

'I think so too, Mary, but you have not told me

your plan yet. I am afraid poor Edward could not
give us much more of his time and attention than
he already does.   While he is so young it would
do him harm to keep him very close to his books.
You know the little hymn,—

> ' In books, and work, and healthful play,
>   Let my first years be past.'

' The healthful play is as necessary to make him
a strong man, as the books are to make him a wise
one.'

' Yes, Mamma, but I am not thinking only of
Edward, at least not only of teaching him now.
My chart, and my problems belong to a double
plan ; they will help Edward a little when he is old
enough to understand them, but in the meantime
I might teach some other children, whose parents
could afford to pay me a very little ; and I would
lay up all I could gain in this manner for Edward,
when he is old enough to go through college.   Do
you like my plan, Mamma ?'

' I should approve highly of your plan, Mary,'
said Mrs. Spencer, tenderly kissing her, ' if you
were a few years older, but you are far too young
at present.'

' But, Mamma, I have been taught a great many things which other girls have not had an opportunity of learning, and I think I could remember how the masters, and more than all, my own dear father used to teach me, and I would be very patient, and kind to my pupils.'

' And if other mammas knew my Mary as I do, I should not doubt of your success in obtaining pupils; but who would entrust the education of their children to a girl not yet quite fifteen?'

' Oh, mamma, I quite forgot that,' exclaimed Mary; ' No one would ever take the trouble to find out if I could teach anything; and they would perhaps think me very presumptuous and silly for trying to begin such an important task. I am afraid several years must pass away before I can lay by any money for Edward.'

After this conversation, Mary tried to banish her plan, as she called it, out of her mind: it did not appear to be God's will that she should accomplish it, and she knew that vain wishes indulged were a great snare to the soul, and that the foolish habit called ' castle-building ' is really sinful; so she had just resolved to think no more of being a teacher ; when a circumstance occurred which gave her an opportunity of trying her powers, though in a very humble and subordinate capacity.

Miss Collins, their landlady, kept a day-school, in which she gave the usual superficial education, afforded by the lower class of academies, to about twenty girls. A week after Mary had spoken to her mother about being a teacher, Miss Collins was taken ill, and at Mary's earnest entreaty, Mrs. Spencer reluctantly permitted her to superintend the school for a few days.

' It would be such good practice for me,' said Mary, in the joy of her heart, but her courage almost gave way as she opened the schoolroom door, and heard about a dozen voices all talking together, evidently without one older, or wiser head to govern their noisy tongues. She had some difficulty in introducing herself as their new teacher, and when she had done so, the stare of surprise or curiosity on every face, and the scarcely suppressed titter from the corner of the room, where two or three of the elder girls were sitting, completed her confusion.

But she was not to be so easily overcome ; she

had undertaken this task for a good purpose, so
when the sound of the rude laugh made her tremble, her heart rose in prayer for strength in this
time of need, her courage returned, and she went
on with her task. The labour was more wearying
than she had expected, for she had to follow the
rules laid down by Miss Collins, all grounded upon
a plan at once irksome to the teacher, and dull
and uninteresting to the learner. Mary felt very
tired of hearing long pages of grammar, and
columns of the dictionary, long before this part of
the business was really over.

She determined, however, to give relief to her
own jaded mind, and to call back the wandering
attention of her pupils, by making the pleasure of
the geography-lesson compensate for the monotony
of the rest. Three well-worn maps were all she
could find in the room ; she selected Europe, and
after making her young charge point out the situation of the principal places on it, she endeavoured
to connect some historical anecdote with each, and
to draw from it a lesson of warning, or a confirmation of scripture truth.

Who built Petersburgh ? was a question that

passed rapidly down her class, till at last one little girl replied,—' The Czar Peter the Great.' And then Mary told them, that he built it at a vast expense of human life, because the place on which its foundations were laid, was a swamp, or marsh, which made the air so full of unwholesome vapours, that many thousands perished while they were building it, for as fast as one party of labourers died, he sent orders to bring others from more distant parts of his empire.

' It was very cruel of the tyrant emperor,' she continued, ' to bring them away from their own home, to labour at his fine city, and die in that strange place. Can you tell me any verse in the Bible, which reproves this wicked conduct of the Czar Peter?'

A look of wonder was the only answer: no one could remember such a verse, so Mary opened her Bible, and read the twelfth verse of the second chapter of Habakkuk. " Woe to him that buildeth a town with blood, and establisheth a city by iniquity." Then she told them that this man is called Great, because he improved the wild country over which he reigned, and taught his subjects,

who were almost savages, how to build ships, and
a great many other clever things which they did
not know before; but, she added, with all his improvements he never reformed himself; he continued a miserable slave to his own guilty passions,
so that a poor man who fears God, and keeps his
commandments, is greater than the Czar Peter
ever was, for you know we read in the sixteenth
chapter of Proverbs, " He that is slow to anger,
is better than the mighty; and he that ruleth his
spirit, than he that taketh a city."

Several of the little girls could show her
the islands in the Mediterranean sea, but not
one of them knew that Candia was the same
as Crete, of which Titus was the first bishop.
And there was a glow of interest on the young
countenances around her, as she showed them the
bay, called ' the fair havens,' on the coast of Candia, and pointed out to them the city of Phenice,
which the crew of the ship of Alexandria vainly
endeavoured to reach, during the fearful storm
that overtook St. Paul and his companions, on
their way to Italy.

The barren and rocky isle of Patmos in the

Archipelago, was looked at again and again, for here, Mary said, St. John was banished, and here he saw the wonderful visions contained in the book of Revelation.

Just as this lesson concluded, the clock struck three, so she dismissed her school, and returned to her mother's apartment. She found the difficulties of her new office greater than she had expected, and she remained silent and thoughtful throughout the rest of the day. When they were sitting together in the evening, Mrs. Spencer said to her, 'Mary, you must not go back to the schoolroom to-morrow; you will only wear out your own strength and spirits, before they are sufficiently established to enable you to go through a duty so arduous with safety to yourself, and benefit to others.'

'Oh, Mamma,' exclaimed Mary, 'do not take part with my foolish fears, and selfish wishes against me. I can hardly conquer the strange dislike I feel to the thought of going again into Miss Collins's schoolroom. But I know I ought to go, for I only dislike it if I begin to think how the older girls laughed when I first went into the

room, and when I remember how long and stupid
those spelling lessons were. But, ah! if I am so
easily discouraged, I shall never do anything to
help you, or dear Edward, and what is worse, I
shall be a very timid, useless servant of the Lord
Jesus Christ.'

Her mother did not answer, and Mary said
again, ' If you please, Mamma, I will try and think
no more about the school to-night. I will get my
chart, and write out a few dates, if I can remember them, and perhaps I can put my troubles quite
out of my head until the morning; you know,
" sufficient unto the day is the evil thereof," and
when the morning comes we can pray for grace
to uphold us through the ·day.'

' And do not forget to pray for your scholars
too, my child, it will be a good means of increasing your interest in them.'

' There was one sweet little girl, Mamma, whom
I am sure I should love dearly ; she is only seven
years old, and she listened more attentively than
any of the other girls did; her name is Emma
Clifford. But I must not talk about them now, or
I shall still fancy I see the sneering smile that

Lucy Wilkins had on her face nearly the whole morning. I will get my chart now.'

As she said this, Mary took out a large sheet of paper which she had carefully ruled in distinct lines, each headed with the names of the principal kingdoms in Europe; in these lines she was writing from memory, the names of the sovereigns, and the most remarkable events, without any assistance but a small volume on prophecy. As she had reserved one broad line for prophetical dates, she found this little book very useful in ascertaining the period commonly fixed upon as that in which some prediction was fulfilled.

She sat for a long time writing in silence, occasionally stopping to consider, or applying to her mother for assistance. At length she exclaimed, ' I am going to write the pouring out of the first vial now Mamma; my little book places it in 1789, the same year with the opening of the sixth seal. The first vial contained the grievous and noisome sore of infidelity. I think I will write among my remarkable persons opposite to this vial, Voltaire, Rousseau, and Thomas Paine, who lived about this time. This grievous sore fell upon those who had the mark of the beast ; but, Mamma, I have heard you say that it spread greatly in England, and we were quite a Protestant nation then, you know.'

' Our government and laws were Protestant, my child, and the greatest part of the people were so in name ; but the number is very small, I fear, who in any country really protest against the errors of Romanism. I often think that the mark of the beast will be found upon many who never wore it openly upon earth. Do you think that all those poor men whom we used to hear crying out, " No Popery," and who took pains to write those words in large chalk letters upon the walls, really knew what Popery was ? '

' I am afraid not, Mamma ; or perhaps they may know a little about it : I dare say they know that the Papists call the Pope the head of the church, and that they say part of their prayers to the Virgin Mary, and other Saints ; but I think they do not all know that Popery begins by deny-ing that Christ is able to save us completely, and so putting something of our own in the place of his merits. I suppose when people believe like

this, Mamma, that not having true faith they are
not able to do real good works, because their hearts
remain wicked and averse to the commandments
of God; and then they begin to think of all manner of strange works to please God with, such as
penances, and fastings, and wearing hair-shirts to
hurt their bodies.'

'There are others who would not think these
things good works, Mary, and yet trust in their outwardly moral life, their regular attendance at
church, and their liberality in giving alms to the
poor. Now let us think, Mary, what are called
good works in the Bible?'

'I think, Mamma, one of the good works
commended in Scripture is the most difficult of
all. Our Lord Jesus Christ calls it " cutting off
the right hand," or " plucking out the right eye."
Oh, I am sure it is harder to take out one sin
from the heart that has long kept it hidden there,
than to do a hundred penances, or fast through
twenty Lents: such sins as selfishness, and pride.'
Mary stopped and remained for a few moments in
deep thought, and then taking up her pen she
began writing again. 'Mamma,' she said, ' how

fearful the outpouring of the second vial was; Do you remember it was said that during the reign of terror, blood streamed in such quantities through the streets of Nantes * that it was necessary to make an artificial conduit to carry it off.'

'The very name of that town gives the stamp of retribution to those fearful judgments, Mary; it was by the revocation of the Edict of Nantes that Louis the fourteenth began his wicked persecution of his Protestant subjects, and you know what the "Angel of the waters" was heard to say; "Thou art righteous, O Lord, which art, and wast, and shalt be, because thou hast judged thus. For they have shed the blood of saints and prophets, and thou hast given them blood to drink: for they are worthy." Rev. xvi. 5, 6. But we must not go on with this interesting subject; it is late, and you will require a good night's rest to prepare you for the arduous duty of to-morrow.'

Mary did not speak of to-morrow, but went quietly to rest, and rose early, that none of her

* See Habershon.

E

pleasanter duties might be left undone. She made no allusion to her task until, about ten minutes before ten, she came to her mother for a farewell kiss before she went into the school-room.

After this morning she appeared more cheerful, and went day after day until Miss Collins recovered, and found her school had been so well attended to, that she asked Mary to continue as her assistant, offering her a very small yearly sum for so doing. Mary had by this time become attached to several of the children, especially to little Emma Clifford ; so she accepted the proposal Miss Collins made, with less reluctance than she would have thought possible a month before, and having obtained her mother's sanction she went on quietly and conscientiously in the same monotonous round of duties, for the long period of three years.

CHAPTER IV.

WE must give only a brief and hasty sketch of
the next few years in Mary's life, during which
she went on with her toil in the little school; and
though no heavy trial overtook her in that period,
it was a season of continued discipline.

Miss Collins knew that her young teacher's
store of knowledge, and method of imparting it to
others, greatly surpassed anything which she herself possessed, and therefore, she was anxious to
retain her services; yet this desire was not sufficient to control the harsh temper, and rude speech,
which often embittered poor Mary's task. Miss
Collins especially disliked the pains she took to
bring the truths of religion into the daily instruction of her young charge. Sometimes she was
contented with muttering, that, 'she had no great
fancy for saints;' at others she would roughly

stop the lesson, and say in a loud and angry tone,
' she would have no more cant for one morning
at least.'   And then the sneering smile would
come back on Lucy Wilkins' face, and the titter
that went to Mary's heart when she first came to
the school, rung in her ears again ; for children
soon learn to " sit in the seat of the scorner."

The tears often came into Mary's eyes ; but
there was prayer in her heart, and strength was
given, and the tears dried, while she felt a recompense for all her trouble in the artless and increasing love of little Emma Clifford.

Emma did not quite understand what Miss Collins was angry with her dear Mary Spencer for,
but she knew that she was angry, and that Mary
was very sad, and then her little cheek would glow,
and a sob be hardly repressed, while she came
closer to her teacher's side, showing by the movement, how much her heart sympathized with all
her griefs.

Emma Clifford was the daughter of a gentleman
then residing in India.   Upon the death of his
wife, he had sent their only child to England in
the charge of a respectable female.

When she arrived in England, she was placed under the joint guardianship of two near relations of his own. One of these, his eldest sister, took the little stranger under her roof—we cannot say under her care, for Miss Clifford was wholly devoted to literary pursuits, and had no time to spare for the child of her absent brother; but she hired a nurse, and fitted up a room as a nursery, where she placed poor Emma, with strict orders that she should be taken out to walk every day, and keep perfectly quiet when in doors.

The nurse, however, loved Emma, and showed her love by spoiling her so much, that Miss Clifford's injunctions about quietness were often quite forgotten. This would not do at all; her mind was disturbed by loud shouts of laughter in the midst of a learned metaphysical treatise; or perhaps the threads of her ideas snapped by the sound of running and jumping on the nursery floor, just as she was on the point of solving a difficult problem: so to school Emma must go; 'and it does not much signify where for so very young a child,' soliloquised Miss Clifford, ' the nearest day-school that can be found where she will be kept

during the morning hours.' The lady's maid
mentioned Miss Collins, and Miss Collins was
fixed upon, without much trouble being taken by
the learned lady to find out whether her school
was respectable, or her own qualifications in any
way suited to her important office.

Emma had been two months at the school,
when Mary Spencer first became her teacher; and
now as the days and months rolled by, she was
gradually improving under better instruction than
her aunt had cared to provide for her; but one
day, when she had been nearly three years at the
school, Miss Clifford remarked to the nurse;
'How greatly Miss Emma is changed for the
better; she is so docile and tractable now, that it
is almost a pleasure to have her in the room with
me. Miss Collins must have an excellent method
with children.'

'I believe she has very little to do with Miss
Emma's improvement, Ma'am,' said the nurse, 'a
poor young lady who attends there as a sort of
teacher may take all the credit, as she has all the
fag of it. Miss Emma says that Miss Collins is very
cross to her, and often makes the poor thing cry.'

' If that be the case,' said Miss Clifford, ' we must try and engage the teacher to attend Emma at home. Do you know her name ? '

' Miss Spencer, Ma'am, I believe. I saw her once or twice when I went to fetch Miss Emma ; she is quite a lady in her manner of speaking : so kind and gentle ; but Miss Collins is a cross vulgar-looking woman.'

Miss Clifford did not encourage the nurse to talk any more, and the subject dropped, and would probably have been altogether forgotten ; but Emma, to whom nurse told the glad tidings as soon as she returned from school, soon found an opportunity of petitioning her aunt to carry her kind intention into execution, and in a short time Mary Spencer relinquished her engagement with Miss Collins, and commenced the more pleasing task of teaching her best-loved pupil in her aunt's residence.

She stayed with her every morning from ten till one o'clock ; and when through Miss Clifford's interest with another lady, her afternoon hours were also occupied, Mary was enabled with a grateful heart, to give many comforts to her mother and brother, of which they had long been deprived. All her hard earnings when with Miss Collins, were carefully put by, for the purpose of promoting Edward's future advancement. College, would occasionally come into Mary's mind, though she tried to shut out the ambitious thought, as something far too high for her to aspire to: but College remained in Edward's mind, as the settled goal of his wishes,

Though still very young, his talents were beginning to give fair promise of future brilliancy, under the skilful guidance of his sister, who devoted the evening of her days of toil, to his instruction. But her tender and subdued spirit was often pained by his expressions of early longing after the fame of human knowledge, uttered with much boyish petulance, and even impatience at those hindrances to his future career which poverty would hold up before his eyes. His fancy however, generally overleaped them all, and made him by turns the chief of English philosophers, a poet of the first order, or Archbishop of Canterbury. And when Mary would say to him ; ' Better far to be a missionary, telling the poor heathen

about the Lord Jesus Christ; using all the talents
God has given you to promote his kingdom; or,
if it be his will, to toil for your daily bread, unknown
and unregarded by men, than to shine in their
eyes until perhaps you would be dazzled with your
own brightness, and so be one of those whom the
god of this world blinds, "lest the light of the
glorious Gospel of Jesus Christ should shine into
them," he would throw his arms about her neck,
and say; ' Well, I will be the missionary like Bu-
chanan or Henry Martyn, but not the trade—not
the humble trade, Mary.'

Yet Edward was a lovely and a loving child.
His mother and Mary both hoped that the good
seed had taken root, and was springing up, though
many weeds remained to obstruct its growth. He
listened with deep attention whenever they would
converse upon some character in scripture history;
and he would return from a missionary meeting
with his mind full of the sublime object of the in-
stitution. Many a scheme of future usefulness
was then planned, which though for the most part
impracticable, nourished Mary's fond hope that he
would be a devoted and a holy man. She did

not at that time remark how soon the impression
died away, and the schemes were laid aside when
some new idea took possession of his fancy. A
better supply of books, which Mary's purse could
now occasionally add to, afforded him the pleasure
of variety; and the dreams of the poet, and the
tales of the historian, generally effaced the remembrance of the holier wonders which he heard
at the missionary meeting.

By this time he had completed his fourteenth
year, and had acquired a good knowledge of those
languages in which Mary was able to instruct him;
but the prospect of ever being able to prepare for
a learned profession did not grow brighter, and
the necessity of his learning to support himself,
and relieve Mary (who for his sake had added to
the number of her daily engagements) weighed
much upon her mother's mind.

An advertisement for an out-door apprentice to
a bookseller, attracted her attention: the little
store Mary had hoarded up to defray college expenses would just pay the fee, which was moderate,
and the situation of the shop was within a short
walk.   Mrs. Spencer saw that no time was to be

lost; she made every necessary inquiry, and completed all her arrangements with Mr. Singleton in a few days; and it was settled that Edward should commence this new course of life in one fortnight from the day Mrs. Spencer had read the advertisement aloud to her anxious children.

Mary looked upon the event as an indication of God's will, and cheerfully acquiesced in the overthrow of all her cherished plans; but her sorrow was very great when she saw the pale cheek of her brother, and missed his merry laugh, and animated conversation. Edward on this occasion gave way to all the selfishness of disappointed ambition. He did not reproach his mother, but he murmured at his lot; and Mary feared that he drew comfort from the very same shadows which had stolen from him the peace of a contented mind; for she heard him say (as if trying to repress the bitterness of his feelings) 'Well, well, Kirke White carried a butcher's basket for some time, but he soon found means to throw away such base employ, and so perhaps may I.'

But his grief was forgotten, and Mary's sorrow on his account completely swallowed up in the far

heavier affliction which overtook them a few days
before Edward should have begun his new employ ;
—this was the loss of their beloved mother.
Her death was not the work of gradual decay, as
their father's had been, but the sudden stroke of
a malignant fever.   An illness of five days, during
the greater part of which she was under the influence of delirium, terminated her earthly course,
and admitted her into the " rest which remaineth
for the people of God."

The days of this mourning seemed yet more sad
than those which followed the death of Mr. Spencer.   There was no longer a surviving parent
needing the devoted care of her affectionate children, and Mary's faith, though it rested calmly on
the assurance that her mother had, long before
her last illness committed the salvation of her soul
to " Him who is able to keep that which is committed unto him against that day," yet wanted
the additional support which her father's happy
foretaste of victory gave. But Edward did all in his
power to comfort her ; he seemed to forget self for
a time, and went to Mr. Singleton's a few days
later than had been appointed, without a murmur,

and with feelings subdued in some measure to the lowly career marked out for him.

And now poor Mary felt the pangs of loneliness and bitter bereavement. Edward, though he returned home in the evenings, dined with Mr. Singleton, and when she came in from the long morning's toil to eat her simple meal alone, how much she missed the kind hands that used to unfasten her bonnet and shawl, and bring a comfortable pair of slippers to give ease to her tired feet; how often she longed to hear the gentle voice whose tender welcome had been the sweetest reward of all her increasing labours. Yet these hours of loneliness became holy hours to Mary Spencer. As soon as she had swallowed her hasty dinner, she flew to her bible, and eagerly sought to check, with its words of perfect peace, the almost convulsive sob that was ready to rise; and by degrees peace returned, and she felt that her Father's chastisements had wrought her spiritual profit.

The brother and sister met every evening, and Edward always looked forward to that hour with the anticipation of much domestic comfort. When

he reached home he was sure to find the tea-table
spread, and Mary ready to receive him with her
own dear smile, even when that smile was chastened with a feeling of sadness.   She did her utmost to cheer, while she improved, his leisure;
and they often pursued together those studies in
which she had been his teacher, and in which she
still far excelled him.

One evening he laid down Robertson's history
of Charles the Fifth, which he had been reading
aloud, and said abruptly, ' It is very strange how
such bad tools worked out the Reformation.   Our
blood-thirsty Henry the Eighth, and that artful
Maurice of Saxony, were detestable characters.'

' Worked out the Reformation, Edward!' exclaimed Mary, ' these were not the men who
achieved that glorious work.   The Lord indeed
made use of their swords to curb the powers that
opposed the spread of his truth, and to overthrow
the sanctuaries of a polluted worship, thus making
way for the voice of his servants, and preparing
room for them to dwell in.   You have only to look
to the history of idolatrous Israel for similar actors
under similar circumstances.   Jehu's courage and

valour were used to bring the " seven thousand" out of the caves and dens of the earth, in which they had hidden themselves during the dreadful days of Jezebel's sway, and to punish the wicked powers that had forced them to make their home in the desert. But Jehu was not a good man. You remember the witness of scripture, " Jehu took no heed to walk in the law of the Lord God of Israel with all his heart, for he departed not from the sins of Jeroboam who made Israel to sin." I often think I can trace a strong similarity between the principal characters and events of those times, and other wonderful events and great characters that marked the period of the Reformation. Israel had her Elijah, her Elisha, and her Obadiah, and we'——

'Our Luther, and our Calvin, and our Cranmer,' interrupted Edward. 'I wonder did the two latter think they were justified by a heavenly commission in the murder of poor Joan Bocher, and the Arian Servetus, because the prophet Elijah, at the express command of the Lord, slew the prophets of Baal at the brook Kishon.'

Mary laid down her work, and looked up at

Edward to see if his countenance would explain
the sarcastic speech he had just uttered; but she
thought, by the flash of excitement that was fading from his cheek, that he had hastily spoken the
suggestion of some other person, in order that she
might, in her own gentle and skilful manner, clear
those characters upon which he was wont to look
with reverence,

' Edward,' she said, ' when I first read a complete
biography of Cranmer, and came to that part of
his life which is stained by the condemnation of
poor Joan Bocher, I burst into tears and closed
the book with a feeling of bitter disappointment,
such as you would scarcely think a record of past
ages could bring. A dense cloud seemed to pass
over all my imagination had before regarded as
perfect light; and so assuredly the Lord's truth,
which was published in that important age, remained, though very fragile were the earthen vessels that contained it. However, I concluded at
once, that Cranmer was not, could not be a child
of God, for it is written, " We know that no murderer hath eternal life abiding in him." But a little
after-thought led me to consider this fearful crime

as the fruit of that system under which Cranmer
had been early trained. Wherever the Church
of Rome was dominant, death was the reward of
heresy, and Cranmer's mind had been so long
inured to this edict of papal tyranny, that he regarded the execution of the sentence pronounced
upon a heretic, as a simple act of justice.'

' You might make the same plausible excuse for
Queen Mary, and her atrocious tools Bonner and
Gardiner.'

' I do not say it to excuse Cranmer, but to
prove that his deed was the foul fruit of the same
Popery that instigated their still more malignant
actions. It will do more good, I believe, to condemn a corrupt creed, than a corrupt character;
for see how deeply even a remnant of that creed
served to criminate an otherwise holy man. Our
venerable martyr was, we trust, fully freed from
the Romish yoke, before his blood was shed by
Romish malice; but the wicked Queen, and her
priests (as far as human knowledge can ascertain)
lived and died with the mark of ' the Beast' deeply
branded on their foreheads. You have forgotten,
while condemning some of the royal upholders of

the Reformation, the fairer example of the young
king who so long refused to sign Joan Bocher's
death warrant, and Frederick of Saxony, whose
name is more intimately connected with the Reformation, than that of his less worthy nephew.
But I do not know why we are disputing on this
subject at all. The truth of God depends not on
the fidelity of its professor, and though we must
know that many who gave public countenance to
its faithful heralds, did so without having their
own hearts affected by it, we know too, that far
more than seven thousand of God's people came
out of the idol-church of Rome, and confessed a
pure faith before men.'

Edward did not reply, but seemed satisfied with
what his sister had said, and went on reading.
But Mary was not satisfied; she would have been
more so, had Edward's strictures on the characters
of the Reformers, appeared to be the spontaneous
expression of his own mind, grieved to find dark
spots where he had thought all was fair; for she
was convinced it is always safer to know the whole
truth, even if that knowledge bring with it much
disappointment and distrust of man. It would still

teach the divine lesson, "Cease ye from man, whose breath is in his nostrils, for wherein is he to be accounted of?" But she thought by her brother's words and manner, that he spoke the suggestion of another, perhaps of a traitor to the cause of truth, and she laid her head on her pillow that night with so many uneasy thoughts that the midnight hour had long past by before she found rest in quiet sleep.

CHAPTER V.

THE next morning, while Mary and Edward were seated at their quiet breakfast, a note from Miss Clifford was given to the former, requesting that she would omit Emma's usual morning lesson, and, with her brother, spend the evening at Bath Terrace, 'to meet (she concluded) Lady Sophia Benson, who thinks she shall discover in you the children of a distant relative.'

The name of Lady Sophia Benson brought back many childish joys and sorrows to Mary's mind. 'I remember her kind smiling face,' she said, 'almost as vividly as if I had parted from her but yesterday, and I know my dear father considered her as a very devoted Christian. I am not generally impatient, but I do quite long for this evening.'

'I scarcely recollect Lady Sophia,' said Edward,

' but it will be a great blessing to have some one
who will own us as relations. I think, Mary, we
need not tell her that I am a bookseller's apprentice.'

' I am sure Miss Clifford has already told her
all she knows of our circumstances,' replied Mary,
' and why should we seek to conceal that God has
thought fit to keep us poor, and, I was going to
say, humble ;—but Oh ! my Edward, I fear we
have yet to seek that meek and lowly spirit which
is in the sight of God of great price. Why should
we be ashamed to own the lot that he has appointed for us ? '

' Well, well,' said Edward, taking up his hat,
' perhaps if she does know, she will not like
her relation to be an apprentice-boy,—and perhaps'—he stopped and coloured, ' good bye,
Mary ; I must e'en set off to that vile shop now,
but I do not despair of entering college yet.'

Mary had a few hours of quiet leisure this morning, which she generally enjoyed, and improved
to the utmost ; but to-day they appeared tedious ;
she was to see her early friend, her ' father's friend '
in the evening ; and though she had some lurking

fears, that Lady Sophia Benson might not look so kind and smiling as her memory painted her, yet she longed for an interview which would recal pleasures she had enjoyed with her unfortunate parents. The evening came at last, and the brother and sister set out on their way to Bath Terrace.

'I have been thinking lately more than ever,' said Edward, 'how high and honourable the office of a clergyman is. To be one of a privileged class, set apart by God himself, to minister in holy things; to stand as it were between God and the people.'

' Only as Ezekiel did of old,' interposed Mary, ' when the Lord said unto him: Son of man, I have made thee a watchman to the house of Israel: therefore hear the word at *my* mouth, and give them warning from *me*.' *

' Who would be slothful in such an office, or untrue to such a cause ? ' said Edward, and then added with a glow of his wonted fervour ;—

> " Ye who your Lord's commission bear,
> His way of mercy to prepare ;
> Angels he calls you, be your strife
> To lead on earth an angel's life.

---

* Ezekiel iii. 16.

Think not of rest, though dreams be sweet,
Start up and ply your heavenward feet;
Is not God's oath upon your head,
Ne'er to sink back on slothful bed?
Never again your loins untie,
Nor let your torches waste and die,
Till, when the shadows thickest fall,
Ye hear your Master's midnight call."

'Where did you meet with those lines, Edward?' asked Mary, after she had listened with silent interest to the last line; 'they are very, very beautiful.'

'I do not know by whom they were written, Mary, but I met with them in a little book which passed through my hands to-day. Mr. Singleton gave me the book to pack up with some others, and I looked at a few of the poems, but quite forgot to remark the name of the author. It was their being so beautifully appropriate to the office of the ministry that made me remember the lines, for my heart went along with them.'

'Then do not exclusively appropriate them to the ministerial office, Edward; the admonition they convey applies to the Christian in every station. To the poor bookseller's apprentice, as well as to the highest clergyman in England; and there

is not much hope that the disciple, who would not
serve his Master to the utmost in a lowly condition, would remain faithful to his cause in a more
exalted one.'

As she finished speaking, they reached Miss
Clifford's house, and having gained a speedy admittance, were met on the stairs by Emma, whose
delight at the anticipated meeting between her
dear Mary Spencer and Lady Sophia Benson was
unbounded. 'I had not an idea,' she exclaimed,
'that you knew Lady Sophia, or I could have told
you about her long ago; though I do not know
much about her either. My father appointed her
as well as my aunt to take charge of me when I
came to England, and I saw her once or twice
when I was a very little girl; but as aunt wished
me to remain with her, I suppose she grew tired
of coming so far to visit me.'

This communication was made in Emma's usual
lively gleeful manner. She knew Edward, for she
had often heard Mary speak heartfelt encomiums
on her 'kind and clever brother,' and she had received him two or three times at her schoolroom
parties, when by Miss Clifford's special invitation,

a few young persons spent the evening with her, while her aunt was engaged with a more fashionable coterie in the drawing-room.

On these occasions, Emma had taken him under her special protection. Mary's age and acknowledged superiority made the young guests treat her with respect, but Emma had often to check the whisper which would circulate about Edward's humble circumstances, by saying 'Oh! he is so good and clever, just like poor Kirke White; and he writes poetry too.' And if, in spite of her gentle defence, the malicious whispers still continued, she would wax warm in defence of the injured one and say,—' He has not a superior in the room. He is our equal in birth, and far surpasses us all in everything that can render high birth valuable.'

Edward was quite ignorant how much he owed to her kind interference in his behalf, but he returned the friendly greeting with which she met him, with real pleasure, and followed her and his sister into the drawing-room, where Miss Clifford, and Lady Sophia were waiting to receive them.

The former met them with her usual stately

courtesy, but Lady Sophia hastened towards them with a look of eager curiosity, and seizing a hand of each, looked earnestly in their faces till poor Mary's eyes filled with tears, and her lip quivered, so that she could not speak the tender words of recognition which her heart dictated. At length Lady Sophia exclaimed, ' Oh yes, there can be no mistake, I should know Charles Spencer's children any where. Mary, do you not remember me ?' she added tenderly embracing her; ' how much you must have suffered, my dears, since I last saw you : but brighter days are in store for you : you are not so utterly destitute as you think; but more of this anon. We will take our tea now, and to-morrow I must have a little quiet talk with Mary in her own lodgings.'

They drew round the table, a cheerful, happy-looking group, Emma's inclination for mirth scarcely restrained even by the presence of her learned aunt, for whom she generally felt a due degree of awe. Mary looked serene, thoughtful, and satisfied, and on Edward's cheek there was a bright flush of hope, as if college honours were already wreathed around his brow, and a pleasant parsonage house threw open its doors at his approach.

The conversation was general, during tea; Lady Sophia studiously avoiding any reference to the situation of the young orphans, lest by any means she should wound their feelings. When the urn was removed, Miss Clifford contrived to drag the elder guest into a discussion on some scientific point, on which she was sure of an easy victory over her opponent. The three younger people listened to their arguments for some time with interest, till Emma, half in earnest, half in merriment at the thought of commencing a literary debate between her two companions and herself, said in a low voice, 'Now, my dear Mary, while you take such pains to cram " all the ologies " into my poor brain, why did you leave out that most venerable of them all—mythology ?'

' Do you quite know what mythology is, when you venture to call it venerable, Emma ?'

' To be sure I do; it is the full and authentic account of all the gods, and goddesses : muses, graces, nymphs, naiads, and satyrs that ever flourished in old Rome, or on the classic shores of

Greece : and I call it venerable because it bears
the high stamp of antiquity, which happens to be
very much the fashion just now.   We had a party
of ladies here a few evenings ago, and you would
have thought we had travelled back into the early
ages. Indeed most of them were discussing ancient
church-discipline, with various customs and ceremonies, in use during the fourth and fifth centuries.   They sounded to me a little superstitious,
but then I was the only modern among them.
Some were quoting passages from the old Fathers ;
and I longed for you, for you could have out-
weighed all that they culled from those musty
tomes, with a few sound sentences from our own
noble Reformers. But there was one lady who
amused me more than all the rest. I began to
think she must have been educated in Athens itself during the palmy days of that city, for she
kept repeating scraps of odes to Apollo, invocations
of the muses, addresses to the graces and'—

' Emma, my love, you forget,' said Mary, ' that
in the multitude of words there wanteth not sin ;
is it right thus to ridicule the faults and weaknesses of others ?   Let us return to our subject,
the utility of mythology.'

' I think,' said Edward, ' it can be of very little use in the education of ladies : but men must be intimately acquainted with the old heathen writers, and of course conversant with their system of mythology.'

' " Must," and, " of course," are words that should be connected with some matter of absolute duty, Edward ; to me it appears a fearful mistake to make the abominations of idolatry the necessary study of a christian man. It seems as if Satan, enraged at the glorious and public victory that Christ's religion won over the chief of his strongholds, determined by subtle means to mar the beauty of the triumph, and therefore devised the scheme of making pagan learning necessary in christian schools. Did not this knowledge contribute its aid towards the full development of the great apostacy ? No, Emma, you must put mythology quite off the list of useful " ologies," and forgive me for not instructing you in it.'

' One cannot help knowing a little about it though,' replied Emma ; ' the names of heathen deities occur so frequently in ancient history, and our own poets have generally been so fond of

introducing those worthies to our notice, that
we become familiar with them before we are aware
of it.'

'Yes, indeed, Mary,' said Edward, 'even your
own favourite Cowper could say,

> " Why, stooping at the noon of day,
>   Too covetous of drink ;
> Apollo, hast thou stolen away
>   A poet's drop of ink ? "

'I know it,' replied Mary, ' he also spent some
of his time, and splendid talents, upon the doubtful work of translating the productions of heathen
poets. But we need not consider what any man
has done, but what we ought to do. Would any
of us think it right to sit down and compose an
ode to Baal or Ashtoreth ?'

'Oh, no, indeed,' said Edward laughing, ' but
the gods of the Phænicians were sensual gods ;
those of the Greeks and Romans are somewhat
more refined, and therefore more worthy to be remembered in an intellectual age.'

'I can prove their dreadful identity one with
the other, Edward,' said Mary, with much solemnity, ' not by showing you from ancient re-

cords that the Jupiter of the Greeks, the Osiris of the Egyptians, and the Belus or Baal of the Babylonians meant one and the same being of the imagination : but by simply reading to you the 19th and 20th verses of the 10th chapter of St. Paul's first epistle to the Corinthians. Remember, the Corinthians were a Greek church. Now listen to the passage. " What say I then ? that the idol is any thing, or that which is offered in sacrifice to idols is anything ? But I say that the things which the Gentiles sacrifice, they sacrifice to devils and not to God, and I would not that ye should have fellowship with devils." May we not also say the pæans which the Gentiles sang, they sang to devils ?'

' Oh Mary,' said Emma, while an expression of deep thought passed over her beautiful countenance, ' this is an awful view of the matter. How much of heathen guilt may be found in our christian nation ; and I suppose the devil in establishing his worship in various countries, changes his name and attributes to suit the taste of each particular people.'

' And thus,' said Mary, ' the demon who was

worshipped by the Israelites under the name of Ashtoreth, might change his name to Diana when he claimed Greek homage, and personate the Virgin Mary, when he summoned apostate christendom to his shrine.'

' Is it right, Mary,' asked Edward, ' to speak in that way of the blessed Virgin ?'

' I am not speaking of the Virgin herself, Edward : but surely the evil one who can to serve his purpose assume the form of an angel of light, may wear the name of the holiest saint, if by so doing he can beguile the hearts, and bend the knees of the unwary.'

' I shall never respect the ancients, or their antiquity again,' exclaimed Emma, ' except a few bright stars, that only make the surrounding darkness more visible.'

' Except—my own too-hasty Emma, there is a vast exception. Your own valued Bible is a record of antiquity. Abraham, Isaac, and Jacob are the Lord's Ancients, and eighteen centuries ago——'

' Nay, Mary, but I mean the old Spartans, and Athenians, for whom I had always a sort of fancy, though you tried to show me how very shallow all their greatness was ; but the fact of their worshipping devils never struck me so forcibly before.'

The elder ladies had been attracted by Emma's exclamation, and continued silent while the young people finished their remarks, and then Miss Clifford said, with much of dignity and importance in her manner; ' I hope, Miss Spencer, I do not understand you right. Surely your peculiar religious opinions have not led you to impress the mind of my niece with feelings of contempt for the worthies of other days, or to look with anything short of the highest reverence upon the classic shores of Attica ! Do not the sons of that soil deserve our heartfelt gratitude for all their labours in the cause of learning, science, and virtue ?'

' Emma could not despise genius, Ma'am ;' replied Mary, ' and I think she may keep her admiration of the enterprize, talents, and industry of the Greeks, while she sees that every thing connected with their religion was utter darkness. You know the Apostle says ; " the Greeks seek after wisdom, but we preach Christ crucified, to the Jews a stumbling-block, and to the Greeks foolishness."

G

And foolishness the same holy doctrine appeared,
to the learned Miss Clifford.   A smile of derision
passed over her face, and then a look of displeasure while she turned her eyes towards Emma, as
if considering whether it were safe to continue her
long-neglected niece under such tuition.

This was almost the first time Mary had had an
opportunity of confessing Christ in the presence of
her employer, and now she felt greatly encouraged
by Lady Sophia Benson, who said to her with tears
in her eyes; ' Mary, my love, it gives me great
joy to find you are your dear father's child in spirit,
as well as by nature.   He used to say, the christian should look back to what Christ has done,
and forward to what he will surely do, and the
twofold gaze will keep our feet in the narrow way.'
It cost Lady Sophia an effort thus to second
Mary's confession of her dying Lord; but the
courage and example of the young disciple helped
her to overcome the dread she always felt of Miss
Clifford's disapprobation.

It was growing late, and Mary and her brother
rose to leave.   Lady Sophia repeated her promise
of coming to their lodging the next day, and Miss

Clifford's courtesy was even more stiff, or what she called dignified, than usual. Emma accompanied them to the anti-room, where Edward (who was indignant at the slight his sister had received) remarked, ' it was strange Miss Clifford tolerated the party of ladies who talked so much about the primitive church, and the ancient fathers.'

' Oh,' said Emma, ' old churches, old creeds, and old fathers, ay, and old monasteries too ; anything but Jesus Christ and him crucified.'

' Emma,' interrupted Mary, tenderly kissing her, ' the heart's abhorrence of that keystone of all true religion is too fearful a thing to be lightly spoken of. Let us take care that our faith be firmly fixed upon it, or a storm may come which will sweep all our profession away.'

CHAPTER VI.

LADY SOPHIA BENSON did not fail to keep her appointment : she was early with her young friends, who, on their part, fully appreciated the affectionate interest that she evidently took in their concerns. She was, indeed, a sincerely pious, benevolent woman, natural active and enterprising : and for many years she had devoted her energies to objects worthy of all their strength, though a dislike to deep reflection, or long consideration, before she acted, sometimes caused her to promote schemes which she would afterwards have gladly forgotten. But on the present occasion, justice, benevolence, and religion, united to sanction the speedy act of friendship, which her feelings prompted her to perform ; and she had scarcely seated herself in the little room, and glanced round its faded and half-worn furniture, than she told Mary

of the long and fruitless search she had made for
them, from the day of their father's funeral, when
Edward saw her stop, and inquire (as he supposed)
where they lived. The person of whom she sought
information, had undesignedly misled her, and she
gave up the search as utterly vain, till about two
years later, when a mutual friend of her ladyship
and their father died, and left a small property to
the children of Charles Spencer.

This friend had appointed Lady Sophia execu-
trix to his will, and she once more renewed every
effort to find the youthful legatees, ' I tried,' she
continued, ' inquiry, advertisements, every method
I could devise, but never could discover your
hiding-place, until a few days ago Miss Clifford
mentioned your name, Mary, coupled with just
praise of your attention to our Emma. And now
your money has been accumulating, and you have
each a yearly income of nearly a hundred pounds:
it is not very large to be sure, but it will enable
you to live in comparative comfort. I must tell
you what Emma and I have been planning—but I
had forgotten—what is to be done with Edward ?
his apprenticeship is not yet I suppose half out.'

' I have only four months longer to serve behind that '—Edward hastily began, but a sorrowful look from Mary prevented the conclusion of
his speech.

Lady Sophia did not regard it, but went rapidly
on ; ' Only four months ! perhaps Mr. Singleton
may be prevailed upon to give you up at once ;
a new apprentice will bring a new fee; and then
I think I know a very pious clergyman, compe-
tent to give you a course of instruction, previous
to your entering college.   Emma says your highest wish is to enter the church. I hope (and Lady
Sophia's voice became more solemn) the desire
proceeds from the right motive of love to the Lord
Jesus, and an earnest desire to be instrumental in
saving souls.'   Mary almost wished her Ladyship
had not been quite so precipitate, in chalking out
before the eager mind of her brother the course
she supposed he would wish to pursue. She
looked upon the ministry, not as one of a set of
professions, to be chosen by taste, or caprice ; but
as an office requiring qualifications altogether un-
connected with earthly considerations. She knew
that a man might be a clever lawyer, or a valiant

soldier, without being a renewed child of God ;
but an unconverted minister !—she dreaded to
think her Edward might be led to say, he
thought himself moved by the Holy Ghost, when
perhaps ambition had urged him to enter the holy
office.

But Lady Sophia did not give her much time to
think on this solemn subject, for she went on.—
' And soon after Edward sets out for Devonshire,
in which county Mr. L.'s parish is, I must carry
you and Emma away with me to Fernely. Come,
come, I must have no hesitation. I was your
father's friend, and I must be your friend. I do
not want to make you dependent : you have now
enough money to prevent that. But I want society ; and I think by what I heard last night, that
we shall agree very well. Then you can help me
in a work I know you love. There are so many
poor people to visit ; so many societies to beg
for ; besides two or three schools that require
constant attention. You see I have much need of
an assistant, and Miss Clifford has given me free
permission to take Emma now, and what would
she do without you, poor thing ?'

Mary could not resist the last inducement, and
the whole plan was arranged, and completed in a
shorter time than even Lady Sophia had thought
possible.

Mr. Singleton was easily prevailed upon to renounce any farther claim to Edward's services, so
that in three weeks from the day on which they
met Lady Sophia at Miss Clifford's, he was on his
way to Devonshire; and shortly afterwards, Mary
and Emma set out with Lady Sophia for her coun-
try-house at Fernely.

Mary's heart was filled with thankfulness, and
chastened joy. She had wept much when parting
with her brother, but they were not bitter tears,
for she had long felt that he required a guide whom
he could reverence, and to whose opinion he could
look up with more confidence than he possibly
could to hers—his sister, his equal; and she felt
that he had found such a friend in the good clergyman, who was to prepare him for entrance upon
a scene of life more crowded with temptation than
any he had yet gone through. ' Now,' she thought,
' his principles will be strengthened, his views
made clear, and the trials of college will but inure

him to all he must go through in life, if be but faithful to his heavenly Master.'

These thoughts were passing through her mind as they turned into the demesne that surrounded Roebrooke-hall. Everything looked peaceful and happy, and most of all, Mary admired the healthy cheerful faces of the poor people who came to welcome their benefactress,—or rather one of their benefactresses,—for before Mary had been many days at Fernely, she was introduced to others who had a just claim to the same sacred title.

About three months before Lady Sophia's visit to London, the village had sustained a heavy loss, in the death of Mr. Warner, the aged and pious rector, who had lived and served his God at Fernely for forty years. His successor had not yet come to the parish, though it was believed the living was already given away, and during the interval between the death of Mr. Warner, and the arrival of Mr. Norman, the new rector, the pulpit was occasionally supplied by the neighbouring clergy, chiefly by Mr. Sidney, the rector of an adjoining parish. He had conscientiously sought and found a curate fitted to share with him the responsibility of ministering to a large congregation, and was thus at liberty to come over and help the inhabitants of Fernely, during the period of time they remained without a minister. The latter parish being comparatively small, the rector was in the habit of doing his own duty, and consequently there was no curate at Fernely.

Mary soon became intimately acquainted with Mr. Sidney and his wife; the latter, as her children were young, did not often leave home, but Mr. Sidney was a frequent visitor at Roebrooke Hall.

'I love Mr. Sidney,' said Emma Clifford one evening when the friends had retired to their own apartment :—' I love Mr. Sidney; he is just what a clergyman ought to be. His sermons remain in the mind the whole week after we have heard them; and then his conduct—his conversation; there is no trifling talk, no wasted time when he comes. Who among all our new friends at Fernely, do you like next best to Mr. Sidney, Mary?'

'I will not even say next best, Emma, for I think I feel equal veneration for good old Mr. Graham, our nearest neighbour.'

' Yes,' returned Emma, ' and his two sensible, matronly daughters: nothing ever seems to turn either of that trio out of the straight path of duty. Wet, or dry, you may see Elizabeth and Jane Graham setting out to teach in the school which they have established, dressed in a manner that scarcely even religious ladies would like to be dressed in; their bonnets, cloaks, and clogs, all suited to the roughest weather. How very useful that school must be.'

' Yes, it is placed in a district that is almost destitute of any other means of grace; it is beyond the bounds of this parish, and so far from any place of worship, that the poor people seldom go to church; except two or three families, who, Lady Sophia says, were always in the habit of coming to hear Mr. Warner.'

' And they continue to come now Mr. Sidney preaches here,' said Emma : ' what a pity that his own church is so far on the other side of Fernely. I wonder what kind of minister Mr. Norman will be.'

' Let us try and stop wondering about Mr. Norman till he comes,' said Mary, taking up her Bible, ' oh that we could more than ever obey the spirit of those two sweet verses; "Cease ye from man, whose breath is in his nostrils, for wherein is he to be accounted of;" and, "Trust ye in the Lord for ever, for in the Lord Jehovah is everlasting strength."

Lady Sophia soon found Mary Spencer a very valuable and useful assistant in all her schemes, for promoting the good of the surrounding poor; for she carried them on when that lady's zeal began to cool. Any good work that could be achieved at once, even at a great expense of effort and self-denial, Lady Sophia was admirably fitted to perform; and when calamity or sickness suddenly overtook any of those who looked up to her for assistance, she became, for a time, a tender and skilful nurse, and an invaluable comforter; but she wearied of keeping the petty accounts of a Bible and Missionary Society, which she herself had established among the poor; and her Sunday and day schools were too often left to less able teachers, because Lady Sophia was settling the rules, and arranging the machinery of 'something new.'

It must be remembered, that the Miss Graham's time was more particularly devoted to the school before mentioned. They also visited the poor, but not merely when death or misfortune gave interest to some particular case. They sought out those among the peasantry, who were the most excluded from other avenues to the light; among these were the inhabitants of that dark district, in which their school stood; and where their father possessed a small portion of land, and also one or two Roman Catholic families in Fernely. To the latter, they found that access was daily growing more difficult.

Mary profited as far as she could, by the example of these sisters. She had, even in her days of poverty and sorrow, been accustomed to teach a class in a Sunday-school; but Mary was always a learner, and she was in the constant habit of " esteeming others better than herself;" so on her first coming to Fernely, she had craved permission to accompany the two sisters (who were some years her seniors) to their school. The request was readily granted, and she went with them once or twice, and by so doing, gained much valuable aid in the management of her own class.

Emma too was a teacher. Though young for that important office, she was a useful one, for she sought to make her scholars think for themselves, and to feel that no one can explain the scriptures, so as to influence the heart, unaided by the Holy Spirit. Whenever any difficult passage occurred, she made them look for other parts of the Bible, bearing on the same subject, and thus explained Scripture by Scripture with as little mixture of her own teaching as possible.

Mary did not in general like the plan of giving up a class of poor children to a young Sunday school teacher. Perhaps uninfluenced themselves by the truths they attempted to teach, and mixing their own opinions with the course of instruction they were to impart, she had often pitied both teacher and learner; the former for presumptuously incurring a great responsibility, for which she was wholly unequal; and the latter for looking up with implicit confidence to her little blind guide. But she knew Emma was influenced by what she taught; that she was humble, and carried on her work in the spirit of godly fear, and therefore, though she was but seventeen, Mary had felt no hesitation in recommending Emma to Lady Sophia, as an assistant in her Sunday school.

Besides the school, Mary and Emma visited together the poor families in the neighbourhood of Roebrooke Hall; and in a very short time they became intimately acquainted with the inmates of every cottage. Among these, one young couple stood foremost in their favour. Both William and Martha Thompson had been brought up under Mr. Warner's ministry, and both were humble, consistent christians. Martha was daily expecting the birth of her first child, and she obtained Mary Spencer's promise to stand godmother : the latter fully understood the deep responsibility of this office, and from the moment her consent was given, she never failed to remember her future charge in her prayers.

While her days were passing thus peacefully and usefully at Fernely, Mary's heart was gladdened by the superior tone of Edward's letters. They spoke indeed the language of a child of God so clearly now, that his sister's anxious fears on his account were fast melting away, under the influence of the brightest hope a christian's heart can know.

CHAPTER VII.

Ye clergy, while your orbit is your place,
Lights of the world, and stars of human race;
But if eccentric ye forsake your sphere,
Prodigies ominous, and view'd with fear.—COWPER.

AT length Mr. Norman came to Fernely. Late
one Saturday evening, a travelling-chaise drove to
the door of the parsonage, and Mr. Norman and
his sister alighted; but the inhabitants of the
village had to restrain their curiosity, for they saw
no more of their new rector, till they all met in
church the next day.

The service passed on as usual; Mary at first
missed the solemn and impressive voice of Mr.
Sidney; but her heart rose with the beautiful and
holy Liturgy, and she soon ceased to feel disturbed
by the manner in which it was read, which was
rather that of a whining chant, than the earnest
tone of a praying heart.

In the morning sermon, Mr. Norman inculcated
the christian graces of brotherly love, and humility; in the evening, the unity of the church,
and the deadly sin of schism, formed the subject
of his discourse. Very few remarks were made on
either, in the family circle at Roebrooke Hall.
There was a savour of holiness in the one, and an
apparent reasonableness in the other, that prevented any expression of disapprobation; while each
felt, that there was still a want—a gloomy want,
in both discourses, that made the preacher's words
fall coldly on the heart, though the imagination
was pleased with ideas of devotion, and spirituality.
Mary knew, that the work of the Spirit had been
nearly omitted, as the cause of that life of holiness
which the preacher recommended; and she strove
to call to mind any part of the sermons, in which
he had mentioned the Atonement; and though she
did not succeed, she tried to excuse, in her own
mind, the great omission, by remarking, that he
had only preached twice, and though it would
have been better to begin at the right end, she
was sure he, who could speak so beautifully upon
christian holiness, and so feelingly upon Christ's

sufferings, would also, with equal plainness, tell
how these sufferings avail for our justification, and
how the justified sinner is to be made holy.

On the whole, Lady Sophia was pleased. She
was always attracted by novelty, and there was
something novel in Mr. Norman's manner ; she,
therefore, mildly reproved Emma, for saying, with
her usual vivacity, ' He seemed to have a great
reverence for the communion-table : taking immense pains, whenever he could do so, to avoid
turning his back upon it. And I think,' she went
on, ' he was not quite easy, all the time he was in
the reading-desk, for he could not keep his face
towards the communion-table then.'

The next day, Martha Thompson's child was to
be baptized. It had been Mr. Warner's custom
to perform the sacred rite of baptism, as it should
be done, on the Lord's day, and in the midst of the
congregation ; but various circumstances prevented
this, during the three months that the parish was
left without a stated minister ; but Martha's child
being more than a month old, the parents were
anxious that there should be no further delay.

Mary's principal morning engagement was at the

baptism, and a solemn morning she felt it to be, while again and again, she dedicated the unconscious infant in prayer to God, and asked strength, and guidance, to perform her own duty towards it.

Emma wished to accompany her to the church, and Lady Sophia determined to call on Miss Norman, during their absence. At the appointed hour, the parties separated, and the two younger ladies arrived at the church-door, just as their humble friends reached it, carrying with them the little object of all that morning's thoughts and prayers. They had only to wait a few moments for Mr. Norman. He went through this service in a solemn manner, so that Mary's heart involuntarily exclaimed, ' Surely this ·is a holy man of God, that is come among us.'

When the rite was over, he looked again at the tender babe, and said as he walked out of church, by the side of Emma and Mary, " Happy child! just cleansed in the laver of Regeneration, the sacred waters of baptism glistening on her infant form. She is meet for the company of angels now ; but sin will perhaps soon stain that robe of purity, and then who can tell how it shall ever be restored ?   A dark, but wholesome doubt rests on every thing beyond : ' the pardon on repentance, for those who have forfeited their baptismal pardon, is slow, partial, gradual, as is the repentance itself ; to be humbly waited for and to be wrought out through that penitence." ' *

' What can he mean ?' said Mary, as Mr. Norman hastily left them at the church door, ' what can he mean, Emma ?   Does he not know that, " if any man sin, we have an advocate with the Father, Jesus Christ the righteous, and he is the propitiation for our sins ?" '

' I am afraid you will often find it difficult to make out what he means,' replied Emma, ' for I have a strange misgiving that we have got a very traitor among us.   I heard a good deal of the sort of people called Puseyites, during the latter part of my stay with my aunt Clifford.   I did not pay much attention to the subject then, for I had never met with one of them, and only supposed they were some obscure sect with whom I had nothing to do.   But the gentleman who described them,

* Dr. Pusey.

said they were always talking about schism, and
the great wickedness of dissent, and that they
held some strange doctrines upon Baptism. I feel
sure that Mr. Norman is one of them.'

'Nay, Emma, that cannot be. I am sure Mr.
Norman is a very good man, and the people of
whom you are speaking are said to be doing all in
their power to lead others back to popery.'

Just at this moment, they met Lady Sophia returning from her visit to the parsonage. She was
highly delighted with Miss Norman, and expressed
her joy at the valuable addition to the society of
Fernely. 'This brother and sister will be quite a
treasure,' she exclaimed, 'The Grahams are very
good plain people, but in Mr. and Miss Norman
we have deep piety, a highly cultivated mind, and
much of the polish of refined society united. They
were travelling on the continent, when Mr.
Norman was appointed to this parish, and that
was the reason they did not at once come to
Fernely.'

'But suppose Mr. Norman should be a Puseyite?' said Emma, in an inquiring tone.

'A Puseyite, my love!' exclaimed Lady Sophia,

' what can have put that idea into your head ?
Mr. Norman is evidently a servant of God, endeavouring to promote his glory.   You could not
have listened to his sermons yesterday, and make
such an absurd supposition.   Why the Puseyites
are a set of foolish young men, just come from
college (where some who ought to be wiser, have
turned their heads) and they set up crosses in
their churches, and keep candles burning on the
communion-table.   They call the Romish Church
their venerable mother, and abjure the name of
Protestant altogether.'

' But their teachers did not begin with those
things, I suppose, Ma'am.'

' Emma, you ought to have a little more of that
charity which " thinketh no evil."   You are, by
your rash suppositions, injuring one of the Lord's
own people.'

Mary remained silent.   She thought both her
friends wrong, Emma in giving words to a supposition, which as yet, she could not possibly prove ;
and Lady Sophia for pronouncing so warm a
eulogy on two persons, whom she had seen for
the first time on the preceding day.   Emma, how-

ever made no farther observation, and the conversation changed.

In the course of the week, Lady Sophia's visit was returned by the inmates of the parsonage, and Mr. and Miss Norman dined at Roebrooke Hall. The next day, Mary and Emma were talking over the subjects that had been discussed the preceding evening; when Mary suddenly stopped and said, ' It is a long time, Emma dear, since we called on the Grahams. Let us go to them now, it will do us good, after so much unprofitable conversation.'

' Unprofitable, Mary! why we travelled all over the world last night, without the aid of either steam-boat or steam-carriage. Mr. Norman is certainly the most amusing man I ever met with; and then we hung on the rear of Mahomet Ali's army, and watched all the movements of that humbler of the Turkish power, and settled what England will be likely to do, and' ——

' I did not refer to Mr. Norman's conversation last night, Emma, but to the idle manner in which we were talking it over. There was so much information in what we heard then, that I could not call it unprofitable.'

'Only confess that Mr. Norman is not a Le
Brun, or a Sidney, and I will be contented. We
could not have passed a long evening with Mr.
Sidney, without gaining some lesson for eternity. I
could admire Mr. Norman as an accomplished
traveller, but I cannot revere him as a Christian
minister, Mary.'

'We did gain one valuable lesson last night,
Emma. We were taught to keep a watch over
the tongue, and to guard against bitterness of
spirit, as being contrary to the law of Christ.'

'Because I ventured to impugn the motives
and the mission of the Sisters of Charity,' said
Emma, 'in whose praise our rector was particularly eloquent. I was beginning to think over,
and profit by the advice he gave, when a few
minutes afterwards, he thrust the whole body of
dissenters altogether beyond the bounds of the
Christian church, and condemned them as having
lived and died in a state of sinful schism. He
spared not one, for Lady Sophia pleaded hard for
Watts, Doddridge, Baxter, and Robert Hall; but
she pleaded in vain. So I saw that the bitter
tongue and the unchristian spirit were only for-

bidden when we speak of Romanists, but that the excellent of the earth were the lawful prey of both, when found in communions not Episcopal.'

'Still Emma, the lesson of self-government was a good and a scriptural one. Let us obey it, for it is the Lord's: and remember that he said himself; "The scribes and the Pharisees sit in Moses' seat; all therefore that they command you to observe, that observe and do; but do not ye after their works: for they say and do not."'

'Oh poor Mr. Norman, which is he, Mary, a Scribe or a Pharisee?'

'Emma, Emma, we must not trifle thus. If poor Mr. Norman be indeed such a character, his state is too awful to be spoken of in jest; but if not, we wrong him deeply by our suspicions; so let us for a little try to forget him; but not at the throne of grace; do not forget him there, Emma.'

Mary spoke solemnly, and Emma's vivacity was instantly checked. She was not a thoughtless girl; on the contrary, her religious convictions were deep and real. Mary had been the instrument of leading her to God, and she still loved her gentle guidance, and continued to follow her bright pattern as Mary followed Christ. But Emma could more easily see the faults and inconsistencies of professors ; not that Mary possessed less natural discernment, but her love " believed all things," and she always honoured those who confessed Christ with the lips, until proofs that she could not gainsay, convinced her that it was with the lips only.

Mr. Graham's grounds reached Roebrooke demesne, so that in a few minutes after the two friends set out on their proposed visit, they found themselves in his large, but plainly-furnished drawing-room. Jane and Elizabeth Graham were busily employed, cutting out some coarse clothes for their poor scholars. After giving their guests a very warm welcome, they resumed their employment, and soon asked and received assistance from both Mary and Emma.

' You must come, and see our schools again soon, Miss Spencer,' said Jane Graham, ' we have just appointed two teachers from among those girls who formed our first class, and we have given them each a class of the younger children.'

' Do you think,' inquired Mary, ' that poor children derive much benefit from the instruction of those, whom they have been accustomed to look upon as companions, and to consider as almost their equals in knowledge ? '

' Oh, Susan and Sarah Miller are not children or very young people,' replied Elizabeth Graham, ' they have been in my sister's class for ten years, and during four of that number have been training for their present office. I think Susan is about twenty-three, and her sister a year younger : and they have the best qualifications. I do not mean, that they read in a very superior style, or even that they spell quite correctly ; but they are humble, self-forgetting Christians, who will labour devotedly among the little ones they are appointed to teach, I think I may say, without a thought that their new office adds to their own importance, but simply that it makes them more responsible in the sight of God. They have one brother, a partaker of the same faith, and they all three remind me often of that happy family at Bethany, whom our Lord loved.'

' But John Millar is not with them just now ;'

said Jane Graham. 'My father has sent him to
be trained, or rather examined by the committee
of the Scripture Readers' Society, and when he
returns, he is to become Scripture Reader in the
place where he lives. My father wishes him to
be under the Society, though he will pay him himself. I anticipate much good from his labours
among the poor neglected people.'

Just as Jane Graham finished speaking, her
father came into the room, and, without observing
their visitors, said to his daughters; 'The workmen will be here in two hours, girls, to take down
that partition-wall, and turn the two drawing-
rooms into one; so you had better desire the servants to remove the furniture as soon as possible.'

'Take down the wall, father!' said Elizabeth,
in a tone of surprise, 'surely you are not in earnest. This drawing-room is very large already;
large enough for all the company we ever see
in it.'

'It is not nearly large enough for all the company we shall see in it, please God, on this day
fortnight. There is no other room in the parish
now, for the Lord's servants (who come from the

continent to tell us what their Master is doing
there) to meet our villagers in: so we must have
them here.' Then perceiving Mary and Emma,
he said, taking a hand of each; 'I beg your pardon, my dear young ladies; I did not till this moment see you; and now will you tell all your
friends, far and near, that I shall be happy to see
them all at the Continental meeting, this day fortnight in my large new room. It will hold more
than the parish school-room where they were formerly held.'

'But the school-room held all who came, father;'
said Jane Graham, 'and it will make this room a
very inconvenient size. Why can we not use the
parish school-room as usual?'

'Because Mr. Norman wills it not, Jane, and
surely my daughter will sacrifice a little of her
convenience in such a cause. A minister of the Reformed Church in France coming! a descendant—a
representative of that noble martyr-church that so
long witnessed with its voice, and its blood, against
the abominations of Popery! God forbid that I
should sin against my own soul, by refusing to throw
open my doors wide to welcome such a guest.'

'Oh, not one room, father; every room in the house should be given up if it were needed,' exclaimed Jane, 'I do not care for the inconvenience, but I scarcely thought' ——.

'You scarcely thought that I could oppose my minister, I suppose, Jenny; and I would not lightly do so. I would rather go far out of my own course, than throw one obstacle in the way of a true-hearted parish minister, and would yield my own will to further his in anything that conscience would allow. But not when the choice is between the minister, and his God.' He stopped and then said, half to himself, half aloud; 'Schismatics indeed! Beyond the pale of the Catholic Church!' well, be it so—they are the choice jewels of Jehovah. His chosen ones whose blood bought them, and we will give them a warm welcome, let who will forbid it. But come, girls, these are no times for talking: let us act now.'

So saying, he rang the bell, and desired the servants to begin removing the furniture; his daughters at the same time, neatly folding up the garments they had been making, prepared to lead their friends through the beautiful grounds which surrounded their dwelling.

As they walked through the shrubbery, Mary who had not previously spoken since they left the house, said in a thoughtful voice; ' I did not think a Protestant minister could be found, who would oppose the Continental Society. I wonder on what grounds Mr. Norman does so ? '

' I think,' answered Elizabeth Graham, 'it is because the Reformed Churches on the continent, which that Society aids in publishing the truths of the Gospel, are not Episcopal, and that he looks upon the agents of that Society in France, as schismatics or separatists.'

' But, my dear Miss Graham,' answered Mary, ' they are only separatists from the Church of Rome. Holy and devoted men trying to lead a few even in infidel France, to serve God " in spirit and in truth." Mr. Norman must surely be ignorant of the state of religion on the continent, and now acts under a mistake.'

' You forget, Mary,' said Emma, ' how much he seemed to know about every part of the continent, that he visited with his sister. They tra-

velled through the south of France and Italy. He
must have seen the Romish system in its darkest
colours; and he might have seen (had he been
willing) the fair contrast, that some at least of
the Reformed pastors, show to the idolatrous
priests of Rome. Felix Neff and Oberlin must
have left successors, and you do not forget your
own Le Brun.'

'I do not think Mr. Norman acts, in this instance, from mistake,' said Jane Graham; ' it
would be false charity to say so, for he had a long
conversation with my father, the day he called on
us, and he spoke much about the sin of dissenters,
and said, that churchmen should hold no communion with their ministers, lest they also should
perish in the " gainsaying of Corah," of whose
sin, he affirmed, all nonconformist ministers were
guilty; and he classed most of the reformed
churches on the continent with dissenters.'

'How,' inquired Emma, 'did he prove the
poor dissenter to be guilty of crimes so dreadful,
as those of Korah, Dathan, and Abiram?'

' He said, that they opposed our ministers, who
received their authority in a direct line from the

apostles, and wanted to usurp their office, just as Corah, Dathan, and Abiram did that of Moses and Aaron.'

'He must have forgotten,' said Mary, 'that Corah and his companions were themselves ministers, set apart to minister before the Lord; and that Moses rebuked them, by saying, "Seemeth it a small thing unto you, that the God of Israel hath separated you from the congregation of Israel, to bring you near to himself, to do the service of the tabernacle of the Lord, and to stand before the congregation to minister unto them? And he hath brought thee near to him, and all thy brethren, the sons of Levi with thee: and seek ye the priesthood also?"'

'Why do you keep saying, "He must have forgotten," Mary?' said Emma: 'he is not like a man who forgets much. He is always on the watch—always on his guard. I do not think Mr. Norman ever forgets anything.'

'My father reminded him (interposed Elizabeth) that the rebellious Levites were ministers already, and therefore, their sin must be one of which a lawful minister could be guilty. "And in our

own day, (continued my father) I believe those in
the Church to be acting the part of Corah, who
are copying so closely the example set them by
the priests of Rome.   Moses was the lawgiver,
and Aaron the High Priest of Israel; both types
of Christ, who is now the only lawgiver and High
Priest of his people : but those misguided men
who call themselves the successors of the Apostles,
without possessing their spirit of meekness and
lowliness, usurp the sovereignty of Christ while
they talk loudly of ministerial authority, and are
fain to bind a yoke upon the neck of their disciples
in the name of a fallible Church ; and think you
not, he went on, they might, if their ears were
not closed, hear their Master saying to them, " And
seek ye the priesthood also ? " for his eyes can
see their communion-tables turned into altars, and
his own appointed feast of remembrance gradually
becoming a propitiatory sacrifice, that they may
stand by as officiating priests."   I never heard my
father speak with such solemn severity before.'

   ' And what did Mr. Norman say in reply ? '

   ' He did not say one word, but rose up with an
air of injured—what shall I say ? I cannot call it

dignity,—for if my father were wrong, he should have patiently shewed him a more excellent way; and I cannot call it meekness, for contemptuous silence is not meek; but he rose up, and bowing profoundly to us all, left the room without saying one word.'

Jane and Elizabeth Graham had now conducted their friends to the limits of their own grounds, where after a loving farewell they parted from them, and Mary observed to Emma,—' We have never called on Miss Norman; let us do so now. I am not fond of spending a morning in paying visits, but this one may perhaps be our duty.'

' Surely, Mary, you are not going to attempt to persuade Miss Norman, that she and her brother are in error ?'

' I am going to invite her to accompany us to the Continental Meeting, Emma. They must be under some wrong impression concerning that Society, for otherwise no Protestant having free access to his Bible could object to it.'

' No Protestant would, I am sure,' said Emma laying particular stress on the principal word in the sentence.

I 2

They gained admittance at the parsonage, and the servant ushered them into the drawing-room, and, saying at the same time, she was not sure that her mistress was at home, she went in search of her.   Emma in the meantime, looked round the apartment with more curiosity than she generally felt in the drawing-rooms of her friends.   A few books attracted her eye, and she rose up to ascertain their titles.   They consisted chiefly of the lighter literature of the day, travels, voyages, and poems.   She read their names aloud, and ended with Froude's Remains, Sewell's Christian Morals, and the Autobiography of Archbishop Laud—' Do you know any of these, Mary ? they sound like strangers, and I would fain put Usher or Leighton in the room of poor superstitious Laud. But what have we here,' she said, turning to the work-table, on which lay two or three tracts, and a small open volume, the tracts were ' The sin of schism,' and ' Reasons why I dare not go to a dissenting meeting-house.'

' I suppose these are for lending through the village,' observed Emma ; ' Mr. Sidney, or Mr. Warner would have given the parishioners a better reason, why they *need* not go to a dissenting meeting, than any this kind of production is likely to offer.'

Mary sighed; 'Yes, dearest Emma, the gospel in our own church, is the best antidote to our wandering wishes, should any such be felt. But the gospel is often preached plainly and fully in the meeting-house, and I should not exactly like to say that I *dare* not go wherever God's word and God's people are to be found; at the same time, there are so many sects holding every varying shade of false doctrine, that a wandering spirit is certainly a dangerous one.'

'I wish,' replied Emma, 'some person would write a tract entitled, 'Reasons why I dare not go, where the gospel is not faithfully preached;' and perhaps it would strengthen many of us for a long walk every Sunday morning—but this little book that Miss Norman has been reading, is 'The Imitation of Christ,' by Thomas a Kempis.

'It is strange,' said Mary, 'that so many even good people have been found to republish, and recommend the writings of men, who though partially enlightened themselves, and perhaps serving

God in spite of all the hindrances their church lays in their way, yet lived and wrote under the gloomy shadow which she throws over her votaries. What do we want with Pascal, or Thomas a Kempis, who have the works of our own Reformers, besides a bright constellation of later writers.'

The servant now returned to say, that her mistress, whom she had supposed to be in the garden, was not at home, and Mary reluctantly left the house without accomplishing her errand. She however found an opportunity, before the day of the meeting came, to press her christian invitation upon Marcella Norman, but all her scriptural persuasions were in vain; all her long-remembered tales of piety she had witnessed in Provence, were utterly unavailing to remove the deep feeling of dislike, which that young person showed towards those, who she said, were not in communion with the Church Catholic!

CHAPTER VIII.

By the unavoidable interference of other arrangements, the meeting in aid of the Continental Society at Fernely, was fixed to take place in the evening. A little before seven o'clock, numbers of decently-dressed villagers were seen walking at a quick pace towards Mr. Graham's hall-door, which was thrown wide open to welcome all who would enter on that important evening. Several carriages from neighbouring parishes drove up the avenue, and Lady Sophia acknowledged with joy, that this meeting seemed likely to equal in numbers and interest any that had ever been held in Fernely.

There was ample space in the large room that Mr. Graham had prepared, for all who came. A small table and a few chairs at the upper end supplied the place of a platform, while the rest of the room was filled with forms, so placed as to accommodate the largest number of guests.

As Mary entered, her mind, always alive to feelings of devotion, rose on the wings of faith to that scene, when " a great multitude which no man could number, of all nations, and kindreds, and people, and tongues, shall stand before the throne, and before the Lamb, clothed with white robes, and palms in their hands." The very opposition which seemed to be stirring up against the servants of God, who obeyed his command and endeavoured to send the everlasting Gospel, even " where Satan's seat is," called back to her memory the angel's question ; " What are these which are arrayed in white robes, and whence came they ? ' and her heart, aided by prophetic feeling replied ; " These are they which came out of great tribulation, and have washed their robes, and made them white in the blood of the Lamb." ' God only knows (she internally said) how long we may be permitted to meet in peace, when ministers of the English church can be found already to oppose a work like this !'

They had not been seated many minutes, before

the gentlemen who were to address the meeting
came in accompanied by Mr. Graham. Mr. Sidney was one of them ; the other an old man with
white hair. Mary started when she saw him ; she
knew his face, it brought back a crowd of recollections which she could not account for ; she
looked again and again, and her heart beat with
agitation, but she had whispered to Emma, 'It is
—it must be Pastor Le Brun,' just as Mr. Graham, who occupied the chair, introduced him to
the assembly.

It was some time before Mary could so far
command her feelings, as to be able to listen
calmly. Her father, and mother ; her absent
Edward, all were present to her imagination, and
memory travelled back with mournful delight to
the Pastor's dwelling in Provence, and she seemed
to listen again to those lessons of Christian holiness
which he there used to impart.

At length her wandering ear was attracted, and
her attention fixed, while he told of all the Continental Society has done, and is still doing, though
mediately by the agency of the Societes Evange-
liques of Paris and Geneva. He spoke of the Col-

porteurs, who travel as the Vaudois used to do,
and sell Bibles to all who are willing to buy them;
of the Evangelists, who resemble our Scripture
readers, and who read and explain to the Roman
Catholic peasant, the sacred word of God ; and then
he spoke of the regularly-ordained ministers, some
of whom first heard and believed the words of
everlasting life from the lips of the apostolic Neff,
and were now treading in his steps, working
" while it is day," with a constant, and perhaps
salutary feeling that the shadows of night may
soon again come over their beloved country ; and
prohibition and persecutions stop the way of the
Gospel of peace.

He told of the deep thirst for the word of God,
that urged even the poor Italian in his land of
dense spiritual darkness, and in spite of the terrible prohibitions of Antichrist, to purchase the
Italian Bible, which has been printed and published for him by the British and Foreign Bible
Society.* ' Perhaps (he said) even now some
child of God in that country is pining for a copy

---

* See Speech of the Rev. A. Sillery, at the Continental Meeting in
Dublin—Reported in the *Statesman*, May 5, 1843.

of God's word which he cannot obtain, or suffering in a dungeon the punishment of having eagerly grasped the treasure when it was within his reach.'

While he was speaking, many hearts yearned for the power of sending more cheap editions of the Bible into Italy, that the cup of cold water might be drunk by some parching lips. Mary felt deeply interested for the state of Protestant Sweden. Of the same Gothic race with ourselves; professing the same pure and scriptural creed, but dead, cold, and lifeless. ' Oh for some Whitfield,' she mentally exclaimed, ' to send the Lord's warning to Sardis with power to the church in Sweden—it would be listened to, would be obeyed, and then would Sweden aid more largely than she now does, in sending the light of truth to the heathen world.'

When M. Le Brun sat down, Mr. Sidney spoke. He said but little comparatively of the Society, but made use of the golden opportunity, and once more preached the Gospel to a congregation, whom he knew to be deprived of it. The only way to induce any people to send God's truth to others, is to let them feel the power of it on their own souls; and the words of deep and loving

warning which they heard that night, were long
remembered by some of the inhabitants of
Fernely.

The meeting did not break up until a late hour ;
but the instant it had concluded, Mary told the
delighted Lady Sophia, that her own Pastor Le
Brun was indeed present, the friend and teacher
of her early youth, and they waited with impatience till the crowd dispersed, and none remained
but their own circle of friends.

When Mary spoke her name in a trembling
voice, Le Brun gazed eagerly at her. He well
remembered the little English girl whose faith and
love shone out so brightly in her tender years, but
it was some time before he could identify her with
the tall and serious-looking young woman who
stood before him ; but when he did so, he returned
her warm greeting with Christian tenderness, and
his inquiries for her long-lost parents, and absent
brother, made her weep at the crowd of hallowed
remembrances that rushed into her mind.

It was ten o'clock, but the friends could not
resist Mr. Graham's pressing entreaties to remain
and partake of some refreshment together, before

they separated for the night. Mary told her old friend much of the way in which the Lord had led her, and heard in return many strengthening tales of patience and Christian endurance under the deepest sufferings.

She took no part in the general conversation that evening ; once only was her attention arrested by hearing Mr. Graham say, as if in reply to some observation of Mr. Sidney's—' Oh, you clergy are so fettered by ecclesiastical laws and points of etiquette towards each other, that you will not, or perhaps cannot do in other men's parishes, what it is absolutely necessary should be done by some one ; therefore, I say, that these are the days for the laity to act with firmness and decision. Let them refuse to receive popish instruction for themselves, and their children, and it will soon cease to be offered to them.'

Mary did not hear Mr. Sidney's reply, and Lady Sophia rose to go home, at the same time inviting M. Le Brun (who was to remain that night at Mr. Graham's) and the whole friendly circle to dine with her the next day. Her invitation was accepted by Mr. Sidney and M. Le Brun, but Mr.

Graham and his daughters declined on the plea of a pre-engagement.

The next morning as they were sitting at breakfast, Lady Sophia mentioned her intention of asking Mr. and Miss Norman to join their party that evening; ' Miss Norman,' she said, ' is a truly fascinating creature, and I should much like Mr. Norman and M. Le Brun to meet. Having visited the same places on the continent, and being familiar with the same scenes, I think they will both derive pleasure from the interview.'

' You forget, Lady Sophia,' said Emma, ' that M. Le Brun visited those scenes as a humble agent of the Societé Evangélique, that he is familiar with the cottages of the poor, and the dwellings of very lowly pastors ; while Mr. Norman visited them as a —— priest—I was going to say—well, minister of the church catholic, and would talk so much about the nave, chancel, and transept of every popish cathedral in France, that poor M. Le Brun —Nay, Mary, do not look so entreatingly at me: I will not spare him to-day; for the minister of the church of England, who could oppose the efforts of French Protestants to spread truth among those who were long their oppressors, must be a traitor and a renegade, let who will gainsay it.'

'Emma, dear,' said Mary calmly, 'if your violent rebuke would bring poor Mr. Norman to a sense of his error, or deter others from following it, you would be justified in uttering it. But remember while we are commanded to "contend earnestly for the faith once delivered to the saints," we must take care that no word of bitterness, no sound of reviling be suffered to escape from us, lest we harden the fallen in their evil way, or tempt others from a false feeling of sympathy and pity to follow them into the paths of delusion.'

'Besides,' said Lady Sophia, 'we do not know the motives which induced Mr. Norman to absent himself.'

'Motives, (exclaimed Emma) motives! oh, a very fervent zeal for Episcopacy, and, what I believe his party call "church principles," makes him refuse even to serve his God, when the occasion for doing so does not come in regular clerical order.'

Mary looked at her watch. 'It is time for us

to go to our school, Emma, and let no motive induce us to be late in so doing, lest we neglect the
order in which we ought to serve our God.'

' Indeed, I wish to be especially early there this
morning ;' replied Emma, rising hastily, ' for I
heard a rumour that Miss Marcella Norman intends taking the management of the school quite
into her own hands, and our constant presence
may prevent this at least for a time : she spent
yesterday evening with Mrs. Chambers, who agrees
with her in condemning all religious meetings,
though from dissimilar motives. Miss Norman
thinks they infringe on the prerogatives of the
church ; Mrs. Chambers, that they too strongly
oppose the world.'

Mary did not reply, but at once began to make
preparation for her walk, and they were soon seated
in the schoolroom, surrounded by children who
loved them both and looked up to them with confidence for instruction. Mary soon forgot every
thing else, and bent the whole power of her well-
regulated mind to fulfil the duty then before her.
She did not wait to forbode what evil influence
might yet mar all the good that had been done in

Fernely, but with a heart uplifted to God for aid, she strove to lay a foundation which could not easily be shaken, and remembering the promise, " My word shall not return unto me void," she went on with her Bible class without the interruption of wandering thoughts.

Not so Emma. She too was zealous in the cause of God, and very anxious for the welfare of the little ones she was trying to instruct, but her mind was straying from her present duty, and her indignant fancy was often internally remonstrating with Mr. Norman upon the injustice of taking the superintendance of the school from Mary, and giving it up to his sister ; she almost went so far as to imagine Marcella Norman teaching a catechism of doubtful name to the children who now stood only half taught before Emma Clifford.

The superintendance of the school was all that devolved upon the young ladies, though they usually spent some hours of each day in it. A pious woman had been engaged as schoolmistress some years before the death of Mr. Warner, and she for the present retained her situation.

When the two friends returned home, Lady

K

Sophia put into Mary's hand a little packet from
Edward, which had arrived that morning soon
after they set out for the school.   It contained a
beautifully-bound little volume, and a letter written
in the same strain which had latterly given his
sister so much pleasure, and concluded with a
reference to the book which he sent for her acceptance. ' I know you will like the Christian Year ;'
it was given me by a gentleman who stopped here
for a few hours on his way to London two or
three months ago.   He had been on the continent,
and being slightly acquainted with Mr. L——, he
took our house on his road from Plymouth.   I
was much delighted with his talents, and piety,
but I believe he differed from Mr. L—— on some
doctrinal points.   The poems in the little book I
think beautiful, and would scarcely have parted
with his gift, but that I happened to discover in it
those lines which you remember I met with at Mr.
Singleton's, beginning :

" Ye who your Lord's commission bear."

' I recollected how much you were pleased with
them, and tried to procure another copy, but could
not do so in this stupid country town ; so having

an immediate opportunity of sending my packet, I thought I could not do better than enclose the one I had by me. I am longing for Oxford, dear Mary : they say the author of these poems is a leading man there.'

When she had finished reading the letter, Mary began to look over her book, expecting to find it a little treasure ; but she soon felt disappointed. Sometimes indeed, a few bright lines spoke the language of genuine piety; over the rest there was a dreamy mist which would not allow her clearly to discover the author's meaning. She read on till her eyes fell on the Ave Marias of the Annunciation, and then she closed it, laying it carefully by with the letter, and as the hour at which their guests were expected drew near, she soon rejoined Emma and Lady Sophia in the drawing-room.

Mr. Norman had never met Mr. Sidney before, and he now returned his greeting in a friendly, almost a brotherly manner, while Emma thought his low bow to M. Le Brun was very ceremonious, and more polite than friendly. The conversation became general, and dinner passed over without any very animated discussion taking place. There was a great difference between the new rector and the two other ministers, which, though not alluded to, was felt, and for some time prevented any easy conversation on subjects immediately connected with religion. On other themes, Mr. Norman shone; and he now contrived to engage the attention of all present, while without seeming to oppose the introduction of higher topics, he dextrously changed the subject whenever Le Brun sought to speak of holy things.

We cannot tell what deeper discussion took place during the short time that the gentlemen remained alone after dinner; but Mr. Norman's speedy appearance in the drawing-room, gave reason to suppose the argument had been deeper than he approved. Yet Mr. Norman did not avoid all religious conversation; he only seemed anxious to choose his own time and manner of introducing it, and (at least in the company of ladies) to avoid touching doctrinal points, while he brought forward the externals of religion in such a manner as would please the imagination, and excite feelings of devotional fervour.

CHAPTER IX.

WHEN the tea-equipage was removed, Mary took her seat by pastor Le Brun, with a feeling similar to that which an affectionate child experiences who, after a long absence, once more feels she is beside a beloved parent. Emma too, who looked at the old man with deep veneration, contrived so to place her chair that she might hear some of those beautiful lessons, which, in other days he was wont to impart to Mary Spencer.

But Emma was disappointed in this hope, for the good pastor was silent, and even Mary seemed wholly engrossed by the eloquent conversation of Mr. Norman. She had been much interested during dinner, with his store of lively historical anecdotes, and she now listened with pleasure while he accurately described some wonderful discovery of modern art; pointing out the manner in which the complicated machinery was made to effect its useful purpose, and then turning to Mr. Sidney, he said, 'Yet after all, this age of cold utility, always seeking to compute the return to be expected from every expenditure, has a chilling influence upon the heart; and I often long to see that spirit of piety once more gladdening the earth, which induced our more generous ancestors to spend their wealth in building and adorning temples meet for the worship of the Most High; temples in which the people of God have, in each succeeding age, bowed in meek devotion before his shrine.'

'I would not,' replied Mr. Sidney, 'attempt to defend that spirit of the present age, which holding before the eyes of man some plan of selfish aggrandizement, or commercial enterprise, would impel him to strain every nerve, and bend every faculty in a service whose highest reward is on this side of the grave, and too often consists of heaps of that gold, whose "rust doth eat as a canker." But let us take the word *utility* in its just and fair sense; and surely an age of *utility* is far more worthy of admiration than an age of romance and superstition, to which many of our Cathedrals owe their erection. We may consider that the reign of utility began just as that of chivalry drew to a close. The last of our great feudal Barons was slain at the battle of Barnet in 1471, and the same year the first printing-press was brought into England. By means of this chef-d'ouvre of utility's right hand, Tyndal's edition of the Bible was widely circulated, and from the seed of the word of God the glorious harvest of the Reformation sprang quickly up. It is needless to trace the slow progress of utility to the present time ; but now, when the Lord has given peace, does not the spirit of usefulness act as a willing handmaid in the cause of religion ? Her steamboats and her railroads may yet give greater speed to the message of peace, which is being sent in this age of utility through the whole world. Surely for the children of God to devote their wealth to that purpose, is a higher and holier aim than to lavish it upon the useless adornings of some gorgeous cathedral. I grant that we have much need to hear the rebuke of the prophet Haggai, " Is it time for you, O ye, to dwell in ceiled houses, and this house lie waste ? " But it is not the building in which we worship, that we suffer to lie waste. The temple in which God would be worshipped is the congregation of his people. Have our zeal and energy been engaged to gather out of the world's waste, assemblies of faithful men to glorify his name ? Has our money been given to defray the expense of the missionary's voyage, to prepare school-houses for the education of the young, and to build capacious churches for the public service of God ? Perhaps we may not be able to say, we " have done what we could," though we need not go back to the age of Abbey and Cathedral-building, for instances of self-renunciation in the bestowal of property.'

' And yet,' rejoined Mr. Norman, ' God did not disdain to sanction and approve the magnificence of the Temple which Solomon had built for him, or the splendid preparations for carrying on his worship. We read, that the glory of the Lord filled the house ; and who can enter one of our Cathedrals—York-Minster for instance—and tread its tesselated pavements, without feeling that an " all-hallowing spirit of holiness seems to preside

over, and breathe around the venerable place ? ''
The grandeur of the whole; the receding line of
vast-clustered columns; the immense height of
the gothic dome; the mellow light streaming into
the nave of the Cathedral through the multiform
compartments of the painted windows; all, all
conspire to fill the mind with an awe and reverence, somewhat akin to what the Israelites must
have felt when their king summoned them to the
great consecration.'

'The Temple of Solomon,' interposed pastor Le
Brun, ' owed all its glory to the typical nature of
its services and decorations, and to the visible
presence of God manifested in the holy. of holies.
The altar on which were sacrificed oxen and sheep
without number, was sacred only as it shadowed
forth Him who is both the sacrifice, and " the
altar that sanctifieth the gift." It was not the
lily-work that adorned the pillar Jachin, nor the
beauty and columnar form of Boaz, that filled
the thoughts of the pious Israelite, but the promise
and the strength which their position and their
names recalled to his mind. When these shadows
had accomplished their purpose, and the disciples,

in the presence of the great Antitype, uttered their own feelings upon the size and proportions of the latter temple—" See what great stones and what buildings are here ! " our Lord took no farther notice than to give them a sure word of prophecy ; " There shall not remain one stone upon another that shall not be thrown down." Another temple was in his heart, and occupied his cares. The builders-up of rites and ceremonies utterly rejected the foundation-stone of his temple ; nevertheless he laid it with his own blood, and the work is going on from year to year, from day to day. No sound of axe or hammer is heard there ; the living stones are shaped and prepared on earth, but He will soon " bring forth the top-stone with shoutings, crying, grace, grace, unto it ! " '

' I believe,' said Mr. Sidney, ' no man possessed of a refined taste, and a keen perception of the sublime and beautiful, could go into most of our Cathedrals, without having his senses powerfully affected ; and, as they have been for three hundred years consecrated to a purer worship, these feelings will be, in some measure, sanctified by the association ; but when the lover of antiquity tra-

vels back into the eleventh and twelfth centuries,
(the great period for enlarging and beautifying
cathedrals), and holds fancied communion with
the worshippers of the dark ages, does not the
" dim religious light" of the vast building wax yet
more dim, while historic truth calls up around him
a crowd of prostrate worshippers, all turned towards one spot, where the contemptible idol of a
degraded Church was held up for their devout
adoration.'

At these words, Marcella Norman made a movement of impatience, and something like a shudder
passed over her; but she did not speak, and Mr.
Sidney went on.

' I never stand in the chancel of a cathedral,
without remembering, with deep humiliation, that
this spot, which some blasphemously presume to
call the Holy of holies, was to our fathers, but the
inner court of the temple of Baal : that on their
altar, (a name I would not willingly apply to the
simple communion-table of the Church of England),
was deposited the strange God of apostate christendom, and that here the holy supper of the Lord
Jesus was degraded into a Pagan rite.'

There was a pause of some moments : Mr. Norman did not seem willing to pursue the subject,
but Lady Sophia, in whose good graces the new
rector was rising every moment, wishing to give
his side of the argument all the support in her
power, uttered a warm eulogium on cathedral
music, and its power to lift the soul from earth to
heaven. 'I have attended (she said) the cathe-
dral-service but once or twice, and I experienced
on those occasions, an elevation of mind, and an
unearthliness of spirit, which I never felt elsewhere.'

Mary Spencer thought, (but she did not say),
' Surely Lady Sophia forgets the moments, when
she has held communion with God in her closet,
or joined our own beloved congregation in a simple psalm of thanksgiving ; ' but Marcella's eyes
sparkled, and her cheek glowed, with an expression, responding to all Lady Sophia said : ' I too,'
(she exclaimed), ' have knelt with something of
ecstatic joy, while the melodious voices of the
choristers replied, in holy melody, to the plaintive
chant of the officiating minister, or while the deep-
toned organ accompanied the Church in her holy

aspirations. Never but once were these feelings surpassed. About two years ago, my brother and I visited Rome ; we were there during Lent, and were induced to be present at some of the services of the Church during that solemn season ; never, never shall I forget the first strains of the Miserere !'

Marcella spoke with enthusiasm, and did not, until she had nearly concluded the last sentence, perceive her brother's eye fixed upon her, with an expression of rebuke, or caution. Emma, who was a silent observer of all that was passing, could scarcely tell which ; but Marcella instantly checked herself, and, slightly colouring, said, ' What a pity it is, that the Church of Rome, while she offers so much that is high and holy to her erring children, yet sees them turning with undue devotion to the shrines of saints and angels. Even the very garments of her widowhood are polluted by their transgressions, and we may truly say with our sweet poet,

> ' At Rome she wears it as of old
>   Upon the accursed hill ;
> By monarchs clad in gems and gold,
>   She goes a mourner still.' '

' My dear Madam,' exclaimed M. Le Brun, ' If we must give the sacred name of Church to the upholders of Romish delusion and crime, let it be that of an apostate and degraded one. The titles and dignity of the spouse of Christ, belong only to the Church triumphant—the whole body of the ransomed and the glorified. Rome a mourner over the sins of her children ! Rome weeping, because they are following idols! She nurtures them in delusion, puts idolatrous litanies into their mouths, and by requiring their subscription to the vile dogma of transubstantiation, forces them to a worship, as unholy as that of the Pagan world.'

Le Brun spoke with a warmth which he seldom used, but it was the warmth of holy indignation at this lingering upon the borders of destruction, this trifling on the brink of a fearful pit, and (without regarding Marcella's look of horror) he went on.

' One of the most powerful lures that she makes use of to beguile unstable souls, is the intoxicating charm of music. What is it that induces the heedless Protestant, in your metropolis, to spend a part of his Sabbath in the Roman Catholic Chapel ?—The music—the voices of selected sing-

ers (often chosen from the *élite* of the theatre)
there pour forth their sweetest and their richest
notes. The stranger listens, and begins to feel his
bosom swell with emotions, which, perhaps, he
mistakes for devotion ; the music ceases, and he
turns with a longing, half-fearful eye, to the splendour of the ceremonies which succeed, and forgets,
in the excited state of his senses, the worse than
vanity of all those bowings, and prostrations, in
the eyes of Him who will be worshipped in spirit
and in truth. He then begins to imagine, there
is a depth in Catholic devotion, which his own
liturgy wants, and—but I need not go on, the idol
is in his heart, and he will soon be on his knees
before it, if God in his mercy prevent not.'

While Le Brun was speaking, Mr. Norman regarded him with a look of anger, but, mastering
his spirit by a violent effort, he said, in a cold and
constrained voice ; ' How rare are the qualifications
necessary for a wise reprover ! So little meekness
and charity are used in our dealings with the Church
of Rome, that it is no wonder the Catholic is confirmed in the faith of his fathers, and that others are
led, by pity, to join the ranks of the persecuted.'

Le Brun replied not; the venerable man, accustomed, upon all occasions, to search his own spirit, now sat silently, asking his heart if it had conceived aught to justify the reproof of his opponent, and praying to his God, to impart more of His own Spirit of lowliness and meekness. But Mary Spencer, stung to the quick at hearing her reverend friend so unjustly rebuked, gained courage from the righteousness of her cause, and said, with a firm voice, 'And yet, Mr. Norman, our Lord himself commends those churches especially that evinced a strong abhorrence of evil doctrines and practices—you remember, he says to one, " I know thy works, and thy labour, and thy patience, and how thou *canst not bear* them which are evil." And to another he says; " But this thou hast, that thou *hatest* the deeds of the Nicolaitanes, which I also hate." Surely it agrees better with the spirit of true charity, to rebuke the apostasy of Rome, than to throw a veil over her deformities, and " speak gently," or (as I would understand the poet who Miss Norman quoted) speak slightly of her fearful fall, and so lead the young, and ignorant, to tamper with her lures, and perhaps to think that separation from her was an act of schism.'

Mr. Norman did not vouchsafe any answer to his presumptuous parishioner's defence of her schismatic friend, (for such he really regarded the pious Le Brun,) but rose abruptly, and went over to that part of the room where Lady Sophia and Marcella Norman were engaged in close conversation, in which he joined at once, with all that graceful ease, and gentle manner, for which Lady Sophia so much admired him. We cannot record the subject of this converse, for it was heard only by the parties concerned ; but Marcella Norman looked eager, and enthusiastic, and Lady Sophia seemed surprised, and half-convinced.

In the meantime, Mr. Sidney addressing Le Brun, observed, ' I hope, sir, you do not condemn the use of music in the public worship of God ; and by music, I mean something more than the tuneless, charmless noise, with which his praises are sometimes accompanied.'

' I am so far from condemning the use of music in public worship,' replied M. Le Brun, ' that I believe such use to be the special design of this

L

much-abused talent. But to be of any value, it must be the real music of the sanctuary ; the union of tuneful and harmonious voices, pouring forth the feelings of holy and grateful hearts; not the skilful performance of the paid singer, or the pleasing effect of amateur melody. I stood in a cathedral once, during the performance of an exquisite anthem. I observed many of those who were around me, listening with wrapt intensity. I saw the flushed cheek, the eye filling with tears, the bosom heaving with emotion, and my heart rose at once in prayer, that these persons might not mistake the delight of their senses, and the depth of their passion for music, for the devotion of the soul. The anthem spoke of heavenly things, and so rich was the enjoyment, that the audience seemed to fancy they were already on the wing for paradise ; but I fear with many, it was a paradise of their own creating ; not the holy place, into which nothing that defileth can enter ; for as soon as we left the noble edifice, I heard the giddy laugh, and the earthly converse going on as freely as ever, and I saw the gay equipage drive off to some fashionable place, there to vie with others equally rich and gay ; and I thought how the heart might remain unchanged, and the life unsanctified, of those, who a few moments before looked as if they had forgotten earth altogether.'

The conversation now terminated, by the departure of the guests. Emma Clifford's laughing eyes followed Lady Sophia Benson and Marcella Norman, with an expression which Mary Spencer did not approve, and when at last she turned to her friend, and whispered, 'Poor Lady Sophia's heart is completely won,' Mary checked her by one of those grave, mild looks of reproof, which often recalled the lively girl to thought and seriousness, when some merry imagination of her own was leading her to transgress the rules of courtesy if not of Christian charity.

CHAPTER X.

The moment Emma and Mary were quite alone, the former exclaimed ; ' I do not know how Mr. Norman could find in his heart to behave so coldly, and sternly, to dear old M. Le Brun. Only that it would have looked very like committing the same fault myself, I could have found courage to bid him, " Rebuke not an elder, but intreat him as a father." But then, I suppose, he does not consider M. Le Brun to be a minister.'

' That would make very little difference in the application of your text, Emma. St. Paul, you remember, gave that rule to a bishop; and the elders whom he was not to rebuke, were to be found among his own flock ; either they were ministers holding a subordinate office to his own, or they were what we should call aged laymen. I have often thought of it, for even in my slight in-

tercourse with society, I have heard young clergymen, in all the pride of "ministerial authority,"
rebuke men, whose piety far transcended their
own, and whose white hairs at least entitled them
to respect.'

'I hope you will see M. Le Brun again. It was
a great pity he would not stay all night, for those
Normans completely destroyed all the pleasure
and benefit we hoped to gain from his company
to-day.'

'He has promised us one hour to-morrow,
Emma. You know he is on a mission, and must
not delay his important work, even to please his
friends; but he is going into Devonshire, and I
trust he will go and see my dear Edward.'

'You heard from Edward this morning, and
have scarcely told me one word about him : that is
not like you, Mary, for in general, when you receive
a letter from Devonshire, it is '—

'My theme, the whole day afterwards, you
would say, Emma; but this time I did not feel
quite so happy as I usually do on such occasions.
Edward writes nothing but what might give me
cause of gratitude, but I am vexed that he had not

discernment enough to see the pernicious tendency of the little poems he sent me; I should have thought a very babe in Christ could do so.'

' Perhaps,' replied Emma, ' it is the same with books, as with persons; when there is a pretty disguise of piety thrown over them, the Christian who believes all things, and hopes all things, does not readily discover the traitor underneath, and too easily gives the writer, or the speaker, credit for qualities which neither possess.'

Mary did not notice the gentle lesson, that Emma's words were intended to convey; her heart and thoughts were with her brother, and she said, ' I hope it may be so; but now, dear, I will not keep you up, it is already late, and I must write to Edward to-night, for I am very uneasy about him, Emma; not that I think he has fallen into any error, but he is so young, and inexperienced, and so easily attracted by any one possessing sufficient talent to dazzle his imagination.'

Emma would have offered to remain up with Mary, but she felt that her friend had rather be alone, and long after she had sunk into a deep sleep, Mary was on her knees, earnestly seeking grace and wisdom for her beloved brother, and then with her open Bible by her side, she sat down and wrote him the following letter.

' MY DEAR EDWARD,

' To thank you warmly and gratefully, for parting with a gift you valued, in my favour, was the first motive that prompted me to reply at once to your welcome letter, but I will not spend my time now, even in telling you how every proof of your affection is treasured by your fond sister. I have a higher duty to perform ; it is to warn you, Edward, against the writer, and the giver, of that little book. I would not for a long time believe it possible that clergymen of the Church of England, our own beloved scriptural church, could be employed in advancing the pretensions of the Church of Rome, and casting up a flowery path, by which their unwary flocks might gradually return to all the delusions which she spreads for wandering feet : but now I am convinced that it is even so, and that the little volume you enclosed to me, is one of the many baits which allure to the first step in dangerous paths. I read it nearly through this morning; met with my favourite verses, and others equally beautiful; and greatly I wondered, that one who could write such holy words, should have contrived to twine the "serpent error" through all his beautiful garland, so that those who will linger to pluck its flowers, may scarce escape unhurt by its deadly fangs.

'The era of the Reformation is condemned, in the very first poem, as a season of "light without love;" this is but a consistent beginning for a book, which contains so much of Romish devotion and sentiment; for then follow in due order Guardian Angels, Ave Marias, and all the impious usurpation of priestly prerogative; and no holy language, no lofty imaginings, can for a moment extenuate the guilty blasphemies, contained in some of the latter poems. I would not say so much about one book, when I know there are numbers of similar works now issuing from the press, but I have heard that this "Christian Year" is a favourite with the party who circulate them, and I am grieved to the heart, my brother, that your own mind was not sufficiently enlightened by the Spirit of God, to enable you to discern its errors.

' You intend to be a minister of Christ's church.
For this office, great talents and brilliant powers
are not required, but real and enlightened piety is;
and enlightened piety will see through the fairest
guise, that false doctrine can robe itself in. Rejoicing only in the righteousness of Christ, and
actuated in all he does by love to his Redeemer,
the true Christian, though his heart would respond
to the call—

> " Think not of rest though dreams be sweet ;
> Start up and ply your heavenward feet."

would obey it in the path of an evangelical obedience, not by a life of religious sentimentalism, and
monastic fervour, such as this whole volume teems
with.

' You are to be a minister of Christ's church ;
not a priest officiating at an altar ; not a mere per-
former of sacred ceremonies : and not, ah certainly
not, one who can give efficacy to sacraments, or
pardon to the guilty soul. All these offices are
claimed by some who call themselves Christ's
ministers ; but for your future commission, Edward, study the epistles to Timothy and Titus,

and with them—" Refuse profane and old wives'
fables, and exercise thyself rather unto godliness."
" Take heed unto thyself, and unto the doctrine :
continue in them ; for in so doing thou shalt both
save thyself, and them that hear thee."   " Hold
fast the form of sound words, which thou hast
heard of me, in faith and love which is in Christ
Jesus."   Study to show thyself " approved unto
God, a workman that needeth not to be ashamed,
rightly dividing the word of truth."   " Preach
the word : be instant in season and out of season ;
reprove, rebuke, exhort, with all long-suffering
and doctrine. For the time will come, when they
will not endure sound doctrine ; but after their
own lusts shall they heap to themselves teachers,
having itching ears. And they shall turn away
their ears from the truth, and shall be turned unto
fables."

' These are some of St. Paul's rules and warnings for a christian minister ; but every word of
the three epistles should be written on your memory, that their plain and simple directions for
your future conduct may never be forgotten.

" Seek, dear Edward, to have your mind so

stored with the word of God, that you may be
always able, without delay, to test every opinion
and practice that you meet with by it. Above all,
seek to lay your own foundation deep in the everlasting rock, and then you will not be carried about
with every wind of doctrine that sweeps over the
visible church, but treading your stedfast way up
the narrow path that leads to eternal life, "the
way of the just, shall be indeed, as the shining
light, shining more and more unto the perfect
day."

' You say you are longing for Oxford. I vene-
rate Oxford for what it has been, and I am sure
there are many servants of God preparing in its
ancient halls for their great mission : but there is
a fearful work doing there, Edward, and when
you do go, let it be with the prayer in your heart,
" Lead me not into temptation." Seek to have a
clear knowledge and a deep feeling of the doctrines of grace. The mere assent of the understanding, to a set of scriptural principles, unaccompanied by thorough heart-work, will easily
give way before the sophistries of falsehood. A
little deviation from the truth will not be quickly

observed, by one whose heart has remained cold
and indifferent, while his creed was quite sound.
I believe this has been the reason why so many of
those from whom better things were looked for,
saw no harm but much good, in the first numbers
of the Tracts for the Times, and were thus gradually prepared to receive the full-blown heresy
which has just appeared in Tract 90.

‘ “Light without love,” will indeed gradually
sink into a fading twilight, till the shadows of the
night succeed in all their twelfth-century gloom,
only lighted up by the false glare of another me-
teor—Love without light, groping for some object, on which to lavish its fervours, till at length
it gives them to saints and angels, wandering on
through vast chambers of imagery, but farther
and farther from Him who is light, and in whom
is no darkness at all.

‘ And now I know that my dear brother is beginning to wonder, why I scarcely ever spoke or
wrote before on a subject with which I seem to be
familiar. But I thought the subject very unprofitable, and believing the danger far off, I felt no
need of special warning against it. Besides, I was

afraid of offending against christian charity; but now the heresy has come near us, even at our doors, and I am convinced that true charity will listen to her Master's voice, and obey the command which he spoke by the mouth of his Apostle Paul, " Now I beseech you, brethren, mark them which cause divisions and offences, *contrary to the doctrine* which ye have learned; and avoid them." Rom. xvi. The doctrine which the Roman converts had learned, is to be found in the whole episto that church.

' In the spirit of that command, dear Edward, I would repeat the earnest entreaty with which I commenced my letter; avoid the givers and writers of such books as that which you sent to me, for they do cause divisions contrary to sound doctrines. We are not commanded to avoid those who differ from us in forms: of these, the word of God speaks lightly, " One believeth that he may eat all things, another who is weak, eateth herbs." Rom. xiv. 2. The very attempt on the part of these men to make the breach wider, between Churchmen and orthodox dissenters, is a proof, that christian unity is not the thing they seek, but papal uniformity—the unity of the dark ages. "Oh my soul, come not into their secret." And Edward, that you may join me in that determination, is the prayer

'Of your fond sister,

'MARY.'

The midnight hour had struck, long before Mary wrote the last words of her letter. The only being awake in that large mansion, eternal things seemed present to her mind, with all the vital power of dread reality. She hated religious gossip, and more especially that species of it, that seems to take delight in recounting the numbers of the fallen,—in perhaps exaggerating the progress of error, for the sake of the strange kind of excitement it produces. She knew that this habit almost insensibly leads to the fearful sin of "rejoicing in iniquity," and though she did not wish to blind Emma's eyes to what was wrong in Mr. Norman's teaching, she wished to discourage her from talking of his errors, merely for the sake of talking.

She had been indeed slow to admit the conviction that he was really a teacher of false doctrine; but, now she could doubt no longer, she determined, by God's assistance, to keep a jealous watch over his intercourse with all she loved, and an air of thoughtful determination was stamped upon her placid brow, as she folded her letter, and prepared to take a few hours' rest.

But the vigil of the preceding night did not prevent Mary Spencer from rising early the next morning. She expected M. Le Brun would be with her before breakfast, and she would not for worlds have suffered even necessary sleep to deprive her of one moment of that precious interview. At eight o'clock she, with Emma, was receiving the last parting counsels of her dear old friend, and praying, as Christians only can pray, who understand what the Psalmist means, when he says, " My soul thirsteth for God, for the living God."

They spoke of the future, as those whose next place of meeting would be before the throne of God; and M. Le Brun especially, reminded his young friends, of the probable difficulties of their future course. ' In France, poor thoughtless

France, (he said) a reaction is even now rapidly taking place. Popery, bowed down for a time, but not destroyed by the iron hand of infidelity, is again rising to all its former greatness, and we scarcely expect that our years of tranquillity will be many. In noble Protestant England, the foul apostacy is so far gaining ground, aided by traitors in her own church, that the true disciples have need to trim their lamps, and stand on their watchtowers, lest the enemy surprise them when they are off their guard. Remember, " ye have not yet resisted unto blood, striving against sin." Be ready always for this mortal strife; it may not come in your day, but be assured, persecution in some form will, if you really " live godly in Christ Jesus." Already the name of Evangelical, (which for some years past, has been considered honourable even by those who had little right to wear it) is beginning to be used as a term of reproach. Professors rather covet the appellation of Churchman, or Catholic. Remain evangelical in name, heart, and life, and the world will not long suffer you to do so with peace and reputation.'

M. Le Brun could not remain longer than his

promised hour, and as they exchanged a sorrowful farewell, Mary repeated her earnest petition, ' Do not forget Edward, when you pass through Devonshire.' His affectionate reply soothed her fears, and with a countenance, on which tears were struggling with a smile of peace, she hastened with Emma to join Lady Sophia at the breakfast-table.

Lady Sophia was reading a letter with deep attention, and did not for some moments notice the two younger ladies. At length she exclaimed, ' You must forgive my rudeness, my dear girls, but this sweet enthusiast has for a moment completely absorbed me. She has written to give me early notice, that her brother intends commencing the daily service next week, in order that I may so arrange my engagements, as to be able to attend regularly. She says, " Let our afflicted church adopt at least this one blessed practice of better times ; and while the morning devotions of her children rise to the throne of God, and their vesper-hymn is heard again at the evening-hour, we may hope the day is not far distant, when their faith and love may equal that of their pious forefathers, in the deeper sentiments of adoration, of

M

mystery, of tenderness, of reverence, and of devotion." I shall certainly go,' continued Lady Sophia, ' and I hope you, my dears, will unite with me in availing yourselves of a privilege so great.'

' I should be sorry to refuse to join in the worship of God at any time,' said Mary, ' and will go if God permit, provided you think Mr. Norman will confine himself strictly to the forms and liturgy of our church.'

' Oh, as for that,' exclaimed Emma, ' you need feel no uneasiness about his using any other prayers; happily he dare not go quite so far.'

' Dare not, is a harsh expression, Emma : ' (said Lady Sophia with some warmth) ' I am sure Mr. Norman would not, if he dared, change one word of our scriptural service. It was zeal, perhaps I should say an extravagant zeal for our Church, that made him refuse to be present at the meeting on Thursday.'

' Nay, dear Lady Sophia,' interrupted Mary, ' not surely zeal for our Church, if by that expression, we mean the spirit of her services, the doctrine of her articles, and the faith of her reformers. You know, that from the Reformation, until late in the reign of Charles I, the Church of England was so truly united with the Reformed Churches on the continent, that our ambassadors at Paris were in the constant habit of worshipping in their assemblies, till Archbishop Laud forbade the sweet communion, and ordered the English envoy to take with him a chaplain, episcopally ordained.'

'Poor Laud,' said Lady Sophia; 'he certainly was a weak old man, and by his arbitrary measures, helped forward the cruel fate that overtook him at last. But I did not mean to justify Mr. Norman's non-attendance at the meeting. I think he was wrong, but that he erred from excess of zeal, and is therefore entitled to our pardon.—And now, Mary, I want you, like a dear good girl, to settle my Church Missionary accounts for me. I have promised to spend some hours this morning with Marcella Norman, and cannot possibly find time to do it myself, and I believe we are to have a deputation from that Society here in a few days. That is a Society which Mr. Norman will aid, I am sure, with heart and hand.'

Mary willingly consented to undertake the task,

Lady Sophia proposed to her; but she looked
grieved, and unhappy. She did not like to urge
her own advice upon Lady Sophia, who was very
much her senior, and although not her benefactor
in a pecuniary point of view, she felt that she
had a claim upon her gratitude. Lady Sophia
saw the struggle that was passing in her mind,
and rising from the table, she kindly patted her
cheek, and said, laughing, ' Now don't be jealous,
my dear Mary, because I am going to spend one
morning with poor solitary Marcella Norman, or
perhaps you fear that your old friend will be caught
by some novel opinion, which that interesting
young person holds; but you need not fear. I
trust my principles are too firmly fixed, to be so
easily unsettled by a romantic girl.' As she
finished the last sentence, she left the room, and
Mary said aloud, while the tears stood in her eyes,
—' Dear Lady Sophia, if you feared for yourself,
I should not fear for you.'

'I am sorry, Mary, (said Emma, after a few
moments' pause) that you so readily consented to
go to the daily services; I would have as little as
possible to do with Mr. Norman, a man who

would scarcely speak to that faithful servant of
God, M. Le Brun.'

Mary had felt much hurt, that Lady Sophia
made no effort to see M. Le Brun, during his
early visit. She had indeed invited him to remain
her guest, the evening before, but she was easily
satisfied with his refusal, and Mary could not help
attributing her coldness towards him that morning,
to the influence of Mr. Norman's example ; but
she had never dreamed of so closely uniting Mr.
Norman, and God's public worship, as to let the
bigotry of the one, make her neglect the privilege
of the other, and she now turned to Emma, with
a look of astonishment, saying at the same time.
' The conviction, that " thou, God, seest me,"
should so fill our minds, Emma, when we go to
the house of prayer, that the defects or the per-
fections of the minister should be quite forgotten.
There are far stronger objections to attending
Fernely church on the sabbath-day, for Mr. Norman preaches then, and he says so much about
fasting, bodily mortification, and the various fes-
tivals of the church, that there is some danger of
forgetting what most we should remember ; the

absolute necessity of "a new birth unto righteousness." But I had better fulfil my promise to
Lady Sophia, and arrange all the missionary accounts, before there is any fear of interruption
from visiters.'

She had nearly completed her task, before her
fears of interruption were verified: but Jane and
Elizabeth Graham were always welcome visiters,
and Emma's eyes sparkled with delight, when the
former said, ' We are come to invite you to join
our party to-morrow; we intend, if it please God,
to walk to Mr. Sidney's church.'

Mary looked grave and thoughtful, for a few
moments, and then replied, ' I should like it so
much that I fear it would be gratifying my inclination at the expense of duty. We shall be
forced to leave our schools.'

' We shall be back in time, both for your
school, and our own,' said Elizabeth Graham,
' by fixing the hour of attendance at them, a
little later in the afternoon ; and we are to have
no carriages—no unnecessary working of horses
on the Lord's day. Where is Lady Sophia ? we
must invite her to join us.'

' I fear she will not go,' answered Mary, ' she does not see Mr. Norman's errors as others do.'

' Then you must not let friendship or politeness induce you to stay with her,' said Jane Graham ; ' my father says we must not feed upon the un-wholesome bread which is offered us in our own parish, for want of courage or energy to overstep its bounds.'

' Do you think, said Emma, ' that these men who are taking so much pains to spread Popish doctrine throughout England, are really Jesuits, in league with Rome, for the purpose of bringing this country again under the papal yoke ? '

' The tree is known by its fruit, Miss Clifford,' said Jane Graham, ' and a Jesuit's deeds may fairly be supposed to proceed from Jesuit craft ; but whether all these unhappy men are in actual league with Rome, we cannot determine, nor does it make much difference in ascertaining our duties of self-defence. That they have led others, and may lead us to Rome, we know ; and even if they stop short of this, their religion is built upon quicksands of human merit, and man's ordinances, and would soon give way under our feet, and precipitate us into perdition. It is our first duty to watch our own hearts; to take care (as my father says) that our religion be sound, and solid, not sentimental. And next to ourselves, we must watch all, over whom we have influence: our servants, the poor, and most of all, our Sunday schools.'

Mary sighed, when her school was brought to her mind. Already she had felt the pain of losing two or three of her favourite scholars, who had been taken from her, to form a class for Marcella Norman; but she did not mention them, and Miss Graham went on: 'Each in his station must do his best against the hosts of the unclean spirit, that are mustering to the battle. It will be a sharp conflict, but it must be fought; for if we sit quietly down, while Popery is preached to Protestant congregations, it may at last be said of us, "The prophets prophecy falsely, and the priests bear rule by their means, and my people love to have it so, and what will ye do in the end thereof?"'

CHAPTER XI.

'Though not a grace appears on strictest search,
But that she fasts, and, item, goes to church.'—COWPER.

EARLY on the Sabbath morning the little party set
out on their way to Mr. Sidney's church. It consisted only of Mr. Graham and his two daughters,
Mary Spencer and Emma Clifford. A few villagers followed their example, and with these they
occasionally interchanged such converse as suited
the sacred season.

It was a time for holy communion and meditation; a meet preparation for the worship of the
sanctuary, in which they were going to join. The
subjects of their conversation were such as raise
the mind above earth, and shed peace and light
through it; and they forgot Puseyism and every
other distracting *ism*, until they met a party of
villagers belonging to the parish to which they

were going, walking hastily towards Fernely, with excited looks, ' Well, my good friend,' said Mr. Graham, ' Where are you going with all this speed ? Something of great importance must surely induce you to turn your backs upon your own church.'

' Oh, (replied some of the men laughing,) we are going to see the images, and the candles, and the holy water which you have got in Fernely church now.'

' Images, and candles, and holy water !' repeated Mr. Graham, ' No, no, we have not got them yet. Nor are we likely to have them, until idle curiosity, such as yours, shall have led people to listen to doctrine that may prepare the way for such trumpery. And when you are ready to look at them with reverence, then perhaps Mr. Norman, or some one who thinks as he does, may treat you to a sight of the images, and candles, and holy water.'

' No fear of that time ever coming, sir,' answered one of the men, ' we are all good protestants ; but it is certain that something new is going to be done in Fernely church to-day, and

we want to see what it is. You know we can
guard better against a danger, after we have seen
it for ourselves, than if we only take it upon
hearsay.'

' To guard against a danger, by running head-
long into it, is a new method of defence, my
friends, and I think a mockery of Him to whom
you pray, " Lead us not into temptation." Be
persuaded by me and return to your own church,
where you may hear to-day, what will make you
wiser and happier all your life. Remember the
admonition of holy writ, " Cease, my son, to hear
the instruction that causeth to err." '

' Oh, but Sir,' said the man, ' if the images
are really there, we mean to get up and come
out of the church, the moment he shows his head
in the pulpit, so we shall not hear any bad instruction.'

' If Fernely church were the only place of worship within your reach, I should say you were
right to try, if even a part of God's worship could
be joined in, without your becoming a partaker in
other men's sins. But as it is, you are only
breaking the Sabbath, and endangering your own

souls, by persisting in your intention. You leave
the blessings of the gospel behind you, for the sole
purpose of showing contempt to the minister of
another church. There is no zeal for God in all
this, my friends, and I can assure you, there will
be nothing visibly new in Fernely church to-day.'

Two or three of the men listened to Mr.
Graham's advice, and turned back ; the rest went
on, saying carelessly, ' Oh never fear, we are too
sound Protestants to be easily caught by Popish
trash and nonsense.'

Just at that moment, Mrs. Chambers' carriage
drove rapidly past. She bowed low to Mary
Spencer and Emma, while the latter exclaimed,
' I suppose Mrs. Chambers is going to see the
images too.' But Emma was wrong in this conjecture. Mrs. Chambers had heard nothing of
images, but she had heard a little of Mr. Norman's
doctrine from Marcella, and she thought there was
something very comfortable and easy in his religion ; very preferable to the terrible sentence
that Mr. Sidney was always ringing in her ears,
" Except a man be born again, he cannot see the
kingdom of God." She would more readily bear

the long life of painful penitence, (or as Mrs. Chambers read it, penance,) that Marcella spoke of, than submit to a religion which required her to renounce every long-cherished sin, and to restrain and deny every wandering wish. She had never, even for fashion's sake, (as it is to be feared too many have done,) frequented the yearly meeting, or gone out of her way to hear a popular preacher. Dancing, and cards, even private theatricals, which had been the amusement of her youth, had never been discontinued in her house; and in her seventieth year she was as devoted a slave to the world, as when she began her gay career in her seventeenth. But grey hairs, and failing strength, reminded her that some religion would be necessary, as she approached the brink of the grave, and having conceived a favourable impression of Mr. Norman's talents, she came to try if his preaching were equally pleasing to the ear, and if it proved to be so, she determined to become a constant attendant at Fernely church. Our party met with no farther interruption to their tranquillity, and the ordinances of the sanctuary gave strength for the other duties of the day, and of the week.

At seven o'clock the next morning, Mary Spencer and Emma, (the latter half reluctantly,) accompanied Lady Sophia to church, and Mary joined, with her accustomed devotion, in England's beautiful liturgy. Nothing new was introduced, and any peculiarity in Mr. Norman's manner she did not observe. The congregation was very small. Few among the pious country people could attend, without infringing on the time they had long devoted to private prayer, or family worship; others indeed there were, whose general distaste to all religious services, helped them to a ready excuse from the farm, and the merchandize. Some of these Mr. Norman persuaded by the merit of the act. A religion that holds out a heavenly inheritance, as the reward of an exact attendance upon outward forms and observances, seems so pleasant and easy, that even the ungodly are often willing to give so low a price for eternal glory.

The Grahams were not there, at which Mary felt some surprise, for she knew their early and active habits, and thought that no slight reason, no mere objection to the minister, would keep

them from worshipping in the house of God,
whenever its doors were opened for that purpose.

Mrs. Chambers was there; this also was matter
of surprise to Mary Spencer, and she hailed it as
the beginning of future good to the poor old lady,
who could thus retrench the hours of sloth, and
self-indulgence, and drive so far every morning to
church. But while Mrs. Chambers' carriage stood
at Fernely church-door, morning after morning,
the gaieties of the evening did not decrease; balls
and card-parties quickly succeeded each other in
her house, and even when her acquaintances
whispered, that she had added to her other observances, the austerity of a Friday's fast, they
remarked also, that these things had put no restraint upon the bitter spirit and the censorious
tongue.

Nothing more occurred during this week to
alter the usual course of things, except the Church
Missionary meeting, which took place towards the
end of it; and at which Mr. Norman was present.
Emma wondered, and Mary rejoiced; for the hope,
that ' something good towards the Lord his God'
might yet be found in the minister of Fernely, had

not yet left her heart. But when the meeting was over, and they were walking home, Emma observed, ' This was the coldest—most uninteresting meeting at which I ever was present; the deputation seemed afraid to speak, lest they should stumble upon something which Mr. Norman would call dissent; and I am certain our rector took his seat in the chair, with the full determination that Mr. Sidney should not speak, lest he should preach the gospel.'

' Emma, (said Lady Sophia with some asperity), you remind me of those persons of whom Jeremiah complains; " All my familiars watched for my halting." Mr. Norman thought fit to absent himself from one meeting, and you expressed great indignation at his absence; he attends another, at which every good Churchman should be present, and you are still dissatisfied.'

' Because, in attending it, I believe he only acted upon that principle which I saw advocated in one of the papers, or pamphlets, that Marcella Norman sends us. The editor, or correspondent of the paper, advised, that those who hold church principles, (as they are called,) should not withdraw from the committees, and meetings of the various societies, but remain in them, and endeavour to leaven them with their opinions. I forget the exact expressions, but there was a hint given, that it would be well when these societies could be done without altogether;—here comes Mr. Sidney; let us ask him what it really was that spoiled the meeting.'

'Now Mr. Sidney,' (said Lady Sophia shaking hands with him,) 'Emma is anxious to have your sanction for condemning the meeting. For my own part, I think it was well attended, and ably addressed. But my two young friends are determined not to be satisfied with any thing poor Mr. Norman does.'

'Twenty years ago,' said Mr. Sidney, 'When I was quite a boy, I was spending a few days with my dear old friend Mr. Warner. The first Church Missionary Meeting that ever was held in Fernely, took place then, and I shall never forget it. To me there appeared to be a halo of glory round the place in which it was held. The clergyman who addressed the meeting, was on the eve of sailing to India as a missionary, and there was a holiness,

N

a self-consecration that pervaded the little assembly, which I look in vain for now. The jeer of the scorner, the disapprobation of the worldling, even the charge of dissent was not heeded then, and we came away resolving to spend, and be spent for Christ. How has that resolve been fulfilled? Perhaps, had our first love not decayed—our distinctiveness from the world continued, the blight that seems settling on our holy things, would have been dispersed when first it appeared. " Let us search and try our ways; and turn again to the Lord." '

Lady Sophia felt that her question was answered. She too remembered that meeting, and the eagerness with which she formed a juvenile association in the good cause. From that day she had been a friend to missions in general, and secretary to the auxiliary societies in Fernely. But when she repeated to herself ' twenty years ago,' she knew that the brightness of her zeal had worn off, and the fervour of her first love decayed, and a feeling of sadness prevented her reply.

After a few moments silence, Mary said, ' Do you think, Mr. Sidney, the plan lately proposed for

collecting all contributions, and'—she hesitated—
' giving them to the Bishops, to be disposed of as
they think fit, a wise and useful plan?'

' Why could you not say, laying them at the
Bishop's feet, Mary?' asked Emma laughing.

' Before that plan could be carried out, in a
manner that would please the proposers of it,'
replied Mr. Sidney, ' the whole bench of bishops
must hold unanimous opinions, and those opinions,
to say the least, must be very high church, and
I should greatly prefer the present method of devoting money to the service of God, to the probable destination of the vast heap, which might
then be collected on the communion-table. It
would perhaps—'

' Prove a fine addition to Peter's pence,' interrupted Emma.

' I am not sure of that,' (returned Mr. Sidney
smiling.) ' But whether the new doctrines are
opening the way for return to Rome, or whether
they are intended to make the chair of Augustine
and Lanfranc vie with that of St. Peter, it matters little, if man, and man's authority be permitted to thrust themselves between the sinner

and his Lord, and any one Church, (be it the
apostate of Rome, or the hitherto scriptural one
of England,) presume to say, " beyond my pale
there is no salvation." Out of Christ there is no
salvation. In him there is a safe refuge for all ;
for Jew, and Gentile ; Episcopalian, Presbyterian,
Independent, or Methodist.'

When Mary reached home, she found a few
lines from Edward, in answer to her long, and
anxiously written letter. She read them eagerly,
but though she felt pleased with his warmly expressed disapprobation of the errors she most
dreaded he might be led into, she thought his
words savoured of self-confidence, and was but
imperfectly reassured, although he said—' Fear
not for me, dear Mary ; I am too thoroughly
alive to the follies and mistakes of the Tractarian
party ever to be caught by them. The errors in
their works are too glaring for there to be any
danger in my plucking a few flowers from among
them. So rest satisfied, my own sister, a Puseyite
I never can be, but I trust before many years
have rolled over our heads, you will have the

comfort of knowing that I am an ordained minister of the Lord Jesus Christ. This is still the first, best wish of

'Your affectionate brother,

'EDWARD SPENCER.'

CHAPTER XII.

" ICHABOD."

THE summer had past away, and autumn too was far advanced. In Fernely everything was undergoing a gradual change. Mary and Emma had by degrees been dismissed from the Sunday-school, though Lady Sophia Benson still retained some influence there, and continued to teach a class herself. The former schoolmistress had been parted with, in favour of a person on whom Mr. Norman could rely, and our two friends instructed a few children of both sexes, who came to them on Sabbath-evenings ; for they still persevered in their morning attendance at Mr. Sidney's church.

Lady Sophia's affectionate heart could never be quite estranged from her younger companions, but Marcella Norman contrived to engross most of her

time, so that she was much less with them than
she formerly had been.

She did not reject the doctrines of grace, but
their influence on her life and conduct was evidently weakened, and though she professed no
alteration in her creed, she seemed half-pleased
with Mrs. Chambers' charge. ' So I hear you are
quite a high churchwoman now.' She had learned
to call all dissenters schismatics, and spoke of the
works of the Fathers, and the Book of Common
Prayer, with a reverence too high for productions
merely human.

Though she was far from adopting Mr. Norman's maxim, that ' to assert the Bible, and nothing but the Bible, is an unthankful rejection of
another great gift equally from God; '* yet was
her Bible read with less constancy and attention
than it had formerly been, while she eagerly de-
voured all the trash that Marcella Norman lent her
in the shape of stories for the young, tales and
novels, which in an open or covert manner, aimed
their shafts at vital religion, throwing an air of

* Tract 71.

ridicule over its professors, and depreciating those
societies which God has raised up and made an
instrument of good to the whole earth.

Besides the books, little elegantly-written and
sweetly-scented notes were constantly passing between Lady Sophia Benson and Marcella Norman,
and the friendship promised to be as close and as
romantic as an attachment between an enthusiastic
girl of two-and-twenty, and an equally (though
less perniciously) enthusiastic woman of five-and
forty could possibly become.

Mary saw the progress of this friendship with
pain, and her efforts to win Lady Sophia back to
her own and Emma's society, were attributed by
that lady to a latent feeling of jealousy, while they
really proceeded from an earnest desire for her
eternal good. ' I am twice as old as Marcella,
(Lady Sophia would reason) and of course, Mary,
there is more chance of my bringing her back to
the right way, than that such a mere girl should
lead me into error.' But Mary knew that this
was not ' of course.' She knew that Marcella had
the advantage of her friend whenever they conversed on any contested point, for she drew all her

resources in argument from her brother, while Lady Sophia, in consequence of the vast concessions she had already made in favour of High Churchism, was perplexed and bewildered. The aid of every text, which she could have called to her assistance, was weakened by ' the church says thus,' though had she calmly and prayerfully inquired into the matter, she would have discovered that her own and England's church drew all her authority, all her doctrines from the Bible, and says expressly, ' Holy Scripture containeth all things necessary to salvation, so that whatsoever is not read therein, nor may be proved thereby, is not to be required of any man, that it should be believed as an article of the faith, or be thought requisite or necessary to salvation,' *

These contests rarely took place in Mary Spencer's presence, and Lady Sophia did not often mention them unless she had gained a controversial victory over her friend, or had on the other hand been so particularly pleased with something that Marcella had advanced, that she thought it

* Article VI.

would influence Mary in her favour. On these occasions, Mary's quick appeal to Holy Writ, although it did good by keeping Lady Sophia in some measure on her guard, was at the same time not so acceptable to her as it should have been, and she gradually became more reserved upon such topics.

But Mary still continued to seek Lady Sophia's society, when the effort to do so had become extremely painful, and she would frequently invite her to walk with herself and Emma, in spite of the indignant remonstrance which the latter would offer, that 'there is something terribly mean in pressing our company upon those who are averse to it.'

During one of these walks in the grounds about Roebrook Hall, when conversation had begun to flag from an evident attempt on the part of Lady Sophia to avoid all disputed subjects, and Emma had become quite weary of the chilling restraint, the monotony of the scene was for a few moments changed, and her curiosity excited by seeing Mr. Norman walking at some distance in close conversation with a strange gentleman, who leaned fami-

liarly upon his arm. As they drew nearer, Mr.
Norman suddenly perceiving the three ladies, returned Lady Sophia's bow of recognition, and
then turned off in a contrary direction.

On coming out into the village, towards which
our party had directed their steps, they again saw
Mr. Norman and the stranger walking in the
same confidential manner. They stopped before
the church-door, and seemed to be examining the
form and situation of the building, and after a few
moments thus spent, Emma observed Mr. Norman unlock the door, and usher his friend into the
interior of the church.

The three ladies called to see some of their poor
people, and could not avoid hearing their various
accounts of the strange foreign gentleman, who
was stopping with Mr. Norman. As they returned home, Lady Sophia ventured to express
several conjectures as to who he could possibly
be, and much she wondered that Marcella had
not mentioned him in the note she had received
from her that morning.

'We will call him the Abbé, ma'am, if you
please,' (said Emma playfully) ' for since Miss

Norman will not introduce us to him, we must
have some shorter mode of designation than ' the
strange foreign gentleman, who is on a visit at
Mr. Norman's.''

' Then choose a more charitable one, Emma,'
returned her Ladyship. ' Why may he not be a
second Le Brun, who from being Mr. Norman's
equal in years and talents, has obtained a salutary
influence over our dear minister, which that good
man had no opportunity of gaining.'

' Oh, don't name Pastor Le Brun and our rector together. Mr. Norman would not be at all
grateful to you for so doing. But I really should
like to know what that minute examination of the
church portends, and why the stranger was so
carefully introduced into our sanctuary.'

The foreigner who had excited so much curiosity in the village, remained for some days at the
parsonage, and during that period, Mr. Norman's
time was wholly occupied by his guest : Marcella
too did not once visit Roebrook Hall until after
his departure, and when she did so, she merely
mentioned the stranger as her brother's friend,
who was travelling through England, and who

had been greatly pleased with the beauties of Fernely. Yet she seemed ill at ease, as if she longed to communicate more, for Marcella was naturally frank and ingenuous. She really loved Lady Sophia, and would gladly have told her all that was in her heart, but her brother's lessons of reserve were not wholly lost upon her, for though painful to learn, she tried hard to bring herself under their chilling restraint.

' How delightful must be a life wholly devoted to God, (she exclaimed without seeming to notice a question that Lady Sophia had ventured to put to her respecting the mysterious guest.) 'It is strange that the Church of England has made no provision to satisfy the longings of such of her children who desire to renounce the world, and to consecrate their days and nights to devout meditation, watching, and prayer.'

' If you talk thus, Marcella,' replied Lady Sophia, ' my young friends will accuse you of a partiality for convents and monasteries, those convenient resorts of sloth and ignorance during the middle ages.'

' Rather say those holy abodes of peace and

piety, dear Lady Sophia. The Catholic practice of retiring from a vain and selfish world, was followed by the most devoted Christians long before the arrival of those much maligned middle ages.'

' Massive walls and iron gratings will not keep the allurements of sense out of the heart of the worldling, however deeply he may incarcerate himself behind them, Miss Norman;' said Mary; ' Neither can all the efforts of the god of this world shut Christ out of the heart of his believing people, while they are serving Him amid the active duties of life. We do not find the Apostles recommending, or their immediate hearers choosing a life of dreaming solitude.'

' And yet,' (said Lady Sophia, who was now anxious to aid her friend,) ' the practice was adopted in the very early ages of the church, and by the best of men. Paul, the hermit, for instance, who lived in the third century, passed nearly the whole of his long and holy life in the desert.'

' And Anthony the Egyptian,' interposed Emma, ' I wonder so good a man as Athanasius could write the life of such a fanatic.'

' Paul the hermit,' said Mary, ' first sought the

desert, as many in his time did, to avoid the
Decian persecution, and then pleased with his calm
retreat, he kept his candle under the bushel, notwithstanding our Lord's admonition. Paul the
apostle, took the nobler part, and literally obeyed
his Master's injunction, " When ye are persecuted
in one city, flee ye into *another*." '

' But Mary,' inquired Emma, ' are not the disciples of Christ described, in the epistle to the
Hebrews, as " wandering in deserts, and in mountains, in dens, and caves of the earth." '

' Forced thither by their enemies, Emma; denied a dwelling among their fellow men; not
surely living there in all the barbarism, and in-
anity of a twelfth century recluse. We have directions in the Bible for the duties connected with
every relation of life; but certainly none for nuns
and hermits.'

' St. Paul, at least, recommends the " angelic
life" of nuns and monks before any other;' said
Marcella Norman, ' he says, " She that is unmar-
ried careth for the things of the Lord, how she
may please the Lord." '

' Because she serves the Lord, Miss Norman, in

her generation ; devoting her leisure, and her
freedom from those cares which disturb the mistress of a family, to the advancement of His cause
upon earth, and in her own heart too.   But why
are we disputing about the value of custom and
institutions which have been such a foul blot upon
the Christian religion ?   I believe many of the
Lord's people were to be found in the first
monasteries ; that they unwittingly encouraged an
evil, the greatness of which they did not foresee.
But to plead the cause of monasteries now ! with
open Bibles in every house and hand.   Oh ! Miss
Norman, take such vain fancies to the foot of the
cross, and the glory of Immanuel's dying love will
constrain you to renounce them all, and to devote
the energies of your youth to His active service in
the world—in the midst of those He died to redeem.   Or if you are at last found taking refuge
in the solitary places of the earth, let it be as one
" of whom the world was not worthy," and has
therefore hated, and driven far away from the
abode of her servants.'

Marcella rose with a look of impatience and disappointment.   She came armed with many fine

and flowery speeches, in praise of the life of a nun, which had taken firm hold on her imagination, and she had indulged a secret hope, that Mary Spencer would be attracted by a glowing description of the austerities practised by the early ascetics.

She had heard from Lady Sophia, and from sure witnesses among the poor, of Mary's devoted piety ; and the number of sick and destitute aided by her very moderate income, convinced Marcella, that if she had not taken a vow of voluntary poverty, she, at least, lived in such a manner, that the vow itself would be no very heavy yoke. Other things she had learned, which Mary thought were known only to herself and God. The hours spent in early devotion ;—her habits of deep study, and meditation, united with a life of constant and unwearied self-denial. This true description of Mary's character, had strangely enough made Marcella imagine that if she could introduce subjects which are attractive to a contemplative mind, she might succeed in winning over Mary Spencer to the new opinions she had herself imbibed. She did not know that Mary had taken her station at

o

the foot of the cross—that she lived there—that all the glory of her young life was but the reflection of those beams which surround her crucified Lord, and that whenever temptation in any form assailed her, she looked up to her risen Saviour, and cried, " Hold up my goings in thy paths, that my footsteps slip not."

Mr. Norman, though he almost despaired that either of the friends would ever come under his influence, had far more hope of gaining Emma, than her calm and reflecting companion. But Miss Norman cordially disliked Emma, having often suffered from the satirical rebukes which the latter could not help administering, when the grossest follies of Popery escaped from the lips of one who still called herself a member of the Church of England. On these occasions Mary generally interposed. She knew that ironical words might only harden the poor apostate, while they injured Emma herself, by checking those deep longings for this wanderer's return, which she really shared with Mary.

As Marcella Norman left the room, she pressed Lady Sophia's hand with some emotion, and expressed much concern that their personal inter-course would soon be interrupted for a long time. She was going, she said, to spend the winter with a friend in the south of England, and the period of her return to her brother's house would be very uncertain. " But you will write, dear Lady Sophia, you will surely write ! Distance, you know, cannot destroy the communion of souls ; and we who have so many thoughts—so many dear cherished dreams in common, can never be really separated; nothing but the grave could divide us.'

' Or convent-walls ; ' said Emma in a low voice ; but there was no irony in her remark then. She had observed Marcella's eyes fill with tears, and worlds would not have tempted her to hurt her feelings. She scarcely knew that the words of warning had escaped her lips, till Marcella's in-dignant look and distant curtsey, made her fear that she had unintentionally added to the passing grief which troubled that young lady.

' I would not have said an unkind word to her on any account, Mary,' she said, ' but she spoke of the separation of the grave, and I thought of the living tomb in a convent cell, and I spoke my thoughts without— '

'Without thinking, dearest Emma ; but we must think, and love, and act too, as dear good Mr. Graham would say, if we will do anything towards stopping this fearful evil, which is gaining ground every day.'

CHAPTER XIII.

'The breach, though small at first, soon opening wide
 In rushes folly with a full-moon tide,
   Then welcome errors of whatever size.'—COWPER.

WHEN Marcella Norman had left Fernely, Mary
Spencer devoted herself with affectionate earnestness, to make up to Lady Sophia the loss of her
friend. Emma too joined Mary in the kind endeavour, and they might soon have had the satisfaction of seeing their hopes realized by Lady
Sophia's gradual return to the habits of better
days, and by her laying aside the pernicious trash
she was wont to read with Marcella Norman; but
there was another equally anxious to fill up the
void occasioned by his sister's absence. Mr.
Norman had seen, with complacency, the growing
friendship, and feeling sure of Lady Sophia as a
convert to the Romish party, he did not often
come to Roebrook himself, devoting his time and

energies to the establishment of what he considered a just, ministerial authority among the
villagers of Fernely.   But now that Marcella was
gone, he determined not to leave Lady Sophia to
the sole companionship of two young persons,
whose views and feelings were so utterly dissimilar from those which he wished her to possess.
He called frequently ; conversed on every subject
that he thought likely to excite an interest in her
warm imagination ; lent her books of a deeper
kind than those she had obtained from Marcella,
and even consulted her about some little plans and
alterations, which he wished to make in his parish.
This, from a man who laid a very great stress upon
clerical dignity, was so great a compliment to her
understanding, that Lady Sophia was won by it,
and she became (while she fancied he showed
great deference to her opinion) a tool in his hands
to spread the very doctrines which she continued
to condemn as contrary to scripture.

The cold and damp of November mornings did
not prevent Mary and Emma from persevering in
their attendance upon the early service in Fernely
church.   This was the only link that still bound

them to Mr. Norman's ministry, and they felt no
wish to break it, until a circumstance which occurred shortly after Miss Norman's departure,
forced them to do so.

'The church is lighted up more brightly than
usual;' (exclaimed Lady Sophia as they drew near
to the sacred edifice,) 'How pleasant and cheering
it looks amid the surrounding darkness?'

'And how solemn and delightful, to be called
to worship God together at such an hour, when
everything is hushed and at peace,' remarked
Mary.

Emma was walking a little before her companion,
and had advanced some paces up the aisle, when
she suddenly stopped—paused for a moment, and
then walking hastily back, she exclaimed, 'Oh
Mary, we have got the images at last. Surely
you will not worship any longer here!'

Mary looked in the direction of the communion-
table, from whence proceeded the greatest blaze
of light, and there she saw two massive silver
candlesticks, with their appropriate lights, on
either side of the table. In the centre stood a
large alms-basin of the same metal, and behind

this appeared the crucifix. When she saw them, her heart sank within her, and she turned towards the door, concluding at once that Lady Sophia would not think of remaining where such objectionable novelties had been introduced.

But her Ladyship did not seem surprised at what she saw, and merely said, in reply to Mary's remonstrance,—'Nonsense! child, what difference can a pair of candlesticks placed on "the altar" make in my devotions? I shall not think of them, I can assure you. Emma was quite wrong in calling such simple ornaments, images.' With these words she went into her pew, and closed the door, while Emma and Mary left the church.

As they were going out, Mary observed the countenances of the few villagers who attended. Some, as they caught sight of the decorated communion-table, exhibited feelings of pleasure and surprise; others expressed a kind of amused curiosity, and the words of Holy Writ flashed into her mind, " Keep thy foot when thou goest into the house of God, and be more ready to hear, than to give *the sacrifice of fools*, for they consider not that they do evil."

They did not see Mr. Norman, who was in the vestry, robing with more than ordinary care, to give all the solemnity in his power to the scenic part in that morning's performance, but though the hour was a very early one, they met Mr. Graham at a short distance from the church, and immediately communicated to him the reason of their hasty return homewards.

'I knew it would be so,' he said,—'I was convinced from the first that a man holding Mr. Norman's views would not take so much trouble, without having some intention which we could not then see, and therefore, neither I nor my daughters cared to disarrange appointments to join what otherwise we should have looked upon as a real privilege.'

Mary looked towards the church, and sighed. Wherever she was in the habit of worshipping, there her heart built an altar to the Lord her God, and the hour of morning prayer had become very dear to her during the short period of her attendance. 'It was a privilege indeed,' she said, 'but it must be given up *now*.'

'But Mr. Graham,' (inquired Emma) 'when

you thought it wrong to attend, why did you not give us warning ? '

' I did not think it wrong, my dear ; and should have been very sorry to dissuade any one from attending public worship. I knew you would refrain from going as soon as false doctrine, or superstitious practices marred the privilege ; to me (as being introduced by a Tractarian) it did not appear in the light of one, but rather seemed designed, according to the plan of that undermining system, to supersede family worship at home, and faithful sermons in the church.'

When they had parted from Mr. Graham, the two friends walked on in silent thought for some time, and at last in order to free their minds from a subject which much disturbed them, Mary proposed to go and see her little godchild ; this visit, and one or two others which, notwithstanding the unseasonableness of the hour, they contrived to pay to some sick people on their way home, detained them until the clock struck nine.

As they quickened their steps up the avenue, towards Roebrook Hall, Emma exclaimed, ' Who can that gentleman be that is coming to meet us,

Mary ?   Some very affectionate friend he must be,
for his motion towards us is accelerating with
every step he takes.'   While she was yet speaking, Mary had bounded from her side, and was in
her brother's arms, before Emma had time to
recognize Edward Spencer.

The joy of this meeting was as great as it was
unexpected, and as they walked slowly on together,
Edward explained that the absence of Mr. L——
from home, for some weeks, had given him a
period of leisure, and that he immediately availed
himself of Lady Sophia Benson's general invitation, and set out for Fernely.   'But come,' he
continued, 'we had better make haste, as her
Ladyship is waiting for us.   She despatched me
in search of you with a message, that the hour for
family prayer had arrived, and she was anxious for
your presence.'

The happiness that glowed on Mary Spencer's
countenance, as she sat at the breakfast-table,
cannot be described.   Edward—her own Edward
was there, and improved in every point; chiefly,
she thought, in those things which always were
first—foremost in her estimation.   He spoke of

Mr. L—— with enthusiasm :—His holy, devoted
life :— his clear and sound views of truth, in
which Edward appeared to join with all his heart,
were all brought forward, and talked over with
real delight; and the distressing event of that
morning was nearly forgotten, till Lady Sophia
recalled it to their recollection, by telling Edward
of ' the weakness of her two friends, who could
not stay in a church with a cross in it, without
supposing that they must be guilty of idolatry.'

' And yet, Mary,' said Edward, ' I remember
going several times with you to St. P——'s
church near London, and in it there was a fine
painted window of four of the apostles as large as
life. I was a very little boy at the time, and I
amused myself during the long sermon with St.
Peter and his keys, and wondering why they had
painted St. John so like a beautiful girl.'

' And the cross on the top of St. Paul's cathedral ;' said Lady Sophia ; I suppose, Mary, you
would not for worlds go into that venerable
building ?'

' I should not feel the slightest objection to go,'
(replied Mary,) ' The cross on St. Paul's is merely

considered as an ornamental part of the building, and no superstitious idea is connected with it. As for the painted window, I think Edward himself has shown some reason against it, by the effect it had in drawing his mind from the solemn realities to which he should have listened, and beguiling it into forming idle imaginations about the personal appearance of the apostles. I did not at that time see any harm in painted windows ; but I think now, that in a place like London, where men of all nations and all religions meet, the evil of such things may be much greater than we can tell. A stranger to the Christian religion going into St. P——'s church, would be apt to form a very wrong, perhaps a fatal notion of the use which the English worshippers make of the four figures in the window. But perhaps you will say this is an extreme case ; and I do not think *exactly* the same objection applies to old—scarcely thought of—ornaments in churches, as to the novelties that are being introduced.'

' Well then never mind the old painted windows ;' said Emma, ' but settle about the cross and candlesticks in Fernely church ; we have most concern with them.'

' I think you need feel no concern about them Emma, (replied her Ladyship) and then they will have no worse effect, at least upon you, than the old painted windows, or the cross upon St. Paul's could have.'

' Have you not in those words, " at least upon you," helped us to one important objection to our attending any church, when such things are introduced ?' asked Mary—' Will you allow me to read an applicable passage in scripture ? ' She read the 8th chapter of first Corinthians, stopping for a moment on the words, " *We* know that an idol is nothing at all, and that there is none other God but one ;" and again reading slowly, and impressively; " But take heed lest by any means this liberty of yours become a stumbling-block to them that are weak. For if any man see thee which hast knowledge sit at meat in the idol's temple, shall not the conscience of him which is weak, be emboldened to eat those things which are sacrificed to idols; and through thy knowledge shall the weak brother perish, for whom Christ died."

' But the cross is not an idol,' observed Lady Sophia.

' It was the idol of Christendom for many ages,' said Edward, ' and continues to be so wherever the church of Rome retains her sway ; therefore our Reformers who " had knowledge," treated it as Hezekiah did the Brazen Serpent ; and we ought not (by setting this Nehushtan on its pedestal again) to confirm the poor papist in his fatal error ; to assist in making weak and unwary ones offend —I think the chapter which Mary read exactly applies to the case.'

' And several weak ones have already gone back to the darkness of Popery,' said Emma. ' I suppose the cautious introduction of Romish forms and observances smoothed their way back. Do you think, Edward, that this sudden rise of popery in England, was the result of a scheme preconcerted by the Jesuits, or only the natural fruit of unwatchfulness, formality of heart, and a restless seeking for something new ?'

' I know,' replied Edward, ' that Mr. L—— thinks that it has at least been greatly assisted by the reaction resulting from a vast amount of empty evangelical profession. He says, that while the army of the spiritual Israel has been increasing, a mixed multitude has for a time marched under the same banners; that their Egyptian nature and habits being little satisfied with the heavenly manna, " they fell a lusting," and have even decoyed some of the people of God to join in their lamentations after the " flesh-pots of Egypt;" for such indeed, is the thirst after Romish practices and ordinances.'

' This is perhaps, the wisest view for us to take of the matter;' said Mary; ' as it will tend to make us watch ourselves, which will be more useful than the discovery of a plot among others.'

' Nevertheless,' replied Edward, ' I am inclined to think that such a plot really exists. I was much struck the other day, by a passage from a letter written by Campian the Jesuit to Elizabeth's privy council. I met with it in a recent publication, and it ran thus—" Be it known unto you, that we have made a league, all the Jesuits in the world, whose *succession*, and multitude, must over-reach all the practices of England, cheerfully to carry the cross that you shall lay upon us, and never to despair of your recovery while we have a man left to enjoy your Tyburn, or to be racked

with your torments, or to be consumed with your
prisons. Expenses are reckoned : the enterprise
is begun, it is of God : it cannot be withstood.
So the faith was planted : so it must be restored.'

'Oh, that such a spirit of union, and deep resolve, were found in the children of light! (exclaimed Emma fervently) and then might all the
Campians of the present day, be brought to the
true knowledge of God's will, and their nobler
natures and martyr-spirits be given to a cause
more worthy of such self-devotion.'

'Devotees may be found to every cause however corrupt;' said Mary; 'but do not, dear
Emma, count those as martyrs whose death was
as much the reward of their treasonable practices,
as it was willingly dared in defence of the cherished errors to which they clung. But you cannot really think, Edward, that the Puseyism of the
present day, is but the carrying out of a design,
formed and resolved upon in the reign of Elizabeth. Satan, indeed, might propose such a plan,
and find tools in each succeeding age to carry it
into execution; but poor short-sighted man must

P

expect more immediate results from his endeavours, be they for good or ill.'

' I do not certainly mean,' replied Edward, ' that Campian and his compeers laid out a plan which they supposed it would occupy three centuries to accomplish ; but they resolved to reconvert England—died, and handed down the resolution, together with the well-framed rules for its fulfilment, to those successors of whom Campian spoke.'

' Then let us (said Mary with emotion) make Campian's resolution ours, and strive to accomplish a more blessed purpose, even to recover our country from this terrible snare, and to force the spirit of Popery completely to evacuate our island. We can more truly say—' Expenses are reckoned: the enterprize is begun ; we have counted the cost; it is of God ; it cannot be withstood !" '

' Yes, (said Edward, smiling at her warmth) but the Jesuits would be willing to pay a price you could not afford for the furtherance of your nobler design. With them, remember, the end sanctifies the means, and crimes may be committed, their own souls jeoparded, the lives of others, and the well-being of communities—all lightly put aside as small obstacles in the way of their one grand scheme.'

'We need not such weapons; (said Mary solemnly.) When our expenses were reckoned we found we had an exhaustless treasury, even the grace of our Lord Jesus Christ ; and when we are opposed by the formidable weapons of craft, and stratagem, we can say as David to Goliath—" Thou comest to me with a sword, and with a spear, and with a shield : but I come to thee in the name of the Lord of Hosts, the God of the armies of Israel, whom thou hast defied." '

'Yet even in this little village, the foe has already in some measure prevailed,' said Edward, 'though besides you three he had Mr. Graham, (of whom you have often written to me) and his two good daughters to oppose him. Your Rector must be a clever man ; you have never told me anything about him in your letters, Mary. What is his name.'

'I did not like to tell you anything about him, Edward, because there was so little that was pleasant to communicate. His name is Norman.'

'Norman !' said Edward starting, and a hasty

flush passed over his face. He was going to
explain, but seeing Mary had not observed his
surprise, he checked himself, and merely asked,
how long he had been in the parish.

'About one year,' replied Lady Sophia. 'And
you must not let Mary completely set you against
him. I do believe he acts upon strictly conscientious principles; and then he is so very talented,
so exceedingly clever, that'—

'No Jesuit could possibly outshine him, (interrupted Emma) he has already put down all the
religious societies in the parish; shut up the
Bible-depository; succeeded (I am pretty sure) in
coaxing two or three old women to auricular confession, and lastly, accomplished his master-stroke
this morning, by setting up his Popish abomination in the church.'

'Now let us speak of Mr. Sidney,' (said Mary,
seeing the cloud about to gather on Lady Sophia's
brow, and anxious to turn the conversation to a
more profitable subject) 'we must introduce you
to him, Edward. He is an old friend of Lady
Sophia's, and a minister resembling your own Mr.
L— so far as I have heard his character from you.'

'Suppose we put on our shawls, and walk through the park, while you discuss Mr. Sidney's merits,' said Lady Sophia, 'we must show Edward all the beauties of Fernely, and a pleasant walk may relieve the monotony of a long eulogium on Mary's favourite minister.'

There was some degree of bitterness in her Ladyship's words, that made Mary glad, that the preparation for a walk would relieve her from the necessity of resuming the conversation, and she determined to mention Mr. Sidney's name no more, but to wait patiently till an opportunity occurred of introducing Edward to one, whose society she thought would be so desirable for him, during his stay at Fernely.

CHAPTER XIV.

They pursued their way through Roebrooke Park and the adjoining village of Fernely, without again attempting a general conversation. Emma walked by Lady Sophia, and Mary leaned upon her brother's arm in all the confidence of deep affection. Very dearly as she loved Emma, Edward certainly held a higher place in her heart ; and now she looked at him with a feeling closely allied to pride. She saw in him an accomplished gentleman ; she believed him to be a devoted Christian ; and on that day the hopes of years appeared to be realized.

As they drew near to the parsonage, they saw Mr. Norman just coming out of it. He seemed at first inclined to shun their party, but when he perceived Edward with them, he advanced towards him with all the familiarity of a long-established

friendship. ' Why, my dear fellow' (he exclaimed), ' this is indeed an unexpected pleasure.
The gratification of meeting you in Fernely was
altogether so unlooked for, that at first I almost
doubted the evidence of my sight. How long
have you been here? and why did you not give
me notice of your arrival?'

Edward explained that he only reached Fernely
that morning, and that until his sister mentioned
Mr. Norman's name a few moments before, he
was not aware that he resided at Fernely. ' But
now you are here,' resumed Mr. Norman, ' we
must renew our acquaintance, which to me at
least has been the source of much pleasure. I
suppose I must not take you from Miss Spencer
to-day (he continued, looking at Mary with more
cordiality than his countenance generally expressed
towards her) but to-morrow—you must breakfast
with me to-morrow.'

Edward accepted the invitation at once, and
then walked on with his sister. He felt a little
surprised at the degree of warmth with which Mr.
Norman had welcomed him, as their acquaintance
had only been that of a few hours, and he had

almost forgotten the name of his quondam friend
till Mary told him who was rector of Fernely.

Mary was surprised, and almost terrified at the
appearance of such a close friendship between her
brother, and the man whose influence over him she
most dreaded; for she thought that in this matter
Edward must have acted with a disingenuousness
which was foreign to his nature.

Lady Sophia was delighted, and Emma, indignant at the discovery they seemed to have made,
but the surprise of all was lessened when Edward
said he had only met Mr. Norman once before,
and then for so short a time, that the friendship
had not continued even by means of epistolary
communication. 'You remember (he said, addressing Mary) when I sent you the " Christian
Year." I told you it was the gift of a gentleman,
who stopped with us on his way from Plymouth to
London. Mr. Norman was that gentleman. I
was greatly charmed with him then, and notwithstanding all you have said, am not sorry to renew
the acquaintance. You must at least confess that
he has a very warm heart.'

'Edward, it was God who " is love " that by

his Apostle gave the command, " Mark them
which cause divisions, and offences contrary to the
doctrine which ye have received, and avoid them."
I wish you had thought of this command, and not
so inconsiderately accepted an invitation to confirm a friendship which must be dangerous to a
young and inexperienced person.'

' Oh,' answered Edward, ' the text which you
have quoted was intended to guard the Church
against such heretics as the Arians and Gnostics.
If a man were to be shunned for using a few absurd ceremonies, and ornaments in the Church,
why such men as Chrysostom, and Ambrose must
have been avoided by the primitive Christians.'

' If God's rule had been attended to, and the
introducers of self-righteous doctrines, and idolatrous observances had been separated from the
ancient church, such men as Ambrose and Chrysostom would never have been defiled with them.
God's way is always the way of safety, Edward.'

' Well, I cannot see any great harm in decorat-
ing the communion-table,' replied Edward, 'though
I own it is extremely foolish and unworthy of so
wise a man as Mr. Norman appears to be.'

'It is more than foolish, Edward. I wish you would read the Homily against Peril of Idolatry, especially the third part of it. I know you will say, that it applies to the worship of images, but remember your own declaration, that the cross was the idol of Christendom. The Homily speaks thus: "What shall I say of them which will lay stumbling-blocks where before there was none, and set snares for the feet, nay, for the souls of weak and simple ones, and work the danger of their everlasting destruction for whom our Saviour Christ shed his most precious blood. Better it were the arts of painting, plastering, carving, graving, and founding, had never been found nor used, than one of them whose souls, in the sight of God, are so precious, should by occasion of image, or picture, perish and be lost. And thus it is declared, that preaching cannot stay idolatry, if images be set up publicly in temples and churches.'"

Edward promised he would read the Homily, and then changed the subject of conversation. The next morning he breakfasted with Mr. Norman according to appointment, and from that time was a constant visitor at the parsonage during his stay at Fernely.

In spite of her anxious fears, Mary continued to hope that his principles were not fatally injured by this intercourse. She observed, indeed, that whenever the subject of Tractarianism or Romanism was introduced, he studiously forbore to take any part in the conversation, but the plausible reason which he gave for this marked silence, induced her to think that it was indeed the law of charity, and the abhorrence of evil speaking that ruled his tongue. She forgot that he was not equally silent when the peculiarities of dissenters, or even the faults of the evangelical part of the Church of England were mentioned. She forgot also that he was quite as forbearing towards the general errors of Tractarianism, as towards the personal character of the men who introduced, or supported them.

Still, he was ready, and even eager to go with them when they visited the poor and the distressed, or would gladly be their messenger when other engagements kept them at home. Mary could not, however, help remarking, that Emma's word and wish had now more weight with him than her own had. At Emma's request he would sometimes decline a pressing invitation to spend the day with Mr. Norman, and by Emma's advice he would even return unread a volume which the Rector had especially recommended to his notice.

This circumstance gave Mary no pain, (for she was above every feeling of jealousy) save that it betrayed a shallowness of principle, when the highest acts of self-denial were but instances of obedience to the wishes of a lively and beautiful girl. Emma, who almost unconsciously became aware of the growing influence which she possessed, always exerted it on the right side, but even her efforts availed not to make him give up Mr. Norman's society,

Mr. Sidney had left his home on the day Edward came to Fernely, and did not return during his stay there: Mr. Graham, and his ' old maiden daughters ' he cordially disliked. He said, they had neither talents, knowledge of the world, nor sufficient polish to make them endurable, and when Mary would try to point out the beautiful consistency of Mr. Graham's character, he would answer, ' Yes, Mary, I know it is only as a matter of duty that you like, or wish me to admire that tiresome old man. But when you speak of him, I always begin to draw a contrast between him and Mr. Norman, which never fails to terminate in favour of the latter. I am sure I should like your Mr. Sidney exceedingly, but you know my own Mary, that my first idea of a loveable character was drawn from your own, and I never can be happy with dull plodding people, however I may esteem them.'

The affectionate flattery with which Edward's speech was sweetened, did not make it less distasteful to Mary. She knew that Mr. Graham was neither dull nor plodding, though his conversation was not so attractive as that of Mr. Norman. But he had (which she did not know) reproved Edward's close intimacy with a Tractarian, and from that time (though he came to Fernely with a determination to love all whom his sister loved) Edward became decidedly cold and reserved in his manner to Mr. Graham.

' I am almost glad, Emma,' Mary would sometimes say, ' that the day is drawing near for my

dear brother's return to Devonshire. He would
be safe there. I must believe that our Edward is
a child of God, but he would be far better out of
the reach of this blighting wind of false doctrine,
or all those promising buds of true religion will
wither, and die.'

Emma hoped, and believed with her, and fully
entered into all her anxieties on Edward's behalf ;
but she did not, for some time, tell her that Edward had tried to draw from her a promise that
she would, when years, and advancing prosperity
should give him some title to assert his claim, consent to become his wife.

Edward himself had indeed long considered the
humbling station in which his early youth was
passed so indelible a stain upon his escutcheon,
that it was scarcely possible the daughter of
Colonel Clifford would for a moment listen to his
plea. His joy was therefore almost beyond
bounds, when Emma, after remaining a few moments silent, said calmly, and deliberately ; ' We
are too young to determine for ourselves yet, Edward. My father is to return from India soon,
and I cannot promise anything without his sanc-

tion, so at least for the present do not think any more of it.'

He considered Emma's evasive answer as a tacit consent to his proposal, little thinking that in the moment she took for quiet deliberation, the uncertainty that veiled his religious profession was uppermost in her mind. Though her feelings pleaded strongly in his behalf, she kept her mind fixed on the apostolic rule, " only in the Lord," and would not bind herself in any way to one who seemed ready to be " carried about with every wind of doctrine."

Of this interview Emma did not speak to Mary until future circumstances gave her occasion to do so. But Edward, in the gladness of his heart, told his fond sister of all his happiness, and when the moment of parting really arrived, and he saw the tears on Mary's cheek, he whispered to her, ' In three months I shall go to Oxford. The time will pass very quickly there, Mary ; and you will take care of your Emma—our Emma, till I am ordained ; after that we three will never part again.'

CHAPTER XV.

THREE months had passed away, and the inmates of Roebrooke Hall were anxiously watching the arrival of the post. At length letters were brought in for Lady Sophia Benson, and Mary Spencer. Mary's was from Edward, giving a joyful account of his removal to Oxford. That to Lady Sophia was from Marcella Norman. She had heard from her but once since she left Fernely, and her expressions of joy at the sight of the well-known handwriting were soon hushed into complete silence as she pondered over the long and closely-written letter.

Emma took up the newspaper to pass the time while her friends were engaged, and after a few moments the quiet was interrupted by her sudden exclamation—' Oh, Mary, how very dreadful ! It must be Marcella Norman, it can be no other.'

And then she read the following paragraph in the paper :—

' Another victim to Tractarian delusion has just devoted herself at the shrine of Antichrist. Miss Norman, only daughter of the late Sir Dudley Norman, and sister of the Rev. H. Norman, rector of Fernely, in ——shire, publicly renounced the Protestant faith on Sunday last, in the chapel belonging to some Benedictine nuns in the neighbourhood of C——. She has commenced her noviciate with the intention of taking the veil in that convent.'

Lady Sophia's grief was great, and her perplexity extreme. She seemed like one who had wandered in a dream to the brink of a precipice, down which she was every moment in danger of falling. Her expressions of dismay and concern almost surprised Mary, who, in the fanatical language of the poor nun, only discovered the same sentiments (more plainly stated perhaps) that Lady Sophia had often listened to with interest, when they were uttered by her as a professed member of the Church of England. Her letter contained a florid description of her happi-

Q

ness in being at length received into the bosom of
her ' venerable Mother Church' for which ' safe
abode of peace and rest,' she said her heart had
often yearned.   ' And oh, my beloved friend, (she
added) what can I do less than devote the rest of
my days to prayer, and penance, in order to atone
for the Protestant errors of my childhood, and
youth.   But the life of a nun is a blessed life.   I
shall live now under the constant protection of the
Mother of our Lord, (whose service I so long
neglected) and of holy St. Benedict, who founded
our order. Would that I could prevail on you too,
my friend, to fly from the world, and cast in your
lot among us. My brother would have persuaded
me to remain a little longer in the Anglican
Church, which he looks upon as a part of the true
Church, though degraded, and afflicted by her
separation from the rest of catholic Europe. He
thinks (as you do) that it is better to remain
where he is, and endeavour to wean the English
Church gradually from some of the errors into
which she has fallen. But I could not endanger
the safety of my own soul by remaining any
longer beyond the pale of the only church in

which salvation is to be found. I longed to hasten into the true ark, and the uneasiness of my mind increased so much, that my brother at last consented to invite Cosmo Bernazzi, (a priest with whom he had contracted an intimate friendship on the sacred soil of Italy) to come to Fernely. This holy man, he said, would counsel me how to act so as most to promote the interests of the Catholic Church. My own wishes, and my brother's would rather have pointed to an Italian convent as the home of my future life; but when Bernazzi came, he advised me to make my open profession in England, and enter one of the few abodes of piety and peace to be found in this sterile ground. He said that even the example of one Englishwoman might do much in the good cause, and I willingly sacrificed my own wishes to the will of holy Mother Church.'

'Cosmo Bernazzi was then the foreigner whom we noticed in company with Mr. Norman,' said Mary, 'how active—how vigilant are the emissaries of ill! "The children of this world are indeed at the present crisis, wiser than the children of light."'

' But the English Jesuit was in this instance wiser than the Italian one ;' said Emma. ' Perhaps poor Marcella's apostacy openly declared in England may warn some who are trifling on the borders of Tractarianism, and prevent their ruin ; but her profession in Italy could have been kept secret till her brother and his fellow traitors had succeeded in spreading their corrupt principles. Oh, Mary, is it not a scheme worthy of the father of lies ?'

' But he does not think those principles corrupt, dear Emma, (said Lady Sophia, mournfully) for with all his failings I am persuaded Mr. Norman is a strictly conscientious man.'

' My Bible, my precious Bible, (said Mary, taking it up) what a privilege in these days of delusion, dismay, and doubt, to have an infallible guide to the conscience.'

Mr. Sidney, who had entered the room unperceived by the party, and had heard Lady Sophia's remark, and Mary's reply, gently took the Bible from her, and turning to the second chapter of second Thessalonians, he read from the middle of the tenth verse. " Because they received not the love of the truth that they might be saved. And for this cause God shall send them strong delusion, that they should believe a lie."

'I am afraid,' he said, 'this strong delusion, this belief of a lie, accompanied by practice consistent with such belief, is often dignified by the appellation of conscientious conduct. A conscience purged by the blood of Christ, from dead works, to serve the living God, is indeed a valuable monitor when we err, and approver when we go right; but a defiled and deluded conscience may lead into all manner of superstition, and depths of idolatry. Let us bear in mind the reason that some are thus given over to delusion; " Because they received not the *love of the truth*." '

'The truth has been very generally preached in the present time,' observed Mary.

'And very generally received, Miss Spencer,' replied Mr. Sidney, 'but not always in the love of it. Some have received it for fashion's sake, or because their ears were pleased by the eloquence with which it was preached; these will for fashion's sake accept the anglo-catholic principles, and follow their leaders to Rome, because their ears are

pleased with solemn music, and the echoings of
depraved antiquity. Others have received, and
even dared to hold it in unrighteousness; these
will more readily listen to a creed which once
taught men to found monasteries as an atonement
for sin, or to purchase absolution from those who
assume the right to grant it.'

'But "some of them of understanding may
fall," ' said Mary.

'Assuredly they may,' replied Mr. Sidney; 'and
therefore have we now especial need to "keep the
heart with all diligence, for out of it are the issues
of life." '

'But can nothing be done to stay a plague
which is so rapidly increasing?' said Emma.
'Why do not the bishops '—

'Nay, Miss Clifford, 'resumed Mr. Sidney,
' we must not arraign the bishops; some of them
are contending earnestly for the faith once delivered to the saints, against this pernicious heresy;
and of all we must say, "To their own Master
they stand or fall." It is for you and I to consider
what we may do to check the evil. Many of the
Tractarians are said to be men of blameless morals,

and holy life. True holiness of heart and life cannot exist apart from " faith which worketh by love ; " but a devout demeanour, and strict outward rectitude may. We should all study to outlive the abettors of false doctrine.'

' But Sir,' said Emma, ' do you think we should be justified in imitating the austerities which they practise? Surely they belong to that kind of piety, or pietism, which St. Paul describes as " having indeed a show of wisdom in will-worship, and neglecting of the body, not in any honour to the satisfying of the flesh." '

' Imitate them ! ' said Mr. Sidney, ' Oh no. I would not set their example before mine eyes, even where they may have done right; it would but prove a certain lure to ill. I remember hearing a sentence repeated in my youth, which often returns to my mind with a more sanctified import than it was then intended to convey. " The arrow which is aimed at the highest mark, will take the loftiest flight." Now while Tractarians are searching the mouldering records of the early Church for examples by which to shape their conduct, let us look from them entirely, and keeping our eyes fixed on "Jesus the author and finisher of our faith," let us aim at the higher, holier life which St. Paul describes, in contradistinction to that of the will-worshippers condemned in your quotation. Thus he goes on in the very next verses,— " If ye then be risen with Christ, seek those things which are above, where Christ sitteth on the right hand of God. Set your affections on things above, not on things on the earth. For ye are dead, and your life is hid with Christ in God. When Christ who is our life shall appear, then shall ye also appear with him in glory. Mortify *therefore* your members which are upon the earth.'"

' " Risen with Christ ! " ' repeated Mary. ' How completely the ransomed people of the Lord are united to their glorious Head. It is strange that any can be found trying to undervalue that atoning blood, and perfect righteousness, by contriving a new justification by baptism, by our own works, the eucharist, and a number of absurd mortifications that can but add to our guilt.'

' Lacerating the body,' remarked Lady Sophia, ' seems always to have been a part of false worship. We read that the worshippers of Baal, when summoned to the great decision between their senseless god and the Lord of Hosts, "cried aloud and cut themselves *after their manner*, with knives, and lancets, till the blood gushed out upon them."'

'The mortification which the word of God commends differs from that used both by Pagans and Papists,' said Mr. Sidney, 'It consists in subduing our sinful inclinations, correcting our evil tempers, and denying every wish that attempts to wander.'

'Harder work,' said Emma, 'than living for forty days together upon dry bread and salt-fish.'

'Yes,' returned Mr. Sidney smiling, 'I believe Miss Clifford would have sometimes found it easier to follow Miss Norman in her long fasts, and self-imposed penances, than to suppress the merry laugh, or satirical remark, with which she often heard some new absurdity defended by the poor devotee.'

Emma coloured, and replied. 'Indeed, Sir, I believe an earnest entreaty, or solemn remonstrance would have better suited my Christian profession, and have been more likely to do Miss Norman good than the thoughtless laugh with which I sometimes greeted her. I fear she only numbered me among the scorners, and considered my merriment as part of the sufferings she must endure as she worked her way to heaven.'

'Yet satire in wise and serious hands is often a useful weapon against error and vice,' remarked Mary, 'the well-directed strokes of our favourite Cowper for instance.'

'"Answer not a fool according to his folly, lest thou be like unto him," replied Mr. Sidney, 'should set a watch upon young and inexperienced lips, when they attempt as it were to play with sin. But the paradox in the following verse, "Answer a fool according to his folly, lest he be wise in his own conceit," may encourage the wise reprover to rebuke the absurdity and inconsistency of every false way. Such rebukes will always be serious, and earnest, not flippant. There is a solemn grandeur in the mockery with which Elijah addressed the fanatical worshippers of Baal, "Cry aloud; for he is a god; either he is talking, or he is pursuing, or he is in a journey, or peradventure he sleepeth, aud must be awakened.'

'Do you think,' asked Lady Sophia, 'that we have no Scripture warrant for the practice of fasting? Our Lord says, " But the time will come when the bridegroom shall be taken from them, and then shall they fast in those days." '

' I understand our Lord's words rather as a prophecy than a command, but in whichever way they are taken they certainly refer to a fast which is not unscriptural. Fasting is an outward expression of inward sorrow and humiliation. As a means of bringing the carnal nature under the dominion of the spirit it has been practised by servants of God in all ages ; but then it is a secret service, known only to God, and the repentant heart engaged in it. Far different this from the fasting of those who in their superstitious zeal for the observance of " days and months, and times, and years," would leave the ignorant and the young, perhaps even the vicious, to a practice which is more likely to injure than benefit any but the believer firmly established on the Rock Christ.'

' Public national fasts,' said Mary, ' for national sins, or public calamities, are, like those of an individual, the expression of repentance, and have nothing superstitious in their nature.'

' We are forgetting my poor friend,' said Lady

Sophia, ' Can nothing be done to rescue her from
her present delusion. I will write to her at once,
and urge every motive, every command contained
in the word of God to induce her to return.'

' I fear,' said Mr. Sidney, after a few moments
deep thought, ' your letters would never reach her.
Convent cells are too closely guarded to allow
their inmates free communication with heretics ;
but I would not dissuade you from making the
attempt. Even the words of inspiration seem to
fall powerless on ears palsied with this Tractarian
system. I have spent hours in the vain endeavour
to press home the fundamental truths of Christianity upon Miss Norman and her brother.'

Lady Sophia was surprised. She had heard
both from Mr. Norman and Marcella much of the
bigotry and spiritual pride which kept Mr. Sidney
from associating with his brother minister, but of
these earnest attempts to win them back to the
light and hope of the Gospel, she had never heard.

As an intimate friend, Mr. Sidney could not
receive Mr. Norman. He would not through any
latitudinarian principle of liberality acknowledge as
a brother minister of the Church of England, a

man whose sympathies and exertions seemed all to be enlisted in the service of the idolatrous Church of Rome. 'Those who amuse themselves with what they are pleased to call the unwritten word,' he continued, 'that is, the traditions that have come down from a high antiquity, accumulating all the defilement of intervening ages, are sure to get so entangled in the foul snare, that they cannot even discern the strait and narrow way which the written word marks out for them to tread in.

CHAPTER XVI.

'Thus, by degrees the truths, that once bore sway,
And all their deep impressions, wear away;
So coin grows smooth, in traffic current pass'd,
Till Cæsar's image is effaced at last.'

                                        COWPER.

WHEN Mr. Sidney was gone, Lady Sophia commenced writing to Marcella Norman, but her task was hard. When she began to speak of the bright hopes of the Gospel, she found that she could no longer, with a steady hand,

'Point to that redeeming blood,
   And say, Behold the way to God.'

She had listened to the "instruction that causeth to err," and though she had never formally given up the foundation-doctrine of Christianity, justification by faith, yet her views had insensibly become cloudy, and confused.

Copy after copy of her letter she destroyed,

ashamed almost to appeal to the Bible, whose voice
she had so often suffered to be overpowered in her
mind by Marcella's arguments, drawn from the
decrees of what she called the Church Catholic.
When at length she so far succeeded as to please
herself, the letter which she read aloud to Emma
and Mary appeared so flimsy and compromising,
that the latter secretly determined to write herself, and denounce to poor Marcella Norman the
faith she had chosen upon the broad ground of
that text, "I am the Lord : that is my name, and
my glory will I not give to another, neither my
praise to graven images." *

When Lady Sophia had folded her letter, Mary
thought the opportunity favourable for urging her
utterly to renounce Mr. Norman's ministry—'He
has connived at his sister's apostacy,' (she said,)
he is the bosom friend of Jesuits and Italian
priests ; at any rate he is a blind leader of the
blind, and fearful indeed is the abyss into which
he will guide.'

Lady Sophia hesitated, but at length said she

* Isaiah xlii. 8.

would on the following Sunday accompany the Graham's to Mr. Sidney's church. Mary's joy was great at what she considered the probable recovery of her kind friend. But Emma was less sanguine, and when they were alone, said she feared Mr. Norman would readily profit by her reluctance, and persuade her to remain under his ministry.

Her fears were realized, and Mary's loving hopes all disappointed, for when the Sabbath morning came, Lady Sophia said, she had a decided objection to leaving her parish church: that she could join in the sacred service, and guard against anything erroneous that might be in the sermon.

' My parish church !' repeated Emma, as she left the hall; but she checked herself, and would not give expression to the ludicrous idea that took possession of her mind, when she reflected on the folly of clinging to the walls of a building, when all that made it sacred had departed, and nothing remained, but a lifeless worship and a growing superstition.

Lady Sophia watched long and eagerly for a reply to her letter; none ever came. To all her inquries about Marcella, Mr. Norman returned evasive answers. Sometimes he spoke with disapprobation of the step she had taken, but generally dropped the subject so soon as he conveniently could. He advised her to consider Marcella as one who had, for the sake of Christ, renounced all the comforts of life, and with them the ties of earthly friendship ; and in order to fill up the void occasioned by her loss, he contrived to bring about an intimacy between her ladyship, and Mrs. Chambers and her fashionable daughters.

The effect of this intimacy was the return of Lady Sophia to many scenes of worldly amusement, which she had given up in her early years, and had continued outwardly at least to condemn ever since.

She silenced the voice of conscience in this instance, as she had done when it bade her not listen to a preacher of heresy—'What harm can my being in a room when dancing is going on do to me ? I certainly shall not dance.'—'There can be no sin in merely going to a private theatre. I am too old, and my religious principles too firmly established to be injured by such trifles.'

R

But what religious principles had Lady Sophia now left that could sustain injury? The vast gulf that separates Protestant truth from Tractarian Popery, she called mere 'difference of opinion,' and was no Puseyite, simply because she was now prepared to say with the infidel poet—

> 'For modes of faith let graceless zealots fight,
> His can't be wrong whose life is in the right.'

She would, at the same time, endeavour to prove the worth and efficacy of Mr. Norman's ministry by triumphantly pointing out to Mary and Emma "the great change," which, she said, had taken place in Mrs. Chambers' feelings with respect to religion. They could discern no change in her, save a little more attention to outward observances. But the village was changed indeed. Two or three Christian families there were among the peasantry, who held fast their profession, and continued in their walk and conversation to adorn the gospel of Christ. Among these were William and Martha Thompson; but Mary (fearing for her godchild) had sought and obtained employment for William in Mr. Sidney's parish, whither she advised and

assisted them to remove. Mr. Norman had succeeded n impressing a very few with such a sense
of his authority, and the power of the Church, that
they were prepared to follow him wherever he
chose to lead. The rest raised indeed the cry of
' No Popery,' but without knowing what they fled
from, or whither they ran, seldom went either to
church or meeting, many of them falling an easy
prey to rebellious Chartists and loathsome
Socialists.

Mr. Norman denounced his straying flock,
threatened, and rebuked, but all to little purpose;
he did not preach the Gospel to them, and nothing
else will change the sinner's heart, or guide his
feet into the way of peace.

Mr. Graham did what he could to stem the
flood of iniquity, and his steady opposition to evil
of every kind sometimes prevailed to stop the
chartist meeting, and to keep the emissaries of
socialism out of the parish. Often too he would
prevail on the poor habitual neglecters of God's
ordinances to assemble in his large room, when
they were addressed by any faithful minister whom
he could prevail upon to meet them. He tried to

bring a scripture-reader to Fernely, but Mr. Norman's opposition to this step was so great, that he was obliged to relinquish it; in doing so, however, he determined with God's help to accomplish another design which would require a greater sacrifice of wealth on his part.

He laid the foundation-stone of a church in that district of the adjoining parish where his daughters kept their school, and cheerfully devoted £1,200, to the completion of the sacred edifice. The Bishop (who was anxious to encourage church-building in his diocese,) readily gave his promise to consecrate the new house of prayer, and to sanction Mr. Graham's appointment of a clergyman.

Mary and Emma rejoiced in the prospect of good that this noble design afforded, but their own home was changed. One or other of Mrs. Chambers' daughters was constantly a guest at Roebrooke Hall, and the domestic arrangements were altered to suit the taste of the new favourites. Large parties were given, and frivolous gossip indulged in; while family prayer was discontinued, because Mr. Norman considered that morning and evening attendance at church rendered united prayer at home quite unnecessary.

About this time a letter from India announced that Colonel Clifford intended soon to return to England, and spend the rest of his life in his native land. These tidings would, at such a time especially, have been matter of great joy to Emma, but that a separation from her beloved friend would be the probable result of her father's return. She did not remember her father, but her love for him had been kept up by a constant and affectionate correspondence, and weary of Lady Sophia's guardianship, she felt that a paternal home would be indeed a refuge to which she would gladly go if she could have taken Mary Spencer with her.

Mary knew that Lady Sophia had ceased to value her society, and now considered her presence an irksome restraint; she determined therefore not to remain after Emma left Fernely, but to seek some temporary home until Edward's ordination. And then she hoped to find a permanent and a happy one. Edward did not often write, but he pleaded arduous study, and multiplied engagements, and Mary was satisfied with the excuse.

CHAPTER XVII.

" Oh that Ishmael might live before thee."—Gen. xvii. 18.

' How awfully the darkness is increasing;' exclaimed Emma; ' I am afraid popery will rise to a
great height, before the millstone is plunged beneath the waves, to rise no more for ever and ever.'

' And before that time,' said Mary, ' we may
perhaps be called to stand in the ranks of a
martyr-church. I have been thinking much of
David's words, " My soul is even as a weaned
child." And I am afraid I cannot say so yet,
Emma; there are some sources of earthly delight
from which my soul is not yet weaned. But the
postman is just coming to the hall-door. I always
tremble when I see him now, for Edward does not
write as he used to do, except when he mentions
you, Emma, or some little affectionate solicitude
about me, for he is warmhearted, and loving as
ever; but he has contracted intimacies in Oxford,

which tend, I think, to foster his natural pride,
and to leaven his feelings with the poison of
worldliness, for his letters have now no savour of
spiritual religion.'

The servant brought in a letter for Mary, and
Emma, (though anxious for tidings from Oxford)
suffered her for some time to read in silence. But
when at last she looked at her friend, Mary was
sitting with her open letter in her hand, her eyes
fixed and her lips parched, and pale. Emma flew
to her side, and by every tender endearment strove
to bring her back to consciousness. At length
she pressed her hand upon her brow, and gazing
at Emma with a look of piteous grief, she said in
a low voice, " Trees whose fruit withereth, without fruit, twice dead ; plucked up by the roots."
She paused a moment, and then added, " Wandering stars, to whom is reserved the blackness
of darkness for ever."

' Oh do not speak so fearfully !' cried Emma,
restraining her own grief that she might strengthen
the despairing sister. ' Remember the prophet
says, " Rejoice not against me, O mine enemy ;
when I fall I shall arise again." If Edward has

fallen, he will be restored, Mary, you were not wont to despond.'

' Oh no,' said Mary, ' the words of the apostle have rung in mine ears all day, a dreadful foreboding, Emma,—" twice dead"—" plucked up by the roots"—no, there can be no hope that the writer of words like these will return and seek the God of our salvation.'

Emma took the letter from her hand.—It was dated thus :—

> ' *Baliol College,*
> ' *Feast of St. Andrew the Apostle.*

' My letters to you, dear Mary, have been of late mere chronicles of unimportant events, the records of my lighter hours; and the importance which I seemed to attach to the acquisition of a new acquaintance among the noble or witty in this venerable city of Oxford drew from you, at length, the gentle reproof administered in your last epistle. I must therefore throw aside the gay covering, beneath which I have long concealed strange and deep thoughts. I will not fear you any longer, my beloved Mary, but at once

open my whole soul to your enlightened and un-
prejudiced mind. You know of the friendship
which I felt for Mr. Norman. It deepened every
day while I remained at Fernely. I saw in him
a man of extensive talents, and exemplary virtue,
bearing with scarce a murmur, the calumnies that
were heaped upon him. Stigmatized as a heretic;
cast out from the society of your Grahams and
Sidneys, he followed in one steady course those
great luminaries of learning and piety whom he
had set as exemplars before him. When I left
Fernely, he solicited the favour of my correspondence, with the humility of a little child. Could I
refuse ? Mine indeed had been the loss if I had
suffered bigotry to mislead me into so doing; but
I did not, and the letters of that suffering saint
have opened my eyes to discern the religious prejudices in which I, and you, my sweet sister, were
brought up. Gladly indeed I accepted his offer
of an introduction to three or four choice spirits
among the students and professors at Oxford,
They are kindred with his own.

> ' With whom the melodies abide,
> Of the everlasting chime.'

' I cannot in the compass of a letter go through
all the arguments which have induced me to
renounce the prejudices of ultra-protestantism,
while I still own myself an unworthy member of the
Anglican church, yearning indeed for more perfect
reconciliation with the venerable Church of Rome,
our mother, who sent from her bosom the blessed
St. Augustine, to bring us her immoveable faith.'

' The eyes of all Christendom are at this moment
turned to England, so long separated from the
rest of Catholic Europe ; everywhere a presenti-
ment has gone abroad that the hour of her re-
union is at hand, and that this island, of old so
fruitful in saints, is once more about to put forth
new fruits worthy of the martyrs who have watered
it with their blood. It has been clearly proved in
a late publication that the Church of Rome fell
into no formal error in the Council of Trent ; that
the theory of that Church is pure, although there
is a system authorized by it, which practically instead of presenting to the soul of the sinner the
Holy Trinity, heaven, and hell, substitutes for
them the holy Virgin, the saints, and purgatory.
It is true that all this does not form an essential

part of the faith of the Church, but the system loudly calls for reform ; it would be impossible for the Anglican Church yet to cast itself into the arms of that of Rome.

'I have heard that two orders of monks have just arrived in England to labour for our conversion ; let them but show us that we have not the image of a Church perfect in discipline, and in morals ;—Let them chant day and night the praises of our Saviour;—Let them go into our great towns and preach to that half-pagan population ;—Let them walk barefoot in sackcloth and ashes, carrying mortification written on their brow ;—Let them, in fine, have among them a saint like the seraph of Assissium, and the heart of England is already won. Yours, my sweet Mary, would be one of the first to pay the tribute of conviction to devotion so unearthly. But the time for this perfect union is not yet come. " We are still the children of that afflicted Church which has drunk the bitter cup to the dregs." *

'In the meantime I still pursue my studies in

* The principal part of this Letter appeared in the *Univers* (Paris journal,) dated, ' Oxford, Passion Sunday.'

this venerable college, that I may be ready for my future destiny whatever it may be. Should the arrangements for a union between the Churches permit marriage to the clergy, my humble name may yet be enrolled among the august priesthood of England. But if in the great Council of the Church Catholic, the indignant spirit of St. Anselm should be present to oppose such a concession to earthly feeling, I trust I shall be forgiven if I sacrifice that highest wish of my ambition, and with my beloved Emma kneel down at the sacred shrines among the humble ranks of the laity, receiving with her the bread of life from the holy hands which shall then minister at our restored altars. Tell her I am looking joyfully forward to the time when I shall again be permitted for a season to walk with you and her through the beautiful woods of Fernely; then I shall be able to give you both a clearer account of our views. But I ought to mention that I have promised to pay a flying visit to one or two of the French cathedrals with an intimate friend of Mr. Norman's. His name is Cosmo Bernazzi, an Italian; a man of blameless life, and profound learning; how-

ever, my sister and my Emma cannot appreciate
his worth just yet, on account of certain little
prejudices which will quickly disperse before the
brighter beams of true Christian charity.

'Your own attached brother,

'EDWARD SPENCER.'

Edward did not understand Emma; he thought
that the lively and merry-hearted girl would be
easily won over to his new opinions, or at least
that her prejudices (as he termed them,) would
easily give way before her affection to him. But
her religion was deep and real. Her God reigned
in her heart, and every human affection succumbed
to that allegiance. An expression of something
like scorn passed over her beautiful countenance,
as she laid down the letter. 'He shall not need
to sacrifice his priestly honours!' she said in a low
voice, but instantly recollecting herself, she threw
her arms round Mary's neck, and said, 'Is anything too hard for the Lord? Mary, Mary,
where is your faith in the promise, "Ask, and it
shall be given you:" but Mary answered not,
neither did she regard it: for once her soul re-

fused to be comforted, and health and life seemed likely to give way before the fearful stroke.

Day after day Emma watched by her bed-side, and sought by every act of fond affection to win her back to peace. Lady Sophia too, at times attempted the task of comforter, but she could not sympathize with the grief. She even remarked that it was strange Mary should suffer so much, merely because her brother had chosen to adopt opinions differing from her own.

Religion at length achieved what friendship could not effect, and Mary's strength began to return. Though it was evident she suffered still, she suffered in silence; not even to Emma did she often speak of her sorrow; but one day coming unawares into the room where her young companion was seated at her writing-desk, she sat down by her, and with the perfect confidence of friendship leaned lovingly on her shoulder, and eagerly watched as she traced the words.

' I should ill brook to be the only impediment between you and the altars of Baal; such impediments were wont to be lightly cast aside during the archepiscopate of that man whose spirit you expect to preside in the future councils of your Church. No! Edward, God being my helper, my place shall rather be among the Joan Boughtons and Anne Askews who may then stand condemned before your august tribunals.'

The tears that dropped from the sufferer's eyes upon the open letter, first betrayed to Emma that Mary was by her side; for, lost in the intensity of her own feelings, she had not even felt her gentle caress. 'Mary, how could you!'—she began, but Mary stopped her with a tender kiss. 'You are right, Emma, she said, quite right; I had foolishly begun to think a union with you might save him from total apostacy, but it would not do so, and you must not leave the path of duty.' She remained in silent thought for a few moments, and then added, 'I am afraid that your final rejection of him will induce Edward to spend the whole of the college recess on the continent, with that Jesuit Bernazzi.'

'We must just do God's will, and leave with Him the consequences,' replied Emma, and the resolute girl shut out from her mind the temptation that struggled hard for admittance.

' I have been thinking much, (said Mary, without noticing Emma's last words) of the heavy grief that Aaron must have felt when his two sons, Nadab and Abihu were cut off in their sins; " and Aaron held his peace." Oh, Emma, I have not held my peace; my heart has often rebelled against the Lord; and yet Edward is not cut off; he is still in the land of—.'

' Prayer and hope,' interrupted Emma. ' We have still bright hope, upheld by many promises, to cheer us, Mary.'

' Ah, yes; but " hope deferred maketh the heart sick" (said Mary, her eyes again filling with tears), and I have hoped for Edward through so many long years. You cannot think, Emma, how vividly I have lately seen the goodness of my heavenly Father, in giving me you to fill the void; —but your father will soon arrive in England, and then I must almost lose you, my more than sister.'

' No, Mary, you never will,' exclaimed Emma, ' you must come with me—live with me—we never can be separated.'

Mary shook her head, ' It is the will of God to

divide us, Emma, and I CAN be separated from those I dearly love. I can almost say "my soul is even as a weaned child" now. But if my God permit, I will pitch my solitary tent near your dwelling, Emma, and we may still be daily companions: more than this we must not expect, and you, dear, will have many weighty duties to fulfil as the mistress of your father's house.'

'Oh yes, (said Emma, with much emotion) but we will walk together, read, and pray together, and visit the poor together, Mary, as we used to do in our happy days.'

'And we will watch together for the wanderer's return,' said Mary.

THE END.

L. SEELEY, THAMES DITTON, SURREY.